"POWERFUL, LUSTY, HONEST"

—Worcester, Mass., *Telegram*

Like MANDINGO and DRUM, MASTER OF FAL-
CONHURST shatters the genteel image of the Old
South and lays bare the savage truth about slavery
and slave-breeding . . . about plantations like Falconhurst where the cash crop was black flesh, where
human beings were stripped bare in the market
place and sold like cattle.

In this great new bestseller, Kyle Onstott unfolds
the turbulent drama of Falconhurst caught up in
the violence of the Civil War. It also is the story of
Drummage, the virile and handsome slave who rose
to become not only ruler of Falconhurst, but master
of the selfish, sensual woman who owned it.

Kyle Onstott

MASTER
OF
FALCONHURST

A FAWCETT CREST BOOK

Fawcett Publications, Inc., Greenwich, Conn.
Member of American Book Publishers Council, Inc.

I wish to acknowledge the collaboration of Lance Horner in the writing of this book and extend to him my gratitude for his valuable assistance.

THIS BOOK CONTAINS THE COMPLETE TEXT OF THE
ORIGINAL HARDCOVER EDITION.

A Fawcett Crest Book published by arrangement with The Dial Press
and the Denlinger Publishing Company, Middleburg, Virginia.

Library of Congress Catalog Card Number: 64-20214

Ninth Fawcett Crest printing, March 1969

Published by Fawcett World Library,
67 West 44th Street, New York, N. Y. 10036
Printed in the United States of America

BOOK I

Chapter I

IT WAS DARK up in the loft and chilly, for the heat of the day did not last through the night, now that autumn had come to the Alabama countryside. Olly, as usual, had almost the whole quilt wrapped around his huge form and Drummage snuggled up closer to his half-brother, feeling the animal warmth exuding from the big fellow. Olly's snores, deep and sonorous, sawed through the still air. As Drummage's eyes became accustomed to the wan light of morning, he could see the vapor ascending from Olly's mouth as the powerful black chest rose and fell, the thick lips quivering with the force of the exhalation, and the wide nostrils vibrating. He dug his elbow into his brother's side, heard him grunt as he heaved his body away, taking the rest of the quilt with him.

"Gimme some o' dat goddam quilt." Drummage sat up on the pallet and tugged at the worn "Rising Sun" piecework. He managed to get a considerable portion of it for himself, during which process Olly turned to face him again. Now by lifting one of the inert arms, he was able to slide under the quilt and snuggle up against the warm chest. Olly's other arm slid under Drummage's neck and the big hand clutched him close so that he felt warm and secure once more. Sleeping with Olly was like bedding down with a mountain but it was a warm, smooth, comfortable mountain and he closed his eyes to go back to sleep. He was just drifting off when a voice from under him called out.

"Hey yo', Ol' Mista Wilson, and yo', Drummage! Gits yo'-sel's up. Brekkus ready, time yo' gits down here and washed up."

There was a plodding of heavy feet across the uneven floor, a creak of boards and a banging of pans. Wood smoke drifted up between the cracks of the boards which floored the loft and as Drummage lay there, dreading the moment when he must get up and climb over Olly, slide down the ladder, and go outside to plunge his face into the rain barrel, he felt a wave of resentment against his mother.

"Goddam that Big Pearl, h'isting hersel' outa bed 'fore daybreak." Maybe if he just ignored her he could go back to sleep again.

"Drummage, you' 'wake?" Big Pearl's voice had the edge of impatience. She knew better than to call Ol' Mista Wilson, more familiarly known as Olly. Getting Olly out of bed in the morning was a monumental task, which usually involved climbing up the ladder with a gourdful of cold water and splashing it in his face.

"Drummage, mind yo' ma!" This second voice, older, quavering and insecure, belonged to Lucy, Big Pearl's mother and the boys' grandmother.

"I'se 'wake—jes' lingerin', tha's all." He was hoping for another few minutes. Sometimes in the press of getting breakfast, tending to Lucy's querulous wants, and propelling her own huge body around the cabin, Big Pearl forgot about him long enough for him to doze off again. He snuggled down closer to Olly, luxuriating in every stolen moment.

"If you' a-pesterin' Ol' Mista Wilson, yo' stops it this minit and gets yo'sel' down here or I'se a-comin' up. No wonder Ol' Mista Wilson ain' got no sap in him—yo' a-pesterin' him alla time." Big Pearl shook the ladder. "I'se a-comin' up and if'n I h'ists myse'f up there, yo' shore goin' to be sorry. Yo' ain' so big yet but what I kin whop yo'— yo' and Ol' Mista Wilson too. Reachin' for the ash shovel right now, I is. Yo' comin'?"

Olly was still sleeping soundly and Drummage had to struggle to get out of his tight embrace. Sometimes he wondered why Big Pearl and Old Lucy always called Olly Ol' Mista Wilson. Masta Hammond Maxwell did too, but everyone else on Falconhurst had shortened Ol' Mista Wilson to Olly, just as they called him Drummage instead of Drum Major, which was his real name.

Grabbing his breeches and shirt, he crept to the side of the loft, and let his long legs dangle over the edge while he pulled his trousers on. Big Pearl, walking below him, tickled the pink soles of his feet and he drew up his legs so sharply his pants fell off. They plopped down on the floor and he slid down the ladder to retrieve them.

"Shame on yo', a-comin' down here buck-assed nekkid,"

Big Pearl chided him, " 'fore yore grandmaw too."

"Seen everythin' that boy got since de day he birfed." Old Lucy chuckled from the propped-up pillows of the bed as she stared at Drummage, whose early morning tumescence had not entirely subsided. "A-goin' to be jes' like his pappy. Mede shore was a man."

"Mede not this'n's pappy, Maw. Mede Ol' Mista Wilson's pappy but not this un. This un's pappy Drumson, who got hisself kilt the night o' the fire. Don' yo' 'members, Maw?"

" 'Members? Co'se I do. That Drumson looken 'nuff like Mede to be he's brother." She kept her eyes on Drummage, who was pulling on his pants and struggling to get into his shirt, which had shrunk so from repeated washings that he was unable to get the crude wooden buttons into the torn buttonholes. "Come over here and kiss yo're grandma, son." Lucy's hands slid along Drummage's smooth arms as he leaned over and pecked at her forehead. "Gits yo're full growth," she said. "Yo' goin' to be so big as Ol' Mista Wilson. How ol' this boy, Big Pearl?"

"Don' rightly 'member, Maw." Big Pearl was kneeling before the fireplace, stirring a kettle of grits. "Cain' think but seems like he's gotten 'bout fifteen Chrismuses." She got up and laid the wooden spoon down on the hearth, and went over to a notched log near the bed. "Le's see. That long one, that's Ol' Mista Wilson." She ran her fingers over the notches, ticking them off one by one on the fingers of her free hand. "Dat Ol' Mista Wilson now got more 'n twenty-five Chrismuses," she announced finally. "And this Drummage"—she made another calculation from a shorter line of notches and held up one lone finger which remained after her counting— " 'pears like he's gotten sixteen but ain' quite shore."

"Masta Hammond a-comin' this mornin'?" Old Lucy queried, running her pink tongue over her toothless gums as though searching in vain for the teeth that had once been there.

"Yas. He say Drummage not go out to de fiel' dis mornin'. Drummage wait here till he come. Think mebbe he's a-goin' to send Drummage in de caffle to New Orleans to be sold." She looked up, trying to hide the tears in her eyes. "If'n Masta Hammond say pore Drummage goin' off in de caffle to be sol' we goin' miss dis boy powerful awful, Maw."

"Goin' ter miss him awful, Big Pearl. Ain' never had none of my kin sol' 'fore. 'Course Masta Hammond kilt po'r Mede and that worse 'n sellin' he but al'ays had yo' 'n' Ol' Mista Wilson. Masta Hammond ain' never sol' yo' ner me ner Ol'

7

Mista Wilson. Goin' to miss this boy much as Mede." She pointed to the bleached skull and the bones up over the fireplace.

Drummage was unperturbed. "Ain' mindin' goin' ter be sold. Hears tell that N'Orleans mighty fine place. Hear tell that Masta Maxwell goin' ter sell me fer a stud nigger. Tha's what I wants. Better 'n stayin' here, a-sleepin' with Olly. Wants ter go, I does."

"If'n yo' ain' got no mo' sap 'n Ol' Mista Wilson, yo' ain' a-goin' ter do much studdin'." Old Lucy giggled in an ascending series of laughs. "Masta Hammond done tried Ol' Mista Wilson on 'bout every wench here at Falconhurst and he ain' took onct. All beef that boy, but no sap in him at all."

"Plenty in me," Drummage boasted. "Masta Hammond knows 'at. Done had me cover that Clarissa wench and she get knocked up in a week."

" 'N yo' still braggin' 'bout it," Lucy mocked him from the bed. "Kinda fergettin', ain' yo', that Masta Hammond never done tol' yo' to cover her? Kinda fergettin' that yo' pestered her in de high weeds 'hind de corn crib. Kinda fergettin', ain' yo', how Masta Hammond paddled yo' ass fer coverin' one o' his wenches 'thout his say so?"

"Take more 'n one to prove yo' gots sap in yo'." Big Pearl made little of Drummage's boasting. "Yo' ain' de only one been a-pesterin' that Clarissa wench. Boys after her thicker 'n houn' dogs after a proud bitch. Why'n't that Ol' Mista Wilson stir hissel'?"

Lucy reached for the gnarled cane which lay beside her on the bed and pounded on the wall.

"Ol' Mista Wilson, yo' a-goin' ter get up or I sendin' Drummage up wid a gourdful o' water?"

A long snore was her only answer.

Drummage, now dressed, opened the cabin door, feeling the impact of the fresh, cool morning on his face after the fetid air of the cabin with its mingled odor of smoke, fried pork, collard greens, sweat, urine and slops. He breathed deeply, glad of the sharp coolness, and ran to the corner of the cabin, where he seized a gourd and poured water over his head. It did not seem to soak the tight curls but merely bedewed it with tiny crystalline drops which sprayed out in the sunlight as he shook his head. The end of his shirt tail served as a towel to wipe his face. Then he dunked the gourd in the water and carried it brimming full into the house.

"Yo' wants Olly up?" he asked.

"Better splash 'im." Big Pearl nodded as Drummage, holding onto the ladder with one hand and trying not to spill the brimming gourd, climbed up. He knelt on the edge of the loft and called to Ol' Mista Wilson. When there was no answer he raised the gourd and threw its contents over the sleeper's face. The big body moved and sat up as the water trickled down over Olly's face and chest.

He grinned. There was no anger, no resentment. Ol' Mista Wilson was almost entirely devoid of emotions.

"Time ter git up." Drummage started to back down the ladder.

Ol' Mista Wilson yawned and threw back the covers. He pulled on his pants and without bothering to use the ladder eased himself over the edge of the loft, supporting himself with his hands until his feet almost touched Lucy's bed. He dropped, landing on the foot of her bed, and grinned as widely at the old lady as he had at Drummage. Ol' Mista Wilson loved everyone because his simple mind had never known what it was to hate. He spoke but seldom, never had an idea of his own, did absolutely what he was told to do, and had resentment towards nobody. Even when he was fighting he had never felt any ill will towards the man he was fighting with. He could gouge out an eye with his big thumb, rip open a man's mouth from ear to ear, twist his scrotum in his big hands, and never feel the slightest degree of animosity towards the man he was torturing. He fought because his Masta Hammond told him to, and if Masta Hammond wanted him to kill another man, that's what Ol' Mista Wilson did— cheerfully.

His huge frame betokened his enormous power but his handsome, rather brutal face was absolutely devoid of expression. He reacted only to purely physical impulses. When he was hungry, he ate; when he became sleepy, he slept; when he desired a woman, he seized the first one that came to hand, threw her to the ground, and took his satisfaction from her. He fought whenever his master arranged fights for him and in his fighting he was almost always successful because of his entire singleness of purpose, abetted by his huge size and superior strength. He had received a minimum of injuries—one ear lobe was missing and a little finger had been chewed off—but these defects, outside of a few scars, were the only evidences of some twenty fights, which had gained his master over thirty thousand dollars. He was one of the showpieces of Falconhurst Plantation—Hammond Maxwell's pure Mandingo fighter—along with the glory of the big house, the broad, carefully cultivated acres, and the six

9

hundred-odd slaves which Hammond Maxwell raised for sale.

Just now Ol' Mista Wilson was hungry. He eyed the wooden bowl that Big Pearl heaped with grits, noted with satisfaction that she doused them with a generous quantity of ham fat, and then started to eat, relishing his food and thanking Big Pearl with his eyes.

Drummage ate more moderately but managed to put away almost as much as Olly. Although not as large as his half-brother, he promised, even in his adolescence, someday to acquire equal proportions. His face, however, was quite different. Ol' Mista Wilson had the rough-hewn strength and beauty of the real African, with his flattened nose, wide nostrils, and large lips, although his skin was not the prune color of the bush Negro but a warm, burnished brown with a tinge of red. Drummage's face lacked the savagery of Ol' Mista Wilson's. His nose was shorter and not so wide-spread, descending from his brow in a straight Grecian line and the nostrils were more sensitve and less flaring. His eyes, so dark-brown as to be almost black, were larger and not so deep set as Olly's, and his lips—full, dark, and moist—were finely outlined, parting to show strong white even teeth. In color he was somewhat lighter and his skin had greater luminosity, highlighted to almost copper. It was his hair which made the greatest difference. Where Olly's was a mat of kinky coarse wool, coming down to a straight line across his forehead, Drummage's was black, shiny, and clustered around his head in tight dark curls that had to be clipped back with shears at least once a month.

"Yo' think Masta Hammond goin' ter send me in de caffle dis year?" He asked the question of Olly, not expecting he would answer, but to his surprise he did. "Don' know, boy. A-wishing' he sen' me. Ev'y un else here been sent and I don' go. Sees 'em marchin' off and I stays. Whaffor I never goes, Maw?" He regarded Big Pearl with some animation.

" 'Cause Masta Hammond has yo' fer his fightin' nigger. Has yo' to entertain he's frien's when them come a-visitin'. Knows yo' cain' be whopped. Makes money on yo' too. Tha's why."

It was almost possible to see the slow mechanics of Olly's thinking. He had achieved an idea, dimly to be sure, but he was now wrestling with it and finally he was able to express it in words.

"If'n I don' fight no mo', den Masta Maxwell, he sell me."

"Yo' jes' try dat, Ol' Mista Wilson. Yo' jes' try dat!" Lucy

10

shook her stick at him from her bed. "Yo' tries deceivin' Masta Hammond and I whops yo' wid dis. Bashes yore fool head in. Looka what Masta Hammond done fer us. We uns got our own cabin. We ain' sold. We Mandingos, we is. Yo' pure Mandingo, boy. Las' pure Mandingo in de whole world. Drummage here, he ain' pure Mandingo. He jes' half. Part Royal Hausa he is on the other half and part white. Masta Hammond say Royal Hausa jes' as good as Mandingo but it ain'. No, it ain'. We's full Mandingo, we is, me 'n' Big Pearl 'n' yo'."

"Ol' Mista Wilson sure a handsome boy." Big Pearl let her hand rest affectionately on his wiry wool. "And Drummage, he more purty even if'n he not all Mandingo." She went to stand in the doorway, shading her eyes with her hand.

"Masta Hammond, he a-comin'. Stop hoggin' them grits and git out here afore de cabin."

"Wants to see him, I does. Wants to see de masta." Old Lucy was trying to get her rheumatic legs out onto the floor. "Masta ain' never forgot Old Lucy." She sank back, exhausted by the effort.

Olly and Drummage left their bowls on the floor and went to stand outside the door. Hammond Maxwell, owner of Falconhurst Plantation, came riding down the dusty lane that led between the slave cabins. His progress was impeded by adoring wenches, saluting bucks, and ecstatic children who raced alongside his horse, screaming his name in their anxiety to be noticed. He flicked his whip at the children, touching them gently on the shoulders; waved back to the men and women, greeting them mostly by name as he passed. His body servant, Brutus, part valet, part major domo, part butler, rode along a couple of paces behind him. Hammond Maxwell was a fine-looking man of about forty-five who looked more youthful than his years, as his blond hair did not show the streaks of gray. His face was florid with good living but his waistline was as athletically trim as a man of twenty-five. Richly, even magnificently dressed in a trim white linen jacket and fawn-colored breeches, he sat his horse with a surety that betokened daily use of the saddle.

At the end of the lane he pulled up in front of Old Lucy's cabin and dispersed the frolicking press of children with his whip, snapping it over their heads without touching them. They retreated, but only for a distance of several yards, where they turned to form a gaping semicircle around the front of the cabin. When Masta came there was always something to see.

11

Brutus, a bright-skinned man, younger than his master but with prematurely grey wool which fitted his head like a steel casque, slid down from his horse and helped Hammond, who had some difficulty dismounting. When he stood on the ground, he leaned heavily against Brutus, and as he walked up the dusty path to the cabin, he limped painfully, putting most of his weight on the Negro. Big Pearl disappeared from the doorway and came back with the one chair her cabin possessed—a rush-seated ladderback with a mended leg. This she placed in the shade of a tall group of sunflowers growing beside the cabin.

"Welcome, masta, welcome. Great day, Masta Hammond suh. Great day when yo' comes to pass de time ob day wid us. Great day!"

Hammond, with Brutus' help, eased himself down into the chair.

"How're yo' Big Pearl and how's Lucy's rheumatiz? Hope it better 'n mine. Guess I'll have to git me a little nigger to dreen it off like my papa did."

"Lucy a-usin' taller for hern. Heats it up I do and rubs it on. Rubs and rubs. Relieves her, it does."

The amenities over, Hammond regarded Drummage and Ol' Mista Wilson, standing in front of him.

"Olly boy, yo' in condition? Some Mista Scott—a Mista John Scott—from up Chattanooga way writ me he's a-comin' by this way to Mobile. Got him a fightin' nigger and heard 'bout yo'. Craves to stop off for a day at Falconhurst and put his boy up 'gin you'. Thinks yo' kin whop him?"

Olly dug one huge black toe into the dust and squirmed in his effort to bring forth his answer. "Yes suh, masta suh. Thinks I whops him."

"Then git yo'se'f over to that grove by the river and start totin' them logs. Gotten to harden yo' up. An' no women! Un'erstan'? No wenchin' fer yo' till after yo' fights. Never could understand why a big gyascutus like yo' ain' got no sap in him. Had yo' cover over fifty wenches, 'sides those yo' covered 'thout my knowin' it, and never did git me a foal from yo' and yo' the only Mandingo lef' in Alabama. Wha's the matter with yo', Olly?"

The big fellow squirmed again.

"Got me plenty o' sap, masta suh. Got me too much. Don't know why it never takes. Gives it to all the wenches but never do no good." He managed a grin. "But they likes it, masta suh. Shore likes it good."

12

Hammond had not been listening. He was appraising Drummage.

"Gettin' to be a big boy, ain' yo', Drum Major. Lessee, yo' 'bout fifteen now. Remembers 'cause yore pappy kilt the night of the fire in the old house and he'd been a-coverin' Big Pearl afore that." He turned to the enormous woman in the doorway.

"Looks like his sire, don' he?"

"That Drumson shore was a purty boy, Masta Hammond suh. 'Members him I do. He more purtier than Mede was."

"Come over here, Drum Major." Hammond's riding whip indicated a spot about two feet in front of him. He waited until Drummage reached there, then held up a hand for him to halt. "Shuck down."

Drummage regarded the not far distant circle of boys and girls who, with rapt attention, were following his every movement. He looked at Big Pearl and at Mamie-Ann, who was leaning out of the one window in her cabin, intent on not missing anything that happened at Old Lucy's.

"Right here, Masta Maxwell, suh?"

"Co'se right here. Where in hell yo' think. Come on—outa them breeches. Ain' got all day."

"Yo' a puttin' Drummage in de caffle dis year?" Big Pearl knew she was overstepping but she relied on the favored position she occupied in her master's good graces.

It was on the tip of Hammond's tongue to answer, "None of your goddam business," as he would to any other slave, but seeing Big Pearl reminded him of so many things in the past, which included some of the happiest and saddest moments of his life, he was willing to overlook her impertinence.

"Who said anythin' 'bout Drum Major goin' in the caffle? Ain' 'tendin' to put him in. Ain' never sold Olly did I? Ain' never sold yo' or Old Lucy did I? Ain' thinkin' o' sellin' Drum Major. Jes' a-lookin' him over. Got things in mind for him, I have. Miz 'Gusta complainin' that I take Brute out o' the house so much these days. I needs him, but Miz 'Gusta say work fer him to do at the big house. That Benoni boy not much good at work, so I'm thinkin' of takin' Drum Major over to the big house and have him housebroke. Miz 'Gusta mighty fond of his sire, she was, and wants me to do somethin' fer Drum Major."

The single button that held Drummage's pants came undone in his slow fingers and the pants fell down into the dust. The wooden buttons slipped out of the torn buttonholes of the shirt and the shirt joined the pants on the ground. Drummage stood naked before his master and—it seemed to him—before everyone else on the plantation. But suddenly he recovered from his embarrassment. He knew his body was something to be proud of in its long, clean lines and its promise of great power to come. He could tell by the expression on his master's face that he had found instant approval. Hammond beckoned him a step nearer and with a practiced hand ran his fingers down Drummage's flanks, squeezed the calves of his legs and circled his ankles. He picked up Drummage's feet, one by one, and examined them in detail, toe by toe, then wiped the dust off his hands on the boy's skin. Finally he cupped the genitals, weighing them, and the boy unconsciously responded with a quick reaction to the warmth of the hands. Hammond Maxwell laughed.

"Quick on the trigger, ain' yo', boy? 'Members now I had to paddle yo' cause yo' were pesterin' that Clarissa wench. Any marks on yore ass?" His hands turned Drummage around to feel the smooth skin of his rump. "Didn' think so—didn' have yo' paddled very hard."

"Hurt though." Drummage dared to speak. If that had been a light paddling he hoped he would never have a hard one.

"Meant it to." Hammond scowled. "Cain' have yo' wastin' yo' sap on scrawny runts like that Clarissa. Good blood in yo', boy. Got to see that it make more good blood. I picks the wenches and I tells yo' when yo' covers them. 'Member that!"

"Yes suh, Masta Hammond suh." Big Pearl didn't intend that Drummage should be punished again. "He min' yo' now, Masta Hammond. He don' fergit that paddlin'. Didn' set down fer three days, he didn'."

Hammond's scowl turned into a grin. "How many times yo' pestered that Clarissa wench?" he asked of Drummage.

"Three times, masta suh."

"Pretty good to git her knocked up. Potent boy, mighty potent. But, yo' keeps yore pants buttoned up over to the big house. Understand?"

"Yes suh, Masta Maxwell suh."

"Yo' says Masta Hammond now, boy. Yo' house servant. Come over when the noon bell rings. Come round to the kitchen door. 'Cretia Borgia lets yo' in and Brute he take care of yo'. Go down to the creek and wash yo'se'f, all over, 'fore yo' come. Got to wash all over every day now. Cain' have no musky niggers in the big house."

"He ain' musky, Masta Hammond suh. Ol' Mista Wilson he mighty musky—smell like a goat sometime—but Drum-

14

mage he never stink." Big Pearl was determined to add to Drummage's distinction.

"Hope he don'. Cain' stand no musky nigger. See that he gits there, Big Pearl." Hammond motioned to Brutus to help him back up on his horse. It was quite a difficult process but Hammond managed to get his leg over the saddle and, with a flick of his whip at the grinning circle of children, he turned and rode down the street.

Big Pearl stepped inside the cabin.

"Masta Hammond, he didn' come in ter see me," Lucy was whining.

"He mighty busy this morning, Maw. But I'se got good news fer yo'. Drummage a-goin' over to the big house to get hisself housebroke. Ain' goin' to be sold."

Old Lucy suddenly and without any apparent reason burst out into tears.

"Death and destruction," she moaned. "Death and destruction when a nigger goes inter the big house. Ain' no fittin' place for 'em. Pore Mede! Got hisself kilt messin' round in de big house. Pore Drumson, got hisself kilt too. Now pore Drummage."

"Hush, Maw, don' take on so. Mighty fine fer our Drummage to git hisself in de big house. We quality niggers now."

Old Lucy hoisted herself up on the pillows, her eyes blazing with indignation. She shook her cane at her daughter.

"Al'ays was quality niggers. Al'ays. We Mandingos, we is."

Chapter 2

DRUMMAGE didn't bother with farewells when he left for the big house. He merely went out and closed the cabin door behind him. Everything he owned was on his back—the ragged trousers and the torn shirt were the sum total of his possessions, except for the broken stub of a comb which he had found on the dump behind the big house. Among all his family, only he had hair that could be combed, for no comb could ever penetrate the thick, kinky wool which covered Olly's skull or the frizzy mop that decorated Big Pearl.

He did not have any regrets about leaving the cabin and his folks. While there, he had enjoyed the protection and dumb companionship of Ol' Mista Wilson; he had received love and affection from Big Pearl and Old Lucy, mingled, to be sure, with a certain amount of discipline and a great number of slaps from Big Pearl's ham-like hand; but there was little in the cabin that he minded leaving.

For the first ten years of his life, Drummage had been a sturdy little animal running around the plantation buck-naked in a herd of other plantation young ones, boys and girls together. Those were halcyon days; with no work to do and no duties to perform, the pack had played from dawn to dusk. Neither playthings nor toys were necessary for their amusement—a stick of wood to float in the stream, stones to throw, trees to climb, mud puddles to splash through and dust to wallow in were enough. They ran, fought, pushed, laughed, cried, and mauled each other as they grew strong and healthy. Then, as they became older, the boys separated and formed groups of their own, which preyed upon the girls.

From as early as he could remember, Drummage knew that boys and girls were different and he knew why. The reproductive processes were never a secret on a plantation whose prime business was the breeding of slaves. Even the children knew what buck was covering what wench. Drummage himself had seen bucks come to his mother's cabin at night and he had peeked down through the cracks in the floor of the loft as he watched the firelight gild their skins while they clutched, wrestled, and moaned on the bed below him. He had early learned the method of self-gratification from his older playmates and had practiced it alone and in groups as well as with Olly in the loft, on those nights when his half-brother was not out wenching or when he was supposedly in training for a fight and was ordered to keep away from women.

When Drummage reached his early teens, he was given a pair of patched breeches which, by their very concealment, had served to make him more conscious of himself. The breeches betokened his approach to manhood, and now the attacks of the male packs on the girls became more frequent. Gradually he became more interested in making certain experiments with the girls than in continuing on with his practices with the boys. But although he found the wenches more interesting and exciting, he still took an active part in the all-male groups when they were swimming in the creek, still found relief and comfort from the warmth of Olly's big hands when he snuggled up to him on chilly nights.

Like all the other children, Drummage had often stared at the big house, awe-struck, from a safe distance, and specu-

16

lated on what glories it might contain behind its white-pillared portico. Huddled together, the children concocted fanciful ideas of what it might be like inside. It represented an unknown world to these little blacks. Nor were they able to glean any information from that lofty race of Negro slaves who were house servants—that high and mighty group of individuals in their sleek black suits and white aproned dresses and their soft polished shoes, their shiny skins and their elegant affectations of gentility. They were indeed a race apart, considering themselves as superior to the rough field hands as the great folks who inhabited the big house felt to them.

Drummage knew the names of the big house people—Masta Hammond Maxwell and Miz 'Gusta, his wife; Miz Sophie, Masta Maxwell's daughter, and Masta Dudley, her husband, together with their two children. He also knew the big house servants by sight. First in importance came old Lucretia Borgia, the cook, whose reputation as a tartar had penetrated to the whole plantation. Then there were Elvira and Cassie, big-busted, small-waisted women who occasionally condescended to walk over to the slave cabins in their clean calico dresses for little social calls in the afternoon. There was also Regine, who was rarely seen and whom Drummage had always thought a white woman until his mother had told him that she too was a Negro, and her son Benoni, who had never been allowed to play with the other children. Then there was Ajax, who drove the shiny barouche, and the men, Merc and Jupe, who worked on the lawns and in the gardens. The plantation slaves stood in deferential awe of these house servants, treating them with almost the same respect and fawning deference they gave to the white folks. To be a servant in the big house was a slave's patent of nobility, even more important than the cherished lightness of color.

"Now, yo' be good boy," Big Pearl had warned Drummage as he stepped out of the house.

"And come back ter see us," Old Lucy had added, recognizing in the boy's new position a constant source of gossip from the big house.

Drummage walked diffidently down the road between the slave cabins, past the blackened masonry posts which alone had survived the burning of the old house and now protruded from the weedy ground like so many broken and discolored teeth. Beyond this, he skirted the burying ground, where a white marble slab with the word "Drumson" on it, marked his father's grave, so Big Pearl had told him. He jumped

17

over the low stone wall to stand before the stone and let his fingers trace the carved letters. Since he could not read, they meant nothing to him, but he knew that his father's name had been Drumson and that these strange markings in some way stood for that name.

It was quiet here, under the cool shade of the live oaks with their festoons of grey moss moving in the gentle breeze. The grass was close-cropped and cool to his bare feet and he marveled at the white-painted iron urns with their wealth of brilliant flowers spilling over the edges. A hitherto unexperienced feeling of pride possessed him to think that his father was here—the only nigger in the white folks' burying ground. He was not too sure of exactly what a father might be, because fathers, as such, were comparatively unknown in a slave community, but he knew that he had some connection with this legendary Drumson who had saved Masta Maxwell's life the night the slaves had revolted and burned the old house. He knew, too, that the all-powerful Miz 'Gusta had insisted that Drumson be buried right alongside the white folks. It was an oft-repeated tale on the plantation, giving satisfaction to the Negro tellers to know that one of their number had achieved such a position.

Reluctantly he left the quiet of the burying ground and skipped down the clean-swept sandy path, through the copse of trees at the bottom of the hill and over the fanciful little high-arched bridge that spanned the slow-moving creek. In a white-painted summerhouse which adjoined the bridge on the opposite side, Miz Sophie—Masta Hammond's daughter—was sitting with her two children, the boy Warren, about ten, and little Amanda, still an infant, along with their black nurse, Blossom, and the boy, Benoni, who was little Masta Warren's body servant. Drummage wanted to look at Miz Sophie because she had such yellow hair but he didn't dare lift up his eyes as he passed her. However, as he was coming down the side of the bridge that faced the summerhouse, gripping his big toes onto the cleats so he would not slip, Miz Sophie halted him.

"Whar yo' a-goin', boy? Don' yo' know fiel' niggers cain' use this bridge? Only house servants. Yo' crosses by the plank down there." She indicated a narrow sway-backed plank, a little way down the stream.

Drummage dared to raise his eyes. He had never been this near to Miz Sophie before and now that he was actually looking at her, he could not take his eyes away from her. Miz Sophie, that glorious yellow-haired creature from the other

18

world of the big house, was cross-eyed—gootch-eyed, the folks called it—and he could not be quite sure whether she was looking at him or not. Allowing for this one glaring defect, she was pretty, but the errant eye so fascinated him that he could think of nothing else.

"I'se a house servant now, mist'ess. Goin' over to de big house jes' now 'cause Masta Maxwell done tol' me to come over. I'se Drummage, Big Pearl's boy." He said it with some amount of pride.

"Come over here." She beckoned to him and he clambered down the bridge to stand at the entrance to the summerhouse.

She eyed him carefully, appraising him with eyes that seemed to strip off his shirt and trousers. Again she beckoned, and he ascended the step and she reached out and laid a hand on his head.

"Yo' Big Pearl's boy, huh? Yo' pappy was Drumson and he the purtiest nigger boy I ever did see. 'Members him afore I went away to school. Shore was a purty boy but think yo're goin' to be purtier. Comin' over to the big house to serve?"

"Yes, mist'ess. Masta Maxwell done sent fer me."

"Then yo' 'members I'm yore Miz Sophie, this here's yore little Masta Warren and this yore little Mist'ess Amanda. This wench, Blossom." She pointed to the young nursemaid, whose head was covered with a multitude of short pigtails, each wound with red yarn so that she bristled like a scarlet hedgehog. "And this, Benoni." She indicated the boy behind her, who, unseen by her, stuck out his tongue at Drummage.

"Yes, mist'ess." Drummage made a jerky little bow which he had seen the other slaves make when talking to a white person.

"Now yo' runs along. Go to de back door and ask for Lucretia Borgia. She set yo' to work. Run along, boy."

And Drummage ran because he had been told to run. He ran up the hill and across the field, past the new cabins which had recently been built behind the big house, until he arrived panting at the kitchen door. Unlike many of the big houses of the South, the kitchen at Falconhurst was an integral part of the house, not a separate establishment. Here he hesitated, not knowing whether to knock or just enter, but his difficulty was solved by the opening of the door and the presence of a huge, melon-breasted black woman with hair like ripe cotton, who filled it.

"Yo' that Drummage boy?"

"Tha's me."

"Yo' answers me 'Lucretia Borgia ma'am' and don't fergit

the 'ma'am,' respectful-like, and de fust time yo' fergits, I clobbers hell outa yo'."

"Yes ma'am, Lucretia Borgia ma'am, ma'am."

She eyed him suspiciously to see if the last "ma'am" had been added in ridicule, but decided his intentions were good.

"Well don' come inter the house till yo' washed all over."

"Washed all over this morning, 'Cretia Borgia ma'am."

"Yo' all sweaty from runnin'. Needs to wash 'gain. 'Sides, we ready to serve dinner and don' want yo' a-clutterin' up my kitchen." She disappeared inside the door and came back in a few moments with a neatly folded parcel of clothes over one arm, a tin cup of soft soap, a big rag and a rough towel in the other.

"Wash yo'se'f good," she admonished. "Cain' have no musky niggers round dis house. Wash under yore arms and in yore crotch. Then put on dese clotheses. They's Benoni's but guess they fits yo' though yo' bigger'n he. When yo' comes back leave them dirty rags in de shed but bring this yere stuff back wid yo'."

"Clothes ain' dirty, 'Cretia Borgia ma'am. My maw she jes' washed 'em."

"Clotheses dirty if'n I says they's dirty and no more back talk. Git!" Her strong hands turned him and faced him back towards the creek. " 'N' see that yo' washes down in that clump o' elders whar Miz Sophie don' see yore nekkedness."

He trudged off, thinking of all the mean things he would like to say to that 'Cretia Borgia ma'am. Once his paw, so Big Pearl had told him, had been head man at the big house. All the servants there were under him and ol' 'Cretia Borgia ma'am didn't even have her stinkin' big ol' foot in the house then. She was still over to the old house, jes' a-cookin' vittles for Masta Maxwell's nigger wench Ellen and his nigger kids. Then, after his paw was kilt and the old house burned with Masta Maxwell's nigger fambly along with it, ol' 'Cretia Borgia ma'am worked herse'f into the new house and there she stayed like a goddam settin' hen, a-runnin' everythin' jus' like she goddam pleased. Some day, Drummage promised himself, he'd be head man at the big house and he'd make ol' 'Cretia Borgia go out and hoe in de fields. He' shore like to see that fat ol' ass of hern a-waddlin' down the rows of corn and maybe he'd jes' take the day off from bein' boss-man at the big house and go out and oversee ol' 'Cretia Borgia and whop her if'n she didn' hoe fast 'nuff. Who was she to be so biggity? She jes' an ord'nary nigger, not Mandingo like his maw and gran'maw. The very thought of humiliating ol' 'Cretia Borgia made him happier.

The elders, reaching out over the water, gave a deep green shade to the sandy-bottomed pool, and the quiet water was cool and limpid, reaching above Drummage's knees. White arabesques of lather covered his adder-slim young body and he splashed in contentment, watching the bubbles float away in the current in swirling, milky eddies. Once out of the water, he found it was chilly under the trees and he shivered as he wiped himself quickly with the rough towel. When he was dry, he slipped into the long trousers of thin black wool and the white shirt, which had a clean smell of laundry soap and hot iron. Both were too small for him—the trousers sausage-tight around his thighs and the buttons of the shirt straining across his chest; he was bigger than Benoni. The clothes brought back the memory of the stuck-out tongue. He'd show that yellow-skinned li'l bastard jes' what's what. To convince himself, he doubled up his arm, feeling the bulge of his biceps with satisfaction. Drummage knew something which perhaps Benoni didn't know, something that Big Pearl had told him. Benoni was his brother. Drumson had sired them both.

He salvaged the broken comb from the pocket of his old pants and ran it through his hair, now tightly curled from the water. The snaggle teeth tore at the tight curls, pulling at the snarls, but he persisted until his hair was plastered to his head in a series of undulations that gleamed in the light. Remembering to get rid of his old clothes, he stopped on the way back and left them in the shed. When he again appeared at the door of the big house, he decided not to knock and boldly pushed the door open, inwardly trembling at his own temerity but outwardly composed and a little pugnacious. He was "in."

"Yore feet clean?" Lucretia Borgia loomed up from the shadows by the stove. "Cain' have yo' a-trackin' up my clean floor. Have ter git Masta Hammond ter have yo' shod cause ain' fittin' ter go round de big house barefoot, 'specially not wid them big feet o' yourn."

"Yas'm, 'Cretia Borgia ma'am, feet's clean and I'se clean all over. Wants to smell me?"

"Don' wants to smell no musky nigger. All yo' Mandingos musky. Kin smell yo' maw a mile away and that Olly"—she held her nose and made a grimace—"whew! He shore stinks, that boy. But come over here. Yo' et?" Her tone became more friendly. There was nothing Lucretia Borgia

21

enjoyed more than to see someone eat the food she cooked.

"Had brekkus," Drummage answered, his nose attuned to the savory smells that were coming from the stove.

"White folks already et and vittles put away, so yo' better have a bite to tide yo' over till supper." She rummaged in a cupboard and handed him a cracked, handleless china cup. "Go out to de spring house and pour yourself a cup of milk. Bring it back here."

When he returned, there was a tin plate with two hot cookies, rich with molasses and raisins and oozing a most delicious odor, sitting on the table.

"Them's yourn." Lucretia Borgia pointed to the plate and Drummage set his cup of milk down on the table. He tasted of one and it was like nothing he had ever tasted before, rich, sweet, and spicy. If this was the kind of food he was going to get at the big house, he was already glad he had come, and he regarded Lucretia Borgia in a new light. Somehow, with the taste of her cookies in his mouth, she did not seem to be quite the ogress he had pictured her. After tasting her cookies, she seemed almost human.

"Thankee, 'Cretia Borgia ma'am, mighty fine bread yo' bakes."

"Tain't bread, cookies. Now yo' better git yo'se'f to work. Don' jes' rightly know what Masta Hammond have in min' fer yo' to do but can' have yo' a-settin' roun' doin' nothin'. Here." She brought a tray full of wooden-handled steel table knives over and put them down on the table. She left them in front of him and returned in a moment with a brick, a small pan of water, and a rag which she placed beside them. "Shine these up, yo' kin. Knows how?"

Drummage shook his head.

Lucretia Borgia showed him how to rub the steel blade against the wet brick to shine it and then how to give it a brighter gleam by polishing it with the rag. The noon meal was over, the dishes washed and put away and the kitchen quiet. Lucretia Borgia collapsed her huge bulk onto a wooden chair and kicked off the misshapen carpet slippers she always wore. With a deep sigh she leaned back, fanning herself with a corner of her apron.

"Brute, he a-comin' back soon from Masta Hammond's room and he tells yo' what he wants yo' ter do. Yo' a-goin' to he'p him—someday maybe yo' be butler too, if'n yo' smart and takes a-holt. Hope yo' not like that Ol' Mista Wilson— he not very bright."

"But he strong"—Drummage was quick to defend Olly—

22

"and he a fighter." The sound of the pantry door opening caused him to turn around. It was Benoni. Drummage's eyes followed him as he closed the door slowly and walked across the floor, making little noise in his soft black-leather shoes. He noted the boy's well-fitting fine clothes, the handsome ivory-colored face with the sullen pouting lips and the long black hair which curled to the boy's shoulders. Benoni in turn regarded Drummage with suspicion and animosity.

"That nigger a-goin' to stay here in the house?" he inquired of Lucretia Borgia, his finger pointing to the newcomer.

"He Drummage, come over to be house servant here."

"Field nigger!" The boy's lips curled in utter contempt. "Awful black, ain' he?"

"He not black." Lucretia Borgia's tone betrayed that she had little affection for Benoni. "And 'sides, he yore brother. He Drummage."

"Ain' no brother o' mine, that black nigger. My mama's other chil'ren all been sol'—Masta Holcomb bought 'em when they's little."

"Don' matter," Lucretia Borgia insisted. "He's pappy same as yourn—Drumson. Yo' two might's well git 'quainted." Lucretia Borgia turned to Drummage. "This yere's Benoni. He Regine's boy but his pappy same as yourn. This boy Miz 'Gusta's pet."

Drummage remembered having thought this Benoni a white boy when he had seen him playing alone around the big house. He looked up at Benoni and grinned, willing to be friendly despite the stuck-out tongue in the summerhouse.

"Pleasured ter know yo', Benoni."

"Yo' two's a-goin' ter bed together." Lucretia Borgia kept on fanning herself. "Li'l Masta Warren a-sleepin' now, Benoni?"

He nodded.

"Then yo' he'ps Drummage wid de knives. When yo' finishes, yo' takes him up on the top floor and shows him whar he sleeps."

Benoni glared at Lucretia Borgia, resenting her authority and resenting even more the fact that he should have to share Drummage's menial work.

"Ain' a-goin' to help nobody with no knives. Ain' called to do no kitchen work. And ain' a-goin' to sleep wid no stinkin' fiel' hand neither. He kin bed hisself down wid Ajax out in de barn. I come here fer Miz 'Gusta. She 'quires that you git her a pitcher col' water from the spring house."

"Miz 'Gusta say dat?" Lucretia Borgia sat up straight in her chair. "She say fer me to fetch it? Yo' a-lyin'. Miz 'Gusta never did say dat."

Benoni was no match for Lucretia Borgia, whose years of authority predated those of Augusta Maxwell, Hammond's wife. He hung his head, not daring to repeat his lie.

"Then yo' gits yo'se'f out to de spring house and fetches de water yo'se'f,"—Lucretia Borgia pointed a long black finger at him—"an' don' yo' tells me what ter do, yo' yellow-skinned imp o' Satan. Masta Hammond says yo' bed wid Drummage, yo' beds wid him. I say yo' show Drummage whar he sleeps, yo' shows him, else'n I paddles yo' ass. Now, go a-runnin' to yo' mama and start a-cryin' and she go to Miz 'Gusta and tell her I 'buse yo'. Den Miz 'Gusta she come to me and say, 'Be good to Benoni, Lucretia Borgia, he delicate.' Delicate! umph! Yo' strong as a mule, yo' is. Den I tells Miz 'Gusta what a lyin' little no-good-fer-nuffin' yo' is an' she paddles yo' ass her own se'f. Go fetch de water fer Miz 'Gusta if'n she wan's it. She say so?"

"Not jes' exackly," Benoni confessed, frightened at Lucretia's wrath for he, like everyone else on Falconhurst Plantation, stayed clear of her when she was in a temper. Even Hammond Maxwell kept out of her way. One swipe of her hand, powered by her quick temper, had been known to floor a field nigger.

Without moving from her chair, she pointed to the tray of knives and the brick. Benoni sat meekly down beside Drummage and reached for a knife and moved it listlessly along one side of the brick. Under Lucretia Borgia's stern eye, he expended more energy on it, and glanced from under his long lashes at Drummage, who was applying himself industriously. Benoni leaned towards Drummage and sniffed.

"He smell clean. Don' stink like no fiel' hand."

"Co'se he don'." Lucretia Borgia's good will towards Drummage was being won over by his humility.

"Then don' min' if'n he beds with me." Benoni applied himself vigorously to the knife. "Takes him up and shows him, I will."

"Thought yo' would." Lucretia Borgia relaxed. Her word had not been disputed. Once more she was the real mistress of Falconhurst, entirely in command.

They continued to work under her watchful eye until the whole tray of knives gleamed brightly. As the work progressed, they entered into competition, trying to see which could finish a knife before the other. The hostility between them gradually relaxed and when they were finished Benoni jumped up from his chair and beckoned to Drummage.

"Come along nigger. I shows yo' whar us'ns beds."

Chapter 3

FALCONHURST was undoubtedly the most unusual plantation in Alabama during that period. Unlike the other big and once flourishing plantations which surrounded it, Falconhurst alone presented a prosperous appearance. Its elaborate big house, with its tall white columns gleaming against the dull pink of the brick walls, commanded a long avenue of trees that led out to the gateposts at the main road, and its gardens and lawns were carefully tended. The other big houses of cotton plantations were shabby and in bad repair, sitting forlornly in the midst of their straggling acres. Their slave quarters were tumbling down and their slaves growing old and decrepit along with the dwindling fortunes of their white masters. Not so Falconhurst! Its slave quarters were well built and cleanly whitewashed and the slaves themselves, some six hundred of them, were young, vigorous, and, for the most part, fine specimens of manhood and womanhood. The well-kept acres surrounding the big house were lush with corn, grass, and carefully cultivated fields of vegetables, and its pastures were filled with sleek cattle. But there was a conspicuous absence of cotton—only a few fields whose yield was used for the spinning and weaving of plantation cloth.

This was because Hammond Maxwell and his father before him had long ago abandoned the cultivation of cotton on their worn-out acres and concentrated on a new and unique cash crop which rose in value every year—slaves. With no new slaves being imported into the country from Africa (Goddam the abolitionists up North and in England.) except the paltry number smuggled through from Cuba, the demand for human livestock had risen and Hammond had been foresighted enough to cash in on it. He bred his slaves as carefully and as selectively as some men bred fine horses and blooded cattle. The big ledgers in his office contained complicated genealogies of all the slaves, and before he allowed any of his stud bucks to cover a breeding wench he made a careful search of the bloodlines of each. For this reason there was no indiscriminate breeding on his plantation, nor were family groups encouraged. A buck was given some three months of nightly companionship in a cabin which housed two, three, or even four other couples. If at the end of that time there were no results, Hammond tried both wench and buck with others and then, if they were still unproductive, they were sold. Within a week, or at the most two, after the child was born, it was taken away from the mother and raised in a common nursery. In only a few cases were children allowed to grow up under maternal care and these rare cases were usually "fancies," which Hammond had decided to keep for himself rather than sell.

As a result of his care and the unassailable excellence of his stock, Falconhurst slaves bore a hallmark of quality and their reputation was known through the South. Men bragged of having Falconhurst slaves on their plantations, and, since they were as expensive as such fine cattle would of course be, they were usually used to improve the breed on other plantations. The yearly auction in New Orleans, to which Hammond Maxwell sent his selected caffles of from sixty to a hundred slaves, were always well attended, with every slave sold at high price and eagerly bid for. Male slaves were usually sold as they approached the age of twenty, nearing the peak of their virility; female slaves were as a rule bred at the age of thirteen or fifteen and allowed to produce some four or five children before being sold. As befitted valuable merchandise, they were well treated, well fed, and well housed. Only on rare occasions was a slave flogged, for the welts that whips left on his back ruined his value. Punishment for most offenses was short rations, separation of a man from his woman, or confinement in the slave pen. The entire plantation at Falconhurst centered around its cash crop—its slaves. The produce of its fields was to feed them, its dairies gave them strength and vigor, its hens laid eggs for them to eat, its spinning and weaving sheds produced clothes for them to wear, and this complete, concentrated endeavor produced the finest specimens of Negro manhood and womanhood that ever stepped up onto an auction block.

The big house, built some fifteen years before, stood at some little distance from the main plantation outbuildings which had clustered around the house that had burned down soon after the new house had been built. In addition to the old slave quarters, the new house had its own street of slave cabins, where selected males and females were kept. Hammond Maxwell employed no white overseer. His only delegation of authority was to trusted slaves who had become bossmen in their respective trades. Nobody at Falconhurst worked very hard or was driven very hard. The Falconhurst slaves were not work horses and one of the greatest difficulties was to keep them all busy.

Drummage found the work at the big house considerably more difficult and onerous than the light work to which he had been accustomed in the fields. There were so many new things to learn; he had entered into an entirely new way of life, far different from the easy, free and primitive existence he had hitherto known in Old Lucy's cabin. There life had been simple. One ate, and slept, and worked in the fields. When one felt the call of nature he went behind a bush. It was a life unhampered by the many and complex appurtenances of civilization. It required no particular thought or concentration to chop corn, to carry water for the field hands, to slop pigs or to milk a cow. Eating meant conveying food to one's mouth in the easiest and quickest way, usually with one's fingers or, as in the case of Old Lucy's ménage, with a wooden spoon from a wooden bowl. Clothes were no problem when they consisted of a pair of rough osnaburg breeches and a tow linen shirt, and shoes were nonexistent.

Work was only from sunup till sundown and never very difficult. After one was finished, he was free to join the group of friends, talking about the wenches, anticipating the trip in the caffle to New Orleans, or bragging about the prowess he'd show when he became stud man on a big plantation.

Such was the easygoing life of the plantation slave at Falconhurst where there was little cotton to be chopped and picked and no white overseer to curse and whip. But once inside the big house, Drummage found himself surrounded by a multitude of seemingly useless things, all of which occupied important places in the complicated lives of white people. There were so many of these fanciful things and so many special places where they had to be kept; so much care had to be taken in handling them, so much work expended on their upkeep. In Big Pearl's cabin a wooden candlestick held a tallow dip, but here in the big house the candlesticks were of brass or silver and must be polished every day. The wooden spoons that Big Pearl used were certainly as efficient as the ornamental silver spoons, and if one were lost or broken it was a simple matter to whittle out another. But the silver spoons must be continually polished, handled with great care, wrapped up in flannel, and treated as tenderly as a setting of eggs. Here in the big house there were lamps which must be filled with oil, chandeliers which had to have candles replaced daily, china chamber pots to be emptied and washed, draperies, rugs, pictures, and a thousand other cluttering things which must be washed, swept, brushed, shined, polished, put away and taken out, and could neither be lost, broken, nor misplaced.

All of this complicated procedure meant rising before daybreak and working sometimes until after midnight. It meant a continual repetition of "Yes, masta suh," and "No, mist'ess ma'am." It meant wearing black pants and black shoes and a spotless white shirt and white coat. It meant staying inside the oppressive walls of the big house for days at a time, when one didn't see the outside world or hear any of the gossip of life that went on outside. It meant scuttling down to the creek on chilly mornings and stepping into the icy water for a quick wash and then having Lucretia Borgia sniff one's armpits to see that he had not cheated.

But most of all, to Drummage, it meant the loss of youthful companionship. He missed the free give-and-take of his friends and their jokes and ready laughter. The severely monastic life dammed up a torrent of unspent forces within him, creating an unbounded energy which enabled him to do all his daily tasks and then peopled his dreams with voluptuous fantasies.

His official position in the house was that of apprentice to Brutus, the butler and nominally the head of all the servants, although Brutus' domain stopped abruptly at the kitchen door where Lucretia Borgia reigned supreme. Actually her influence extended into every phase of life at the big house. For a time, between the elder Mr. Maxwell's death and Hammond's return from temporary exile in Texas, she had run the entire plantation herself, building up a stock of slaves which had been instrumental in giving Hammond his position as a man of great wealth rather than a well-off slave breeder. Lucretia Borgia had never relinquished a tittle of the authority she had so laboriously acquired, and she never intended to. Although Brutus was butler and to all intents and purposes the head of the house, it was she who really ran it. Fortunately for Drummage, he had early established his place in her good graces, partly because of her own preference for such a handsome lad and partly because of the dislike she shared with him for the boy Benoni.

All the servants knew that Benoni had been spoiled. His

mother was the octoroon Regine who, before Hammond Maxwell's marriage to Augusta Devereaux, his second wife, had been Hammond's bed wench. After his marriage she continued on in the house as Miss Augusta's maid, giving birth to a posthumous child by Drumson, Drummage's father. This was the boy Benoni, who had inherited his mother's lightness of color, her beauty and her physical charm and might have had a disposition to match, had he not been so overly humored and petted. Not only his mother but Miss Augusta herself and later, after she was married, Miss Sophie, had all contrived to indulge the lad, making him selfish, wilful, and conceited to such a degree that it was now almost impossible to live with him. His tattling tongue and his dislike of all the other slaves whose darker color, he thought, made them inferior persons to himself, had produced in him an air of superiority and nasty snobbishness which was balanced by a fawning subservience to all the whites. His particular animosity was now directed towards Drummage, to whom he had taken an instant dislike on their first meeting. Another youth, his own age, right in the big house, would surely be a rival, and he made it plain from the beginning that he would accept no claimant for his position. Benoni's enmity was apparent and Drummage returned it in kind, although inwardly he would have welcomed Benoni's friendship.

Of almost equal age and sired by the same father, they were in distinct contrast. Each partook of the genes of his mother although there was a decided resemblance between the two boys, inherited from their common father. Benoni was smaller, lighter, and handsome in a pretty way, with regular Caucasian features, belied only by a slight thickening of the lips and widening of the nostrils. Drummage was bigger, taller, heavier, and much darker, with a nobility to his Negroid features which far exceeded the prettiness of Benoni. Neither had kinky hair—Benoni's falling in long locks to his shoulders, Drummage's covering his head with a glossy cap of black curls.

Because of his size, Drummage appeared the older of the two, although in truth he was only a few weeks senior to Benoni. Had he dared take advantage of his physical superiority over the smaller boy he certainly would have had the advantage. But Benoni was protected by his mother, Miz 'Gusta, and Miz Sophie, so that he enjoyed immunity. As it was, they were like two gamecocks, and whenever they encountered each other there was a rising of hackles, an appraised eying of each other, and a sharpening of spurs.

Through his determination that nobody should usurp his position in the affections of the whites, Benoni did everything possible to discredit Drummage in their eyes. His fertile imagination was constantly embroiling his rival in one difficult problem after another. A cup which Drummage had only moments before hung from its hook in the pantry would be found shattered on the floor. Drummage's fault! A silver spoon was missing in the nightly inventory that Brutus always made. Drummage's fault! A spill of wine on the fresh table cloth where he had only moments before placed the cut-glass decanter. Again Drummage's fault! Regardless of how painstaking he tried to be with his chores, many things of which he knew himself to be innocent were laid to him and earned him punishment. Had it not been for Brutus, who really liked him—having worshiped his father—and Lucretia Borgia, who always covered up for him as much as she could, poor Drummage would have been subjected to so many whipping that his back would have been permanently scarred. As it was, neither Miz 'Gusta nor Masta Hammond ever heard of most of his supposed indiscretions. Outside of the mental anxiety which he experienced—and Benoni's frustrations in realizing that his carefully laid plans for his rival's downfall so often went awry—things proceeded with an apparently calm surface.

The nights were the times that Drummage hated the most. Despite their constant antagonism throughout the day, the boys were forced to spend their nights together in the same bed. Their mutual animosity produced a strained silence which seemed intensified by their physical nearness. To avoid even touching Benoni, Drummage sought the very edge of his mattress, yet he always awoke in the morning in a tangle of arms and legs with his bedmate. When he first woke up, the contact seemed warm and pleasant, reminiscent of such hours with Olly, and he found himself sensually satisfied with Benoni's nearness. But when he was fully awake and conscious of the fact that it was Benoni who was pressing against him, he was revolted at the thought of touching him and moved as far away as possible. Drummage had the feeling that if he yielded, their enmity might change to intimacy but yield he would not and his refusal widened the breach between them.

Drummage was lonely for a friend, but the only two of his own age in the big house were Benoni and Blossom, who had been brought in and trained as a nursemaid for little Miz Amanda, Sophie's daughter.

Blossom, he sensed, would like to be friendly with him, although he saw very little of her for she spent most of her time in Sophie's big room on the second floor with little Miz Amanda, Masta Warren and Benoni. But on those rare occasions when he met her in the halls or in the pantry, Blossom always had an inviting smile and a pleasant word for him. Once, when they met in the deserted corridor of the third-floor servants' quarters, she had invited his embrace and allowed him to push her up against the wall where they clung together in mutual anticipation until they heard footsteps coming up the stairs. Drummage had to duck into his own room and close the door, to hide the visible evidence of his excitement.

Since that day nothing had happened between them, but the remembrance of their one embrace gave him hope for an alleviation of his enforced celibacy, even though Blossom, with her flat rather stupid face, did not attract him. Her room, with its closed door down the hall from the one he shared with Benoni, presented a nightly temptation. Even greater, however, than the pressing need which impelled him towards that door was the remembrance of the paddling he had received for his association with Clarissa, and Hammond's strict injunction that any wenches to be covered were to be designated by himself.

So for many nights when he first came to the big house Drummage lay awake, staring into the darkness, listening to Benoni's regular breathing, and wishing he were back in the loft over Big Pearl's cabin. There at least he had had the companionship of Olly. He tried to console himself by remembering that Blossom was not pretty, or even provocative as Clarissa had been. Still, she was female and her body had other compensations than her face. He needed her. But all he had near him was Benoni, whom he hated.

Eventually he became accustomed to sleeping in the big house and managed to fall asleep from sheer exhaustion. And, since enmity cannot forever keep its sharp edge, the feeling between himself and Benoni became dulled, and they managed a few words of conversation with one another. There was still no intimacy of friendliness between them, but they were able to discuss trivial things of mutual interest. Drummage found himself so tired after the long day's work that he fell asleep as soon as his head touched the pillow; it took several poundings on the door by Lucretia Borgia in the morning before he could arouse himself sufficiently to slip out of Benoni's arms and get dressed.

One evening, after a particularly difficult day when he had first taken up his duties with Brutus in the dining room, he went up to his room around midnight, so completely weary that he could hardly keep his eyes open while he shucked off his clothes. During the long meal which the white folks ate he had stood beside Brutus, scarcely daring to move for fear he would do something wrong. He had kept his eyes on the big fan over the table, which was being pulled by a young lad out in the kitchen, and its motion had so hypnotized him that he had found himself swaying back and forth on his feet in a synchronized motion with the fan.

He had already taken off his shoes and socks when Benoni, whose duty it was to stay with young Dudley until he was soundly sleeping, entered. While Drummage was slipping out of his clothes, Benoni spoke to him. His voice lacked the usual irritation.

"Yo' shore sleeps sound, don' yo'? Sleeps jes' like a fiel' hand. And how yo' snores."

"Snores if'n I wants to. Yo' snores too."

"How yo' know I snores. Yo' ain' never awake."

"Hears yo' sometimes."

"Hear anythin' else?" Benoni put the question cautiously.

Drummage shook his head, too weary to reply, and slipped into bed. He was asleep before Benoni blew out the candle and crawled over him to his place by the wall. But that night he awoke soon after dropping off to sleep. The room seemed strangely quiet and he missed the regular sound of his bedmate's breathing. Slowly, so that he could withdraw his hand if it encountered the other's flesh, he reached along the bed, but Benoni was not there. Well, so much the better, he thought. But the unaccustomed luxury of having the bed all to himself and the possibilities it offered for private self-indulgence which had so long been denied him kept him awake. Yet even when he had accomplished that which he desired, in a quick spurt of relief, he was still unable to go back to sleep, for he was consumed with curiosity as to where Benoni might be. He might have gone to the servants' privy outside the house behind the barn but this seemed quite impossible, for even had the call of nature been peremptory, there was always the chamber pot under the bed. He might have felt ill and gone to his mother's room, but as she occupied the small room beside Miz 'Gusta's on the second floor it would necessitate Benoni's walking through his mistress's room. Then where could he be? Drummage considered other possibilities. Out to the spring house for a drink

32

of water? No, that would be the last place that Benoni would go, for he was scared to death of snakes and dreaded to go to the spring house even in the daytime. Could he have gone down to Brutus' room on the second floor? No, because Brutus was covering a wench who came nightly from the quarters and Benoni would not dare to disturb them. Lucretia Borgia? Benoni disliked her as much as she did him. Merc and Jupe? Benoni always pinched his nose together with his fingers when he came near them for he said they smelled musky. Elvira and Cassie? Their dislike of him was as evident as was Lucretia Borgia's.

That left only Blossom, and if Benoni was with her he had certainly stolen a march on Drummage, who had been dreaming of just such an expedition for some time. But would Benoni dare such a thing? If there was one thing that Masta Hammond was strict about it was a buck covering a wench without his consent.

Yet . . . Benoni must be with Blossom. Drummage was consumed with anger, jealousy, and curiosity. He slipped out of bed and into his pants and carefully lifted the latch of the door. The long corridor with a window at each end was shrouded in darkness, relieved only by a wan light that entered the far window from a late-rising moon. It was enough to show the outlines of the doors along the hall. In his bare feet, making no noise, Drummage tiptoed down the hall. He heard Lucretia Borgia's stertorous breathing coming from her room, heard the deep breathing of Merc and Jupe, listened at Elvira's and Cassie's door and heard them chattering inside. The next door was Blossom's.

Quietly he knelt before the door, applying his ear to the hole where the latch-string passed through. There was a sound of movement inside, the rustling of the corn-husk mattress accompanied by a series of little soft moans which he recognized as Blossom's and a heavy breathing which must be Benoni's. As he listened the moans increased in intensity and the thrusting of the mattress became more violent. There was a hoarse gasp and a little cry of urgency, and then quiet.

Drummage sensed that it was all over. His curiosity had been satisfied—at least he knew where Benoni was. But his need, satisfied so shortly before, had returned with his eavesdropping, and this need increased his jealousy and his anger against Benoni. He was tempted to wait until Benoni came out and give him a trouncing, but he realized that this would wake the entire servants' floor. Better to bide his time and return to bed. As he passed Lucretia Borgia's door, a floor board

33

creaked under his feet and he stood still, frozen in terror, but no sound came from her room other than her labored breathing. He reached his own room safely and crawled back into bed. In a few moments he heard the creaking of the board in the hall and the door opened slowly. Benoni's hand on the latch eased it down carefully and in another moment he was beside the bed. Drummage feigned sleep while, with the utmost care, Benoni crawled over him to the extreme edge of the bed beside the wall.

"That goddam li'l bastard," Drummage thought. "He gits ever'thin'. Al'ays gits ahead o' me. Now he's got hisself that Blossom wench and I hope he gits hisself caught."

Should he tell on him? No, he could not prove it. Besides, the more nimble-witted Benoni would somehow manage to turn the tables on him and then he would get paddled again. He clenched his fists as he listened to Benoni's satisfied snores and hated him more than ever.

Chapter 4

THERE FOLLOWED a couple of months of feverish activity, which extended to everyone on Falconhurst Plantation, even to the white folks and the house servants. Hammond Maxwell was making up his fall caffle of slaves for the New Orleans market—an annual event toward which all the work, planning, and strategy of the entire plantation had been directed for a whole year. This was Falconhurst's cash crop—the strong-limbed and handsome, the dark-skinned and brown-skinned, the wenches heavy with child and the tall bucks with unlimited potentials in their loins.

It was an event eagerly awaited by whites and blacks alike. To the Maxwell family it meant a sojourn in the city with the luxurious delights of the Saint Louis Hotel awaiting them. To the blacks it signified that final great day, so long anticipated, when they stepped out into the world, beyond the limits of Falconhurst and all they had known of life within its narrow confines. Not a single one of the blacks who made up the caffle regretted his or her lot. From childhood each buck had looked forward to this day, for it had been discussed, lauded, and embroidered upon ever since he could remember. The Falconhurst caffles were never shackled.

There was no need for it, for there was not one of the bucks who did not anticipate a life of Elysian ease as a stud nigger on some large plantation, with a continuous round of wenches to cover, no work to do, and plenty of time to sleep, together with enormous meals to replenish his strength. The wenches looked forward to being covered by strange, unknown bucks and to prolific breeding which would enhance their esteem in the eyes of their new masters. Falconhurst had been good and Masta Maxwell had been a kind master but something better was ahead. Ee-yah!

For weeks before the caffle departed the whole plantation took on a holiday air of anticipation. Armed with his enormous calfskin-bound ledgers, Hammond sat behind a deal table in the shade of a magnolia tree. The entire male population of full-grown bucks was assembled before him, and as each approached the table at the calling out of his name Hammond looked up his entry in the studbook, considered the boy's age and breed, and then looked the boy himself over carefully to decide whether he should be sold or not. If he had any apparent physical imperfection he was slated to be sold to the first itinerant slave dealer who came to Falconhurst—an ignominious and bitter end which every boy dreaded. But there were few who did not pass this first test, for over the years Hammond had carefully weeded out any who did not meet his high standards, and these had long since departed, stumbling along in a caffle behind some slave dealer's buckboard.

In addition to records of sire, dam, and date of birth, the book contained each man's stud capacity and how many children he had sired. If it showed that he had sired none, he still might be sold with the caffle, but it would be stated when he stood up on the block that he was not a potential breeder. Such was Hammond Maxwell's way of maintaining his reputation and the trustworthiness of his merchandise. The average age for sale was between eighteen and twenty, when most bucks had propagated eight or ten foals before they were sold and when they were in prime condition to sire more for their next master. As each man was chosen, a small red wooden disc attached to a string was hung around his neck—a decoration as coveted and as proudly worn by these black boys as a gold and enameled star in the courts of Europe.

After this general selection of the men—a process which was never hurried because Hammond thoroughly enjoyed this yearly inventory—the same procedure was followed with the women, particular care being taken to choose wenches for the caffle who either were obviously pregnant or who, before the sale took place, would give birth and be able to mount the block with infants in arms. In this respect Hammond never cheated. Some breeders, in order to get rid of a barren wench at a high price, would substitute the child of another woman as proof positive of her breeding capacity, but those of Hammond's wenches who were barren were sold with a plain statement of the fact. Buyers all over the South had great respect for the superiority of the Falconhurst breed and for the word of its owner.

Once the initial selection had been made a more thorough inspection ensued. All the men who wore the red discs were assembled in the big barn on a bright sunny day where once again Hammond Maxwell confronted them from an armchair, placed with its back to the light which came in through the big wide-opened doors. Each man shucked down, stripping himself of shirt and pants, and waited for his final inspection. Here again Hammond was slow and meticulous and his examination of each man was a painstaking procedure. No Falconhurst slave was ever sold with a welted back as evidence of his unruliness or with scars betokening that he was a fighter. Slaves who had such marks were disposed of to those same itinerant slave dealers and disappeared from the plantation overnight. It was a mark of pride to Maxwell that he had never sold at public sale a slave with a disfigured back. In his zeal to see that each man was as perfect as possible, every inch of the fellow's skin was carefully examined and the smallest pimple caused a look of consternation on Hammond's face. The fellow's teeth were checked by Hammond's own finger, his buttocks were spread apart for assurance that he was not suffering from piles, and his genitals were scrupulously examined, the foreskin pulled back and the testicles weighed. He was made to jump up in the air, run and fetch a thrown stick, and measure up in all ways to the Falconhurst standard. Only then did the coveted red disc become his certified possession. Naturally the examination was confined only to the fellow's body—his mentality was never questioned except for the fact that he could understand and follow orders. The Maxwell breeding was entirely selective—the deformed and the idiotic had all been disposed of at birth or soon after.

Weeks of almost complete idleness for the lucky ones chosen followed the final selection, which this year had resulted in over a hundred males, and some forty females of whom thirty were big with child. No work was required of the men with the red discs, except for long periods of strenuous exercise during which they ran, wrestled, and carried heavy logs to build up their bodies and harden their muscles. They were, however, much to their regret, separated from the wenches they were covering and taken to a special shed for this last period of conditioning, where they were locked up every night and carefully watched over during the day. Each evening they rubbed each other's bodies with goose oil, to make their skin soft and pliant, and each morning they were herded down to the river where they scrubbed themselves with soft soap and grass until their bodies shone. Nails were pared close and even; such hair as needed cutting was clipped close except on those few pates where an adulteration of Negro blood with white had resulted in longer hair, which was allowed to grow long and combed and oiled until it glistened.

Even the big house felt the stir of increased activity. Miss Augusta and Miss Sophie copied out entries from the studbook and enclosed each separately in an envelope to be given to the purchaser. Lucretia Borgia was in a tizzy of activity, getting together garments for the men and women to wear, and Drummage made innumerable trips between the big house and the sewing house with piles of new garments and patched old ones. Every slave who left Falconhurst departed in well-worn breeches and shirts or osnaburg dresses, but the wagons were loaded with hampers in which there was a completely new outfit for the great day when each man or woman would ascend the block and become, for a brief moment at least, the cynosure of all eyes.

Elvira, Cassie, and even the elegant Regine were put to stitching seams, sewing on wooden buttons, and making buttonholes. Brutus was in constant attendance on Hammond throughout the day and far into the night, which left all the household duties for Drummage, in addition to the extra work which the preparation of the caffle entailed. Even the indolent Benoni was given duties in the cobbler's shop where the workers were preparing the rough shoes and the heelless slippers that the men and women would wear. Benoni grumbled about working outside the house and came back from the shop each time complaining to his mother about how the rough hides hurt his hands. But although she petted him and greased his hands with mutton tallow, she dared not speak to the master about it.

The only person who was not caught up in the hustle and

bustle was Blossom, whose ailing of late had served to lighten her duties. One morning, as the other slaves were sitting down to breakfast and Lucretia Borgia slid a plate of grits dripping with ham fat before her, Blossom jumped up from the table, her hand over her mouth, and scuttled out the back door. Those at the table stopped eating to listen to the sounds of retching outside. When Blossom returned her face was drawn and livid. Unable to face the sight of food, she did not return to the table but slumped down in a chair by the door, shoulders hunched, her face buried in her hands, ready to dash out again should it be necessary.

"What's the matter wid yo'?" Lucretia Borgia looked up from her plate and surveyed the luckless Blossom with little sympathy. "Ain' no place round here fer ailin' folkses. Better git yo'se'f on yore feet and carries li'l Miz 'Manda's brekkus up to her."

"Cain'."

"What yo' means 'cain'!" Lucretia Borgia got up from the table and lumbered over to her, her hand raised in a menacing gesture. "Yo' means 'Cain', Miz Lucretia Borgia, ma'am,' doesn't yo'? Ain' yo' a-fergettin' how to 'dress yore betters?"

"I'se too sick to 'member. Awful sick, Miz' Cretia Borgia, ma'am. Sick like to die I am and if'n I die yo' be sorry."

"Humph! Yo' ain' a-goin' ter die." The big black woman cupped the girl's chin in her hand and yanked her face up. Her big lips pursed themselves in an unasked question while she scrutinized the girl's face, her eyes like boring gimlets. But Blossom twisted her face away and refused to meet the older woman's eyes. Suddenly Lucretia Borgia's big hand reached out, clutched a handful of the girl's dress and lifted her up.

"Yo' knocked up?" she demanded.

"What yo' mean?"

"I mean has yo' been a-spreadin' yore laigs fer some buck 'thout Masta Hammond's a-knowin'? Yo' been lettin' someone a-pester yo'? Yo' in foal?"

"Ain' let nobody a-pester me." The denial lacked the ring of truth. Blossom hung her head, refusing to raise it to look at her accuser.

"Yo' knocked up! I knows it. Gal like yo' a-gettin' sick afore a plate of vittles in the morning sure sign. Yo' missed yo' period?"

"Ain' been a-sleepin' with no one." Blossom was astute enough to realize that this one sweeping denial covered everything.

"Ain' no wench ever did git knocked up jes' a-lookin' out the winder. On'y way she gits herself knocked up is to let some buck push it inter her." She got a surer hold on the girl's dress and propelled her across the kitchen to the door that led upstairs to the servants' quarters, kicked open the door, and pushed her up the stairs ahead of her. Those seated at the table had stopped eating, and now the women smiled knowingly while the men grinned and winked at one another.

"Yo' been a-pesterin' that kid?" Brutus asked of Merc.

"Ain' had me no leanin's toward that Blossom wench. She too flat-faced fer me," Merc said. " 'Sides, Masta say Jupe 'n' me kin pester Elvira 'n' Cassie when we craves to."

"She too li'l fer me." Jupe shook his head in denial. "Gits me a li'l one like that, she screams so she wake up the whole house. I too heavy fer a li'l thing like that."

"He shore is." Cassie giggled, looking at Jupe with an air of possession. " 'Sides, if'n I kotch him a-crawlin' in wid dat Blossom wench, I smacks him good."

"Don' look at me," Ajax said as Brutus looked in his direction. "Ain' had nothin' to do with her. Yo' knows I bin a-coverin' that Clementina wench Masta Hammond done give me, out'n de barn. Got her knocked up good fer de caffle. 'Sides, how's I goin' ter git in de house nights from de barn?"

Brutus accepted Ajax' explanation and now there were only two males left at the table—Drummage and Benoni. Strangely enough Brutus bypassed Benoni.

"Looks like yo', Drummage. Yo' sleeps alongside o' Blossom. Easy fer yo' ter git to her."

Drummage had no opportunity to deny, for just then Lucretia Borgia appeared dragging the weeping Blossom behind her.

"Ain' no need fer yo' to ask Drummage," she said with an accent of authority that ended all further discussion. "He done it. Blossom say so and she shore knocked up."

Drummage looked from Lucretia Borgia to Brutus, to the weeping Blossom and then back to Benoni, who met his gaze with an absolutely blank expression on his face. He waited, expecting Benoni to confess that he had been the one with Blossom, but he made no move to speak and merely appeared an interested spectator.

"Didn' do it." Drummage himself felt the lack of conviction in his denial. He could see by the expression on all the faces looking at him that he was already condemned and mere words would not remove their certainty.

Lucretia Borgia pushed Blossom roughly down into a chair and then ordered the others to finish their breakfast and get about their work. One by one they skipped out and Benoni was the first to leave. When they were all gone, Drummage walked over to the stove where Lucretia Borgia was standing.

"Didn' do it, Miz 'Cretia Borgia ma'am. Wanted to awful but didn'. Knows who done it though. Benoni, he done it."

"Hush yo' mouf. That li'l squirt, Benoni, he ain' got no sap in him. He jes' a boy. Cain' knock up no wench nohow. He so li'l-peckered he ain' got 'nuff to stick in her. Don' go a-sayin' Benoni done it." She shook an admonitory finger at him. "Now yo' waits here. Don' yo' leave. Masta Hammond got ter see yo' n' Blossom soon's he finish he's brekkus. 'N' don' yo' go a-tellin' Masta Hammond that Benoni pestered Blossom. He know better and he know yo' a-lyin' and if'n they's one thing Masta Hammond hates it's fer a nigger to lie to him. Better a nigger chop off'n his own hand 'n to lie to Masta Hammond."

"But Benoni did, Miz 'Cretia Borgia ma'am." Drummage felt he must make her believe him.

"Yo' saw'd him?"

"No, not 'zackly but I heared him."

"Hearin' ain' a-seein'. Hearin' don' mean nuffin'. Yo' set here with Blossom and don' yo' skip out. Yo' wait."

And wait Drummage did, staring across the room at his still weeping accuser who refused to meet his gaze.

"Whaffor yo' wants to lie 'bout me, yo' flat-faced, big-nosed homely wench yo'?" he yelled across at her. "Yo' knows it were that Benoni. Whaffor yo' wants to lie 'bout me?"

"Wan't Benoni. Was yo'!" She lifted her head long enough to glare at him. "Yo' knows it was. Comin' to my room at night a-rapin' me. Didn' want ter do it but yo' made me. Yo' think that li'l Benoni make me? Clobber him if'n he try. Yo' too big so cain' clobber yo'. 'N' yo' hurted me awful too."

"Hush yo' moufs, both o' yo'." Lucretia Borgia appeared in the pantry door, hand upraised. "Don' crave ter hear 'nother word out'n yo'. Masta Hammond he settle yo' when he comes." She looked up to see Benoni at the open door. He had a wide grin on his pretty face and he delivered his message with a malicious verve which was not wasted on Drummage.

"Masta Hammond wants to see both of yo' in his office 'fore he eats his brekkus. Right now! Say fer yo' to hop to it."

Lucretia Borgia yanked Blossom up from the chair and gave her a shove towards the pantry door. Drummage followed on reluctant feet, dreading the necessity of facing his master and knowing full well that he would not be believed. Once again Benoni had stacked the cards against him.

With Benoni skipping a few steps in front of them, they walked through the dim mahogany-paneled dining room and the airy lightness of the big parlor with its chandelier of glittering crystals, through the pillared archway that led into the big central hall and across the polished boards into the pale green-and-gold splendor of the ladies' drawing room, then through the elaborate rosewood Belter of the gentlemen's room and into the small room at the back of the house, which Hammond had used as a bedroom before his marriage to Augusta Devereaux but now used as the plantation office.

He was sitting behind a green baize-covered table and looked up only momentarily from his ledgers as Benoni opened the door and ushered Drummage and Blossom in. Hammond's face was grim as he glanced up at them, then he returned to his laborious writing in the book. Neither Drummage nor Blossom spoke, standing awkwardly before the presence of the man who owned them.

"Here that Drummage and Blossom." Benoni stated a most evident fact.

"Then yo' go." Hammond pointed to the stairs at the side of the room which led up to the second floor. "Miz Sophie a-waitin' fer yo'."

His pen scratched on the paper and he frowned at the slow intricacy of his writing. The pen sputtered and a jet of ink crossed the page, causing him to curse under his breath. With a gesture of impatience, he flung the pen down on the desk and regarded the two abject figures before him. Blossom had once again given way to tears.

Hammond leveled his finger at Drummage.

"Gettin' yo' ass paddled once ain' 'nuff fer yo', is it? Cain' yo' keep them pants o' yourn buttoned up? Thinks yo' kin pester any wench yo' wants. Well, goddam it all, yo' cain'. When I wants a wench pestered I'll tell yo'. Yo' ain' big 'nuff yet to start breedin'. Young boy like yo' ain't got strong 'nuff sap in him yet. Kids like yo' a-coverin' my wenches we gets scrawny suckers. Come yo're eighteen, nineteen, lets yo' cover so many wenches as yo' kin but I picks them out. Un'erstand?"

"Yes suh, Masta Hammond suh, but I didn' cover this wench. Ain' a-pestered her, I ain'."

"What yo' mean yo' ain' a-pestered her? Lucretia Borgia

41

says yo' did. This Blossom says yo' did. What more yo' wants? Yo' knocked up Clarissa didn' yo'?"

"Yes suh, Masta Hammond suh, I did suh."

"An' I paddled yore ass fer it, didn' I?"

"Yes suh, Masta Hammond suh."

"Damn little good it did. Yo' too goddam horny like all them Mandingos. Cain' have no horny boy like yo' round the house. No tellin' what yo' do. White women ain' safe with no half-Mandingo buck a-rampagin' through the house a-bustin' out o' his breeches. Damned if'n I goin' to geld yo' but yo' got to keep that pecker o' yourn out o' the wenches." He turned to Blossom. "Yo' say this boy a-pestered yo'?"

Blossom sniffled and tried to compose herself.

"Raped me he did. Come to my room one night and jumped up on de bed. Say if'n I don' he shore goin' ter kill me. He strong. Bore me down. Didn' dare scream 'cause he say he kill me if'n I do."

"Doubt he rape yo'. Seen yo' wiggle yo' ass front of the boys. Yo' jes' as much ter blame's him. Probably more 'cause yo' been a-tantalizin' him, but that don' excuse him. He got to larn to stay away from the wenches."

"Yo' ask her if Benoni done it." Drummage forgot himself in his anxiety to prove his innocence.

Hammond half rose from the table, his face flushed with anger. "Yo' a-tellin' me what to do, boy?"

"Regretful, I is, Masta Hammond suh. Mean to say it Benoni and not me, suh."

"Benoni only a boy. Ain' 'nuff sap in him yet. He still a-playin' with hisself. Don' try to tell me that Benoni did it." He got up from the table and went to the foot of the stairs and called up. "Benoni!"

There was an answering "Yes suh, Masta Hammond suh" from the floor above.

Hammond returned to this desk and waited for Benoni to come down the stairs. He looked up at the boy, admiring his beauty and his easy grace of movement, for Benoni had long been a special favorite of his.

"Drummage say yo' been a-pesterin' Blossom."

The proper look of shocked surprise spread across Benoni's face. His eyes opened wide—guiltless.

"Drummage know better 'n that. Sleeps with him I do and Drummage know I ain' never had a wench yet. Sleepin' with Drummage don' need none." His eyes lowered in modesty over the confession, then lifted triumphantly to stare at Drummage.

42

"Don' know what he talkin' 'bout, Masta Hammond suh." Drummage glared back at his enemy. "Ain' pesterin' no boys, not leastwise Benoni."

Hammond's lips settled in a grim line as he waved Benoni back up the stairs.

"How much time yo' along, Blossom?"

" 'Cretia Borgia she say I 'pears 'bout three month 'long."

"Then yo' git yo'se'f over to the women's shed and stay over there. Cain' have yo' a-swellin' up round the house here. Go, now!"

Hammond waited for her to leave and then spoke to Drummage.

"Goin' to have yo' strung up, I am, and goin' to really whop yo' this time. Jes' paddlin' yo' ass ain' 'nuff. Goin' to give yo' ten strokes. Ain' a-wantin' yo' to get welted but shore am goin' to teach yo' a lesson."

Drummage edged closer to the table, thoroughly frightened now. Ten strokes of the cowhide paddle was a punishment that strong men had quailed under.

"Please, Masta Hammond suh. Benoni done it. He climb outa bed and go to Blossom's room. Heard 'em I did through the latch hole."

"Benoni don' lie. Never know that boy to lie. An' lyin' won't get yo' out o' it. Likes yo' I do, Drummage, but yo' got one fault. Yo' too goddam horny but yo' pappy he a horny bastard too and them Mandingos they all hung so heavy they cain' help bein' horny." His voice dropped lower and became strangely confidential. "Yo' see, Drummage, it's this-a-way. Falconhurst is a stud farm fer niggers. Breeds 'em we do. Got to get us good foals o' we don' git good bucks 'n' wenches. Cain' have young boys like yo' a-rampagin' all over the place, pesterin' what wenches they wants. If'n they do, we gets a lot of in-breedin'—bucks a-coverin' their sisters and mayhap even their mothers. 'Nother year or so, I gives yo' plenty o' wenches to cover and won' give yo' no flat-faced wench like that Blossom. Brought her over here to the big house 'cause I didn' want to breed her, she so goddam ugly."

Taking advantage of the friendliness in Hammond's voice, Drummage was encouraged to plead his case.

"Never pesters no more till yo' tells me I kin, Masta Hammond suh, if'n yo' don' whops me."

"Has to whop yo'. Has to make a 'zample of yo' 'fore all the rest o' the boys. But this time, I'se goin' to whop yo' jus' as

43

much for lyin' to me as for knockin' up Blossom. Don' ever lie to me agin."

Drummage realized that any repetition of his assertion of innocence would only bring more wrath down upon him. Benoni had conquered, Benoni had won. But the day would come when he would get back at Benoni. He made a silent vow that he would.

Hammond's standing up was a signal of Drummage's dismissal, and he walked out. He passed Regine in the hall and she stared at him, her eyes heavy with sadness.

"Feel sorry for you, 'deed I do, Drummage."

He was on the point of telling her that her own Benoni was the culprit but something about the woman's eyes kept him from saying anything. He suddenly felt sorry for her. She came to him and put her hand on his shoulder.

"You look like your father, Drummage. Perhaps you are like him and if you are, you could no more help doing what you did to Blossom than breathing."

She sighed and left him. He stood for a moment watching her. She had known his father—Benoni was proof of that. Drummage wondered what this man who had sired him must have been like. He would like to have known this legendary Drumson.

Chapter 5

DRUMMAGE spent the rest of the morning in fearful anticipation of what seemed inevitable—his flogging. He had had a little taste of it once and he knew that it was certainly nothing to look forward to. The physical pain of the first had been excruciating and this time, he knew, he would be more severely punished than before. He trembled at the thought of the pain but, even more than the dreaded pain, the sharp blows of the whip, the hornet's sting of flame biting into his body and the almost unbearable discomfort afterwards, was the galling thought that he was being punished for something he had never done. Benoni had had all the pleasure, yet he was to go scot free. The sense of injustice rankled within Drummage. Benoni had managed to get Blossom to swear to his innocence; obviously she was infatuated with him. And yet, in the brief encounter Drummage had had with her in the hall she had not been indifferent, for her fingers as well as his had explored and he knew that hers had been satisfied. If only he had had a further opportunity to demonstrate his superiority over Benoni, he could have made her doubly infatuated with himself. But the job was already done.

Drummage knew that further appeals to Hammond Maxwell would be of little use. Hammond was in no mood to be talked to. For him to back down now would be a sign of weakness on his part. Although he was a fair man, Drummage knew that he would never alter his decision once it was made. The more he protested his innocence, the more punishment he would receive. Who would believe him? Who could help him?

Brutus? Perhaps, but Brutus was as far up to his ears in work as was Hammond. Miz 'Gusta? No, because although she had always been kind to him, Benoni was her particular pet as he was also Miz Sophie's. He'd go to his own mother, but Big Pearl would be powerless to do anything. She and Old Lucy and Olly were only slaves—their pleas would be useless. Lucretia Borgia? There was a possibility for Drummage knew that she disliked Benoni and he sensed that she liked him. Yes, Lucretia Borgia was his court of last resort, for although she might be a slave, Hammond Maxwell, like everyone else at Falconhurst, listened to her when she talked.

He cleared off the breakfast dishes from the table in the dining room and brought them out to the kitchen, scraping off the food as he had been taught to do and assembling the plates, cups, and saucers together in separate piles on the long table. It was not his regular job to wash the dishes any more since he had started to assume Brutus' duties but, as they were shorthanded in the kitchen this morning, he took it upon himself to get out the big dishpan. He filled it with hot water from the kettle, then carried it over to the table.

Lucretia Borgia welcomed every opportunity to relieve her feet of her enormous weight. Now she came over to the table and slowly let her huge bulk down into a kitchen chair. It groaned and squeaked under her as she fitted her overflowing rump into the rawhide seat, and when she was settled she looked up at Drummage. Handsome male flesh had always had an appeal for Lucretia Borgia, and she was not so old but that she could still admire it. Drummage, with his promise of lusty virility, was something to look at as he stood with his sleeves rolled up over his arms, his shirt open at the neck, and his face, now grave and without his usual smile, lowered

45

to concentrate on his task. She knew that had she been twenty-five years younger, she would have wheedled him into her bed as she had once, albeit unsuccessfully, tried to entice his father. As it was, her fingers itched to fondle the bulge in his breeches where he leaned against the table.

"When Masta Hammond a-goin' to hang yo' up and strip yo' down?" she asked. Although her question was a blunt one, Drummage seemed to detect a note of sympathy in her voice.

"Dunno, Miz 'Cretia Borgia ma'am. He don' say, but hopes he do it soon. Likes ter gettit over with, I do."

Despite the fall coolness in the air outside, the kitchen was hot and redolent of the fried ham which had been served that morning in the dining room. Lucretia Borgia picked up a corner of her dress and fanned herself with it, revealing a wide expanse of brown thigh. Slipping her feet out of her worn carpet slippers she moved her bare toes back and forth on the stone floor.

"Yo' an awful fool, Drummage, a-pesterin' that Blossom wench. Didn' yo' know she a-goin' to git caught sooner ner later? Don' yo' know Masta Hammond goin' ter strip yo' down, onct he fin' out. 'Sides, yo' a quality nigger—too good fer that Blossom trash. She jes' a mongrel, some Bantu o' Ashanti, I guess. How yo' manage ter pester her 'thout a-gettin' caught?"

"Didn' do it, Miz 'Cretia Borgia ma'am, jes' didn'.'"

He was conscious of her hitching her chair a little closer to him. She wanted to hear the most intimate details of his encounter—whether Blossom had been a virgin; if she had been willing or if he had had to force her—and any other prurient details of the actual fornication which she could drag out of him. She reached out and grabbed his arm, and pulled him close to her, spreading her knees wide so that his body pressed against her breasts. Her voice sank to a whisper —syrupy and confidential.

"Don' have to deny it to me, Drummage boy. Don' care if yo' did o' if'n yo' didn'. Yo' jes' go ahead and tell ol' Aunty 'Cretia all about it." Her arm encircled his waist and she pulled him closer, letting her other hand wander over the thin black stuff of his trousers.

He sensed that he was buying Lucretia Borgia's partisanship. Well, it was a cheap and not unpleasant way to purchase it. He rested a hand on her shoulder to steady himself, and closed his eyes. Afterward, Lucretia Borgia leaned back in her chair and smiled up at him.

"That Blossom wench shore a lucky girl." She wet her lips with the tip of her tongue. "Don' blame her 'tall."

"But I didn', Miz 'Cretia Borgia ma'am." He stood before her, fumbling with his buttons, depressed by the thought that, despite what he had permitted, she would not believe him. "Why'n yo' believe me? Why everyone think I pestered her? Jes' 'cause I done it to that Clarissa wench, now everyone think I done it to Blossom. Didn', didn', didn'! Don' care if'n yo' believes me or not. Don' care if Masta Hammond whops me 'til I dead, won' say that I did." He brought his face to within inches of Lucretia Borgia's. "Yo' hears me, ma'am, I didn'."

She pulled his face down close to hers, a little ashamed now of what she had done. She'd never done anything like that to a young boy before. But his acceptance of her was a bond between them. Suddenly she believed him and released him.

"Then who did? Not that li'l runt Benoni?"

"Yes, Benoni." And Drummage told her in such minute detail about the night that he had awakened to find Benoni gone that she was now convinced he was telling the truth. But she had only his word for it, and his word, even substantiated by her belief, was not enough to convince their master of his innocence. She'd have to prove it.

"Mayhap I believes yo', Drummage." She did not take her eyes from him as she spoke. "Mayhap I he'ps yo'. Don' know if'n I kin but kin try. Yo' a good boy. Made yo' ol' aunty happy jes' now. Does what I kin but, if'n I cain' do nothin', jes' don' whimper to Masta Hammond. He shore hates a boy that whimpers when he a-goin' to be whopped. Stan' up and take yore medicine."

That Lucretia Borgia actually seemed to believe him somehow made it a little easier for Drummage. But he had no time to think about it. There was a rap at the back door and Lucretia Borgia motioned to him to answer it. He dried his hands on the dish towel and went to open the door. Olly, as the biggest and strongest buck on the plantation, was the official whipper, and he stood outside, tongue-tied for having to come to the big house. His big toes scrumbled in the dirt and, with the awe and reverence with which the field hands treated the house servants, he now bobbed a little nod of deference to his brother and managed to recover his tongue.

"Masta Maxwell done sent me here to fetch yo', Drummage boy."

Drummage knew why Olly was there, but he wanted to put off the moment of leaving as long as possible.

"Whaffor Masta Hammond wan' me?"

"Masta Maxwell say I to hang yo' up and strip yo' down. He say to paddle yo' good but not leave no marks. Yo' better come along by me."

Drummage felt a hand on his shoulder and half turned to see Lucretia Borgia behind him. She gave him a gentle push.

"He a-goin' wid yo', Ol' Mista Wilson," she said. "He ain' a-feard of gittin' whopped. Lay it on hard's yo' want, he ain' a-goin' to whimper. He my boy!" The hand on his shoulder reached around and embraced him with rib-crushing tenderness.

Olly was unable to show his sympathy by words, but he put one of his big hands on Drummage's shoulder and they walked along together silently. Their way led down the path into the creek hollow and across the little bridge, then up the hill past the burying ground where his father's stone reared its white and phallic finger, past the foundations of the old house and down to the big barn where the doors stood open. As they neared the barn, he heard the bell tolling, calling all the slaves in from their work in the fields and the various shops and buildings. On the rare occasions when Hammond punished a man, he insisted that all the population of Falconhurst, with the exception of the house servants, be present. Not only was the culprit himself punished but every other slave received full warning of what would happen to him should he be guilty of the same crime or misdemeanor. It was a form of entertainment that they all enjoyed, and they all came running to the barn. The sight of suffering satisfied those sadistic impulses in their African background, which had been buried and were now permitted to come to the surface. They enjoyed the helpless figure as it writhed in pain beneath the lash that each man pictured himself as wielding. Ee-yah! They hoped that whoever was to be the culprit today would put up a good show.

Those who were already present willingly parted their ranks and gazed in wonderment as they saw Olly leading Drummage along. Those who didn't know him recognized by the well-fitting black trousers and the white shirt that he was one of the house servants; not one of them had ever seen a house servant punished before. They knew without being told that the case must be something serious. But they had to admire the high-headed way Drummage walked beside Olly. Mindful of Lucretia Borgia's admonition, he would not whimper, and not one of those goddam niggers would see him cringe. Some strength which he had not realized he possessed came to him and enabled him to plant his feet in their light

48

slippers down firmly, even as firmly as Olly's big bare feet plowed through the dust.

They walked through the press of half-naked sweating bodies up to the doors of the barn. Hammond Maxwell was sitting inside, partly obscured by the shadows, waiting for them. Olly led Drummage up to him, abandoned the boy, and stepped back, leaving him alone in front of his master.

"Whops me if'n yo' wants, Masta Hammond suh, but wants to say once more I never done it."

"Yo' goin' to keep on lyin'? One thing I cain' stand is a lyin' nigger—mos' as bad as a thievin' one. So," he glared up at Drummage, "goin' to give yo' five more strokes fer that. Lie to me 'gain and I'll give yo' five more."

"Didn' do it, Masta Hammond suh."

"Tha's five more, Drummage. Yo' keeps on and I'll slice all the meat off'n yore back."

Drummage realized that it was best for him to keep his mouth shut. He had already earned himself ten extra strokes and he was fully aware of the suffering that each additional stroke entailed. Of one thing, however, he was secretly glad. None of the house servants had been summoned, least of all Benoni. Benoni could not stand there, gloating over him while Olly slapped the paddle on his flesh. Benoni would be cheated out of that.

"Git that paddle, Olly." Hammond pointed to a piece of thick cowhide that was attached to a wooden handle. He waited until Olly walked across the barn floor and took it down off the hook where it hung on the wall. Ordinarily Olly was not reluctant to use it. He derived a certain sensual satisfaction from bringing it in contact with naked flesh and in hearing the scream that ensued as it bit into the skin. The lash was seldom used at Falconhurst because its thin thongs bit too deeply into the flesh and caused wounds that were difficult to heal. Instead, the paddle of thick cowhide, perforated with holes, was used. It did not bite so deeply but it caused wicked punishment. After a few applications, with the full force of Olly's arm behind it, the tender flesh was so lacerated that blood spurted from the holes. Twenty strokes reduced a man to a screaming bundle of pain. Fifty might well prove fatal.

But this time Olly realized that he was using this instrument on his brother, and the thought of the paddle eating into the flesh he loved caused him to hesitate. He returned with it to stand beside Drummage in front of Hammond.

"Needs he'p to git this boy strung up, Masta Maxwell suh."

49

"Ain' a-goin' to string him up. Take too much time and we too busy. There." He pointed to a pile of meal-filled sacks on the barn floor and then signaled to two boys standing in the front row of onlookers. "Yo', Tamerlane, and yo', Tacuba, come over here and hol' this boy down there. Drummage, yo' shuck yo'se'f down."

Drummage undid the buttons on his clothes and they slithered to his feet. He stood naked and unprotected before them all, seeing them nudge each other with their elbows and hearing them snicker. The two blacks stepped forward and grabbed him, one by each arm, and propelled him across the floor to the pile of grain sacks and pushed him down on them. He was angled up from the floor, his head and shoulders some three feet above, his toes braced against the floor.

"Better spancel his feet." Hammond pointed to the wall where the leg irons hung. "He a-goin' to kick something awful and cain' hold him. Spancel his feet and yo' boys hold his arms."

Drummage felt the rough jute of the bags under his belly and smelled the clean, nutty smell of the middlings they contained. He felt the soft grain give under the weight of his body and for a brief moment he felt comfortable and relaxed. The spancels were clamped over his ankles and then his wrists were clutched by strong hands and his arms spread out at his sides, securely anchored by the men who were now crouching beside the pile of bags.

"Don' got to pull my arms out o' the sockets," he said to the one man he could see.

"Shut up!" Hammond put an end to Drummage's remonstrances.

There was nothing more that Drummage wanted to say, except again and again and again to protest his innocence which he knew would avail him nothing. Although he could not see behind him, he knew that Hammond had got up from his chair and was walking across the floor, for he could hear the noise of his boots on the boards. The steps drew nearer and Hammond was now directly behind him, speaking to Olly.

"Wants yo' to take care with this boy, Ol' Mista Wilson, but wants yo' to lay 'em on good. Don' spare him jes' 'cause he yore brother. He's a-goin' to git twenty strokes but don' want them all in the same place. He too val'able to git scarred up but he got to git punished. Thinks yo' kin whop him that way?"

Drummage felt a hand, which he imagined to be Hammond's, on his back, and then a finger outlining certain areas.

The finger stopped its tracing and he heard the sound of Hammond's heels as he stepped back, and then his voice.

"Yo' boys know I'm not much of a one fer whoppin'. Don' believe in it and don' take no pleasure in a-hurtin' any one o' yo'. But sometimes it's the only way I kin knock sense into yo' thick heads. Two things I cain' stand—one for a boy to cover a wench 'thout I gives her to him. The other, and that's even worse, is for a boy to lie to me. No matter what he does, he tells me the truth, I like it better. Now this Drummage here, he a good boy but he got two bad faults. He too goddam horny and he always after the wenches. Got his ass paddled onct and that didn' teach him a lesson so he goes and gits after another wench. This time he goin' to get whopped fer it. Ten strokes fer pesterin' the wench. Then, he lied to me, said he didn' do it, so he gits ten strokes more. Yo' boys watch and yo' who stays on after the caffle leaves remember to leave the wenches 'lone less'n I gives yo' leave and if yo' does anything bad, not to lie to me." The footsteps receded and Drummage heard the chair creak as Hammond sat down.

With the mealy odor of the middlings in his nose and their yielding softness under him, he waited. He could not believe that this could actually be happening to him when he had done nothing to deserve it. Surely a person wasn't punished for being innocent. But it was happening, for he felt the grip on his wrists become tighter and he heard a faint swoosh in the air. It struck . . . and it was as though his flesh had been scorched with a living flame. The skin itself was seared with it and down in the depths of his muscles such an intense pain plucked at his nerves that his flesh twitched with a life of its own. The pain was so intense that his brain impulses almost failed to register it as pain. It was more like a complete disintegration of every sensation he had ever had, exploding in a volcano of molten lava which engulfed him, wrapping him in fire. Although he had determined that he would not cry out, he heard his own scream soaring into the rafters and the echo of it returning from the depths of the barn. He gasped for breath to scream again but before he could gulp the air into his lungs it struck again.

Like a trapped animal he tried to escape from his tormentors. He pulled at the restraining hands, flailed his helplessly chained legs, ground his body into the yielding meal. And then it came again and he heard his master's voice say "three" and then it was "four" and now the fire moved all

51

over his body, licking up and down his back, onto the soft cushions of his rump, down the fleshy part of his thighs, and still the torture continued, throwing his whole body into twinging convulsions as he writhed under the onslaught.

From some other world than the scarlet one of pain which he alone inhabited, he heard the words:

"He's had ten, Olly, give him a rest. Want to talk to him, I do."

In his anguish it made little difference to him that the blows had stopped. Nerves and flesh and skin could suffer no more, and yet the blow which he had steeled himself for did not come; instead, he could see, by raising his head a little, the rough cloth of Hammond's trousers.

"Tha's your punishment for pesterin' Blossom." Hammond leaned over to speak to him. "Yo' got ten more a-comin' fer lyin' to me but, if'n yo' tells the truth now—admits yo' did it —jes' might fergit 'bout them other ten."

Slowly and with infinite labor, Drummage raised his head until he was able to look into Hammond's eyes. He was surprised to see no anger in them, only pity and compassion. Although in his crucifixion he could not realize it, Hammond was not punishing him through any sense of sadistic pleasure or senseless desire for revenge; he was merely meting out what he thought to be justice. But wracked as he was by torment, Drummage knew only that he was being mercilessly punished for something he had never done.

Drools of clotted saliva spun from his mouth and the phlegm in his throat was thick as he tried to speak. It was too much of an effort to hold up his head, and it sank down again. Hammond had to lean forward to distinguish the words that came through the dry lips.

"Ain' lied to yo', Masta Hammond suh. If'n yo' wants me to say I did it, I be a-lyin' to yo'. Benoni done it."

"Stubborn little fool!" Hammond stood up and made a sign to Ol' Mista Wilson. "Let him have it. Pour it on good. Start up to his shoulders and work down agin." He turned to the assembly of slaves, some slavering with delight and some ashen-faced with terror. "If'n yo' lies to me or yo' new masters, yo' kin see what yo' gits. All right, Ol Mista Wilson, pour it on."

The brief surcease from agony did not mitigate the force of the next blow, as Hammond said "eleven." After the respite it seemed far worse. Once again Drummage shrieked, howling with the frenzied yelps of a whipped dog. "Twelve!" And through the stinging nerves of his rump he felt a wet slithering of the oxhide as the paddle dragged across the skin and he knew that he was bleeding. "Thirteen!" He could never live through another. "Fourteen!" The world inside his glazed eyes began to dim from the scarlet of pain into a grey limbo of senselessness.

But although the word "fifteen" was spoken, the remorseless sting of pain did not follow. Drummage was dimly aware of a commotion in the barn. Through the engulfing waves of unconsciousness he struggled for recognition of what was happening.

"Masta Hammond suh, Masta Hammond, yo' makin' a mistake." It was Lucretia Borgia's voice and only Lucretia Borgia would have the temerity to accuse Hammond of making a mistake. That she was now doing it, and doing it before the assemblage of men, betokened the direness of the emergency.

Hammond half stood in his anger as he shouted at her.

"What yo' mean, Lucretia Borgia, comin' in here like this? Git yo'se'f back to the house and take them two varmints with yo'."

"Ain' a-goin' 'til yo' hears me fust. Whops me if'n yo' wants. But yo' got to listen."

"Listens to yo' when I gits through here, not before. Go on, Ol' Mista Wilson."

But Olly hesitated. The blow did not fall. He was staring at Lucretia Borgia.

Drummage raised his head with difficulty. He saw Lucretia Borgia standing before Hammond, one hand clutched in Benoni's long hair, the other with a firm grip on Blossom's dress.

"Git up there, yo' miz'rable weasel!" She gave Benoni such a push that he landed on his face at Hammond's feet. "Git up on yo' feet and tells yo' masta what a low-down polecat yo' are. Tells him how yo' lied 'bout Drummage. Tell him o' I wallops yo' 'gain like yo' never walloped afore." Her hand free, she brought it down on the weeping Blossom with a resounding slap across the girl's cheek that caused her to wail in a higher key. "Stop yore blubberin' o' I give yo' something to make yo'."

"What this mean, Lucretia Borgia?" Hammond regarded her and the crumpled form of Benoni at his feet.

"He'll tell yo'." Lucretia Borgia took a step towards Benoni, one fist doubled up like a ham, the other one dragging Blossom. "He'll tell yo', the sneakin', crawlin' little cottonmouth. Make him git hisself up on his feet and tell you."

"Benoni!" Hammond's voice brooked no delay.

Benoni struggled to his feet, as mindful of Lucretia Borgia's clenched fist as he was of his master's grim visage.

"She a-lyin', Masta Hammond, and that Blossom a-lyin'. Drummage he a-lyin' too. Didn' do nothin' to Blossom, Masta Hammond suh."

"If'n I draws off and lets yo' have it," Lucretia Borgia menaced him, "yo' won' live to tell him."

"Blossom, she made me do it to her, Masta Hammond suh. She did, it her fault. Didn' want to do it, but she made me. It her fault."

"Made yo' do what?"

"Pester her."

Drummage was breathing easier now. His body was a quivering mass of pain but he felt certain his punishment was over. He was being vindicated. It flashed through his mind that the price he had paid for Lucretia Borgia's championship had been a small one.

Benoni had sidled up to Hammond, confident of his charm and Hammond's liking for him.

"She bad, that Blossom. She a-sayin' she give me good time and sayin' she never tell no one."

"He still lyin', Masta Hammond suh." Blossom twisted under Lucretia Borgia's grip. "He guv me this." She fumbled inside her dress and brought out a gold locket, suspended from a piece of string. "He say Miz 'Gusta guv it ter him and he guv it ter me if'n I let him pester me and if'n I say that Drummage done it."

At Hammond's nod to Lucretia Borgia, she wrenched it from the girl's neck, breaking the twine, and handed it over to him. He examined it for a moment, then slipped it into his pocket.

"Yo' Tamerlane and yo' Tacuba, take this here Benoni boy down to the pen and lock him in. We's takin' him in the caffle to N'Orleans when we go. Ain' a-goin' to whip him 'cause he too delicate-skinned and spoil his value. But a-goin' to sell him. Cain' have no lyin' thief round here. This Blossom she a-goin' in the caffle too. She knocked up good and proper and it's a good time to get shet of her."

Benoni dropped to the floor, crawled to Hammond and clasped his knees.

"Masta Hammond suh, yo' ain' a-goin' to sell me. Don', Masta Hammond, don' sell me. Cain' live 'thout my mama and 'thout yo' all." The boy's body shook with hysterical

54

sobs, but Hammond merely unlocked the clinging arms from around his knees and pushed him away with the toe of his boot. He looked to Lucretia Borgia, silently asking her approval of his move, and she slowly nodded her "so be it."

Then Hammond did a strange thing. He got up from his chair, stepped over the wailing Benoni, and came to where Drummage was still stretched out on the feed bags. His fingers touched Drummage's shoulders lightly and ever so faintly ran their course down the puffed, swollen, and discolored back.

"Believe yo' now, Drummage." Hammond hesitated a moment, not daring to speak the words that had come into his mind. He could not admit, even to himself, that he had erred in judgment, and especially he could not admit to Drummage or to the assembled slaves that he had been wrong. No white man was ever wrong in his dealings with niggers. But he could mitigate his error.

"Olly a-takin' yo' over to Big Pearl's. She goin' to look after yo' fer a few days. Old Lucy she know herbs that ease yore back." In a whisper that was meant for Drummage's ears only, he said: "How yo' likes to go to N'Orleans, Drummage?"

"Yo' a-goin' to sell me 'long with Benoni?"

"Hell no, boy. Ain' a-goin' to sell yo.' Needs that Mandingo blood yo' got fer breedin'. Yo' goes 'long as my body servant. Think I leave Brute this time and take yo'."

"Likes it fine, Masta Hammond suh. Likes to go with yo'. Likes to be yore body servant."

Hammond came even nearer and whispered even lower.

"When we gits back, goin' to pick out a wench for you to cover. Guess yo' 'bout ready now."

Despite the burning pain in his back, Drummage was happy. He turned on his side, reached up for Hammond's hand, and brought it to his lips. The pain that he had suffered was as nothing compared to the joy that was in his heart.

Chapter 6

A STRETCHER was hastily fabricated of croker sacks stretched between pitchfork handles. Olly, who had so recently inflicted pain, now gently lifted Drummage's aching body from the pile and placed him, belly down, on the stretcher, which he and another boy then carried from the barn to Big Pearl's cabin. As Drummage was carried out, he saw Tamerlane and Tacuba hauling the weeping, struggling Benoni away to the calaboose, an isolated little building at some distance from the other cabins. It was here that recalcitrant slaves were confined—those who had run away and been brought back by the patrollers; those who were awaiting punishment; and those who, by virtue of recent purchase, were feared to be possible runners. To the credit of Falconhurst, it was a building which was used but seldom. Just now there was only one occupant, a big buck by the name of Nero, whom Hammond had recently purchased because of his apparently almost pure Ibo bloodlines, from The Coign, a nearby plantation. Hammond liked Ibo blood and wanted to breed the boy, but Nero couldn't forget his woman over at The Coign and had a habit of taking off, without permission, to visit her. Although he had returned to Falconhurst voluntarily after two days at The Coign, and was not a runner, Hammond had shut him up in the calaboose to cool him off. Benoni would be the second occupant.

Despite his pain, Drummage was happy. He had been vindicated. Masta Hammond now believed him and knew him to be innocent. Best of all, he was going to New Orleans with the caffle not to be sold like Benoni but to enjoy all the sights and the exciting life of the city, with the surety that he would return to Falconhurst and the wench that Masta Hammond had promised him.

With the sound of Benoni's screams fading in the distance, he lowered his head, cupping his chin in his hands and seeing only the wrinkles in Olly's pants and the big black hands on the pitchfork handles. He would not have to be up at dawn and hard at work all day. He would be fussed over, pampered, and petted. To Big Pearl, Old Lucy, Olly, and the other slaves, he would be the hero of the day. Eeyah!

Big Pearl saw him coming from the door of her cabin and with a cry of fright dashed headlong out to meet him, weeping hysterically until she had assured herself that he was alive and not seriously hurt. She was all for dispossessing Old Lucy from her bed, but Drummage assured her that with Olly's help he could negotiate the ladder to the loft. Once in his old bed, which, truth to tell, was not so comfortable as his bed at the big house, and with a smelly but

56

warm, comforting poultice of herbs on his back, he slept, his body recuperating, his spirit at ease. Throughout the long afternoon he dozed, waking only to drink the chicken broth which Lucretia Borgia had sent over from the big house, along with a whole roast ham and one of her famous pound cakes. Then he slept again until he awoke to find it dark and to hear Olly coming up the ladder. After that there was the warmth and softness of Olly's big hulk and the protection of his strong arms.

But neither Benoni nor his mother Regine slept that night. In his loneliness and fear, the boy wept on the rough boards of the calaboose until Nero, who could stand the walling no longer, slapped him into silence. In the big house Regine paced her little room up over Hammond Maxwell's office.

That which she had always feared was about to take place. How many nights she had awakened from the nightmare of having Benoni taken from her, and found comfort in reaching across the bed to touch her son sleeping beside her. Later, when he had grown up and moved away from her to the third floor, she could still reassure herself, knowing that he was in the big house, safe and secure. She had used every method possible to ingratiate him into the favor of Hammond Maxwell and his wife, and later, when Hammond's daughter Sophie had arrived with her two children, she had had her handsome son installed as a companion to the young Master Warren. But now all her carefully laid plans had failed. The heart-clutching anguish of her dreams had become a reality. Benoni was to be sold; they were to be parted. He would leave her, marching down the road in the slave caffle, and she would never see or hear from him again. There was nothing she could do about it—Hammond would sell him as impersonally as a colt, a calf, or a setting of eggs.

How could she, a slave, change the inevitable? Yet from the very moment when Lucretia Borgia had dragged Benoni and the howling Blossom from the house that morning and she had followed them, she had tried. She had stood on the outer fringes of the crowd of men, knowing that she had no right to be there, and she had heard Hammond's pronouncement. Wild-eyed with terror, she had stumbled back to the big house and thrown herself before Miss Augusta to plead for Benoni. She had found tears and sympathy but little help from her mistress, who could only admit her helplessness and her inability to sway her husband's mind once it was made up.

In vain Regine had then pleaded with Sophie. Although she was fond of the boy and little Warren worshiped him, Sophie too gave her little encouragement. The boy was a slave—pretty and engaging though he might be—and if he were to be sold, he would be sold. That was that. Both Augusta and Sophie nevertheless tried to influence Hammond and Sophie even exhibited a weeping Warren to clinch the argument, but Hammond remained adamant. Then, when all intercessions had failed, Regine herself approached Hammond, hoping he might remember the nights she had shared his bed, and the pleasure she had tried so hard to give him. She had been a beautiful girl when he purchased her in New Orleans, with dark curling hair and a tea-rose complexion that only hinted at the faint trace of Negro blood. She had been educated to read and write and her deportment was equal to that of any white woman. Even now, fifteen years later, approaching thirty-five, she was still a beautiful woman, but neither her beauty nor her sorrow nor the remembrance of times past could influence Hammond.

Benoni was to be sold! It was final. Hammond agreed that he was a fine-looking boy, well mannered, agreeable, and valuable—too valuable to be put up on the vendue table. But he was a liar and a thief and that ended it for Hammond. As a concession to the weeping Regine he promised that the boy would be sold privately and not put up on the auction block or sold as a field hand. But Regine's request to see him while he was in the calaboose was denied. Yes, of course she would go to New Orleans with the caffle—wasn't she Miz 'Gusta's woman? She would go this year as always but she would have no contact with Benoni on the trip. He would have to go with the rest of the boys to the slave jail, awaiting sale.

All Regine's pleadings could procure nothing more. She left Hammond sitting at his desk and walked slowly up the narrow stairs to her own room, which had a connecting door to Hammond's and Augusta's room. Benoni was the only thing that she had ever loved, except his father Drumson, and she had known Drumson only the night of his death, when Benoni had been conceived. Without her son, life would have no purpose for her. Without Benoni there could be no life for her at Falconhurst or any other place. Take him away and she would die. Yes, she would surely die.

She went to the window that looked out across the fields to the slave cabins and the sheds that had clustered around the old house before it burned down. Beyond them, she could pick out the solitary, isolated building where Benoni was.

Her heart ached for him in his misery, and in her grief her respect for Hammond turned to hatred. And slowly, from the confusion of her thoughts, there emerged a plan—a plan which just might work—although it carried considerable risk.

She washed her face with cold water to remove the puffiness from crying and descended the stairs to the office below. Augusta was now seated at the desk, copying entries from the studbooks. Her look was warm and sympathetic, for she realized what Regine must be suffering. Perhaps some sort of occupation would help her.

"Regine, you write so much better than I do." She laid down her pen. "I'm going to let you copy out these entries for me." Augusta indicated the big book beside her. "You've done it before and I should see Lucretia Borgia about the dinner tonight—the Gasaways are coming, you know. Here are the names of the boys being sold and you know how to look them up in the book."

"Yes, Miz 'Gusta ma'am." Regine was all too willing, for it coincided with her plans.

Augusta relinquished her seat and Regine slid into the chair. Augusta's hand on her shoulder was meant to be consoling, but Regine resented it.

"I'm so sorry about Benoni. I wish there was something I could do. I shall miss him as much as you do."

"Yes, Miz 'Gusta, ma'am." Regine bowed her head to the open books. As Augusta stopped in front of the mirror, she turned to the next name on the list—Neptune—and looked it up in the book. She started to copy in her fine, copperplate script.

> Neptune, out of Erminia by Paddy. Buck, born
> January 31st, 1833, at Falconhurst. Sired:
>> Out of Flavia, buck Nahum
>> Out of Candace, wench Cleopatra
>> Out of Rosabell, buck Lorenzo
>> Out of Veronica, buck Pip
>> Out of Roxanna, wench Rhoda.
> Tall, strong, healthy. Color, light brown. Cicatrix on
> upper right arm. Some Ibo blood from dam, Ashanti
> from sire. Disposition good. Trained as a mason.

She tried to place this Neptune but she knew very few of the other slaves on the plantation. However, as she wrote her hatred for Hammond Maxwell grew. Animals, just animals! And she and Benoni were just as much animals as the rest of them. She finished copying out the entry just as Augusta left, and she flipped through the pages until she came to her son's name. The entry was equally brief.

Benoni, out of Regine by Drumson. Buck, born October, 1843. Good looking, housebroken, trained as house servant. Hair, long black and curly. Disposition good. Fair percentage of human blood from dam who is octoroon. Royal Hausa, Jaloff and some human blood from sire. Note: This buck not to be sold but to be used for Falconhurst breeding.

Damn Hammond Maxwell! So, Benoni was not to be sold. That was as much as his word meant. No! Benoni would not be sold, not if she could help it. She rummaged in the desk drawer and removed a sheet of the printed stationery which Hammond used for his business correspondence and bills of sale. A florid heading, with the word *Falconhurst* so completely buried in scrolls as to be hardly legible, served to identify it, and Hammond Maxwell's name, followed by *Prop.*, gave it authority. Although the occasion might never arise for using a document of the sort Regine had in mind, it would be well to be on the safe side. She dipped the pen in ink and wrote with careful strokes, hoping that what she wrote would be couched in the right phrases:

To Whom It May Concern:
Regine, servant for life to Mr. and Mrs. Hammond Maxwell of Falconhurst Plantation, near Benson, Alabama, together with her son, the boy Benoni, is traveling with full consent to Cincinnati, Ohio, to join my sister Mrs. Martin Oakes of that city.
        Mrs. Hammond Maxwell.

She read it over and, although she had no way of knowing how correct it might be, she remembered a similar pass that had been written out for her by Augusta when she had gone to New Orleans once to accompany Miss Sophie and the children back. It seemed to her that the wording was familiar and, although she hoped she would not have to use it, it was well to have it with her. Once more she read it over, dotted the "i's" in Cincinnati, folded the paper, and put it in an envelope which she hid in her pocket. Then she resumed the copying of the Neptune entry.

How little it said. He had been born of a union between

some buck Paddy and a wench Erminia. It said nothing as to whether Paddy cared for Erminia or their mating was merely routine. Only the result of their union mattered —this male child Neptune—except, of course, that he was not a child. When he was born he was called a sucker or a foal and now that he was grown he was not a man but a buck. This unknown Paddy had not been his father—merely his sire—and the Erminia who had been his mother and had carried him in her womb was not his mother—only a dam. Neptune had known neither of them, nor had they known him. He had been taken away from the woman who had borne him after she had suckled him for a week or two. He had been bred as an animal and sold as an animal. Even Benoni, with his so-called *human* blood, was nothing more than an animal and she herself, with an attenuation of Negro blood that was so minor it was not discernible, was nothing but an animal, although, as she knew, on her father's side she was related to some of the great families of Louisiana. What did it matter? If Hammond took a notion to sell her in some moment of anger or temper, she would mount the block as quickly as any of her black sisters. Oh, how she hated him, and how sweet revenge would be!

When Augusta returned Regine was busy copying. She had finished Neptune and gone on to Tad, who was sired by Rufus out of Celestina, and then to Rollo, who resulted from a temporary joining of Hannibal and Ettie. She was just starting on Zachary by Sebastian out of Flora when Augusta came to stand beside her.

"Let me finish these and you go and fix a toddy for Hammond. He's coming in now and he's pretty much upset. Don't mention Benoni to him. Perhaps, after a few days have passed, I shall be able to do something about it."

Regine heard the words and knew that Augusta was trying to be kind, but they were words, nothing more. Augusta was as helpless in the situation as she was.

"Yes, Miz 'Gusta ma'am." Regine rose from the desk and walked out. She no longer walked with bowed head. There was a new determination within her: Benoni would not be sold. When she arrived in the kitchen she disregarded Lucretia Borgia, who had precipitated the crisis; mixed the corn, sweetening, and hot water to the well-known proportions that Hammond liked; placed the glass on a silver tray; and carried it through the house back into the office.

Hammond did not look up as she entered, and she was glad, not only because she did not want to meet his eyes but

61

because there was something in the room she was looking for. It was the plantation key board, on which every key to every building hung from a numbered hook. Many times she had returned the keys to their proper hooks and she knew the exact location of the key to the calaboose. It was hanging there now where Hammond had just replaced it—a long iron key with two smaller ones hanging over it, which she knew must be the keys to spancels although she did not know why there should be two. She was ignorant of the fact that Benoni was sharing the calaboose with Nero.

With Drummage at Big Pearl's, Blossom in the birthing house, and Benoni in the calaboose, the big house was shorthanded, and Regine volunteered to look after little Amanda while the rest of the family were having dinner. Fortunately the baby was sleeping in her crib and Regine had an hour-and-a-half of uninterrupted time in which to complete her plans. She went about them in a methodical way. The pass was to be used in case of extreme emergency only, but Regine had no intention of remaining a slave. She was certain that she could pass for white—many of the Creole families of New Orleans with an admixture of French and Spanish blood had the same creamy complexion as hers —and although Benoni was too dark to pass he could well be her servant. However, there was one prop she needed. As a widow she would receive the solicitous homage which Southern men conferred on a bereaved woman, and Augusta's mourning dress and crepe bonnet, which she wore only to funerals, would add this touch of respectability and authenticity. Augusta's clothes fitted Regine, and the dress, of rich black taffeta with a garniture of dull jet, would give her the quiet distinction of a bereaved widow, while the veiled bonnet would screen her face from too close a scrutiny. She was sure Augusta would not miss the dress. It hung in a percale bag in her wardrobe, and Regine took it, along with the bonnet, and hung it in her room. There was one other thing needed: she ransacked Augusta's jewel case for the broad gold band which Augusta seldom wore and which could well be mistaken for a wedding ring.

With these things safely hidden in her own room, she packed the carpetbag she had carried before on her trips to New Orleans with the family. Her own clothes—hand-me-downs from Augusta—were all of good material and style, and fortunately she had some of Benoni's which she had been mending. The bag packed, the dress and bonnet hanging on a hook at the back of her wardrobe, she felt that all had been done which could be done at present. The more difficult part of her escape would come later, under cover of darkness.

After dinner was finished Hammond spent some time with Augusta and Sophie in the drawing room, discussing their forthcoming trip to the city. Around nine o'clock they ascended the stairs to their own room, and Augusta's bell tinkled for Regine to help her undress. When Augusta was ready for bed, Regine went in to check on Sophie and the children, found them already in bed, and then went down to the kitchen to mix Hammond's nightcap—his usual hot toddy, which she brought upstairs and placed on the table by the bed. She waited for him to sip it and nod his approval, and then, at Augusta's request, turned out the lamp and went back to her own room.

She must wait until they were sleeping. This would be the most nerveracking time, for there was nothing to occupy her mind except such minor things as she could think of—a bit of lace to be tucked into the bag, a bottle of laudanum in case of sickness, and other trifles she might need. She forced herself finally to sit on a chair, but although her body was quiet her mind was racing—toward freedom for herself and her son. The little clock on the wall slowly ticked off the minutes which she hoped would be her last moments of bondage.

Chapter 7

THE CLOCK ticked on and after what seemed an interminable period, but which was scarcely more than an hour, Regine stood up and cautiously, one step at a time, went to the door that opened into the Maxwells' room and, with her finger on the latch, slowly opened it. She listened. Hammond's deep snores and Augusta's regular breathing testified that the emotional problems of their slaves did not rob the masters of their own sleep. Regine closed the door as carefully as she had opened it. Now at last she was ready to act.

She lit a candle and lost no time in getting into Augusta's gown and putting on the veiled bonnet. With her carpetbag in one hand and the candle in the other, she went down to Hammond's office and let the light of the candle fall on the key board. The keys were still there—a long iron key and two smaller ones. She took all three and slipped them into her reticule. Then she went to Hammond's desk, opened the top drawer, and found the tin box which was always kept there. She took five gold eagles, a number of silver dollars, and a quantity of bills which she did not bother to count. There was no further need for the candle and she extinguished it, listening in the dark to hear any move overhead which might betoken her discovery. But the house was quiet except for the night noises that any house develops—a creaking and groaning of beams and joists as if it were settling down for the night. Without turning around she opened the back door and stepped outside. There was a faint light from the rising moon and she ran from the shadows of the house to the shadows of the barn, then along the path that led to the darkness of the little woods that bordered the creek, across the footbridge and up the hill to the lane between the cabins. The weight of the carpetbag impeded her and she was forced to stop frequently for rest, choosing the protection of a crape myrtle bush or the deeper shadows between the houses. After what seemed like a long time, she reached the isolated calaboose whose whitewashed exterior gleamed with a strange phosphorescence in the darkness. The heavy plank door was secured with a padlock and the one small grated window was far too high for her to reach. She did not dare to call out and awaken Benoni, but she sensed that in his sorrow and loneliness he might not be sleeping. Risking her visibility against the whiteness of the building, she crept close to the window, straining up to bring her face as near to the grating as possible, and called out, keeping her voice low:

"Benoni! Benoni, boy! It's Mama."

She heard a noise of shuffling inside and saw broad black fingertips with strong, wide, broken nails on the windowledge. They were far different than Benoni's delicate hands.

"Who that?" It was a strange voice, its deep tones magnified by the walls of the calaboose, but it was followed by the beloved voice she anticipated.

"Mama, Mama, take me out a-here."

"Yo' Benny's mama?" the strange voice asked.

"Yes, but don't talk."

The key grated in the lock and she entered into the darkness, close with a musky male scent. She felt Benoni's arms around her, and for one swift moment she held him close, trying to quiet his sobs. But there was another figure behind him and now she felt a powerful hand gripping her arm.

"I's Nero. Yo' a-goin' to help me too, missy?"

The hand clutched frantically, the fingers pressing painfully into her skin. The unknown voice continued. "Better yo' he'p me git 'way too, missy. Easier fer yo' if'n yo' have a man along. How yo' 'n' a boy a-goin' ter git 'way? Come daybreak yo' not more 'n' five miles 'way. Paddy rollers sho' fin' yo'. I knows runnin'. Goes to de Coign ter see my woman Phoebe and don' get caught. Yo' takes me, missy. We takes a horse 'n' goes fast."

"Don't talk to him, Mama." Benoni was pleading. "He's a bad man. He did bad things to me, Mama. He hurt me awful."

Her hands, caressing Benoni, hushed his words. Eyes now ...stomed to the darkness could see the outline of a power- ...an. But what he had said had caught her attention, ...she recognized a certain feasibility in his suggestion.

"What do you mean we can get a horse? How?"

"Steals one from the barn. I'se a hostler, knows all them horses. Hitches to a buckboard and we goes by the road." He pulled her to the door of the cabin and lifted the crepe veil to stare at her in the moonlight. "Yo' white, missy! If paddy rollers come, yo' say I yo' servant, a-drivin' yo'. Boy sit in the back and yo' say he yo' slave too. Whar yo' a-headin', missy?"

"Wants to get to Westminster so's we kin take de steam-cars."

"Don' know Westminster."

"Kin tell you. Been there before." She remembered the trip she had made alone. Ajax had driven her from Falcon-hurst, and the glorious feeling of freedom she had had on that trip had impressed every detail of it on her mind. If this Nero could get a horse and wagon his idea would be a good one. Walking, she and Benoni would take days to get to Westminster, and their progress would not only be slow but dangerous. Riding, she might be able to brazen it out with some fabrication of how she was being driven by a planta-tion slave to the depot. Once on the train, with Nero aban-doned to his own resources, she and Benoni would have passed the most perilous part of their flight.

Regine turned a deaf ear to Benoni's pleadings to abandon Nero. "I'll take yo' with us," she said.

"We'se spanceled, missy."

She reached in her reticule and brought out the two keys. With her fingers she felt for the spancels on Nero's feet and located the lock. The key turned with difficulty but Nero snatched her fingers away and turned it easily. In the mo-ment of freeing himself he brushed against Regine and she dropped the other key to the floor. Precious minutes were lost in trying to locate it, but it was found and Benoni's spancels were loosened. Regine took his hand, again cautioning him not to speak, and led him out the door. Nero followed and closed the door behind him, snapping the padlock. Regine laid the big key on the stone step outside the door, but Nero picked it up and flung it far out into the field.

"Let the bastards look fer it," he said, stepping in front of her and Benoni to lead the way.

All that Regine had been through, all the chances she had taken were as nothing compared to what now lay ahead of them, but she felt more confidence with Nero along. His looked strong and handsome and he strode ahead with fidence. It was good to have a man with her.

Nero led the way to the barn, and when they got there pointed with satisfaction to the big doors, which were open. Once inside he moved with the stealthiness of a big cat towards the restless horses in the stalls. He located a harness on the wall and chose a gentle mare which made no fuss over being harnessed, threw the harness over her and tightened the straps, then backed her out and hitched her to the light buckboard which stood near the door. They climbed in and Regine held her breath. The wheels creaked over the wooden floor and the sound of the horse's hooves rang out with a hollow sound, but once out of the barn and in the lane the horse and wagon made little noise.

Regine breathed more deeply when they gained the main road and Nero touched the whip to the horse. She had a fair idea of just how to get where they were going. They would follow along the big Tombigbee River until they came to a small town which had a bridge that crossed it. Once on the other side it was not far to the town of Westminster, where she had caught the morning train for Mobile. In Westminster she would let Nero go on by himself with the horse and she and Benoni would be safe on the train. Hammond would never think to look for her there.

With the horse trotting steadily along and the pale white ribbon of the road passing beneath the wheels, she had a chance to talk with Benoni.

"We're running, Benoni child," she said. "Even if we are caught, it will be no worse for us. You'd be sold anyway and if I am to be sold, it makes no dif'rence to me."

"Whar we goin', Mama?"

"Goin' to git us a train for Mobile and then to New Orleans and gits us a boat up north. One thing yo' got to understand now. While we runnin', I'se the mist'ess, yo' the servant. Got to do it that way 'cause yo're darker'n me. I kin pass for white and yo' cain'—leastwise not down here. Up north yo' kin. Yo' got to play-act for a while, Benoni. Don't fergit and call me 'mama.' Got to call me mist'ess now. Yo' kin remember little Miz 'Manda's name. Call me Miz 'Manda."

"Yes ma'am, Miz 'Manda ma'am." Benoni wanted to display his ability.

"Better he gits in de back." Nero turned and looked at Benoni, half sitting in Regine's lap. "If'n de paddy rollers comin', ain' fittin' fer no white woman holdin' a big nigger lummox like dat." He drew up the reins and the horse stopped. "Git out and git in de back. Yo' kin let yore laigs hang over."

"Must I, Mama?"

" 'Pears better that way, if, as Nero says, the patrollers come along."

Benoni sought the back of the buckboard, resenting Nero's presence on the seat but realizing the necessity for his move. How he hated that damn Nero nigger, when he rememberd the humiliating things the big buck had made him do. And yet, in retrospect those things now became almost pleasant. If only it had not hurt so!

They drove on through the night, passing through sleeping hamlets, passing the white wraiths of big houses, set back from the road behind long avenues of trees. Long after midnight they came to the big bridge which spanned the Tombigbee, and Regine sighed with relief, for she knew that they were on the right road and that their trip was nearly over. The darkness, the rhythmic motion of the wagon, and the click of the horse's shoes relaxed her. Every passing moment put more distance between them and Falconhurst and increased their chances of escape. She missed Benoni's presence beside her but was grateful for Nero who had made all this possible. The nervous tension of the day subsided and she felt the welcome oblivion of sleep coming upon her. But before she allowed herself to doze off, she reached one arm over the seat to touch the top of Benoni's head.

"Yo' all right, boy?" she was hardly able to form the words in her fatigue.

"All right, Mama." He hesitated. "Miz 'Manda, I means. Wisht I was up there with yo'."

"Curl up under the seat and try to go to sleep. We've got a long day tomorrow and you'll need the sleep."

67

The word brought home to her consciousness just how tired she really was; she could no longer fight to keep her eyes open. She closed them, grateful for Nero, and immediately dozed off. In her sleep she was aware of a softness and a hardness that were comforting—a comfort she had not enjoyed in many years. When she awoke, after a few minutes' sleep, she found that the softness was Nero's chest and the hardness the pressure of his arm around her.

"Yo' bin a-sleepin'," he said. "Bin a-lookin' at yo' and wishin' yo' didn't have that thing over yore face."

The scent of his body was strong with musk but it was not distasteful to her nostrils. It had a strange exhilaration about it that sent her senses pulsing. The weight of his arm around *r* shoulders was heavy but it gave her a feeling of security *\ strength. She lifted the heavy crepe veil and looked up at *m*. He was not handsome as Drumson had been—his square face was rough-hewn and Negroid, with a flattened nose, large nostrils, and prominent lips. A low forehead shaded deep-set eyes, shadowed now in the dim light. No, it was not a handsome face, but it was entirely masculine and its rugged strength had an erotic appeal.

He looked down and smiled, the white line of his teeth showing clear in the darkness. His head lowered and his lips came close to hers.

"Yo' a mighty pretty gal, missy. But yo' white. Fancied yo' mebbe yella but didn' know yo' white." He smacked his lips which were close to hers and moistened them with his tongue. "Always hankered to have me a white woman. Ain' had no woman fer a long time and shore would like me a white woman."

Regine felt the soft pressure of his lips against hers and she did not turn away. The softness became hard, brutal, pressing her lips against her teeth, and his searching tongue sought entrance but she did not open her mouth. She desired him, and yet with Benoni so close she did not want him. She wanted freedom, and now this strangely welcome presence was diverting her from her thoughts.

His voice had become low and husky now.

"I'm a-kissin' yo', pretty missy. Goin' to keep on a-kissin' yo'."

Again his lips pressed against hers and the temptation to return his kiss in all the abandoned passion with which it was given was strong within her, but she turned her face away. She almost regretted that she had repulsed him when he straightened up, but it was only to wind the reins around the whip socket. His face was again close to hers, more demanding now, and his arm around her tightened while the searching fingers of his other hand were caressing her neck and shoulders, seeking an entrance into her bodice. He undid the first few buttons and his hand slipped inside. The calluses of his palm felt rough against the softness of her flesh but his touch sent a stream of desire through her body and her nipples hardened under the painful pressure of his fingers. This time when he kissed her, she abandoned herself to him, unwillingly but through a compulsion she could not resist. He ripped down the front of her bodice and she could feel the warm part of his tongue as it crept away from her mouth and moved along her throat to come to rest on her breast. She remembered his saying that he had not had a woman for a long time. Good God! She had not had a man for over a year and that had been a white man, stopping overnight at Falconhurst, to whom she had been surreptitiously offered by Hammond as a part of Falconhurst hospitality. His puny attempts had not satisfied her. The ardor of this Nero reminded her of Drumson.

The soft blandishment of his mouth almost prevailed, but reason conquered. Their escape was far more important than the demands of their bodies. He must realize that; she must make him realize it. She pushed him away and managed to separate herself from his embrace.

But Nero was too far gone to be reasonable. His hand fumbled with his own buttons, then returned and clasped hers and pressed it to him. Once again she was tempted to yield and the temptation was now overwhelming, for this was no puny white man but a strong, hard man with all the virility she remembered from Drumson. Her hand was loath to leave and the longer it lingered the more difficult it became to repulse him.

Just as he felt that he had succeeded and that she was thoroughly quiescent, she pulled away from him, struggling to slip out of the subtle trap he had set for her. Her denial angered him.

"Wha's de matter? Don' yo' like me?" The hoarseness of his voice rasped the words in his throat.

"More important that we gets free," she countered. "Plenty of time to get frolicsome afterwards. Jes' now we got to get away from Falconhurst. 'Sides, patrollers might come along. Don' look fittin'. I supposed to be a white woman. How it looks if'n they sees me gittin' raped by a nigger. They string yo' up fast and I have to say yo' tryin' to rape me."

She sensed that she had frightened but not persuaded him. However, he did release her, and took the reins back in his hands.

"Got to have yo' though," he said as he slapped the reins against the horse's back. "Ain' never had me no white woman and yo' as close as I'll ever git."

She adjusted her dress, pinning it with a brooch where he had torn the buttons off, and when he did not seem inclined to close his own garments she reached over and fitted the crude wooden buttons into the buttonholes herself. She straightened up, moved over to the far side of the seat, and sat primly, glad that Benoni was sleeping. Inwardly she cursed herself for her inability to repulse Nero and determined that it would not happen again. Once they had reached the depot in Westminster, she would send him along, alone with the horse, and she would be free of him.

They came to a small stream—one which flowed into the Tombigbee—and Nero slowed the horse. The road divided. A main part crossed a wooden bridge but a grass-grown cart path led down from the road to a ford in the stream. Nero deliberately chose the path.

"Got ter let the horse drink," he said in justification of his move. "Got ter treat the horse good else she won' last till we gits to de place yo' want ter go." When they reached the middle of the shallow stream, he slacked the reins, letting the horse drink from the running water. Slowly they passed through the water, onto the sandy bank on the other side. Close to the water there was a thick grove of pines and bushes. Instead of letting the horse proceed, he reined her in and stopped.

"Cain' go no furder less'n I takes yo'," he said urgently. "Cain' think 'bout nothin' else. Got ter do it now."

She was angry at him—angry at his stupidity and at his overwhelming maleness, which was more important to him than his freedom. She wanted it, too, but she was not going to succumb to it, wasting precious minutes. That could come later. Mayhap she'd take this big buck with her to New Orleans. Having a man along with her would be good in many ways.

"Why are you stopping?" she demanded. Her anger and impatience were evident in her words. "What are you going to do?"

He was climbing down from the wagon. "Dark here." He was whispering so as not to wake Benoni. "Way I feels takes on'y couple o' minutes. Come on, get down." He pointed urgently to the pine trees. "Groun' soft under dem trees, and 'sides, do de horse good to res' a little. She been a-trottin' purty steady."

"Get back up here." Unconsciously Regine adopted the role of mistress. "Get up here and get started and put that foolishness out of your mind." In her anger she forgot her desire for him and his stupidity made her detest him. An ignorant field hand! That's all he was. Why had she let him fondle her? She was as stupid as he to have allowed him and even encouraged him.

"Yo' a-goin' to come down with me, missy, o' mus' I take yo' down?"

"Neither." She reached for the whip, wrenched it from the socket, and struck wildly with it. She heard a yelp of pain and the whip was snatched from her hand.

"Who yo' ter be whoppin' me? Think yo' a white woman? Think yo' my mist'ess? Yo' nigger same's me. A-goin' to have yo' if'n I wants yo'. Needs a woman bad, I do." His voice changed and the anger departed in a wheedling cajolery. "Come down, missy. Yo' a-goin' ter like Nero. He somethin' special. Gits it over quick an' then I drives on."

Regine grabbed at the reins and the horse started so quickly that Nero had to jump back to keep out of the way of the wheels. But he was quick to leap ahead of the horse. Catching the bridle, he quieted the animal and pulled the reins from Regine's hands.

This time he wasted no moments in words. He reached up and lifted her from the seat. She kicked and beat her hands against his chest and face, but all the strength she was able to put into her blows made no impression. He carried her from the wagon to where the pine trees made a blotch of ebon blackness on the ground. He had gone only a few steps when Benoni, awakened by the commotion, jumped down from the wagon and came running after them.

"What yo' a-doin' with my mama?" He clung to Nero's shirt but even with Benoni clinging to him and Regine beating him, Nero did not falter.

"Mama!" Benoni was wailing as he stumbled along behind them. "Don' let him do it to yo'. It hurt awful. He did it to me back there and like to kill me, he did."

"What yo' do to my boy?" Regine added new strength to her struggles and managed to get her feet on the ground. She faced him defiantly in the tight circle of his grasp, and in the moonlight she saw his slack mouth and his eyes glazed with desire.

71

"Jes' pestered him a little in the calaboose. Liked it he did, but pesterin' a boy ain' like pesterin' a woman."

"He hurt me, Mama, hurt me bad."

With one hand Nero reached out and grabbed Benoni, but the boy, fired now with some strange courage he had not realized he possessed, threw himself on the man, scratching, beating and clawing at him. In his attempt to keep the boy off Nero relaxed his hold on Regine. One of his powerful hands caught Benoni and the other slapped him hard, but Benoni was not to be frightened. He redoubled his efforts while Nero, like a horse pursued by a gadfly, tried to shake him off. His hand reached out and clutched Benoni's throat, tightening around the slender adolescent neck. Benoni's hands ceased their pummeling and his knees buckled under him. Regine raged against Nero, her hands beating a steady tattoo on the man, but even her maniacal attack accomplished nothing. Benoni slid to the ground and Nero was upon him, his knees straddling the supine body, his hand still gripped around the boy's throat. Benoni's body stiffened, there was a convulsive twitching of his legs and he lay still. Nero sat back on his haunches and stared at the limp form, quite unaware of what he had done. Regine threw herself down beside her son.

"You've killed him. Oh my God! You've killed my boy." She was suddenly quiet, numbed. In her shock she had forgotten all about safety, flight, and freedom. The first insane thrust of her grief had emptied her mind of everything. Now there was no longer any reason for anything.

Nero gave little consideration to what he had done. That Benoni had died made no impression on him. That afternoon, captivated by the boy's beauty, he had enjoyed him, holding his hand over Benoni's mouth to stifle his screams. Now the same hand, equally ruthless, had squeezed the breath from his body, and Nero regretted the one action as little as he did the other. He was glad that Regine had stopped screaming, and he shifted himself away from the dead boy. Still on his knees, he forced Regine to the ground.

In vain she struggled and fought him, ripping his worn shirt and raking his chest with her nails; he seemed insensible to pain. Unconsciously, to stop her screaming, his hand sought her throat as it had Benoni's and with his other hand he freed himself from his own clothing. She became quieter, and as his body pressed against hers she ceased to struggle. Although she did not respond to his coarse words of endearment, he twice delayed his moment of ecstasy until, unable to constrain himself any longer, he thrust mightily and fell prone across her.

For a moment he lay there, slobbering over her still face with his big lips. Then he stood up, adjusted his clothing, and reached a hand down to her.

"Better we gits a-goin' now, missy. Sorry 'bout the boy, I am. Didn' mean ter kill him. Has gotten to leave him here, we will."

Her hand was limp in his and when he released it it fell to the ground. Slowly it dawned on him what he had done. He had killed her, too. Frightened, he backed away from the two bodies and went to the wagon.

He was alone! The fact that he had killed two people did not plague him as much as the realization that he was alone with their corpses. What could he do? Where could he go? His limited intelligence, which had never formulated an independent thought except to follow the dictates of his own animal passions, now left him helpless. Regine had been the guiding brain; without her he did not know what to do. There was only one thing he could think of—one refuge. Go to his woman at The Coign Plantation. She would be glad to see him. She always welcomed him and hid him; fed him and released him from the demands of his body. He would go to her. He would be safe there.

He climbed up in the wagon and turned it in the direction from which they had come. Standing up in the buckboard he whipped the horse, and they splashed through the water and up the bank to the road. Still standing, he lashed at the horse, speeding on through the night, oblivious of the fact that the road he was taking led him past the gates of Falconhurst. He could accommodate only one idea at a time in his mind. That afternoon it had been Benoni, tonight it had been Regine, now it was his woman at The Coign. Neither the struggling boy nor the unresponsive woman had satisfied him, and he felt a fire mounting in him. He wanted the wild gyrations of black limbs, the animal grunts, the inciting cries and the overpowering ecstasy which only his own woman could give him. He sank back onto the seat, letting the horse run without guidance. Finally the animal slowed to a trot and then to a walk, but Nero did not notice. The first faint streaks of the new day appeared in the east, lighting the sky as the tired horse plodded on.

Chapter 8

WHEN HE AWOKE the next morning, Drummage thought at first that he was still in the big house. It was only when he saw that the person beside him was Olly and not Benoni that he remembered he was at Big Pearl's, and not in his room at the big house. There was no Lucretia Borgia to get him out of bed at dawn. He could go back to sleep again. Olly's arms were warm and protective, and although the corn-husk pallet was not as soft as his mattress in the big house, he found it comfortable. But when he tried to turn over he became aware of the lameness in his back. It was so sore and stiff he could scarcely bear his weight on it. But the herbal poultice had already accomplished wonders and when he got onto his stomach again he managed a degree of comfort. Soon, warmed and relaxed by Olly's nearness, he was asleep, and when he awoke some three hours later the sun was shining, Olly was up and gone, and the odor of fried fat-back hung heavy in the cabin.

Crawling on his belly to the edge of the loft he looked over, down into the cabin below. Old Lucy was still in bed, propped up with a multitude of pillows, and Big Pearl was sweeping the ashes off the hearthstone with a turkey wing. She heard his movement and looked up.

"Yo' ain' a-gittin' out a bed today!" she said. "Masta Hammond say yo' to stay here till yo' gits well and I'se a-plannin' on keepin' yo' a few days. Seems good ter have ma boy back."

"Ain' a-plannin' to git up," Drummage yawned, "but I'se mighty hongry. Man cain' stay up here all day 'thout'n no vittles."

"Since when yo' calls yo'se'f a man?"

"Proved it, ain' I? Done knocked up one wench and everyone thought I done knocked up 'nother. Wat more yo' wan'?"

Big Pearl snickered. She was proud of this boy of hers, even if he had just been whipped.

"Gits yo' brekkus and brings it up ter yo'. What yo' wants?"

"Wants grits and ham 'n' eggs and white biskits with butter 'n' honey. Wantin' coffee too with milk and sweetnin'."

Big Pearl's snicker turned into a derisive grunt.

"Hear that, Maw?" She turned to Old Lucy. "He house nigger now. He mighty fussy. He want white folks' vittles now."

"Gittin' uppity, ain' he? Give 'im grits 'n' hog belly 'n' he fills hisself up. Mawnin', Drummage." She waved up at him. "How yore back?"

"Better. Feels mighty good this mawnin'. Feels like gittin' up and goin' to the big house. Needs me there, they do."

"Well, yo' ain' a-goin'. Masta Hammond say fer yo' ter stay here." Big Pearl had kept his breakfast warm in the ashes and she was now dishing it out. From her squatting position on the hearth she was facing the open door. Something caught her attention and she laid down the wooden spoon, staring with rapt attention outside.

"Whaffor ol' Cissie a-leggin' it down to mah cabin? Mus' ha' picked up some news. That ol' Cissie's jaw like an ol' Black Minorca hen. Cackle, cackle, cackle! She got tongue's long as her foot and keep it waggin' alla time." Forgetting Drummage's breakfast, she stood up and went to the door.

"Mawnin', Cissie." Big Pearl was as avid for gossip as anyone. "Happy to see yo', Cissie. Out early, ain' yo'?"

Cissie, a prune-black Negress, tall and lanky as a broom handle, hurried up the path between the sunflowers, her big feet scuffling in the dust.

"Mawnin', Big Pearl." She was panting from her dog-trotting. "Mawnin', 'n' how yer all and how's that pore boy Drummage? How's yer maw too?"

"We all fine and Drummage, he better." Big Pearl knew that the formalities must be complied with before any news that Cissie possessed was divulged. "How yo', Cissie? 'N' how de rest of de wenches down to de birthin' house? Hears yo' got a new one—that Blossom from de big house."

Old Cissie nodded wisely. "Came yistiday, she did. Got knocked up by that Benoni boy over to de big house. Spindlin' little feller. Don' see how he have 'nuff sap ter do it but she shore knocked up."

"Come in an' set, Cissie." Big Pearl stood aside to let her in and waited for her to go through her greetings to Old Lucy and to Drummage, who was still looking down from the loft. Once Cissie was ensconced in the cabin's only chair, with a cup of Old Lucy's catnip tea sweetened with molasses, she was prepared to divulge her news.

"Hied m'self over to de big house dis mawnin'." She assumed the air of importance which an errand to the big

75

house incurred. "Saw Miz 'Cretia Borgia, I did. Had to git that Blossom's things 'cause she ain't 'lowed outa de birthin' house. She a'goin' in de caffle."

Big Pearl waited patiently, knowing that Old Cissie would take her time.

"Yo' knows that uppity Miz Regine over to de big house. She de one dat's a mustee—de one dat Masta Maxwell pestered after his Ellen died."

"Seen her," Big Pearl nodded, "but don' knows her."

"She Benoni's maw." Drummage, interested, leaned over a little further. "What happen to Regine, Cissie?"

Cissie took a sip of her tea, savoring it, rolled her eyes back, and shook her head dolefully as a fit accompaniment for her words.

"She runned las' night."

"What yo' mean, 'runned'? Ain' never no woman runned from Falconhurst." Old Lucy was sure that Cissie was lying.

"Runned I said and runned she did." Cissie waggled her long, bony finger at Old Lucy. "Stole he'se'f some o' Miz 'Gusta's clotheses, stole a gol' ring, stole Masta Hammond's money, stole a horse 'n' wagon and stole that boy Benoni. Got clean away she did and she tooken dat Nero buck what was in de calaboose wid her boy. Miz 'Cretia Borgia she say Masta Hammond he so mad he g'wine ter kill her if'n he find her. G'wine ter hang her up 'n' strip de meat off'n her back and strip dat Benoni boy too."

Drummage's bare legs were dangling over the edge of the loft now and he was drawing his pants on with some difficulty. With his shirt and shoes in his hand he descended the ladder.

"Whar yo' think yo' a-goin'?" Big Pearl demanded.

"Goin' over to de big house. Masta Hammond he need me. If'n that Regine runned 'n' if'n Blossom in de birthin' house and if'n Benoni he go with Regine, ain' no one over there to he'p Masta Hammond 'n' Miz 'Gusta."

Old Lucy agreed.

"Better yo' he'ps him, Drummage."

And Big Pearl also agreed.

"He take it right likely if'n yo' comes back."

Drummage knelt on the floor before Cissie while Big Pearl soaked the remains of the poultice from his back with a cloth wrung out of warm water. The skin on his back was not broken—only that on his rump, which made sitting difficult, but he was able to walk. When Big Pearl had patted his back dry he managed to get his shirt on, and although he could scarcely bend over to put on his slippers he finally managed to get them on with Big Pearl's help.

It took him some time to walk from the cabin to the big house—each step was painful—and when he reached the back door and let himself in he was so exhausted he had to rest. Sitting down was out of the question, so he knelt in front of one of the chairs, leaning his elbows on the seat. The kitchen was deserted, but he heard footsteps descending the staircase and knew by the heavy tread that it was Lucretia Borgia. She opened the door and stepped down into the kitchen, took a second look to assure herself that it was Drummage in that unusual position, and came over to him.

"Grateful to yo', I am, Miz Lucretia Borgia ma'am. Mightily grateful."

"Yesterday should have got'n over to the barn afore I did but took me some time to clobber that Benoni and that Blossom. Got the truth outa them finally 'cause they know I kills 'em if'n they lie. Too bad it too late to save yo'."

"Masta Hammond know now I didn' do it. That's what I glad of. Tell me, Miz Lucretia Borgia ma'am, Regine runned with Benoni?"

"Shore did, and with that Nero nigger too. Miz 'Gusta madder 'n a wet hen 'cause she stole her moanin' dress 'n' hat. Stole Masta's money too. Took that Benoni and went in a wagon wid a horse wid that Nero. Masta Hammond he mighty mad-tempered."

"Like to see him. Think he see me?"

"He in his office. He glad to see yo'. Likes a boy what don' whimper."

Drummage made his way slowly through the big house to the door of Hammond's office. He heard voices inside and hesitated to knock, but it was his right to do so. As a house servant he had the right of entry, provided his knock was acknowledged. He heard Hammond's voice from the other side of the door.

"Who there?"

"Drummage."

"Drummage?"

"Yes, Masta Hammond suh."

"Come in."

Drummage entered to see Hammond sitting behind his desk, talking with a tall, red-bearded man who stood in front of him. Hammond acknowledged Drummage's presence merely by lifting his eyebrows, and continued his conversation with the bearded man, thumping his fist on the desk to emphasize his words.

"Yo' shore yo' only caught that Nero, Mista Skaggs? Cain' believe he travelin' 'lone. Ought to be two more with him—a mustee wench and a quadroon boy. Had three run last night and shore they all run together."

"Jack Phelps and Uriah Simpson done a-holdin' him over at de ol' barn, Mista Maxwell." Skaggs bobbed his head with every word in deference to Hammond. "We cotched him a-comin' 'long de road 'bout two mile t'other side o' Benson. Sleepin' he was and horse a-walkin'. Saw he a-headin' fer Falconhurst and wid de rig and all didn' think he a-runnin' but Uriah say better we question him. No pass he had and he a-lyin' 'bout how yo' say yo' a-sendin' him to de Coign to cover his woman thar. Knowed he a-lyin'. Fust place, he on de wrong side of Benson ter go to de Coign and secon' place, knows yo' ain' a-sendin' out no nigger wid a horse and wagon jes' to go cover his wench."

"Been keeping that bastard in the calaboose." Hammond rose from his desk and started for the door, followed by Skaggs. With his hand on the latch, he turned and took notice of Drummage.

"How yo' feelin', boy? Thought I tol' you to stay over to Big Pearl's till yo' a-feelin' better."

"Feelin' better now, Masta Hammond suh, and thinkin' with Regine 'n' Benoni 'n' Blossom all gone, yo' needs me here. Short-handed now in the big house, we are."

That Hammond appreciated Drummage's willingness to return unasked was not apparent from the expression on his face, but there was a certain gruff tenderness in his voice.

"Needs yo' I reckon. But yo' better come with me now. Patrollers foun' Nero but didn' fin' Regine nor Benoni."

"Who Nero, Masta Hammond suh?"

"Buck I a-keepin' in the calaboose till time to go with the caffle. Troublesome buck! Regine must a-loosened him last night when she took Benoni. He a randy buck, that Nero. Always headin' for The Coign to his woman there." Hammond shook his head, puzzled. "Don' understand it, Skaggs. Nero always run to The Coign but what he doin' the other side of Benson? Cain' figure it out, but git it outa him. May have to strip him down some."

"Sure hopes yo' do, Mista Maxwell. Take the meat right offa his bones. Runners bad they is. Gittin' a-hold o' that 'bolitionist talk from up North, they are. Figurin' they kin git up there and git free. What them goddam Yankees a-thinkin' of, Mista Maxwell? They's women won' be safe a minute with these randy varmints a-roamin' the country."

"Gits some o' their wives 'n' sisters raped, they won't be so crazy to have these nigger bucks up there. Them damn Yankees jes' a-tryin' to ruin the South, that's all, Mista Skaggs."

They left the house, still castigating the northern abolitionists. Drummage understood little of what they were saying. No nigger could be free, he knew that, and he was just thankful that he had Masta Hammond for a master and that he was living at the big house and that soon Masta Hammond was goin' to get him a wench. Jes' couldn't figure out why anyone would want to run. 'Course he had a mighty sore ass but that wasn't rightfully Masta Hammond's fault. Couldn't hold that against him. He hurried his steps, painful though it was to keep up with the two white men.

When they arrived at the barn there was a group of slaves milling around the doors, and inside, on the barn floor, Nero was still sitting in the buckboard, one hand manacled to the iron armrest on the side of the seat. The horse had been unharnessed and put in the stall. Two white men, dressed scarcely better than the slaves, were standing guard, armed with flintlocks. As Hammond approached, the crowd parted to make way for him, and the two white men bowed respectfully.

"Mista Simpson," Hammond bowed to the younger of the two men, "would yo' 'blige me by unlocking that varmint and bringin' him down from the wagon?" He turned and surveyed the group of slaves as though searching for someone in particular. When he recognized Olly among the black faces, he beckoned him to his side.

"Get a-hold o' that nigger, Olly, and don' let him go."

As soon as the manacle had been unlocked, Olly dragged Nero down out of the wagon and pulled him over before Hammond.

Nero's bravado had entirely left him. He cringed before Hammond, protesting his innocence in a gush of mumbled words. Tears streaked his cheeks and his powerful hands clawed at the air. But he was unable to answer Hammond's questions with any degree of coherence or intelligence. He finally admitted that a woman had come to the calaboose the night before and that she had released him along with the boy he called Benny. At first he maintained that she and the boy had left him at the door of the calaboose and that he had come alone to the barn and stolen the horse himself. As to why he was driving in the wrong direction, he made a feeble excuse of losing his way in the night. He insisted that he had been going to The Coign and had only wanted to see his woman, and that he knew nothing about the other woman who had come to open the calaboose door. She and the boy Benny had just slipped away into the darkness and he had never seen them after that. The more Hammond questioned him, the more confused his story became. Finally he said that he had driven the woman and Benny to The Coign and that they were still there. No, he had driven them some place where there was a steam train. At length he became so muddled that his answers were entirely incoherent.

During the questioning Drummage had seen something which apparently had escaped Hammond's attention. He waited anxiously for a chance to speak to Hammond but he did not dare to interrupt while his master was speaking to Nero. At length, when Hammond, in utter exasperation, paused to catch his breath and allow his choler to subside, Drummage came close to him and whispered:

"May I speaks to yo', Masta Hammond suh?"

Hammond nodded abruptly.

"Look under the seat of the wagon, Masta Hammond suh. 'Pears like they something there belongin' to Miz Regine."

"Looks like a carpetbag." Hammond shaded his eyes to squint at the shapeless mass in the shadows under the wagon seat. "Shore 'nuff is. Go fetch it, Drummage."

Drummage returned with two objects, not only the carpetbag but Regine's black silk reticule. Hammond opened the reticule first and found the money and the pass that Regine had written. Then, upon opening the carpetbag and discovering Regine's and Benoni's clothes, he confronted Nero again, holding them in front of the black fellow's face.

"She was wid you," he declared. "She was a-runnin' wid yo' and now where is she? If'n she not a-runnin' wid yo', she be sure to take these. Why she leave them behind?"

"Don' know, Masta Maxwell suh." Nero had recovered some of his aplomb. "Jes' don' know nuffin' 'bout that woman. Ain' never seen her. She wan' wid me no time. No suh, Masta Maxwell." Nero's big hands clutched each other so that the knuckles showed pale under the black skin. His face was contorted with guilt and fear but he stuck stubbornly to his assertion that he had had no part in Regine's disappearance.

"Shuck yo'se'f down." Hammond's patience had been exhausted.

"What yo' mean, Masta Maxwell? What yo' a-goin' to do to me?"

"Rip his clothes off'n him, Olly."

Olly didn't bother with buttons. His huge hand gripped the collar of the shirt and tore it down the back. He reached for the waistband of the pants, and the button parted and the trousers fell down around Nero's ankles.

He stood there, trembling in Olly's grasp, sobbing now and still imploring Hammond through his sobs to save him.

"Git another boy, Olly, and string this varmint up."

Olly, without relinquishing his hold on Nero, beckoned to another buck, and together they forced Nero to his knees and then down onto the floor, flat on his belly. While Olly sat on his back, the other boy ran to the side of the barn door, untied a rope from an iron ring, and lowered the end of the rope, which ran through a pulley fastened to a beam in the ceiling. He brought the rope end to Olly, who fastened it securely around one of Nero's ankles; then he ran back to the other side of the door, untied another rope, and lowered it so that Olly could secure it to the other ankle. With the help of volunteers from the crowd they hoisted Nero up, feet first. He howled as his belly was dragged along the splintery floor, trying to support himself with his arms until he was hoisted so high that he could no longer touch the floor with his fingers. His legs were spread-eagled apart, and his body swung slowly as he tried to lift his head from its pendent position, still hoping that his pleas for mercy might be heard.

Hammond walked slowly over and examined the knots, and then came back to where the three patrollers were standing.

"We ain' lashed a nigger at Falconhurst for more 'n ten years. Uses a paddle most of the time. But I'm a-goin' to lash this one till the meat falls off'n his back. Olly, get that lash off'n the wall."

The lash, a long thin piece of oxhide, long ungreased, stiff from disuse, was like a rod of thin black metal in Olly's hands. As he practice-swung it through the air, it did not bend and he looked questioningly at Hammond.

"Grease it up on this varmint's back. It'll loosen up." He turned to the circle of bucks around the barn door.

"Goin' to tell yo' why I'm a-lashin' this boy. He a runner. Got out o' the calaboose last night, stole my horse and wagon and runned. Wan' yo' all to see what happens to runners."

Nero's eyes, staring curiously upside down, tried to concentrate on Hammond.

"Don' whop me, Masta Maxwell suh. Don' know nuffin'

'bout them others. Didn' see 'em. Believe me, Masta Maxwell suh. Ain' a-lyin' to yo'. Ain' . . ." He was unable to finish his sentence. Olly, obeying Hammond's lifted finger, had raised his arm, and the stiff lash with all Olly's power behind it came stinging through the air, biting deep into the fleshy buttocks. Nero's body swung forward with the blow, and the flesh, laid open in a cruel gash, spurted bright carmine blood which ran down his back, channeling through the spinal cleft in a bright stream, reddening the black wool of his head and dropping onto the floor. As the pendulum swing of his body slackened, Olly hit again, placing the blow a few inches above the other, and this time the whip, more resilient, bit deeper.

Nero howled, jackknifing his body up until his head almost touched his knees. He straightened out, waving his arms frantically.

"I tells yo' Masta Hammond. I tells yo' if'n yo' not hit me 'gain. Don'."

"Goin' to tell me the truth this time? 'Cause if'n yo' don' we kin keep on whoppin' yo' till there ain' no meat left on yo'."

"Tells yo' if'n yo' let me down."

"Keeps yo' a-hanging there till I knows yo' tellin' the truth."

Between gasps and sobs, Nero told them. Told them how Regine had freed him and Benoni and how they had fled together in the wagon and how she had headed for the railroad. Told them how she had wanted him, begged for him, and finally persuaded him. Confessed how she had insisted he stop the wagon at the ford and how he had yielded to her entreaties and stopped and taken her. Then he swore that she and Benoni had fled into the night. He told them he was returning to Falconhurst to give himself up as he had done twice before when he had run to The Coign.

Hammond almost believed him. He doubted, knowing Regine and her fastidiousness, that she had wanted this field hand, and yet he remembered from his own intimate knowledge of her that she was hot-blooded. It might be that she had wanted this man and had taken him, but when he looked down at the black satin reticule and the carefully packed carpetbag he knew that Regine had not fled from Nero and abandoned the money that would secure her freedom. But he needed Nero and he could not afford to incapacitate him further.

"Let him down," he ordered Olly. "Put him in the back of the spring wagon and spancel him good. Hitch a team to

the wagon." He turned to the three patrollers. "If he's tellin'
the truth and Regine was a-headin' for the steamcars, she
was goin' to Westminster. Knowed the place, she did. We'll
go there and take him along. Thinkin' we may find her and
Benoni 'long the way."

Nero was dumped, still sobbing with pain, into the back
of the wagon, where he lay, belly down on the floor, his
wrists and ankles spanceled to the four corners of the wagon.
Hammond had his horse saddled, and motioned to Olly to
get up on the wagon seat and drive the team. He noticed
Drummage.

"Yo' wants to go?" he asked him. "Feel like sittin'?"

"Shore do, Masta Hammond suh."

Hammond jerked his thumb to the empty space beside
Olly, and Drummage climbed up over the wheel. Hammond
and the red-bearded Skaggs rode ahead, followed by the
wagon with Olly and Drummage on the seat and Nero still
howling in back. The other two patrollers rode behind the
wagon.

Chapter 9

HAMMOND rode hard and the others kept up with him. After
about three hours of almost steady trotting, they arrived at
the bridge which spanned the Tombigbee, and Hammond, up
ahead, turned his horse and rode back to the wagon. He
cantered alongside and prodded Nero with his riding crop.

"Git up! Look round! Yo' ever bin here before?"

Nero lifted his head over the side of the wagon, surveyed
the scene and seemed unable to identify it.

"Ain' never bin here afore, Masta Maxwell suh. Ain' never
bin this far off'n home. My back hurt somethin' awful, Masta
Maxwell suh. Ain' we a-goin' home soon?"

Hammond's crop slashed across the fellow's face and he
yelped.

"Don' yo' remember goin' over this bridge?"

" 'Pears like I do, Masta Maxwell suh, but it night and I
cain' just tell. 'Members we went over a long bridge, but cain't
tell if'n it's this un."

"Only long bridge round here. Yo'd remember it." Hammond raised the crop again.

" 'Members it now, Masta Maxwell suh. 'Members a-hearin' the hoss's shoes on the boards. 'Members it, suh."

Hammond rode alongside the wagon and after they crossed the bridge and rode a short distance on the other side, Skaggs stopped and pointed to the waters of a creek ahead.

"Yore nigger said somethin' 'bout a ford. Think this un's it?"

"Could be." Hammond pointed to the fresh tracks which ran down from the road and were now filled with ribbons of water where they crossed the sand. "Been a wagon here not long ago." He motioned to the others to follow him and they left the road, going down the bank and across the stream.

Even from midstream they saw them!

A woman's body was sprawled awkwardly under the pine trees, her skirt and petticoats covering her head, her naked legs spread apart. Not far away from her was Benoni's body, the face swollen and empurpled, covered with a crawling mass of green flies.

Hammond leaped from his horse even before it had reached the shore and ran up the bank to kneel beside Regine's body. He pulled down the black skirt, recognizing the black taffeta of his wife's dress. It was Regine's face, as indeed he had known it would be.

Drummage and Olly arrived in the wagon with Nero still stretched out behind, and they were joined by the patrollers. All gazed down at the two bodies silently, except for Nero, who had raised himself up, and was now loudly wailing his protestations of innocence to which nobody paid the slightest attention.

Hammond stood up and pointed to an unpainted but commodious wooden cabin with several barns and outhouses, only a short distance across the fields.

"Who lives over there?" he asked Skaggs.

Simpson volunteered to answer. "Kinfolk o' mine," he said, jerking his thumb in the direction of the house. "Jim Getty married my cousin Almira Simpson."

"Think he might have a length of rope 'n' a shovel?" Hammond queried.

"Might," Simpson answered cautiously. "Mos' probably does."

"See if'n yo' can borrow them fer a while. Pay him well."

Simpson bristled at the implication that his cousin, a property owner, would accept payment. "Jim won' take no pay jes' fer bein' neighborly. Be honored he would, to help yo', Mista Maxwell. Falconhurst well thought of round here."

"Obliged if'n yo' ask him and request him to kindly come over here."

Simpson lit out over the fields to the house and was soon back, followed by Getty and his two gangly, tow-headed sons, accompanied by three slaves. One was an old man, crowned with a pate of white wool, who limped badly from rheumatism; the second, a middle-aged man, powerfully built and intelligent-looking; the third was a young buck of about Drummage's age. It was readily apparent that they were three generations of the same family.

Forgetting momentarily the business at hand, Hammond appraised the young fellow with his eyes. He was always an admirer of slave flesh, and whenever he saw an unusually fine specimen he wanted to buy it. This was the type of buck he admired, and his eyes took in the sleek muscular frame, the intelligent face. Looked like almost pure Ibo, he thought.

Each of the slaves carried a spade, and Getty, tall, tow-headed as his sons, but with a beard stained brown around the mouth from tobacco juice, had a coil of new rope around his shoulder.

"This yore property here, Mista Getty?" Hammond asked after Simpson had introduced them.

"Shore is, Mista Maxwell, and mighty proud I am to have yo' on it. Them yore two servants that was killed?" He pointed to the bodies of Regine and Benoni, and at Hammond's nod he stepped nearer for a closer look. " 'Pears to me that the lady got herself raped."

"Not a lady, Mista Simpson, jes' a mustee, but she did get raped."

"He done it?" Simpson pointed to the trembling Nero in the wagon.

"Shore did," Hammond agreed. "Goin' to hang him, we are. Askin' yore permission if'n we kin hang him to one of yore trees, Mista Getty." Hammond looked up into the tree and pointed to a branch that seemed to be both high enough and sufficiently strong-limbed.

Nero had raised himself on his elbows and was peering over the side of the wagon. Drummage, beside the wagon, was conscious of Nero's face suddenly raised up beside his own. He turned to see the muddy grey of Nero's cheeks, the eyes lackluster from fear, and the trembling bluish lips. Knowing that the man was going to die, Drummage felt something akin to pity for him. He laid his hand on Nero's wiry poll.

"Wh' they a-goin' ter do ter me, boy?" Nero spoke in a hoarse whisper; fear had robbed him of his voice.

"They a-goin' ter hang yo' up."

"Goin' ter strip me down again?"

Drummage shook his head. "Ain' got no whip here."

"Then what they goin' ter do ter me?"

Drummage could not tell him.

"Dunno, man, wait an' see."

"They a-goin' ter kill me?"

Drummage could not answer him.

"Yo' gits me a hatful o' water," Nero begged as he pointed to the stream. "Powerful dry I am."

"If'n I gets yo' de water, yo' tells Masta Hammond yo' done it?"

"Think it do any good?"

"Dunno, but yo' kin try." Drummage took off his straw hat and went down to the stream, filled it, and brought it back spurting water in all directions, but there was enough left for Nero to drink.

Hammond noticed.

"Whaffor yo' a-babyin' that nigger, Drummage? Won' need no water where he a-goin'."

"He want ter talk to you, Masta Hammond suh. Says his throat so dry he cain' talk."

"Don' want to lissen to him."

"I done it, Masta Hammond." Nero had managed to find his voice. "I done it. Tells yo' all 'bout it but don' whop me no more. Don' whop me, Masta Maxwell suh." He had risen to his knees and was kneeling with arms outstretched. Drummage stepped back.

"Ain' a-goin' to whop you. Stan' up." Hammond unlocked the spancels.

Slowly and painfully Nero got up, balancing himself with difficulty on the wagon. He seemed somewhat more composed over Hammond's assurance that he was not to be whipped, but his eyes were riveted on the unusual operations which were taking place. He watched Getty, who, with sure hands, was tying a noose on the end of the rope and winding the rope-end carefully around the noose above the knot. When Getty was finished Nero raised his head to see the end of the rope flung over the high limb of the pine tree, and watched the youngest of the Getty slaves crawl slowly out on the limb to loop the rope over the limb and remain there, legs twisted around the branch.

Nero had never seen a hanging and probably had never

heard of one, but he sensed that something was about to happen to him as a result of these preparations and it dawned on him that it might be far worse than the flogging which he had dreaded. His knees collapsed and he sank to the floor of the wagon.

Hammond ordered Olly up into the wagon and told him to hold Nero upright, while Getty jumped up beside them and placed the noose around Nero's neck. When he had adjusted it he called up to the boy in the tree, whom he addressed as Jubal, to tighten the rope so there would be no slack and then to tie it securely to the branch. By the time Jubal had finished fastening it, Nero's head was stretched up sideways and he was standing on tiptoe to ease the strain.

"Yo' a-goin' ter hang that buck stark nekkid?" Simpson asked.

"Lef' his pants behind at Falconhurst," Hammond answered, "and he shore ain' a-goin' to need 'em where he's goin'. 'Sides, we off'n the road and won't offend no white ladies a-passin' by."

"Shore do seem a waste a-hangin' that nigger up. He well built and well hung. Admires having a buck like him myself." Skaggs gazed enviously at Nero. Merely owning such a slave as Nero would give a red-neck such as Skaggs an enviable place in the community.

"He a runner and a raper." Hammond sensed the hint in Skaggs' admiration. "He a danger to the community. Rapes a slave one day, rapes a white woman the next. Kills a slave one day, kills his masta the next. Only one thing to do with this kind."

Now Nero sensed that he was to die. A hysteria of fear possessed him, causing the flesh of his naked body to quiver and his knees to give way, so that Olly had difficulty in holding him up. He released him and Nero sank down, but the tightening of the rope forced him to stand up again. He clung to Olly in desperation.

It was Hammond's turn to step up onto the wagon and he adjusted the noose so that the bulky knot came just under Nero's ear.

"Yo' ain' a-goin' ter hurt me no more, Masta Maxwell?" Nero managed to mumble the words but Hammond did not answer. He jumped down from the wagon and motioned to Drummage to get up in the driver's seat. He then ordered Olly to stand a few paces behind the tailgate of the wagon.

"Yo', Drummage." Hammond placed the whip in Drum-

nage's hand. "When I counts to three, yo' use the whip
on them horses. Let 'em have it good."

"Yas suh, Masta Hammond suh."

"And yo', Olly, when that Nero come a-swingin' out
o' the wagon, yo' grabs him 'round the belly and hang on.
Lift yore feet up off'n the ground and swing with him."

"Yas suh, Masta Hammond suh." Olly spread his arms wide
apart and braced his feet.

"One." Hammond brought down his right hand.

Nero was sobbing incoherently.

"Two."

The patrollers were grinning widely. Entertainment such
as this was a rare occasion for them. Getty's three slaves
stood in the background, fear making their faces livid.

"Three."

Drummage brought the whip down on the backs of the
horses and they lunged forward. Nero's body was swept out
of the wagon into Olly's arms, and he fastened himself around
Nero, lifting his feet high so that he swung free. The wide
arc of their bodies slowly diminished and Olly released his
grip, letting Nero swing alone until he hung straight and still.
The head was bent at a strange angle and a stream of white
semen crawled slowly down one black leg. Already the face
was empurpled, but still the muscles of his body twitched
and the fingers of one hand moved.

"Take a-hold of his legs agin, Olly." Hammond found
difficulty in speaking. "Put yore whole weight on him and
pull."

Olly grabbed the knees of the body and gave a final mighty
downward wrench. The hand stopped moving.

"Guess that bastard won' rape no more wenches." Hammond scrubbed his hands together as though trying to clean
them of something. Seized by a sudden nausea he plunged
into the bushes, and they could hear him retching. When
he returned, white-faced, he sat down on the ground, his
elbows on his knees and his face in his hands. Although
he spoke directly to Olly and Drummage, who had returned
with the wagon, he glanced up at the three Getty slaves to
include them in his warning.

"Yo' see what happens when a buck covers a wench 'thout
permission."

Both Olly and Drummage bowed their heads. They
watched the body that only moments before had lived
and breathed and spoken. Now it hung motionless.

Hammond reached into his pocket and drew out a gold eagle.

"Be 'bliged to yo', Mista Getty, if'n yo' has yo' boys dig three graves for my servants on yore property."

"Cain' rightly take no money fer that, Mista Maxwell." Getty shook his head. "Pleased to help yo', neighborly-like. We planters has ter stand tergether and I'm honored to serve the master o' Falconhurst. Honored, suh."

Hammond realized that the man's pride and the fact that he was a slave owner himself made him his peer. To press payment on him would be an insult. By refusing Hammond's money he placed Hammond in debt to him, and from now on he could boast that he and Hammond Maxwell were equals.

But there was one way that Hammond could repay him. He had not forgotten Getty's young slave, and he now looked up at the boy and motioned to him to come over to him. Jubal advanced with long strides to stand in front of Hammond.

"Likely-looking boy yo' got there, Mista Getty. Ever think of sellin' him?"

"He a good boy, Mista Maxwell." Getty shook his head. "Raised him myself I did. Ol' Joab there his grandpappy, and Stone here his pappy. His dam, she Clotilda from over to Taunton Plantation. Mista Holderness o' Taunton wanted Stone to come over and stud some o' his wenches 'cause Stone pretty near pure Ibo and he guv me Jubal when he a sucker for payment. Clotilda she a fine wench—part Ibo herse'f—and Stone he a good boy. Jubal mighty strong but gentle. He gentle as a kitten. Ain' never thought o' sellin' Jubal. He like one o' the fambly."

"How ol' is he?"

" 'Bout sixteen, seventeen years. Him an' Stone and Joab all live in the house with me and my wife. Eats with us too. Ain' got no slave quarters we ain', and ain' got no wench now since Stone's woman died."

"Admire mighty well to finger him, even if'n I don' buy him. Yo' mind, Mista Getty?"

"Proud ter have yo', Mista Maxwell. Shuck yo'se'f down fer Mista Maxwell, Jubal. Yo' kin feel mighty proud that Mista Maxwell fingerin' yo'. He know more 'bout niggers 'n any man in Alabama."

Jubal smiled as he loosened his clothes and let them fall to the ground. He was proud of his body—the only thing he possessed—and he was glad to exhibit it. Hammond went

89

over it with trained fingers, noting the smoothness of the skin, the flow of the heavy muscles, and the strong solid bones beneath them. This was the kind of boy he liked— strong, healthy, intelligent, with a multitude of offspring burgeoning in his loins. He wanted this boy but he recognized Getty's attachment for him. He did not press the matter but he could not resist adding: "Had thought I might use him for a house servant, seein' as how you say he's housebroken. That boy there"—he pointed to Benoni's body—"was body servant to my grandson. Got to train me 'nother boy right away 'fore us goes to N' Orleans. That's why I a-thinkin' o' yore Jubal. Seems like a right smart boy. Could use him for breedin' too. Likes Ibo blood, I do."

Getty hesitated a long minute.

"If'n yo' wants him, Mista Maxwell, I sells him ter yo'."

Jubal was struggling back into his clothes and now Joab and Stone came up. Both were crying and both took him in their arms. They all clung close together.

"I sells him ter yo', Mista Maxwell, on one condition. Sells him only if'n Jubal willin'. Ain' never sold none of my boys and ain' 'tended to but knows yo' be good ter him."

"How much I bring, Masta Jim?" Jubal extricated himself from his father's and grandfather's arms.

"Don' rightly know, Jubal. Mista Maxwell ain' made no offer."

"If'n I bring 'nuff, Masta Jim, yo' could get a wench ter help Miz 'Liza." Jubal waxed enthusiastic. "She ailin' and she need help. Then pappy he have himself a wench ter cover and he get yo' a lot o' new suckers. Ain' wishin' ter leave yo', Masta Jim, but thinkin' of Miz 'Liza."

"Jes' as Jubal say, Mista Maxwell. My wife she mighty porely and ain' had no wench ter help her since Aggie up and died. Jubal willin', it's a deal."

"Ever bred this boy, Mista Getty?"

"Ain' never bred him 'cause we ain' got no wenches. Was a-goin' ter ask Mista Holderness if'n Jubal could cover one o' two of his wenches jes' ter give the boy a chance ter know a wench, but he still pretty young fer breedin'. Should have plenty o' good sap in him, Mista Maxwell. Ain' never wasted none."

"Looks like he might," Hammond agreed. "Offerin' yo' one thousand two hundred dollars fer the boy. That 'lows yo' to git a good wench fer round eight hundred and gives yo' a cash profit o' four hundred."

"Sell me, Masta Jim! I worth a lot of money." Jubal was both laughing and crying.

"Like to take him with me now." Hammond stood up and offered Getty his hand to seal the bargain. "But ain' brought no 'mount o' money like that with me."

"Yo' kin send it to me." Getty swelled with pride to think he was involved in a business deal with Hammond Maxwell. "Yore word's good as yore bond. Be honored if'n yo' all stay ter eat with us. Cain' offer yo' nothin' fancy but yo' welcome to what we has."

"Thank you, Mista Getty, but we needs to get back to Falconhurst. I speakin' for myself only. Perhaps these gen'lemen likes to stay with you to eat."

"We shore would," Skaggs answered. "Ain' had no vittles today."

Hammond waited for Jubal to finish his farewells and then motioned him up onto the wagon. Joab and Stone still clung to him after he had seated himself in back beside Drummage.

Hammond placed his foot in the stirrup preparatory to mounting his horse, but hesitated and took it down. He walked slowly over to where Regine and Benoni were lying, and stared down at them for a long minute. Then he walked over to where Nero's body swayed slightly in the breeze. Again he felt ill, and a dry retching contracted his throat but he overcame it. Now he realized why he had been so anxious to buy this boy Jubal. Regine and Benoni and Nero represented death, but Jubal was life. Jubal's loins would add more husky bucks and wenches to Falconhurst. Hammond was not going back empty-handed. He never had. Even when he disposed of his caffles in New Orleans he always took new slaves back with him. Today he had lost three, but the fact that he had one to replace them mitigated the loss. He walked over to his horse, waved to the men, mounted, and cantered off, through the shallow ford and up the bank onto the road, without turning back.

But when Olly started the wagon, Drummage looked back. He could see the men now digging with their spades and the elongated body of Nero still swaying slightly as Stone climbed out on the branch to cut him down. He turned to Jubal beside him. The boy was crying.

"Yo' shore goin' to like Falconhurst, boy. Tonight if Masta Hammond say so, yo' kin sleep alongside o' me in my bed. Not so lonesome-like that way."

Jubal lifted up a tear-stained face and smiled.

"What yore name?" he asked.

"I Drum Major but they calls me Drummage, they do."

"Yo' shore got a funny name but I likes yo'. We be frien's, Drummage."

"Yes, Jubal, we be frien's."

Chapter 10

MUCH TIME had been lost at Falconhurst, but Hammond's scheduled arrival in New Orleans had to be met. The Falconhurst sale had been widely advertised throughout the slave-holding South. Many buyers would be congregating, and it could not be postponed.

This year, owing to the lateness of perparations, Hammond decided to try a new means of transportation to get his caffle from Falconhurst to New Orleans—the steamcars. Before, they had always started out with the shiny barouche carrying the family, at the head of a long caravan of wagons to tote the wenches, followed by the marching caffle of boys on foot. But such travel consumed precious days, and, although Hammond had made the trip many times in the past, there was always some uncertainty about overnight accommodations. When they were able to accept the hospitality of some affluent planter, it was easy enough to feed and bed the slaves in his barns or quarters, but sometimes they were forced to stay in taverns overnight and then there was always the problem of a place to keep the slaves. In good weather they could sleep in the fields, but Hammond would not allow them to stay out in inclement weather. He had put too much money and work into their rearing to take chances of their contracting lung fever. So the week or more that it took to go overland, gauged always by the footpace of the caffle, was a problem. They always arrived tired, and as a result the slaves had to be conditioned in the slave jail for several days, to be fed, fattened, and rested up after their long journey.

Other slave dealers had used the railroad, and this year Hammond decided to try it. After negotiations with the station agent at Westminster, he arranged for a special train to take them to New Orleans without having to change trains in Mobile.

They were scheduled to leave Falconhurst in the evening,

directly after their last meal, and walk through the night to Westminster where the train would be waiting for them in the morning. A gala atmosphere pervaded the plantation on that last day before leaving. True, a few of the boys and more of the women regretted to leave the familiar surroundings in which most of them had been born and reared, but they had been so thoroughly conditioned from the time they were children to look on this day as a big turning-point in their lives that not one of them, regardless of sentimental ties, would have volunteered to remain at Falconhurst. It was, in a way, their baccalaureate. It signaled their passing out into a larger world and as such it was a mark of distinction. Only the best were included in the caffle. The marred, the misfits, the maimed and the ugly had been weeded out and gone their way with itinerant slave drivers. This was the cream of the crop, the strongest and handsomest of the bucks, and the prettiest and most fertile of the wenches. Their future had been painted to them in glowing terms, and every boy anticipated becoming a stud on some big plantation while every wench looked forward expectantly to being a brood mare. They knew that they were Falconhurst slaves and, as such, prime flesh—the aristocracy of southern servants. Their pride in themselves, their anxiety to see the big city, and their future prospects all combined to make them tractable and docile.

Hammond, on his horse, headed the procession as they started down the lane from the quarters to the main road. Next came Ajax, driving the shiny barouche, with Augusta, Sophie, and the children inside. Following them came the spring wagon, piled high with trunks and valises, and after it a long row of wagons for the wenches, with the boys marching four abreast behind and Brutus bringing up the rear. Drummage and Jubal, as house servants, rode behind the barouche as footmen.

The high spirits of the bucks, plodding along the dusty roads, continued throughout the night. Hammond allowed them frequent short rests, and during the journey along the roads they timed their steps to songs, in which the wenches joined them from the wagons. Around midnight they stopped for a lunch of bread and hot coffee and sat around the dying fires for an hour, then started off with renewed vigor. Dawn found them crossing the bridge of the Tombigbee, and it was fully light when they passed the ford where only a short time ago Nero's body had hung from the big pine tree.

This was home territory to Jubal and he delighted in pointing out to Drummage spots which held particularly poignant memories for him. His black finger indicated the spot where he and Joab had treed a raccoon one night; there was the swimming hole where they bathed in summer; there was the Getty cabin, with a plume of grey smoke curling from the chimney and there—he turned and waved until Drummage thought he would disjoint his arm—was Stone, out behind the cabin chopping firewood. Stone waved back, but Jubal never knew whether Stone had really recognized him. He hoped he had, but just seeing his pappy across the fields made him happy.

When they arrived at the little wooden Gothic railroad station in Westminster in the early morning, they had another meal of bread and coffee, fortified by big chunks of cold meat, before the train arrived.

To all of them except the white folks it was a frightening apparition. The big engine, belching sparks and smoke from its over-sized smokestack, the clanging of the bell and the toot of the whistle—all made it appear like some unearthly monster coming to devour them. Bucks as well as wenches showed their terror. But when it stopped it was not quite so fearful, and they got over their fears and bragged among themselves that they had known all the time it would not hurt them.

It took some time to get the barouche up onto a flatcar and lashed securely. Then the frightened horses had to be led up a ramp into another car. Finally it was time for the slaves to board, and they walked up the same ramp the horses had used, into open gondola cars. The floors of the cars for the wenches had been spread with straw but those for the bucks were bare. They were crowded in, tightly packed against each other with only two cars for the hundred and twenty bucks in the caffle. At the end of the train was a saloon car for the white folks, with plush seats, ornate brass lanterns, and glazed windows. Drummage and Jubal were the only two servants to ride in such splendor. Jubal was there to take care of the children, who already worshiped him far more in the short time they had known him than they ever had Benoni. Drummage was now waiting on all the white folks. Miz 'Gusta had decided not to replace Regine from among the plantation slaves and take upon herself the onerous duty of training a girl to the niceties of being a lady's maid. She preferred to wait until she could purchase a girl in New Orleans who was already trained.

With a lurch the train started and Drummage, trying hard to cover up his fear, looked out of the window to see the depot of Westminster receding and the landscape hurrying by at a speed which he had never thought possible. It was so different from the slow motion of a horse. Here he was, most comfortably seated on a luxurious, albeit rather gritty chair of red plush, watching through the window and seeing the telegraph poles hurrying past. At first it looked as though the speed of the train were actually mowing the poles down, as a scythe mows grass, for as the train passed they seemed to fall, but they didn't fall, as he was able to ascertain by looking back.

There was little for him to do. Miz 'Gusta curled up on one seat and went to sleep and Miz Sophie slept in another. Even Hammond leaned back and dozed off. Little Miz 'Manda slept and after running back and forth in the car for half an hour, Masta Warren slept also. But neither Jubal nor Drummage closed an eye. Tired as they were from the long night's traveling, they were not going to waste a moment of this precious experience, and they sat, eyes glued to the window, watching the fertile farmlands of lower Alabama rush past, as trees piled upon houses, fields engulfed forests, and rivers rushed past them. The tracks ran beside fields which were black with workers and as the train sped by they stopped long enough to straighten up and raise their hands in greeting, and then went back to work again. Even above the roar of the train Drummage could hear the shouted greetings of the boys in the open cars ahead and he knew that they were feeling far superior to the bent-backed workers in the fields. Why not? They were Falconhurst bucks, a-riding in style to the big city for their own brief moment on the vendue table.

Between stops to feed and water the slaves in the open cars, and the time consumed for switching the train from track to track to get it through Mobile and on its way to New Orleans, the entire day passed and night came on, but still they sped on at what seemed to Drummage a hurtling speed. Long hours in the car had accustomed him to the new experience; now, in the darkness, he was no longer able to look out the window, for he could see nothing but his own dark face, peering back at him. The oil lamps had been lighted and he had the job of unpacking the big hampers and setting up a meal of cold chicken and ham along with biscuits and coffee for the white folks. After they had eaten, he shared the left-overs with Jubal. The two children were put to bed, each occupying one of the plush divans, and Miz

95

'Gusta, Sophie, and Hammond made themselves comfortable with rugs and pillows. Drummage and Jubal had seats of their own at the end of the car, where they managed to sleep fitfully through the night until the train arrived at New Orleans, just as dawn was breaking over the city.

The slaves, regardless of the fact that some were lighter-skinned than others, all looked uniformly black as coal from the smoke and cinders, as they came down from the cars and formed into a long line to march to the slave jail under Brutus' authority. The horses and the big barouche were un-loaded and Ajax finally managed to get the frightened animals into their harnesses. Drummage and Jubal climbed up on the footman's seat, Ajax spoke to the horses, and the carriage rattled over the cobbles of the just awakening streets of New Orleans. The only people on the streets were the house servants, yawning and stretching as they sluiced the banquettes and scrubbed them clean with long brooms made of twigs.

To Drummage, accustomed to a lifetime of plantation living, the city was a never ending miracle. House after house after house where people lived, stores, shops, and all sorts of establishments passed one after the other in a bewildering kaleidoscope which seemed to go on forever in a pageant of life and color.

And . . . women! In his brief trip through the streets, he saw, even at that early hour, more wenches than he had ever seen before in his life. Whether it was the novelty of the situation or the fact that the New Orleans wenches had a well-deserved reputation for beauty, he knew that he had never seen so many desirable women before. They were certainly different from the wenches at Falconhurst, for these, many of them, were dressed in the cast-off finery of their mistresses. Even in their second-hand elegance they seemed like creatures from another world, with their gayly colored madras turbans and their flounces and ruffles. They were a far cry from the country wenches in their shapeless osnaburgs.

Ee-yah! How he ached to try one of them. He even considered disobeying Hammond's command to leave them entirely alone. Surely such glorious creatures could not give him any of the dreadful diseases he had been warned of.

Jubal suddenly nudged Drummage and pointed to the banquette at his side. It was then that Drummage saw her.

She was possibly his own age—maybe even a year or two older, for her breasts were well-developed rounded globes that strained at the thin material of her dress. Her wide skirts, with an inner layer of ruffled petticoats, were tied up around her waist with a length of twine, leaving her slender, curved legs bare, so that the water which she was splashing on the banquette would not soil her gown. As she bent over her hiked-up dress revealed a far greater expanse of brown thigh than she had ever intended, and it was this sleek expanse of flesh that had attracted Jubal's attention. Drummage had had only a moment to surfeit himself with these tempting charms when she straightened up, brushed a lock of curly black hair away from her forehead with a dripping hand, and looked directly at the two boys sitting on the high seat behind the carriage.

Her eyes slipped over Jubal and came to linger on Drummage, and for an instant their eyes met. And in that one moment he knew that never again would he see a wench he desired quite as much as this one. She was tall and slender with an oval face, and even at a distance he could see that her eyes, instead of being brown, were darkly blue. Her color! Ah, it was difficult to describe. She was not the pale tea-rose color of Regine; she was more the color of translucent amber—an all-over golden hue that gave the impression of an inner light shining through her skin. Now, standing with her young breasts pushed even more tightly against the bodice of her gown, she was conscious of Drummage's stare, and she forced her chest forward. She smiled impudently and provocatively, curving her upper lip over a row of small, even, white teeth. As Drummage, still gazing at her in open-mouthed wonderment, continued to stare, she called out:

"Ain' yo' never seen a gal before, pretty boy?"

By turning in his seat he managed to keep her in view. Just as they were about to turn the corner he called back: "Not as pretty a one as yo'!"

They drove on, but all the way to the Saint Louis Hotel Drummage fondled the unknown girl in his thoughts, pressed his lips against that perfect mouth, let his hand glide along that sleek expanse of revealed skin, and brought himself to such a state of tumescence that when the carriage stopped in front of the hotel he was ashamed to climb down and face those inside the carriage. Fortunately they were all too exhausted . . . too relieved to reach their destination, to notice. By the time he was ready to carry his luggage through the tall doors, across the marble tiled lobby and up the carpeted stairs, his appearance had subsided to normal.

Yet that long, slim-legged, amber-hued vision that he had seen slopping water on the banquette had taken up a permanent residence in his thoughts. Try as he could he was not able to get her out of his mind. Talking about her with Jubal did not help matters. Jubal merely regarded her as another wench, whose small, well-rounded buttocks had momentarily attracted his attention. His attitude puzzled Drummage. He knew that Jubal had never had a woman and this should have made him more anxious to discuss them in prurient and lascivious details. But Jubal did not even know the words. Never having had any prospect of having a wench, he had thought little about sex. Sure, he admitted, he had anticipated it, but he could not get as hotly aroused as Drummage, for whom women were the most important things in life.

After two more or less sleepless nights and the long journey on the steamcars, the white folks wanted nothing more than to stretch out on the cool white linen sheets of the big beds, have the jalousies closed to dim the light in the large, high-ceilinged rooms, and nap until late afternoon. They didn't even want their trunks or boxes unpacked for, as Miz 'Gusta said, "Nothing matters now except to rest." Once Drummage had closed the jalousies and Jubal had made an exploratory trip to the kitchens to get milk and cookies for the children, the boys were dismissed and were free to seek out their own quarters on the high top floor at the rear of the hotel, where a long dormitory with evenly spaced cots accommodated the visiting male servants; the female servants slept on a lower floor.

The long dormitory, stiflingly hot under the roof slates and insufficiently ventilated by the tiny dormer windows, was empty now, except for one middle-aged colored man sitting on his bunk with an open book in his lap. He seemed oblivious to the heat, so engrossed was he in his book, but as the boys entered he looked up from his reading and greeted them pleasantly.

"Yo' boys new here?" he asked, closing the book but keeping his fingers between the pages.

"We Masta Hammond Maxwell's servants from Falconhurst Plantation," Drummage answered the man respectfully. "We jes' 'rived this mornin'. Come by the steamcars, we did. I Drummage and"—he jerked his thumb in Jubal's direction—"this yere is Jubal. Where we supposed to sleep in this yere oven?"

"Pretty well filled up here. Lots of planters here for the Falconhurst sale. Yo' two bein' sold?"

Drummage drew himself up proudly. "Co'se we ain'. We Masta Hammond's house servants. All the bucks and wenches

98

to be sold over to the slave jail. Mighty tired we is. Been a-travelin' two nights. Masta Hammond say we kin sleep now till four o'clock. Cain' sleep tho' 'cause we hungry. How yo' called, man?"

"I am Parnassus, body servant to Mista Beauchamp of Medford Plantation up near Natchez. He here to buy some, of yore Falconhurst bucks." He pointed to the two neatly made bunks beside his own. "These two bunks aside me ain' being used. Yo' kin take them. Ain' yo' got no clothes wid yo'?"

"Got 'em but they still out in the kerridge. Got to bring 'em in. Don' know where to find the kerridge though and we mightily hungry."

"Then I'll go with yo'." Parnassus placed the book he was reading inside a canvas bag and slid it under the cot. "First off we'll go down and I'll show yo' how to git yore' breakfast in the servants' dinin' room. Then I'll take yo' out to the livery stable and show you where yo' kin find yore carriage. After that yo'll know yore way around."

With Parnassus as a guide they were served the servants' breakfast in the plain, white-walled room off the hotel kitchen, and afterwards they found Ajax and got their small boxes from the barouche. By this time they were practically asleep on their feet and could hardly manage to slip out of their pants and their thin slippers and throw themselves on their cots.

Parnassus reached under the bed and withdrew the book from the canvas bag. He found his place and started to read.

Drummage opened one eye and looked at him curiously.

"What yo' a-doin', man? Readin' that book?"

"Uh-huh."

"How come yo' kin read?"

"Taught myself, I did. Masta don' know I kin read."

"What dat book say?"

"Dis book written by a gen'lemun up North, name o' Garrison. He say slavery wrong. Say that all colored people should be free jes' like white people. Say that soon all white masters, a-goin' to have to give us our freedom."

"Whaffor?" Drummage was curious.

"Don' yo' wants to be free?"

"Ain' never thought nothin' 'bout it. Got me a good masta, I have. Got me a good home. I'se house servant. Eats good, sleeps good, don' have to work hard. Masta goin' to git me a wench too. Whaffor I wants to be free?"

"So's yo' kin be yore own masta," Parnassus replied.

It was a new idea to Drummage. To be his own master! To

belong to himself! The idea was so stupendous, so seemingly impossible that he could not quite comprehend it, but it opened up infinite possibilities.

"Kin I learn to read 'bout stuff like that?" he asked.

"Take a little time but if'n yo' wants, I teach yo'. Mustn't tell yore masta yo' a-learnin'. He won' like it. Colored folks not supposed to read. Colored folks not supposed to know nothin' 'bout abolition."

" 'Bout what?"

"Abolition. Dat means no more slavery. Dat means to abolish slavery. Dat means yo' jes' as good as yo' master, even if'n yo' black and he white."

"Abolition." Drummage repeated the word. "Likes to know more 'bout it, I would. Likes to know how to read words, I would. Likes to. . . ." His eyes closed, and in another moment he was sound asleep.

Chapter 11

IT WOULD HAVE BEEN difficult for Hammond Maxwell to analyze his feelings towards his slaves. His whole life, ever since he could remember, had been devoted to the breeding and raising of Negroes for market. While other boys were spending their adolescent years in school, hunting, fishing, and following other boyish interests, Hammond had been dogging his father's footsteps, devoting his time to learning all that his father could teach him about his business. Outside of a few hours each day with his family, all his time was spent among them. Certainly he felt more at home with the Negroes than he did with any white men. He loved his "niggers" with the same affection another man would have for his dogs or horses; he rejoiced in a fine male or female Negro which he had raised himself as other men took pleasure in a hunting dog or a winning race horse which had resulted from careful breeding. To Hammond Maxwell his Negroes were valuable cattle, but in many ways they were far superior to cattle—they could think, talk, act and respond, and thus they transcended the dumb beasts and became companions.

Of course he considered their intelligence to be limited. They were only interested in eating, drinking, sleeping, and whoring. They laughed when they were happy—which was most of the time—and they wept when they were sad. They suffered when they were in pain and they could sicken and die like humans. But they were not really human. Naturally not—they were "niggers"! In Hammond's opinion they never would attain human intelligence, regardless of the amount of *human* blood they might possess. But they were his. He had supervised the implanting of their seed; he had brought them into the world; he had watched them grow up and develop. And now that they had reached fruition he was forced to dispose of them, but not without regrets. Frankly, he hated to have them leave, for he had become accustomed to them and each one had left some impression of his personality on him. But sell them he must, because there would be a crop coming along next year and another one the year after that, and he certainly could not keep them around just eating their heads off until they became old and useless. Yes, "niggers" were his business—the raising of them and the selling of them. But although he enjoyed the former, he did not relish the latter. After watching them grow up and develop from squalling suckers into fine strong boys and sleek-skinned wenches, it was hard to part with them, despite the fact that they increased his bank accounts by many thousands of dollars.

With so many leaving each year, the few whom he permitted to remain at Falconhurst—house servants such as Drummage—were those he depended on and clung to with far more affection than he would be willing to admit, even to himself. Lucretia Borgia, in spite of her advancing years, was almost as much a power at Falconhurst as Hammond Maxwell himself, and he often depended on her judgment. Brutus, who had been with him now for nearly twenty years, was his own right hand, capable of exercising authority and certainly capable of trust and confidence.

But it seemed to Hammond that most of those whom he had cared for he had destroyed either knowingly or unwittingly. Those twin sons of Lucretia Borgia's whom he and his father had once petted and coddled had met their death indirectly through Hammond. The lovely octoroon Ellen, whom he had loved far more passionately than any other woman and who had borne his children, had perished with them in the fire that destroyed the old plantation house. Mede, his superb Mandingo fighting nigger, on whom he had lavished pride and affection, had been destroyed by Hammond's own hand. Regine, who had shared his bed before his marriage, and whose pretty face had so appealed to him, was now dead, along with her son Benoni. Drumson, Drummage's father, had given his life to save Hammond's own. And lately, in a fit of anger and disbelief, he had punished Drummage—a boy who had the promise of becoming the most superb slave he had ever owned.

Of course he had every right to punish Drummage! But Hammond knew that he had punished the boy wrongly. Drummage had never lied to him before and he should have known that he was not lying then. One might beat a hunting dog in a fit of anger or lash a favorite horse in a drunken stupor but one could regret it afterwards even though the beast bore no resentment. Apparently Drummage had forgotten, but Hammond had not, and now, although he would never have admitted it to himself, he felt like an indulgent father trying to make it up to the boy. Drummage became his constant companion in New Orleans.

Not that there was anything unusual in this. Every prosperous planter, throughout his waking day, was followed by his favorite black man or boy, and the handsomer and more impressive that boy was, the greater the prestige that accrued to the master. Wherever the master went, the servant followed two steps behind, and no higher compliment could be paid an owner than to admire and praise his servant. "Finelooking boy you've got there"—it was a eulogy that reflected on the owner's wealth, position, and good taste. Any master would glow with pride and, when in entirely male company, he would need no urging to show off his boy. Invariably he would call him over and order him to shuck down so that everybody might see and admire his naked strength and perfection from the crown of his head to the soles of his feet. The servant, accustomed to such exhibitions, would comply willingly and even enthusiastically. Occasionally they resulted in a sale, and then would come a time of parting and a time of uncertainty for the slave, but he could always be comforted by one thought. He had brought a high price, which proved that he was valuable, and that would be something to brag about among the other servants in his new home.

Most of these "boys"—and they were called that regardless of their age—were young, handsome, well built and well dressed. Just as horse fanciers willingly spent money on silver-studded saddles to dress up their horses, so now were well-to-do planters dressing up their body servants. In some cases the gaudy accoutrements of the servants far outshone the conservative clothes of the master. Gone were the days of the torn shirt, the osnaburg trousers, and the dusty bare feet. These young bucks—black, brown, sepia or cream-colored—were ornaments to their masters' vanity, and their sartorial elegance put Drummage's well-worn and decidedly outgrown black suit to shame. That was one thing Hammond could easily remedy, it was entirely fitting that the boy belonging to the master of Falconhurst should outshine any other. Not for him were the gaily striped coats and the fantastic pantaloons! The two suits that Hammond ordered were of the finest quality bottle-green mohair, with short-cut jackets and high-rising skin-tight trousers. His shirts were of fine linen, with wide collars that came out over the jacket, and his well-cobbled shoes were polished to shine like mirrors.

Dressed in these new, well-fitting clothes, Drummage strutted just a little more than usual, fully conscious of the striking appearance he made. He enjoyed the admiring glances which came his way, especially those of the wenches whom he passed in the street. Not only the fine clothes but the height, strength, and broad shoulders he had inherited from his father and more especially from Big Pearl's Mandingo blood arrested all eyes and brought a closer inspection of the well-shaped face, the cap of curling black hair, the wide-set eyes, and the short, well-formed nose over the curling dark-red lips. He did not envy the paler-skinned mulattoes except for their ability to grow hair on their faces, for he would have welcomed the elongated sideburns that some of the yellow boys sported. Alas, neither his youth, nor his black blood allowed for those hirsute adornments.

If there was one thing which both Hammond and Drummage detested it was their enforced attendance at the French Opera House, which Augusta demanded. It was not so bad for Hammond, who managed to sleep, despite the high notes of the soprano, on one of the uncomfortable little gilt chairs. But for Drummage, standing in the back of the box first on one foot and then the other, the long performances were a trial. Augusta never missed a performance and Hammond never attended one if he could avoid it. In this Drummage aided and abetted him, thinking up excuses when Hammond could not.

Thus it was, one evening, that Drummage announced, before Augusta and Sophie, that Brutus had sent word that Hammond's presence was required at the slave jail, and Hammond, quick to catch on, said that it would be impossible for him to accompany the ladies to the Opera. He would send them in the barouche with Ajax, and Jubal would remain in the hotel rooms with the children. Naturally he regretted his inability to accompany them, but as soon as they had left he winked at Drummage and told him to get ready to leave also. Although he knew that Brutus' request for him to come to the jail was merely a fabrication on Drummage's part, Hammond felt that he might as well go there anyway. A hired fiacre drove them over and Hammond hung around, discussing the health and well-being of his property with Brutus until it was time for the slaves to be bedded. After that there was nothing for him to do.

Even in his younger days the sporting houses of New Orleans had had little appeal for Hammond, and now they had even less. He had never desired any other white woman than his own wife, and his taste for colored flesh was amply gratified at his own plantation. Nevertheless, he was now faced with an evening to kill and, with Drummage correctly two steps behind him, he started out to walk back to the hotel, dawdling along the streets and letting the life of the city flow past him. It was nearly dark when they reached Jackson Square, but far too early to return to the hotel, so, instead of crossing one of the diagonal paths of the square, Hammond kept to the left, under the galleries of the Pontalba Buildings, until he reached Bourbon Street, then turned left along it on his way to the Old Absinthe House. The lamplighter was coming along—a blazing tallow wick in one hand and a short ladder in the other, and as the street lamps were lit, casting pools of yellow light on the banquette, the city seemed to awaken. Once arrived at the Absinthe House, Hammond entered and walked to the long marble bar, with a motion to Drummage to take his seat on the wooden bench at the back of the room, where servants sat awaiting their masters. As the bar was practically empty, there were only two boys sitting there, each one far more showily dressed than Drummage, but their fine clothes could not compensate for his superior physique and good looks. Both were outlandishly attired with red-and-white peppermint-striped jackets and white pantaloons and both sported gold earrings which glinted brightly under their long, curled hair. It was evident that they were well acquainted with each other, for they were talking together in lisping whispers. When Drummage appeared they grudgingly made room for him, appraised him carefully, and then discussed him openly with covert glances from under long lashes. He ignored them completely. Their airy mannerisms disgusted him.

There were three men at the bar—two foppish young blades with well-padded coats, stovepipe trousers and brocaded vests with a plenitude of gold fobs, who were carrying on a desultory conversation with an older man who was plainly but richly dressed.

Hammond signaled to one of the bartenders and ordered his favorite drink, a hot toddy. The man behind the bar looked up at him with surprise, as hot drinks in New Orleans were a rarity, but he recognized the Master of Falconhurst and set about supplying the strange request. While he was waiting, Hammond became interested in the conversation of the three men.

"Ain' no more real fightin' niggers in New Orleans today," the older man was saying. "Nigger fightin' sure seen its best days. These nigger fights today jes' slaughter. Kill or be kilt—tha's all. Why don' they jes' give the boys razors and let 'em hack each other to pieces if it's jes' blood they wants. Thirty-five, forty years ago, it was different. Then we had real fighters."

One of the younger men lifted a languid hand, heavy with rings.

"'Yo' talk jes' like my papa, Dr. Masterson. He says nigger fightin' a waste of time and money today. Lost three fighters myself in the last three months. Papa says I cain' have no more. Says he won' let me waste good bucks on nigger fightin'.'"

"Lost two myse'f." The other fellow lifted his frosted glass and sipped delicately. "Paid three thousan' dollars for one and he didn' last ten minutes. Other nigger broke both his legs and then strangled him. Heard 'bout 'nother boy though, up in Richmond. Thinkin' I'll send up for him and bring him down by boat, sight unseen."

The older man shook his head reminiscently.

"Greatest nigger fighter we ever had lived right here in New Orleans. Name o' Drum. Used to belong to ol' Madame Alix, what had a fancy house over on Dumaine Street. Never was a nigger like him. Never lost a fight but got himself kilt in a street brawl. Everyone said it must of took ten to kill him." He looked up at Hammond as though to draw him into the conversation. "Yo' 'n' me 'bout the same age, suh"—he bowed slightly—"yo' ever hear tell about that boy Drum?"

Hammond laid some coins down on the bar to pay for his drink, which the bartender had just brought, and nodded to the man who had spoken to him.

"Heard 'bout Drum? Certainly have, but never seen the

105

boy fight. Wish't I had though. Say he was the best fighter in the South."

"Best in the world," the other man agreed. "Real fighter, that boy, not jes' killer." He looked carefully at Hammond, pursed his lips, and nodded his head knowingly. After a long minute, he held up his hand.

"Don' tell me, suh, don' tell me! It'll come to me in a moment. Sure I know yo', suh. No . . . don' tell me. Memory seems to be slippin' but it'll come to me." He brought the flat of his hand down on the bar. "Now I know. Yo're Mr. Maxwell o' Falconhurst. Attended many of yore sales."

Hammond bowed, and smiled.

"Yo' have the advantage over me, suh."

"Dr. Masterson of this city, suh. Used to be with ol' Doc Roberts and when he died took over his practice." His finger drummed against the bar and he scrutinized Hammond again. "Falconhurst! Falconhurst! Comes to me now. Yo' shore should remember Drum! Yo' bought his son from ol' Madame Alix."

One of the younger men put his glass down on the bar and extended his hand. "My papa knows yo' well, Mista Maxwell. He's Jean Brulatour of Chantilly. I'm his son, Pierre."

"We got several of yore boys at our place, Mista Maxwell," the other said. "I'm Georges Michel of High Point."

Hammond accepted the proffered hands but it was with the Doctor that he spoke.

"Yore memory's a good one, Doctor. How come yo' knew I bought Drumson?"

"Tended to ol' Madame Alix 'til she died. She'd always been a patient of Dr. Roberts and yo' might say as how I inherited her. After she died and her place closed down, I bought Drum's woman Calinda from the ol' lady's estate along with her man Blaise and their wench Dorothée. Got me a wench outa Dorothée—pretty little thing by the name of Candace. Calls her Candy, we do."

Hammond smiled slowly and knowingly, lifting his glass deliberately, taking a sip of his toddy. He turned to face the back of the room and called out.

"Drummage, git yo'se'f up here, boy!"

Drummage leaped up and came over to the bar. He eagerly awaited Hammond's next command.

"Turn round, boy, and face the light so's these men can git a good look at yore face."

"Fine-lookin' boy yo' got there, Mista Maxwell." Dr. Masterson examined Drummage. "But then, that ain' to be

106

wondered at, seein' as how yo' have the pick of the Falcon-hurst crop."

"This boy for sale?" Brulatour seemed to lose some of his affected languor. "Admire to buy him, Mista Maxwell, if'n yo' but names yore price. Young yet, but got the build of a good fighter."

"Sure has," Hammond agreed. "Powerful young buck, but regret he ain' for sale."

"Like to see him shuck down." Michel moistened his al-ready damp lips with the tip of his tongue. "Don' often see young bucks so well-set-up as he. Cain' be more'n sixteen, seventeen."

"Jes' 'bout." Hammond held up a restraining hand as Drum-mage started to undo his shirt collar. "Be glad to 'blige yo', Mista Michel, and have the boy shuck down if'n it not so public here, but first I'd like to ask Dr. Masterson to look at him right carefully." He turned to the Doctor. "Yo' said yo' remembered Drum. See anythin' in this boy that might remind yo' of him?"

"Well, he's bigger if anything—taller and broader and he blacker'n Drum too, but . . ." He came closer and put on a pair of steel-rimmed spectacles and squinted at Drummage's face. "Yes, Mista Maxwell, this boy sure looks like I re-member Drum. He looks a little more niggery but he's got Drum's good looks."

"Ain' surprisin'," Hammond said. "He Drum's grandson. His sire Drumson and his name Drum Major, but we calls him Drummage. Like yo' say, suh, I bought his pappy, Drumson, from ol' Miz Alix and bred him to a pure Man-dingo wench I got at Falconhurst. Ol' Miz Alix say that her Drumson was part Royal Hausa and part Jaloff with some human blood. That makes this boy half pure Mandingo and half Royal Hausa and Jaloff with a little human blood too."

The Doctor leaned a little closer to Hammond.

"And yo' know what that human blood be?"

Hammond shook his head.

"Madame Alix herself."

Hammond shook his head in disbelief. "Yo' mean . . . ?"

"All came out after the old lady died, suh, but not many knew 'bout it. Lef' some papers she did 'n' I saw them. Drum sure 'nuff her son, sired by some black *bozal* in Cuba. Don' think he ever knew it himself 'cause she always passed him off as son of her servant Rachel but there's no doubt 'bout it. He her own son."

"My papa tol' me 'bout that Madame Alix," Pierre Brulatour interrupted. "Wish she still a-runnin' that whorehouse of hers down on Dumaine Street. My papa said she used to put on shows down there. Called 'em *mêlées* she did. She'd have some big nigger buck a-standin' up in the center of the room and have four-five wenches a-fightin' to strip his clothes offa him and take him on. Said it was sure worth seein' the way them wenches fought over him, scratchin' and a-gougin' and a-pullin' hair to be the first to take him."

Michel wet his lips again. His eyes had a faraway look as he envisioned Drummage in such a role, with himself as one of the women fighting for Drummage's service. "Think mayhap I try that out when I go back upriver," he said.

"Seen them *mêlées* myself," Dr. Masterson said. "Sure was worth seein', too. My boy Blaise, which I bought from Madame's, used to be the boy they fought over till he lost his arm. Blaise he's a-gettin' on in years now but he 'members about it." He laid a hand on Hammond's shoulder. "Mista Maxwell, why'n yo' come over to my house. Ain' far —jes' a few blocks. I'd like to have ol' Blaise 'n' Calinda see this boy of yours. Les' see—he's my Calinda's grandson. Like to put him up alongside my Candy and see if'n they look alike. Yo' all welcome too." He invited Brulatour and Michel more or less perfunctorily with a wave of his hand.

Michel adjusted his hat. "Perhaps if we go to your house, Dr. Masterson, Mista Maxwell be willing to have his boy shuck down." He looked at Hammond hopefully and, although not encouraged by any acquiescence on Hammond's part, both he and Brulatour called their own boys from the bench and the party started out, Dr. Masterson and Hammond leading, followed by Michel and Brulatour with the three servants trailing behind.

It was, as Dr. Masterson had stated, only a short walk, and when the Doctor paused at the small door in the porte-cochere to withdraw his key and unlock it, Drummage stared at the façade of the house with his heart pushing up in his mouth. Yes! It was THE house. He remembered it. It was the identical house where he had seen the girl out on the banquette the morning he had arrived.

He turned to one of the boys beside him.

"Yo' ever been here afore?" he asked.

The mulatto looked at him disdainfully and shook his head so that his gold earrings swung. He had noticed his master's interest in Drummage and his jealousy was apparent.

"My masta, he don' take up with town folk, less'n they's Creole. He don' never come to this part o' the city. Yo' shore are an ignorant nigger. Quality folkses don' live on this street."

Drummage was far too happy to take umbrage at the boy's words. He detested the lisping little runt anyway because he reminded him somewhat of Benoni, whom he wished to forget. His only interest now was in the house. Once inside he might see the girl. He was certain that she lived here. He followed the others inside, through the dark passageway into the interior courtyard. Two candles in tall glass hurricane shades did little to illuminate the plants and shubbery but they revealed a staircase that led up to a second-floor balcony. Drummage and the other two boys sat on a bench inside the doorway and the three men went up the stairs. But no sooner had lights appeared on the second floor than Hammond came out into the balcony and called to Drummage to come up.

"I regret that this is now Bachelor's Hall," Dr. Masterson apologized, "but since my dear wife passed away last year, I have been living here alone except for the servants, and the place lacks a woman's touch." He walked to the wall by the door and pulled the bellcord. Somewhere down below in the court they heard the jangle of a bell and then footsteps sounded on the stairs. Through the open door walked an elderly Negro, tall and well built, with one coatsleeve pinned up to the shoulder. His pate was crowned with a cap of pure white wool.

"Yo' rang, Masta Docta?"

"Yes, Blaise. Bring wine for the gentlemen—my best Madeira—and when you return bring Candy and Calinda up with you."

Drummage was standing in the background, his face and upper body in shadow, when the old servant returned. With him was a woman with hair as white as his but with an air of almost aristocratic beauty on her fine features. Between them—and Drummage caught his breath when he saw her—was the very girl he had been dreaming about. She was even more beautiful than he had remembered. The old servant walked with sedate steps to a small mahogany table, placed the silver tray on it, and then filled the glasses with wine from the tall decanter. Not until he had handed the glasses to the Doctor and his guests did the Doctor speak.

"Got a little surprise for you and Calinda, Blaise." He motioned for the three servants to step nearer into the circle of lamplight. "Calinda, tell these men 'bout Drum."

"He my firs' man, Masta Docta." She seemed saddened by

109

the recollection. "Drum a fightin' man, suh. He fit for Madame when we lived over on Dumaine Street. He sired my firs' born. Drumson we called him, after his pappy."

"And what became of Drumson?" Dr. Masterson asked.

"Madame she sol' him to a Mista Maxwell. Ain' never seen my boy after Madame sol' him."

"Well, here's Mista Maxwell himself, Calinda. He's the man who bought your Drumson." He turned to Hammond. "This here's Drumson's ma, Calinda, and this her man, Blaise. He used to train with Drum, he did."

Both Blaise and Calinda bowed low in Hammond's direction and there was a brightening of Calinda's eyes.

"How my boy Drumson?" Calinda asked. "Please to hear about him, suh."

Hammond did not have an opportunity to answer before the Doctor spoke.

"Mista Maxwell's got something to show you, Calinda."

"Drumson here?" She peered into the shadows where Drummage was standing.

"Not Drumson, Calinda, but Drumson's boy, Drummage. He's yore grandchild, Calinda. Thought yo' might like to see him."

Hammond had been interested in seeing one of Drummage's forebears, and now he reached behind him and plucked Drummage's coatsleeve to bring him out into the light. Calinda came closer and reached up a slender hand to stroke his cheek. Her voice trembled a bit.

"Yo' shore look like Drum, boy, only yo's darker. Drum he bright-skinned and prettier'n yo'."

"No, he weren't, Calinda," Blaise interrupted. "This boy prettier'n Drum. Bigger too! He fine-looking boy, Calinda. Credit to you, he is. Wishin' now that Drum might a-seed him. Drum al'ays proud he was." He bowed to Hammond. "Hope he a good boy, Masta Maxwell, suh. Hope he don' give yo' no trouble."

"He's a good boy, Blaise. Only trouble I have with him, he gets pretty hot after the wenches. Sired one sucker already and now he's waiting for a wench I promised him."

"He Drum's gran'chile all right," Calinda smiled. "Drum like that too."

"And now, Candy, step out and stand up here alongside yore cousin." The Doctor spoke. "We wants to see if'n yo' two look alike."

It was Candy's turn to step up and she took a position beside Drummage, her eyes demurely cast down but not so

110

low that she was unable to see the sleek lines of Drummage's legs in his tight trousers. Although she reached only to his shoulder and her skin was several shades brighter, there was a decided resemblance between them.

"Shore looks alike, they do," Hammond agreed. He got up from his chair and walked over to where the two were standing. With an inquiring look to the Doctor, to which the Doctor nodded acquiescence, Hammond ran his hands expertly over the girl's body. She shrank from his touch, but Blaise reprimanded her.

"Stan' still, girl. Mista Maxwell ain' a-goin' to hurt yo'."

"She 'bout eighteen?" Hammond asked.

" 'Bout," Dr. Masterson answered.

"She be eighteen come December, Mista Maxwell suh," Blaise corroborated.

Hammond walked back to his chair and sat down.

"Drummage, whyn't yo' go down below with yore grandmaw and yore little cousin Candy. They wants to see yo' and get 'quainted with yo', and Dr. Masterson and I have some things to talk about." Hammond was hoping that Brulatour and Michel would take the hint to leave.

"Thought we was a-goin' to see the boy shucked down." Michel plainly showed his disappointment.

"Tell yo' what, gentlemen." Hammond became conciliatory, for these men's families were good customers. "If'n both of yo' come over to Sly's Vendue House tomorrow, I'll be there round eleven. Got me some fine bucks over there that'll interest you. Shucks 'em down for yo' and gives yo' plenty o' time to 'zamine them. Should be some there which'll interest you when they comes up on the vendue table."

They realized that they were being dismissed, albeit politely, and became effusive in their thanks to the Doctor. Both promised to be at the jail on the morrow. When they had left Hammond seemed to be more at ease. He was scarcely sympathetic to their type and realized that they had only one desire in seeing Drummage shucked down. Ordinarily he would not mind, would even be proud to display his boy, but tonight he was disinclined to satisfy their curiosity. The boys who were up for sale were actually on public display and could therefore be examined freely, but Drummage was a different matter.

Hammond waited until he heard their footsteps going down the stairs. "Kinda hates to see my bucks goin' to men of that sort," he said. "Jes' a waste o' good breedin' stock when one of 'em buys a buck. Hard on the boys, too."

The Doctor shook his head in agreement and waited patiently. He knew that Hammond had something in mind but he was not anxious to precipitate matters.

"About that Candy wench," Hammond began. "Like to know who sired her. Knows her dam came o' good stock but who's her sire?"

"Good blood there too." Dr. Masterson refilled his glass, noticing that Hammond had not touched his wine. "Yes, good blood. Victor Sacre-Coeur, a free man of color, probably an octoroon because he was almost white, got his tail up for Dorothée. She used to slip out and meet him and he knocked her up. Victor's still here in New Orleans. Owns a second-hand furniture store the other side of the canal. Fine-looking chap and it's said that many white ladies have developed a taste for second-hand furniture jes' on account o' Victor. Be that as it may, I never held it 'gainst him that he knocked up Dorothée. Happen to know that Victor's the son of a man from one of the best families in the city and a quadroon girl who was famous for her beauty. Sorry I can't mention no names, but my information is in confidence, Mista Maxwell suh."

"Respects yore confidence, suh, and takes yore word. What became of this yere Dorothée."

"Gave her to my own daughter in her dowry. My daughter married and moved to Georgia. Kept the child here, we did, thinkin' it better that my daughter not be troubled with an infant. Calinda and my wife brought the girl up."

"Seems like we ought to keep all that good blood in the strain. She 'n' my boy be well mated. Ever bred her?"

Dr. Masterson shook his head in denial. "Been pretty closely watched, she has. My wife trained her as a body servant 'n' she always slept off our room. Since my wife died, Calinda's kept a strict watch over her and ain' 'lowed no bucks near her, though plenty waiting the chance. She only too anxious for 'em but Calinda watches her carefullike. Sure she ain' had no buck."

"Well, there's several ways we could do it." Hammond leaned forward in his chair. "I could sell yo' Drummage which I don' want to do; yo' could sell me that Candy, which I would like yo' to do; or, failin' that, yo' could let my boy cover her while he's here and if'n he gets her knocked up, yo' could let me buy her sucker when he gets 'bout a year or so old."

Dr. Masterson sat back in his chair, thoughtfully considering the matter.

"Ain' never considered sellin' Candy. Calinda'd take on somethin' awful."

"Mos' of 'em do," Hammond agreed, "but they gets over it in a few days. Ain' as though they's human."

The Doctor scratched his head in indecision. "Yes, she'd get over it, jes' like she did when Dorothée left. Come right down to it, I don' need the girl and she's jes' another mouth to feed. Blaise and Calinda'll take care of me as long as I live." He looked up expectantly at Hammond. "How much yo' offerin' me for her?" he asked.

"Twelve hundred and fifty. Good housebroken wenches like her goin' for anywhere from seven hundred up to a thousand. Extra fancies goin' 'round twelve hundred. She not an extra-fancy but I shore want her. My business is breedin', Doctor, and I always try to git finest blood strains I kin. Ain' often I kin git 'em these days 'cause mos' niggers jes' mongrels but I know about my boy Drummage and yo' knows about this wench. And," he added as a parting argument, "Miz Maxwell here in New Orleans 'thout a servant and she a-lookin' fer a wench. Treat her good, she will."

"Think I'll take yo' up on it." The Doctor finished his glass. "Wouldn't sell her to everyone, Mista Maxwell, but know you have a good reputation. I'll tell her to get herself ready to leave with yo'. 'Spects it's better for Candy too. Better for a nice clean young buck like yours to cover her than for her to get raped by some of these city niggers." He reached out his hand to Hammond and they shook hands to seal the bargain.

"Tell yo' what." Hammond pointed to the bellcord and the Doctor pulled it. "We a-goin' to be here 'bout another week more till after my sale. Candy kin stay right here till we go, if'n she comes every day to the hotel 'round eight in the mornin'. That gives my wife a chance to break her in. Give Calinda a chance to get used to her goin' and she'll not take on so when the time comes. Drummage kin bring Candy back at night."

Blaise appeared in the doorway in answer to the bell.

"Tell my boy Drummage I a-leavin' now and have him wait fer me at the door," Hammond said. " 'Pears to me I remember yo' now, boy. 'Members seein' yo' at Miz Alix's when I bought Drumson."

"Yes suh, Masta Maxwell suh, 'n' I 'members yo' too. Yore boy Drummage a fine boy. Mighty thankful to see him, we

113

are, suh. He's a-gettin' along fine wid our Candy. Seem to take to each other, they do."

"That's good, Blaise." Dr. Masterson silenced him with a wave of his hand. "I've just sold Candy to Mista Maxwell here. He's buyin' her for his Drummage to cover. Should make you and Calinda mighty happy to have a man like Mista Maxwell buyin' Candy and make her happy gettin' a fine strong young buck like Drummage."

"Yo' sol' Candy, Masta Docta suh?" Blaise's voice shook with emotion.

"Better break it to Calinda, Blaise. Tell her I don' want no goin's-on either. Best thing in the world for Candy. Couldn't have done better for her if'n I'd tried. She goin' to be Miz Maxwell's own servant and she a-goin' to stay here till the Maxwells leave for Falconhurst, so Calinda'll get used to her leavin'."

"Yes suh, Masta Docta suh." Blaise was trying hard to control his emotions.

Hammond rose and the Doctor accompanied him down the stairs. Drummage was waiting in the courtyard. There was fire in his eyes and his restless feet moved in little dancing steps on the flagging. He could not keep still during the time Hammond and the Doctor concluded their leave-takings, and once outside on the banquette he had the temerity to match his steps to those of Hammond.

Hammond frowned.

"How come yo' so full of bezom, boy? Git back where yo' belong."

"Yas suh, Masta Hammond suh. I gits back. Jes' happy tha's all. That Candy shore is a pretty wench. She shore likes me, she does."

"And what do yo' think o' her?"

"She pretty, Masta Hammond suh. Prettiest wench I ever seen. Prettier'n any wench we got at Falconhurst."

"How yo' like pesterin' a wench like her?" Hammond's frown had disappeared.

"Shore like it, Masta Hammond suh, but ain' a-pesterin' no wenches 'thout yo' say so. Ain' aimin' to get my ass paddled 'gain. Learned my lesson I have. Shore hopin' yo' finds one pretty soon and gives me leave, Masta Hammond suh." Drummage skipped up a step and then quickly retreated.

"Jes' bought me that Candy wench." Hammond pretended to be talking to himself. "Been a-wonderin' who I'm a-goin' to git to cover her. Think I'll put her to Jubal. Looks like he got plenty o' sap in him."

"Ain' got so much as me." Drummage skipped up alongside Hammond again. "Look, Masta Hammond"—He pointed to a damp stain on his pantaloons—"Got so much I'se a-wastin' it, jes' thinkin'."

Hammond looked down and started laughing.

"Cain' waste it, boy. Guess I'd better give her to yo' after all. But yo' better be sure yo' gets to work and gets me some good suckers outa her."

Drummage was speechless. He managed to stammer one word.

"When?"

"Careful," Hammond cautioned, noticing the lack of the accustomed "suh."

"When, Masta Hammond suh?" Drummage came to his senses.

"We a-goin' back to Falconhurst in 'bout a week. Guess yo'll have to wait 'til then. Cain' very well take her up and bed her down with all those men and ain' got no place for yo' off'n our rooms."

"We not goin' for a week, Masta Hammond suh?"

"Thought yo' liked it here in the city?"

"Likes it fine, suh, but mighty anxious to git home. Wishin' we was there now so's I could kick that Jubal boy outa my bed and git that Candy wench into it."

"Candy goin' to stay at the Doctor's house till we go. She's a-comin' over to the hotel every morning to help Miz 'Gusta and yo' has to take her home every night so no other buck gits at her." He pondered a minute although he was well aware of what he was going to say. "Don' know if'n I minds if'n yo' stay over to the Doctor's house too, him bein' willin'."

Drummage's skipping steps took him ahead of Hammond this time. His face was beaming, his feet dancing on air.

"Yo' mean, Masta Hammond suh, I has yore permission?"

"Sooner yo' gits started the better," Hammond grinned. Somehow he felt he had paid his obligation to Drummage. By this act he had wiped his conscience clean of the un-merited punishment he had meted out to the boy, and at the same time he had done a good stroke of business. He expected some prime and fancy suckers from this union. Damn few bucks and wenches left with such good bloodlines.

Drummage reached down and grabbed Hammond's hand and lifted it to his lips and kissed it.

"Yo're the best masta in the whole world."

Hammond pulled his hand away and cuffed Drummage soundly.

"What the hell yo' think I am, boy—a-kissin' my hand. Think I'm like those two we met in the bar? Don' go round a-kissin' no men's hands, leastways not mine. Ain' fittin'."

Drummage was abashed.

"Jes' cause yo're such a good masta, suh. Didn't mean nothin' by it, Masta Hammond suh. Jes' respectful-like it was, suh."

Hammond relented and stopped for Drummage to come alongside him. Very gently he placed his hand on the boy's shoulder.

"Yo're a good boy, Drummage. Ain' mad at yo', I ain'. Understand, I do." He started walking again and Drummage followed, but whereas Hammond Maxwell's feet trod on the flagging of the banquettes and the cobbles of the streets, Drummage's were walking on air.

Chapter 12

DRUMMAGE lay awake most of the night, far too excited over his prospects to sleep. Masta Hammond had bought a wench for him; had given him permission to pester her. And the most wonderful part of it all was the fact that, were the whole world to parade before him, this one girl—this Candy —would most certainly be the one he would have chosen. Ee-yah! How could he ever live through all that night and all through the next day and keep his wits about him until the time came for him to take her back to the Doctor's house? True, she did not seem to be as crazy about him as he was about her, but that didn't bother him too much. She was now Masta Hammond's wench and if Masta Hammond said for him to pester her, pester her he would and she'd have nothing to say about it.

Supposing . . . a terrible thought, but just supposing the Doctor wouldn't give him permission to stay at his house with Candy. No, he would not think about such an eventuality, because he certainly could not hold out another week until he got back to Falconhurst. But Masta Hammond would arrange it for him. Masta Hammond could do anything in the world. Masta Hammond was just like that god that the white folks were always talking about. At any rate, as far as Drummage was concerned, Masta Hammond was God. How

116

he loved him! No other nigger had such a fine masta as Masta Hammond—no suh!

With the calming assurance that Masta Hammond would handle everything in just the right way, Drummage finally drifted off to sleep, only to be awakened by Jubal when he came stumbling down the dormitory aisle, after the ladies had returned. He made so much noise that he awoke Drummage and, once awake, Drummage had to tell him all about the wonderful thing that had happened. When their talk disturbed the other servants, Drummage crawled over onto Jubal's cot where they whispered together for another hour. Although Jubal pretended to be glad that his friend was to get something he so passionately desired, he was really consumed with jealousy, for he realized that Candy would come between them. Eventually Drummage ran out of words and fell asleep alongside Jubal, but when he awoke in the morning his excitement mounted all over again. How was he going to survive the whole long day until the time came for him to walk home with Candy to Dr. Masterson's?

Candy arrived early in the morning, having been escorted to the hotel by Blaise. Her timid knock on the Maxwell's door admitted her to their apartments. Drummage, who had brought up breakfast for the family and was setting the table, thought she looked more beautiful in daylight than she had the night before, and he was happy to see that both Miz 'Gusta and Miz Sophie evidently approved of her, for Miz 'Gusta smiled at her and tried to make her feel at home. Drummage used every subterfuge possible to remain in the rooms after the meal was over and his services were no longer required. He brushed Hammond's hat with meticulous care, picked infinitesimal pieces of lint off the carpet, and made himself so much in evidence that Hammond finally sent him off to the livery stable with orders to have Ajax harness the horses for their trip to Sly's Vendue House, which was their usual morning program.

"Yo'll be wantin' me to go with yo', Masta Hammond suh?" Drummage was hoping that for some reason Hammond would not require his attendance.

Hammond turned on him.

"Listen, boy, wha's come over yo'? Course I want yo'. Haven't yo' been with me every day since we came here? Why shouldn't I want yo' this mornin'?"

"Jes' askin', Masta Hammond suh. Jes' wantin' to be sure I does what yo' wants me to do." He let his eyes wander to Candy, who was sitting in a low chair by the window,

117

attaching a bit of lace to one of Augusta's bonnets.

Hammond saw the look and smiled to himself while he continued to frown at Drummage.

"Knows what yo' a-wantin' to do and it ain' what I'm a-wantin' yo' to do right now. Plenty of time fer that. Now, git!" He pointed to the door. "An' don' think if'n yo' don' behave yo'se'f, I cain' do what I said I might do. Ain' forgettin' what I said 'bout Jubal. If'n yo' don' min' yore manners, Jubal's a-goin' to get what yo' wantin'."

It was enough for Drummage. The very thought of Jubal falling heir to his Candy was too much for him. As if that big lubber would know what to do! Yet he hated to go. He had not had a single moment to talk with Candy alone, and whenever he had caught her eye across the room she had avoided looking at him. In fact, although he was reluctant to admit it, she had not even seemed glad to see him. Last night, during the few moments they had stood alone in the courtyard, he had hoped he was making a good impression on her, for he was not unmindful of his own good looks and the way other wenches always admired him. He had been so close to her he could see every line of her body under her thin dress, could feel the warmth of her flesh and smell the clean odor of soap and water mingled with the faint musk of her skin. How he had longed to press his lips to his in the dim shadows of the courtyard. He had advanced one halting step, his eyes bright, his lips parted, his hands outstretched. She had not retreated. His hands had felt the warm flesh under the thin cloth and his eager mouth had sought and found hers. For a brief moment she was in his arms, and then suddenly he had felt the sting of her palm across his cheeks.

"Who yo' think yo' are, black boy?" she said angrily, and she walked swiftly across the courtyard to where the kitchen doorway framed a rectangle of light. "Ain' no black nigger a-foolin' 'round wid me. If'n I cain' have a bright skin, don' want nothin'. Yo' wid yore big mouth and yore big lips!" She spat on the ground.

Yet once they were in the kitchen with Blaise and Calinda she became charming again, smiling and stressing their cousin-ship. And now, this morning, she looked at him with the same animosity she had displayed while they were in the courtyard, or ignored him completely as if he did not exist. If only he could be alone with her so that he might tell her how much he wanted her, how many times he had thought of her since he first saw her. But there was no opportunity. Now Hammond was going out and he must go with him. Drummage looked across the room at Candy, who still sat by the window, head lowered and eyes demurely occupied with her mending.

"I'll go and tell Ajax, Masta Hammond suh." He spoke loudly, hoping that the fact that he was leaving would spark some response, if only a quick glance, but she continued to ignore him.

"Then git started! Whaffor yo' waitin' round here?" Hammond was impatient. There was nothing left for Drummage to do but go, dragging his feet behind him, casting one backward look at Candy, who never lifted her head.

Throughout the day he followed Hammond from place to place, but although he was in attendance on his master his thoughts were on Candy and what he would do with her if they were alone in the old Doctor's house. He desired her so, surely she must feel the same way about him. And if she didn't, he would teach her to. He was certain he could.

The hours and the business at the jail were tedious. It seemed to Drummage that Hammond was more demanding than ever. But finally the morning wore away and they returned to the hotel for dinner. Alas, he was cheated of even a glimpse of Candy, for Miz 'Gusta and Miz Sophie had decided to eat in the hotel dining room. That meant that Candy and Jubal were together upstairs, minding the children. As he ate alone in the servants' dining room, Drummage pictured the intimacies that might be going on between them until his food became dry in his mouth and choked him. Yet, Jubal, he tried to reassure himself, had not been particularly interested in his long description of Candy's beauty the night before. Jubal did not seem to be particularly interested in any wench. He sure never gets excited over them the way I do, Drummage thought. Just one look and things started to happen to him which were often embarrassing.

He kept his eye on the long bell board which ran alongside one wall of the servants' dining room. The Maxwell suite was Number 31 and Drummage wished the bell would ring and summon him, but it remained mute throughout his meal. Tormented with jealousy he pushed aside his plate of warmed-over chicken from the guests' meal served yesterday in the dining room and went upstairs to the dormitory.

Each day during the afternoon siesta time, he had been studying letters with old Parnassus, and when he arrived at his cot in the dormitory the old Negro was sitting there with his book open. Drummage had made considerable progress—he was naturally intelligent and quick to learn—and

119

was already able to distinguish the different letters and put them together into simple words. But today he could not put his mind on learning. He was far too tense to concentrate on the intricacies of the miserable little letters. If he could not be with Candy, he wanted to be alone to think about her. Parnassus soon realized his inattention and put away his books and left the room. Drummage did not even realize he had gone. Involved in his fantasy of Candy, he lay back on his cot until Jubal came into the dormitory.

Drummage was surprised to see him at this hour. Usually Jubal stayed with the children to watch over them during their afternoon nap.

"Whaffor yo' a-doin' here?" he demanded. "An' what yo' been a-sweet-talkin' to my Candy wench?"

"Comed here cause Miz 'Gusta say Candy goin' to lie down on the bed 'longside little Miz 'Manda. Ain' been a-sweet-talkin' her neither. She too uppity fer me. She ain' spoken nary a word to me. Look down on me she does and say I stink like a fiel' hand." He lifted his arm and sniffed his armpit. "Don' stink, I don'. Washed myself all over this mornin'."

"Sometime yo' mighty musky. That's cause yo' so goddam black." Drummage felt a great relief to know that Jubal had been snubbed.

"How come yo' a-callin' me black? Ain' no blacker'n yo'. Don' stink no more'n yo', neither."

Drummage rolled up his sleeve and pulled Jubal's arm down alongside his. The tobacco brown contrasted with the darker black.

"Yo' jes' a goddam ignorant stinkin' black nigger—that's all yo' are. Ain' had no shoes on those goddamn big feet o' yourn come a month ago. Jes' an ignorant fiel' hand, a-choppin' cotton 'til I edicates yo'. Come to Falconhurst and piss outa the window the fust night yo' there. Ignorant yo' was and ignorant yo' is."

Jubal worshiped Drummage, but Drummage had never spoken to him this way before. He resented it.

"Ain' so ignorant but what I kin take a poke at yo'."

"Takes a poke at me and I messes yo' up good, black boy."

"Stan' up and say that."

"Stan's up and I don' say it, I does it." Drummage sprang up and landed a telling blow to Jubal's face. It hit him full on the cheek but, instead of raising his hands to protect

120

himself or fight back, Jubal merely looked at Drummage. Tears appeared in his eyes.

"Whaffor yo' a-fightin' me, Drummage? Ain' done nothin' to yo'. Ain' a-goin' to fight wid yo'. Ain' afeared o' yo' but jes' ain' a-goin' to fight yo'. We frien's. Al'ays been frien's. What's the matter wid yo' now?" The tears were rolling down Jubal's cheeks and the blood was dripping from the bruised skin where Drummage had hit him.

The sight of blood brought Drummage to himself.

"Didn' mean to hit yo', boy, but yo' provoke me. Feelin' techy, I am. Thinkin' 'bout that Candy wench and thinkin' perhaps yo' a-pesterin' her up there while the folks eatin' dinner. Gets me almost crazy, a-thinkin' on it."

Jubal laid a big-fingered hand awkwardly on Drummage's arm.

"Listen, man! Don' wan' yore Candy wench. Don' wanna pester her none at all. Ain' admirin' to pester no wench at all. Jus' hopin' Masta Hammond don' make me do it. Don' know how. Don' know what to do, gets me a wench in bed with me."

"Don' have to know." Drummage's anger had disappeared. "Yo' jes' goes ahead and does it. Man, yo' don' know what it's like. Once yo' pesters a wench, yo' not interested in jackin' off no mo'. Hundred times better."

"Knows one way and don' know the other and ain' anxious to try. Likes sleeping wid yo' better'n any wench." Jubal grinned.

"Ain' a-sleepin' wid me no mo' onct we gits us back to Falconhurst. Yo' sleepin' alone 'cause Candy sleepin' alongside me." He noticed Jubal's eyes brimming with tears. "Perhaps maybe I goes out to the spring house wid yo' sometimes. Perhaps I lets yo' pleasure me if'n it gives yo' fun. Ain' sayin' I will 'cause mayhap don' have nothin' left for yo' onct I git Candy. Thinkin' tho' I have some left over for yo'."

Jubal was gratified for even the slightest favor.

"Yo' always good to me, Drummage. Yo' my frien'. Ain' never had no fun till I comes to Falconhurst and yo' learns me to have fun with yo'. Mighty happy yo' learned me."

"Olly learned me, he did. But some day goin' to learn yo' to pester a wench. Goin' to show yo'. Yo' likes it much better. Ee-yah, boy! What we do now jes' kid stuff." He reached out a finger and tenderly touched the spot on Jubal's cheek. The blood was beginning to congeal but the dark-purple mark under the skin was now very evident. Drummage was sorry for what he had done and also a little frightened. Masta

121

Hammond wouldn't like it, him a-messin' up Jubal. He regarded Jubal thoughtfully. "Ain' forgettin' that I said yo' could pleasure me sometimes when we gits back to Falconhurst but shore won't ever let yo' if'n yo' tells Masta Hammond I hit yo'."

"Tellin' him I slipped on the stairs and hit my head, if'n yo' lets me." He turned around and saw that the dormitory was empty. "Lets me now, I mean."

"Cain' let yo' now, Jubal boy. Yo' knows I a-goin' with Candy come evenin'. Needs all the sap I'se got. But I ain' a-forgettin' my promise. Lets yo' soon if'n yo' tells Masta Hammond yo' slipped on the stairs. Yo' wants to sleep?"

"Wants to. Ain' slept much last night with yo' a-talkin' to me."

"Ain' a-sleepin' myself. Cain' sleep," Drummage said. "Goin' out in the barn to talk with Ajax and the boys."

"Comes with yo' and puts cold water on my face."

The afternoon passed slowly. They talked with Ajax and the other coachmen and hostlers and listened to their prurient accounts of their weekly conquests in Congo Square. They applied cold compresses to Jubal's cheek, which somewhat relieved the swelling. Slowly the long hot afternoon dragged on until they were summoned to the family's apartment, where each took up his duties, Jubal to watch over the children and Drummage to set the table and prepare to serve supper, while Candy was busy dressing Miz Sophie's hair and adding the finishing touches to her toilette. She did not leave Miz Sophie's room while Drummage was serving supper. It was not until he had cleared the table, carried the trays back down to the kitchen, and returned to the rooms that he saw her again.

She was standing just inside the door and, when he entered, Hammond spoke to Drummage, handing him a sealed white envelope.

"Yo' a-takin' Candy home now. Give this letter to Dr. Masterson. Askin' him, I am, if'n yo' kin stay over to his house this night, so's yo' kin be with Candy."

"You do the most ridiculous things, Hammond Maxwell." Augusta was not angry but her voice had an edge to it.

"Keeps my word, I do," Hammond replied. " 'Sides, sooner this boy gits started the better."

Augusta flounced off into the other room, leaving them alone. Drummage took the letter and opened the door for Candy. Hammond called to them as they started down the hall. "Git her back here 'fore half-past seven tomorrow morning, and all in one piece too."

"Yas suh, Masta Hammond suh." Drummage took her arm with a gallant gesture but she shook it off. Without speaking they walked down the hall, down the servants' stairs and out the back door of the hotel onto the streets. During the several blocks which stretched between the hotel and the Doctor's house, Candy did not open her mouth, as Drummage walked alongside her, vainly trying to think of something that might open a conversation. He was far too excited to think of words. He was uneasy, too. He had not anticipated such frigidity from someone he desired so entirely and so ardently. This was not at all as he had hoped it would be.

When they arrived at the back door of the Doctor's house, Blaise let them in and took them into the kitchen where Calinda had kept the remnants of the Doctor's dinner hot for them. But Drummage had no taste for food. Blaise took Hammond's letter up to the Doctor's rooms and when he returned he drew Calinda aside into a far corner and whispered to her. She left the kitchen, only to reappear in a few moments with her arms full of clean linen and then leave again, and Drummage could see her going up the stairs of the *garçonnière* in the rear of the courtyard. When she returned she called Candy into the small back room off the kitchen and Drummage heard loud words, mingled with the splashing of water coming from behind the closed door. He could not distinguish what Calinda was saying but he could hear Candy's rising remonstrances, shrill with anger and defiance.

"I won' and nobody kin make me! Don' care if'n I'se sold to the Maxwells."

Drummage noticed that Blaise was listening too, a disturbed expression on his face. The old man finally got up from the table where he had sat out of courtesy to Drummage and walked into the room where Calinda was talking with Candy. Drummage heard the sound of a slap and then Candy's wails.

"Yo'll do 'zactly as yo're told," Blaise said. "And yo'd better be glad Masta Docta sol' yo' to the Maxwells. Drummage a fine boy. He yore own kin. Yo' treats him good and, if'n yo' don', I strips yo' down myself and tells Masta Maxwell to give yo' a good lashin' too."

Blaise reappeared in the doorway, spreading his hands apologetically.

"Little skittish, she is. Gals always like that at fust. She come roun' though. Always do. If'n yo' wants help, jes' call me. I fix her good."

Drummage bowed in appreciation, but he could not hide his smile of confidence.

"Thinks I make out right well, man. Masta Hammond say I do, I do. Ain' doin' nothin' 'thout he say so. Knocked up a wench at Falconhurst 'thout his sayin' so and got my ass paddled. Now he say so, I do so. Come mornin', yo' see."

"Yo' shore like yo' grandpappy Drum. Shore is. Jes' like him. Remembers once him 'n' me we picks up two quadroon fancies in Congo Square. He keep ridin' both them gals all night long after I quit. He sure crazy over bright-skinned gals. But they the death o' him." Blaise's face saddened. "He a fine man, that Drum. Never got over missin' him. Yo' looks a lot like him. Shore do. But if'n yo' hung like him, better go easy with Candy. She young 'n' tender. Don't hurt her."

"Won' hurt her," Drummage grinned. "Likes her too much to hurt her. She pretty, Candy is. Goes slow 'n' easy with her."

"Hurts her jes' the same. Candy she never had no man. Jes' got to break yore way in slow and easy, boy. Don' go after her like a bull. Easy does it. Calinda'll give yo' some bacon grease, she will. Helps."

The door opened and Calinda led a sullen Candy out from the back room, half pushing her into the kitchen. She had on a long-sleeved, high-necked, white cambric nightgown which fell to the floor. Little drops of moisture bedewed her hair and she exuded the clean damp soapy smell of newly scrubbed skin. With her head lowered she refused to lift her eyes to look at Drummage, and as Calinda nudged her along to the center of the room where Drummage was standing, Blaise arose and took a lighted candlestick from the table.

"Don' want no foolishment out'n yo' tonight, gal. This yere's yo' man and a good boy he is. He yore own cousin and yo' should be damn glad to have him. Masta Maxwell a fine man and he be a good masta to yo' so yo' do whut he say. He say for Drummage to pleasure yo' so Drummage have to. Take him up to yore room." He placed the lighted candle in her hand. "Now, git!"

Slowly, without raising her head, she started for the door and Drummage followed. He turned around to see Calinda crying, but Blaise winked at him and handed him a small jar of grease. He followed Candy's slow steps out into the courtyard and along one side to where a flight of wooden steps led to the *garçonnière,* the wooden structure at the back of the courtyard which housed the slaves' quarters. She started up the steps and he followed behind her. Each step raised the long nightgown a little, so that he had a glimpse of a shapely brown ankle, a tantalizing foretaste of what was in store for him. When she reached the landing, she proceeded down the narrow balcony and opened a door. Had he not been directly behind her with his foot in the door it would have slammed in his face. He pushed it open and followed her inside, closing the door behind him. She placed the candlestick on a chair and turned to face him.

"If yo' a-thinkin' yo' goin' to bed with me, yo'd better think 'gain, Mista 'Bama Nigger, 'cause I ain' a-havin' no truck with yo', understand?"

"Masta Hammond done say I to pleasure yo' and if'n Masta Hammond say so, I do."

"Don' care what yore ol' Masta Hammond say. He ain' a-told me, so ain' a-goin' to."

"He yore Masta Hammond now and if'n he say I do, he mean yo' do too. If'n yo' don', he shore goin' to strip yo' down. Way he flog the wenches at Falconhurst shore is a caution. Shucks 'em down and hists them up in the air feet first and then slices the meat right off'n they backs."

"He ain' a-goin' to strip me down. Ain' a-goin' to Falconhurst, I ain'. I runs, I will. Got me a boy here—bright-skinned too, not black like yo'. He in love wid me. He'll help me, he will. So's yo' better jes' bed yo'se'f down on de flo' and don' come a-crawlin' up into de bed. Ain' havin' nothin' to do wid yo' nohow." She pulled down the top sheet and eased herself up onto the bed, taking care to keep herself completely covered with the nightgown. "An' don' yo' take off yore clothes neither. Ain' a-wantin' to see no coal-black nekkid nigger."

Drummage was hurt by the epithet "coal-black nigger." And her reference to another man aroused his jealousy.

"Who this boy yo' say a-lovin' yo'?" He did not intend to share Candy with anyone.

"Yo' thinks I'se a fool to be tellin' yo'?" She tossed her head airily—as well as she could on the pillow. "Ain' a-goin' to tell yo' 'cause then yo' knows where I runs to." She stuck out her tongue and made a disparaging noise. "He handsome he is, mos' white too. He got yella hair that's curly."

"He ever pleasured yo'?" Drummage advanced a step towards the bed and Candy recoiled from the scowl on his face. She swallowed hard, staring at him.

"Co'se not. Whut yo' think I am?"

Without answering her, Drummage took off his jacket, un-

125

did the string tie, unbuttoned the shirt and folded it carefully across the back of the chair. He kicked off the loose slippers and reached down to slip off his black cotton socks. Candy covered her face with her hands but Drummage thought he saw her fingers move as he slipped off his trousers and unbuttoned his linen drawers. Yes, the fingers did move and he knew that she was peeking between them. Let her look! Maybe he didn't have curly yellow hair and maybe he wasn't a white-skinned mustee, but he had something to exhibit that was far more important. Let her look! He wouldn't even blow out the candle. He took it from the chair and placed it on the floor, then removed his clothes and placed them in a neat bundle on the floor, and braced the chair under the latch of the door. He caught the reflected light of her eyes between her fingers and knew that she was watching him. The knowledge that he was under surveillance increased his desire and heightened his excitement. Slowly and deliberately, so that she could get a good look at him, he walked back across the tiny room and stood beside the bed. His hand reached down and swept her fingers away but she turned, burying her face in the pillows.

"Yo' 'fraid to look at me?" he questioned.

She shook her head, burying it deeper into the pillow. One of his arms slipped down under her shoulders and his other hand turned her head towards him.

"Look at me, I says!"

She kept her eyes screwed tight.

He relinquished her and let her fall back onto the pillow. Things were not going the way he had planned and he was nonplussed. Even stronger than his own mounting desire was the fear of what Hammond might say to him for failing to do what he had ordered. His disappointment and his frustration combined to make his anger rise with his passion. He had anticipated this moment for too long to be cheated out of it. Violently he yanked at the sheet, tearing it from her clutching fingers, and threw it to the foot of the bed, uncovering the clinging folds of the nightgown. Now he pushed her chin back until both hands could creep inside the neckband, and with a mighty downward tug he ripped the thin garment open, tearing it from neck to hem.

"Take that goddam thing off." His face was close above hers now, so close he could feel her breath on his cheek.

Her answer was suddenly to fasten her teeth on the lobe of his ear. The sharp pain made him recoil. With his strong

126

fingers he forced her jaws apart. Blood dripped from his ear onto her face.

"Jes' don' understand yo', gal. Whaffor yo' act so stubborn? Ain' a-goin' to hurt yo', least no more'n I got to. Yo' my gal. Wants yo' more'n any yella boy ever could." He sank down, stretching his limbs alongside of her and feeling the warmth of her flesh against his own. She would have wrenched away from him but he held her close.

"Yo' ain' a-goin' to," she insisted, struggling to get away from him.

"Gittin' sick o' foolin' round." He gritted his teeth and flung himself across her. She squirmed under him but he found her hands and pinioned them against the bed, then rose on his knees, crouching over her. "Ain' wantin' to hurt yo' but yo' shore goin' to git hurt if'n yo' don' change." He waited hopefully for some response from her but she remained rigid. Her silence inflamed him. He raised his hand and brought it down across her cheek, and she cried out, but her frightened scream did not deter him. He struck her again even harder. Seizing her by the shoulders he lifted her up, shaking her furiously until her head bobbed back and forth, as if disjointed from her slender neck. Finally he flung her back onto the pillow. Panting from his exertions, Drummage heard her low moans, saw the red mark slowly spread across her face where he had struck her. She had ceased to struggle but kept her face turned sideways on the pillow, her eyes closed as though to blot out his presence. He noticed a tear oozing out from under one of the tightly pressed lids and watched it trace a wet path down her cheek. He seemed to sense that for the first time in her life she had come face to face with her own bondage, with the realization that her body no longer belonged to her. A second tear followed the first one and the resentment he had felt for her softened into pity. Very gently, without speaking, he released her and lowered himself to the bed, stretching out alongside her again and slipping his arm under her so that her head rested on his shoulder.

Their faces were so close that their lips touched, but she did not move away from him; neither did she betray by any token that his nearness was welcome. With his free hand he twined his fingers in her dark curls while he pressed her face even closer to his own. His lips opened to nuzzle hers but his darting tongue encountered the rigid blockade of her teeth. Yet after a moment, although seemingly without volition on her part, her teeth parted and his searching tongue found entrance to the dark mysterious warmth of her mouth. Soon he felt her own tongue responding. Hardly able to contain his excitement, he lifted his lips from hers.

"Kissin' yo' I am, Candy," he whispered. "Thinks perhaps yo' likes my kisses. Thinks yo' likes my kisses better'n any mustee boy's."

She did not answer but her hands, which had been clenched into tight little fists against his chest, started to open, until he could feel the warm pressure of her palms against him. Her fingers traced a warm line across his sweaty skin and came to rest on the rounded tip of one of his nipples, examining it and then pinching it so hard that he winced. Her mouth opened wider and she burrowed her head into the pillow the better to accommodate him. He pulled her closer and with one hand traced delicate little arabesques down her back while his other hand caressed her breasts.

She trembled and pulled her mouth away from his, but only for the brief second required to whisper his name. The one hoarse word reassured him, and now his tongue sought her cheek, roaming over it in little circles until it reached her ear and his teeth closed around the lobe, not enough to cause pain but enough to make themselves felt. Breathing heavily, she squirmed against him, then moved away and lay on her back, feeling his tongue explore the warmth of her skin until it crept between her breasts. She was moaning again but the moans were different now—little animal-like sounds that crept between her lips, interspersed with words that denied while they implored.

"No, Drummage boy! No, no, no, no, no!"

He ignored her protestations for he knew she did not mean them, and as his lips moved over her breasts his hands sought the hidden recesses of her body, gently at first and then boldly and forcibly to make her protest further. Her hand, timidly inching over his skin, traced a hesitant path down over his body until it reached his sex. Quickly she drew back, as if she had been burned, but now he was so aroused that only one caress could satisfy him. Seizing her wrist he forced her hand to return. At first she struggled to get away, but he held her wrist firmly until he felt the resistance go out of her hand, and felt the welcome clutch of her fingers.

Drummage sighed with pleasure. But now the clutching fingers were avid. Their moving caress was so vigorous that he felt endangered, and had to pry her fingers away. For a second he turned from her, his whole body tense, his breath

128

coming in gasps, trying to overcome the imminent spasm which he so greatly desired and yet wished to halt. She could not understand his momentary lack of interest and tried to force her fingers back but he held them firmly.

"Don', Candy gal, don' do it," he groaned.

"Wants to, Drummage, why cain' I?"

"Yo' spoils everything if'n yo' do. Wait a minute, Candy baby."

Now their roles were reversed and she became the aggressor. Her mouth, a few moments before so unwilling, became an instrument of joy and torture to him. Suddenly she had become all searching fingers, all warm moist mouth, smooth skin, pressing against him, manipulating him, fondling him and torturing him.

"Candy baby, stop!" He found words to speak. "Les' not hurry it. Les' make it las'."

She was unable to understand the emergency that had caused him to abandon her but he flopped over onto his stomach and pushed her hands away. Soon his breathing became more normal and he turned towards her, enveloping her in his arms and pressing his mouth against hers.

"Now, Candy, now!" he panted, and without realizing what she was doing, she accommodated him. Immediately his thrusting body found entrance and she screamed, pushing his face away from hers and striking out at him furiously. But he was as oblivious to her pain as to his own punishment. Nothing could stop him now, and he continued until with one last mighty plunge he spent himself and fell prone across her, gasping for breath. She tried to extricate herself from under his heavy body but he was immovable. Minutes later he slid from her and lay panting alongside her. With his remaining strength he gathered her into his arms, pillowing her head on his chest, seeking the welcome quiet of complete relaxation, but she, still tense, would not leave off her importunings. The very movements which he had welcomed so ardently a few moments before now failed to move him and for a moment he wished he could make his bed on the floor as she had suggested. But as the moments passed the amorous movements of her hands and lips began to arouse him again, and before he realized it he was responding to her with renewed ardor. He arched his body towards her, reveling in her aggressiveness.

"Yo' likes me, Candy baby?" he whispered, beside himself with excitement.

"Likes yo' well 'nuff," she said. "Yo' awfully dark-skinned

but I likes to have yo' pleasure me. Les' do it 'gain, Drummage man."

She was repeating the same sentence when the first streaks of dawn crept in through the small window. But her begging was useless. Drummage was sound asleep beside her.

Chapter 13

AFTER A WEEK of constant activity, during which Drummage dogged Hammond's footsteps throughout the long days and spent his ecstatic nights at the Doctor's house, the last day of their stay in New Orleans arrived—the day of the auction sale of the Falconhurst slaves which was to take place under the stained-glass dome of the Saint Louis Hotel. Instead of being exhausted from his nights of love-making, Drummage seemed to have a store of boundless energy that enabled him to keep going all day, constantly on his toes to anticipate his master's every wish, and still have enough left over to satisfy Candy, whose needs, despite his eager willingness, were sometimes almost beyond his capacity.

New clothes had to be issued for all the slaves who were to be sold—black trousers and white shirts for the men along with well-cobbled shoes; black dresses with white fichus and headcloths for the women. Falconhurst slaves were never sold in tattered hand-me-downs of tow linen or osnaburg. They were quality cattle and as such they were decently dressed. Hammond even rehearsed them for their brief appearance on the vendue table. The men were taught to take the few steps that led up to the platform with a brisk and elastic stride; to stand there smiling and debonair, their shoulders back, their bellies sucked in and their feet apart with hands on hips, flexing their muscles so that their chests strained against the thin white shirts and their arms bulged under the rolled-up sleeves. The women were expected to be more modest. They were to ascend the steps slowly and with dignity and stand before their appraisers with downcast eyes which did not, however, entirely negate their smiles. Those who were big-bellied with pregnancy were to arch their backs to emphasize their appearance, and those with

130

babies in arms were to present a fond picture of maternal solicitude.

Both bucks and wenches were now entirely accustomed to the lengthy examinations and fingerings which had gone on at Sly's slave jail since their arrival, but Hammond warned them to be prepared for even more when they were to be sold. None of them, particularly the exhibitionist bucks, minded this constant parade of their nakedness; most of them gloried in it. If, as they had been led to believe, they were being purchased as studs, it was only natural that they should have to display their equipment. Like fine-blooded bulls and stallions, few of them were to be disappointed, for Falconhurst slaves, over the years, had acquired such a reputation for fine breeding that few plantation owners relegated them to the menial tasks of field hands. With the slave mania which was raging in the South during those last few years before the War between the States, fine slaves were the South's most valuable possession—more valuable than all the crops of cotton, rice, or sugar combined. They were the wealth of the South. Therefore, to put a Falconhurst buck in the cane fields where he was certain to die within three or four years from overwork was merely a waste of good money. Field hands could be picked up for far smaller sums than these highly bred specimens.

Although his prime reason for being in New Orleans was to dispose of his year's crop, Hammond never neglected the unexcelled opportunity which the city offered to add to his own stock. He attended all the auctions and private sales, ever on the lookout for children and adolescents which his trained eye told him had the promise of strength, intelligence, and good bloodlines. With Drummage at his heels he visited the many slave dealers in the city.

Scarcely a day passed but Hammond was approached with offers to purchase Drummage. He took a special pride in showing off the boy, watching prospective buyers gloat over his perfection while their hands glided over his sleek limbs. At first Drummage had been fearful of these frequent inspections, particularly when he overheard some of the prices offered for him. He was experienced enough to know that the prices were fantastic but with Hammond's continued refusal to accept them he gained confidence as he strutted before the would-be purchasers. He was convinced that there was not enough money in New Orleans to buy him and indeed there was not. With good luck and a careful selection of dams, Hammond anticipated twenty-five or more fine bucks

131

and wenches, all sired by Drummage. If prices on slaves kept going up as they had, the boy stood to gain him some fifty thousand dollars instead of the paltry two or three thousand he was offered.

So Hammond paraded Drummage for others' envy and enjoyment but kept an eye out for merchandise for himself. Whenever he came across a promising young one, which he could buy at a reasonable price, he purchased the boy or the girl. Men brought the highest prices. Outside of house slaves, women were primarily for breeding. That any crop which might be conceived this year would not be marketable for a goodly number of years to come did not worry Hammond. His stock at Falconhurst was practically self-supporting and it cost him little to raise a slave to maturity. Fortunately he could not look into the future and realize that his careful investments would be worthless when they were ready for sale because, in that unforeseen future date, there would be no buying and selling of slaves. Despite the growing abolitionist movement in the North, this was something Hammond could not envisage.

True, there were rumors in the South, but nobody paid much attention to the ravings of Northern agitators. As far back as man could trace his history there had always been slaves. There always would be. Wasn't slavery sanctioned by Holy Writ itself? The black man was born to be in bondage to his white brother. That's the way it always was and the way it always would be, despite those mewling Northerners with their holier-than-thou attitude. Goddamn it! They even preached that niggers were human beings! How ridiculous! Everyone knew that a nigger was only an animal—perhaps a superior one, because he could talk and reason to a limited extent, but an animal nevertheless.

How would it be possible to run a plantation without these work animals? The whole South reared itself on its broadcloth-clad legs and asked that one question to which there was no logical answer. Let the grubby, money-mad Northerners stick to their whirring looms and sooty factories filled with pale, tow-headed child workers: the South would never change. Not by a damned sight!

But regardless of the pounding of tables and the slapping of broadcloth thighs, the South was changing. The fertile lands which had produced cotton year after year were fast running out. Each year the crops were getting smaller while the black populations of the plantations increased. Plantation warehouses stood empty while their slave quarters were filled to bursting. But that's the way it should be! A planter's wealth was not in the crops he produced but in the human cattle he boasted about. Any planter who could brag of having six hundred slaves was in a class by himself, regardless of the fact that his petered-out fields produced scarcely enough to feed the burgeoning crop of blacks, and that the blacks themselves, along with the plantation, were mortgaged from woolly pates to callused soles. In a lesser aristocracy, there were three- and four-hundred slave men; but even the man who claimed only a hundred head did not relinquish hopes of achieving more in the years to come. That these goals would never be reached was hidden from Hammond and his peers. Like the tulip mania which had once crushed the economy of Holland, the slave mania thundered on to its own destruction. Meanwhile, as all agreed, what a pleasant way it was to make money! One coupled a buck and a wench, let nature take its course, and in twenty years or so there was another slave worth from a thousand to two thousand dollars. "Like money in the bank, suh, jes' like money in the bank."

And Hammond was making money. His father had buried their capital of gold eagles in iron kettles at various spots on the plantation, but Hammond had now outgrown leaving his money in the ground. Out of sentimentality, he still allowed the kettles with their contents of gold pieces to remain in their burial places known only to him. He had so much money in the banks of Mobile, New Orleans, and Natchez that he could look on these antique kettles as souvenirs of the past. Today, Hammond Maxwell of Falconhurst Plantation near Benson, Alabama, was one of the richest men in the whole South. He was accepted as one of the top-drawer Southern gentry and the label of slave-trader which had, at one time, limited his social ambitions, no longer clung to him.

The fruit of his combing of the slave markets of the city totaled eighteen young slaves—twelve males and six females to be exact, ranging in age from eight years to sixteen. In each case Hammond had struck a good bargain, for the market for children and adolescents was not an active one. His purchases were all strong, healthy, smooth-skinned, and good-looking. After purchasing them he allowed them to remain wherever they were until after the sale of his own slaves, when they would be collected and taken back to Falconhurst.

On the day of the sale, he was up early and together with

Drummage he went to Sly's for a last minute inspection of the bucks and wenches in their gala clothes. Hammond saw to it that they all breakfasted well. After breakfast he issued a small glass of corn to each of them to increase their spirits and prepare them for the day, although, truth to tell, any artificial stimulant was quite unnecessary. For the first time since they had arrived in New Orleans they were to be outside the jail, and all were gleeful and in high spirits as they lined up, four abreast in the street outside Sly's, behind the banjo-strumming, horn-blowing, drum-banging band which Sly had hired for the occasion. Two of Hammond's tallest and most prepossessing bucks carried the poles that supported the banner advertising the sale. With a beat of drums, a fanfare of the trumpets, and a twanging of the banjo strings, the procession started—a forerunner of the minstrel parades which were to come fifty years later.

The music, the freedom, the novelty of the city and the stares of the populace excited the boys and girls, and when Hammond left them, high-stepping down the street in rhythmic cadence, they were attracting attention from all sides. Drummage was almost sorry he was not in the parade. He would have enjoyed the trip through the city, timing his steps to the music and ogling the wenches who stopped on the banquettes to watch him pass. Ee-yah! He'd give them an eyeful, he would! It would be something for them to talk about for months to come—the goddamndest handsomest nigger buck they'd ever seen. Ee-yah!

Sly and Brute were in charge of the slaves and Drummage did not see them again until, standing by Hammond's side under the dome of the Saint Louis Hotel, he saw them take their places on the vendue table. He was aware of his master's nervousness as each one of his boys and girls mounted the steps and several times he heard Hammond repeating the slave's name, almost like a regretful good-by.

One by one the slaves mounted the steps and stood for a brief moment, the cynosure of all eyes, while the bids rose, until the final knock of the hammer signaled that the sale was over and the boy or wench stepped down into another life. Drummage had known all of them since he could first remember. He had played with them, slept with them, fought with them. They were all members of one big family, inextricably related to one another either by blood ties or long intimacy. He heard their names called, their pedigrees read, their virtues extolled, their prices shouted, and then saw them disappear, knowing that he would never see them again. Big Saturn, a tower of strength; heavy-handed Plato, the champion plowman; lithe Tonio with his race-horse limbs who could run faster than any buck at Falconhurst; pretty Jimmy-Boy with long-lashed eyes, olive cheeks, and curling hair; Naxos of the scowling brows, who looked mean but was as gentle as a kitten; Tamerlane who had sired twelve suckers in as many months; Tobias and Raphael and Leo and Giles and Dominick and Octavius—each had his moment of glory. There were prune blacks with the purple sheen of Africa; tobacco browns; sepias; yellows; ivories; and even a mustee, so near white with his blue eyes and blond curls that he appeared more Nordic than Negro. After them came the Junos, the Betties, the Fannies, the Claudines, and all the other wenches with children born or unborn.

Then it was all over and the shouting crowd dispersed, their afternoon's entertainment over. Sly gathered up his papers and his gavel and went over the accounts with Hammond. The vast rotunda under the dome of the Saint Louis became quiet again and the long bar gradually filled with men, completely erasing all evidence, except for a faint musky odor from the bodies that had been there, that through this room in New Orleans' most fashionable hotel, a procession of cattle had passed to be sold.

Drummage, waiting for the tedious details of business between Hammond and Sly to be over, felt that he had lived through a nightmare. It was over now and he was glad that he had not been one of the high-steppers behind the band. Yes, it was over and his friends were gone and somehow it didn't seem possible that these familiar faces would be missing from Falconhurst when he returned. But he still had his own Masta Hammond and together they climbed the stairs to the Maxwell suite above, where Hammond threw himself on the bed and had Drummage draw off his boots and mix him a toddy.

The next morning, there was a tearful parting between Candy and her family. Drummage was in such a hurry to get back to the hotel and down to the railroad station to take the train for Mobile that she had little time for good-bys. She had only a glimpse of the city from her seat between Drummage and Jubal as they drove to the station, but already she was missing New Orleans more than she missed her parents.

The return journey was far from comfortable. Now there was no special train, and Drummage, along with Candy, Jubal, Brutus and Ajax, had to use the freight car, along

135

with the frightened children Hammond had purchased as well
as the horses for the carriage. It was a long, gritty journey,
with an exasperating wait in a smoke-filled back room of
the railroad station in Mobile while the two cars—one for
the slaves and the horses and another for the barouche—
were switched in the yards and coupled onto the train for
Winchester. Again they huddled on the hard floor through
the long night, during which Drummage pillowed Candy's
weary head on his arm while he leaned against Jubal's shoulder.

Chapter 14

IT WAS STILL NIGHT—about an hour before daylight—and
raining hard when they arrived at Winchester depot, only to
stand about disconsolately in the cold dampness while they
waited for the arrival of the wagons from Falconhurst. But
the wagons were little better, for they had no covering, and
Drummage and Candy huddled together shivering under a
sodden blanket all the way back to Falconhurst.

Drummage was so glad to get home he soon forgot the
rigors of the journey. It was warm and comfortable in the big
kitchen; a pot of coffee simmered on the stove and the hot
greasy smoke of frying ham stung the eyes. Lucretia Borgia
had only a moment to nod to them before she was out on the
portico welcoming the family, and there was nobody in the
kitchen but a new kitchen wench—a harelipped slattern
named Marguerite whom Hammond had taken "to boot" in
a slave trade and had never been able to get rid of. She
turned to look at them with eyes still heavy from sleep, her
arms elbow-deep in dishwater, but did not speak.

Candy, cold, wet and miserably homesick, stretched her
hands out to the fire while Drummage went out to the
wagon to fetch her zinc trunk and his own carpetbag. Then,
looking around to make sure that Lucretia Borgia was still
out of the kitchen, he slipped into the pantry and managed
to pour out a generous measure of Hammond's brandy into a
cracked teacup. This he brought back into the kitchen, pour-
ing half into another cup and filling them both with hot
coffee. He and Candy sipped in silence and, when they had
finished, the warmth of the coffee and the brandy had taken

136

away some of the chill. At least Candy's teeth had stopped chattering.

"Better if'n yo' comes up to our room. Gits them wet clotheses off'n yo' les' yo' catches yo'se'f an ague." Drummage propelled her across the kitchen and up the two flights of stairs to the room he had formerly shared with Jubal.

Her face fell at the sight of the tiny room and the one narrow bed. She noticed the dusty windowpanes, the cobwebs hanging from the ceiling, and the entire absence of furniture except for the bed and one rickety chair. There was a coat of gray dust on the rough cotton sheet that covered the bed and the rain dripped disconsolately outside the window. The unaired room still had the musky odor of Drummage's and Jubal's bodies.

Candy wrinkled up her nose. "This where we a-goin' to sleep? Stinks in here. Why, this jes' a cubbyhole. Ain' like my room in N'Orleans. Ain' room 'nuff to swing a cat in here and ain' no place to hang my dresses."

Drummage swept his and Jubal's old clothes down from the wall. "Nails on the wall, ain' there? Little sweepin' and dustin' clean it up. 'Sides yo' won' be here much. Days yo' spen' in Miz 'Gusta's room, this 'un jes' for sleepin' 'n' pleasurin'. Gots us a lot o' pleasurin' to do 'cause Masta Hammond mighty anxious to git a nice sucker off'n us."

"Masta Hammond dis! Masta Hammond dat! He ain' a-goin' to git no sucker off'n me."

"Tha's whut yo' thinkin' gal but I'se goin' to work mighty hard to please Masta Hammond. Now shuck yo'se'f outa them wet clotheses and git some dry ones on. I gotta change too 'cause I gotta wait tables jes' so soon as the folks gits ready to eat. Miz 'Cretia Borgia she got brekkus all ready. This mornin' yo' takes the chil'rens' brekkus up to Miz Sophie's room 'n' feed 'em whilst white folks eatin'. Jubal got to git they's things in the house and he wet." Drummage watched her while she slipped out of her sodden dress and peeled off her stockings. He was out of his own clothes, searching among the garments he had thrown on the floor for his old black trousers. As he came across the room he brushed up against her, and the warmth of her flesh, as always, stirred him. Without waiting for her to protest, he drew her close to him, feeling the hardening points of her breasts against his bare chest.

"We a-goin' to be right happy here, yo' 'n' me, Candy Baby. We lucky, we are. Nice room here all by ourselves.

137

Much better'n the quarters with four, five couples all in one cabin. Yo' shore goin' to like Falconhurst."

"Ain' a-goin' to like it," she wept. "Miz'rable place. This room miz'rable—dirty ol' room what stinks. Ain' no place to go, ain' nothin' to do, ain' nothin' to see. Cain' even go out for a stroll on the banquettes. Ain' none here. What I a-goin' to do here all day?"

"Yo' be busy." Drummage sought her lips but she turned her head.

"Work all day, huh? What we do at night? How we goin' to have any fun?"

"Plenty o' fun." Drummage's voice had sunk to a husky whisper and he managed to force his knee between her legs. It threw her off balance and she fell backward onto the bed, he on top of her. "Plenty o' fun every night, yo' 'n' me."

In her misery and her loneliness, she slapped him, pushed him away, and stood up.

"Work all day! Gits myself pestered all night. Tha's all. Yo' nice boy, Drummage, but gits sick o' yo'. Got to have me somethin' else to do 'sides gettin' pleasured by yo' all the time. Craves me a change onct in a while. Gal gets tired o' the same boy all-a time."

"Yo' my gal! Ain' goin' to have no other buck less'n Masta Hammond say so and he won' say so 'cause he say yo' my wench. Whaffor yo' a-wantin' 'nother boy anyhow? Cain' none o' them pleasure you so good as me."

"Masta Hammond, Masta Hammond, Masta Hammond! I'se sick to death o' hearin' 'bout him. If'n I wants 'nother boy, I take him 'n' Masta Hammond he don' stop me." She stared at Drummage defiantly.

"Drummage!" Lucretia Borgia's voice bellowed up the stairs, putting an end to their bickering. "Git yo'se'f down here. Folks a-sittin' down to de table and they's hungry. Git that wench down here fer to carry up the chil'rens' brekkus. Ain' no time fo' yo' to be a dilly-dallyin' now. Button up yore britches and git down here."

"Better hurry, Candy." Drummage eyed her suspiciously, aware that she had scored a point on him. "We finish tonight what we started now. Better git yo'se'f ready for tonight 'cause yo' shore got it comin' to yo'. Hurry now. When you talks to 'Cretia Borgia, be sure to call her 'Miz 'Cretia Borgia ma'am' 'n' don' git her mad on yo' 'cause she shore hell when she gits mad." Drummage was into his pants and shirt and down the back stairs.

Lucretia Borgia handed him the big silver urn full of steaming coffee.

"Who dat uppity gal and wha's her name?"

"She my gal. Masta Hammond done bo't her for me. She cousin to my pappy Drumson. Name's Candy. Ain' she sweet?"

"Candy!" Lucretia Borgia grunted. "She a-goin' to be 'lasses taffy if'n she don' stir her stumps and git down here goddam fast. Goin' to pull her apart like'n I do 'lasses taffy."

Drummage was reassured by Candy's steps on the stairs. He took the urn and carried it through the open door into the pantry and then through the free-swinging door into the dining room. A fire crackled in the grate and the table shone with white linen and silver. It all looked so familiar that it was hard now to realize he had ever been away. He was glad to be home and that Candy was with him. She'd love Falconhurst as much as he did and she wouldn't want any other boy but him. It was just a lot of talk—just foolishness. When he had finished passing the cups that Augusta poured, he came to stand behind Hammond's chair. His hand went up to feel his cheek; it still stung from Candy's slap. He liked a girl with a little bit of spunk, he did, but he knew how he could take it out of her. Get her knocked up and she wouldn't be wanting any other boy.

Throughout the service of the meal, each time Drummage appeared in the kitchen from the dining room, Lucretia Borgia awaited him, breathlessly poised to spring through the doors.

"They through eatin' yet?" she would ask impatiently.

It was not until he returned with the silver tray after serving coffee, to mix Hammond's after-breakfast toddy, that he gave Lucretia Borgia the nod.

"Miz 'Gusta and Miz Sophie, they done gone upstairs and Masta Hammond he a-settin' at the table all alone. Talk wid him now if'n yo' wants. But I a-stayin' and listenin'. Wants to hear what yo' a-been a-doin' since we gone."

"Yo'll hear! Plenty!" She strode through the pantry into the dining room to stand before Hammond.

"Masta Hammond suh." With hands on hips, Lucretia Borgia was a formidable sight. "Masta Hammond suh, shore am afraid yo' a-goin' to have me strung up and stripped down. Jes' done somethin' never done in my whole born days."

Hammond looked up at her and laughed. "Cain' think o' nothin' yo' ain' never done, Lucretia Borgia. Thought yo'd a-done 'bout anythin' any female could. But first, tell me what's

139

been a-goin' on here since we left. Have any trouble with the boys or girls?"

She gave him a disparaging look that told him he had underestimated her ability.

"Ain' never had me no trouble with niggers," she said. "I speaks—they jumps. If'n they don', they gits the back of my hand. 'Ceptin' for those yo' left in de cabins, ain' been no pesterin' here at Falconhurst. The boys stay put and the wenches stay put and ain' no changin' off. Gits 'em all up and out in de fields come five o'clock in de mawnin'. Works 'em till sundown I do, till they so dog-tired ain' no sashayin' roun'. Got me more work outa them lazy niggers 'n yo' ever did. Gotten us twenty cords o' wood, sawed, 'n' split, 'n' piled. Gotten all de corn shucked and sacked ready to go to de mill. Birfed us three suckers we did 'n' got that good-fer-nuthin' Priam 'n' he's frien' Curtius all lined up fer yo' to strip down fer sassin' me back. Ain' takin' no sass from no niggers. No suh, Masta Hammond suh. Ain' no nigger born what a-goin' to sass Lucretia Borgia. I tells 'em yo' whops 'em and yo' whops 'em."

"Whops 'em if'n they needs it, don' whop 'em if'n they don'." Hammond intended to judge matters himself. " 'Pears like everythin' went along tolerable whilst we 'way."

"Went fine, Masta Hammond suh, jes' fine. Ain' never had me no trouble wid no niggers but when it come to white man, shore had me a lot of trouble this time. Got us one locked up in de calaboose. No-good bastard he bin there fer six days a-hollerin' he's fool head off till I think I go 'n' clobber him 'gain."

Hammond rose so violently from the table that he knocked over his chair.

"What yo' mean? Yo' got a white man in the calaboose? What yo' mean a-sayin' yo' goin' to clobber him *again?* Who'n hell yo' think yo' are, a-clobberin' a white man!"

Lucretia Borgia did not retreat an inch from Hammond's fury. "Miz'rable polecat, that's what he is! Strip me down if'n yo' wants ter but shore enjoyed clobberin' that weasel. Shore hated ter give that varmint anythin' to eat. Ain' given him much 'cept bread 'n' water but he lucky ter git that."

Drummage righted the chair and Hammond sat down again. He gulped his toddy and motioned to Drummage to make him another one, and for once Drummage hurried with its preparation in order to get back into the dining room. He felt he had not missed much of the conversation. Lucretia Borgia still held the floor.

" 'Bout a week ago," she was saying, "sent all de bucks and mos' o' de wenches down into de ten-acre fiel'. Corn ripe for pickin' and I has de bucks a-pickin' and de wenches a-huskin'. Tells any wench what husks a red ear she kin kiss any buck she wants and they a-workin' they fool ass off. Goes down 'n' gets 'em all started and lef' Big Randy to oversee and I comes back to de house on de mule. Got back here and foun' dat lazy Marguerite wench ain' washed de brekkus dishes so lets her have it, fust on one ear and den on de other till her head a-spinnin'. Jes' a-soakin' my han's in hot water to take out de sting and listenin' to that Marguerite wench a-yellin' to high heaven when Big Randy he come a-runnin' to de kitchen do'. 'Miz 'Cretia Borgia,' he say, 'yo' better hist yo'se'f up on dat mule and git yo'se'f back down to de ten-acre fiel'. White man done come 'long in he's buckboard and stops all de hands a-workin'. Starts a-talkin' to 'em, he does. Say he goin' to abolishun us. A-goin' to make us free he is!' "

Hammond's face settled into a grim line. "One of them goddam abolitionists from up No'th?"

"Yas suh, Masta Hammond suh! Big Randy he go out in de barn, gits me my mule and hists me up and I take off 'cross de fields. Git me to dat ten-acre fiel' and there was this varmint, a-standin' up in he's spring wagon and all those good-fer-nuffin' niggers gathered roun' 'n' a-listen' to him. He a-goin' on at a great rate, tellin' 'em they's human bein's. Goddam ignerant bastard! Tellin' 'em to run and come up Nawth where they treated jes' like white folkses. Tellin' 'em de undergroun' railway helps 'em."

Hammond was beginning to understand. What had at first seemed a blameworthy action on Lucretia Borgia's part—molesting a white man—now was turning out to be entirely in her favor. The scowl on his face had disappeared and he grinned up at her.

"So what yo' do? Runs him off the place?"

Lucretia Borgia regarded Hammond as though he were not very bright. " 'N' let him go some other place 'n' start yappin' all over 'gain? What right he got a-comin' here a-shootin' off his big mouf, tellin' those ignerant niggers they free? Git ideas into their thick heads 'n' pretty soon cain' do nothin' wid 'em. Gittin' mighty uppity now, some o' 'em."

Hammond nodded in agreement.

"So's I druv de ol' mule right up 'longside he's spring wagon 'n' I gets one foot on de wagon. Den I eases myself off de mule. All a time, he a-turnin' roun' 'n' grinnin' at me.

141

" 'Welcome, moddom,' says he to me, wrappin' bacon roun' every word. 'Low me ter intraduce mysel'. I'se de Reverent Obadiah Stokes o' Boston, Massy-chew-setts. Frien' 'n' dish-i-pull o' de famous Garrison. Hopes yo' a-goin' to help me bring de glorious truth o' freedom to dese pore benighted brethren.' Well onct I got my two feet on de wagon and gits my balance, I walks up to him and"—Lucretia Borgia doubled up one hamlike fist—"I lets him have it. Clobbers that skinny li'l weasel right 'tween de eyes, I do. Den I gives him 'nother in de belly"—she feinted with her left hand—" 'n' he falls down like a poled bull. Den I tells dose lazy niggers to git they'selves back to work and believe me, they gits, all 'cept that Priam 'n' his frien' Curtius who a-wantin' ter argify. Big Randy 'n' Sampson they stays by me and they lays that stinkin' li'l polecat out flat on de wagon. Big Randy take de mule, Sampson he drives de spring wagon and I sets straddle-legged cross de Reverent Obadiah Stokes. We heads fer de quarters 'n' every time he opens his eyes, I clobbers him 'gain. Gets us to de calaboose 'n' Big Randy 'n' Sampson takes him off de wagon and chucks him in. Locks him in there, we do, and there he stay till now. Couldn't let him out if'n I wanted to 'cause ain' a-knowin' 'bout de key what unlocks de calaboose. He bin a-hollerin' 'n' a-psalm-singin' most o' de time. Sayin' he a-goin' ter have de law on us. Sayin' he a-goin' to 'rest us. He kin do dat?" She thrust her chin forward at Hammond.

Hammond got up and put his arm around Lucretia Borgia's shoulders.

"Ain' a-goin' to do nothin', dat meddlin' bastard. He still there?"

"He shore is. If'n yo' stay in N'Orleans six months, he stay in the calaboose 'cause couldn't get him out 'thout a key." Lucretia Borgia beamed under Hammond's approval.

"Guess I saunters over there and takes a look." Hammond signaled to Drummage to accompany him.

"Admires to 'company yo' myself, Masta Hammond suh," Lucretia Borgia said. " 'Pears like I'se got an interest in that there varmint."

"Too far for yo' to walk," Hammond said. "Who out in de barn?"

"Big Randy. I had him a-takin' Ajax' place."

"He yore new boy?" Hammond grinned at her.

"He mighty capable, that boy," Lucretia Borgia snickered, cackled, and crowed all at once. " 'Minds me o' that Mede boy yo' had long time ago. Big Randy he don' look

like such a gyrasticus as that Mede but he shore a *big* boy."
Lucretia Borgia closed one eye slowly.

Hammond was silent for a moment and Drummage remembered the bleached white skull and bones which decorated the shelf above the fireplace in Old Lucy's cabin. That was Mede. A cold shiver passed over him as Hammond turned to him.

"Run out to the barn and tell Big Randy to hitch the horses to the buckboard. We all a-goin' over to the calaboose to see what kind of a varmint Lucretia Borgia done trapped fer us."

Chapter 15

HAMMOND slammed shut the door of the calaboose and snapped the padlock, all the while turning a deaf ear to the howls and protestations which still issued from inside. Quite a crowd had congregated in front of the calaboose, composed mostly of the plantation children, with women from the cabins, and the few men who were not out in the fields. With a wave of his hand Hammond dispersed them and himself assisted Lucretia Borgia to heave her huge bulk back up into the buckboard, signaling to Drummage to hop on behind. During the short distance from the calaboose to the stables Hammond's rage kept him muttering to himself. Although he did not openly congratulate Lucretia Borgia for her capture of the abolitionist, the fact that he did not censure her was a tacit commendation of her treatment of the white man. Ordinarily for a Negro to lay hands on a white man, however low his social position might be, would be a serious crime. But this white man, by his unwarranted presence in the South and his uninvited invasion of the rights and privileges of a slave-owning plantation, had forfeited all rights to any protection his color might warrant him.

When they arrived at the stable, Hammond halted the horses and turned around to speak to Drummage.

"Go in 'n' git Big Randy to saddle a mule fer yo'. Then I want yo' to ride into Benson and I want yo' to stop at every house 'long the way. Yo' goes round to the kitchen do' and inquire respectful-like fer the masta. If'n he ain' there, ask fer the overseer. Then yo' give him this message. Yo' say Masta Hammond Maxwell's compliments suh, and would it be possible fer yo' and yore menfolks to meet Mr. Hammond

Maxwell at the tavern in Benson at"—he reached in his pocket and pulled out his watch—"three o'clock this aftanoon. Tell 'em it's a matter of importance. Kin yo' remember all that?"

"Yes suh, Masta Hammond suh, shore kin." Drummage was standing on the ground, facing up to Hammond. He bowed slightly from the waist as though addressing a stranger. "Mista Hammond Maxwell's compliments ter yo', masta suh, and he desires to know if'n it possible fer yo' and de menfolks here to meet up wid him at de tavern in Benson come three o'clock this aftanoon. Mr. Maxwell a-sayin' it mighty important matter he wishin' fer yo' to come." Again he bowed.

"That'll do." Hammond nodded his head. "Now git a-goin'. Keep on through the town till yo' gits to the Gasaway place an' yo' tells Masta Gasaway that I requests he feed yo' and that he bring yo' back with him to Benson. Guess I better write yo' out a pass 'cause I don' wan' no patrollers a-stoppin' yo'. If'n patrollers do stop yo', tell 'em the same message. Wants every man round Benson to be there this afternoon. Soon's I git over to the big house, I'm sendin' Brute off in the other direction. Now git!" Hammond finished scribbling on the back of the envelope he had taken from his pocket and handed it to Drummage, who dashed into the barn, only to reappear minutes later astride one of the farm mules.

Out alone on the road, freed from all restraint, Drummage experienced a thrill of liberty such as he had never known before. He was on important business for Masta Hammond and, although he did not know exactly what it was, he was proud that he had been chosen to be messenger. It had something to do with the white man in the calaboose—of that he was sure—but just what it was he did not know. Abolitionist! That's what the white man was! Wanted to free all the slaves. Ee-yah! Shore would be nice to be free! He'd like to do just as he pleased and when he pleased—sleep late in the morning, get up and have ham and eggs every day for breakfast. Have a whole stableful of wenches so's he could pleasure whichever one he wanted to. Have himself a house like Falconhurst and a nigger to play the banjo and another nigger to wait on him.

But there was another side to the picture. That would mean no Masta Hammond, no Miz 'Gusta, no big house, nobody to care for him and look after him or tell him what to do. Nobody to look up to and love and respect. Suddenly the prospect did not seem so pleasant. Here at Falconhurst he was safe and secure. Masta Hammond and Miz 'Gusta were here to protect him. Candy was there to sleep with and

'Cretia Borgia was there to cook him three meals a day and if'n he wanted ham and eggs for breakfast, 'Cretia Borgia cooked them for him. When he got Candy knocked up, Masta Hammond'd give him another wench and then another and another. So—what did he want to be free for? Ee-yah! He was better off the way he was. He wasn't any field hand, chopping cotton from sunup till sundown. Let them agitate for freedom if they wanted it. He was Drummage of Falconhurst and that was the finest thing any nigger could be. Masta Hammond Maxwell's own Drummage. Nothing was better than that!

He halted the mule at the driveway to the Twitchell place. It wasn't such-a-much. Nothing like Falconhurst, but Hammond had said every white man and Jed Twitchell was a white man, so Drummage rode up the dusty lane and around the back of the unpainted house. A one-legged slave, with torn and patched osnaburg trousers which only partially hid his wooden stump, eyed him suspiciously from the barn door. With the self-importance he felt from being on home territory and addressing a stranger, he called out:

"Who yo', nigger, and where yo' think yo' a-goin'?"

"When yo' 'dresses a quality colored man, yo' uses *suh,* nigger," Drummage snapped back at him, secure in his Falconhurst authority. "None o' yo' goddam business whereat I goin'." He pulled up at the back door of the farmhouse and dismounted, wading through a puddle of oozy mud, the accumulation of daily dishwater thrown out the back door, to get to the slatternly back porch, where an unshaven man slept with his back to the wall, his two bare feet sticking out in the sunshine. Not daring to wake the man, Drummage rapped on one of the canting posts that supported the roof. Although his knocks did not awaken the man, they sent a couple of hens squawking out of the door and brought a woman paddling from the dark interior in her bare feet, her stained cambric dress hardly able to contain the big, sagging breasts inside. Two tow-headed, snottynosed youngsters, their faces grime-encrusted, peered out from behind her skirt.

Drummage almost gagged on the sour smell that emanated from the open door but he bowed in the courtly fashion he had been taught and repeated Hammond's message. The woman seemed scarcely able to understand what he was saying, but she was obviously awed by the elegance of a Falconhurst house servant in his clean, decent clothes. She went over and prodded the sleeping man with a long, yellow-nailed big toe.

"Wake up, Paw! One o' them Falconhurst niggers here with a word from Mista Hammond Maxwell. Wake up!" She waited for the man to show signs of life and as he sat forward rubbing his eyes, she spoke to Drummage.

"Tell Paw wha' Mista Maxwell a-wantin'."

Drummage repeated the message and much to his surprise the man thanked him and invited him into the kitchen for something to eat, but the foul odor was too much for him. He declined politely, bowed again to both the man and woman, and rode on his way. Not, however, without a threatening look toward the lone slave in the barn.

"Better keep that big mouf o' yourn closed after this."

In the few miles between Falconhurst and the town of Benson, Drummage stopped at perhaps twelve houses, the majority of them little better than the Twitchell place. At the white-pillared Johnstone mansion, he was invited into the kitchen for a glass of cool buttermilk, and from his glimpse through the open door into the dining room he could see the threadbare poverty reflected in the soiled tablecloth, the swarm of flies over the melting butter dish, and the general slackness of the house as compared with the immaculate neatness of Falconhurst. Johnstone Oaks was petered out, its once-rich land depleted, but the Johnstones were quality and the entire Johnstone household of father and five grown sons turned out and followed Drummage to Benson. By the time he reached the town there was a fair-sized scattering of men assembled around the tavern.

On through the town and to the Gasaway plantation on the other side, and once again Drummage saw peeling paint, sagging roofs, and a slipshod descent from affluence to poverty. The big house sat in the midst of overgrown gardens, which showed that there was not enough slave labor to be wasted on nonessentials, and behind it there were many slave cabins now tumbling to ruin. The Negroes that Drummage saw were either elderly or runty young ones—a far cry from the sleek young bucks of Falconhurst. Lewis Gasaway himself—a contemporary of Hammond's—looked little different in his homespun trousers and shirt from the red-necked Twitchell, but his hospitality was lavish and Drummage was regaled with all the remnants of the family dinner.

When they arrived at Benson the crowd at the tavern had increased, and in the center of milling heads Drummage could see Hammond, sitting on his horse beside the abolitionist's buckboard with the abject figure of the man himself

146

crouched on the wagon seat. Hammond was haranguing the crowd.

"Wants to present yo' with a real, genuine, stinkin' polecat," he was shouting. "This little pipsqueak done come all the way from the No'th jes' to tell us that our niggers better'n we are. Says they's human. Tryin' to make out that they's jes' the same as we are 'cept for the color of their skins. What he know 'bout niggers? We've lived with niggers all our lives and we know niggers better'n any man from up No'th. So I'm a-goin' to ask all of yo', and mos' of yo's nigger owners, if'n any of yo' thinks that niggers is human bein's? I bin a-raisin' niggers ever since I kin remember. Likes 'em I do. Ain' nothin' finer in the world 'n a fine upstanding young buck o' a nice purty nigger wench. I got some of the finest niggers in Alabama right here at Falconhurst but ain' a one of 'em human. Ain' never seen a nigger that was a human bein', any more'n I've seen a horse that was a human bein'. Niggers is niggers and white folks is white folks and horses are horses and dogs are dogs. Am I right?"

"Co'se yo's right, Mista Maxwell," a voice called out, echoed by others who substantiated Hammond's views.

"A white man's a white man and a nigger's a servant," someone else called, "always has been and always will be. Says so in the Bible it does. Niggers always been servants. George Washington he had niggers, so did Mista Jefferson. What them goddam Northerners a-talkin' 'bout?"

"Thank you, Mista Holman." Hammond bowed in the direction of an ancient greybeard whose straggly moustache was stained yellow by tobacco. "Them's my sentiments too. But now this varmint comes sneakin' round, talkin' to our servants and tellin' them they ought to be free. Tellin' them they ought to start runnin'. He's a goin' to help 'em run, he says, and yo' know what that means? Every buck that runs means a thousand dollars loss to yo'. He say he a-goin' to take them on the underground railroad up North where they kin go 'round a-rapin' white women if'n they wants. He don' know that a randy nigger buck, if'n he cain' get himse'f a wench, goin' to take a white woman. Oh, no! He think they human bein's. Wonder how he'd like his sister a-raped by a nigger buck."

"That's what he'll git. Ain' a white woman safe when a buck gits randy."

" 'Grees with yo', Mista Worth, certainly 'grees with yo'," Hammond nodded to a young planter. "We knows it 'cause we knows our niggers and we knows how to hold 'em

147

in line. Mayhap it takes a touch o' the whip now 'n' then but we tames 'em. Have whips fer horses we do and have whips fer niggers. One needs it as much as t'other."

"Mos' times niggers need it more'n hosses." A tall thin man, his trousers held up with hempen twine, shifted his cud of tobacco from one side of his mouth to the other as he spoke.

Hammond nodded to the speaker.

"Now look at what we got here." He pointed to the Northerner on the seat of the wagon. "This squirt, what ain' never owned a nigger in his life, come down here with his agitatin' 'n' his abolishunin', a-stirrin' up strife 'mongst our niggers. Caught him red-handed on Falconhurst we did, whilst I was in N'Orleans. Kept him locked up till I got back. Fust off I was a-goin' to kill the runt but didn' want his blood on my hands, so's I brought him over here to yo' folks. Wanted yo' all to see him and wanted to ask yo' all what we a-goin' to do with him?"

"String him up!"

"Hang him!"

"Hangin's too good fer that ornery critter. Our lives ain' goin' be worth a picayune with him a-settin' the niggers 'gainst us."

Several more cries of "Hang him!" came from different parts of the crowd and a clod of dirt sailed through the air to land on the Reverend Obadiah Stokes's cheek. Like a cornered rat, he stood up and opened his mouth to speak, but Hammond gave him a shove that sent him sprawling the length of the manacle on his wrist, whose other end was fastened to the wagon.

"Yo' gits yore chance when we tells yo'," Hammond shouted at him, then turned again to face the ring of upturned faces.

"Hangin's too good for this cuss," he said, " 'n' 'sides, spite of everything, he's a white man and we ain' a-hangin' no white man 'fore niggers. But he bin incitin' the niggers to run; been fillin' 'em with ideas 'bout revoltin'. Bin tryin' to destroy our property and a nigger's just as much property as a horse or a bull. We kin hang horse thieves but we cain' hang nigger-lovers." Hammond shaded his eyes with his hand and looked around the circle of men until he spotted Lewis Gasaway with Drummage behind him. "That yo', Lewis?" he called out, "glad yo' got here. What we goin' to do with this varmint?"

The crowd parted to make way for Lewis Gasaway while

148

he strode up to Hammond. He came directly up to the wagon and leaned forward to look at the man.

"Well," he drawled, " 'Course we could hang the bastard but jus' don' hold with hangin' a polecat like that 'cause after we'd a-hung him, we'd have to cut him down 'n' bury him 'n' don' wan' nothin' as putrid as that a-buried roun' here. If'n we had some tar, could tar 'n' feather him."

"Got plenty of 'lasses," someone cried out. " 'Lasses jes' 's good's tar—stickier too."

Hammond nodded his head in approbation. "Needs us a barrel o' blackstrap 'lasses. You, Jed Twitchell, go over to the store 'n' tell 'em to send over a barrel and charge it to Falconhurst. 'N' yo', Young Bill"—he pointed to one of the Johnstone clan—"go over to Miz Daniels' 'n' ask her for the loan of two of her feather pillows. Tell her Miz Maxwell'll send her two from Falconhurst to replace them. 'N' somebody find a good strong rail so's we can ride this bastard outa town. But we ain' a-goin' to condemn no one less'n they has a chance to speak fer themselves. So yo', Stokes, if'n that's yore name, git yo'se'f up on yore feet and speaks yore mind." He reached over and grabbed hold of Stokes's collar and lifted him to his feet. "Tell these men how yo' tryin' to git their niggers to run 'n' revolt."

The little man was trembling but resolute. He had suffered several days' imprisonment in the Falconhurst calaboose on short rations; he had been pushed, shoved, and mauled by all and sundry; but the fanatical zeal that had prompted him to place himself in such jeopardy in the first place had not been dampened. His eagerness for martyrdom far overshadowed his fear. He waited until the catcalls subsided, then faced his tormentors.

"Don't make any difference what you do to me." He glared at his unfriendly audience. "There's nothing you can do to stop the abolitionist movement. We are growing every day on both sides of the ocean. Sooner or later, in spite of all you do, these poor benighted black brothers are going to be free. We aim to free their souls and their bodies."

"Ain' got no souls," a heckler cried, "and their bodies belong to us."

"Of course they have souls, just like we do." Stokes pointed a trembling finger at the man. "They are men, they are. They suffer, they laugh, they talk, they sing and they weep and in the end they die, just the same as we do. And I say to you that every man of you who owns a slave is bound for hell and damnation in the next world. I see you all burning in that bottomless pit of fire and brimstone. I hear you calling for mercy. I hear you begging some poor black soul whose body you owned during his lifetime to come down and wet your lips with cool water. But he won't do it. No, sirree, he won't! He suffered too much from you while he was here on earth. Oh, brethren, I beg of you, if you want to save your immortal souls, let these poor slaves go. Free them today and rest secure in your beds tonight, knowing that you have done God's will. Free them, and I will lead them to a land of milk and honey up north were every man is free and where there is no more selling and buying of human flesh. You there"—he pointed across the sea of faces to where Drummage's black face stood out—"Don't you want to be free, young man?"

Drummage hung his head but Hammond's voice prompted him to speak.

"That's my boy, Drummage," Hammond said. "Speak out boy. Tell this feller if'n yo' wants to be free or not."

"Ain' a-wantin' ter leave yo', Masta Hammond suh. Yo' good to me."

Lewis Gasaway pointed to his own slave who had accompanied him and who was standing near Drummage.

"How 'bout yo', Chip? Yo' wan' ter run?"

"Ain' aimin' ter run, Masta Lewis suh. Yo' knows dat. Don' wan' to leave Lizzy 'n' the li'l 'uns."

One by one the white masters in the crowd questioned the slaves who had accompanied them. Not one, regardless of what his true feelings might be, but insisted on his love for his master and his desire to remain with him.

"Guess that shows yo', Mista Stokes." Hammond pushed the man down again onto the wagon seat. "Guess that shows yo', yo' jist a-stickin' yo' long nose in where it don' belong. We a-goin' to git shet o' yo', Mista." He squinted over the heads of the crowd to where two men were trundling a barrel of molasses on a squeaking wheelbarrow and another followed them with a couple of fat pillows in blue and white ticking. "An' we goin' to get shet o' yo' damn soon. Bring that gear over here," he shouted to the men with the wheelbarrow, while he reached in his pocket for the key that unlocked the spancel around the man's wrist.

Willing hands lifted the heavy molasses barrel out of the wheelbarrow and stove in the head. Other hands reached up and grabbed the Reverend Stokes and stripped his clothes off until he stood stark naked in all his scrawniness.

"Looks like a picked chicken."

"Goddam small-peckered."

"Bet he never pleasured a wench in his life."

"Had ought to put him next to a hot black one. She'd teach him 'bout her 'mortal soul.'"

Stokes was lifted up in the air and plunged head first into the barrel of molasses. Again and still again he was dunked like a tallow dip, until his whole body was coated with the sweet sticky stuff. Meanwhile, the bed pillows had been ripped open and then feathers spread in a white mound on the grass. Then the dripping victim was rolled back and forth in the feathers until he emerged beplumed like a month-old chick. By now he had recovered his breath and he was screaming hoarsely behind his mask of feathers and molasses.

Someone had wrenched a rail from a nearby fence, and as hands spread open his feathered legs the pole was forced between them and lifted while Stokes clung to the rail, trying to relieve the strain of the sharp edges against his groin. To add to his discomfort they jiggled the pole up and down, steadying him so he would not fall off.

One of the Johnstone boys climbed up in Stokes's wagon and slapped at the horses with the reins, while several other men lifted the pole shoulder-high with the screaming man astride it. They started off, with the laughing, shouting men falling in behind on horses and mules, and the Negroes, including Drummage, bringing up the rear. About two miles out of town the men got tired of toting Stokes and dumped him, then hoisted him up in his wagon, slapped his horse, and sent him on his way. A few of them followed along, whipping the poor horse to make it gallop, until they too tired of the sport.

Hammond had seen enough. He had done his duty and now he was sick of it. He called Lewis Gasaway to him and slipped a gold eagle into his hand. "Take 'em all back to the tavern and stand drinks for the crowd, Lewis. I've got to git home." With Drummage behind him, he sat on his horse by the side of the road until the crowd had left, then took a short cut across the fields to the road that led to Falconhurst. The excitement was over and now the hum of cicadas and the distant songs of slaves returning from a long day in the fields were the only sounds. The thick dust swirled from the horse's hooves and settled on their perspiring faces. Hammond checked in his horse and waited for Drummage's mule to come up alongside him.

"Guess we settled that bastard," he said.

"Yo' shore did, Masta Hammond suh, shore did," Drummage agreed.

Hammond rode on a few steps in silence.

"Yo' mean what yo' say back there? Yo' mean yo' ain' never had no wish to run?"

Drummage shook his head vehemently. "Never wanted ter leave yo' 'n' Miz 'Gusta, 'n' 'Cretia Borgia 'n' that Candy wench yo' got fer me."

Hammond smiled and nodded.

"How yo' comin' with that Candy?"

"She a li'l skittish fust off, Masta Hammond suh, but she a-likin' it now. She shore a-likin' it good."

"Yo' gits her knocked up, goin' to bed yo' with Reba. She a nice li'l wench. Reckon she got either Mandingo o' Hausa blood in her and wants to mate her up with yo'. Have to break her in tho'."

"Yas suh, Masta Hammond suh, but shore do like that Candy wench."

"Kin have her 'gain after she foals. Ain' goin' to breed her to no one but yo'."

"Thank yo' Masta Hammond suh, thank yo'. Sure admire to have Candy for my regular wench, 'ceptin' when she in foal." Hammond started to ride ahead but Drummage clucked to his mule and kept abreast of him.

"Aimin' ter ask yo' a question, Masta Hammond suh, if'n yo' gives me permission." Drummage looked at his master expectantly.

"Well now, if'n yo' asks so respectful-like, permission granted."

"Aimin' ter ask yo' if'n yo' kin git a wench for that Jubal boy. He ain' never had no taste o' tail and he gittin' awful horny like. He mos' eighteen, he say, and he jes' a-wastin' he's sap."

"Been thinking 'bout him." Hammond nodded his head in agreement. "Been thinkin' I mate him up with Jewel. She foaled twice and she a good wench fer starting that boy. She a nice clean wench 'n' she housebroken too so's she kin come nights to the big house and bed in Jubal's room."

"Thank yo', Masta Hammond suh, thank yo' kindly 'n' Jubal he be happy too."

The gateposts of Falconhurst welcomed them.

Chapter 16

A WEEK or so after the episode at the tavern, Augusta sent Drummage out to the barn to see if he could locate a parcel which she was sure she had left in the barouche after her shopping trip to Benson the day before. As she had suspected, it was there, and Drummage found it without any difficulty, but as he started to leave the barn with it in his hand, he spied a piece of white paper, half covered with straw and litter, which he thought might belong in the big house. When he picked it up and brushed off the dust, he was surprised to see the crude representation of a Negro on the front of the pamphlet—a half-naked buck with arms upraised, bursting the chains of his bondage. Its location, under the place where the abolitionist's wagon had been standing during his incarceration in the slave pen, identified it as belonging to the man whom Drummage had seen ridden out of town. As such, Drummage knew it did not belong to the Maxwells, and he decided to keep it for himself. The illustration of the big-lipped black brute intrigued him and although he was not able to decipher all the letters, he felt that with some study and concentration he might make them out. He folded it carefully and placed it in his pocket, for he knew that its possession would be forbidden. As soon as he had delivered the packet to his mistress he went to his own room, removed the pamphlet, and hid it under his mattress. Candy knew how to read and write; he would enlist her co-operation because he was anxious to learn more about the exulting colored man and how he had managed to break his fetters.

He was smoothing back the covers of his bed, trying to approximate the wrinkle-free perfection which Candy always achieved, when he heard Lucretia Borgia shouting up the stairs from the kitchen below.

"Masta Hammond a-wantin' yo' quick, Drummage. Drop what yo' a-doin' and run. He mighty upset, he is."

Drummage raced down the stairs, passing Lucretia Borgia in the kitchen. Her black finger pointed toward the front of the house to direct him.

"In de front hall, he is."

Drummage hurried through the dining room and the drawing room to see Hammond standing at the front door talking with Lewis Gasaway. They both seemed to be in high spirits, talking loud and slapping each other on the back. He sidled up behind Hammond softly in his slippers, standing still and not daring to interrupt until Hammond turned and saw him.

"Where in hell yo' bin, yo' lazy bastard? Been a-yellin' my head off fer yo'. Git yo'se'f out to the barn and tell Ajax to saddle up fer me."

"Yo' a-wantin' me to go 'long wid yo', Masta Hammond suh?"

"If'n I wants yo' I tells yo'. Didn' say nothin' 'bout yore goin', did I? Better yo' stays here and looks after yore mist-'ess."

Drummage was disappointed that he was not going but he sped through the house and out the back door, down the short path that led to the barn. Ajax was sitting in the barn door, polishing the silver ornaments on the harness, but he sensed the urgency in Drummage's haste and together they saddled Hammond's horse. Almost before Drummage reported back Ajax had the horse at the door. Miz 'Gusta was down in the hall now and Miz Sophie too. Drummage was surprised to see that, in contrast to Hammond's high spirits, they were both crying, and he wondered at the reason for their tearful farewells. There was no holding down either Hammond's or Gasaway's jubilance. Ajax gave his hands to them to mount and they galloped down the driveway, yelling to each other and calling back to the house. At the turn into the road, Hammond rose in his saddle and waved back. Then they were lost in the trees that grew along the road to Benson.

Drummage lingered in the hall, hoping to glean some word of the happenings from his mistress's conversation, but she and Sophie ascended the stairs, their arms around each other's waists, apparently consoling each other over some tragedy. Drummage went out into the kitchen, for certainly the omniscient Lucretia Borgia—that fount of all wisdom— would know if anybody did. But she was as ignorant as he was himself and together they attempted to conjecture what had happened, reaching no conclusion until Jubal scuffed into the kitchen. He came over to where Drummage was sitting, letting his big fingers play around the nape of Drummage's neck, tweaking his ears and giggling.

"All hell broke loose upstairs," he said. "Bof Miz 'Gusta

and Miz Sophie a-rampagin' and a-cryin' and a-weepin'. Set the kids to cryin' too. Everyone a-bawlin'. Don' know what's a-goin' on. Masta Hammond a-whoopin' down the road, Miz 'Gusta a-bawlin'. She say as how yo' bring 'em two glasses o' Madeiry to settle they's nerves."

"Wha's the trouble?" Lucretia Borgia lumbered across the kitchen to unlock the wine closet, selecting a key which hung from the ring at her belt, while Drummage brought a small silver tray from the pantry and placed two wine glasses on it.

"Le's see," Lucretia Borgia was muttering. "Port on the left, Madeiry on the right." She took down a bottle and filled the glasses, then replaced it. "Wha's a-goin' on?"

"Don' rightly know but this mawnin' that Masta Gasaway he comed ridin' up a-bellerin' fer Masta Hammond 'fore anyone gits to de do'," Jubal said. " 'Thout knocking he runs in, callin' Masta Hammond and sayin' something about the war he's started. Wha's war, Miz 'Cretia Borgia? What he mean?"

Neither Lucretia Borgia nor Drummage was prepared to answer him. War was a word with which they were both unacquainted. Drummage had a vague idea that it had something to do with two men fighting each other, but he knew that Lewis Gasaway and Hammond were the best of friends and certainly they were in high spirits when they departed and far removed from killing each other. Perhaps, he considered, Brutus or Ajax might know something about this unknown war. He would have set off in search of them, but he had to carry the wine upstairs first.

His rap on the door admitted him. Both his mistresses had now somewhat regained their composure, and Candy had quieted the children. Drummage passed the silver tray first to Augusta and then to Sophie. He lingered, desiring to speak but not daring to do so until Augusta asked him: "What is it, Drummage?"

"Craves to ask yo' a question, Miz 'Gusta."

She looked up at him quizzically and for the first time that morning he saw her smile. Miz 'Gusta had always been a friend of his—he was never afraid of her.

"Wha's this here war, Miz 'Gusta ma'am?"

Her smile disappeared and she spoke rather sternly.

"Something you would not understand, Drummage. It's nothing for the servants to talk about because it's a terrible thing—people killing each other, burning houses and doing awful things."

155

"Yo' means white folks a-killin' the niggers?" He began to be a little fearful himself.

"No, Drummage, white folks killing each other."

He breathed deeply, sensing he was not involved, but he still felt fearful.

"Nobody a'goin' to kill Masta Hammond, Miz 'Gusta. Nobody goin' to burn down our house. I perteck yo' all, Miz 'Gusta. My pappy save Masta Hammond onct, now it's my turn. Don' yo' worry, Miz 'Gusta." He doubled up his fist threateningly. "If'n anyone come here to kill Masta Hammond, I lets 'em have it. Kin fight, I kin. Goin' to learn Jubal how too, I am."

Her white fingers closed over the dark fist.

"I know, Drummage, I know. We have no cause to fear and we pray that nothing will happen to Master Hammond, but we are sad because he may be leaving us soon. We're going to have to get along without him. They're forming a cavalry company in Benson today and they want to make Master Hammond Major."

"I a-goin' with him, Miz 'Gusta ma'am?"

"I don't know. We'll have to wait until he returns to see what his plans are. Maybe he won't even be going. But if he does go, chances are he'll take you with him."

"Yes'm, Miz 'Gusta ma'am. I goes with him to perteck him." Drummage picked up the tray and started for the door. He knew little more now than before, but he could sense the importance of what he did know. Masta Hammond was going away to kill other white men.

His hand was on the door latch when Augusta stopped him.

"Come back, Drummage."

He returned to stand in front of her chair.

"That little packet that you brought to me earlier this morning." She pointed to the tall mahogany chest of drawers against the wall between the two front windows. "Open the top small drawer, Drummage. You'll find it inside. Bring it to me."

Drummage crossed the room softly, his slippers making no noise on the carpet, opened the drawer and found the packet he had that morning removed from the barouche. He brought it back to his mistress and handed it to her. She took it and without opening it placed it in her lap.

"I have something to give you, Drummage. It was broken so I took it into the jeweler's at Benson to have it repaired. For a long time I have meant to give it to you because it belongs to you. I do not know exactly what it is or what particular meaning it has but it belonged to your father and I understand that it belonged to his father before him. So I think that you should have it."

She opened the box and took out a silver chain to which was attached a small filigreed silver box. Motioning to Drummage to come even closer, she bade him kneel down before her and slipped the silver chain over his head, letting the little silver box slide down into the opened "V" of his shirt. It felt cold against his skin and he shivered.

"Shore is pretty," he said as he lifted it to examine it. He could see the small hinges on one side of it. "Kin I open it?"

"You may," she nodded her head, "but there is nothing inside but some bits of cloth and a little cake of earth or something like it. What its meaning is I do not know nor do I know why your father wore it. Hammond said he had it on when he purchased him and his former mistress said he must always wear it."

"I know." Sophie spoke for the first time. "It was some sort of a talisman. Once when I was a young girl, I asked Drumson about it and he said it had come from his father. He said as long as he wore it nothing would happen to him. I demanded that he give it to me but he refused. Then I begged Father to make him give it to me but he told me it belonged to Drumson and I couldn't have it. I remember that I was pretty angry to think a slave could have something which I could not have."

"Drumson lost it the night he was killed." Augusta relived the scene in memory. "I picked it up the next morning. Now it's yours, Drummage. You'd better wear it. Maybe you'll have a son some day and you can pass it on to him."

"Should be havin' one mighty soon, Miz 'Gusta ma'am. Been a-workin' on that Candy like Masta Hammond tol' me." He noticed the frown on Augusta's face and changed the subject. "Thank'ee, Miz 'Gusta ma'am. Grateful, I am." Her frown changed to a smile as he got to his feet and left the room. He could hardly wait until he got downstairs, and once in the privacy of the butler's pantry he took the chain off from around his neck and pried the little case open with his fingernail. As his mistress had said, it contained nothing but some brittle little scraps of cloth that pulverized at his touch, and a tiny cake of some substance that looked like dried mud. His finger pawed at the cake but it did not break and at length he carried it to his nose and sniffed. There was a faint aroma of musk—a ghost of perspiration that smelled

157

like his own. Regretfully he snapped it closed and hung it around his neck again, but now it felt warm and comfortable against his flesh. He must go to Big Pearl and ask her about it. She'd probably remember seeing it around his pappy's neck. With a flannel cloth he wiped his fingerprints from the silver tray and placed it on the shelf, then went out into the kitchen. Brutus and Ajax were both sitting at the table, facing Lucretia Borgia and Jubal. In his new pride of possession Drummage displayed the silver chain, interrupting the heated conversation that was going on.

"Miz 'Gusta jes' done give me this." He swaggered a little. "Said it belonged to Drumson."

Brutus looked up and recognized the silver talisman.

"Shore did. 'Members seein' it round Drumson's neck when we bedded together up there." He pointed to the room above the kitchen. "Drumson set a mighty store on it. Said ol' Miz Alix who owned him tell him it come from his grandpappy and that his grandpappy brought it from Africky. Said his grandpappy was a king there. Said that little box had powerful magic. Said if'n he los' it, he goin' to die. Shore 'nuff died when he lost it."

Drummage replaced the ornament.

"What yo' all been talkin' 'bout?"

"Tellin' 'em that this here's war shore 'nuff." Brute resumed his interrupted conversation. "No'th a-fightin' the South 'count of us niggers. No'th say we'uns ought to be free mens, jes' like white folks. South says we gotta be slaves jes' like we are. South a-goin' to see-sede from the No'th. Goin' to have us a new country. Ain' a-goin' to let them Yankees tell us what we kin do."

Drummage bethought himself of the pamphlet he had picked up that morning with the exultant Negro breaking his chains. He had never been chained so he could not quite understand it. What was this big to-do about freedom anyway? He had never realized that he was not free. Of course he knew that he belonged to Masta Hammond.

"Whaffor it mean to be free, anyway?" He looked up at Brutus. "Yo' a-wantin' to be free, Brute?"

"Hell no! Whaffor I wantin' to have to work my ass off all day a-choppin' cotton for nothin'? Don' have me no fiel' work now. If'n I free, have to plant my own taters, have to plant my own yams, have to plant my own cotton, have to raise my own pigs. Have to live in some li'l cabin. Better off now, I am. Don' wan' to be free, wants to 'long to Masta Hammond here at Falconhurst."

158

"Don' some of the boys 'n' wenches what go to N'Orleans wan' ter be free?" Drummage still pictured the Negro on the pamphlet.

"Ain' no Falconhurst nigger ever complain," Brutus laughed. "Those bucks all a-waitin' to be sold. Everyone a-hopin' he go next year. Wants to be a stud. 'N' mos' Falconhurst bucks gits they wish. Hears though it pretty bad on the big cane fields in Louisiana. Say they work the bucks so hard there, no buck lives more'n four-five years. We lucky here at Falconhurst. I knows 'cause I talked with lotsa fellows for sale. Some mastas pretty mean cusses. Don' blame them bucks fer wantin' to be free, but don' want it myself."

Lucretia Borgia drew herself up proudly in her chair. "I'se Masta Hammond's wench, I am. Nigh onto eighty years old, I am. Aim to die as Masta Hammond's wench. He sol' me onct but I comed back. Ain' knowin' what I'se a-goin' to do if'n I ain' a-livin' here. Ain' wantin' to live nowhere else. Ain' wantin' to be free. White man come to tell me I'se free, clobbers him I will."

"Me, I don' wan' to be free nuther." Ajax affirmed his statement with a vigorous nod of his head. "Al'ays been here and wants to stay here. Knows every horse in the barn. That barn mine. Niggers comin' out to that barn have to step roun' like I tells 'em. Masta Hammond say I in charge of the barn. I head man there."

"Likes it here too," Jubal added. "Got me a good home. Got me a good masta. Got me a good frien' here in Drummage."

Ajax winked at Brutus, who winked back at him.

"Brute 'n' I good frien's o' yo' too, ain' we, Jubal?"

Jubal grinned. "Yo' all frien's. Likes yo' all."

"Ain' wantin' to be free nuther," Drummage spoke.

"Well I do!"

They all turned to look at Candy, standing in the pantry door and waving the pamphlet Drummage had found.

"Yo' all a lot of ignorant niggers. Tha's all yo' are. I ain' a-wantin' to stay here. Whaffor anyone want to stay out here! Me, I wants to be free. Wants to go back to N'Orleans. Gits me a yellow satin dress. Gits me a big carriage with four white horses. Rides to the opera. Rides to the shops. Buys me some diamon' ear bobs. Dresses up in pretty clothes an' lives in a big house with lots o' niggers to wait on me. 'Miz Candy, ma'am,' they say to me and if'n they don' I whops 'em. Whops 'em anyway jes' to hol' 'em in line. Gits me a nigger boy to drive my kerridge; gits

159

me a little nigger boy to hol' up my dress; gits me a high
yella' boy to wait on de table; gits me a nigger wench to
paint my face. Sets me down three times a day to eat off'n
white chiny with pink roses and uses silver forks. Gits me
high-heeled red satin slippers. Shore thing I wan's to be free.
Ain' aimin' to kowtow to white folks all my life. They no
better'n me."

Lucretia Borgia heaved her huge bulk out of the chair
and with a deceptive smile strode slowly and deliberately
across the kitchen to where Candy posed in the door. When
she reached the girl, she drew back her hand. Years had not
robbed Lucretia Borgia of her strength, and the resounding
slap that she delivered to Candy's face rocked the girl's
head. She fell to the floor and Drummage rushed over to
pick her up.

"If'n she wan' to be free, she kin wan', cain' she?" he
shouted at Lucretia Borgia.

" 'N' she kin keep her big mouf shut too. Ain' havin'
no talk 'bout sech things here. Not in my kitchen! Yalla
satin dresses! Humph! She a-goin' to be knocked up soon.
Been a-hearin' the ropes on that bed o' yourn a-screechin'
all night. Makes so much noise cain' sleep. How she a-goin'
to look wid a yalla satin dress over her big belly?"

Candy was weeping and Drummage was trying to console her.

"If'n yo' wants to be free, Candy girl, yo' kin want. Ain'
for Lucretia Borgia to say."

"Goin' to tell Miz 'Gusta on her." Lucretia Borgia's hand
was poised for another slap. "She tell Masta Hammond and
he strip her down. Slice the meat right offa her back. Whops
her good and she won' be yellin' 'bout no diamon' ear bobs."

Candy was frightened. She realized that she had said too
much. She extricated herself from Drummage's arms and
rushed to Lucretia Borgia. Her arms encircled the old
woman and she kissed her, palavering over her.

"Didn' yo' knows I jes' a-foolin', Miz 'Cretia Borgia. Jes'
a-makin' fun I was. Whaffor I wants to leave here? Got me
a nice boy here. Pleasures me right well, Drummage does,
so ain' wantin' no high yella boy to wait on me."

Drummage pricked up his ears at the further mention of a
yellow boy. He thought he had made her forget the one
she had left behind her in New Orleans. Lucretia Borgia,
however, accepted Candy's explanation. The hand that had
so recently slapped Candy now patted her consolingly.

160

"Glad yo' was only a-foolin'. Sorry I clobbered yo'. Shore thought yo' meant it."

But Candy had not fooled Drummage. He knew that she meant it. He knew that she had told the truth. She wanted her freedom and that freedom did not include him. It envisioned some stylish mulatto buck to share her carriage and her bed. Yet when she abandoned Lucretia Borgia and placed herself once again in the protection of his arms, he forgot about the mulatto buck and had only one desire —to carry her up the back stairs and gently place her on the white-sheeted bed. She pressed close to him and smiled up at him.

"Got to go upstairs and tidy myself up. Goin' to change my dress 'fore I goes back to Miz 'Gusta. Why'n't yo' come up for a minute wid me, Drummage?"

Chapter 17

IT WAS AFTER MIDNIGHT when Hammond arrived home, and he was not alone. At least twenty men accompanied him and all of them were gloriously and uproariously drunk. Augusta had instructed Drummage to wait up for Hammond and he had been dozing in a big chair in the lower hall, resentful over the fact that Candy was alone in their bed while he had to stay in the hall. Hearing the commotion in the driveway, he awoke from his stupor, and with the one lighted candle that had been left burning he hurriedly lit the candles in the hall and managed to get the front door open by the time Hammond and the men had dismounted and stumbled up onto the portico. Hammond and Lewis Gasaway entered, their arms around each other, more for physical support than from affection, and once inside the door Hammond, in a gesture of hospitality to those following him, opened his arms wide to welcome them, which caused Lewis to slump to the floor. He sat there, staring blankly at the wall while the others entered.

"Drummage boy"—Hammond staggered over to him and would have fallen also had not Drummage reached out his arms to support him—"Hist yore black ass out to de kitchen and mix toddies for these gen'mun. Bring in Port and

Madeiry fer them as wants it and a jug of corn if any of 'em craves it straight 'n' cold."

Drummage eased Hammond into a chair and slipped out through the dining room into the kitchen, where the tea kettle was still warm over the dying fire. He arranged long rows of glasses on the big dining-room waiter, measured out corn for each toddy, and then poured in the amount of sweetening that Hammond liked to each one, filling them all up with hot water. It took both hands to carry the heavy waiter into the hall and, as each man took a glass, there was no need to return to the kitchen for wine.

Gasaway had managed to get himself up off the floor, and with the other men he formed a circle around Hammond. They lifted their glasses high.

"To Major Hammond Maxwell of the Falconhurst Lancers."

"Bes' goddam major in de Confederate Army."

"Generous o' him, mighty generous, I calls it."

"Three cheers for Major Maxwell."

"E-e-e-e-e-e-YAH!" The rebel yell set the crystal prisms on the chandeliers to tinkling, and Augusta appeared at the head of the stairs, her long blue velvet peignoir sweeping the floor. She descended the stairs slowly to stand beside Hammond, who was on the bottom step.

"To Miz Hammond Maxwell, the flower of Southern womanhood." A reeling gallant raised his glass.

"E-e-e-e-e-YAH!" Again the cheer sounded.

"Purtier'n a magnolia blossom."

" 'N' jes' as sweet 'n' pure."

"Miz Maxwell, we salutes yo'."

She bowed, smiling at them all, but her presence seemed to put a damper on the gathering and one by one they edged toward the doorway—all except one red-neck who doubled over and grabbed his stomach as he started to puke up his liquor on the floor. The others hauled him out, strewing a trail of vomit behind him. When the last one had departed and the sound of their horses had died away, Augusta took Hammond's arm to assist him up the stairs, but he gently disengaged her hand. Suddenly he appeared sober.

"Yo' go on up alone, 'Gusta," he said. "Drummage 'n' me got a little somethin' to attend to 'fore I gits to bed."

"But you must be exhausted, darling. Can't it wait until morning?"

"Night's the best time for what we a-goin' to do," Hammond assured her. "Ain' somethin' I wants all the rest of the niggers to see. We goin' to do a little diggin'."

She did not seem to understand, but Hammond offered no explanation.

"Digging what?"

He came over to her and took her hand. "Some things better yo' don' know 'bout. Might be dangerous for you if'n yo' know. War's here, 'Gusta, 'n' I don' think it'll ever come to Alabama but it might. If'n yo' don' know 'bout some things, yo' cain' be made to tell."

"But you seem to trust Drummage."

"He a nigger. He don' know 'bout sich things. 'Sides, he know I kill him if'n he ever open his mouth." He turned to Drummage. "Yo' hear what I say? We a-goin' to do somethin'. If'n yo' ever says a word 'bout it, yo' a dead nigger. Understand? Even if'n I'm not here. I'm a-goin' to leave word that if yo' ever tell, yo' gets strung up like that-there Nero. 'Member him?"

"Yas suh, Masta Maxwell suh, I 'members." Drummage had a terrible picture of the limp body swaying in the breeze.

"Rope round his neck, a-hangin' till he's dead. Yo' want anythin' like that?"

"No suh, Masta Hammond suh. Whaffor yo' thinkin' I goin' ter tell? Ain' never tol' nothin' yet. Ain' never a-goin' ter."

"Yo' go back up to bed, 'Gusta." Hammond assisted her up one stair. "Be with yo' in 'bout an hour. Fact is I need money. Ain' got no time to send to N'Orleans fer it. They elected me Major of this here cavalry company and I guaranteed to fit out the company at my expense. Goin' to buy horses and uniforms for a hundred or so men what cain' afford to buy 'em fer theirselves. So Drummage and I a-goin' after money tonight and nobody needs to know where it comin' from."

Now she understood, and she leaned over the balustrade and kissed him, then went on up the stairs, waiting on the landing until she heard the door close behind Hammond and Drummage.

It was so pitch black outside that Hammond stumbled going down the steps. He grabbed for Drummage's arm.

"Too goddamn much corn," he mumbled to himself.

"We needs us a lantern." Drummage was excusing his master. "Cain' see."

Together they made their way around the house, stumbling through flower beds and shrubbery until they reached the stables, where a dim light showed between the crack of the wide double doors. Ajax was inside, rubbing down Hammond's horse by the light of a lantern. He looked up as Hammond entered.

"Ain' yo' to bed yet?" Hammond's voice was gruff but he seemed pleased to know that Ajax was attending to duty.

"Jes' cain' put dis animal in a stall, all a-lather like he is. All finished now."

Hammond picked up the lantern and carried it along, while Ajax tethered the horse and started up the ladder to his room above the stables. Hammond pointed to a spade standing against the wall and Drummage picked it up and followed him out of the barn. They took the well-worn path that led down into the hollow and across the creek to where the slave quarters stood, and where an absence of lights and movement testified to the fact that all were sleeping. Not far from the single cabin where Drummage had been born and where Big Pearl and Lucy lived, Hammond stopped and halted by a chinaberry tree and pointed to a large rock, overgrown with bindweed and creepers. It was a familiar landmark to Drummage as it had been one of the favorite playspots of his childhood, and an oft-played game had been for one young stalwart to stand on top of the rock, resisting all attempts of the others to dislodge him.

"Start diggin' here"—Hammond placed the lantern on a spot about two feet away from the rock, in a line with the tree—" 'n' dig careful. Don' have to dig more'n two feet down."

By the flickering flame of the candle's lantern, Drummage drove his spade into the loose sandy soil and had a fair-sized hole excavated before his spade hit something that gave off a metallic ring.

"That's it," Hammond said. "Use yore hands now. Scoop up the dirt careful."

A few handfuls of dirt and the iron cover of a large old kettle appeared. By brushing the soil away with his fingers, Drummage was able to locate the bail. Tugging at the bail, he managed to loosen the kettle from the impacted dirt but was unable to lift it, even by exerting all his strength. It required both his and Hammond's efforts to hoist it up onto the ground.

"Awful heavy, Masta Hammond suh." Drummage wiped the sweat from his forehead with the back of his hand. "What all yo' got in that ol' kittle?"

Hammond's hand crashed heavily against Drummage's face.

"Yo' jes' keep on askin' questions 'n' yo' goin' to feel that rope round yore neck jes' like Nero did." Hammond reached

164

down to lift the kettle. "Jes' keep yore mouth shet and help me bring this to the house."

Drummage, resentful of the slap, which he considered unmerited, reached down for the bail and lifted. He was quicker than Hammond and his end of the kettle came up first, tipping it so that the heavy cover slipped off. Inside Drummage could see the gleam of gold pieces.

"Yo' goddamned clumsy nigger!" Hammond would have slapped him again but he was too busy trying to balance his side of the kettle. "Yo' sure all big mouth and big hands tonight. Cain' seem to do nothin' right. See if'n yo' kin git this to the house with me. Got a mind to string yo' up tomorrow fer bein' so clumsy. Git in step with me so this kittle won' bang 'gainst our legs."

They had to set it down several times along the path on the way home, and by the time they arrived at the kitchen door the thin bail was cutting into Drummage's hands. The back door stood wide open and Lucretia Borgia, enveloped in a voluminous cotton nightgown, was silhouetted against the light that streamed out.

"What yo' a-doin' wid yo' papa's kittle?" she asked. "He a-tellin' me afore he died I ain' never to tell no one 'bout that kittle 'n' the three others. He say they only fer 'mergencies. He say fer me ter tell yo' but yo' never to take them."

" 'Nother big mouth a-shootin' off hot air. Goddamndest 'quisitive niggers round this place." Hammond was in none too good a temper after the liquor and his recent exertions. "What I want to know is, who's masta round here? Fust this yere Drummage a-flappin' his big mouth and now yo'. If'n yo' niggers a-runnin' Falconhurst, jes' let me know but if'n I still masta here, then yo' all keeps yore lips buttoned up. Ain' havin' no sass tonight. Been workin' harder'n a fiel' hand already."

"Heard yo' up and bin a-makin' a cup o' coffee fer yo'." Lucretia Borgia was a firm believer, when it came to white folks, that a soft answer turneth away wrath. "Whole house a-rampagin' roun'. Miz 'Gusta she up 'n' call that Candy wench ter git up. Miz Sophie up 'n' she wake the chil'ren and they starts a-squawkin', so dat Jubal have ter git up to keep 'em quiet. Ain' no rest in dis house tonight, so's I bile up some coffee 'n' yo' all might's well have some. Git that waiter, Drummage, and the chiny coffeepot 'n' cups and take it upstairs fer Masta Hammond 'n' Miz 'Gusta 'n' Miz Sophie. Den git dat Candy and dat Jubal down here and if'n dey craves coffee dey kin have it. Le's git this place quieted down so's a body kin git theyselves some sleep."

Hammond's anger was gone. He grinned back at Lucretia Borgia and motioned to Drummage to come over and help him carry the kettle into his office. By the time Drummage appeared upstairs with the tray and coffee things everything was quiet, and he left the tray on the round mahogany table in the big front bedroom, where Candy was remaking the beds. Jubal had already quieted the children and he went back downstairs with Drummage. They were sitting at the table, drinking coffee with Lucretia Borgia, when Candy came in, entering the kitchen from the door that led to Hammond's office.

"Ain' had a wink o' sleep tonight," she grumbled.

"Dat gal shore like yore a-pleasurin' her." Lucretia Borgia laughed and pointed a finger at Drummage. " 'Less'n she gits it, she cain' sleep."

" 'Less'n I gits it, I cain' nuther," Drummage grinned. "Masta Hammond a-goin' ter give Jubal a wench too. Tol' me so. Jubal got to git hisself a-humpin' ter git some suckers outa her."

"Don' wan' no wench." Jubal was crestfallen. "Wan's ter sleep out in de barn with Ajax."

"Yo' ain' gettin' Masta Hammond no suckers a-sleepin' wid Ajax. Time yo' learned what yo' here for. Let's git up ter bed." Lucretia Borgia poured her coffee out into the saucer and drank it, stretched out her arms and yawned. "Five o'clock come mighty soon. Hankerin' to give that Jubal boy a lesson but I'se too dog-tired tonight. Ain' so ol' but what I kin still learn him de right way to pester a wench."

Jubal, fearful that she might carry out her threat, ran up the stairs to his own room and the rest followed slowly. Lucretia Borgia lumbered down the hall to where she slept, and Drummage and Candy went into their own room and closed the door. Once inside in the darkness he gathered Candy into his arms and pulled her close to him. In her haste to answer Augusta's summons she had merely slipped on her dress, and Drummage could feel the warmth of her body under the thin material.

"Miss me tonight, Candy baby?" His lips nuzzled hers as he undid the buttons of her dress and slipped it off over her shoulders. It fell to the floor, but instead of the soundlessness of cloth he heard a sharp metallic clink and then the sound of something rolling across the floor.

"Whazzat?" Drummage relinquished Candy.

"Ain' nothin'." She fastened her lips to his, confident she could make him forget everything else.

"Is too somethin'. What yo' got in that pocket?"

"Nothin', Drummage boy." She was unbuttoning his clothes as he had undone hers.

He brushed her hands away and reached down to the floor for his trousers to pull out his tinder box. He sparked it and blew on the tinder to ignite the candle on the floor beside the bed. Its light showed a gold eagle on the floor. Immediately he grabbed Candy's dress and discovered three more in her pocket.

"Whar yo' gits these?" he demanded.

"Dunno." She shook her head. "Ain' never seen 'em before."

"Ain' seen 'em? Jes' didn' take legs theyselves 'n' crawl into yore pocket, did they? Yo' knows whur yo' got 'em. From the kittle in Masta Hammond's office. Yo' did, didn' yo'?"

She shook her head.

"Yo' stealin'. Ain' havin' no stealin' wench roun' here. Masta Hammond find yo' stealin', he whops yo' good. Slices the meat right off'n' yo'. Oh, Candy baby, why'd yo' do it? What yo' a-wantin' that stuff fer?" He thought for a moment. "Yo' thinkin' ter run? Ain' yo' happy here?" He pushed her backwards onto the bed. "What wrong with yo', gal?"

She started to sit up but he pushed her back, slapping her hard.

"Ain' a-havin' yo' steal things. Ain' a-havin' yo' gittin' whopped." He was slapping her first on one side of her face and then the other. "Goin' ter learn yo' a lesson. Don' wan' ter hurt yo' but ain' a-hurtin' yo' half so much as Olly hurt me wid that paddle on my ass. Cain' bear ter see yo' whopped." His hand halted in mid-air and he sat down on the bed beside her.

"Got to git these things back 'fore Masta Hammond misses 'em." He gathered up the gold pieces in his hand and tiptoed to the door. Quietly he lifted the latch and stepped out into the hall, then stealthily crept down the stairs to the kitchen. Slowly he made his way across the kitchen floor and into Hammond's office, and there replaced the gold pieces. Once more he negotiated the passage across the kitchen and up the stairs into his own room. The candle was still burning and Candy was weeping on the bed. Drummage shucked off

167

his shirt and crawled in beside her, snuffing out the candle as he lay down.

She crawled up to him, her face damp against his chest.

"Likes yo', I do, Drummage boy," she whispered. "Likes beddin' with yo', but oh, Drummage, I gits so homesick. Ain' never lived out in the country a-fore. Don' seem right out here in all this quiet. Wants to git me back to N'Orleans, I do. What'm I goin' ter do, Drummage?"

Suddenly Candy appeared to Drummage in a new light. He had never seen her before except as an appealing bit of flesh for his own enjoyment. Now it was brought home to him that she too had a life of her own, which existed before and after their frantic clutchings at each other. She had dreams, desires, and thoughts of her own. She was a person. In his realization of this he forgave her for the theft, realizing as he did so that he had never really blamed her. His only fear was that she might be punished. The hand that had slapped her so brutally now became warmly tender as he stroked her cheek.

"Candy baby, what 'love' mean?"

"Tha's somethin' only fer white folkses, I guess. Thought mayhap I love that boy back in N'Orleans 'cause he tells me he loves me, but jes' don' know. Loves yo', Drummage, when yo' pleasures me, then when we gits all through, I wants my mammy and pappy. Guess I loves them, I do."

"Thinkin' I loves yo' too, Candy," Drummage admitted. "Not jes' only fer pleasurin' but all the time. Ain' mad at yo' fer stealin'. Jes' couldn't bear to see yo' whopped. Kill me it would. Don' never steal no mo', Candy baby. 'N' don' think no more 'bout N'Orleans. Yo' here with me 'n' Drummage loves yo'."

That night the wildness of their passion became calmer. Instead of a frenzy of sweaty limbs there was a quiet flow of love from one to another, and instead of separation afterwards they rested in each others' arms. But Candy did not sleep. She missed the noises of the city, the light that filtered into her room from the street lights outside, the lax discipline of the Masterson household. Most of all she missed the excitement of the streets with their passers-by. There was always a young buck to flirt with, a bright-skinned delivery boy to dally with in the alley back of the house, or a Sunday afternoon with Papa Blaise in Congo Square. She snuggled up to Drummage. The warmth of his body was her only consolation.

Chapter 18

THE WHIRLWIND of preparation that followed the formation of the Falconhurst Lancers was even more time-consuming and hectic than the preparation of the caffle for New Orleans. It seemed to Drummage, as he looked back on the last few months of his life, that all he had been doing was to run frantically after his own shadow without ever catching up with it. But at least the New Orleans journey had been founded on procedures which had been perfected over the years; this new venture was entirely without a background of experience. Nobody really knew what to do or who should do it, with the result that as much time was spent on countermanding orders as on initiating them. Hammond, as major, and Lewis Gasaway, as adjutant, held nominal authority, but that did not prevent other elected officers and noncoms from taking off in a direction of their own choosing which might be entirely at variance with all others.

There were over a hundred horses to be purchased for those who could not afford to buy their own; there were uniforms to be designed and tailored, for with the individuality of privately sponsored military companies, the creation of a fanciful uniform in those first days of war was of paramount importance. Then there were arms to be purchased— sabers, side arms, and muskets, and even useless but decorative pennoned lances to substantiate the name of the company. Above and beyond all the minutiae of quartermastering—for most of which Hammond was footing the bills— there were the nightly drills in Benson. When the motley company had achieved some measure of discipline, there were Sunday parades and shooting matches, which the women of the community turned into social events with picnic lunches and a certain amount of style and formality reminiscent of jousting events in the Middle Ages.

While the men were happy with their new toys and the excitement of going to war, the women on the plantations were wondering just how they would manage. Most of the large plantations had white overseers and these worthies were remaining behind. But as Falconhurst had never had a white overseer, Hammond's leaving for the war presented a very real problem.

Augusta would of course be the logical manager in his absence, but Sophie, Hammond's daughter by his first wife, was more or less of a problem. She had inherited her mother's vapid good looks and her nymphomania, along with her limited mental capabilities. An early marriage, with a dowry sufficient, it was said, to overcome Sophie's cross-eye, had resulted in two children, after which her husband, Dudley, had returned to his native England. He had driven into Benson one afternoon on some trivial errand and, outside of Christmas presents which arrived for the children from England, had never been heard from again. Gossip said that Dudley could not stand Sophie's gooch eyes any longer, but the truth was that, weak not only in character but strength, he could not stand her continuous assaults on him.

Sophie had not accepted her "widowhood" calmly, but her memories of certain episodes in her childhood, when she had discovered a far greater degree of virility among her father's Negroes than poor Dudley had ever possessed, helped to solve her problem. As the master's daughter, she could suborn the services of certain of her father's stock whose special good looks appealed to her. Her not too imaginative brain evolved a scheme which had worked out to her satisfaction. Although she detested any form of physical exercise, she had developed an interest in riding which gave her the opportunity to change grooms often. She was wise enough to take proper precautions, so there had never been any visible evidence of her philanderings. That she had been able to accept the services of her grooms over the years without the knowledge of her father or her stepmother was due as much to her publicly professed hatred and fear of all Negroes as it was to the incredibility of any white woman's having sexual relations with a Negro. It was unthinkable to everyone but Sophie. She had no fear of her partners' ever telling. Any admission on their part that they had even as much as touched her hand amorously would have been their death warrant, and they were fully aware of their danger. The secluded spot she picked as the destination of her daily ride, in a dense growth of pines by the river, was one of the most distant parts of the plantation, far removed from the fields and the activities of the hands. And if, by chance, she was discovered, she had only to scream that she was being raped and, regardless of the innocence of her companion, she would be believed. For the last few months before the trip to New Orleans her groom and paramour had been a handsome young buck by the name of Valentine, whose regular, chiseled features were undoubtedly inherited from some Moorish ancestor, but whose strength and virility were purely African.

Sophie had never been taken very seriously by either Hammond or Augusta. She was vain, fond of ostentatious dressing, with a plentitude of mediocre jewelry and sweeping, broad-brimmed hats that minimized her cross-eye. Given her own way and allowed to indulge in her secret sensualities, she was easy to live with, unassertive, and pleasant in a dull-spirited way. Whenever one of her grooms was sold, as Valentine had just been, she became petulant and disagreeable, and this would continue until she wheedled a replacement from her father. Her children meant little to her, outside of the pleasure which she took in dressing them up and displaying them. Care and companionship for them were provided mostly by Augusta and the slave attendant on them—Jubal at present.

Sophie's inability to assume any responsibility left Augusta the only white person in authority at Falconhurst after Hammond's departure. That she was still in love with him was apparent, and his devotion to her was proven by the fact that he had never bedded a colored wench since the day he married her. Over the years, Augusta had smoothed off his rough spots and transformed him into a gentleman. She managed him and her share of Falconhurst with efficiency and acumen. During her residence it had achieved its greatest productivity and wealth. At times she disapproved of Hammond's methods of breeding his stock and his callous indifference to any emotions that might be involved in the relations between his slaves, but she had learned over the years not to see such things and to pretend they did not exist. Now she was going to have to open her eyes and see things as they were.

Although Falconhurst's annual crop did not require such seasonal planting, cultivating, or reaping as cotton did, it was perhaps even more complicated; to obtain future crops it was necessary to sow the seed, cultivate it, and in the end dispose of it. All of these processes would be quite beyond Augusta's ability, for she had never been able to regard Negroes as merely a superior breed of animals. With her in charge, couples would have been permanently mated, children reared by their parents, and no slaves ever sold.

Which was not, most definitely, the way to run a slave-breeding plantation.

However Lucretia Borgia, although a Negro herself, was most adept at the sowing and cultivating of Falconhurst's peculiar crop. During the period between Hammond's father's death and his return from Texas, she had bred slaves as astutely as Hammond himself and there was never any sentimentality in her matings. Although she was growing old, her years did not show and their accumulation did not diminish her activity, her ability, or her authority. The accumulation of weight may have diminished her agility, but not her strength. She could well carry on the delicate matters of procreation which were an essential part of the slave-crop process. They were not distasteful to her as they were to her white mistress—in fact, Lucretia Borgia enjoyed them.

Then there was Brutus, who had been Hammond's right-hand man for many years and who knew as well as Hammond himself all the inside workings of the plantation. Brute was trustworthy, honest, intelligent, and a willing worker, but like Lucretia Borgia he was a Negro and a slave and as such had no authority except what he derived from his master. And then there was Drummage, young, inexperienced, and altogether willing, but untried and scarcely old enough to have any degree of authority.

One morning, just a few days before the Falconhurst Lancers were to leave for Birmingham, Hammond, seated behind the green baize table in his office, dispatched Drummage to the upper floor to summon Augusta and Sophie, then out to the kitchen to call Lucretia Borgia and Brutus, and after that to the barn to bring Ajax. When Drummage returned, Augusta and Sophie were already seated before Hammond's desk, Lucretia Borgia and Brutus were standing behind them, and in another moment Ajax entered. Hammond waited for Drummage and Ajax to take their places alongside Lucretia Borgia and Brutus. That he was nervous was apparent by the way he fiddled with the ornate paper cutter, tapping it on the desk. There was a look of sadness in his eyes which Drummage had never seen before.

"Thought I'd better get all you folks together and explain some things," he said. "We're leaving in a few days. It's goin' to take most of the men from round Benson away. Mos' everything round here'll be in the hands of women folks and servants." He surveyed them all. "Glad I got both. Feels I kin trust yo' all."

"Yas suh, Masta Hammond suh." Lucretia Borgia nodded

172

her head in time to her words. "Shore kin, Masta Hammond suh."

Hammond scowled at her for interrupting but his look of displeasure did not perturb her. She was about to say something more when he silenced her.

"If'n yo' jes' keep yore mouth closed, Lucretia Borgia, till I git finished, yo' kin talk yo' fool head off, or if'n yo' thinkin' yo' masta here, mayhap yo'd better take over the job of Major and I'll stay her 'n' do the cookin'."

She subsided and he continued.

"Falconhurst ain' had no overseer since my papa had one when I was a boy. We ain' no cotton raisers so's we ain' never had no use for an overseer. I always been able to do what bearin' down is necessary. But now, 'thout no overseer, we goin' to have to make some changes. That's what I wants to talk to yo' all 'bout. Niggers is our business and niggers is goin' to be our business—that's what we're fightin' this war fer. Sons-a-bitches up No'th say niggers is free men; we says they ain'. Ain' never heard no talk of freedom fer niggers at Falconhurst an' ain' goin' to be none. Yo' people servants fer life and that's that. We a-goin' 'way to war to keep yo' that that way but, 'fore I go, I want to know if any of yo' got any complaints 'bout being servants at Falconhurst."

As always, Lucretia Borgia was the first to answer. "Yo' knows better'n to ask me, Masta Hammond suh. Onct yo' sol' me and I hikes myself back here. Could've run if'n I'd a-wanted to. Been here all my life; wants to stay here till I dies."

Hammond's look conveyed his gratitude.

"Brute," he asked, "How yo' feel?"

"Same's Lucretia Borgia, Masta Hammond suh. Yo' always been good to me. Ain' got no complaints. Ain' a-wantin' to leave. Yo' tells me what yo' wan's done whilst yo' gone, I do it."

"Knew I could depend on yo', Brute. Yo' always been a good boy. Now yo', Ajax. Am plannin' to take yo' with me. If'n yo' go, plenty o' chances to run if'n yo' got it in yore mind so want to know how yo' feels 'bout it."

Ajax, who was never as voluble with men as he was with horses, was at a loss for words. Finally he managed to stammer out his reply.

"Whaffor I wants to leave yo', Masta Hammond suh? Who take care of yore hosses if'n I leave yo'. Who take care o' me if'n I do. Ain' a-goin' ter run, Masta Hammond suh. Ain'

173

never runned in N'Orleans. Ain' never goin' ter run, never."

Hammond seemed satisfied with his answer and turned to Drummage.

"Yo' jes' a young squirt, Drummage, 'n' yo' only got one thing on yo' mind. But yo' been a good boy and I wants to know where yo' stand. Got to find out these things 'fore I leave. Yo' a Falconhurst boy o' not? Soon's I go yo' goin' to skedaddle?"

Drummage shook his head vigorously. "Ain' wantin' to go nowhere else, Masta Hammond suh, less'n it with yo'. Shore likes to go wid yo' 'stead o' Ajax but if'n yo' wants me to stay here, I stays here, lookin' out fer Miz 'Gusta and Miz Sophie—lookin' out fer Falconhurst too."

Hammond regarded them all, raising his eyes above Augusta's and Sophie's heads. Yes, they were niggers—this elderly woman, these two grown men, and this young man. But he trusted them. He knew they were telling him the truth. They were as much a part of Falconhurst as he was and he was certain that, if necessary, any one of them would die for him as Drummage's father had done. He owned them; they were his. Yet there was something far greater between them and himself than mere ownership. Their loyalty to him was reflected in his to them, and perhaps for the first time in his life he acknowledged that he had love for them.

"Then yo' all listen to me. I'm a-tellin' yo' this front of Miz 'Gusta 'n' Miz Sophie so yo'll all know that they know what I'm a-sayin' to yo'. Miz 'Gusta she a-goin' to be yore masta 'n' yore mist'ess too. She a-goin' to take my place here. 'Spects yo' to do her biddin' same as yo' does mine. She say somethin', yo' jumps. Yo' don' ask no questions; don' wan' no argufying. She know what she a-doin' and when she tell yo', yo' do it." For some reason he was looking at Drummage, so Drummage took it upon himself to answer.

"Yes suh, Masta Hammond suh, we does 'zactly like Miz 'Gusta says."

"Yo'd better," Hammond threatened, " 'cause if'n yo' don', she a-goin' to have Olly whop yo'. 'N' when I gets back I'll have Olly whop yo' all over 'gain." He pointed his finger at Brutus. "All the outside work up to yo', Brute. Yo' gits the crops in, yo' tends to 'em, yo' harvests 'em. Wartime's here and we's goin' to need more food. Got to raise us more hogs, more cattle, more horses, 'n' more mules. Army goin' to need all we kin spare. We goin' to put in a little cotton but jes' 'nuff to keep the spinnin'-house busy. Up to yo', Brute, to

174

get the boys out into the fields, keep 'em workin'. Yo' kin do it. Yo' worked with me long 'nuff to know how things go. Now on, yo' the overseer at Falconhurst."

"Yas suh, Masta Hammond suh."

"And if'n yo' don' know, ask Lucretia Borgia. She thinks she knows goddam near everything. Guess mayhap, she do. Don' yo' go up 'n die on me, Lucretia Borgia. We a-goin' to need yo'."

"Goin' ter live a hunnert years, Masta Hammond suh." She cackled in a series of ascending giggles. "Goin' to have ter shoot me ter git rid o' me. 'N' when I die, goin' ter come back to hant yo' if'n things not right here."

"Bet yo' would too." Hammond laughed along with her. "But as long as yo' here, a-goin' to keep yo' busy. I'm gittin that Reba wench in for Drummage jes' soon's he get Candy" —He stopped, red-faced, and looked at Augusta—"Well, a-gettin' her in anyway 'n' that Jewel wench fer that Jubal boy. Wants that Reba to learn to wait on Miz 'Gusta and wants wants that Jewel wench to do the cookin' after yo' teaches her. Don' wan' yo' to be bothered in the kitchen. Plenty to do to keep yo' busy." Again he looked apologētically towards Augusta. "Wants yo' to take over matchin' up the bucks 'n' wenches, Lucretia Borgia. Got to keep this place a-humpin'. Onct we win this war, goin' to be bigger'n ever demand fer servants. Prices goin' up sky high. Got to have us a big stock ready. Got to keep these bucks busy. Wishin' now I had more wenches fer the boys."

"I tends to it." Lucretia Borgia bobbed her head, realizing the pleasure she would get from her all-important position.

"But yo' ain' jes' goin' to have any buck cover any wench. Got to take it up with Miz 'Gusta so she gits the pedigrees out and looks 'em over and picks out the best combinations. She pick 'em out. Up to yo' to mate 'em. Up to yo' to follow through. Wenches bein' mated fer the fust time, want yo' there to supervise. Yo' follow through. Sucker's born, yo' puts the wench to work 'gain. Think yo' kin do it?"

"Knows ah kin, Masta Hammond suh. Didn' I do it whilst yo' in de Texies? Didn' I have a good crop a-waitin' fer yo' when yo' come back?"

"Shore did, Lucretia Borgia." He turned to Ajax. "How that Big Randy with the horses? He Lucretia Borgia's boy now and if'n he good he kin stay in the stables 'long with Sampson."

"He all right." Ajax managed to get the words out.

"Then yo' put him in charge of the barn. Now then, every-

175

one here know what he's a-goin' to do?" Hammond looked at them for confirmation.

"Yo' didn' tell me, Masta Hammond suh," Drummage said. "Brute he in charge of the fields, Lucretia Borgia she in charge of the birthin's. Big Randy he in charge of the horses. What I do, Masta Hammond suh?"

"Yo' in charge of the house. Yo' in charge o' Miz 'Gusta, Miz Sophie, the chil'ren 'n' the servants in the house. Charge of the gardens round the house too. Want everything kept good."

Drummage was satisfied. He had been given his own sphere of authority.

Hammond drummed on his desk. " 'Bout next year's caffle, don' know what to tell you. Jes' got back from this year's so ain' goin' to worry too much 'bout next year's now. War'll be over by then anyway. Damn Yankees ain' got a chance. We're goin' to take New York in six months. I'll be home in time to take the caffle but if'n I ain', Miz 'Gusta'll handle it. Mayhap she'll get Sly out here from N'Orleans 'n' he kin take the caffle in hisself. Ain' like I a-takin' it but better'n lettin' them bucks eat they's heads off after they ready to go." He dropped his eyes to where Augusta was sitting. "If'n any slave traders come 'long with wenches fer sale, better have Brute 'n' Lucretia Borgia look 'em over. Ain' never much good stock with slave traders but mayhap we gits something. Needs about twenty more wenches. Git 'em ready to foal. Cain' be bothered with young uns now." Hammond stood up from his chair as a gesture of dismissal and they all filed out except Drummage, whom he told to remain.

Augusta walked around the desk and put her arm around Hammond's shoulders.

"I only hope I can do it all for you."

"Course yo' kin. Ain' a-feard yo' cain'. Anything go wrong, jes' ask Lucretia Borgia. She help yo'. And if'n yo' needs money, she tell yo' where to git it quick."

She kissed him and walked out, while Drummage held the door open for her. Sophie had remained in her chair and it was obvious she had something to say to Hammond which she did not want anyone else to hear. The fact that Drummage was still there did not, however, deter her.

"Lookin' fer me another boy to groom me." She stood up, adjusting the lace of her dress nonchalantly. "If'n I don' get out fer a ride ever' day I gits housebound. Go crazy if'n I have to stay in the house all the time and scared to go

176

out with the whole place swarming with niggers less'n I have a boy of my own I kin trust. 'Yo sold my Valentine so now ain' got nobody."

"Yo' got anyone in mind?" Hammond was anxious to get rid of her. He had never had much in common with his daughter.

"How 'bout yo' lettin' me have that Zanzibar boy? 'Pears like a good boy, quiet-like."

"Zanzibar?" Hammond had to think to place the boy she mentioned. "He that hulkin' big flat-nosed boy what's blacker'n the ace of spades—the one we uses fer duck huntin'?"

"Tha's he," Sophie nodded.

"How come yo' a-wantin' him—big black bozal like that?" Hammond was surprised, for Sophie's grooms were usually bright-skinned and attractive.

"He strong 'n he kin perteck me. Hates niggers I do. Cain' stand 'em round me but that's all we got here. Niggers, niggers, niggers! All my life I been with niggers. Scairt of 'em I am. Knows what happened to my mama and ain' wantin' to git raped by none of them. Tha's why I wants me a strong buck to ride behind me. Wid yo' gone, ain' no tellin' when these niggers start rampagin'. They a-feared o' yo' but ain' a-feared o' 'Gusta o' Brute. I want a derringer, I do." She glanced up at her father to see if she was making her story sufficiently dramatic.

"They a-feard o' Lucretia Borgia," Hammond chuckled. "But if'n yo' wants that Zanzibar yo' kin have him. Tell Brute yo' wants him 'n I say yo' kin have him. Have Brute tell him to wash all over 'fore he come up to the barn 'cause he awful black 'n' awful musty, that boy. And if'n yo' wants a derringer, yo' better learn how to use one fust. Git you'se'f one in Benson if'n yo' wants 'n' have Zanzibar teach yo'. He a crack shot, he is."

"Thank yo', Papa." Sophie was exulting inwardly but she did not allow her enthusiasm to show. If Zanzibar lived up to her expectations, she was determined that he would not be included in next year's caffle. Niggers, huh! Wan't no nigger she was afraid of! Sure was easy to fool papa with all that talk of derringers. "Thank yo' kindly, papa." She turned and walked out of the room.

Hammond signaled to Drummage.

"Come on, boy, we got work to do and not many more days to do it in."

Chapter 19

THE TALL ENGLISH CLOCK on the landing at Falconhurst ticked off the minutes and its deep-throated chimes called off the hours until the day finally arrived for Hammond's departure. On that morning, Lucretia Borgia banged on Drummage's door before daybreak. He found it difficult to creep out from the warm shelter of Candy's arms into the chilly darkness, and still more difficult to rouse Candy. The fact that Hammond was leaving that day was of no interest to her—indeed, her glazed eyes seemed to comprehend little as she leaned over the side of the bed, retching. Drummage would have liked to comfort her in her all-too-apparent misery but he realized the importance of this last breakfast—the last time he would serve his beloved master in the dining room at Falconhurst. Unwillingly he left Candy and crept down the back stairs.

The kitchen was ablaze with lights. Lucretia Borgia, that pillar of strength and wisdom, was seated at the kitchen table, her arms outstretched on its clean-scrubbed whiteness, her shoulders heaving with sobs. Drummage had never imagined that Lucretia Borgia had the makings of a tear in her, and it was a shock to him to discover that she was capable of such emotions.

"He a-goin', he a-goin'," she wept. "My Masta Hammond he a-goin' off to de war. My own Masta Hammond that I rocked in de cradle, he a-goin' off ter git hisself kilt and we won' be seein' him no mo', no mo'."

Harelipped Marguerite stood by the stove, sniffling while she listlessly turned slices of ham in the big skillet. Brutus sat at the other end of the table, staring at Lucretia Borgia with lackluster eyes and making little clucking noises of sympathy. Jubal too was sniveling. It was all too much for Drummage. He too started crying, and when the rest of the servants came down the stairs and in from the stables they dissolved into the same general watery gloom.

With a final sob that shook the table, Lucretia Borgia straightened up and surveyed the kitchen through reddened eyes that finally came to rest on Drummage.

"Whar that lazy Candy wench o' yourn? Ain' she up?"

"Candy sick." Drummage swallowed a sob. "Oh, Miz 'Cretia Borgia, ma'am, what we a-goin' ter do 'thout Masta Hammond?"

"Jes' ain' a-goin' ter let the whole place go to hell. Why'n that Candy not down here? Miz 'Gusta'll be a-wantin' her. Ain' easy fer pore Miz 'Gusta, seein' her man a-leavin'."

"But Candy she awful sick, Lucretia Borgia ma'am. Seems like she jes' cain' git herself off'n de bed. She a-leanin' over the side a-pukin' somethin' awful."

"Now ain' that too bad!" Lucretia Borgia heaved herself up and scuffled in her carpet slippers over to the door of the stairs, yanked it open and bellowed, "Candy yo' hist you'se'f outa that bed and git you'se'f down here." She waited, cupping her ear to catch an answer. "I'm a-comin' up there and paddle yore ass if'n yo' don' git down here. Yo' hear me?"

"Cain' come." Candy's voice drifted weakly down the stairs. "Cain' sit up, let alone git up."

"Humph!" Lucretia Borgia snorted and laughed at the same time. "Yo' ain' de first wench got herself knocked up. Won' be the last nuther. At least Masta Hammond have some good news on his last day here." She turned to Drummage, "Guess yo' gone and done it, boy."

"Yo' means . . . ?"

"Gal start a-pukin' in de mornin', sure sign she got a sucker planted in her. Masta Hammond'll be glad. She all right; ain' nothin' wrong with her. Git yo'se'f up there and yank her outa bed and git her down here."

Drummage grabbed a candle and took the stairs two at a time. Candy was lying in a welter of sour sheets, her face ashen, her hair wetly plastered against her forehead. She opened her eyes and managed a stricken glance at Drummage, then closed them.

"Ain' nothin' the matter with yo', Candy baby." Drummage was reassuring. "Have ter git yo'se'f up though. Miz 'Gusta a-waitin' fer yo'. Helps yo', I will." He got his arm under her and lifted her to a sitting position, then swung her legs around until her feet touched the floor.

"Oh, Drummage, I feels miz'rable."

"Ain' nothin'! Yo' jes' knocked up. 'Cretia Borgia done say so and I so happy."

"Yo' happy!" She regarded him with astonishment, wondering how anyone could be happy when she felt so bad.

"Shore I'se happy. We got good news fer Masta Hammond jes' as he's a-leavin'. Goin' ter tell him we's gone and made him a new sucker." Drummage's chest swelled with importance while he reached for her dress and managed to get it over her head. He knelt to slip her feet into her slippers and pulled the dress down around her knees, then lifted her up and let her lean on him as he helped her down the stairs. She reached the kitchen table and slumped into a chair.

Lucretia Borgia had entirely recovered from her moment of sentimentality. She came over to the table and cuffed Candy on the side of the head.

"Git yo'se'f up and git up to Miz 'Gusta's room. Whaffor yo' a sittin' here a-moanin'? Masta Hammond a-leavin' this mornin' 'n' yo' floppin' roun' lak a wet dishrag."

The cuff on the ear brought Candy up from the table. She stood defiantly before Lucretia Borgia.

"Masta Hammond!" She beat on the table with her fists. "Masta Hammond! What I care 'bout Masta Hammond? Damn him; hope he goes 'n' gits himself kilt and never comes back."

Lucretia Borgia bore down upon her, horror and fear written all over her black face. She raised her arm to strike, then lowered it slowly.

"Git!" she screamed. "Git, 'fore I kills yo'. Cain' kill yo' now 'cause Miz 'Gusta a-needin' yo', but git outa my sight. Ain' forgettin' what yo' jes' said. Yo' got' it comin' to yo'. Ain' a-goin' ter tell Masta Hammond on he's las' mornin' here but I'm goin' to strip yo' down myself."

Drummage sided with Lucretia Borgia. He was aghast at what Candy had just said and he too was prepared to punish her. All the other servants in the kitchen regarded her with open mouths. Never had any of them heard such blasphemy. Candy turned her back on them and walked slowly across the kitchen to the door of Hammond's office, from where the stairs led to the second floor. She was afraid now, for she realized the full import of what she had said. Just as she reached the door, she turned.

"Didn' mean it," she said lamely. "Didn' mean a word of it. Jes' feelin' so miz'rable, don' know what I a-sayin'. Loves Masta Hammond I do. He good man. Goin' ter write my mammy a letter in N'Orleans 'n' ask her ter light a candle in de church fer him. Cain' nothin' happen to Masta Hammond wid a candle lighted 'fore Jesus."

Lucretia Borgia had been in New Orleans herself and she had seen the inside of a church, with its stained-glass windows, its plaster saints, and its flickering candles. If anything

180

would guarantee Hammond's safety, certainly this would. Powerful conjure it was! Sufficient to forgive Candy. Lucretia Bogia started weeping again.

"Brute." She wiped the tears from her eyes with the hem of her dress. "Yo' go over to de quarters 'n' get all de boys and de wenches up. Tell 'em to line up on bof sides of de drive in front o' de house. Masta Hammond goin' to know how much his Falconhurst niggers thinkin' o' him. 'N' yo' tells those niggers, I don' wan' a dry eye in de crowd whilst Masta Hammond a-drivin' by."

Brutus nodded to Lucretia Borgia and left. With a cuff at poor Marguerite, who had let the ham burn, Lucretia Borgia sent her sprawling to the floor and took over the cooking herself. She tossed the burned ham onto a platter, reserving it for the servants' breakfast, then sliced several thick pink slices and dropped them into the sizzling fat, watching them carefully to see that they were cooked to perfection. Drummage went into the dining room to set the table with the best gold-edged china, for it seemed a worthy occasion to him. Then, dashing out the front door into the grey-lighted garden, he plucked a bunch of chrysanthemums and put them in a cut-glass bowl in the center of the table. Foot-steps on the stairs informed him that the folks were coming down, so he slipped into the butler's pantry to get the big coffee urn. The scraping of chairs informed him that they were seated and he kicked at the swinging door and entered, holding the big tray with both hands.

"Mawnin', Miz 'Gusta. Mawnin', Miz Sophie." He placed the urn before Augusta and came around the table to where Hammond sat, resplendent in his gold-laced grey officer's coat, with the wide silken sash of yellow around his waist. "Mawnin', Masta Hammond suh." It was too much for Drummage. He fell on his knees to the floor. "Oh, Masta Hammond suh, Masta Hammond suh."

Hammond was touched. He gently put his hand under Drummage's arm and lifted him up.

"Ain' fergettin' 'bout yo', Drummage boy. Yo' good boy! Now yo' serve Miz 'Gusta and Miz Sophie jes' as well as yo' have me. Do as they says. 'N' mind Lucretia Borgia 'n' Brute too."

"Got good news fer yo', Masta Hammond suh. Candy a-goin' ter give yo' nice sucker pretty soon."

Hammond looked across the table at Augusta and saw that she was smiling.

"Then yo' a-goin' ter get started on that Reba wench right soon, huh?"

"Shore will, Masta Hammond suh, shore will."

"Beg pardon, 'Gusta." Hammond smiled apologetically after Drummage went out into the kitchen. "That pore boy jes' a-wantin' to do something to make me feel good, tha's all. Tha's the best thing he know to give me for a present. He proud, he is, 'n' he a good boy. Dependable, Drummage is, jes' like Drumson."

Strangely enough, the breakfast proceeded like any other breakfast. Augusta was composed behind the big silver urn; Sophie ate her usual large breakfast; Hammond talked over matters of the plantation as nonchalantly as though he were going down to the quarters after breakfast, instead of riding into Benson. The only difference was that it was perhaps a more elaborate breakfast than usual—scrambled eggs instead of fried eggs, beaten biscuits instead of corn bread, and watermelon preserves which usually appeared only when there was company for dinner. When the meal was finished everyone rose from the table and there were no tears from either of the womenfolk. Both of them swept up the stairs and left Hammond to go into his office. Once inside, he called in Lucretia Borgia and had a long conference with her. Brutus followed, and Drummage hoped he would be next, but he was merely told to get Big Randy to hitch up the barouche and Ajax to have the horses saddled and waiting out in front.

"Yo' 'n' Jubal rides footman on de kerridge," Brutus said. Drummage was glad that he was going into Benson. It meant that he would be with Hammond just that much longer. He ran quickly upstairs to get into a clean white starched shirt and his new clothes, and met Jubal on the stairs already dressed. When he came back down, Lucretia Borgia thumbed him out of the back door and he ran to the stables just in time to scramble up beside Jubal on the seat in back of the open carriage. Big Randy, who could not get into Ajax' livery, had, however, preempted Ajax' hat, and although his white shirt and tow linen trousers did not look very prepossessing, his monumental size was awe-inspiring.

Ajax, riding his own horse and leading Hammond's big roan and another horse whose empty saddle was piled with blanket rolls, luggage, and saddlebags, was followed by the barouche. Hammond, Augusta, and Sophie and the two children, together with the house servants, were all standing on the portico. Lucretia Borgia was clutching and unclutching

182

her big white apron, and all the rest, Drummage noticed, even Candy, were wailing. Augusta and Sophie, however, though strained were composed. Hammond embraced them and kissed them both, then picked up the children and kissed them. Drummage could see his lips moving but could not hear what he said. Hammond then hugged Lucretia Borgia and kissed her, took Brutus' hand and pumped it, and waved to all the rest as he walked slowly down the steps of the portico and mounted his horse. He clucked to the horse and moved away. Followed then the barouche, with Ajax and the pack horse in the rear.

Drummage, sitting above the ladies in the barouche, could see that they had on their finest dresses—Augusta a violet-colored broadcloth embroidered with bugle beads and a bonnet with a long purple plume; Sophie in light blue with a multitude of rose-colored ruffles and a bonnet of pink roses. Drummage was proud of them. He knew that none of the other plantation ladies could muster such finery. The shiny carriage was far more elaborate than anything else around Benson, and there were not two better-looking boys than himself and Jubal, sitting ramrod straight, their arms folded at the correct angle in front of them, and the brass buttons gleaming on their bottle-green suits. It meant something for a nigger to belong to quality. It meant something to be Major—yes *Major*—Hammond Maxwell's boy of Falconhurst Plantation, to drive into Benson when all the other servants were left behind.

All down the long driveway that led from the big house to the road, the Falconhurst slaves were lined. Even without Lucretia Borgia's instructions, there was not a dry eye to be seen. Big bucks, their arms waving and tears coursing down their cheeks, were bidding their master farewell. Wenches in clean headcloths and white fichus were throwing flowers at him and into the carriage. Once in a while, one more emotionally wrought-up than the others would run out, grab Hammond's boot and kiss it, or trot along beside him for a moment until he placed his gloved hand on the wiry black head. Hammond saluted them all, calling some of them by name as he passed, waving to others, and occasionally singling one out to say some personal thing.

"How yo' likes that Pansy wench, 'Rasmus?"

"Don' ferget to fix the roof on the hen house, Wolf."

"Lookin' for a good sucker out'a yo', 'Melia."

"Keep them gals a-spinnin' 'n' a-weavin', Auntie Belle."

"Tell Miz Lucretia Borgia I say it's time yo' had 'nother wench, Seminole."

"Look after Big Pearl and Old Lucy, Olly."

When he passed Big Pearl, he reined in his horse and held out his hand to her. "Yore boy Drummage a good boy, Big Pearl."

And so down the line of weeping, shouting, sobbing men and women, each of whom regarded him as a superior being, a white god, all-powerful, all-loving, and all-knowing. They feared him and yet they loved him. They were his property to be sold at his will, and yet he was their father. He had raised them, fed them, clothed them, and protected them. Now he was leaving them and they were heartbroken. But the parting was no sadder for them than for him, for these were his children—these simple-minded, uneducated blacks were his own and he loved them, too. As he passed the last weeping buck at the gate, he brushed the chrysanthemum heads and the fall asters from his uniform and his saddle. The most difficult part of his leavetaking was over, and he glanced back at the soaring pillars of the big house as he turned into the main road.

The early morning sun lit up the rose brick, whitened the tall pillars, and glinted on the many-paned windows. A slow procession of blacks wound up the driveway, disappearing into the quarters behind. A flash of waving white on the portico betokened Lucretia Borgia's last farewell. Hammond's lips settled into a grim line and he touched the spurs to his horse, settling it into an easy canter for the trip to Benson. He was leaving Falconhurst—that monument he had built with black flesh. He was leaving his home and his way of life, which, although he was going to war to defend it, could not survive. Falconhurst in all its sunshine glory and grandeur was doomed.

The pillars of the big house receded into the distance and the few miles to the town were covered quickly. When they arrived at Benson the whole place was *en fête*, with all the houses draped in bunting and the Stars and Bars displayed from every porch and upper window. Everyone for miles around had turned out, from babies borne on ample breasts to a few grey-bearded gaffers who were loud in their reminiscences of Indian skirmishes. A band was blaring down in front of the tavern and Hammond led his retinue there, where the company was already mustering in a long line of four abreast, each man on his horse trying to hold the animal in check. Hammond's arrival was greeted with a burst of "Dixie" from the band, a running back and forth across the street of barefooted urchins, and a pelting of more wilted chrysanthemums from four young girls, flower-crowned, in white dresses and yellow sashes, who were supposed to represent the Flower of Southern Womanhood or Virtue Enthroned or some other elegantly allegorical subject.

In the melee, Hammond got down from his horse and stood beside the barouche for a last farewell. His arms reached up and embraced Augusta, and Drummage saw her hand tremble on the gold-fringed epaulette on his shoulder. As Hammond walked around the back of the carriage to embrace Sophie and the children, his hand reached up and grabbed the calf of Drummage's leg to squeeze it. It was his only farewell to Drummage but it meant more to the boy than all the fanfare of crowds, flags, and music. He felt he would never be able to forget that gentle pressure which had sent goose bumps over his whole body. Again the drums rolled. Hammond mounted and rode to the head of the line and the long procession started. Augusta and Sophie bowed to the passing men. When at length, they had all passed, there was nothing to be seen but a group of stragglers, running to keep up with the procession—young boys proudly carrying Confederate flags, the four white-robed Vestals, their flowery crowns awry and their slippers dusty, and one elderly man who was still able to shout and wave his arms. Soon there was nothing but a cloud of dust down the road, raised by the horses, and eventually even that vanished and the bunting and the flags hung limp in the heat.

Augusta spoke to Big Randy and he wheeled the barouche around and headed back to Falconhurst. As soon as they were quit of the town, Drummage and Jubal relaxed their rigid, ramrod-straight, arms-folded pose and slumped down in their seats. Big Randy removed his shiny hat and placed it on the seat beside him, while the horses, instead of high-stepping, cantered casually. The smart turnout lost a bit of its spit-and-polish perfection with each mile of the return journey; casualness was replacing strict discipline. The children stood on the cushioned seats and leaned over the back, the better to see the road. Sophie took off one shoe which was pinching her and wiggled her toes. Big Randy mopped the sweat from his face with a soiled bandana, while Jubal undid his string tie and unbuttoned the neckband of his shirt. Only Augusta sat bolt upright and did not relax, but she did not remonstrate with the children nor the servants for their little slips from rigid discipline. They all seemed so

185

unimportant to her now. But Drummage knew that if Hammond were present, none of these things would be happening.

Back at Falconhurst, he found the kitchen empty and quiet. He could not remember ever seeing it that way before. Lucretia Borgia was not there, and neither was the scullery maid Marguerite. The unwashed plates from breakfast, with their accumulation of hardened grease and dried egg, were still on the kitchen table along with half-empty coffee cups and soiled silver. Never before had he seen dirty dishes left after a meal. He wondered where Lucretia Borgia was, and opening the door into Hammond's office he found her lying on the leather couch where Hammond sometimes napped. She opened her eyes and stared up at him.

"He only bin gone a few hours," she said, sitting up slowly, "'n' it seems like it days already. Don' know how we a-goin' ter git along 'thout him but guess I'd better git somethin' fer de ladies' lunch. Bread 'n' col' meat, I guess." She heaved her body up, slipped her feet into the overlarge carpet slippers, and slowly shuffled out into the kitchen.

Drummage looked around the room, which now, without Hammond sitting at the green baize table, seemed so unfamiliar. A glass tumbler, with about a half an inch of Hammond's last toddy, sat on a saucer at the side of the table. Drummage picked it up and drained the remainder of the toddy. He had not especially desired the drink but merely wanted his lips to rest where his master's had been such a short time before. It seemed almost like a bodily contact and he lapped the complete circumference of the glass trying to *taste* Hammond, but his only reward was a sticky sweetness. Somehow he did not want to wash the glass, so he carried it into the butler's pantry and placed it far back on the top shelf. When Masta Hammond returned, he'd serve him his first toddy out of that same glass. It seemed to promise Hammond's return to him, a visible evidence that his master would be back.

Coming back to the kitchen he was comforted to see Lucretia Borgia stirring around and the girl Marguerite scraping the dishes preparatory to washing them. But somehow it was not the same. A certain air of authority and discipline had vanished. Instead of going up to his room to change his clothes, as he had originally intended to do and as he knew he was supposed to do, he walked into the pantry and took down one of the best china cups and saucers, which he set down on the kitchen table, although he knew it was forbidden for a servant to eat even the scraps which were left from the dining room off the good china. Lucretia Borgia eyed him, but instead of the outburst he expected she kept a strange silence. Without asking her permission he poured himself out a cup of coffee, sweetening it with sugar instead of cane syrup. Still expecting her outburst, he buttered one of the biscuits remaining from breakfast.

She came over with the platter of cold meat she had been slicing for the ladies' lunch and placed it on the table.

"Piece o' this go well wid yo' biskit," she said, handing him one with her fingers.

"Thank yo', Miz 'Cretia Borgia ma'am. Thank yo' kindly. Shore am glad yo' didn' go off to de war." He was buttering her up as skillfully as he had buttered the biscuit. "Ain' no one in Alabama kin cook so good's yo' 'n' I ain' a-goin ter say nothin' to no one if'n Big Randy a-comin' in de kitchen every night and climbin' up to yore room. Ain' a-goin' to say a word 'bout it to Miz 'Gusta."

Lucretia Borgia gave him another piece of the cold meat. "Sendin' fer that Reba wench, I am," she said, "but we's got ter keep that Candy here fo' a couple of weeks o' mo' to teach Reba how to take care o' Miz 'Gusta. Ain' time yet ter send her over to de birthin' house. Bin a-wonderin' whar we a-goin' to bed that Reba."

"Ain' nobody in that room nex' ter mine whar that Blossom used ter sleep."

Lucretia Borgia slowly closed one eye and let her finger twine a ringlet of Drummage's hair.

"Nice 'n' handy fo' yo', huh?" Suddenly her mood changed and she cuffed him, gently, however, and playfully. "Git movin,' boy, 'n' go 'n' set de table fer de ladies. Yo' kin feed yore face after they gits through. 'N' wash that cup out wid scaldin' water 'n' put it back in de pantry." She turned. "An' yo', Marguerite, yo' black slut, yo' step spry with them dishes 'n' if'n yo' breaks one, I breaks yore goddam head"

Chapter 20

THAT UNKNOWN WORD "war," which had seemed so strange and unmeaningful to Drummage when he first heard it that fateful day Lewis Gasaway came to Falconhurst, gradually came to take on a baleful significance as time passed and the weeks of Hammond's absence turned into months and then passed the year mark. At first, he had been bitterly disappointed that Ajax and not he had been the one picked to go with the master. But, on the one brief occasion when Hammond had returned to Falconhurst, he discovered how fortunate he was to have been left behind. The picture Ajax painted of the military camp at Montgomery was far from pleasant; in fact, he was sick at heart over the prospect of having to return. Later, when Hammond had gone to Virginia, occasional letters from him which Drummage heard Augusta reading aloud to Sophie seemed to indicate that conditions were even worse up there.

Drummage had left his adolescence behind. Added responsibilities had caused him to grow up in the year since Hammond had left. He was now the father of three, but none of his offspring had been sired on Candy. Her first child was a nearly fatal miscarriage and after that she had never conceived again. Augusta had allowed Candy to remain in the big house during the first months of her pregnancy and she herself had nursed the girl in the serious days which followed the miscarriage. Only Candy herself knew that it had been an abortion. She had hated pregnancy and its distortion of her body, as she had feared childbirth and its pains, and despised the thought of motherhood. Bits of information which she had picked up from various women on the plantation had caused her to experiment in all the methods she had heard about, and in the end she had suffered far more than she would have in childbirth. The loss of the child did not trouble Drummage, although he feared censure from Hammond and felt that in some way he might be to blame. But his son by Reba, his daughter by Agnes, and his second son by Salome proved his fecundity. He felt no interest in these children other than the fact that he had been able to sire them; he was unable to distinguish them from the twenty or more other babies which squalled in the nursery. A child from Candy might have stirred some feeling of paternity, but the others meant nothing to him.

He and Candy still shared the same room in the attic. But now, with Hammond gone, and with Lucretia Borgia to back him, Drummage was not confined to his own bed; he had adopted a *droit de seigneur* which he used as an unlicensed liberty to take any wench he fancied. There was nobody to gainsay him. Discipline at Falconhurst had slipped. Lucretia Borgia was getting too old to rule with the iron hand she had always used. Augusta, although presumably making all the final decisions, rarely left the house and almost never visited the slave quarters except in the case of some slave's serious illness. Sophie spent her time riding with Zanzibar, of whom she had not yet tired, or resting in her room. Consequently the real management of the plantation passed into the hands of Brutus, who, under Hammond, had been an efficient overseer, but was now an overbearing tyrant when he could get away with it without Augusta's knowledge. Drummage, although he knew nothing about plantation management, had become Brutus' lieutenant, and assumed authority on his own accord, especially that of studding the wenches.

Little by little he had usurped Lucretia Borgia's responsibility of overseeing the breeding of the slaves. There was a certain amount of rivalry between the elder Brutus and the younger Drummage, but on the surface they made a good pair and their differences of opinion never actually came into the open, for each knew that he needed the other's support. Jubal, almost completely untrained, had taken over the management of the house under Lucretia Borgia, and the big house gradually came to present the same slackness that the plantation and the slave quarters did. It all happened so imperceptibly that the change was not at first noticed. But each day saw Falconhurst decay a little more.

Situated as it was in a backwater, the plantation felt little of the overpowering tides of war. Life flowed on seemingly as usual, yet without its captain the ship was floundering. Everything was becoming more expensive and more difficult to get. The white pillars on the front of the house missed their yearly painting because there was no paint; broken china could not be replaced; clothes were a problem not only for the whites but for the servants; the sturdy whitewashed slave cabins turned a dingy grey and the loosened shakes on their roofs were not replaced.

There was still plenty to eat at the big house. The slaves continued to multiply. When it came time for the yearly sale, Augusta professed her absolute inability to arrange for the transfer of human chattels to New Orleans. Even if she had been able to take them, it would have been a worthless gesture. Sly, indeed all the leading slave merchants of New Orleans, were either out of business or facing bankruptcy and the price of slaves had fallen. There was still talk that after the war was over they would be bringing fantastic prices, but now, with the white owners of the big plantations all sporting generals', colonels', and majors' uniforms, and busily engaged in chasing the Yankees from pillar to post up North, there was nobody left to buy the slaves on the market. Of course, after the South had won the war there would be plenty of "niggers" left and once again the business in human flesh would be booming. But what to do with them in the meantime was a problem.

Those at Falconhurst grew, ate their heads off, worked little under Brutus' lash, and either suffered under or enjoyed Drummage's embraces. There were altogether too many "niggers" for a plantation the size of Falconhurst. Little by little those who had suffered under Brutus stole away, running in the night, and with nobody to pursue them their success emboldened others.

Finally word was received from Hammond, which was relayed on to Brutus and Drummage, to hold a slave auction at Falconhurst. It was something which had never happened before. Augusta made all the arrangements for the vendue, hiring an auctioneer from New Orleans and having bills printed and posted around the neighborhood, even mailed to far-off plantations whose owners had, in the past, been avid customers for Falconhurst slaves. But when the day arrived, only a miserable handful turned out—mostly red-neck farmers from the hills who had not volunteered for military duty and who had never owned a slave in their lives. The bidding was desultory. Fine young bucks who had formerly sold in New Orleans for thousands brought only hundreds. Long before the sale was over, on the advice of the auctioneer, Augusta stopped it and sent the bidders away. In all, less than fifty slaves had been sold, which still left an overwhelming number at Falconhurst—idle men with nothing to do. Despite Brutus' whip he was able to get little work out of them.

White authority had disappeared, and black authority, although it was even more drastically enforced, was not felt to be real; it was ignored as much as possible. Unknown to

Augusta, Brutus inaugurated nightly floggings for those who had incurred his displeasure during the day. Formerly, for a field hand to talk back to an overseer was unheard of. Now they bickered with Brutus, disputed him, and often deliberately disobeyed him. The black grapevine had brought news of freedom and independence and with it a stirring of rebellion. A white man still might have controlled them, but not a Negro who was himself a slave. Each day saw Brutus' authority diminishing and more and more slaves left. Their running did, however, solve one problem. They were out of the way and were not lazing around, fighting over wenches and devouring the gradually diminishing supply of provisions.

The black wealth of Falconhurst was fast disappearing. Those stalwart bucks and fecund wenches, formerly so much in demand, were now a drug on the market. Nobody could afford to buy them. The wide cotton fields of the Southern states lay fallow and the canefields were overgrown with weeds. All through Dixie the big plantation houses were crumbling, their Greek pillars sagging, their proud walls scaling with old paint, and their once-fertile fields reverting to bindweed and briars. Within their walls, the women of the South were trying to ignore the tattered wallpaper which could not be replaced, the torn upholstery which could only be mended, the last year's dresses which must be refurbished for this year, and the growing impudence and laziness of their house servants.

Fortunately for Falconhurst there was still Maxwell money in the banks of New Orleans and Mobile and Montgomery. There were Confederate bonds engraved with beautiful goddesses, and brave Confederate bills stamped with high denominations. Then there were the iron pots, filled with good solid-gold eagles, which were still buried in the ground where Hammond's father had placed them many years before. Lucretia Borgia knew their exact location, and Drummage had been present when one of them was unearthed. Augusta, too, knew of their existence, but Hammond had not wanted to entrust their secret to her—not because he lacked confidence in her, but because he loved her. Union soldiers had tortured women in Virginia to find where they had buried their jewels and silver. Rebellious slaves might do the same to Augusta.

She came to feel that she was sitting on a powder keg, with some four hundred Negro slaves gradually getting out of hand. But what to do? Letters to Hammond took so long and were so often lost that it was practically useless to write to him and wait for his reply. One day Augusta called a council of those she felt she could trust, and who had sufficient intelligence to know what she was talking about. Sophie was of course included; although she was not overly intelligent, she was nevertheless white and as such represented a certain authority. There was old Lucretia Borgia, who had carried Falconhurst through one crisis but had lost some of her mind's cunning with advancing age. And Drummage and Brutus, for they were Augusta's liaison officers between herself and the slaves; and Jubal, who could not contribute much in the way of brains but who had the present responsibility of the big house. Then, too, there was Big Randy from the barn; he was stolid and slow but honest and dependable; and finally old Jupe and Merc, the white-polled gardeners who had served at Falconhurst since the big house was built.

For the first time in his life Drummage sat at the big mahogany dining table with white people rather than standing behind it to serve them. It was the first time for the other servants too, and they felt ill at ease seeing their black hands reflected in the polished wood along with the shadows of the elaborate cut-glass epergne. Augusta sat at the head of the table in Hammond's place, with Sophie facing her at the other end, beside Drummage.

They all waited in nervous silence for Augusta to speak. She regarded them one by one, wondering just how much she really knew and understood them—these black faces which she had seen day after day until they were as familiar as her own face in the mirror. Were the thoughts that went on under those kinky polls the same as hers? She realized that they were humans as well as herself. Augusta was one of the few white people who had no illusions about their being nothing but a superior breed of animals. Yet although they were human, she knew that their minds were different from hers. They were controlled by primitive emotions—lust, pride, anger, or revenge, together with loyalty and love. Their thoughts were for the moment only. The present joy or sorrow was what mattered most to them; planning for the future was something they could not comprehend. But they were all she had to work with. They were her only tools.

"Men and women of Falconhurst," she began, realizing that it was the first time they had ever been addressed as men and women, and not as bucks or wenches. "We are faced with a serious problem. I need your help."

"Yas ma'am, Miz 'Gusta ma'am."

"Shore thin', Miz 'Gusta ma'am."

"What kin we do fer yo', Miz 'Gusta ma'am?"

She waited for the various remarks to die down. Somehow these willing assents gave her courage. Although a wide and impassable gulf separated her from these people, they were nevertheless her own family. They might disagree at times, but underneath there was a certain kinship which bound them together.

"This is our home and we want to keep it," she continued. "To do so, we've got to make a big change in our way of living here at Falconhurst. All of the slaves who are in the quarters must go, at least most of them. We can no longer support them all here. There is not enough work for them to do to keep them busy, and the way things are now we have not enough food to feed them or clothes to clothe them So . . . what are we going to do with them?"

"Whyn't we send them all off to N' Orleans 'n' sell 'em?" Sophie asked. "Papa always sold 'em off every year. Let's send 'em all off, git the money on them, and close up Falconhurst. We could go to England 'n' visit Dudley's family." Sophie occasionally remembered her long-lost husband.

"Sophie!" Augusta was disgusted with the younger woman. "We cannot abandon Falconhurst! We cannot sell the servants if there is nobody to buy them any more! We cannot just move out and leave and most certainly we cannot go to visit people in England who have never invited us and who care nothing about us. No, we shall have to do something else."

"We ain' a-goin' ter leave here." Lucretia Borgia looked straight at Sophie. "This yore papa's place and this yore grandpappy's too. Only time I leave here when I dies."

"Then there is only one thing we can do," Augusta said. "We'll have to permit them all to leave. Let them go anywhere they want to go. But first I want to ask if there is anyone here who would rather leave Falconhurst than remain. If so, let me know."

She looked the length of the table on both sides but not a hand was raised nor a mouth opened.

"Then I take it that all of you want to stay?"

Again there was a chorus of "Yes ma'am, Miz 'Gusta ma'am."

Augusta looked first at Brutus. "I want your advice. Hammond always said that the twenty-acre field between the barn and the quarters was the most productive land at Falconhurst. That and the field down by the river. Now, if we plant those two fields to grain and other foodstuff, we'll have enough for the big house and some workers, yes?"

Brutus nodded assent.

"And if we keep the three fenced pastures, we'll have enough for cows and pigs, yes?"

Again Brutus nodded.

"We can sell off the cows and the horses we do not need. Four horses should be enough—two for the carriage and one for each of you, Brutus and Drummage. We'll use mules for farm work. Thank goodness there's a market for livestock. Now, what I want to know is, outside of the men and women here and Candy and young Pip, who is taking care of the children upstairs, how many servants are we going to need to cultivate those few acres, take care of the cattle, and run the place?"

She looked first at Brutus and then at Drummage and then around the table.

Lucretia Borgia was busy counting on her fingers and was the first to answer.

"If'n yo' asks me, Miz 'Gusta ma'am, I'd say we needs 'bout twenty men. Wants us good strong husky young uns, we do. But if'n we goin' ter have twenty men, we's goin' to need twenty wenches too. Cain' have bucks 'thout wenches. Tain' safe."

Brutus nodded. "Thinks 'bout twenty men handle things fine, Miz 'Gusta. Then I thinks we should keep Malachi too. He been trained as a carpenter and we a-goin' ter need 'im. Needs Jude too. He good vet'nary come calvin' time 'n' kin do blacksmithin' too."

"Needs us more'n twenty wenches, Miz 'Gusta ma'am," Drummage spoke anxiously. "We cain' buy cloth no more but we kin buy cotton 'n' tow so needs us two o' three wenches for the spinnin' 'n' weavin' 'n' needs us two more wenches here in the house. That Marguerite, she no good." He looked to Lucretia Borgia for confirmation.

"Worse'n nothin'," Lucretia Borgia agreed. "Let her hike herself off. Good riddance."

Drummage awaited Augusta's reply anxiously. Although he was still as mad about Candy as ever, he had become accustomed to variety. It had always irked him that the hare-lipped Marguerite should be so conveniently in the house and yet so repulsive he could not touch her. He knew a wench he would like to have replace her.

"Hopin' I kin keep young Sampson out'n the barn with me," Big Randy said. "He a good boy and right smart too."

194

"What 'bout Old Lucy, Big Pearl, and Ol' Mista Wilson?" Drummage asked. They were his family and he was concerned about them. "Masta Hammond always say he ain' a-goin' ter sell them."

Jupe spoke for the first time. "Merc 'n' me kin make a kitchen garden near the house if'n yo' likes, Miz 'Gusta ma'am. Kin raise fancy greens fer the house. Better havin' somethin' ter put in our bellies than roses ter smell of."

"If'n yo' lets Zanzibar take one of Papa's guns, he kin hunt." Sophie made her first sensible suggestion. "He shoots good. Gits us coon 'n' possum 'n' deer. Gits rabbits 'n' ducks. Gits quail too. Gits plenty o' meat for all."

Augusta had been quiet through the various proposals. Every suggestion made a certain amount of sense. After a moment of silence, she addressed them.

"You've given me the information I want. I think it is in the main correct. Supposing we keep twenty men and twenty women, letting each man pick his woman, and if she agrees she will stay with him. We'll keep Malachi the carpenter, Jude the cattleman, and Sampson the stable boy. We'll keep Zanzibar for huntsman. Drummage will choose three girls, provided they wish to remain, for the spinning house, and two for the big house."

Drummage felt relieved that his suggestion had been accepted.

"Naturally we'll keep Old Lucy, Big Pearl, and Ol' Mista Wilson. Now, the question remains, what are we going to do with the rest of our people? We can't just send them out into the world with the clothes on their backs."

"Them that wants to go, kin go." Lucretia Borgia almost spat out the words. "They's the shiftless uns anyway. Good riddance to 'em. Thinks they a-goin' ter have a jubilee onct they gits away. They'll find out. They'll find out. Have to work ter fill they's bellies o' they starve." She shook her head ominously.

"But what about the others?" Augusta asked.

There was a long interval of silence.

"Them as wants to stay," Drummage began, "got to know they cain' jes' sit on they"—he hesitated—"on they backsides and let us feed 'em. Why'n yo' take the big fields on the other side of the road 'n' divide 'em up. Give each buck what wants ter stay a little land. Let him pick himself a wench and they builds theyselves a little cabin. Ain' much work ter build a cabin outa logs 'n' Malachi oversee it. Then they raises their own food. Mayhap yo' gives 'em a pig o' a cow and then they gives yo' a shoat o' a calf come next year. They plants the land, gits 'nuff food for theyselves, and mayhap helps the big house too."

"Better 'n lettin' the land grow up to briars," Brutus added. "Workin' the land better fer it than standin' it idle. When Masta Hammond come back, he kin start in again."

Augusta bowed in acquiescence. It was a good idea. Gradually their problems were being solved. She glanced at the English clock which hung over the sideboard. It was nearly three o'clock. Standing up, she turned to Brutus.

"Brutus, in two hours you should be able to get every man and woman on the plantation assembled. Have them all meet here at the front door of the big house. I'll talk to them. Those that wish to leave may leave, those who wish to stay may remain and we'll try to furnish them with a means of livelihood."

"Yas, Miz 'Gusta ma'am." Brutus stood up beside Augusta. "Gits 'em all here fo' yo', I will."

For some minutes Sophie's hand had been caressing Drummage's knee. She stood up reluctantly and gathered the thin lace shawl about her shoulders. Drummage did not dare to stand. He leaned over, ostensibly to fumble with his shoe but really to give himself enough time so that he would be able to stand up without embarassment.

Sophie followed Augusta out of the room but just as she was passing through the pillared archway into the drawing room she paused, looked back at Drummage, and spoke.

"Fin' that Zanzibar boy 'n' tell him, I cain' ride now. Tell him to be ready 'bout five o'clock 'n' ride with me then."

BOOK II

Chapter 21

THERE WAS NOTHING GRAND about the Grand Hotel de Paris et du Monde, which faced the levee in New Orleans, except its name. Even the once-gilt letters which proclaimed that name to the waterfront rabble were now scarcely discernible. The hotel offered lodging of a sort for two bits a night, if a man was willing to share his bed with some drunken sailor or roustabout—four bits if he was fussy and wanted a bed alone or with a woman of his choice. Apollon Beauchair was one of the fussy ones and although the woman beside him was not the woman of his choice—far from it—at least she served his purpose far better than a sailor or a dock worker.

He lifted himself on one elbow, taking care not to wake her. All he could see was the mass of frowsy blonde curls on the back of the woman's head; he had quite forgotten what her face looked like. At least she was white, although the brassy chain around her neck had left a greenish-black mark on her skin. She was sleeping soundly as the result of the empty rum bottle on the floor beside the bed, whose contents he had taken only sparingly. When one was forced to live by one's wits it did not do to stupefy oneself with alcohol. Not that his wits were his only asset. There was his face and his superb body which, together with his cleverness, had supplied last night's lodging and, he hoped, this morning's breakfast.

Apollon Beauchair threw off the sheet and glanced down at his body, quite satisfied with what he saw. His skin, a pale ivory with just a hint of gold, glowed beside the doughy whiteness of his companion. His long legs, strong and heavily muscled, seemed unnecessarily heavy to support such a slender waist, which in turn appeared quite inadequate to carry the wide-shouldered and the heavily muscled chest on which his paps appeared like carefully placed copper pennies. He pulled up a corner of the coarse grey sheet and scrubbed at his body, drying and cleaning it from the night's sweat. Then he laid his head back on the crumpled pillow and stared at the blotched ceiling and the curtain slowly waving in the hot breeze.

With a grimace of revulsion, he moved as far away from the figure of the sleeping woman as possible, yawning and brushing his long hair back from his face. It was straight, black, and oily and his fingers became greasy from the heavy applications of macassar oil which he used to keep the slight suggestion of waviness out of it. The bare back of the woman tempted him to wipe his hands on her skin but he did not want to awaken her and he rubbed them on his belly, feeling a certain pleasure in the contact of his hands with his own hard flesh. He yawned. Already he had made his plans, and now he was faced with the problem of getting up, dressing, and slipping out without waking his companion.

Slowly, so as not to cause the bed ropes to creak, he swung his legs over the edge of the bed and sat up. The ache in his kidneys produced a compelling desire to relieve himself but there was no chamberpot under the bed, and even if there had been he would not have taken the chance of arousing the sleeper. The tiled floor felt cool to his feet and he stood up and tiptoed around the foot of the bed to where his clothes hung on the back of a chair. Still moving with feline grace and caution, he put on the pale, lemon-colored trousers with the stove-pipe slim legs, his white, frill-fronted shirt, socks, and shoes. Stepping even more quietly now, he picked up the black silk reticule which lay on top of her dress on another chair. Turning his back to the bed to hide his movements, he pulled the drawstring and reached inside, pulling out two Confederate bills—one a five-dollar bill, which he was surprised to see, and the other a dollar—with a handful of small silver and coppers. These he transferred to his own pocket, then placed the reticule back on the chair.

So far so good: it was better than he had hoped for. Now to get out as quickly as possible. His black satin stock he crammed in his pocket and slipped on the blue broadcloth coat. With his white beaver hat in his hand, he posed for a second before the shard of flyblown mirror tacked to the wall. No time to go through the elaborate process of combing his hair, so he gathered it up and pulled the hat down on it at a jaunty angle, then smiled at himself in the glass.

"You're goddam handsome, 'Pollon, *mon fils*." He greeted his reflection with a debonair tilt of his head, not realizing that the face that stared back at him was altogether too handsome. There was a softness and a sensuality about it that belied his body's tallness and strength. The eyes were too black and were shaded by too long lashes. The brows were too arched and too regular; the nose too straight and the nostrils a little too large; the lips too red and too full and the cleft in the chin too pronounced. Even the dimples in the cheeks seemed artificial, as though they had been momentarily pressed in with the point of a skewer, and the sleek black *favoris* which extended down onto his cheek seemed to be penciled with crayon instead of hair. But his face satisfied Apollon and he was well aware that it satisfied many other people too. It was a face that one remembered and idealized when away from it, yet when one saw it again there was always something strangely disappointing about it. It never measured up to one's expectations.

His thin shoes made more noise on the tiles than his bare feet and he walked more slowly, lifting each foot cautiously and placing it down with care. He had nearly reached the door when the woman on the bed stirred, stretched her arms wide, and opened her eyes. She stared up at him and he, not in the least disconcerted, smiled back at her, even drawing near enough to the bed to rub the knuckle of his index finger over her sagging cheeks. *Mon Dieu*, but she was ugly; she must be at least ten years older than he was, all of forty. He had certainly earned the pittance he had stolen.

"Whar yo' goin'?" she asked petulantly. "Yo' a-runnin' out on me?"

"*Chérie.*" With the tips of his fingers he drew a line from her cheek to her chin, then down her neck to linger on one of her breasts. "Leave you? *Mais non,* how could I after last night? One does not abandon paradise so easily." He wondered if, in the light of day, he could bear to kiss her, but decided he couldn't. Instead, he allowed his fingers to play with her breast while she reached up and grabbed his hand.

"But yo' all dressed. Even got yore hat on. Ain' yo' a-runnin' out? Ain' yo' a-leavin'? If'n yo' are, I want two dollars. Usually gits five, I do, but yo' pleasured me so much, only chargin' yo' two dollars."

"It's not enough, *chérie*. Ten dollars! That's what I'm going to pay you and even then I shall be cheating you. Yes,

I'm going out but I've no intention of leaving you. Just going to surprise you, that's all. There's a shop two doors down the street and I was going to get coffee and *croissants* to bring back for both of us. Doesn't that sound good? Hot coffee and hot rolls *together* in bed? Then I'll give you a chance to earn another ten dollars. How about it, coffee and rolls for the two of us and then. . . ."

"And then?" She raised her head and kissed his strong fingers, which the sun had turned a light bronze. "Yo' means I'se really worth ten dollars?" She had not had such a compliment for many years. "If'n yo' weren't a gen'leman o' quality, shore would like to have yo' a-pimpin' fer me. Give yo' half of everythin' I make jes' ter know I had yo' ter come back ter." She looked up at him, squinting her eyes in the bright light. "Yo're young, yo' are, and don' git many young uns these days. War bin a-goin' on fer over a year and mos' men yore age up No'th a-fightin' in the war. Mos' the young uns these days only got one arm o' one laig."

"I'm a Frenchman, *chérie*, not an American." He allowed his fingers to wander down her body for a more intimate caress. "Listen, *chérie*, I'm starving. Let me run and get the coffee and when I'm back we'll make some plans while we drink it. How'd you like a little cottage of your own over on Rampart Street?"

"With yo' a-comin' every night, I'd love it. Yo' mean that, man? Say, what's yore name, anyway?"

"Cupid, the god of love, and you indeed must be Venus. Now I go, *bébé*, but I'll be back in a few moments. Turn over and go to sleep and when I bring the coffee, I'll crawl in beside you." His final caress convinced her of his own overwhelming desire and she watched him as he lifted the latch of the door and blew a kiss at her.

Once outside the door he shook his head in relief and took the cracked marble steps two at a time, but he managed to repress his haste and stroll casually through the dirty little office where a corpulent man dozed behind the zinc-covered counter.

"Be right back." Apollon's smile was so convincing that the man did not doubt him. "Just going out to fetch coffee and *croissants*."

"Could've sent 'em up to yo'. Got us a nigger here ter run errands. Whyn't yo' call him?"

Apollon winked one eye, the long lashes making a sooty semicircle on his cheek. "After last night, I need a little fresh air before I start in again." He had edged nearer to the door and now stepped out onto the banquette and strolled casually down the street. Thinking perhaps that the woman up in the room might have come out onto the balcony to watch him or that the hotel proprietor might be looking, he stepped into the open doorway of the coffee shop, but continued on through the courtyard until he reached a black door with the word "Messieurs" nearly obliterated. Thank God! The stench inside gagged him but his relief was worth it. Now he could really get started. When he came out he noticed that there was a rear entrance onto an alley in the back, and he took it, walking faster once he was in the alley. Striding with long steps he headed back from the levee up into the center of the town, stopping once in a doorway to tie his cravat and comb his hair. He had no watch, but the shadows told him it must be around noon; he would be on time to keep his appointment with Cupidon, his half-brother, in Jackson Square.

Now that he was in a different part of the city, with little chance of meeting any of the waterfront characters he had been with during the night, he walked more leisurely. His hand, contentedly roaming his trouser pocket, encountered the two bills and he laughed aloud, wondering if the stupid whore was still waiting for him to return. The slut! She'd have a hell of a wait! He shuddered at the memory of her slobbering kisses and avid pawings. Ahead of him he saw the greenery of Jackson Square, and he turned at the corner, strolling under the long balconies of the Pontalba Buildings until he arrived at one of the entrance gates. Cupidon was sitting on his usual bench, in the shadow of a cabbage palm, and had seen him coming. Apollon sauntered up to the bench and sat down, stretching his long legs on the gravel path. Immediately Cupidon arose to stand before him.

"Ain' had no brekfus, 'Pollon," Cupidon muttered.

Apollon glanced up at him. Despite the difference in clothes, for Apollon's were those of a gentleman and Cupidon's those of a slave, it was like looking into a mirror, for he saw his own features reflected "as in a glass darkly" in his brother's face. Cupidon was a few years younger than Apollon but one would have judged them to be the same age. Were it not for the marked difference in color they might well have been twins. They both possessed the same superlative good looks which in their ultimate combination were too perfect. But where Apollon's skin was the color of ivory, Cupidon's was a deep bronze, and where Apollon's hair had only the hint of wave, Cupidon's was almost kinky. Apollon's lips were full and red, not thick and dark like his brother's and his

201

sensuous nostrils only a trifle magnified, whereas Cupidon's were actually Negroid.

Apollo reached in his pocket and drew out the handful of change, taking care not to disclose the bills.

"Whar yo' git dat money, 'Pollon?"

"Worked fer it, Kewp. Worked damn hard fer it, doing something you wouldn't be able to do."

"Kin do anythin' yo' kin do, 'Pollon."

"But not as well as I kin. Here, take this two bits and get something to eat, but first I want to talk with you."

"What yo' wants, Masta 'Pollon suh?" Cupidon grinned as he lapsed into slave talk.

"We got to make ourselves some money. We're broke—stony-broke. No money, no place to stay, nothing to eat. I've pawned my watch, Papa's ring, and my other suit of clothes."

Cupidon's grin vanished. "Yo' ain' a-goin' ter sell me 'gain, 'Pollon?"

Apollo shrugged his shoulders. "Ain't aiming to but we sure got to do something. First we both got to git cleaned up." He jerked his thumb in the direction of Chartres Street. "Think that wench of yours would let us slip in the back door so we could wash up there?" He felt his chin, glad that he almost never had to shave.

"Which wench yo' talkin' 'bout, 'Pollon? Got me plenty 'bout town."

"That Clotilde wench—the one that's always giving you meals—belongs to old Madame Lamartine."

"Oh, her? She do anythin' fer me but if'n she sees yo', won' never want me 'gain."

"Ain't having no truck with black wenches, Kewp. Besides you kin handle them better than I kin. Come on, we'll go there first. Maybe she'll even give us some breakfast and you kin save your two bits."

"She'll give us the whole goddam house if'n yo' jes' sweet-talk her a bit, 'Pollon. She man crazy, that gal."

"Kewp, if you'd had to sweet-talk a woman like I did last night, you wouldn't want to see another for six months."

"Le's try Clotilde den." Cupidon hitched up his soiled tow-linen pants, tucking the tail of his patched shirt into them. His feet were coming out of his shoes and the straw hat that he wore hardly held together, but even his miserable clothes could not hide the strength and perfection of his body.

"Then we'll figure out what we're goin' to do, boy." Apollo stood up and, now that they were both standing, it was apparent that he was about an inch shorter than his brother. "Sure don't want to have to sell you again but if we'll have to, we'll have to."

They walked along a few steps together until Cupidon fell back behind Apollon. As they walked along there was no doubt who was master and who was slave. At the next corner Cupidon caught up with his master, and for a moment they stood side by side as a carriage passed.

Cupidon was worried. "Look, 'Pollon, if'n yo're a-goin' ter sell me, don' sell me to some no-good bastard like that young Troyon yo' sol' me to las' time. Cain' stand 'nother like him a-pawin' at me 'n' squirtin' perfum'ry all over me. Kep' me locked in he's room fer a week. Thought I'd never git a chance to run away."

Apollon turned on him. "Listen, boy! Ain't you fergettin' that you're my slave and I'll sell you to whoever I damn please?"

"Listen, man," Cupidon answered him without his affected servility, "ain' yo' fergot that yo're my brother'n yo're jes' as much a nigger servant as I am, even tho' yo're white."

Was, boy! *Was* a slave! Ain't one no longer. Ain't nigger either. Papa died and gave me my freedom and gave me you too. Watch out, or I'll sell you down in the canefields where you'll never git away."

Chapter 22

WHEN THE TWO MEN, a couple of hours later, emerged from the back door of the Lamartine house, there was certainly no difficulty in distinguishing between master and slave. Apollon's clothes were in the latest style and good taste. Clotilde, yielding to his charm, had sponged and pressed them. The hour's sleep which he had enjoyed while Clotilde freshened up his clothes had erased the sagginess of the previous night's dissipation, and a hearty meal had given him new courage. Cupidon, by contrast, looked even more bedraggled and unkempt in his flapping shoes, torn shirt, and patched trousers. He had had no chance to sleep; he had to entertain Clotilde while Apollon's shirt was drying in the sun.

The two bills in his pocket were all the money that Apollon possessed and now he realized that a part of these would have to be sacrificed, or rather invested. However, if the small investment he had in mind paid off, it would be well worth it. Cupidon's clothes were a disgrace to his master's style. He'd have to dress him up a little and make him at least presentable.

With Cupidon following a few steps behind, he made his way to the north side of Congo Square, where there was a veritable thieves' market of old clothes and oddments, presided over by free men of color. They bought anything that slaves wished to sell—clothes stolen from their masters or passed on to them as castoffs. Here one could find almost anything in the barrows that lined the banquette. And if one had the patience to haggle, whatever one found could be bought at a price. It was a long walk and a hot one, but they had plenty of time and, by keeping on the shady side of the streets under the balconies and by walking leisurely, Apollon managed to retain his dapper appearance.

The barrows proved productive, and for less than three dollars he was able to outfit Kewp in fairly presentable clothes—at least sufficiently presentable without too close an inspection. For two bits he purchased a pair of freshly laundered white drill trousers, which, although wine-stained, were intact; a dollar bought a blue broadcloth jacket with tarnished brass buttons; another two bits, a white shirt which had been torn and mended in the back; and a half-dollar purchased a pair of re-soled black slippers. As a final extravagance, a few copper pennies purchased a square of scarlet silk, and with all these in hand they repaired to a rough shelter of ragged blankets stretched on poles, which served as a dressing booth for those buying or selling. The trousers proved to be a little too small; the sleeves of the coat were an inch short and it was impossible to button it over Kewp's broad chest; the shirt was too large. Fortunately the old shoes fitted comfortably, and when Cupidon was dressed he made a presentable appearance in what might well have been Apollon's hand-me-downs.

From the food stalls on the other side of the square Apollon purchased some roast spareribs and baked yams, which Kewp carried in a greasy newspaper to a vacant lot nearby where they ate under the shade of a thick-leaved magnolia. During their meal they rehearsed the part Cupidon was to play in the little drama which Apollon was about to inaugurate if conditions were favorable. It needed little rehearsing, for this was the third time they had played it. Side by side, they walked together until they had perfected all their plans.

Kewp was loath to play his part, but he realized he had little to say about it. On the street corner where they separated Apollon had one last word.

"Git away as quickly as you kin. I'll go directly to Les Chenes. If you git there first by any chance, tell Mama I'll be there."

" 'N' if'n yo' gits there first, tell my mama I'll be a-comin' too."

They separated and Apollon walked on slowly, seeking the shade of the overhanging balconies, until he arrived at the Hotel Saint Louis, whose long bar under the dome, at that late hour in the afternoon, was the gathering place for the men of the city. Some might fancy the St. Charles, others the Old Absinthe House, but the elite clung to the Saint Louis. Not that there were so many as had frequented it before the war, for most of the young and able-bodied men were now fighting. But there was always a gathering there—plantation owners stopping over in the city, Creoles from the old families, businessmen, a few riverboat gamblers, and some, like Apollon, who lived by their wits or their good looks.

The dim light, filtering through the varicolored glass dome, was flattering to Apollon's appearance, but it did not cover up the encroaching shabbiness of the Saint Louis Hotel. Here, where formerly the great slave auctions of the city had been held in a setting of splendor which was ill conceived for the tragedies that were enacted on the vendue table, the effects of the war were already beginning to be seen. The gold leaf was starting to peel, the marble tiles in the floor were cracking, and there was a general air of decaying grandeur. Although the barmen were as unctuously polite as ever, the drinks were tepid, for no more ice was coming down the Mississippi from the North.

Apollon had never operated in New Orleans before. It was too near his own home and he had always held in reserve for some future time, some big *coup*. Mobile, Memphis, Pensacola and Natchez had all been productive. Now, in his present emergency, it had to be New Orleans. Fortunately nobody knew him there. True, the once proud Les Chenes plantation was not far from New Orleans and the Beauchair name was equal to any in the old Creole aristocracy. But Apollon had been born on the wrong side of the blanket and had never mingled with other plantation scions whose births had been legitimate . . . . and white. His mother had been, despite the almost infinitesimal attenuation of Negro blood, a slave, and although her manumission at the hands of

Apollon's father had made him a free man, few were aware of his existence. He had been sent North at an early age to go to school, where he had been fully accepted as white and where a lavishment of money had given him expensive tastes. His half-brother Cupidon, the son of a full Negress, had never been anything else but a slave, and on Apollon's father's death had become his property. Despite the difference in their color and station, there was a strong bond of affection between the two and an equal affection between the two mothers, who still lived in the crumbling grandeur of Les Chenes.

Once inside the bar, Apollon, with a confidence born of the worn bills in his pocket, ordered a Sazerac cocktail and sipped it slowly, sizing up the other men who were leaning against the bar or sitting at small tables. He judged he was too early. There were too few people there and those few did not seem likely prospects for the deal he had in mind. Finishing his drink, he set his glass back on the polished mahogany and wandered out into the hotel lobby. Here there seemed to be a little excitement, occasioned by a magnificently dressed woman with two small children—a boy and a girl—and a weak-looking but well-dressed man with pale blond side whiskers. Near them and evidently belonging to them was a male slave whose well-tailored clothes were far superior to Apollon's own. The woman, whose broad-brimmed and plumed hat partially hid her face, was sobbing dramatically, and while Apollon looked on she sank to the floor in a billow of blue taffeta and lace to hug the two children. Apollon was near enough to hear her anguished words as she looked up at the man.

"Jes' cain' bear to part with my babies, Dudley. It's downright cruel o' yo' to take 'em. Wouldn' let 'em go if'n it wasn't better fer 'em in England what with this terrible war on here. But I cain' let 'em go. I jes' cain', Dudley. Oh, whyn't yo' take me with yo'? How kin yo' bear to separate these dear chil'ren from their mama? Take me with yo', Dudley. I'd love livin' in England. Jes' love it, and these babies needs their mama."

"We've been all over that, Sophie," the man answered dispassionately. "We've discussed it a hundred times. We're no longer married."

"Yo' jes' the meanest man in the world, Dudley. Me havin' a chance to be a real Lady and yo' divorcin' me. Ain' right, Dudley, ain' right fo' yo' to take my babies."

"They are my children too, Sophie. Young Warren is now

an earl's son, and he needs to be brought up as one, and Amanda will have a far better life as my daughter in England than as yours in Alabama." He looked up as another Negro slave came to stand beside the first one, equally well dressed and prepossessing. He nodded at the boy. "You know this boy will be free when he gets to England. Are you sure you want him to go along?"

"My babies got to have their Jubal. Be lost without him. He'll stay with them, free o' not."

At a motion from the man, the slave addressed as Jubal picked up the little girl in his arms and took the boy's hand. They walked out the main door of the hotel to a waiting carriage, and the other slave carried the valises, the rolled-up rugs, and the other luggage. The woman followed them and once at the carriage burst into another violent fit of weeping, leaning on the arm of her slave for support.

Apollon turned to the well-dressed man who had come up to stand beside him, a question in his eyes. The stranger read the question and answered it.

"The Earl of Charnwood, taking his children back to England," he said. "Quite an interesting story about it in the *Picayune* today."

Apollon lifted his eyebrows to show his ignorance of what had been happening.

"Yes, that man who just left with the children is the new Earl of Charnwood. Younger son of a younger son and all that, he was about as far removed from the earldom as you or I. But the series of deaths in the family elevated him and he came over here to get his children after divorcing his wife. She's 'bout the richest woman in the South too but I understand he had to pay plenty to get the children. Her father is Major Hammond Maxwell, the owner of Falconhurst. You've probably heard of the Falconhurst breed—best slaves in the South."

"And who has not?" Apollon answered, with a glance at the slave, who was now following the weeping woman back into the hotel. "Could recognize that boy as a Falconhurst slave anywhere. Best niggers in the South, although I've got a boy that's even better."

"You are fortunate, sir." The man bowed to Apollon. "Allow me to introduce myself. Charles Goodwin of Bucks Plantation."

"And I am the Vicomte de Noailles, from France." Apollon saw no reason why he should not raise himself to the nobility; he saw that the man had been impressed with the

English earl. He bowed low and offered his hand. "Yet as regards my servant, perhaps not as fortunate as you might think. It is regrettable but I must part with him. Been hating to put him up for sale because he's far too fine a boy to sell in public and besides, there isn't the market for niggers there formerly was. Am going to have to lose money on him."

"Forced sales are always bad," Goodwin acknowledged. "These low prices are only temporary. Going to go sky-high after the war. Bigger demand for niggers than ever before. I've managed to keep all my stock so far although there's been a lot of running on other plantations. Glad I have, too, because it's practically impossible to buy anything good these days. The finest bucks are all running No'th. Damn those Yankees!"

Apollon felt it was time to switch subjects. He did not want to appear too interested in the matter of selling. Instead he thanked Goodwin for introducing himself, bowed low, and started to depart; then he turned abruptly and came back, smiling his most engaging smile.

"M'sieur Goodwin." Apollon displayed all his charm, which was considerable. "Perhaps I could presume on our very short acquaintance to invite you to take a drink with me in the bar. One gets tired of listening to one's own thoughts and it would be pleasant to converse with a real gentleman. I am a stranger here and know no one."

Goodwin, like most people, was immediately won over by the ingenuousness of Apollon's smile and by his good manners, which were sufficiently respectful towards an elderly man and yet entirely lacking in obsequiousness. He was only too glad to accept the engaging young Frenchman's attention and as Apollon had surmised, he was a little awed by his title. As a gesture of intimacy, he offered his arm to the supposed Vicomte and together they walked into the bar, sat down at one of the tables, and ordered drinks. Apollon entertained with reminiscences about his native Paris (which he had never seen), about the plantation down on the Delta which he had inherited and sold (patterned after recollections of his own home), and about the excellence of the slaves he had purchased and whose services had been so extremely satisfactory. Goodwin, warming to the charming personality of so exalted a personage, expatiated about his own plantation, the difficulty of shipping cotton through the blockade, his anxiety to get new breeding stock for his slaves, and, through a series of subtle questions put by Apollon, on the lady who had been creating such a scene in the lobby.

"The Maxwells are a fine family." he said. "Married into the Hammonds, another fine family. Knew Major Hammond Maxwell, the lady's father, very well. Bought several fine bucks from him 'bout twenty years ago and used them to improve my breed. Bucks' bucks, I call 'em." He nudged Apollon with his elbow. "Pretty good, eh? Bucks' bucks! Been a-wishing I could get more like them. Pretty late to get started now, seeing as how the war is nearly won, but in another twenty years we'll be getting top prices for fine servants. Breed's running out in most places. They've been letting inferior bucks cover inferior wenches and getting inferior stock—weak, scrawny, lazy, and bad dispositions. Was hoping Falconhurst would have a sale this year, but it didn't. Might take a trip over that way sometime soon and see what I can pick up."

"Are they still selling?" Apollon asked nonchalantly.

"Suppose so. Major Maxwell dead and understand that Miz Maxwell passed on too. Major took down with dysentery somewhere in North Carolina and Miz Maxwell went there to nurse him. Understand she was taken sick too. Anyhow, they're both gone and nobody left but Major Maxwell's daughter, she whom you just saw out there." He jerked his thumb towards the hotel lobby. "Richest woman in the South, I hear, and now she's all alone on that big place."

A flickering of Apollon's long eyelashes was the only indication that the information was of interest to him. Noticing that Goodwin's glass was empty, he suggested another drink, demurred politely as Goodwin offered to pay, and then with apparent reluctance allowed him to do so. The bar was filling now and Goodwin pointed out several important men, both civilians and officers in Confederate grey. One or two of them wandered over to the table and Goodwin introduced them, at which Apollon stood up, clicked his heels together in the best Continental manner, and assured them he was honored to meet them.

As they were finishing their third Sazerac, Apollon noticed that Goodwin was staring at something behind his back, and then he heard the words which he had been so anxiously awaiting.

"Beggin' yore pardon suh, but dis yere letter jes' 'rived fer yo' at yore lodgin's. Nigger what brought it a-sayin' it mighty important so's I thinkin' I bes' bring it over to yo', knowin' as how yo'd be a-comin' here."

Apollon turned to find Kewp behind him.

"Your indulgence, M'sieur Goodwin." He took the cocked-hat note which he had written only a few hours previously, unfolded it, and read the few lines of writing. He frowned, shook his head sadly, and stood up to leave, reaching out his hand to Goodwin.

"A thousand regrets, M'sieur Goodwin, that our most pleasant conversation must be interrupted by business, but I fear that I must leave you. If you remember, I told you I was anxious to dispose of my servant here, Cupidon, and I've just received an offer for him. Unfortunately it is a most disappointingly low one, so I shall lose money on him, but I am so pressed for time that I shall be forced to accept the loss. I paid fifteen hundred dollars for the boy some six months ago; now I shall be forced to accept half of that."

Goodwin studied Kewp, standing behind Apollon's chair. With a grin as engaging as his master's, Cupidon smiled back at the planter. "This the boy you mean?" Goodwin continued his study.

"And a fine boy he is." Apollon resigned himself with a sigh. "Wish I could take him to France with me but he'd be altogether too much of a curiosity there and I'd still lose money on him as he'd be free in France. So, I guess I shall have to accept the seven hundred and fifty and let him go. It's been a pleasure talking to you, M'sieur Goodwin. Should you ever come to Paris, do let me entertain you. Anyone in Paris can direct you to the Hôtel de Noailles and you will be most welcome there."

Goodwin also stood up. "Perhaps it will not be necessary for you to leave so quickly, Vicomte. You say this boy is for sale and that you are about to accept a sacrifice price for him. Seems ridiculously low. I'm prepared to offer you more than that, provided the boy is sound of wind and limb."

"He's sound all right." Apollon nodded emphatically.

"Don't suppose you've ever bred him, seeing as how you don't own any wenches?"

"Never have actually, M'sieur Goodwin, although when I was disposing of my plantation he covered one of the wenches there successfully, didn't you, Cupidon?"

"Shore got that one knocked up quick, Masta Vicomte suh."

"Perhaps if I could just examine him." Goodwin continued to inventory Kewp. "There are rooms here for that purpose—left over from the times they held the big sales here."

"Most certainly," Apollon agreed.

"Yo' a-goin' ter sell me, Masta Vicomte suh?" Cupidon

looked terror-stricken. "Don' wants to be sold, Masta suh. Wants ter stay wid yo'. Yo' good masta."

"That's enough, boy," Goodwin cut him off short. "Appreciate your liking your masta but if he wants to sell you to me, he can." He led the way through the maze of tables, Apollon and Cupidon following. Requesting the loan of a candlestick from the bar, Goodwin ushered them into a small bare room with one tiny barred window high in the wall. "Shuck down, boy," he commanded.

Cupidon looked to his brother and at Apollon's nod he undid his breeches and peeled them off his legs, stepped out of them, and took off his coat and shirt. Standing naked before Goodwin, he flexed his muscles, as the planter ran his hands over him, then carefully examined and weighed his genitals in his hand. He seemed satisfied with the examination.

"I'm a businessman, Vicomte," he said, his hands still running over Cupidon's sleek thighs, "and as a businessman I am always looking for a bargain. This boy's a prime nigger. You say you've been offered seven hundred fifty dollars for him. I presume it's from a dealer, who has to make a profit. Well, he'll want to double his money and he'll probably sell at fifteen hundred or maybe hold out for two thousand. That's a big amount of money for a nigger today, although a few years ago it was standard price. But this boy of yours is exceptional—prime! Tell you what I'll do. I'll offer you twelve hundred fifty dollars. That's five hundred more than you've been offered and probably five hundred less than I'd have to pay for him anywhere else."

"Don' sell me, Masta suh." The tears that were rolling down Cupidon's cheek had all the appearance of being real.

"Quiet!" Apollon's hand was raised to slap. "I'm inclined to accept your offer, M'sieur Goodwin, but on one condition."

"And that is?" Goodwin asked.

"I am sailing tomorrow on a packet to Martinique where I shall be able to pick up a ship for France. If you will allow me the services of this boy for tonight and tomorrow to help me with my packing and the other business I must attend to before I leave, I'll sell him to you now." He motioned to Cupidon to dress himself.

"That satisfies me fine," Goodwin nodded. "I'm staying here at the hotel and it will relieve me from having to take care of him. Leaving myself day after tomorrow."

Apollon hesitated. "No, Mr. Goodwin, on second thought we'd better complete our transaction now. I'll make out a

211

bill of sale and you can make me a sight draft on your bank, payable tomorrow. You take Cupidon along with you and I'll manage to get along without him. After all, you do not know me and how do you know but that I might fail to deliver him." He opened the door of the little room, and bowed to give Goodwin precedence.

"Nonsense." Goodwin looked over his shoulder at Apollon. "I know a gentleman when I see one. Your word's good enough for me. Can see why you'd need the boy and I don't need him." He walked over to one of the small tables, pulled out a chair, and signaled for the waiter.

"Bring us pen, ink, and papers, boy."

The waiter brought them almost immediately. The papers were printed forms of bill of sale and bank drafts. Such transactions as the buying and selling of slaves were commonplace at the St. Louis, where sometimes, in the old days, a slave might change hands two or three times in the course of one evening.

While Apollon dipped his pen in the ink and wrote out a bill of sale in his fine, formal hand, Goodwin dashed off a draft on the Planters' Bank. They both waved the papers in the air to dry and exchanged them.

"You can cash this in the morning, Vicomte. Just ask for Mr. Olivares at the bank and he'll be glad to oblige you."

"And I shall deliver Cupidon here tomorrow evening. If he finishes with my work and errands, I can bring him even earlier."

"Six o'clock will be fine." Goodwin nodded his approval. "Or, if you desire to leave the boy earlier, have him wait for me over there." He pointed to a long bench in the back of the room where attending servants awaited their masters.

"Until tomorrow then." Apollon clicked his heels, bowed formally, and left with Cupidon behind him. Once outside the hotel he walked for a block, with Cupidon following a few paces behind. When they had turned the corner into a dimly lighted street Apollon waited for Cupidon to catch up with him, and they fell into each other's arms, slapping each other on the back, laughing until the tears came down their cheeks.

"Yas suh, Masta Vicomte suh." Cupidon went into another gale of laughter.

"Easiest sale we ever made." Apollon managed to control himself. "This time you don't even have to run away."

"Goin' ter pack all your clotheses so's yo' kin go to Yew-rope." Cupidon was off again.

"Hoped I was going to get two thousand for you like I did last time, but prices coming down."

"Shore was worth it having to sleep with that bastard for a week 'fore I could get away."

"Bank opens at eight tomorrow morning. I'll go and cash this draft. Then I'll drop in and tell Mr. Goodwin I'll bring you over at six. That will allay any suspicions he might have—seeing me again. By ten o'clock I'll be finished, with the money in my pocket. There's a diligence leaving for Barataria around eleven. We'll take it, get off at the lake, buy a pirogue there—or steal one—and go down the bayou. Should be at Les Chenes the next day and then I've got some plans."

"What yo' a-goin' ter do, 'Pollon?"

"Going to get ourselves fitted out real smart on this money —new clothes for both of us. Going to get a carriage. Then we're going to take a trip over Alabama way. Don't know just where we're going but I'm going to marry the richest woman in the South. She's kind of fat and from what I could see she's cross-eyed, but something tells me she's itching for a man and I think I've got just what she's looking for."

"Hope yo' don' have to sell me 'gain, 'Pollon. Gittin' tired o' bein' sold, I am."

"Once I get my hands on that Falconhurst money, I'll free you. Look, Kewp, where we going to sleep tonight?"

"That Clotilde wench she shore like you this morning, 'Pollon."

"She likes you better than me and I'm going to sleep to-night. I put in a hard night last night getting our stake. I'll let you handle Clotilde."

They started along in the direction of the Lamartine house, walking side by side along the darkening streets.

" 'Pollon?" Cupidon looked up at his brother.

"What you want, Kewp?"

"Yo' know, 'Pollon, I thinkin' yo' be a lot happier if'n yo' nigger like me 'stead of trying to be a white boy."

Apollon did not answer as they trudged on. But he was thinking, *I am white. God damn it, I am white!*

Chapter 23

THE NARROW PIROGUE glided noiselessly over the oily black water through the green light that seeped through the moss-hung cypress trees. There was an oppressive silence, broken only by the muted song of a bird and the slither of a moccasin making a corkscrew path through the water. Kewp lifted his pole to hit the snake on the head, but he missed and it swam away easily. Apollon shifted his weight carefully and grinned back at his brother.

"We're most there, Kewp boy. Seem good to be getting back home?"

"A-wishin' we was goin' to stay here, 'Pollon. Wishin' we could jes' stay here, huntin' 'n' fishin', doin' a little trappin' 'n' plenty o' wenchin' 'n' a-livin' here with our mamas. Got us a good place ter live, plenty ter eat, right here at Les Chenes. Whyn't we stay here, 'Pollon?"

"If things go right, and they'd better go right, Kewp, I'll never be selling you again. We'll be living high, boy. War gets over, we'll head for New York. Get tired of New York, we'll go to London, Paris, Rome. We'll see the world, Kewp. And,"—his voice dropped lower—"we'll see it like gentlemen."

"Yo'll be the gen'leman, 'Pollon. I'll never be nothin' but a nigger."

"Better to be a rich nigger, Kewp, than poor white trash. Besides, they say that in Paris those French girls are crazy for colored boys like you."

"But I'll have to keep on bein' yore servant." Kewp shoved the boat forward and rested. "Gettin' tired o' callin' yo' Masta 'Pollon suh, o' Masta Antoine suh, o' Masta Hyacinthe, o' Masta Charles. Yo' takes so many names, cain' remember which un yo' answerin' ter. What yo' goin' ter call yo'se'f next time?"

"Next time I think I'll be myself, just Apollon Beauchair of Les Chenes plantation. After all, the Beauchairs are an old Creole family and a quality name."

"Suppose I got to go on bein' yore servant, 'Pollon?"

"That's what you are, Kewp. Servant for life! Not my fault and not your fault. Not my fault that my papa made me white and made you black. Not your fault either. Cheer

214

up, *mon frère*, it's not to bad being my servant, is it? Lots worse masters than I am. Never had you whipped, did I? You do about as you damn please."

"Don' mind bein' yore servant, 'Pollon. Jes' don' like havin' to sleep with the niggers, always havin' nigger wenches, eatin' nigger food, bowin' to white men."

"Mayhap we can change some of that. Where we are going, I'll get you a room by yourself and give you table food, but you can't have a white woman. Besides, you're lucky, boy. You do your pleasuring for pleasure. Remember that. Mine is work and damn little pleasure in it for me. Hardest work in the world, boy, bedding yourself with a woman you don't like, even if she is white."

"Ain' never tried it; ain' a-wantin' ter." Kewp anchored his pole and turned the corner of a point of sandbar to send the pirogue up a narrow inlet. "Water's high 'nuff so's we kin take the short cut."

Here the banks were narrower and the moss hung down so low they had to brush it from their faces. After a quarter of an hour in the narrow stream they emerged onto a wide bayou, red and gold in the setting sun. In the deep water it was necessary for Kewp to paddle, and he sent the pirogue forward with long, deep strokes until the bayou was nearly crossed and they sighted a rough pier on the opposite shore. Behind it, almost hidden by live oaks and thick-leaved magnolias, there were glimpses of a brick house from which smoke emerged in a black column against the red sky. Kewp put new energy into his strokes and brought the pirogue up alongside the rotting pier. Near the shore, where the wood was more solid, he jumped out and pulled the pirogue in, holding it steady for Apollon, then removed the carpetbag, pasteboard box, and several small bundles. Apollon's role of master slipped from him and he carried his share of the bundles.

Shirtless, and clad only in rough osnaburg trousers, their resemblance was more apparent. Cupidon was the peasant. Apollon the aristocrat. Cupidon was the Negro, Apollon the white man. But as they walked up the well-worn path to the house they were no longer master and servant but two brothers, rejoicing in being home.

A turn in the path brought the house into view between the overhanging trees. It had never been an imposing house—not one of the storied Southern plantations—but its architect had had a good idea of form and proportion. It rose a story and a half from a high foundation, with a sweeping roof that projected in the front to cover a balcony the entire length of the house. Long French windows opened out onto the balcony and a row of dormers peeped out of the roof. A period of affluence in the house's history had added a row of Ionic pillars across the balcony, but these were now wood-colored, with only a few scales of white to show that they had once been painted. The pillar at the end of the porch had completely disappeared and had been replaced by a section of tree trunk to which the bark still clung. The steps leading up to the gallery had a handrail of plain wood, but the white palings were now broken like the teeth of a comb. Several of the panes of the windows were broken and had been replaced with cloth or paper. A fallen tree, propped against the side of the house and resting on the wreckage of an upper-floor dormer, testified to a past windstorm. Chickens scattered from the path as the two men walked up to the rotting boards of the steps.

"Haloo," Apollon cried out. "Mama, we're here."

"We'se here, Mama," Cupidon echoed.

They eased their packages down onto the floor of the veranda and stood by the open door. The first to arrive was a distinguished-looking woman, whose white hair was piled high with a large tortoise-shell comb. She was wearing a clean but bedraggled dress of some thin white stuff, set off by a blue sash around her waist. Her tea-rose complexion was heightened by skillfully applied rouge and her dark eyes devoured Apollon.

"My son, my son!" she cried, embracing him, and blocking the doorway temporarily so that the colored woman behind her could not get out. The Negress, herself a handsome woman, several years younger than the mother, sidled past her and threw her arms around Cupidon, hugging him to her ample bosom.

"They're here, Jeanne-Marie, they're here! Oh what a happy surprise." The white-haired woman spoke excellent French, with hardly a trace of accent.

"Shore is, M'dame Beatrix, shore is, 'n' 'bout time too." The colored woman spoke in English, but each seemed to understand the other. "Whar yo' boys bin? What yo'all bin a-doin'? How come yo' didn' let us know yo' a-comin'? Ain' nothin' fitten for yo' all ter eat but guess kin stir up somepin'. Shrimps we got, 'n' chicken too. Made us a gumbo fer our supper so guess we'll make out." She still clung to Cupidon, running her fingers over his sweaty skin.

"And you, Apollon, shame on you for arriving home half-naked." Madame Beatrix held him at arm's length to get a better look at him. "Where are all your fine clothes? I'll have Jeanne-Marie heat up some water and take it up to your room. I want you dressed for supper."

"All in good time, *Maman*," he smiled back at her. "Polin' a pirogue is no place for good clothes. Got to save them. Going to stay a month or so, so you'll have to get used to seeing Kewp and me this-a-way. We're going to hunt, swim, fish, shoot, and take it easy for a while. Then we'll be off again. Remember what I said, Mama? I'm going to dress you in silk and satin someday; going to hang diamonds around your neck; going to set you up in the Pontalba Buildings in New Orleans—you and Jeanne-Marie."

"We're happy here." She touched her finger to his lips. "We'd rather have you and Kewp with us here than live in New Orleans like a queen. Stay here with us, 'Pollon, don't go away again."

He returned her gesture, placing his own finger on her lips while he motioned to Kewp to hand him one of the packages, which he gave to his mother. While she unknotted the string that bound it, he nudged Kewp with his bare foot to hand the other package to Jeanne-Marie. For a few seconds both women were absorbed in undoing the twine, and both gasped with pleasure when the boxes were open. Madame Beatrix drew out a fringed black shawl covered with embroidered flowers, and Jeanne-Marie proudly displayed a sequined magenta headcloth.

"Kewp picked it out for you," Apollon said, to add to the colored woman's pleasure. "And now we'd better unpack our clothes."

Carrying their gifts, the women walked into the house and the boys followed. They waited for Jeanne-Marie to light the candle stubs in the salon. Here, too, were traces of former opulence. Apollon sat down carefully on a gilded chaise longue, mindful of its broken leg, and Cupidon lolled in an armchair, making a dark stain on its worn damask with his sweaty back. Both women found seats, and for a moment they all stared smiling at each other, until Apollon spoke:

"I'm thinking of getting married." He said the words casually, curious to see what effect the announcement would have on his mother, who showed her surprise but smiled happily.

"Time you did, 'Pollon. And who is the fortunate girl who will have my handsome boy for her own?"

"Haven't asked her yet, *Maman*. Mayhap she won't have me. And she's hardly a girl. I'd say she was at least five

217

years older than I am, maybe more. She's"—he stretched his arms wide and shrugged his shoulders—"a little on the fat side and she's cross-eyed."

"Apollon, *mon fils,* stop teasing your poor mother. If you're in love with her, she must be the most beautiful girl in the world because only the most beautiful girl would be worthy of the handsomest man."

"Who said anything about love, *ma mère?* Love doesn't enter into it. But folks say she is the richest woman in the South. Oh, she doesn't know I'm going to marry her yet. She's never even seen me, but that is not important because I'm going to marry her whether she knows it or not."

"And bring her here?" Jeanne-Marie sat forward in her chair expectantly.

Apollon shook his head. "No, we'll live at her place. Ever hear of it—Falconhurst in Alabama?"

His mother slowly nodded assent, trying to connect the name with something she had heard or known about. A light of recognition appeared in her eyes.

"Falconhurst . . . Falconhurst? Yes, I do know." She turned to the Negress. "Remember, Jeanne-Marie, the time Monsieur Beauchair went to New Orleans and bought that buck Vermillion?"

"Shore remembers that Vermillion boy—handsome buck he was. Masta Beauchair mated him up wid Morgana 'n' they had a sucker by the name o' Clovis. Masta sol' them to that man from Arkansas what was a-huntin' here."

Madame Beatrix nodded, looking to Apollon. "Your father purchased that Vermillion boy from Falconhurst. I remember because your father was always bragging about it. Best breed in the South he said. Having a Falconhurst buck on the place just seemed to set him up. My, how he pampered that boy—special food, good clothes, everything. Used to take him everywhere just to show him off. I always said poor Vermillion had his clothes off more than he had them on. Yes, I've heard the name Falconhurst—it was all your father'd talk about after he bought that boy and even after he sold him. Proud he was that he'd had a Falconhurst buck."

"Well, this woman I'm going to marry owns Falconhurst."

"She must be rich then."

"Heard on good authority she is."

"But you don't love her, Apollon." She rose and walked over to where he was sitting and ran her hand along his bare shoulder. "What will your life be like if you do not love the

218

woman you marry? When I think of how I loved your father. . . ."

"And did he love you, *Maman?*"

"Yes, he did." She was emphatic. "And it was I who suggested that he take Jeanne-Marie. It was the winter I was so sick, when you were a baby and I was no use to him. He could not marry me and make you legitimate, but he did send you to school in the North where color is not so important. He freed me and he freed you so that neither of us would ever have to stand on the vendue table. Yes, your father loved me and I loved him."

"He was a good man, 'Pollon," Jeanne-Marie added.

"Never paid no never-minds to me," Cupidon grumbled.

"But he never sol' yo'," his mother said. "Sol' all the rest but me 'n' Ol' Jason 'n' yo'. He let M'dame Beatrix brung yo' up right here in the house. Yo' never treated like no servant —more'n like a son."

Cupidon bowed his head in meek acknowledgment and when Apollon rose to go upstairs to his room, he went up with him.

It was hot in the upstairs bedroom. The closed window was thick with cobwebs in which were imprisoned the dried bodies of flies and wasps. The big double bed with its draped net filled most of the room. Nails on the wall supported castoff clothes which the boys had worn on their previous visits home.

"I a-sleepin' here wid yo', like always?" Cupidon asked expectantly.

"Ain' no other place unless you sleep on the floor." Apollon grinned. "And besides, it will be a relief sleeping with someone who won't be pawing me all night. But if you're going to sleep here, you got to wash. Can't stand you when you smell musky."

"Whyn't we go down in de bayou fer a swim? Yo' takes a bath up here, yo' a-sweatin' bullets when yo' gits through. Water nice 'n' cool in de bayou; sun's down so yo' won' git yore skin dark."

"Good idea!" Apollon had managed to get the window open but there was not sufficient breeze to cool the room. "Tell your mama to give us a tin of soft soap and here . . ." He rummaged in the drawer of a tall Empire chiffonier and found two old towels, one of which he threw to Cupidon. Unbuttoning his trousers, he let them fall in an untidy heap to the floor and stepped out of them.

"Wait till I shucks down." Cupidon undid the button of

his own pants, remembering how often he had done it for the inspection of the curious and for prospective buyers. He was safe at home now; he needn't worry about that any more. Wrapping the towels about their waists they abandoned the hot room, and raced down the uncarpeted stairs and out onto the porch.

They took the path to the water in bounding leaps, ran out as far as they could on the rotting pier, and dove in. Together they sported in the water like two porpoises, then proceeded to lather themselves from top to toe, submerging themselves to leave iridescent circles of soap bubbles on the surface. Now that the sun was down the air was cool and fresh and they clambered out onto the pier, scrubbed each other with the towels, then sat on the edge of the crumbling wood, dangling their feet in the water.

"After supper, 'Pollon, les' take the pirogue and go down to the Landin'. Plenty of nice Cajun girls there fer yo'; plenty o' nice wenches fer me." Noticing the look of indecision on Apollon's face, he continued, trying to make the prospect more enticing: "That Madeleine gal yo' useter like. She probably there."

Apollon shook his head. "No, I'm not going and neither are you. First night home we stops here and talks with our mamas. Then we go to bed early. Besides, I'm not like you. Like I told you, sleeping with women is my work. Now I'm on a vacation. I don't work on vacation, Kewp."

"Yo' mean . . . ?" Cupidon's disappointment showed in the drop of his jaw.

"I mean that this time we're home, no wenching, not even for you, Kewp. We'll do a little hunting, a little fishing, a lot of wrestling to keep us in condition, and a lot of sleeping. I don't want to arrive at that Falconhurst place looking like some dissipated old roué. Got to keep myself fresh and pretty. And if I can do it, you can do the same."

"After a week yo'll be changin' yore mind."

"Won't change it and nothing you say will change it either." His voice became sternly serious. "You just remember one thing. You go sneaking off wenching down at the Landing and I'll get out Papa's snake and slice you up. Jason may be old but he's strong and he and I can string you up. Don't forget one thing, *mon petit frère*, you belong to me and I can do as I want with you."

"If'n yo' say so, Masta 'Pollon suh." Cupidon became servile and fawning. "If'n yo' all dry, Masta' Pollon suh, we goes up to de house, Masta 'Pollon suh."

"Stop it!" Apollon stood up and wrapped his towel around him. "Stop your goddamn foolishness. It isn't my fault and it isn't yours. Blame God who made niggers black. Blame Papa Beauchair because he screwed your mother. Blame these stiff-necked goddamn white bastards who started it all. Kewp, I hate them—every goddamn one of them—and I'm going to screw them all. I'm going to get every cent I can out of them. I'm going to steal from their men, screw all their women, cheat them, lie to them, do anything I can to get every cent I can out of them. And when I do and when I make us a pile, we'll take our mamas and we'll get to hell out of this goddamn country to some place where every white bastard won't take a second look at me while he's making up his mind whether I have nigger blood in me or not."

" 'N' I'll be free too?" Cupidon asked.

"You'll be just as free as I am. I can't make you white but, by God, I'll set you free." He shook his fist at Cupidon. "But until then, boy, you're my slave and you'll act like one and I'm your master and I'll act like one. Keep in mind one thing. You do what I tell you to do and whatever I tell you to do because"—his clenched fist opened and he laid his hand on Cupidon's shoulder—"I'm figuring a way out of all this and I need you to help me."

"Come on, 'Pollon, I'll race you to the house." Cupidon slapped his brother smartly on his rump in the exact spot where a splotch of black skin, the size of an inky hand, stood out sharply against the ivory whiteness of Apollon's body.

Chapter 24

TRUE to his word, Apollon did not leave Les Chenes for a month, except for a number of daytime visits to the general store at the Landing, which performed a sort of mail-order service with some of the larger stores and tailor shops in New Orleans. By supplying his own and Cupidon's measurements to LeClair, the proprietor of the store, Apollon was able to order a complete new wardrobe for himself, and clothing for Cupidon that would be a reflection of his master's glory. Contrary to the general trend in sartorial splendor, Apollon decided to outfit both himself and his servant entirely in black—glossy black broadcloth for himself, set off by the whitest and most immaculate linen; shiny black mohair for Cupidon, with a bit of white lawn at collar and cuffs to accent the dark brown of his skin. Apollon Beauchair was an artist when it came to his own appearance; his decision on all black was based on the fact that the somber hue of his clothes would make his olive complexion lighter by contrast.

During their stay at Les Chenes, both he and Cupidon followed a well-organized schedule, which eliminated all liquor and women and gained them plenty of sleep and good food. For an hour each morning Apollon anointed his face, neck, and arms with a preparation concocted by Madame Beatrix. It was an old recipe which the octoroon women of New Orleans had used for many years and it was supposed to whiten the skin. Madame Beatrix made it of tansy leaves, calomel, glycerine, flax seed, and other ingredients. Although it accomplished little in bleaching Apollon's skin, it did seem to have the effect of refining it and making it more glossily smooth and fine-pored.

Each morning the brothers wrestled on the smooth grass under a giant oak. They lifted a heavy anvil, carried boulders, even lifted each other, until their muscles ached but broadened. Daily they fished in the bayou, Apollon wearing a broad-brimmed straw hat and cotton gloves, or hunted in the low delta scrub, bringing home rabbits, birds, and squirrels for savory stews and roasts. After the sun went down they swam in the bayou, ate an enormous supper, sat with their mothers for a while on the rotting porch, and then went to bed early.

It was also a month of activity for Madame Beatrix and Jeanne-Marie, as they busied themselves with infinitesimal stitches on fine lawn to make new shirts for Apollon. These they trimmed with delicate hand ruffles and insertions of lace salvaged from Madame's petticoats. There were shirts for Cupidon too, equally well made but plain. Then there were small-clothes to be made for both, long nightgowns for Apollon and waistcoats of dull-black brocaded satin (made from an old gown of Madame Beatrix') with gold buttons taken from Apollon's father's clothes.

So the days passed in a quiet peace that erased the lines of dissipation and worldliness from the men's faces. Apollon seemed content, but Cupidon longed for an evening's excursion into the Landing and an opportunity to nuzzle some wench. He knew several who would be only too willing. But Apollon's word was law, and although Cupidon did not believe that his brother would go so far as to have him whipped, he knew his quick temper well enough to realize it would not be wise to tamper with it. The bond of affection between them was closer than either of them recognized, but this affection could be changed, on Apollon's whim, to the relationship between master and slave in which neither their consanguinity, their love for each other, nor their long intimacy mattered.

Within a few days, Apollon announced, they would be starting on their journey—not in the pirogue and the osnaburg trousers in which they had arrived but in the smart black chaise with the white wheels and the pair of high-stepping black horses which he had purchased. The rig had made a big dent in his bank roll, but it was necessary for him to arrive at Falconhurst in style. Once there, he hoped, he would have no need for money. The richest woman in the South! Every penny that he invested now would be worth a hundred times itself if his plans went right. And they would go right! They had damned well better go right!

Together they rode into the Landing to get the clothes which had been ordered from New Orleans. For this trip Jeanne-Marie had refurbished the suit which Apollon had worn in New Orleans, steaming out the spots and pressing it. Now, with fresh linen and the white beaver hat well brushed, he looked like the young dandy he fancied himself to be. The black horse, broken both to saddle and harness, added éclat to his appearance. Cupidon's horse was equally fine, although his clothes were still rough. But then, clothes did not matter particularly to Kewp. In fact, he preferred to divest himself of all clothing as soon as possible and the wenches always liked him better that way.

The Landing was not much of a town. Rotting piers ran out into the river to accommodate an assortment of small craft and the wheezing little steamer which made a weekly trip from New Orleans. The street, if it could be called a street, ran along the edge of the bayou, ankle-deep with dust in the dry season and a mire of gumbo mud after a rain. Facing the street were the usual establishments of a small town. LeClair's general store was larger than the others, because it served not only the town but also many of the larger outlying plantations, as well as carrying a certain amount of river trade. It sat up high off the street, with a roofed veranda which was reached by a number of plank steps. In addition to the store, there was a livery stable, with the usual assortment of male hangers-on seated in its doorway; a blacksmith shop where hammers pounded against iron and sparks flew in the semi-darkness; a dressmaker's whose proprietor was said to offer evening entertainment to drummers; and a millinery shop with an assortment of dusty bonnets behind the fly-specked glass window. Next in importance to the store was the tavern and ordinary, which served liquor and meals and offered beds to drummers and hunting parties.

Everything about the town, with the exception of the store, was unpainted, leaning crazily awry or tumbling down. But despite its decrepitude, there was always a certain amount of excitement to be found there by those who lived out on the farms. It was a place for men to meet other men, a place where women could buy anything that was not raised at home, and so it took on a certain exotic appeal. In short, it was a metropolis to the farm folk. To Apollon it was scarcely worth visiting, for he had no contact with the whites and disdained any with the Negroes. But to Cupidon it was an El Dorado, because in the colored section, on those streets which wandered off the main river road, he would be a welcome guest at many of the shacks; the black girls had not forgotten him.

They hitched their horses at a rail under a big live oak, where the animals would be in the shade, and started walking toward the store along the uneven plank walk. As they neared it Apollon noticed, with some surprise, a smart open barouche approaching. It was a turnout rarely seen at the Landing and he knew it could come from only one place—the big, white-pillared plantation house of St. Denis, some ten miles to the north. He was even more surprised —indeed he gasped—when he caught sight of the young lady in the carriage, sitting under the shade of a black lace parasol which was held by her black girl. Seldom had he seen such a beautiful girl; she could not be over eighteen, he thought. He surmised that she must be the St. Denis' daughter, Denise, whom he had not seen since she was a child. If it was, *mon dieu*, how she had changed! Who would ever have imagined that that leggy colt with the mop of black curls could possibly have grown into this beautiful young lady? Here was a woman it would not be work to sleep with, a woman whose beauty equaled his own. What a pair they would make together!

Immediately Apollon began to change his plans. The St. Denis money might not be as plentiful as that at Falconhurst, but there was no comparison between the Falconhurst woman's overblown charms and this entrancing vision. Perhaps God had been on his side all along. Perhaps it would not be necessary to make the long trip to Alabama with this right here on his doorstep. He was in luck, such delectably wonderful luck. He continued to stare as he brushed the dust from his coat and rubbed his shoes against Cupidon's pants' leg until they shone once more. Settling his shoulders back, and bidding Cupidon follow him at a distance of a few paces, he started walking again just as Denise—and he was sure it was Denise—was being helped from the carriage by her footman, always under the shade of the black parasol held by her slave.

Apollon did not realize how he had been staring at the girl until he felt her eyes on him, appraising him as carefully as he had studied her. While he had noted black curls and ringlets peeping out from under the rose-trimmed Italian straw bonnet, she had seen his sleek black hair and the penciled favoris on his cheeks. While he had noted slumbrous blue eyes under black lashes, she had seen deep brown ones under even longer lashes than her own. His visualization of the firm young breasts under the sprigged taffeta bodice was no more vivid than hers of the two copper pennies hidden under his thin shirt. Each was looking through and beyond the sprigged taffeta and the lemon-colored trousers, sensing the hidden delights. Their eyes met, and she lowered her head in confusion until he could see only the rim of her bonnet, but almost immediately she looked up again and smiled at him. Then, with an imperious gesture, she beckoned to her slave to follow. Spellbound, Apollon watched her go up the plank steps into the store.

In an age when physical desire between a man and a woman was never acknowledged openly, such attraction was called "love at first sight." It became a poetic inspiration for languishing looks, idyllic nosegays, serenades beneath open windows and all the other accoutrements of romance. But there was nothing spiritual or romantic about this mutual desire which had so suddenly come to life between Apollon Beauchair and Denise St. Denis. It was physical desire, hot, lusty, and imperious. Each drew the other like a strong magnet.

Apollon's eyes followed Denise until she was lost from his view in the dim interior of the store. He turned to face Cupidon.

"I'll be here about half an hour. No need for you to come in, Kewp."

"Half an hour ain' long, Masta 'Pollon suh." Kewp remembered his status. "Got ter be pretty quick on de trigger in dat time."

"Thought you always were." Now that he had seen Denise, Apollon could recognize Kewp's need. "Half an hour it is, so you'd better get started quick. Be back here in thirty minutes. I'll wait ten minutes more for you and no longer. If you're not back I'll take the horse and go home. You'll have to walk. Make it a quick one this time."

Cupidon was gone before he finished speaking, his bare feet making little clouds of dust in the road. Apollon ascended the steps slowly and walked into the semidarkness of the store. It took a second for his eyes to become accustomed to the light, after the bright sunshine outside, but he soon saw the girl, standing in the back of the store, talking with the proprietor who was leaning on the counter, all attention to her words. Since his business was also with LeClair, he walked over to the counter and stood beside Denise, so near that by lifting a hand he could have touched her elbow. Her perfume—she used the French heliotrope, heady and pungent—intoxicated him, and he felt that she was as aware of his presence as he was of hers, even though she was pretending to be preoccupied with LeClair. He listened while she spoke to the proprietor in perfect English, with the slightest trace of French accent.

"Oh, M'sieur LeClair"—she looked down to see Apollon's strong, well-manicured fingers gripping the edge of the counter with such force that the knuckles were white—"I am in such a predicament. I do hope you can help me."

"Anything, Mam'selle St. Denis, anything!" LeClair spread his hands wide in a gesture that encompassed the whole store.

"We are having a ball at St. Denis tonight for my friends who are visiting from New Orleans, and at the last moment, the very last moment"—she fluttered her hands helplessly—"*Maman* has discovered that we are short of candles, wax candles, because of course we could not use tallow dips." She lifted her head so that the roses on her bonnet were now just below Apollon's eyes, and as she did so she seemed to lose her balance, so that she leaned, for one fleeting second, against Apollon's arm.

It was sufficient for him to reach out a hand to steady

her elbow, and for her to look up at him. Neither of them noticed that LeClair was scowling.

"Your pardon, m'sieur," she smiled. "How clumsy of me."

He saw the frown on LeClair's face, and relinquished her elbow and bowed.

"*Pardon*, Mam'selle. A clumsy boor like myself should not be standing so close." He bowed again and moved a foot away from her.

But when LeClair left the counter and mounted a stepladder to pull down some boxes from a high shelf, she inched closer to him again.

"I am Denise St. Denis of St. Denis," she whispered, and then apologized laughingly, "As you can see, my father is overfond of the name and it always embarrasses me."

"And I am Apollon Beauchair of Les Chenes." He decided to risk everything, for if she repulsed him now he knew his case was hopeless. He was gambling on the chance that she would not recognize the name. Les Chenes was so small compared to St. Denis it was altogether possible she had never heard of it. Nor of him, since he had been in the North at school and had been away most of the time since he returned to the South. She did not turn away. Instead, she smiled encouragement at him.

LeClair returned, his arms piled high with pasteboard boxes. "We have twenty dozen candles left, Mam'selle, the last ones. We'll never be able to get any more. And if that is not enough, perhaps I could steal four or five boxes from my wife upstairs."

"Oh, would you, *cher* M'sieur LeClair?" Denise was most grateful. "And would you have Hugo, our coachman, come in and get them and put them in the carriage?"

"*Certainement,* Mam'selle." LeClair noted that Apollon was busy examining a display of hair oils in a glass case. He walked the length of the store and opened a door which disclosed a flight of stairs. When the door closed behind him and they could hear his footsteps as he ascended the stairs, Apollon glanced around. Except for Denise and himself, the store was deserted, and two quick steps brought him beside her. Her hand sought his and he brought it to his lips but did not relinquish it. He pressed it lightly and the pressure was returned. Now she was so close to him he could hear the rasp of stiff taffeta as her breasts touched his coat, feel their softness and warmth against his shirt. She looked up at him.

"Apollon!" Her lips were trembling.

"Denise!"

His hand crept around her waist and she braced her body against his. Dared he risk the next move? But he had not been repulsed. Pulling her to him, he lowered his head to hers, questioning with his eyes and finding that her eyes invited rather than repelled. Their lips met, and now there was no question of her willingness, for her mouth sought his as avidly as his sought hers. For a long moment they remained together until he released her, unwillingly.

"You will think I am a shameless hussy, m'sieur," she smiled up at him, "and indeed I am. I do not know why I did this. Believe me, I have never done it before. It was something I could not resist."

"And neither could I." Passionately he drew her to him once more. But now he heard the sound of LeClair's footsteps on the stairs and he drew away, making a pretense of studying the hair-oil labels again.

LeClair stepped down into the store, his arms again piled high with pasteboard boxes, which he carried out to pile on the veranda.

"How glad I am that I am a hussy, *mon Apollon*." She came near him, ostensibly to study the hair-oil labels also. "From the moment I saw you outside, I *wanted* you to kiss me. Now, before he returns"—she nodded in the direction of LeClair—"tell me you will come to the ball at St. Denis tonight."

It was Apollon's turn to hesitate. He wanted this girl more than he had ever wanted anyone before. They were made for each other. But he realized that a chance meeting in a deserted store was far different from appearing at the big house of St. Denis with the scores of guests who would be assembled there.

She noticed his hesitation and pressed his hand urgently. "Say you will come, Apollon."

"I will come, Denise."

"I shall save the first *valse* for you. We shall open the ball together. At nine sharp. I shall be waiting for you on the portico." She pressed a handkerchief, heavy with heliotrope, into his hand and walked to the door.

In a few moments, LeClair returned. Without glancing at Apollon he reached down under the counter and pulled out several large cardboard boxes, tied together with tape. With a flick of his knife he cut the tapes and placed the boxes one by one on the counter, flipping off the covers as he did so.

"The suit of black broadcloth, Apollon."

Apollon winced at LeClair's neglect to address him as Monsieur Beauchair. He allowed his finger to slide over the dull satin of the label.

"The second suit"—LeClair opened another box—"identical with the first."

Apollon lifted it slightly from the box, admiring the expert tailoring.

"The suit for Kewp."

Apollon glanced at the black mohair.

"And the hat, the gloves, the cravats, the handkerchiefs." LeClair indicated the various objects. "And the watch and the ring." He held up a watch with a heavy chain, and a large gold ring with a flashing red stone which appeared as impressive as a real ruby. "If you'd like to try them on before you take them home, boy, you can use the storeroom out back. You can spread newspaper down on the floor so you will not soil the trousers when you put them on."

Apollon knew that LeClair's white customers were always invited to try their clothes on in the LeClair bedroom upstairs. However, he was accustomed to these slights. It was best to ignore them.

"I'll try them on at home, M'sieur LeClair. Now let me settle my bill." He waited for the proprietor to tote up the column of figures he had been writing down.

"Two hundred and fifty-seven in gold, Apollon; three hundred and fifty-seven if you pay in paper money."

"That's all I have." Apollon counted off the bills from the roll he had in his pocket. "Is Confederate money falling?"

"Every day," LeClair said glumly, replacing the covers on the boxes.

"Tie them in two bundles, please, so Kewp can carry one and I the other." Apollon waited until the bundles were made and carried them himself to the door, leaving them there to go out and wait for Kewp. But Kewp was already there, sitting on the hitching rail and grinning.

"That Lucinda, she at home. I jes' went in 'n' she say, 'Yo' back, Kewpie?' 'n' I say, 'shore am but in an awful hurry.' So she jes' shucked down quick-like 'n' so'd I. Then I jumped her. All over in a minute 'n' I been waitin' here fer yo' fer ten minutes a-wishin' I'd a-jumped her 'gain."

"Mayhap you'll have a go at another wench tonight. Ever try out any of the St. Denis wenches?"

"Ain' never been there, 'Pollon."

"Well, we're going there tonight."

"Thought yo' didn' like black wenches, 'Pollon."

"Who said anything about black wenches? I've been invited to a ball there by Denise St. Denis herself."

"But yo' ain' a-goin'!" Cupidon shook his head decisively.

"I damn well am going. And if things come out the way I want them to, we won't have to go to Alabama. To hell with that cross-eyed Maxwell woman. Old man St. Denis may not be as rich as she is but his daughter's a lot prettier. That's one woman I'd *like* to sleep with."

"But 'Pollon. . . ."

"Get on your horse and let's get home. We got ourselves thirty miles of riding to do. Ten miles home on horseback and twenty miles to St. Denis in the chaise. It's three o'clock already."

Cupidon continued to shake his head.

"Yo're shore crazy, 'Pollon."

"Crazy over that girl. I sure am."

"Well, 'Pollon, if'n anyone kin do it, yo' kin."

"Don't worry, Kewp. You pleasure yourself with the St. Denis wenches out in the quarters while I take Mademoiselle St. Denis right out from under her papa's nose. Chances are he doesn't know Apollon Beauchair from a hole in the ground."

"But if'n he do, yo' goin' to end up with a shot o' lead in yore belly."

Apollon grinned, and got on his horse. He tapped the side of his nose and winked knowingly at Cupidon.

"My luck'll hold out, Kewp. We'll have Jeanne-Marie make a conjure for us." He slapped his horse and headed for home.

Chapter 25

IT WAS only a little after eight by Apollon's new watch when they arrived at the big iron gates of St. Denis, now gilded by the light of flambeaux. Apollon, mindful of his nine o'clock appointment with Denise on the portico, drove past them, pulling up beside the road under the shadow of a grove of trees. There, in the almost total darkness, he slipped out of his New Orleans suit and into the new black suit. He had tried it on at home and he knew that it fitted perfectly. Kewp passed a rag over his shoes to remove the dust that had settled on them during the drive, and then turned the chaise and drove back to the St. Denis gates. This time they entered and drove up the long drive, guided by the blaze of lights from every window in the house.

The night was kind to St. Denis. Even the flambeaux did not reveal the overgrown gardens, the grass sprouting in the gravel drive, the sagging shutters, or the scaling paint on the white pillars. A servant in worn livery appeared out of the darkness to hold the horses while Kewp jumped down to help Apollon out. Kewp listened to the boy's directions to tie the horses at a long rail at the left of the house. Apollon remained on the steps for a moment, watching Kewp and the carriage depart and making a note of exactly where they were to be. Much to Kewp's disgust, Apollon had rescinded his permission for him to dally in the quarters, and had given strict orders for him to stay by the chaise.

Apollon knew that he was embarking on a dangerous venture—far more risky than anything he had ever done before. Previously his escapades had been coolly considered and carefully thought out, ruled entirely by his head. But this time his head had very little to do with his planning; something quite different was impelling him. His desire for Denise was so all-consuming that caution scarcely entered into his plans.

The big door of the house was wide open and a blaze of light streamed forth, making an orange path up the brick steps and onto the portico. Inside the house, Apollon could see a crush of people—an iridescent kaleidoscope of women's gowns, the glint of jewels, the black of men's coats, and the grey uniforms and yellow sashes of the military. Outside on the portico there was only the splotch of light and semi-darkness, but the ghostly whiteness of one of the far pillars seemed to move and he saw a billowing mass of white net materialize from behind it. In a second he had crossed the bricks and found Denise. She was all in white—filmy, diaphanous white—with a wreath of white May roses in her hair and a long garland of them extending from her shoulder down onto her skirt. With a little gasp she clutched at him, and he felt the moist warmth of her hand inside his own. With her finger to her lips she led him down the side steps on the portico to a sculptured clump of boxwood, black in the shadows. Once behind this, without a word of welcome, she abandoned herself in his arms, her hands searching his body frantically.

"I have lived through hell these past few minutes." She managed to speak despite his lips against hers.

"And I in heaven," he answered, "knowing that I would soon be with you."

"I was not sure you would come," she murmured. "The way I threw myself at you in the store, I was afraid no decent man would want me."

He laughed, while his finger outlined her lips and traced a path across her cheek. "But I am not a decent man, Denise. You did not throw yourself at me. We both realized that such a moment in our lives might never come again. There was no power on earth that could have kept us apart. I love you."

"Then this feeling I have must be love too, for since I left you this afternoon I have thought of nothing else but you." She separated herself from him, adjusted her dress, and let her fingers stray over his hair. But the separation was only momentary, for immediately they were in each other's arms again, until finally she took the initiative and held him at arms' length. "Come, Apollon, the dancing starts in a moment. I hear the fiddlers tuning up. We shall wait until they start dancing and then go in, making our entrance together."

"Together," he repeated.

The scrape of fiddles floated out into the night and they could see couples gliding past the long French windows. With her hand in his, they emerged from the thicket, and went up onto the portico and into the house through the big front door. Those in the hall made an aisle for them, grey uniforms and black coats bowing low as they traversed the hall and paused for a moment at the wide entrance to the large room, cleared of its furniture for dancing. All eyes were upon them as Apollon opened his arms wide and slipped his right arm around her waist. Their feet caught the tempo of the waltz and they glided out onto the floor. Slowly they circled the dance-floor on the outside of the other dancers, and as they passed the matrons, seated on small gilt chairs along the wall, they heard long-drawn sighs of admiration. Everyone knew Denise St. Denis but none of them recognized the handsome stranger she was dancing with. *Mon Dieu*, but they made a handsome couple!

Apollon and Denise were so close together now that he could feel her heart beating against his chest. He could feel his own heart answering in the same mad rhythm. Her scent of heliotrope was aphrodisiac, the nearness of her body, intoxicating. Feeling too cônspicuous on the perimeter of the dance floor, he guided her through the maze of couples to the center of the room, until they were directly under the big chandelier, completely surrounded by dancers. One by one the other couples faded away, until finally Apollon realized that he and Denise were alone on the floor. A ring of admiring faces had formed around them—a circle of multicolored gowns and uniforms—and as they danced one of the women started clapping her gloved hands together. Others joined in the applause as the waltz approached its coda. But instead of stopping, the orchestra played on, and now, with the knowledge that they were the center of attraction, Apollon struggled to regain his wits, to overcome the effect of the perfume and the nearness of the beautiful girl in his arms. Concentrating entirely on the intricacies of the dance, he wheeled Denise in ever faster and more complicated measures, while the clapping and the "Bravos" from the onlookers increased.

Without warning, the air of the ballroom was suddenly electrified by a sound like a pistol shot. The orchestra struck a false note, and lapsed into silence. Apollon, with Denise still in his arms, saw the clapping circle of men and women fall back and open up to disclose the figure of a man standing in the doorway, a long black whip in his hand. He raised his arm, and the whip snaked out over the floor, cracking again like a pistol. He was a slender man, clad in plum color, with a pointed "imperial" that heightened his likeness to the French Emperor. His scowl, the blaze of anger in his eyes, and the grim set of his mouth were reflected in the group of men, most of them in uniform, who followed him. He strode directly up to Apollon and Denise, staring straight at Apollon.

"Take your dirty black hands off my daughter."

Apollon relinquished Denise and bowed low to the man.

"Do I have the honor to address Monsieur St. Denis?" he asked.

"I am St. Denis, but who are you?"

"Apollon Beauchair, and for your information, monsieur, my hands are clean, and as you can see, they are not black." Apollon stretched out his two hands for St. Denis' inspection.

"A nigger's hands are always dirty."

"*Hélas*, monsieur, but I am not, as you say, a nigger."

"I told you he was Apollon Beauchair and he is," said a young sandy-haired man in the uniform of a lieutenant,

233

who was standing beside St. Denis. "Aren't you a nigger, 'Pollon?"

"I am not," Apollon answered with quiet dignity.

"No?" St. Denis pursued the question. "I believe otherwise." He turned to the young man beside him for confirmation. "Your mother was a slave of Othon Beauchair of Les Chenes."

"You are misinformed, monsieur. My mother was the daughter of the Vicomte de Noailles, staff officer to His Imperial Majesty, Napoleon the First." Apollon was thinking quickly and his words were glibly plausible. "My father was Apollon Beauchair, a *magistrat* of the city of Montpellier in France."

A look of bewilderment caused St. Denis' jaw to sag. "I do not understand. . . ." He hesitated, then added lamely the one word, "monsieur."

"And neither do I understand, monsieur. Your charming daughter invited me to attend a ball at your home. I came here in good faith only to be insulted by my host." Apollon stripped off one white glove from his hand and advanced a step towards St. Denis, his hand raised. Then, seeming to swallow his sense of insult, he lowered his hand. "I shall not ask satisfaction from you, Monsieur St. Denis, because I intend to ask for your daughter's hand and it would hardly seem fitting that I should kill you before I make that request."

"There has been a mistake. I am sorry." St. Denis was embarrassed, and he handed the whip to the young lieutenant beside him. "I thought you were . . ."

"Apollon Beauchair, the mulatto son of my uncle?" Apollon smiled as he drew the white kid glove back onto his hand and meticulously fitted the small pearl button into the buttonhole. "It is indeed unfortunate that my uncle should name his bastard after my father and also unfortunate that the mulatto and I are about the same age. Where the fellow is, I have no idea. I have never seen him as I have but recently arrived here from France. As the only surviving member of my uncle's family, I inherited the plantation of Les Chenes. Had I realized it was such a worthless piece of property I would not have come all the way from France, under such conditions as your war imposes, to claim it. Now that I am here I find it not even worth selling. And it seems that neither my namesake Apollon nor his mother are my property, as my uncle manumitted them before his death. So, I return to France, Monsieur St. Denis, and"—he took

234

Denise's arm—"I had hoped that I would not return alone."

"I shall go with him, Papa." Denise spoke for the first time.

"Are you going to believe this cock-and-bull story, Mr. St. Denis?" The young lieutenant stepped a pace nearer to Apollon. "I tell you this man is Apollon Beauchair, the son of the owner of Les Chenes and the woman they call Madame Beatrix, his octoroon slave. I know! I ought to; I've known 'Pollon since we were boys. Our plantations adjoined. We played together—him and me and his black brother Kewp and my boy Casco. We hunted, fished, and swam together 'most every day." He stopped suddenly, snapped his fingers together, and then exclaimed, "By God, that's it! We swam together! I can prove that this is the same Apollon Beauchair I knew. Yes, gentlemen, he appears as white as any of us. But look at him! Look at him closely! Study him! At first you will not notice any trace of nigger blood but as you study him you will become suspicious. Notice his lips —just a little too wide. His nostrils—a little too broad. His hair—a little too curly in spite of the hair oil he has put on it. Look, sirs, look! But even those points may be open to debate, so listen to me. Nigger blood shows in one way or another, and if this is the Apollon Beauchair whom I know, he has a black mark as big as my hand on his. . . ." He stopped in confusion and lowering his voice, whispered in St. Denis' ear, "smack-dab on his ass."

The color had drained from Apollon's face. He felt Denise's hand withdraw from his own. Inside he was trembling, for he had recognized the young lieutenant as Jeff Farnham, and he was fully aware that Jeff knew his secret. It would take all the bravado he possessed to get out of the present situation. He had already forgotten Denise; now he was concerned only with saving his own skin.

"And what do you propose that I do, messieurs?" He managed a smile which he hoped would pass for complete self-assurance. "Would you that I strip myself before you like a slave ready for the vendue table that you may inspect the more private parts of my anatomy? Surely you can take the word of a French gentleman for who I am and what I am."

St. Denis spoke. "Surely, as a gentleman, you will not mind proving to us that you are not the Apollon Beauchair we thought you might be. The matter of Negro blood is a serious affair here in Louisiana. If you are Apollon Beauchair of France as you claim, not only I, but all of these

235

gentlemen, will offer you our most abject apologies and I shall gladly consider your request for my daughter's hand. If you are not. . . ." St. Denis grabbed the whip he had only moments before relinquished.

"I refuse to submit to such an indignity." Apollon bowed low to Denise, raised her hand to his lips and kissed it, then turned again to the men. "Allow me to depart, messieurs, and on the morrow I shall have papers delivered to you, proving exactly who I am. I did not bring them with me tonight as I did not feel that in a civilized society one must carry one's *carte d'identité*. It will be furnished you tomorrow together with letters from my *procureur* in New Orleans, and letters from my family in France. These I shall send by special messenger for your inspection. And now, with your permission, I shall depart. Please have your servants call my groom."

"Not so fast." Young Farnham put his hand on Apollon's arm, restraining him. "Why should we wait till tomorrow when you can prove who you are tonight? We insist on knowing. You have come here; you have danced with Miss St. Denis; you have had your arm around her waist and your lips have touched her hand. We refuse to wait until to-morrow."

There was a muttering of assent from the assembled men. Several more stepped forward and surrounded Apollon. At a gesture from St. Denis they followed him, with Apollon in their midst, out of the ballroom, down the long hall, and into a large room, lined with book shelves. No sooner had St. Denis closed the door than there was a frantic pounding on the outside. He opened it and Denise would have rushed into the room, but her father's outstretched arm barred her entrance.

"Go to your mother!" he commanded.

"But Papa. . . ."

"Even now you have disgraced yourself and me enough. Think, girl, think! You may have danced with a nigger. We must know."

"Apollon is not a nigger," she sobbed, "and even if he were . . ."

"And even if he were?" St. Denis stared at her.

"I love him."

He pushed her from the door, closed it and locked it, then turned to the men, standing grim-faced around Apollon.

"You shall now accommodate us, monsieur," St. Denis

236

said. "You see I am giving you the benefit of the doubt until proved otherwise."

"And I refuse to strip myself naked before these men. It is a gross indignity which no man should be subjected to. I have offered to give you conclusive proof if you will but wait until tomorrow. Surely you can delay a few hours."

"We do not wait in the South when the honor of our womenfolk is involved," a voice from the rear said.

"What are you afraid of, Frenchy?" said another. "A bare-assed man is no rare sight in the army. We've seen plenty."

Apollon was frightened. His bravado had left him. Alone, against twenty men, he knew he had no chance. His words were useless but he could not stop them.

"Please, messieurs." He was pleading now. "Permit me to leave in peace." But even as he was speaking he realized that nothing he might say would be of any avail. Strong hands grabbed his arms and held them outstretched, rigid. St. Denis himself took hold of the end of his cravat and ripped it off. Other hands stripped off his coat and unbuttoned his shirt. He felt the waistband of his trousers loosen and saw them slide to the floor. The strength of the other men forced him to bend over, and then he heard Farnham's triumphant voice and felt the slap of his hand against his flesh.

"Look! I told you that he was a goddamn nigger. Now will you believe me?"

And Apollon knew that they were looking at the black birthmark which spread like an inky hand on the ivory skin of his rump. How he had cursed it in the past. He had always insisted on blowing out the candles when he bedded himself with a woman, and on getting out of bed in the morning and into his drawers without his companion of the night ever seeing that telltale black mark. Up North it had excited only good-natured comment, but here in the South it was the stigma that proclaimed his ancestry.

"Goddamn nigger!"

"Arrogant son of a bitch, forcing his way in here."

"Hung like a nigger too! No white man ever hung like that."

"Nigger bastard!"

"Let's teach him a lesson so he'll never force himself on a white woman again."

"Hang him."

"String him up."

237

"No, gentlemen." Apollon heard St. Denis' voice. "There'll be no murder here."

"Are you a nigger-lover, St. Denis? He might have raped your daughter. Goddamn randy, these mulattoes."

"My daughter is safe, I assure you of that. She was mistaken as we almost were. But I shall not countenance murder."

The hands that held Apollon did not relax, and it was impossible for him to straighten up. He saw the varnished boots of St. Denis pass behind him and then he heard the screech of the whip as it cut through the air and took its first bite into his flesh. He screamed, and as he did so he realized he was screaming like any other nigger slave under the whip. But all his pretensions were swept away with that one searing pain, and he continued to shriek and implore mercy, just as his African ancestors had done, while the lash descended again and again. He felt the warm stickiness of blood running down his legs but still the blows continued, until a merciful blackness engulfed him and he could feel no more.

He was awakened by the jolting of the chaise. For a moment he could not orient himself, until the searing pain in his back caused him to remember all that had happened. He was on his knees on the floor of the chaise, his elbows on the seat. At last he mustered sufficient strength to look up, and saw Kewp driving. His groans and his movement alerted his brother.

"Yo' all right, 'Pollon boy?" Kewp's voice was warm with sympathy.

"No! No! No! I'm not all right. Goddamn them all. Where are we, Kewp? Are they following us?"

"We 'bout five miles no'th o' de Landing. Ain' none o' dem hot-headed sodjers a-followin'. They was a-comin' but Mista St. Denis he say any man a-followin' yo' 'countable to him. He awful mad but he say he ain' never killed nigger nor white 'n' he ain' goin' ter have murder on his conscience. We be home soon, 'Pollon. Yo' want ter stop 'n' put yore pants on? They threw 'em in on de floor."

"God no! Let's keep going. Am I bleeding much?"

"Cain' see now, 'Pollon, but yo' a-bleedin' plenty when they dumped you in de kerridge. Took a couple o' whacks at me 'fore I could git started. Cut my hand with they's goddamn whip."

"White bastards think they're God."

"Ain' a-goin' ter be God much longer, 'Pollon. Our time a-comin'. Servants all a-talkin' in de kitchen. Sayin' as how de Yankee gunboats a-sailin' up de river. Goin' ter take N'Orleans right soon. Goin' ter set us niggers free."

Apollon groaned as he shifted his weight. "Us niggers! Now I know how you feel, Kewp. I know how it feels to be shucked down and have people paw at your body." He lowered his head on his brother's knee, and there he wept.

Kewp's hand rested on Apollon's head. "Ain' never done nothin' ter me, 'Pollon. Feel sorry fer yo', I do. Mighty sorry. Yo' proud, 'Pollon. Yo' ain' never wanted to be no nigger. Yo' always tried to be white man 'n' yo' are a white man. I'se nigger. Cain' do nothin' 'bout it. Black I am 'n' black I'll al'ays be. But yo' my brother, 'Pollon. When they hurts yo' they hurts me."

"Everything would have been all right if it hadn't been for that goddamn Jeff Farnham. Figured he was in the army but the son of a bitch was home on leave."

"He a worthless skunk, 'Pollon. Ain' half so good as yo'."

Apollon's hand reached up and grasped Kewp's. They rode on through the darkness, each listening for hoofbeats behind them, which fortunately did not materialize. Suddenly Kewp stopped the horses and wound the reins around the whip socket. He unbuttoned his jacket and reached inside, drew out something and placed it in Apollon's hand. An odor of heliotrope scented the night air. Apollon raised himself up while Kewp made a light with his tinderbox. Inside the web of lace there was a folded piece of paper, and by the tiny flame Apollon read it.

"Good-by, Apollon." The fine letters on the note blurred before Apollon's eyes. "I thought I loved you very much and I shall never forget you but it's impossible now."

"Maybe not as impossible as she thinks." Apollon threw away the note but kept the handkerchief. Even in his pain, its scent excited him "Someday, Kewp, I'm going to give her what she wants."

"Yo' goin' ter rape her?" Kewp snickered.

"Can't rape that kind, Kewp, they're too willing. You say the Yankees going to take New Orleans, Kewp?"

"So they a-sayin'."

"Well then, we'll wait and see. Times are changing, Kewp boy. Our day's a-coming. Let's get home. Your mama will know how to heal me up quick. We're going to Alabama and make these white bastards pay for all they've done to us."

Chapter 26

MADAME BEATRIX was well versed in the beauty secrets of her octoroon sisterhood, but Jeanne-Marie had the more practical knowledge of the roots and herbs which cured the flesh. From the dry, pungent bunches which hung in the hot attic, she compounded a vile-smelling poultice which healed Apollon. The pain departed from his body but the scars on his mind remained deeply graven. Formerly the wounds which had injured his pride had been minor ones—the occasional, sudden departure of a man who had been standing beside him at a bar; the neglect of a tradesman to use "Mister" before his name; a puzzled inventory of his face by a stranger; or the treatment he had always been accorded by the whites at the Landing. These he had been able to ignore, although they had stung him deeply. Now he brooded over the public insult to his cherished body at St. Denis, and the taunt of "nigger" which still rang in his ears.

He was fully aware that he had been born a slave, because of that one-sixteenth or one-thirty-second or even one-sixty-fourth (although Madame Beatrix called herself an octoroon she was less than one-eighth colored) of Negro blood in his veins. But he had been sent North in his teens, after careful tutoring by his indulgent father, and in the small private school in Connecticut, where he had been educated, he had been treated exactly the same as the other boys. His French name explained his dark hair and ivory skin; nobody at the school was aware that he had been touched by the tar-brush. To faculty and students alike he was the legitimate son of a wealthy Southern plantation owner—a true scion of Louisiana aristocracy. He had been popular with all his classmates, mostly sons of wealthy Northern families, and had been invited to their homes for Christmas and spring vacations where he had been enthusiastically received by their parents. His manners were perfect, his culture inbred and not superficial; and his determination to be liked made him a welcome guest.

After he had graduated from the lower school he had spent a year at home, mostly hunting and fishing with Kewp. His father was ailing, which was sufficient excuse for them to forego all social activities, and Apollon had enjoyed the easy life of the crumbling plantation. At his father's insistence, he had gone North again, this time to abolitionist Boston, where he had enrolled at Harvard College, renewed old acquaintances, and made many new ones. He was not a good student, but a facile memory coupled with his personal charm had enabled him to get through. During his senior year his father had died and he had received word through a New Orleans firm of lawyers that his tuition and expenses would be paid through his graduation but that that would exhaust the estate. With this communication he had received another formal document, which granted him his manumission from servitude. This he had carefully hidden, while he continued to be popular among his classmates, visit their homes, and make love to their sisters. It was doubtful that any of them would have believed that the dashing Apollon Beauchair had so recently been a slave. With the abolitionist feeling running high in Boston, it was also doubtful that such a fact would have mattered very much.

His power over women and his fascination for them had been early apparent to him, and he had quite taken it for granted that all women would desire him. His conquests were so easy he soon began to feel an arrogance which assured him that any woman he wanted could be his for the asking. Older women especially doted on him, and his last two years in puritanical Boston had shown him the inside of many bedrooms on austere Beacon Street and Louisburg Square, which visits had supplied him with new clothes, abundant pocket money, and even greater assurance of his ease of conquest. Small wonder he came to make women his career.

The only time Apollon had ever been grateful for his slight attenuation of color was when it had kept him out of the army. Negroes were not permitted to serve in the Southern forces. He had no sympathy for the Southern cause and was uninterested in that of the North. Had he himself still been a slave, he might have volunteered to fight for the North solely to obtain his own freedom. But he was no longer a *servant for life*—a slave—and the fact that Kewp, although he was his own half-brother, now belonged to him made slavery seem justifiable.

As a matter of fact, Apollon had never been overly interested in anything or anyone but himself. He was accustomed to getting what he wanted, and so far what he wanted had always come to him. He enjoyed victimizing the whites; it gave him a feeling of power and superiority over them. Until

241

he had met Denise St. Denis, he had never had a real failure, and his inability to have his way with her stung him deeply. Here for the first time was a woman—a white woman—he really desired—perhaps even loved—and he had suffered a most terrible disgrace and humilation at her house. It was a canker that ate into his soul, for not only had he lost her but his own status had been brought most miserably before him.

The first few days, while he had lain, belly down, in the hot little upstairs room at Les Chenes, with his body so filled with pain he could hardly move, he had raved and sobbed in his utter inability to do anything about the situation. But by the time he was able to sit up again his sense of humiliation had become an iron determination to avenge himself. The Falconhurst woman would provide the money that he lacked for the position he wished to occupy. The debt incurred at St. Denis would be paid in full.

This time he was including Kewp in his planning, and together they sat for hours, rehearsing their campaign. Apollon discovered a new side to his brother. The boy was not stupid, only uneducated and untrained, but with a quick intelligence that sometimes grasped a point even before he did himself. Then, too, there was a difference in their relationship now —a new loyalty on the part of Kewp, new affection and consideration on the part of Apollon. They realized, of course, that once away from the plantation their relationship must revert to its former status if their plans were to succeed. But only on the surface. Underneath, the old distinction of master and slave had disappeared.

Came the day of their leaving and, once more in his fine clothes, seated in the smart and shiny chaise with the black horses, with Kewp as well dressed as himself, Apollon felt reassured. There was no longer the problem of having to pass through the Confederate lines, for with the fall of New Orleans to the Northern troops, the entire Delta was in Union hands. He planned to say he was traveling to offer his services to General Butler, the military commander of New Orleans, and he was able to substantiate this claim by his Northern credentials—his sheepskin from Harvard, letters from old classmates in the North, and communications from prominent families in New England—including one from the Sumner family, the most dedicated of all abolitionists, at whose home in Massachusetts he had spent a vacation some few years ago.

But that would be only the first part of his journey. From

Union-conquered territory, he must once more enter Confederate jurisdiction in Alabama. Here again his fertile imagination helped him. Among his father's papers he found the Falconhurst bill of sale for the slave Vermillion and, by a careful forgery of Hammond Maxwell's scrawled signature, he wrote out an agreement whereby he had leased the services of the slave Kewp from the owners of Falconhurst for a year's time for stud purposes, on the express agreement that he return the said slave, Kewp, in person at the expiration of a year. He was not sure of the date of the death of the master of Falconhurst, but it was a risk he would have to take. According to the terms of the agreement, Apollon was only carrying out his part—returning valuable merchandise to its owner at trouble and expense to himself. The goddamn Southerners were great sticklers for a gentleman living up to his agreement. It was one thing they would respect, come hell or high water or even passing through the Confederate lines.

He experienced no difficulty in traveling from Les Chenes to New Orleans, and at Belle Chasse, where there was a ferry across the Mississippi, he met a former acquaintance from the North, a certain Lieutenant Channing who was in charge of the ferry. Accepting the Lieutenant's invitation to dinner and to spend the night at an appropriated plantation house, he further learned, during an evening of reminiscence about mutual friends, that another acquaintance of his, Bob Bradford, was now stationed in New Orleans as Provost Marshal of the city. Things were beginning to look up for Apollon.

Another day's drive brought him into the city. Armed with the safe-conduct pass which Channing had written out for him and a letter of introduction which the lieutenant had given him for the Provost Marshal, he had Kewp drive him directly to the Saint Louis Hotel. He would have preferred the St. Charles, but General Butler had commandeered that hotel for his headquarters. However, the Saint Louis served very well. He was quite certain he would meet none of the Southerners whom he had hoodwinked in the past, for New Orleans, now in Union hands, offered scant hospitality to Confederates. He was right. The hotel was filled with blue uniforms.

Apollon had planned to spend only a day in the city, leaving as soon as possible to get through the Confederate lines into Mississippi and then on into Alabama. He had only the

243

vaguest idea of where Falconhurst might be. The town named on the Falconhurst bill of sale was Benson, but the whereabouts of this obscure hamlet was a mystery. However, inquiries at the hotel gave him the desired information—that it was in the southwestern part of the state, not far from the Tombigbee River. With a landmark as prominent as the Tombigbee to guide him, Apollon knew he would have little difficulty in finding the plantation.

However, the amenities of the Saint Louis with its efficient service, its comfortable rooms, and its perfect meals were so enticing after his months at Les Chenes that he lingered on for a few days, calling on Captain Bradford to renew his acquaintance and through him meeting several other of his friends.

Kewp, with plenty of leisure on his hands, was able to ingratiate himself once more with those New Orleans wenches who had so eagerly sought his favors. Many a back door in the Vieux Carre opened eagerly for him. Through the grapevine that ran from servant to servant and house to house, he was able to hear more gossip than Apollon, and he learned the almost incredible news that Denise St. Denis was not only in New Orleans but that she was being held at Union Headquarters, a prisoner.

"A prisoner? Denise!" To Apollon it seemed so fantastic as to be incredible. "That's impossible. She isn't even in New Orleans."

"Reckon she is, 'Pollon boy." Kewp was sure of his information. "Spen' dis afternoon wid Sue-Betty. She servant for the DesMoulins 'n' they lives nex' do' to the St. Denis house here in de city. She good fren' o' Miss Denise's wench, Gloryann. Yisterday Miss Denise lef' de house wid Gloryann to visit her frien', Miss Babette somethin' o' other. De two gals a-walkin' down ter visit 'nother frien' what lives in de Pontalba Buildin'. Miss Denise 'rested 'n' taken to de Provost Marshal what held her in de jail all night. Folks at de St. Denis house right crazy a-thinkin' she daid. This mornin', ol' Masta St. Denis, he found she in jail 'n' he madder'n a wil'cat. Goes a-high-tailin' it over to de Provost Marshal 'n' dey threw him out. Den he wen' to Gineral Butler hisself. Challenge de Gineral to a duel 'n' de Gineral threw him out. Hell to pay."

Even now it was difficult for Apollon to believe it. But why should they arrest Denise? Certainly she was neither a spy nor a dangerous personage. However, he decided to call

244

on Bob Bradford to see what it was all about. Maybe he'd have the St. Denis family eating out of his *nigger* hand yet.

When he descended the staircase into the lobby, several of the Union officers called out to him and he returned their greetings, walking out the front door to where Kewp was waiting in the chaise. It took only a few moments to drive to the office of the Provost Marshal and, once there, the sergeant on duty recognized him and admitted him to Captain Bradford's office.

" 'Pollon! How nice to see you," Bradford exclaimed, rising to shake hands with his visitor. "Say, how about eating with me tonight? We've a fairly decent mess at the St. Charles."

"Might take you up on it, Bob, but frankly this is not exactly a social call. I'm here to inquire about a prisoner of yours."

Bradford laughed. "Well, that's one thing we've got plenty of; take your choice—black, white, male, female. Which one in particular did you have in mind?"

"Miss Denise St. Denis."

"The little spitfire?"

"But surely you did not arrest her for that?"

"But surely we did." Captain Bradford searched among the papers on his desk, found the one he was looking for, and handed it to Apollon. "Perhaps you have not seen this, although everyone else in New Orleans has. We're at war now, 'Pollon, and war is often unjust although sometimes injustice seems necessary. Since yesterday this is justice or injustice, depending on how you look at it."

Apollon glanced at the sheet of paper Bradford handed him. Large, inky-black letters on sturdy paper showed that it was a public announcement for posting in the city. As he read it he was at first shocked, then pleased. Butler knew how to take the starch out of these stiff-necked Southerners.

GENERAL ORDER NO. 28
HEADQUARTERS DEPARTMENT OF THE GULF
NEW ORLEANS, MAY 15, 1862

As the officers and soldiers of the United States have been subject to repeated insults from the women (calling themselves ladies) of New Orleans, in return for the most scrupulous noninterference and courtesy on our part, it is ordered that hereafter when any female shall, by word, gesture or movement, insult or show contempt for any officer or soldier of the United States, she shall be regarded and held liable to be treated as a woman of the town, plying her trade.

Benj. F. Butler,
Major General, U.S.A.

By Command of
GEORGE G. STRONG, A. A.
CHIEF OF STAFF

Apollon read it and whistled. *"Mon Dieu!* Your general doses them with strong medicine."

Bradford was deadly serious. "It was necessary, 'Pollon. We've had little or no trouble with the men. But the women! They have certainly acted like women of the streets and so we have decided to treat them as such."

"And Miss St. Denis?" Apollon could easily picture her being a ringleader. "Did she insult by word, gesture or movement or otherwise show contempt for an officer or soldier of the United States?"

"Did she? By word, she called Major Gifford a dirty polecat; by gesture she spat in his face; and by movement she kicked his shins."

"She did that?"

"With unholy aptitude and apparent pleasure."

"So you arrested her?"

"As a wanton, a whore, and a prostitute—as a woman of the town plying her trade."

"Good God!" Apollon stared at Bradford with incredulity. "You've stirred up a hornet's nest. Surely you do not intend to hold her."

"We had planned on holding her only a few hours merely as a token punishment. But she acted like the devil incarnate and more than one soldier carries the marks of her teeth and nails. Then her fond papa arrived breathing fire and brimstone. He managed to get in to see General Butler and applied some most unflattering epithets to the old boy. Even threatened to kill him. So Butler started seeing red and told St. Denis off and threatened to keep the girl till the war ends. In the meantime, however, with a little taste of the Parish Prison, she has already lost most of her defiance and is spending her time in tears. Can't say I blame her—it's a pretty grim place."

"Would it make any difference if I were to see General Butler and inform him that the young lady in question is a very good friend of mine whom I hope to make my fiancée?"

"It most certainly would. Provided you would be responsible for her if she is released. It's become an impossible situation. We naturally don't want to hold her, but under present conditions we've got to save face. Tell you what, 'Pollon. Let me see Butler. Come back in an hour." He put his hand on Apollon's shoulder. "My congratulations, old friend. She may be a little spitfire but she's devilishly beautiful."

Apollon accepted Bradford's congratulations and left, only to return again in an hour and find the Captain wearing a broad grin.

"Everything's been arranged," Bradford said. "The fair lady will find the prison gates opening for her under your hand and will depart on your arm. You'll have our thanks as well as hers. You'll conduct her to her home and to her fire-eating papa and you'll have his thanks as well. The whole St. Denis family will fall on your neck and beg you to marry her with their blessing."

Apollon had his own mental reservations about old man St. Denis falling on his neck and blessing him. He had no intention of escorting Denise home, at least not until after she had visited his room at the St. Louis. He waited while Bradford wrote out an order for her release, then called an orderly and told him to conduct Apollon to the Parish Prison.

Once inside the prison gates, he was admitted into the woman's section. It was a bare, sunburned courtyard, which gave entrance to a row of barred cubicles. For a moment he was almost overcome with nausea. The stench of urine and human excrement was increased by the damp heat and mingled with the rancid odor of sweaty garments and lice-ridden bodies. From the small barred windows, the cries and screams of the imprisoned women issued forth, their words filthier than their surroundings.

In the last cell Apollon found Denise.

When the jailer opened the door she was lying in the filth of the floor. Although she had been there less than twenty-four hours her hair was damp and matted, her face streaked with dirt and tears, her thin dress of sprigged organza as dirty as the floor she was lying on. Apollon's shadow fell across her and she looked up numbly, blinking her eyes in the sudden light of the open door. But she soon recognized him as he stood before her so immaculate and clean in contrast to her own filthiness.

She half rose and came toward him on her knees to clasp him around the legs. "Apollon!" He felt the warmth of her face and the dampness of her tears against his thighs.

"I've come to take you out of here, *ma petite*." His hand sought her face and lifted it.

She stared up at him and suddenly released him, to sink back on her heels, eying him suspiciously through the touseled strands of hair. He could see the conflict of desire and repulsion written plainly on her face. Then slowly the corners of her mouth drew down in contempt.

"Get out," she whispered harshly. "Get out. What right have you to come for me, you nigger? I'd rather stay here until I rot than leave here with you."

"Denise," he begged. "I once told you that I loved you and I still do. Come, let's leave this place."

"Apollon." She seemed calmer now, almost ashamed. "I should never have said that I loved you. It was stupid. How could I love you without knowing you? You're good-looking, Apollon, too damned good-looking, and that was all I saw. Now I see more."

"Does who I am or what I am really matter, Denise, if I can take you away from this?" His hand touched her shoulder and lingered there, and he could feel her whole body trembling.

"It is no disgrace for me to be here," she said proudly. "But if I were to leave here with you, I would never be able to hold up my head again. Please go, Apollon." She was suddenly humble, and the tears streaked down her soiled cheeks. "Regardless of what you are, I still want you. I want you more than anything in the world, believe me. I dream about you at night. Probably I always shall. But I had rather die here than have you touch me. Oh, don't you understand? If you touched me, I might yield and that I must never do. Please go."

Now his eyes, too, filled with tears. He held out his arms to her, imploring.

"Denise."

For a long moment she hesitated, torn between desire and denial, but then she backed away from him to crouch in the far corner of the cell.

"Go! Go, Apollon," she cried, "before I start screaming that you are trying to rape me. Even these damned Yankees would protect a white girl from being raped by a nigger. Oh, for the love of Jesus and His mother, go, Apollon, and pray God that I shall be able to forget you."

He stepped backward over the threshold, out into the light, and she flung herself against the door, banging it closed. The jailer was joking with the harridan in the next cell.

Fortunately he had not heard. He seemed puzzled to see Apollon alone.

"She prefers to stay," Apollon said. "She prefers to be a martyr to a lost cause. Let her stay."

"I'll go with you, cutie." The woman in the cell next to Denise reached out a grimy paw. "Take me, handsome, and you'll not be sorry. O-o-o-o, what I couldn't do for you."

He flipped a coin into her outstretched hand and walked away. As he gained the end of the row of cells, he looked back. Hands were waving to him from all the barred windows except that of Denise. Her face was pressed against the bars, staring at him hopelessly.

Chapter 27

APOLLON rushed back to Bradford's office, explaining somewhat incoherently that he had been able to effect nothing in the way of releasing Denise. She preferred, he said, to remain a martyr to the Southern cause. Anything between them was over forever! She had called him vile names, the least of which were Union-sympathizer, Damn Yankee and Nigger-lover. Why, she had even accused him of being Negro himself! A most ridiculous accusation, Bradford agreed, from a hysterical girl who was carried away by her ill-placed patriotism. Well, he advised, let her cool her heels a few days longer with her sisters in the Parish Prison. Would Apollon dine with him at the officers' mess that night? Apollon declined. Now he only wanted to quit himself of New Orleans as quickly as possible. No telling what rumors might start to circulate from the St. Denis family. Even though Bradford and the others would not believe them, he wanted to be far enough away not to have to refute them.

With Cupidon he made fast work of packing and getting out of the city. As he had anticipated, he had no trouble getting through the Confederate lines. Apparently everyone in the South had heard of Falconhurst and its breed, for the young lieutenant who passed him through was far more interested in Kewp than he was in his master. He had, so he said, never seen a Falconhurst slave although he had heard about them all his life. Would Apollon let him satisfy his curiosity and examine Kewp? He'd sure like to see the boy shucked down and know if all the things they said about Falconhurst slaves were true. Apollon agreed and Kewp co-operated. The lieutenant was quite satisfied and indeed impressed when Apollon informed him that Kewp had knocked up over thirty wenches in the year that he had had him. The lieutenant called in three of his fellow officers to marvel along with himself at Kewp's perfection and all congratulated Apollon on the forthcoming crop he would have and the high prices prime niggers would surely bring after the war. Despite the fact that the Union forces now held New Orleans and most of the Mississippi, they were all sure that the war would be over in a few months. Apollon's French name and his manners and good looks passed him without any suspicion on the part of the Confederate officers, who, coming from South Carolina, had a vague idea that all Creoles were olive-skinned.

But his good looks did not tempt him to seek hospitality in any of the big plantation houses he passed in his journey through Mississippi and Alabama. Better by far to stay in the inns and ordinaries along the way, which, though bug-ridden, dirty, and uncomfortable were far more impersonal. He felt it would be wise to revert to his "alien" status and pose once again as a French subject. Even among the rustic and illiterate owners of the inns, his adopted title of Vicomte de Noailles engendered a certain amount of awe and respect. It not only explained the fact that he was not in uniform, but eliminated any suspicion as to his birth. It would, he felt certain, make him doubly appealing to the mistress of Falconhurst.

They reached the small town of Benson just as night was falling. Apollon decided to forego the dubious pleasure of eating in the miserable tavern which seemed to be the only place the town afforded. He stopped only long enough for Kewp to go inside and ascertain the road to Falconhurst, and they proceeded. Now, so near his goal, he was nervous and he sensed a reflection of his own nervousness in Kewp. Everything depended on the outcome of the next few hours. So many things might happen. The lady herself might not be there; she might have married in the meantime; she might even have died. Apollon's money was nearly exhausted and even if, in the last extremity, he had to offer Kewp for sale, where would he find a buyer. The whole state was plainly impoverished.

His hands trembled as he rehearsed once again with Kewp their plan of action. As far as either of them could see it was not only perfect but foolproof, provided—ah yes, *provided*—the mistress of Falconhurst was still alive, still unmarried, and as susceptible to Apollon's charms as he hoped she would be.

The gateposts of Falconhurst came into view and he was heartened to see lights in the house, shining at the end of the long avenue of trees. At least someone besides the servants was in residence. It appeared to be a larger house than he had anticipated, quite as imposing in its dark silhouette as any he had seen in his journey. Family money had built a house like that; there must still be money after the sale of thousands of slaves at high prices. Goddamn it, there had better be.

Kewp halted the horses just inside the driveway and Apollon took off his hat, loosened his cravat, and unbuttoned the collar of his shirt. He stretched out on the seat, slumping down in it, and for an extra dramatic effect let one leg hang over the side of the chaise. With a knowing look at Kewp, he spoke.

"You know what to do, Kewp boy?"

"Shore do, 'Pollon."

"Then let's get started." Apollon laid his head back on the seat and closed his eyes. "Whip up the horses, Kewp, you've got a dying man on your hands, boy."

Kewp touched the whip to them and they galloped up the drive, scattering gravel to right and left. He pulled up at the pillared portico and abandoning Apollon, now stretched out with eyes closed and mouth agape, apparently unconscious, he dashed up the steps and pounded on the front door. He did not have long to wait. A young Negro of about his own age opened the door and confronted him. Kewp quickly appraised him, noting his good looks along with his stained and worn clothes.

"Needs help quick, I do." Kewp gasped out the words. "Masta a-dyin'." He jerked his thumb backwards to where the carriage showed in the light of the door. "Took awful bad, he is."

The boy who had answered the door seemed undecided what to do.

"Ain' there no white folks here?" Kewp pressed the question anxiously.

"Miz Sophie, she here, a-eatin' dinner."

"She yore mist'ess?"

The boy nodded.

"Then run 'n' fetch her if'n yo' kin git de lead out o' yo' ass. My masta a-dyin'."

He waited until he saw Drummage back away, then ran down to the chaise.

"She here, 'Pollon," Kewp whispered, as he hovered over the inert form of his master. "Servant gone to fetch her. Think she a-comin' now." Kewp rushed back, to see a woman coming to the door. He noted her blonde plumpness, her soiled and bedraggled lace gown. Waiting until she arrived at the door, he bowed low. "Servant o' de Vee-comte, Mist'ess ma'am, please. My masta took awful sick. Think he 'bout ter die. Cravin' yore help I am. Don' know what ter do, Mist'ess ma'am. Saw de lights o' de big house a-shinin' 'n' came here."

Sophie seemed to rise out of her lethargy.

"Where is he?"

"In de kerridge, mist'ess ma'am."

Sophie rushed through the door and down the steps of the portico. The lights from the doorway shone full upon Apollon, and Sophie stood beside the carriage, gazing up at him. His face, even with eyes closed and mouth agape, was by far the handsomest she had ever seen, and she noted the long powerful legs, the heavy chest, and the column of his neck, exposed by his head's being thrown back on the cushion of the chaise. His labored breathing was evidence of his extremity. Reaching up, she grabbed one of his limp hands and chafed it between her own.

"He's alive." She turned quickly and called back to the boy, still standing in the doorway; "Drummage, run 'n' get Brute 'n' go out in the barn 'n' get Zanzibar. Tell 'em to come quick. Don' know who dis man is but he mighty sick. Got to git him inside." She kept rubbing Apollon's hand. "Who is he?" she asked Kewp beside her.

"He my masta, mist'ess ma'am. He de Vee-comte de Noailles from France, ma'am. I'se Kewp, his servant. Took awful sudden ridin' 'long de road. He ain' dead is he ma'am?" Kewp started to sob, managing in his excitement to squeeze out real tears. "He de bes' masta in de worl', ma'am. Don' let him die."

There was a commotion around the side of the house and the boy Drummage came running up, followed by two Negroes—a middle-aged man and a boy about Kewp's age. Sophie relinquished Apollon's hand and started wringing her own.

"Git a chair, boys, git a chair 'n' ease him inter it so's you

252

kin tote him upstairs. Whar Candy? Have her spread down Papa's bed. Whar Lucretia Borgia? Have her heat up some water. Needs us stoneware jugs ter put at his feet. Gotta warm him up. Cain' let this man die."

Drummage soon appeared from the hall with an armchair. With Kewp up in the carriage and willing hands below to receive him, Apollon was lowered from the chaise onto the chair, where Kewp held him upright while the others carried him up the steps into the house. Apollon wanted to open his eyes and see what kind of a place it was but he knew he must not. Kewp would be able to tell him about it afterwards. Slowly, they carried him up the broad staircase, down a hall and through an open door. He was laid on a bed.

Sophie was again giving orders.

"Yo' boys kin leave now. Zanzibar, put the man's horses in the stable. His own boy 'n' Drummage will git him into bed. I'll go 'n' get Lucretia Borgia started. Need to git his feet warm to draw the blood from his head." She shuffled out in her worn carpet slippers.

Apollon could hear Kewp talking with the other boy.

"Yore name Drummage?" Kewp was asking.

"Yo' Kewp, that yore name?"

"My name Cupidon but they calls me Kewp."

" 'N' mine Drum Major but they calls me Drummage." He looked down at Apollon. "Yore masta shore a fine-lookin' fellow. Kinda resembles yo', only he's white 'n' yo' black."

" 'N' he French 'n' I bo'n in Louisiana. He a Vee-comte, he is." Kewp was drawing off Apollon's boots.

"Whazzat?" Drummage was removing the coat, lifting Apollon to slip off the sleeves.

"Yo' awful ignorant," Kewp replied. "Tha's like a King in France o' like Pres'dent Jeff Davis here. Mighty 'portant man, my masta is. He a-goin' back ter marry up wid de Queen of France 'n' he takin' me wid him. I a-goin' ter be King o' all the niggers in France. Goin' ter dress up 'n' ride in a gold coach. Now he sick 'n' a-dyin' perhaps we don' go never no mo'." Kewp deposited the boots on the floor. "Yo' go on, git him undressed. I a-goin' down, take de valise out of de kerridge. Whar de barn here?"

Drummage pointed to another door than that from where they had entered. "Down them stairs 'n' yo' goes out another do' to de kitchen, den out de back do' 'n' de barn straight 'head. I finish takin' off his clotheses."

Kewp departed and Drummage continued removing Apollon's shirt, then undoing the buttons of his trousers, and by lifting one leg at a time, he slipped them off, noticing the fine quality of their material and workmanship. He had just folded them and laid them on a chair when the door opened and Sophie entered, a stoneware jug wrapped in flannel under one arm. She hesitated for a moment on the threshold, seeing Apollon lying on the bed in only his linen drawers. Her eyes met those of Drummage across the room.

"He come to yet?" she asked.

Drummage shook his head, "Ain' open his eyes."

Sophie came to the bed and placed her hand on Apollon's forehead, smoothing back a lock of hair that had fallen across it. "Whar's his boy?" she questioned.

"Gone down to fetch de valise from de barn."

"Well, what yo' waitin' fer?" she asked impatiently. "Why'n't yo' a-gittin' him ready fer bed—gittin' him undressed."

"Waitin' fer his nightshirt what his boy gone to fetch."

"A man a-dyin' 'n' yo' waitin' fer a nightshirt? Git his drawers off 'n' git him under the blankets. Needs to git him warm. Catch a chill that way."

Drummage divined her thoughts and grinned up at her with an impudence he would never have dared use in the days when either Hammond Maxwell or Augusta was at Falconhurst.

"If'n I take his drawers off, he be naked, Miz Sophie. Yo' ain' a-wantin' to see dis here man stark naked, is yo'? Ain' respectable, is it?"

Had the bed not been between them she would have slapped him, but her arm did not reach him and he ducked back, grinning. With the same impudent grin he unbuttoned Apollon's drawers and drew them off. He let out a low whistle and observed Sophie's eyes as she stared at Apollon. Drummage knew his present mistress only too well. He was well aware of what happened on her rides with Zanzibar and he himself lived in mortal terror that her fancy would light on him. She had pressed the point several times, but so far he had managed to avoid her. All white women, but particularly Sophie, were repulsive to him. Still grinning at her, he drew up the sheet and blanket over Apollon.

She slipped the hot water jug under the blanket, and as she placed it at his feet she felt the sleekness of his calves and thighs. Then, straightening the sheet, she fluffed up the pillows under his head.

Apollon slowly opened his eyes, stared vacantly into space, then closed them again.

"He better, Miz Sophie." Drummage leaned over the bed. "That hot water cure him already."

Sophie shook her head, listening to the slow footsteps on the stairs. Soon Lucretia Borgia pushed open the door and came in, shaking her head gravely.

"Pore man, pore man. He's a-dyin'."

"He jes' opened his eyes," Sophie said hopefully.

"Maybe dead already." Lucretia Borgia lumbered across to the bed and leaned down, putting her ear against Apollon's chest. "Heart still a-beatin'. Why ain' someone give him some brandy. Ain' no one in this house got no sense? Drummage, git yo'se'f down to de pantry 'n' git de brandy bottle. Fix him a toddy with de brandy. Not too hot, 'n' not too sweet. Who're yo'?" she asked as Kewp came in with the valise.

"Kewp," he answered. "I servant to him." He placed the valise on the floor and rummaged through it, pulling out the long white nightshirt. "Better put this on him." He looked first at Lucretia Borgia and then at Sophie, hoping they would leave, but they remained, staring down at Apollon.

Lucretia Borgia grabbed the nightshirt from Kewp's hand and lifted Apollon gently, slipping it over his head.

"I a-takin' care o' this pore man now. Have him right well soon. Ain' got us no doctor here no mo'. But I fix him." She drew a small black bottle out of her pocket. "First we wakes him up wid brandy, then we puts him back to sleep with dis laud'num. Whar that slow-foot Drummage?"

"Comin', Lucretia Borgia, comin'." Drummage entered with a glass on a silver tray. Lucretia Borgia took it, tasted it, and decided it was not too hot. Slipping her finger inside Apollon's lip, she slowly poured the mixture into his mouth, noticing that he gulped it down. The hot mixture, which was nearly all brandy, so stung his throat and choked him that he could no longer keep his eyes closed. He opened them and this time he looked around, first at Lucretia Borgia who was holding him and then at Sophie.

Feebly and with great effort, he managed to speak.

"Where am I?"

"Yo're safe, suh, 'n' in good hands." Sophie leaned over him. "Now don' yo' worry, mistah. We're a-takin' care o' yo'."

"Thank you." Apollon's voice grew a little stronger. "Sorry to be so much trouble."

"Ain' no trouble 'tall." Lucretia Borgia eased him back onto the pillow. "Falconhurst al'ays ready ter help anyone in trouble."

"Falconhurst?" Apollon asked.

255

Sophie nodded. "I'm Miz Sophie Charnwood, owner o' Falconhurst Plantation. These my servants Lucretia Borgia 'n' Drummage. Yo' in pretty bad shape when yore boy brought yo' here, Mista. Yo' a-feelin' better now?"

Apollon struggled weakly to move his head. "I am . . . I am the Vicomte de Noailles."

"He what?" Lucretia Borgia asked Sophie.

"French, I guess. A Vicomte in France is somethin' like Dudley is in England. Means a lord or somethin'."

"My gratitude ma'am, for taking me in." Apollon managed to concentrate his gaze on Sophie. "Can I prevail on you to feed my servant, Kewp, and put him up for the night? I fear I too must further encroach on your hospitality as I do not feel strong enough to move."

"Falconhurst yore home, suh, lon's yo' wish to stay. Ain' no trouble to us." Sophie was all graciousness. "See to your servant, we will. Drummage take care o' him. We ain' got many servants now, suh."

"Bet yo' hungry too," Lucretia Borgia said. "I'll go down 'n' dish up that chicken soup we havin' fer supper. Do yo' good to git somethin' hot in yore belly. Don' think yo'll be needn' the laud'num now. Color come back to yore face." She plumped up the pillows behind him.

"*Oui, oui*, I am feeling better," Apollon admitted. "Kewp'll go with you to fetch the soup."

"Drummage fetch it," Sophie said.

"Fetch it myself." Lucretia Borgia flounced out.

Sophie drew up a chair beside the bed and sat down. "Yo', Drummage, go 'n' show this Kewp boy where he git his supper and where he bed fer the night. I'll watch over him till yo' come back." She turned to Apollon. "Jes' cain' recollect yore name, suh."

"Call me Apollon."

"Apollon! My, that's a pretty name."

Kewp followed Drummage out of the room, casting a backward look at Apollon. Things were working out well. They were inside Falconhurst, welcome to stay as long as they wished, and, Kewp knew, nothing brought out a woman's possessive instincts as much as a sick man. Sophie was already as happy as a fox in a chicken yard.

After they left, Sophie reached over and placed a hand on Apollon's forehead. "Yo' ain' got no fever."

His hand reached up to clutch hers. The big red stone in his ring flashed like a burning coal in the light of the oil

256

lamp as he placed his hand over hers. "You have saved my life, madame. I am truly grateful."

"Ain' nothin' 'tall." Sophie did not draw her hand away. "Nothin' we wouldn' do fer anyone. Glad yo' a-feelin' better."

"Must have been my heart." Apollon sighed and patted her hand. "The doctors in Paris told me I must be very careful. I've had these attacks before and I fear I shall continue to inconvenience you for several days unless there is an inn or a tavern near here."

"Wouldn' sen' a dog nor a nigger to that tavern in Benson. Yo' a-stayin' right here where Lucretia Borgia 'n' I kin take care o' yo'. Ain' a-gettin' out o' that bed. Falconhurst pretty lonely these days. My papa's dead, Miz 'Gusta's dead, 'n' my babies in England. Here all 'lone I am, 'cept the servants. Mighty glad to have company."

Apollon struggled to sit up, but fell back on the pillows exhausted, gasping for breath.

"What yo' tryin' to do, suh?" Sophie was genuinely concerned.

"I must leave, madame. I would be compromising you if I stayed here."

Sophie smoothed the bed covers up over him, laughing while she did so. "Shush! Cain' compromise me, Mista Apollon. Been married, had two children, been divorced. Cain' nothin' compromise me. I'm Sophie Maxwell o' Falconhurst. Don' give a damn for nobody." She gave him a knowing look.

Kewp appeared at the door with the bowl of soup and Sophie rose reluctantly to leave. As she stood beside the bed Apollon took her hand, brought it to his lips, and kissed it.

"Shall I see you in the morning, madame?"

"Shore will." Sophie smiled. "My room jes' nex' do'. If'n yo' want anythin' in the night, yo' jes' sing out. I hear yo' 'cause I sleep light. Better have yore boy leave the lamp turned down." Slowly she withdrew her hand and, gathering the frowsy flounces of the lace gown around her to leave the room, she halted in the doorway for a moment to smile back at Apollon, who returned her smile wanly.

"Good night, madame. You are as gracious as you are beautiful."

The door closed slowly behind her. Kewp stood poised with the bowl of soup. Apollon sat up, hanging his legs over the edge of the bed.

He winked at Kewp and whispered: "Well, here we are boy, so far so good. Give me that soup, I'm hungry."

Kewp shook his head from side to side. "Yo' a-goin' ter make love to dat woman, 'Pollon? How yo' a-goin' ter do it?"

"Business, Kewp, business. She's rich; we're poor. She wants loving, I want money. It's a fair exchange. She's going to pay for what she gets. I'm going to work for what I get. It won't be easy, I assure you."

Kewp was still shaking his head.

"Mighty pretty gal down in de kitchen. Her name Candy. She dat Drummage's woman 'cause he showed me whar they beds together in de nex' room to whar I sleeps. Shore wishin' I was a-beddin' with her. She right beautiful, 'Pollon."

"When I get to be master here, Kewp, you can have her. Tell me, what's the place like?" Apollon surveyed the room, the heavy, expensive mahogany furniture, the bed with the tall carved posts, the mirrored armoire, the rich carpet and draperies. All of them bespoke wealth despite the dust and the general slovenliness.

"Big house," Kewp answered. "Look mighty fine. Big stables with a big kerridge too. House look kinda dirty though. All 'cept the kitchen. That big woman, that Lucretia Borgia, she one yo' got ter watch out fer. She ain' no fool like the white woman. Yo' make love to the white woman but yo' make up to the colored one too. Somethin' tell me she runs this place 'n' Miz Sophie do 'bout as she say. She awful old but she mighty pond'rous."

There was a knock at the door. Apollon swung his legs back into the bed, waved his hand in a warning to Kewp and closed his eyes. Kewp opened the door and Sophie reappeared. She had changed her gown for a more elaborate one—cleaner also—and tidied up her hair.,

"Jes' wanted to make sure yo' all right." She hesitated on the threshold.

Kewp put his finger to his lips and whispered his reply. "Thank yo', mist'ess ma'am. Masta done fallen asleep. He much better now. Kin I sleep on de floor aside him? He might be a-needin' me in de night."

"Don' 'low no servants ter sleep in these rooms, boy." Sophie turned to go. "My room jes' nex' do'. I hear him if'n he call out."

"Thank yo' kindly, mist'ess ma'am." Kewp turned down the light and followed her out. "Guess my masta mighty sick man."

"He be better in the mornin' but don' think he oughta move round much for a week or so. Look boy, yo' tell that Candy wench down in the kitchen to come up 'n' help me. Yo' go to bed. Drummage tell yo' whar yo' sleep?"

"Yes ma'am, mist'ess ma'am."

"Then go to bed." Sophie waited until she heard him traverse the length of the stairs and go into the kitchen. Quietly she opened the door of Apollon's room and walked over to the bed. He seemed to be sleeping soundly and she stood over him, devouring him with her eyes. Quickly, for a woman of her size, she bent down and touched his brow lightly with her lips. Without turning, she backed out the door, keeping her eyes on Apollon.

"He shore a lot prettier 'n' that Zanzibar," she said to herself, " 'n' jes' as strong, 'n' jes' as big. I do declare, he the prettiest man I ever did see in all my life. Wishin' he wasn't sick though. No, I'm glad he's sick. Jes' hope he never gits well. Jes' like to take care of him always 'n' keep him right there in Papa's bed."

Chapter 28

IT WAS A QUESTION whether Apollon would have suffered any more in the ensuing week had he been really as ill as he feigned. For a healthy man to confine himself to a week's inactivity in bed and be watched, nursed, and babied was quite enough to make him feel almost as ill as he pretended. The only moments of privacy he had were when he insisted he must sleep. Then, with Kewp guarding the door, he would get out of bed and pace up and down the room like a caged animal. He was never entirely safe, for a rap would sound on the door and Sophie would arrive with a bowl of invalid pap or some delicacy which she and Lucretia Borgia had concocted. The latter, quite as assiduous as Sophie, was in constant attendance on him.

No longer was his room dusty or ill-kept. Candy, supervised by Lucretia Borgia, kept it shining, and Drummage, at Sophie's orders, rubbed the furniture daily with lemon oil and turpentine until it gleamed like a mirror. Lucretia Borgia would appear with clean linen sheets and pillowcases, while Sophie kept the vases filled with roses and oleander. With such a constant coming and going, Apollon felt he would have had more privacy had his bed been set up in the lobby of the Saint Louis Hotel.

He and Kewp had little opportunity to talk, and when they did they had to converse in whispers. Apollon was anxious to know more about Falconhurst and its resources. His window gave a view of an overgrown flower garden and a lawn grown high to grass and weeds—nothing else. From what little he could see, it certainly did not look like the abode of the richest woman in the South. But even the greatest of the Southern homes were showing signs of wear and neglect, owing to the shortage of slaves and the scarcity of materials. Before the war an establishment such as Falconhurst would have been cultivated by hundreds of slaves. Kewp reported that the house was large and expensively furnished, with a dining room agleam with silver and a drawing room with ornate and costly crystal chandeliers. Outside there were extensive barns, workshops, and slave quarters not far from the big house.

"And the famous Falconhurst slaves?" Apollon asked.

Here Kewp was in a quandary. There were some, he assured Apollon. About—and here Kewp had to count on his fingers—twenty of the slave cabins were occupied, with a man and a woman and a number of children in each. The long dormitories for single men and women were, however, deserted, as was the birthing house. The occupants of the slave cabins were engaged in cultivating a few fields only. Out in the stables there was a fellow called Big Randy who was in charge, and with him another fellow called Sampson. The real boss of the barn, however, Kewp informed Apollon, was Zanzibar, who was Miz Sophie's groom and who rode with her nearly every day. Then there was a group of three or four wenches who did spinning and weaving, a man called Malachi, who was a carpenter, and another called Jude, who had charge of the flocks. These were all under the jurisdiction of Brutus—who was called "Brute" —a middle-aged man with greying hair. A big, fine-looking woman, who was called Big Pearl and who was Drummage's mother, lived in a cabin by herself with another son, Drummage's brother, called Olly. This cabin, Kewp said, was better than the rest, as Drummage had furnished it with castoffs from the big house.

But where were the Falconhurst slaves; those who were sold every year in New Orleans and who commanded such fabulous prices?

Kewp thought he had the answer. Down the road a stretch,

260

there was a settlement called New Quarters. It was composed of more small cabins than Kewp was able to count and contained a large number of men, women, and children, all of whom worked on Falconhurst land. These then must be the Falconhurst slaves, Apollon decided. Sophie must be holding them for sale after the war, letting them earn their own keep in the meantime. It was a smart idea and she must have been a smarter woman than he had given her credit for to have thought of it. By so doing she kept her stock at no expense to herself, and once the war was over she would be able to dispose of them at the high prices everyone claimed they were going to bring.

That accounted for the outside slaves. The big house, Apollon knew, had Lucretia Borgia, Drummage, a boy by the name of Pip, Candy, and, according to Kewp, a kitchen wench by the name of Marguerite, who hurt his eyes everytime he looked at her. Drummage said they had tried to get rid of her but couldn't; he had even taken her to Benson once and abandoned her there but she had managed to find her way home. Kewp shook his head sadly. Goddamn ugliest girl he had ever seen; couldn't even talk straight because of a harelip. He shuddered. It appeared the wench had taken a liking to him, but he had eyes only for Drummage's Candy. She had let him know that his attention would not be unwelcome if only Drummage was not around.

So Apollon learned of Falconhurst from what he heard through Kewp. Yes, there was wealth here, no doubt about that. Each day Sophie appeared in a costly toilette, with different jewels which Apollon could see were genuine. Her sloppiness had disappeared along with the bedraggled lace dress she had worn the night he arrived. Now she always appeared tightly corseted, her hair elaborately coifed and her dresses immaculate. She no longer took her usual daily horseback rides with Zanzibar in attendance, Kewp reported.

Even a less practiced eye than Apollon's would have had no difficulty in discovering that Sophie was already madly infatuated with him. She had not, as yet, made any move to reveal her feelings, but that was hardly necessary. It was quite apparent that she could be had for the asking. But Apollon was not anxious to rush matters. With the memory of Denise's kisses still on his lips, it was going to be more difficult than ever to make love to this older woman. Still, she was not too bad-looking; not so repulsive that it would be impossible. She had a certain air of the aristocrat about her, and this to Apollon was always a challenge.

After a few days of custards, soups, and gruels, he was ready for something more substantial to eat and longed for the gumbos, pilaus, and temptingly seasoned foods of his Creole home, or even the baked beans and chowders of Boston. It was Lucretia Borgia who came to his rescue and insisted that he eat more nourishing food to regain his strength. He blessed her, and thereafter he reveled in ham and chicken and a wide variety of vegetables, bolstered up with an assortment of hot breads and topped off by rich pastries and slices of Lucretia Borgia's famous pound cake. Apparently there was no dearth of food at Falconhurst, as there was beginning to be at so many places in the South.

Came the night when he was considered able, by his two nurses, Sophie and Lucretia Borgia, to come downstairs to dinner. With Kewp on one side of him and Drummage on the other, he descended the wide staircase slowly, step by step, and then, after a rest in one of the high-backed chairs in the hall, he was again assisted into the dining room, where the immense mahogany table was laid for two.

Now, with his own eyes, he could see the glories of Falconhurst. Remembering Kewp's first impression of dirt and slovenliness, he was surprised to find the place clean, polished and shining. He was glad he had not yielded to the temptation to buy the elaborate dressing gown he had seen in New Orleans, for an even more elaborate one of garnet brocade, which had belonged to Hammond Maxwell and had apparently never been worn, had been found for him. It was a trifle short in the sleeves but its satin lining felt smooth against his skin.

Sophie was resplendent in a gown that would have done justice to the Opera in New Orleans—a garish concoction of orange taffeta and black Chantilly, which did, however, provide an effective contrast to her blonde hair. She was wearing a necklace and earbobs of diamonds and topazes. Even Drummage's soiled clothes had been cleaned and pressed and he looked nearly as smart as Kewp. In fact, Apollon was forced to admit to himself, this Falconhurst Drummage was even better-looking and more prepossessing than his own Kewp—taller, stronger, and better featured, with curly hair instead of Kewp's kinky skullcap.

Lucretia Borgia, with the help of her slattern Marguerite, had produced a creditable meal, but Apollon was more interested in the heavy silver on the table. The huge glass and silver epergne was filled with roses. The immense coffee urn steamed with a rich aroma and the massive candelabra supported a dozen candles each. Everything testified to Falconhurst wealth, and this wealth was now concentrated in the fluttery, posturing woman across the table from him, who was so obviously trying to impress him. She was a plum, ripe for the picking—if somewhat overripe—and he was going to pluck this prize.

After dinner he was helped out to a rocking chair on the front portico, where Sophie sat beside him while Drummage served her a jewel-like glass of liqueur and Apollon a hot toddy. He was rather nonplused at the warm drink, until Sophie informed him it was an established custom of her father's and grandfather's. After sipping it he agreed that it was pleasant and potent, with a cooling effect in spite of its warmth.

"This place a big responsibility for a lady what's all 'lone in the world." Sophie languidly waved her hand to indicate the overgrown garden and the fields beyond. "Needs a man here, it does. My papa always kep' things good 'n' 'Gusta always overseein' the house. Now I got to do it all. 'N' things diff'rent now. Ain' got the servants we useter have 'n' cain' seem to get no work outa those we got. Lucretia Borgia she a-gettin' old. Drummage he a good boy but he more int'rested in wenchin' 'n anything else. Brute he manages the fields but he pretty hard on the hands. Say he cain' get nothin' outa them less'n he whops 'em 'n niggers gittin' so independent they runs if'n they gits whopped. Olly good with the whip though. Mayhap he lay it on too hard sometimes. Whopped one boy so hard he died." She shook her head sadly. "Don' know how much longer this war a-goin' to last. Don' know how I a-goin' to get started 'gain onct it's over." She brightened up. "Don' guess I'll ever start in again. Don' really need to. Papa lef' me well off." She glanced up at Apollon to see what effect this might have made on him.

"A great responsibility, madame, a very great responsibility," he agreed. "Far too much for those dainty hands of yours."

Sophie looked down at her blunt fingers with the square-cut nails. Dainty hands! Nobody had ever said that to her before.

"Was your father killed in the war?" Apollon asked.

"No." Sophie relinquished her fan and dabbed at her eyes with a bit of lace. "He taken sick up in Raleigh. Word came to us 'bout it by his boy Ajax. Soon's 'Gusta—she my step-mama," Sophie explained "—hear 'bout it, she go by train to Raleigh. Papa still 'live when she git thar but he died 'n' then she took sick too 'n' she die. That leave me all 'lone here wid my babies, 'n' then their papa, what live in England, he sen' for them. Say with the war and all it better for 'em in England. Begged me to go too but never was in love wid Dudley so's I stayed here. 'N' Dudley, he divorce me 'n' I glad. Never could stan' Dudley. He a weak, pukey sort of man. But he a fair man. Paid me ten thousand pounds, English money, but cain' use it 'cause it in England in a bank there with some of Papa's money. 'Fore he lef', Papa sol' a big caffle in New Orleans 'n' sent mos' of the money to England. Say it safe over there. But he put mos' o' his money in banks in New Orleans 'n' Mobile."

Apollon made a quick mental note. Ten thousand pounds in England along with the unknown quantity of Papa's other money. He reached over and patted Sphie's hand. "You might be happier in England, what with the war going on here."

"Don' dare to go alone." Sophie reached up and took off one of the heavy earbobs. "Pulls on my ear somethin' awful," she explained.

"May I?" Apollon reached out his hand and she placed the earring in it. He examined it, noting the size of the diamonds and that the topaz was of gem quality. Silently he returned it to her, pressing her hand slightly as he dropped it into her palm.

"I am leaving for France soon," he said. "Must get back home, for I too have many responsibilities there. I came over here to settle up an inheritance—plantation down in the bayou country. Wasn't worth much. Niggers don't bring much any more."

Sophie nodded in approbation. " 'N' gettin' mighty uppity too. Like that Drummage boy o' mine. Reckon I'm goin' to have him whopped. Impudent, he is."

"Poor dear lady." Apollon clasped her hand again. "I marvel at how you manage here all alone."

"Tain' easy," Sophie agreed, pleased with the touch of Apollon's strong fingers on her own, which seemed strangely abandoned when he took his hand away.

"Perhaps, in the short time I shall be here, thanks to your gracious hospitality, I can be of some help to you. A man usually has more authority with servants than a woman. Now I am glad I came this way. With the Union forces in New

Orleans, I thought it better to get a ship from Mobile—some blockade runner going to Havana or Port au Prince. From there I can get a ship home. Now just what can I do to help you while I'm here?"

"Well, f'rinstance, yo' could take some of the sass outa that boy Drummage 'n' let him know he ain' a-runnin' Falconhurst. Missed a chair from Papa's office. Wan't nowhere in the house 'n' found Drummage he toted it over to his mama's cabin for her to sit in."

"Perhaps I can help you with Drummage," Apollon nodded. "I've had far more experience with the peasants on our estates in France than I have with your Negroes, but managing one is about like managing the other."

"Them peasants white men?" Sophie asked.

Apollon nodded.

"Then they ain' like our niggers. Niggers ain' human even if'n they has human blood in 'em like that there Drummage. Beasts they are. Wishin' I never have to see a nigger 'gain. Bin wid 'em all my life. Sick o' black faces, I am. Wisht I was a-goin' to France."

Apollon winced inwardly. Even with human blood, he was a beast! Well, sooner or later Sophie would find that out. His feelings did not change his air of sophisticated urbanity, however, and he managed to continue without a tremor in his voice.

"Ah, dear madame, France is a most delightful country, so different from this one. Ah, Paris. . . ." Apollon closed his eyes and began a fantastic description of that city. He had never seen it, but his imagination gave him full rein. He described the immense Hôtel de Noailles where he lived when in Paris. He discoursed on the elaborate balls, the glitter of the court, and his own *entrée* there. He spoke of Napoleon III as a close friend and of the Empress Eugénie as an old acquaintance. Name-dropping came easily to him and he thrilled Sophie with his intimate revelations of the court of the Tuileries. From Paris he took her to the non-existent Château de Noailles in the south of France and introuced her to the *fêtes champêtres,* to which all the French court came by special trains from Paris. He described at length the marvelous jewels which belonged to his mother and were now stored in a vault, awaiting another wearer. He told of his aged and ailing father and the glorious title of prince which would become his on his father's death. With unlimited imagination, he pictured his life in France as a continuous round of champagne-spilling, money-flowing, social activity, in which he was the central figure.

Sophie sat enthralled, drinking in every word, picturing Apollon as always the center of a group of elegantly costumed females, any one of which he could have for the asking. There was one question she must ask, but so much depended on it she feared to ask it. She gathered up her courage and made the attempt.

"'N' yore wife, Apollon? Yo' never mention her."

Again his hand sought hers. "There is no Vicomtesse de Noailles, dear madame. I have never married."

Sophie pressed his hand. "How come?"

"Perhaps because I have never found a woman I really cared for. French women are beautiful, *oui!* They are charming, *oui!* They make lovely companions, *oui!* But marriage," he sighed, "ah, that is something different. For marriage one wants a wife who is not only beautiful but wise; not only charming but intelligent; not only a companion of the moment but a companion for life. So far I have never found such a woman."

"Never, Apollon?"

"No, dear madame, but I am still searching. I must remember that the woman I marry will some day be the Princesse de Noailles and I must choose carefully." He relinquished her hand and sat erect in his chair. "But I shall find her, dear madame, yes, I shall find her." He smiled at her in the growing dusk. "And now I weary, dear madame, and I believe I shall retire with your permission. I anticipate the day when I shall be able to see your plantation. It will be good to get out again although I do not feel able to mount a horse yet."

Sophie smiled indulgently, her mind recalling something which had been gathering cobwebs upstairs in the stables for many years.

"Tomorrow I shall have a surprise for you, Apollon."

"Your kindness to me day after day has been a constant surprise to me. . . ." He paused and looked at her fondly. "May I call you Sophie?"

She lowered her head, as if overcome by his intimacy. "You may," she whispered. "I'll call yore boy 'n' Drummage to help yo'."

He rose by himself and waited for her to stand.

"It will not be necessary, dear Sophie. With you to lean on, I shall be able to dispense with the boys." He placed his arm over her shoulders so that his hand touched her breast just above her décolletage. Emboldened, she put her arm around his waist, feeling the strong muscles of his back through her father's brocaded gown. Together they walked into the hall. Only one candle burned there, its flame straight and unflickering in the big glass hurricane shade. With his free hand Apollon lifted her face until her lips were close to his. Then he lowered his lips to hers and kissed her lightly. He sighed.

"It is unfortunate that my illness forces me to say good night, dear Sophie."

"But yo're a-gettin' better, Apollon. Yo're a-goin' to be well soon." Sophie was exhilarated. Things were going just the way she wanted them to go.

"Better call the boys, dear Sophie." Apollon gently disengaged her arm from his waist. "Being so near you is a temptation a sick man should not have to resist. Yes, I am feeling better, but there are still some chances I do not, as yet, dare take." He lowered himself into one of the hall chairs while she pulled the bell cord. She returned to him and this time it was she who was the aggressor. It was her lips that sought his and claimed them, even while Kewp and Drummage stepped from the drawing room into the hall.

They both stopped, fully aware of the implications of the embracing pair. Kewp grinned: Apollon was making progress. But Drummage scowled. This stranger presented a threat to his own security. He certainly didn't want him for a master. There was something about him and his boy Kewp he distrusted.

Chapter 29

THE NEXT MORNING Apollon, with Kewp's help, dressed for breakfast. Damn! He was feeling as weak as though his sickness had been real. He needed to get out of doors; needed some sunshine. If only he could get his feet on the ground or a horse between his legs. He was sick to death of the big bed, of being fussed over by two women; tired of pretending to be an invalid, and bored with the big upper room where there was nothing to read except the saccharine stories in Godey's. Still, boredom was small recompense for what he hoped to get; it was necessary to maintain his convalescence a while longer. Sophie was ready but he wasn't. He wanted to be sure before he committed himself further.

Again he made the descent of the stairs, this time leaning on Kewp alone. When he reached the dining room he was surprised to find Sophie already there, dressed in a green velvet riding habit, complete with plumed hat. She looked radiant this morning, far different from the woman he had surprised in her bedraggled gown the night he arrived.

"Heard yo' a-gittin' up 'n' figured yo' might be a-comin' down to breakfast." She smiled from behind the coffee urn. "Tol' yo' I'd have a surprise fer yo'. Afta breakfast, yo' a-goin' out, but don' ask me no mo' 'bout it." She waggled a finger at him.

He made his way around the table, lifted her hand and kissed it, then returned to his place. Drummage brought in the meal—tender fried pink ham, eggs with delicately ruffled brown edges, fluffy biscuits to be drenched with butter or molasses, and coffee rich with cream. He ate heartily, and when the meal was finished he asked Drummage to call Lucretia Borgia in. She entered, to stand smiling behind Sophie's chair, rubbing her work-gnarled big hands on her apron.

"A most delicious breakfast, Lucretia Borgia"—Apollon inclined his head slightly—"most delicious indeed. I'd like to take you back to France with me. How'd you like to live in Paris, Lucretia Borgia?"

She shook her head decisively. "Thank you, Masta Apollon suh, thank yo', but cain' go. Cain' leave Miz Sophie; cain' leave Falconhurst. Goin' ter die here, I am. Miz Sohpie's grandpappy done sol' me onct to New Orleans but I comed back. Cain' leave here, masta suh."

Apollon glanced at Sophie while he answered Lucretia Borgia. "But if your Miss Sophie were to go to Paris wouldn't you want to go with her?"

Again she shook her head. "Ain' a-leavin' here, Masta Apollon suh, less'n Miz Sophie a-sellin' me and won' go den. She ain' a-goin' nuther. Ain' a-goin' to no Paris. Whar dat place?"

"A long ways from here," Apollon laughed. "Well, don't worry, Miss Sophie won't sell you to me. If you want to stay here, you can."

"Le's go out de front do'." Sophie rose from the table and gave Apollon her arm. "Anxious fer yo' ter see the surprise I got fer yo'." They walked out slowly, through the hall and onto the portico. Zanzibar was holding Sophie's mare, and behind him was one of the strangest contraptions Apollon had ever seen. Two stalwart Negroes were carrying a hammock, swung from a long pole which rested on their shoulders. Above it a fringed canopy kept off the sun. It was a litter reminiscent of pagan Rome.

"Belong to my Grandpa Maxwell," Sophie exclaimed proudly. "Ain' bin used in years. Boys cleaned it all up las' night 'n' put new cords on it. Jes' right fer yo' now. Gits yo' out in the fresh air. Them boys what's carrying it good 'n' strong. They's Big Randy 'n' Sampson. Yo', Kewp, help yore masta git in. Whar that Drummage? He ain' never round when I want him."

"Kewp will be enough, Sophie." Apollon descended the steps and lowered himself into the hammock while Kewp held it steady. Surprisingly enough it was comfortable, and he relaxed while Sophie mounted her horse. His bearers started to follow her and Apollon lolled back, enjoying this new mode of transportation.

They were evidently on a tour of inspection of the plantation. Sophie kept her horse at a walk, with the mounted Zanzibar following her. Apollon had an opportunity to study the groom with his flat-nosed, big-lipped African face, and he wondered why Sophie had chosen him. Compared with Kewp or Drummage, he seemed a savage—a crude *bozal*. From time to time, Sophie stopped to point out various places of interest—the stables, the little summerhouse, the creek. After they had traversed it, fording it instead of using the ornamental little bridge, they stopped at the family burying ground, where Sophie pointed out her mother's grave and a white marble monument with the name "Drumson" on it.

"He a nigger," Sophie explained. "Sire of Drummage. But he a special nigger 'cause he saved my papa's life onct 'n' 'Gusta had him buried here. My pore papa 'n' 'Gusta not here. They up in No'th Cahlina someplace. Ain' never seen whar my papa buried."

Further on, at a tangle of overun roses and shrubbery, she stopped and pointed to the crumbling foundations of another house.

"Ol' house useter be here." She pointed with her riding crop. "I bo'n here 'n' useter live here onct."

It was evident that the old house had been the center of activity for the plantation. Sophie stopped at most of the surrounding buildings, acknowledging the greetings of the men working there. They progressed down the street of slave quarters—solidly built cabins of squared logs which had once been whitewashed. Many of them were now vacant, their doors closed and the windows boarded up, but some of them were still occupied. Whenever they stopped, crowds of children stood in a circle about them as Sophie greeted the women who came out. There were no men around for, as she explained, they were out working in the fields.

Everywhere there were signs of neglect. Grass had grown over the once well-traveled street. Cabin ridgepoles were sagging and shakes were missing from the roofs. Here and there a chimney had fallen or a crude fireplace had caved in. The women who came out were poorly dressed in worn, patched, and faded osnaburg dresses. The children, even the adolescents, paraded their nudity without shame. A sour smell came from the open doors of the unoccupied cabins and the front yards were littered with offal.

At the end of the street Sophie again stopped, this time at a cabin whose spruce smartness separated it from the rest. It was neatly whitewashed, and someone with more imagination than skill had fashioned crude imitations of the big house pillars to support a miniature portico. Rocking chairs similar to those at the big house were on the little veranda, and the front yard was a bower of roses and crape myrtle. Sophie waited for Apollon's litter to come up beside her.

"Yo' ever seen a pure Mandingo?" she asked.

Apollon shook his head. He was aware that the Mandingos were an African tribe and he supposed that Sophie meant a slave of that extraction. No sooner had they stopped than an enormous fellow of about Apollon's age lounged out of the door and stood before the cabin bellowing, "Maw, Miz Sophie's heah." A woman, almost as large as the fellow, poked her head out of the door. Where the other women along the street had been dressed in tattered and shapeless clothes, this woman was neat and clean in a dress of brown calico and with a spotless white headcloth.

"This Big Pearl." Sophie seemed to take a delight in showing off the woman. " 'N' this her boy Olly. She mother to Drummage too. She pure Mandingo 'n' so's Olly. Drummage he ain' 'cause he part Hausa 'n' li'l bit human."

Apollon had never had much appreciation for "nigger flesh" but he realized that he was looking at something unusual. The woman, although huge, was perfectly formed. If she was the mother of the man beside her, her years sat lightly on her; she might easily have passed for his sister.

For the first time in his life, Apollon recognized the true

beauty and majesty of Africa. The woman's face was smooth and unlined, regally beautiful. She stood straight and erect and, although proportioned on a heroic scale, she was as perfect as a bronze statue. Her breasts strained at the fabric of her dress, large and overripe, but not sagging nor pendant. Her flat belly spread into wide hips and thighs, which tapered into straight strong legs with beautifully rounded calves. Large bovine brown eyes, like pools of swamp water, stared back at him. Her son, if it was possible that such a young looking woman could have a son of that age, was the most perfect male specimen he had ever seen. He wore no shirt, and his torso and arms seemed to be made of copper, they were so hard and smooth. He was a most impressive display of brute strength, monumental and heroic, but his face, although as handsome in all its lineaments as his mother's, was blank, as though the intelligence behind it did not comprehend all that was happening.

Big Pearl descended the one step and walked towards Sophie, halted and made a slight curtsey. "Ain' seen yo' fer a long time, Miz Sophie ma'am. Bin a-missin' yo' 'n' feared yo' ailin'. Won' yo' all come in 'n' set?"

Sophie accepted her greeting but did not dismount. She pointed with her crop to Olly.

"Ain' he a gyascutus? Papa useter use him fer a fightin' nigger but ain' no fightin' no mo'. He do the whoppin' fer us now. Likes to whop, he do. Papa say Big Pearl 'n' Olly 'n' Drummage cain' never be sol'. Ain' never sellin' 'em. If'n yo' feels like it, Apollon, go 'n' see Big Pearl's cabin. She right proud o' how Drummage fixed it up fer her. If'n I don' look out, Drummage cart the big house all down here."

Apollon was certainly not interested in the interior of a slave cabin, but the woman herself fascinated him. He wondered how one could bed oneself with such a giantess. It would be a most unusual experience, something one would never be able to duplicate.

"If'n yo'd like ter come in." Big Pearl took a step towards Apollon's litter.

"Yo'uns'll have to help him. He bin sick. Yo' take one arm, Big Pearl, 'n' Olly take t'other." Sophie still sat her horse. "I wait fer yo', Apollon, but she be right proud if'n yo' go in."

Between Olly and Big Pearl Apollon felt himself lifted like a bit of thistledown, and they practically carried him up to the house and through the door. Inside, he was amazed to see the cabin was immaculately clean and in good order.

The floor was scrubbed white, the big bed was spread with a patchwork coverlet and the pillowcases were stiffly starched. Castoff furniture from the big house had been repaired and now gleamed with a high polish. The most arresting sight, however, was the grinning, white, human skull on the mantelpiece and the white thighbones beside it. Apollon was curious about them, but the nearness of Big Pearl and the faintly musky but clean smell of her body were having an effect on him. He slipped his arm around her waist, the better to steady himself, luxuriating in the feel of her firm flesh under the thin calico.

"You have a pleasant home, Big Pearl," he said. "When I get to feeling better, I'd like to come and see you again."

"Yo' welcome, Masta suh. Yo're mighty welcome. Jes' come any time. Big Pearl al'ays glad to see de white masta."

And something in her words told Apollon that she had sensed his feelings for her. Strange, he thought, that she should appeal to him when he had never wanted a colored woman before. But she was different. She would be something to remember. He turned towards the door and she and Olly led him out, back to the hammock where they deposited him. During the rest of the journey, he thought only of her.

From Big Pearl's cabin they rode down into the fields and Sophie pointed out the cattle pasture with its grazing cows and the field where the hands were working. He was politely interested, although his thoughts were back in the cabin he had just left. Noticing his apathy, Sophie turned and headed back for the creek, where again she waited for him.

"Don' wan' yo' ter git tired out, yore first day out o' de house." She smiled. "Thinkin' perhaps yo' a little peaked-lookin' 'n' yo' better go back 'n' lie down fer a while. Have Drummage mix yo' a toddy 'n' lie down in Papa's study— couch there. If'n yo' don' mind, I think I will take a little longer ride. Bin kinda housebound myself."

Apollon nodded his acquiescence and watched her touch her crop to her mare. She trotted off, Zanzibar following behind her. Both Big Randy and Sampson, who bore the litter, were sweating, their shirts plastered to their skin, when they arrived back at the big house and deposited Apollon at the front door. Kewp was waiting for him but, instead of leading him up onto the porch, he pointed to a marble bench, half hidden under a tangle of shrubs.

"Want ter talk, 'Pollon. Cain' say a word in that damn house. Some one al'ays a-listenin'. Le's go over there." In case anyone might be peering from a window, Kewp took

Apollon's arm. Once seated on the bench, surrounded by shrubbery, they both relaxed.

"What's troubling you, Kewp?"

"Cain' stay here no longer less'n I kills that goddamn Drummage."

"What's the matter with Drummage? Seems like a nice boy."

"He nice 'nuff, but he shore ornery. He got that Candy wench what he sleeps wid every night. 'N' he got three wenches down in de spinnin' house what he a-layin' all the time. 'Sides dat he got hisself a woman over in de New Quarters whar he go when her man out in de fields. He got all dose wenches 'n' he won' let me have none. Not a single one! Know what he say to me?"

"No, what?"

"He say I kin have dat goddamn Marguerite with de split lip and de snotty nose. Says I kin pleasure her if'n I wants a woman. She 'nuff to make me puke, she is. Gittin' mighty horny but not 'nuff to pester her. No suh!"

"You just keep your pants buttoned up and forget about killing Drummage." Apollon regarded a suspicious bulge in Kewp's breeches. "What you got there?" He reached over, fumbled in Kewp's pocket, and pulled out a small derringer.

"Where did you get that gun?"

"Foun' it in de ol' masta's office under yore room."

"And what were you going to do with it?

"A-goin' ter scare that Drummage inter givin' me one o' his wenches."

Apollon slapped Kewp on the side of his head with the full force of his hand. Kewp winced but did not retaliate. Apollon hit him a second time.

"You goddamned stupid nigger! That's all you are, Kewp. All you think about is bedding yourself with a wench. Well, you listen to me. I've got too much on my mind to worry about you. I don't give a damn if you never have another wench. Get along without one. I do. But you're not going to make any trouble here. There's too much at stake. If you do, by God, I'll call in a veterinary and geld you. I'll cut the goddamn thing off and you'll not be itching any more. Believe me, Kewp, I mean it."

"Yo' wouldn't do that, 'Pollon?"

"I would and I will if you don't keep in line. You play along with me and I'll buy you any wench in the world that suits your fancy, black, brown, or high yellow." Apollon slipped the derringer into the pocket of his coat.

"Such like Candy?"

"Her if you want her. Now behave yourself and don't let me hear of you getting into any trouble because if you do"—Apollon stuck out his index finger and sliced through the air with it—"you'll be wondering where your knockers went. Understand?"

Kewp knew that Apollon meant it. He was instantly contrite. "I understan', 'Pollon. Won' make no trouble. But I got somethin' else ter tell yo'."

"More deviltry that you've gotten into?"

"No, 'Pollon, something 'bout yore Miz Sophie. Yo' know why she go a-ridin' wid dat Zanzibar buck? She go mos' every day till yo' come. Know whar she go 'n' what she do wid him?"

Apollon shook his head.

"She a-lettin' dat big buck pleasure her. Big Randy he tol' me. He say all de people here know 'bout it. He say Zanzibar mighty scared too 'cause he don' wan' ter go wid her but she make him."

Apollon smiled, then pursed his lips together.

"Sort of suspected it, I did. Thought she was anxious to get away this morning. Glad you told me, Kewp. May come in handy." He reached over and patted Kewp's leg. "Sorry I hit you, Kewp. Kind of forget sometimes. Look, Kewp boy! I saw a nigger wench today like I never saw before. Something about her made me want her and you know I never want wenches. She the biggest goddamn wench you ever saw and I'll bet she'd give you your money's worth. She'll dreen you, boy. Whyn't you try her. She's Drummage's mama so he won't be wanting her anyway."

"Yo' meanin' that Big Pearl what live in de pretty cabin wid Olly? Ain' thought 'bout her." Kewp grinned. "Jes' like climbin' onto a mare. Thinkin' I'll try it."

Apollon got up to leave. "If you don't, boy, there's only one thing left for you until I get things straightened out." He made a suggestive motion with his right hand.

"Hell, I already done it, 'Pollon, but that ain' much fun."

"Fun will be coming later, Kewp. Plenty of it. Just be patient."

Kewp stood up to help Apollon.

"Yo' goin' ter keep that li'l gun, 'Pollon?"

"That too might come in handy."

Together they walked up the steps of the portico and into the house.

Chapter 30

APOLLON had not wanted to rush his courtship of Sophie, preferring to let her take the initiative. He had no intention of her later accusing him of being a fortune hunter. In her anxiety to add to her attractiveness as a good "catch," Sophie was wont to boast about her wealth, and he was only too willing to listen to her stories. With the excuse that she did not know which of two necklaces better suited the dress she was wearing, she called him into her room to decide for her, and this gave her an excuse to bring out not only her own jewel casket but also that of her stepmother, for him to examine.

Much of Sophie's jewelry, he discovered, was more ostentatious than valuable—lava cameos, semiprecious stones, and even frank imitations. Augusta's jewels, chosen with more discrimination, were really valuable. Maxwell had evidently enjoyed indulging his wife, because the diamonds were fine and their velvet and morocco cases bore the names of New Orleans' most famous jewelers. All in all the jewelry at Falconhurst must be worth well over twenty-five thousand, he figured, which was a substantial sum for the womenfolk of a plantation owner.

Then too, Sophie was not unwilling to consult Apollon about matters of business. She had a clutch of long envelopes which contained financial documents she had not been able to understand and brought these to him also for his advice and assistance. He found, from bank statements, deposit books, and other data, that she was indeed a wealthy woman, but outside of the Charnworth settlement of ten thousand pounds, which had been added to her father's account of fifty thousand pounds in Brown's Bank in London, all her money was invested in Confederate bonds. It was disappointing. Already Confederate money was at a discount and it was decreasing in value daily. What a shame! So many hundreds of thousands of dollars all in worthless paper. However, he did not disillusion Sophie as to their value, but tried to convince her that a conversion into other assets might be advisable—turning them into real estate and tangible assets. Sophie demurred. Such nice round sums! Such absolute security!

Weren't they in the big banks of the city and didn't her papa put them there?

Yet even without the Confederate, there was enough money, Apollon figured, to give him financial independence. He would find a way to get rid of Sophie once he had his hands on the money. Perhaps, he thought, he had delayed long enough. There was nothing to be gained by playing the invalid any longer. Sophie, without Zanzibar's services for a period, would be all the more susceptible; he must supplant Zanzibar by taking the daily ride with her. Apollon was playing his cards as wisely as any Mississippi steamboat gambler.

Sophie, he saw, lived in splendid isolation at Falconhurst. During the weeks he had been there, she had never received a caller or gone to another plantation. She did not join with the women of the village who were busy scraping lint and rolling bandages, nor did she seem to have any church affiliations. This made things easier for Apollon. He had no competition, for no other eligible males ever appeared at Falconhurst, set on courting the rich mistress. Not that he would have feared them had they come—he knew the power of his good looks and his charm. However, for the present he let the days slip by in a *dolce far niente* of procrastination.

May gave way to June and June to July, when the full heat of the Southern summer descended upon them. The vicious heat penetrated even into the darkened rooms and through the thick brick walls of Falconhurst. The big fan over the dining-room table, pulled by a long string attached to the big toe of a boy in the kitchen, made eating fairly comfortable, but the other rooms were hot and airless. Even the servants carried big palmetto fans and sweat poured from white and black alike. As the heat of the house concentrated in the upstairs bedrooms, Apollon and Sophie were accustomed to sit until nearly midnight out on the portico, waiting for the cool breezes of evening to fan the heat from the house.

These were difficult evenings for Apollon, for Sophie's conversation was limited. She had been away at school, he knew, but evidently learning was not stressed at the particular female academy she had attended. He doubted that she had ever read a book—at least there were none in the house; she had traveled only as far as New Orleans but knew nobody there; she had no pastimes or interests. Apollon had perforce to do most of the talking, but although his fertile

276

imagination served him well, he tired of the sound of his own voice.

The sound of music from the distant New Quarters finally solved his problem of boredom. One of the hands had a guitar, another a fiddle, and the rich voices of the Negroes blended beautifully with the soft, fragrant air of the night and the silvery music of the strings in the darkness. Through Brutus, he invited them to come to the big house evenings and prevailed on Lucretia Borgia to make these evenings festive occasions by the preparation of big crocks of switchel —a drink compounded of water, molasses, and vinegar, flavored with ginger, to which Apollon himself added a small quantity of corn. Nightly they would gather in the dusk, sitting in a wide semicircle around the steps to the portico while he and Sophie sat in rocking chairs and the house servants occupied straight chairs behind them.

Their songs were spontaneous, starting sometimes after a long period of silence, when a hand would sweep across the guitar strings to inspire some man or woman with a melody. A voice would be raised, a chorus would support it, and the night would be filled with a primitive music that would drift away into nothingness and then return. Often the words, detailing as they did the daily gossip of the plantation, would be innocently obscene, as they told about the matings of this couple or that. Drummage and his plenitude of wenches came in for much good-natured ribbing, but Drummage did not mind; he rather enjoyed his reputation for virility. At times the songs condemned Brutus and Olly for brutal whippings. All seemed to take it for granted that there was a license of speech in the songs that would not be permitted in conversation. Sophie was constantly lauded, and Apollon received his share of praise, being often referred to as the "pretty masta." The switchel was appreciated, and gourdfuls of it passed around.

Thus they would continue until the night coolness had dissipated the heat of the day, when the people could bear to return to their hot cabins and the white folks could go upstairs to their beds. It was a pleasant way of passing what would otherwise have been tedious and interminable evenings.

After a while Apollon himself took up the guitar and sang a number of French songs, then followed them up with college songs he had learned up North. Gradually his contributions came to be the highlight of the evening's entertainment and were enthusiastically received by Sophie, who felt that his love songs were directed exclusively to her, as Apollon intended.

One evening, after they had returned from an all-day trip to an auction at a neighboring plantation, Apollon decided that it was time for an understanding between himself and Sophie. He had squandered his last remaining dollars on buying her a hand-painted fan with mother-of-pearl sticks. He had delayed long enough; the step must be taken.

He brought his chair closer to Sophie's and his offering to her that night was an impassioned love song. After he had concluded, and handed the guitar back to the boy who owned it, he let his fingers seek hers in the darkness. He was not surprised when hers clutched at his as though she would never let them go. He returned the pressure, knowing that it would have the desired effect. After the singing was over he helped her out of her chair and took her arm in his. As they mounted the stairs he slipped his arm around her waist, encountering the stiffness of whale bone and thinking how different it was from the voluptuous flesh of Big Pearl. At the door of her room she lingered for a good night, inviting him with her eyes but hesitating to say the words that would ask him across the threshold.

Once in his own room, he undressed quickly and dismissed Kewp immediately, not without loudly instructing him to leave his door open because of the heat. He did not don his nightgown but stretched out naked on the sheets. Nor did he blow out his lamp, but turned it down so that the low flame gilded his body, changing its ivory to gold. He was determined not to sleep, but let his mind drift off into a phantasy in which he pictured Big Pearl beside him, with a bleached skull grinning down from the mantelpiece. He could hear Sophie in the next room; heard her tell Candy to go; and listened to the girl's footsteps as she traversed the stairs. With the doors open, he could even distinguish Sophie's breathing in the next room. She was restless, and he could hear her mattress rustle and the bed ropes creak as she tossed from one side of the bed to the other. He knew she was desiring him as much as he was wanting the black Juno that was Big Pearl.

Gradually Sophie quieted down and his phantasy about Big Pearl produced the desired effect upon himself. Now, he decided, was the right time, the culmination of months of carefully planned movements. At first softly, and then more audibly, he groaned like a man in pain. He heard a movement as of somebody sitting up in the next room, and his groans gave way to gasps and then to one long high-keyed howl. His artifice brought results. Sophie appeared at his door, and through the slit of his nearly closed eyes he saw that she had on only her nightgown. Feigning sleep, he saw her come to the bed and stare down at him. For a long moment she looked, feasting her eyes, then plumped down on the edge of the bed, her hands reaching for his shoulders, shaking him into wakefulness.

"Yo' sick 'gain, 'Pollon? Yo' ailin'?" There was worry in her voice.

He opened his eyes. Seeming to force himself awake, he shook his head, reaching out for her, clinging to her.

"Un chauchermar!" he shuddered.

"What yo' say, 'Pollon?"

"A nightmare, Sophie! A terrible dream! I'm glad you woke me, but sorry to disturb you." Apparently aware of his nakedness, he pulled the sheet up around him.

"Didn't bother me, 'Pollon. Fearful 'bout yo', I was. Shore yo' ain' sick 'gain?"

"No, my dear, just a bad dream. I thought something terrible was happening to you and I was trying to reach you but couldn't." He reached for her hand. "What a bother I am to you, dear Sophie, and you are so good to me. I should not be accepting your hospitality any longer, but I hate to leave you. Falconhurst is beginning to seem like home to me. It is going to be difficult to leave and know that I shall not see you any more."

"Don' talk 'bout goin', 'Pollon. Cain' bear to think o' bein' here 'thout yo'."

Slowly, like a creeping tortoise, his hand inched over the sheet to encounter the warmth of her thigh under her thin nightgown. It did not stop, nor did she make any move to resist it. Her hand, equally bent on seeking and finding, crept under the sheet and came toward him. For long moments they sought, found, and discovered, then he reached up and drew her down to him, pulling the nightdress up over her head. She snuggled close to him.

His half-waking dream of Big Pearl had prepared him and his continence of the last weeks now stood him in good stead. He was prepared to make love with all the animal passion which his body demanded, although his mind stayed aloof, directing his body in a practiced performance of love. Poor Sophie, who had never learned to distinguish between love and passion, was quite satisfied with his *coup de thêâtre*, which was not, however, of long duration. He released himself from her embrace and lay rigidly beside her, letting the cool air from the windows blow over him. She too was silent, not understanding his frigidity but not daring to question it. He had shown such an excess of fire, it was hard for her to understand his indifference. In her extremity she began to sob. It was what he had been waiting for. His hand reached over to touch her lightly with sympathetic assurance.

"Can you ever forgive me, dear Sophie? I have wronged you greatly." Suddenly he jackknifed up in bed. "Oh, my God, Sophie, what have I done? What a terrible thing! What an abuse of your hospitality and your goodness to me. Oh, Sophie, what can I ever do to wipe out this terrible disgrace I have brought upon you?"

"Ain' nothin' so very bad, 'Pollon. 'Sides, yo' not all to blame."

"I deserve to be whipped, Sophie. Scream! Call the servants! Have me lashed! Call Brute and have him take me to the whips. I'll not resist, dear Sophie. I deserve it for having taken advantage of you" He reached over and turned up the wick of the lamp.

She regarded him numbly, beseechingly, a look of utter sorrow on her face.

" 'S much my fault as yourn. Guess maybe I wanted yo' more 'n yo' wanted me, 'Pollon."

It was his turn to sob and he did it effectively, knowing that nothing moves a woman like a man's tears.

"But that does not make it right, dear Sophie. I came to your house a sick man; you took me in, nursed me in your kindness, and I have done this to repay you. But I can make it right to you, dear Sophie. I can make it right. There is one thing I can do."

"What's that?" She feared he was going to say he would leave her forever.

"Marry you, if you will have me. That is the only way I can right this terrible wrong. If we become husband and wife, this awful thing will be erased. Sophie, I beg of you, marry me."

She was dumbfounded. This was something that even in her wildest dreams she could not have hoped for. To have this man above all others as her husband! To occupy this bed with him freely and forever, without restraint! To hold that glorious body in her arms; to be the willing victim of his demands! The heavens had opened up for her. She could only look at him, sobbing before her, offering himself to her, and marvel that this miracle could have happened to

280

her—poor, fat, cross-eyed Sophie Maxwell, who had been neglected and unloved all her life. She knew she had little to offer such a man as Apollon. He was younger than she was, far handsomer than any man she had ever seen before and . . . wonder of wonders . . . he had asked her to marry him. The image of Zanzibar came before her and she regretted him and the legion that had preceded him.

Her silence worried Apollon. Had he overplayed his part? He had thought she would dissolve in his arms, all gratitude and willingness. Again he implored her.

"Sophie! I asked you to marry me. Are you so angry at me for what I have done that you cannot let me make it right? Oh, dear Sophie, speak to me."

She sat up beside him, pushing her hair away from her face. Her hand reached out tentatively like a child's seeking something which had always been forbidden but was now within reach.

"Yo' means it, 'Pollon? Yo' means yo' really wants to marry up with me?"

"I am a gentleman, Sophie. It is the only decent thing I can do."

She had hoped he might say he loved her but that was asking too much. That he wanted to marry her was sufficient.

"Yes, I'll marry yo', 'Pollon. I'll marry yo' 'n' I'll love yo' and I'll be proud to be yore wife."

A gesture on his part seemed to be called for; something more than words. He gathered her to him and kissed her, not on the mouth but on the cheek, and then released her. Slipping the red-stoned ring from his finger, he placed it on hers. While she looked down on it, admiring it in the lamplight, he climbed over her to stand on the floor. With one hand he reached down for her nightgown, placing it over her head.

"We must not be tempted to do this again until we are married," he whispered.

"When will that be?" she asked.

"Just as soon as we can find a priest."

"Ain' no priests round here. Everyone Protestant here. Jes' got ministers, tha's all."

"But there is a church in Benson. I saw it."

"Baptist."

"Then we'll be married by the Baptist minister."

"If'n yo' wants, 'Pollon."

"It matters little who does it as long as we are married,

Sophie." With one arm around her and the other carrying the lamp, he led her to the door of her room.

"You have made me very happy, Sophie." Again he kissed her on the cheek. "So happy I cannot sleep. I'm going to slip on my pants and my shirt and sit down on the porch for a while."

"I'll come wid yo'."

"No, dear Sophie, you sleep. My ring on your finger will bring you happy dreams. I have much to think about. There are changes I must make in my plans, for now I must include you in all of them and I must be alone to think about them. A man cannot think calmly when the woman he is going to marry is sitting beside him."

"God bless yo', 'Pollon"

Still carrying the lamp, he went back to his own room, pulled on his trousers, and slipped into low shoes. Turning out the lamp, he tiptoed back into the hall and down the stairs, but the chairs on the front portico did not tempt him. Instead he took a path through the tangled shrubbery round to the back of the house and then found the path that led down to the creek and over the little bridge. On the other side, at the crest of the hill, the tombstones in the cemetery rose ghostly-white in the moonlight, and he hurried on past them. All the slave cabins were dark as he half ran, half walked down the dusty street. At the single cabin where Big Pearl lived, he halted. The door under the crazy little pillared portico was open. From inside he could hear the sound of regular breathing.

"Pearl!" His voice sounded strangely loud in the silence of the cabin.

There was a rustle of the corn-shuck mattress and a male voice came from the bed.

"Who dar?"

Apollon recognized Kewp's voice.

"Me . . . Apollon!"

"Who dat a-talkin', Kewp boy?" Big Pearl had awakened.

"My masta."

"Him?"

"What yo' a-wantin' o' me, 'Pollon?" Kewp's face appeared in the doorway.

"Get to hell out of here, Kewp. I want Pearl. Need her."

"Yo' kin have her, 'Pollon. Like yo' say, she dreen me long time 'go. Bin sleepin'." Kewp came close to Apollon and whispered. "Yo' shore a-goin' ter like what yo' a-goin' ter git, 'Pollon. M-m-muh!" He disappeared into the darkness of

282

the cabin and reappeared, pulling on his breeches. "She a-waitin' yo', 'Pollon." He sped away in the darkness and Apollon stepped inside.

A square of pale moonlight from the open window illuminated a section of the bed and a spot on the floor. He could see the darkness of Big Pearl, turned on her side, facing him.

"What yo' a-wantin' o' me, masta suh?"

"Been wanting you ever since I saw you."

"Meanin' yo' wants ter pleasure me, masta suh?"

"Meanin' I wants ter pleasure myself," Apollon found himself answering her in her own slurred words.

"Ain' had no white men sence Masta Hammond done guv me a sucker long time 'go. Yo're welcome though. Admires ter have yo'. Kewp gone?"

"Yes."

"Whyn't he stay? Cud've slep' with Olly rest of the night. He nice boy, that Kewp."

A voice called down from the loft above.

"Who yo' talkin' ter, Maw?"

"Yo' go to sleep, Olly."

Apollon walked toward the black shape on the bed. A hand came out to guide him and with his free hand he disengaged his one garment and kicked off his slippers. He lowered himself onto the mountain of soft flesh, sinking into it like a man caught in a quicksand. His hands, excitedly exploring, sought the wild tumultuous body beneath him, feeling it arch under him and draw him down, down, down until it engulfed him. Always before he had been the aggressor, now he had to fight against being overwhelmed by the primitive power beneath him. That infinitesimal part of him which was Africa now dominated him, erasing all the veneer of civilization on which he had prided himself. He was no longer Apollon Beauchair but some nameless Ibo warrior, rutting in a grass hut beside a black river where crocodiles slept in the moonlight. He matched the heaving mass beneath him with a power he did not know he possessed, and then shuddered in a cataclysm so violent that it left him sucking in his breath with deep thirsty gasps. He remained where he was, unable to move, content forever to rest, spent and exhausted on this heaving mountain of warm flesh.

Gone were his frustrating desires for Denise; forgotten was his cruelly forced passion for Sophie. Here he found such satiation as he had never experienced before. There had been no necessity for any conscious urge to please and satisfy

283

his partner. There had been no dalliance, no soft little words or tender touches. And now that it was over there was still no need for them. He rolled away, allowing himself to catch his breath for a few moments, and then stood up, searching with his toes for his breeches and his slippers.

"Don't say anything about this, Big Pearl."

"Won' say nothin', masta suh."

"And Olly?"

"He 'sleep. He a-thinkin' yo're Kewp anyway."

"Can I come again?"

"Don' have ter ask me kin yo' come. Come when yo' wants, masta suh. Ain' never had no one pleasure me like yo' sence Mede."

"Mede?"

"That him." Big Pearl's moon-silvered hand pointed to the skull on the mantelpiece. "Mandingo, he was."

Apollon shivered, seeing the dim outlines of the skull, and walked out into the square of moonlight that was the doorway. The night air was heavy with the rich scent of dying roses and the rank odor of burgeoning growth and fertility. Instead of feeling weakened he felt strong, with a power in him which he had never recognized before. After he had taken a few steps he was tempted to return to the cabin, but he decided against it. He knew Sophie would be waiting for him to return and he did not want to answer any questioning. He could think about Sophie dispassionately now. His marriage, brief and transient as he planned it to be, did not seem such a difficult chore. Tonight, in Big Pearl's arms, he had found himself, and for the first time he did not blame his father for planting his seed in his mother and again in Jeanne-Marie. Now he could understand Kewp and Drummage and all the other of his dark-skinned brethren. No wonder they had only one thing on their minds, if it was anything like what he had just experienced. Those few drops of black blood in his veins had triumphed. For a few moments—yes, for a few fleeting moments—he would allow himself to be proud of them. Through them he had found himself, and he rejoiced in what he had found.

Chapter 31

APOLLON and Sophie waited in the blinding sunlight on the sloping veranda of the Baptist parsonage in Benson while someone inside made frantic efforts to turn a key in the rusty lock. When the door finally opened, they were greeted by a tall spare young woman, her tow-colored hair pulled back so tightly from her head that her eyebrows were arched in a perpetual expression of surprise. She was holding a squalling infant in the crook of one arm, while a brood of young tow-heads peeped out from behind her draggled skirts. Quite overwhelmed by the appearance of the Falconhurst barouche, with coachman and footmen, at her door, she was tongue-tied except for a barely audible "Come in." After ushering them into a small, dark parlor whose sour airlessness mingled dust, collard greens, and babies, she backed out through another door which allowed a momentary glimpse of the kitchen, with piles of dirty dishes on the table.

They waited, seated on a sagging sofa stuffed with prickly horse-hair, while muffled sounds of a whispered conversation and a hurried scuffling to and fro came to them from the adjoining room. A child was slapped with a resultant howl, a door slammed, and then there was comparative quiet for several minutes while they sat, allowing their eyes to become accustomed to the semidarkness, and stared at a small, marble-topped table which supported a large gilt-edged Bible. A framed black lithograph of some stern-visaged cleric stared down at them with disapproving eyes from the wall.

The door opened at length to admit the Reverend Silas Hazzard, a puny, youngish man with stooping shoulders, whose bushy red beard and numerous progeny testified to a greater virility than his appearance might indicate. He had donned a long black coat over his osnaburg trousers but whether he wore a shirt under the coat was debatable, as his whiskers covered the opening between the greasy lapels. His small green eyes gleamed catlike in the semidarkness, burning with a fanatical zeal at the possible conversion of the mistress of Falconhurst. Apollon, whose hearty masculinity completely negated his own puniness, he disregard as much as possible, addressing himself to Sophie.

"May the blessing of Almighty Gawd 'n' His sweet son Jesus Christ be 'pon yo', Missis Charnwood. Honored I am by yore callin' heah. Any pore pilgrim a-searchin' fer Gawd al'ays welcome ter come to ouah spiritual teas' spread out fer all sinners ter pertake of. Welcome in de name o' de Lawd."

"Thank you, Mr. Hazzard." Although he had been omitted from the welcome, it was Apollon who answered. "We have come to inquire about a ceremony which we would like to have preformed."

"Yo'all a-goin' ter be baptized?" Hazzard almost jumped up and down in his zeal. "Yo' felt sweet Jesus a-stealin' inter yore hearts? Bless yo' all, oh, bless yo' all. Sweet Jesus, al'ays a-lookin' fer stray lambs ter lead inter de fold."

No, Apollon said, they had not come with baptism in mind, a pronouncement which caused the Reverend's face to fall. A rich church member like Sophie would have done much to alleviate the personage's daily diet of sowbelly and greens. He sighed and slumped down into a chair, his disappointment showing plainly.

"We're a-wantin' ter get married." Sophie nodded the plumes on her big hat. "An' we a-wantin' yo' ter do it. This my husband-ter-be. He the Vee-comte de Noailles of France."

The Reverend Hazzard stared belligerently at Apollon, exactly as though Sophie had introduced Beelzebub himself.

"Yo' one of them papists," he asked, "spawned by the whore o' Rome?"

Apollon lied glibly, shaking his head in denial. In fact, he had not the slightest idea of what he was or might be. Having been born a slave, he had never been baptized, but he had attended Mass with his mother. While at school in the North, attendance at the school's Congregational chapel had been compulsory and he had spent a half-hour there daily without ever having paid any attention to the fountains of meaningless words which had spewed from the headmaster's lips. While at Harvard he had attended a Unitarian church several times but his motive in going had merely been to escort a certain lady home. It mattered little to him what he was. Anything convenient would do.

"Yo' bin baptized?" Hazzard looked first at Sophie and then at Apollon. Both answered "no" at the same time.

"Marriage a holy ceremony." Hazzard became pontifical. "Cain' marry no one less'n they been baptized. Has to be immersed in water ter be baptized. Cain' be jes' sprinkled. Jesus himself baptized in Jordan river. Immersed he was.

If'n yo' all wants ter join up wid us here in Benson; if'n yo' all wants ter become membahs, kin 'range it. Cain' talk no more 'bout it 'til then but we kin pray 'bout it. Le's all kneel 'n' pray 'bout bringin' yo' inter de fold. Sweet Jesus, He a-standin' at de open do', jes' a-askin' yo' all ter come in." He slipped onto his knees from the chair and raised his black-clad arms high.

"Oh, mighty 'n' everlastin' Gawd. These pore sinners a-comin' to Thee, hongry 'n' a-thirstin' for Yore blessin'. They pore travelers in de wilderness o' sin but they a-seekin' Yo' 'n' we craves Yore blessin' 'pon them. We craves that Yo' look inter their hearts 'n' takes out de blackness o' sin 'n' washes them white as de driven snow. We craves that Yo' gather them to Yore table that they might eat de feas' o' joy 'n' salvation Yo' has prepared fer them. Let 'em see de light. Let 'em know that sweet Jesus done died for them. Let 'em feel the healin' waters a-flowin' ovah 'em 'n' come ter jine Thy church 'n' support Thy word 'mong de heathen. Let them know the wants of Thy church 'n' Thy servant. They jes' pore sinners a-lookin' fer light in de darkness 'n' they've come to Thy servant fer guidance through de valley o' shadow."

On and on he proceeded, painting an ever blacker picture of all the sins of Babylon which he insisted were present in his two listeners. From their iniquities he went on to call down blessings upon his own church and his parishioners, expatiating in glowing terms on their safety and happiness in the Everlasting Arms. He did not neglect to mention the need of his church for an organ and to pray that it might be forthcoming. Nor did he neglect his condemnation of all human vices and passions which he enumerated with mouth-watering, tongue-rolling descriptions. In the field of politics and war, he was certain the Deity was on the side of the South but he was not niggardly in his advice of how the war should be won and a quick victory granted to the Confederate armies. Then with a final impassioned plea he urged Apollon and Sophie to come to the arms of the Lord and ended with a sonorous "Amen."

Apollon felt the boards of the floor through the broadcloth of his trousers and his knees ached. He arose stiffly and helped Sophie up, and once again they confronted the little man. Sophie who had also felt pins and needles in her legs, stamped her feet to banish them, and pulled at the strings of her reticule. She fumbled for a moment and drew forth a crisp new Confederate fifty-dollar bill.

"Guess we'll have to go to a justice o' the peace. Willin' to pay fer a marriage." She folded the bill in half, creasing it crisply between her fingers. "We not only willin' ter pay fer the marriage but we'd be glad ter 'tribute to the church, say 'bout a hundred dollars a year even if'n we not members."

Hazzard eyed the bill greedily. Fifty dollars was more than he had ever had at one time in his life. Fifty dollars now and the promise of a hundred dollars every year! It was a lot more than a quarter of a hog or a bushel of corn meal, which were the usual contributions. He hesitated.

"Gittin' married by a justice o' de peace ain' gittin' married in de eyes o' Gawd." He frowned. "Understan', Missis Charnwood, that yo' a dee-vorced woman."

"Legal though," Sophie answered. "Got the papers at home. Makes me free to marry 'gain. Yo' kin see 'em if'n yo' wishes."

" 'N' yo' free ter marry?" Hazzard asked Apollon with a cocky belligerency toward this man who seemed to have so much more than he had ever possessed.

"Naturally," Apollon nodded, "seeing as how I have never married."

Hazzard came closer to Apollon, studying him carefully for a long moment. "Co'se yo' a white man? Law requires me ter ask yo' that. Cain' marry no one wid a nigger o' that has nigger blood in 'em."

"If I did not know you were required by law to ask that question I would consider it an insult both to Mrs. Charnwood and myself. I am Apollon Beauchair, Vicomte de Noailles, son of the Prince de Noailles, aide to His Imperial Mastesty Napoleon III, Emperor of France."

Even the Reverend Hazzard had heard of Napoleon III and was impressed.

"Saint Paul a-sayin' 'tis better ter marry than ter burn." He reached out his hand for the bill. " 'Pears like it my duty ter marry yo' even if'n yo' not baptized. Cain' have yo' all a-burnin' through all eternity." He forced a smile, trying to establish his little joke. The fifty-dollar bill crinkled in his pocket. "Was yo' a-wantin' ter get married today?"

"We were," Apollon answered.

"Needs us two witnesses." Hazzard opened the door into the kitchen. "Missis Hazzard," he called, "kin yo' run ovah to Missis Ballard's 'n' ask her if'n she could step ovah heah fer a few minutes?"

There was a sound of footsteps and while they waited in strained, frozen-smiling silence, they heard the footsteps returning and Mrs. Hazzard entered with a neighbor woman, still wiping her floury hands on her apron. Hazzard tried to raise one of the paper shades at the window but it fell with a clatter. Any other man would have cursed it, but he rolled it up carefully and placed it against the wall. Sunlight, streaming into the room, made its shabbiness even more apparent. In the sudden light the two women studied Sophie and Apollon, noting the richness of their clothes and particularly Apollon's appearance. Each mentally compared him with her own mate and envied Sophie.

Hazzard faced the marble table with the Bible and motioned to Sophie and Apollon to stand before it, with his wife beside Sophie and Mrs. Ballard beside Apollon. Sophie had saved the wedding ring Dudley had given her—there had been no time to buy another—and Apollon had it in his pocket. Fumbling in the pocket of his coat, Hazzard brought out a small book and started mechanically to read the wedding ceremony, which seemed strangely brief, but after it was over he indulged in another even longer prayer with all of them on their knees. The second prayer was more or less a repetition of the first, but it gave Hazzard another opportunity to advise God how to handle the world and all its affairs. At length he had to close, having run out of phrases, and they all creaked back into a standing position. Mrs. Hazzard presented a leathery cheek for Apollon to kiss and Hazzard's bushy red beard brushed Sophie's face. Mrs. Hazzard made a tentative move to kiss Apollon but her husband frowned and she desisted. Mrs. Ballard, however, kissed him full on the mouth and he had a feeling that her lips would willingly have lingered there, but she dissolved into tears and damply gathered both Apollon and Sophie into her embrace before she left the house, wiping her eyes with the corner of her apron.

Hazzard was effusive in his good-bys, calling down the blessing of the Lord upon them as they left the house, and even accompanied them down the dusty path where they were helped into the barouche by Drummage and Kewp. Big Randy touched the whip to the horses and they started for home in the hot sultry afternoon. Throughout the trip Sophie insisted on holding Apollon's hand, and he soon tired of its sweaty clasp. They returned to Falconhurst in time for the evening meal and gorged themselves on Lucretia Borgia's festive efforts, which Apollon washed down with several hot toddies.

He was ready for bed, exhausted from the long prayers

and the tiresome ceremony. But the thought of sharing his bed with Sophie on this hot and breathless night, when the temperature in the upstairs room was truly unbearable, was more than he could stand. He realized that she would expect a *tour de force* from him on this her wedding night, and he hoped that there would be no scene when she found out it would not be forthcoming. Tonight would govern their future marriage relations, and he certainly did not intend to spend the remainder of his time at Falconhurst trying to satisfy Sophie. Diplomacy and subterfuge would be the best course to follow. It would be easier in the end than violent scenes, recriminations, and weepings. Better to settle the matter now. After the hands arrived for the evening singing, there would be little opportunity. He must erase that expectancy from Sophie's eyes.

He looked at her across the table, softening the coming blow with his most engaging smile.

"Madame la Vicomtesse," he began, "my wife Sophie. Did you realize that in addition to being a vicomtesse of France you are also Mrs. Apollon Beauchair?"

"How come I got two names, 'Pollon?"

"Only one, Sophie. My *name* is Apollon Beauchair; my *title* is the Vicomte de Noailles. You see it's like this. Your father's name was Hammond Maxwell, yes?"

She nodded.

"That was his name. But he was also Master of Falconhurst; that was his title. Now do you understand? Falconhurst was not his name any more than Noailles is mine. So, your name is Beauchair even though are a vicomtesse and will some day be a princess." He was glad that hurdle was successfully over. Now any documents could be made out in his own name.

In her preoccupation with Apollon himself, Sophie had paid little attention to the fact, as she believed it to be, that she had become a woman of title. It meant little and much to her; little because she did not really understand what titles of nobility actually signified, but much because even in her ignorance they conferred a certain grandiose distinction.

"If'n yo' say so, 'Pollon. But don' matter much ter me what they calls me, long's I yore wife."

"Thank you, Sophie." Apollon's charm waxed more than adequate. "But now that we are man and wife, there are certain things we must both understand. I am not, as you know, a man of robust health. With my weak heart, I must always

290

be on my guard against overexcitement. So that limits me. Do you understand, my dear?"

"But I'm here, 'Pollon, always here to take care o' yo'."

"And the mere fact that you *are* here, Sophie, makes matters more difficult for me. Sophie, darling, we shall have to go carefully. We cannot be exactly like other husbands and wives."

"Yo' mean . . . ?" The enchantment was fading from her eyes.

"I mean, my dear wife, that although we shall have to limit our indulgences, it does not necessarily mean that we shall love each other less."

She shook her head in incomprehension.

He realized that it would be necessary for him to be less subtle. "About our making love to each other, Sophie. Now of course, it is the normal thing for a husband and wife to occupy the same bed."

The look of expectancy returned to her eyes.

"But in our case it would mean that you would soon be a widow. Being near you would naturally excite me to do things which would be harmful to me and make me ill again. There is nothing so dangerous to the heart as the violence of love. Perhaps that is why, dearest, the heart has always been considered the seat of love. Some night, in the very act of loving you, I might die in your arms."

"Oh, 'Pollon, no!"

"Yes, it is true, Sophie. So, as much as I want to be with you, it is not safe. It would be better for me and for you, if you do not want to be a widow, to continue to occupy our separate rooms."

"And we won' have no . . . ?"

"But of course, my silly one, and we shall set aside one special night each week for it. In that way we shall both have something to anticipate and my health will continue good. We'll be so happy together, wait and see."

"If'n yo' say so, 'Pollon." Her disappointment was obvious. " 'Course I wouldn' wan' ter do nothin' to hurt yo'. Jes' mus' keep yo' well 'n' happy. Goin' to be hard on me tho', 'Pollon."

"But twice as difficult for me, Sophie." He stood up and walked around the table to where she was sitting, and kissed her lightly on the forehead. "After all, dear Sophie, there is much to marriage that does not take place in bed. By limiting it to once a week, we shall enjoy it all the more. With good food and plenty of rest I shall conserve my strength for that one special night each week. Shall we say Saturday night?"

She made a mental calculation. This was Monday. That meant five more nights. Surely it would be worth waiting for. But she herself must save face.

"Yo're right, 'Pollon 'n' yo're most sensible. Truth is only wenches wants ter be pleasured ever' night. White ladies not like wenches 'cause they more delicately constituted. Guess that's why so much human blood in our niggers today. Always heard that a pretty nigger wench in the house saves a mist'ess lots o' sufferin'. Glad I am that yo' not one o' them demandin' husbands. But"—she looked up at him and smiled consolingly—"come Saturday night, I'll 'commodate yo', 'Pollon." She was compensated in her thoughts by the fact that even though the state of his health kept him from her, he was not giving some nigger wench that which she so desperately wanted.

"Thank you, dear Sophie, you are most understanding."

Outside they heard the plink of strings as a guitar was being tuned. With Sophie on his arm, Apollon led her out to the assembled people, who, although they were not quite sure what the marriage of their mistress signified, had made this evening an even more festive occasion than usual. They were all dressed in their best, and as Apollon and Sophie appeared on the portico one of the women from the New Quarters, attired in starched white, came forward with a wreath of field lilies and ferns, which she presented to Sophie. Cheers and handclappings came from the semicircle, with loud cries of "Miz Sophie, Miz Sophie."

Holding Apollon's hand, she advanced to the steps that led down to the lawn. With her hand raised for silence, she surveyed the group below her.

"I wan' yo' all should meet yore new masta." She pushed Apollon a little ahead of her. "Yo' all 'members yore Masta Maxwell. Yo' 'members how yo' loved him and 'beyed him. Well this yore new masta. Yo'll call him Masta 'Pollon. He yore masta now. Gotta 'bey him jes' like'n yo' did yore Masta Maxwell."

Again there was cheering and this time Apollon heard his own name repeated along with Sophie's. It sounded good to him and assured him that finally he was the Master of Falconhurst, that these were his people. Too goddamned bad, he thought, that he couldn't sell them all off and turn them into money, but even if he could sell them, they would bring only worthless Confederate script. He had arrived too late

—too late by several years. But all was not lost, not by a damn sight.

After waving to the hands in acknowledgment of their cheering, he led Sophie back to her chair. That night he did not sing but fidgeted in his chair until the evening was over and the hands had left for their quarters. When they were gone he led Sophie upstairs, kissed her good night at the threshold of her room, and left her with the words "Saturday night" on his lips.

Kewp was waiting for him inside his room and Apollon stood for Kewp to slip his coat off. When Kewp had undressed him, Apollon called him over and whispered in his ear.

"Yo' keep away from Big Pearl tonight. Understand, boy?"

"Yo' a-goin' thar, 'Pollon?"

"Just as soon as she gets to sleep." He nodded in the direction of Sophie's room.

"Then if'n yo' a-goin' ter take Big Pearl, kin I have Candy?"

"Been waiting for a piece of that for a long time, haven't you, Kewp? Well, go ahead. Take her. I'm master here now. What I say goes. Take her if you want her."

"What 'bout Drummage, 'Pollon? He goin' ter be mighty mad."

"Mad?" Apollon raised one eyebrow. "Haven't you forgotten one thing? It doesn't make a goddamn bit of difference whether he gets mad or not. Drummage is a servant for life, a slave, a nigger. From now on, Drummage does as I tell him. Go ahead, take Candy if you want to, and say that those are my orders. Tell Drummage to go to hell. But before you go, Kewp, take out a pair of old pants for me. No use messing up my good ones walking through all that dust."

Kewp pointed to the other door in Apollon's room and winked. "Better yo' use the back stairs, 'Pollon. Them front ones creak somethin' awful."

Apollon grinned back at him.

"Right thoughtful of Miz Sophie to give me a room with a back door, what, Kewp?"

"Right considerate." Kewp grinned back.

Chapter 32

THE NEXT MORNING after breakfast, as befitted his new position as master, Apollon ordered a horse saddled. With Kewp accompanying him, he planned to start on a round of the plantation. Just as he was leaving the house, Drummage appeared. Apollon noticed the bitterly resentful look in the boy's eyes. He could see that Drummage was doing his best to stifle his anger but was not succeeding too well. The boy, Apollon decided, had been getting a little too big for his breeches. Even Sophie had complained about him. However, when Drummage addressed him he could not complain about his words, even though his surly manner belied his respect for his new master.

"Masta 'Pollon suh, kin I speak wid yo'?"

"Why certainly, Drummage. You can always speak to me anything you want, provided you ask permission. Shall we talk now?" Apollon held up a finger to warn Kewp that he should hold the horses a moment longer, and seated himself in one of the rocking chairs on the portico. He pointed to a spot in front of him, and Drummage stepped over to where Apollon had designated.

"Now, Drummage, what's on your mind?"

With the opportunity to speak, Drummage could not collect his thoughts into words. He rubbed one foot slowly back and forth, clenched and unclenched his hands, looked back over his shoulder to see if Kewp could hear, and then finally gathered up his courage to address Apollon.

"It's 'bout Candy."

"That's no way to address me." Apollon's abruptness did little to encourage Drummage. "I'll make allowances this time, for I am newly your master. The next time you're disrespectful to me, I'll punish you."

"Yes suh, Masta 'Pollon suh." Drummage had not meant to be impolite. His urgency had caused him to blurt out the words improperly. "It's 'bout Candy. She my woman, Masta 'Pollon suh. She my woman 'n' las' night yore boy Kewp he come upstairs a-sayin' that yo' say Candy she ain' my woman no more. He a-sayin' Candy kin bed wid him. Ain' a-saying' nothin' last night, Masta 'Pollon suh, 'cause yo' a-gone ter bed 'n' ain' that I could talk ter yo'. But Candy she my woman, Masta Pollon suh, 'n' yore boy . . ."

Apollon held up his hand and the gesture silenced Drummage.

"Now let's just get one matter straightened out, Drummage. You say that Kewp's my boy. Well he is, but don't forget one thing. You're my boy too."

"I'se Miz Sophie's boy, Masta 'Pollon suh. When Masta Hammond die, that make me Miz Sophie's boy."

"And when I married Miss Sophie yesterday, that makes you my boy now." Apollon stood up quickly, staring straight at Drummage. "Understand that, Drummage! You're no longer Miss Sophie's boy, you're mine and the sooner you get that through that goddamned thick head of yours the better. From now on, you do as I say whether you like it or not."

Drummage stared straight back at Apollon.

"Masta Hammond done bo't Candy fer me long 'fore yo' come here. Masta Hammond he say she my woman. Masta Hammond never took'n her 'way from me. Candy my woman 'n' she a-goin' ter be my woman."

"From now on, Candy's going to be Kewp's wench. And that, Drummage, ends our discussion."

"Yo' ain' got no right, Masta 'Pollon suh. Masta Hammond done give her to me. Yo' ain' de masta here. Miz Sophie say what I kin do."

Apollon raised his hand and the noise it made when it struck Drummage's cheek surprised even Apollon himself. He saw Drummage clench his fists tighter and tentatively raise one.

"If you hit me, Drummage, you'll be a dead nigger." Apollon realized that this was a test of his authority—the first one, and he meant it to be the last. "And for your even thinking you could hit me, you're going to be punished."

"Yo' ain' a-goin' ter whop me! Yo' ain' my masta!" Drummage turned and ran down the steps and continued on down the drive, looking back over his shoulder. He had no idea where he was going or what he was going to do but he was determined that he would not submit to being whipped.

Apollon leaped down from the porch and onto his horse. "Come on, Kewp, we'll catch him. Got to teach that nigger a lesson."

Drummage was no match for the horses. They came up, one on each side of him, but he still kept on running. Apollon motioned to Kewp and they brought their horses close together, squeezing Drummage between them. Apollon reached down and got a fistful of Drummage's coat at the same time that Kewp did. Between them, they lifted him off his feet.

"Want to run, do you?" Apollon eased his horse over, still holding onto Drummage. "Well run, goddamn it! Run just as far as you want." He took a firmer hold on Drummage's jacket. "Come on, Kewp, we'll teach this bastard how to run." With Drummage suspended between them, they forced their horses to a gallop. Drummage's feet scarcely touched the ground but it was necessary to move them to avoid being dragged. He fought for breath.

"Stop, Masta 'Pollon, stop. Cain' go no mo'."

"Oh yes, you can, Drummage. You like running, so you're going to see what it is to run."

At the gates that led to the main road, Apollon released him and he fell to the ground. Abandoning him for the moment, they rode on until they could slow the horses down and then returned to where Drummage was still huddled in the road.

"Guess by the time he runs back, he'll have had enough running for a while." Apollon leaned over and slapped Drummage with his quirt. "Come on, boy, you like to run so we'll run a little more. Up on your feet."

But Drummage could not move. He was utterly winded. Apollon's quirt bit deeper this time. "Guess you didn't hear me. Up on your feet, I said."

Drummage managed to pull himself up, using Kewp's stirrup. Still unable to get his breath, he hung there, panting. Again they grabbed his shoulders and started their horses, but Drummage could not make the attempt. They carried him, his feet dragging on the ground, his shoes left behind, making two black splotches on the drive. They continued with him up to the house and then around the driveway to the back. Brutus, mounted and ready for his morning tour of overseeing, was just leaving the barn. Big Randy and Zanzibar were standing in the doorway.

" 'Fore you go, Brute, I've got a job for you to do." Apollon and Kewp rode up to the barn door and released Drummage. "Want you to take this boy and have him whipped."

"Drummage, Masta 'Pollon suh?" Brute could scarcely believe it.

"Yes, Drummage! Threatened to strike me, he did."

Brutus dismounted and came to stand alongside the other men. He stared down at Drummage in disbelief. This Drummage, cringing on the ground, was no longer the lordly cock-o'-the-walk of Falconhurst. He was just a very frightened boy, but his fear was as nothing compared to the misery in his heart. He felt that his own world had collapsed about him. This tall, confident man, who sat so securely on his horse, was his new master, but he would never be the master that Hammond Maxwell was. Drummage had loved his Masta Hammond; he hated this man.

"Where do you whip around here, Brute, and who does it?" Apollon slapped his quirt against his boot.

"Whops ovah in de odder barn, Masta 'Pollon suh, 'n' Olly does de whoppin'. Don' use whips though. Uses a paddle."

"Then take him over there and get Olly. Give him fifty strokes." Apollon got down off his horse and started for the back door.

"Fifty strokes'll kill him, Masta 'Pollon suh." Brutus knew the strength behind each of Olly's strokes.

"Then kill him!" Apollon banged the back door. There was nobody in the kitchen but the harelipped Marguerite, who glanced up at him as he ran through. He took the stairs in the office up to his room and found the derringer in a drawer in the armoire. Some premonition told him he had better be armed. These niggers were not his own and might resent his authority.

Once on his horse again, with the loaded derringer in his pocket, he felt safer, and led the way for the straggling procession that was half dragging, half carrying Drummage. Apollon was aware from the grim look on their faces that they were resentful of his authority and that they did not want Drummage punished. But his own future position at Falconhurst—temporary though he intended it to be— depended on his present course. Outside of his authority over Kewp, who had always co-operated, Apollon had had no real experience in dealing with slaves, but he knew that a heavy hand and strong discipline were necessary. What he did not understand was the fact that Falconhurst slaves, having had a taste of lax discipline, had already had the opportunity to enjoy independence.

They crossed the bridge and went up the rise on the other side of the creek, down to the old barn. Here Brutus pointed to the ropes and pulleys which were used to hoist a man up. At the wave of Apollon's quirt, Drummage's clothes were stripped from him and the ropes were tied around his ankles, but the men did not hoist him up. For a moment Apollon hesitated. The pure perfection of physicality before him was so arresting that it seemed a crime to damage it. But any sign of mercy on his part would be a show of weakness. He had to go through with it.

"Why don't you pull him up?" he demanded. "What are you waiting for?"

"Waitin' fer Olly." Brutus was hoping to gain time. "He de whopper. Sent fer him but he ain' come yet. No sense in pullin' him up till Olly come."

"No sense in waiting either," Apollon insisted. "Up with him, and let the bastard hang there. Where is that Olly?"

As if to answer his question, Olly appeared, loping down the street from Big Pearl's cabin.

"What yo' a-wantin', Brute?" he questioned. "Goin' ter whop? Who a-goin' ter git it?" His wide grin evidenced his pleasure in the forthcoming event.

Brute pointed to the hanging figure in the doorway. The ropes around Drummage's ankles had raised him up high, his legs spread widely apart, his dangling arms a few inches from the floor. He swung slowly back and forth as he tried to raise his head. With his back to the light and his head down, Olly did not recognize him.

"Who dat?" He squinted at the swaying figure. "Ain' no one else here so big as dat but Drummage. Dat Drummage?"

"It's Drummage." Brutus pointed.

"Whaffor yo' a-whoppin' Drummage?" Olly went over to the hanging figure and stepped around it, kneeling down to look at his brother's face. "Drummage ain't never done nothin' bad. Whaffor yo' a-whoppin' him, Brute?"

"I ain' a-whoppin' him. Masta 'Pollon done give de orders. He say Drummage a-goin' ter hit him and den run."

Olly shook his massive head as though to collect his brains inside. Slowly, as though he had some difficulty in sending the impulses of his mind to set his limbs in motion, he strode to the side of the barn where the ox-hide paddle hung, took it down and slashed the air experimentally with it. Then, still in doubt as to what his next move might be, he ran his hands over Drummage's hanging body, caressing the sleek flesh with a tenderness that seemed alien to his big hands. After a long moment of indecision, he turned and walked over to where Apollon was sitting on his horse.

"Ain' a-goin' ter whop him." He stared up at Apollon. "He ma brother. Ain' a-goin' ter whop Drummage."

"You damn well are going to whip him because I'm telling you to."

"Ain' a-goin' ter whop him." Olly threw the paddle down on the ground and turned slowly to walk away.

"Olly!" Apollon's command was high-pitched and tense. It caused the big fellow to stop and turn around. He stared blankly at Apollon, watching him while he drew the derringer out of his pocket and aimed it at him.

"Pick up that paddle and get to work."

Olly shook his head slowly from side to side, mechanically, repeating the same phrase. "Ain' a-goin' ter whop Drummage."

"You'll be a dead nigger if you don't."

The little piece of metal in Apollon's hand did not frighten Olly. He was only dimly aware of what it might be and its miniature size did not seem to threaten his hugeness. "Ain' a-goin' ter whop Drummage," he repeated again.

The explosion of the tiny derringer was magnified by the silence. For an instant nothing seemed to happen, then a small spot of red appeared on the left shoulder of Olly's shirt. Still he continued to stand there, looking blankly at Apollon as though trying to connect the pain in his body with the noise. The spot grew larger until the whole shirt was incarnadined, and then Olly fell on his face to the ground, crumbling like a collapsed building. Apollon jumped down from his horse and ran the short distance to where he lay, stretched out in a distorted heap of arms and legs. With the toe of his boot he tried to turn the body over, but it was too heavy. He called Brutus and Zanzibar and together they heaved Olly over onto his back. His eyes were still open but there was no movement of the chest, no breathing. The movement of his body had caused a small geyser of blood to spurt from the wound. Olly was dead.

Apollon looked around at the circle of hostile faces which were now staring at him. He was frightened by their looks and their menacing gestures. The one bullet in the derringer was spent and he had no more with him. He wondered how many of the men knew it and if they would be cowed by the sight of the gun alone. At least none of them moved toward him.

Now the sound of screaming behind him caused him to turn. Big Pearl was running down the dusty street and the muttering slaves made way for her, opening up a path that led to Olly's body. She spied it and threw herself down on the floor and gathered the huge bulk up into her arms.

"He daid," she shrieked, "Ol' Mista Wilson daid! Who dun it?"

Nobody spoke but the circle of eyes all looked to Apollon.
"Yo' kilt him, masta suh?" with one hand she wiped the
tears from her eyes. With rough gentleness, she laid her
son's body back onto the ground and stood up. "Why yo'
kilt Olly, masta suh? He good boy. He not very bright, but
he a good boy."

Her half-crazed appearance and the slow movement of the
slaves to surround him kept Apollon from answering. He
edged toward his horse, never taking his eyes away from the
threatening press, and when he gained the stirrup Kewp
was there on the ground to help him mount. The circle of
eyes followed him.

Turning, Big Pearl saw, for the first time, Drummage hanging in the doorway. With another cry she ran to him.

"Let 'im down!"

Still staring at Apollon but obeying Big Pearl, two of the
men disengaged themselves from the group and untied the
ropes from the sides of the doorway. Playing them out in
their hands, they lowered Drummage's body until, by placing
his hands on the barn floor and walking forward on them,
he was able to crawl along and flatten his body onto the
floor. Willing hands untied the ropes from his ankles. With
an effort, he turned himself over and sat up. Big Pearl pulled
him to his feet and he stood, naked in his mother's arms.

"What goin' on here?" a voice from the back of the crowd
demanded.

Everyone turned to confront Sophie. Lucretia Borgia was
puffing along a few steps behind her. For the first time since
he had arrived at Falconhurst, Apollon was overjoyed to
see Sophie. He slipped down from his horse and stood beside her, feeling a strange sense of security in her presence

"Your slaves are not very amenable to discipline, Sophie."

"What's happened, 'Pollon?"

"Drummage threatened to hit me and then ran away. Kewp
and I caught him and I ordered him to be punished. Olly
refused to do the job and he too defied me. It was necessary
for me to shoot him." He pointed to the body on the ground.
"These people had better learn who's master around here
now, Sophie."

She nodded in agreement.

"Masta 'Pollon yore masta now." There was a ring of
authority in her voice. "Yo' all do like'n he say."

There was a murmur of dissent among the men, and from
the women who had come out from the cabins to join them.
Lucretia Borgia stepped in front of Sophie. She took in the

situation quickly and pushed Apollon back, to shield him from the hostile, muttering crowd.

"What all yo' crazy niggers a-doin' here? Work ter be done 'n' yo' all a-lolly-gaggin' round de barn. Git 'em back to their work, Brute. 'N' take him 'way"—she pointed to Olly—" 'n' bury him if'n he daid. Cain' have no stinkin' carcass round here a-drawin' flies. 'N' yo', Malachi, git back to yore shop. Kewp, git down off'n that horse 'n' walk Miz Sophie 'n' Masta 'Pollon back to de big house. Big Pearl, yo' hist yore fat ass back to yore cabin 'n' stay there. I'll come ovah later 'n' help wash 'n' lay out Olly. Now, git, all o' yo'! Dis is still Falconhurst 'n' niggers not a-runnin' it. Serve Olly right. Masta 'Pollon he yore masta; Miz Sophie she yore mist'ess. Yo' do's they says. If'n yo' don', I a-goin' ter strip yo' down myse'f. Pull d' meat right off'n yore backs in hunks 'n' feed it to de hawgs. Now git! 'N' yo' Drummage, git yore breeches on, what yo' a-doin' a-standin' round here buck-nekkid afore Miz Sophie? Lotsa work ter be done ovah to de big house 'n' I ain' a-doin' it all. Git yore breeches on 'n' help me back." She waited for Drummage to put his pants on and then took his arm. With deference she motioned for Apollon and Sophie to precede her, then, still on Drummage's arm, she fell into step behind them.

The hands stood still, watching her go, but she had gone only a few steps when she turned and yelled back at them:

"Didn' yo' hear me, yo' wo'thless niggers? I said git 'n' I means *git*."

Slowly they separated, fanning out from the tight little circle they had made. Their menacing looks gave way to grins and chuckles. The crisis was over. They were willing to return to work now, all except Big Pearl, who knelt over her boy's lifeless body, sobbing.

Chapter 33

WHETHER it was because of Apollon's deed, or Lucretia Borgia's words of authority, respect for the new master was engendered among the hands. Not that they loved him or felt any loyalty to him, but they at least obeyed him, if not with willingness, at least with alacrity. Drummage, going about his tasks in the house as usual, paid respectful lip service to Apollon. The loneliness of his bed at night without Candy still rankled when he pictured her on the other side of the partition with Kewp and listened to the creaking of the bed ropes, but he tempered his anger with the thought of the girls in the spinning house and a recent conquest he had made in the New Quarters. Only none of them were like Candy, for whom he felt love as well as desire. They served his purpose but they did not take her place. Still, he was unwilling to risk his life for her. He saw what had happened to Olly. Life was still sweet to Drummage, even without Candy, and he had no desire to face Apollon's anger or his derringer.

The incident was never referred to in the big house, either by Sophie or Apollon, and least of all by Lucretia Borgia. The one person who might well have borne Apollon ill will —Big Pearl—seemed little affected, at least openly. He had been hesitant about going to her cabin and had stayed away for several nights until Kewp told him she was asking for him and wondering why he did not come. He went, and found that Big Pearl's emotions over the loss of her son were entirely separate from the demands of her body. She welcomed Apollon as warmly as ever and responded to him as wholeheartedly as before. As few words had ever passed between them previously, there was no need for words now. After all, Apollon assured himself, she was his property and she had to do as he desired. But as she responded with a warmth which could not be commanded, he decided that she did not hold him responsible for Olly's slaying. He was white and he was the master; therefore his right of life or death was not to be questioned. So Apollon crept into her cabin at night, occupied her bed, and departed as usual, without a word being spoken between them, leaving Big Pearl free, after his departure, to return to her grief. On Saturday nights he manfully did his duty by Sophie, which was exactly as wordless and far more mechanical than what he did with Big Pearl. He enjoyed it not at all and came to dread the recurrence of those Saturday nights to which Sophie looked forward with such obvious expectancy.

At his own suggestion she had resumed her rides with Zanzibar and, although they were no longer of daily occurrence, he watched her go and bade her a willing good-by with the wish that she might have a pleasant ride. She did not insist that he accompany her and he was well aware of her reasons. It was all a part of his plan, and so far, with the exception of the Drummage-Olly incident, his plan was working out even better than he had hoped. The affair with the Falconhurst slaves was of minimum importance to him. He intended to be there only a short time, so why bother about a lot of worthless niggers who would only bring a few paper Confederate dollars if he found an auction block to stand them on. Their drop in value had been a great disappointment to him when he figured out their prewar value in so many hundreds of thousands of dollars. But he felt better when he remembered the good solid English pounds securely banked in London.

Indeed, it was time to think about those English pounds, time to get them into his own hands and feel their security behind him. It might not prove easy, but he would try. Sophie would need a little softening up but that would not be difficult. He knew the way to do that. Although it was only Tuesday he would surprise her, and when she appeared for breakfast in the green velvet riding habit he did surprise her.

"Riding again today, dear?" Apollon's charm was turned on, making poor Sophie flutter.

"Got ter git outa the house, 'Pollon. Stayin' inside all the time makes me fidgety."

"And me too, my dear. I feel so well today, so strong and full of life. Guess I'll go with you this morning. It just occured to me that I've never kissed my dear wife out of doors in the sunshine. Why don't you dismiss Zanzibar, wait for me to change my clothes after breakfast, and we'll ride together today. We've never had a *lune de miel*— what do you call it here—a honeymoon. Let's have a little taste of one today."

She was overjoyed—quite beside herself with enthusiasm —and after breakfast they set off alone. She led him across the plantation fields to the secluded spot where she was wont to go with Zanzibar. Once there, they dismounted to sit on the soft needles under the pines. It was a pleasant, peaceful spot, and although it held many memories for Sophie it had never seemed quite so idyllic as today. Apollon stretched out on the ground, patting a place for her beside him. When she had seated herself, he lay back and pillowed her head in his lap. His fingertips drew little circles on her neck and then started to undo the buttons of her bodice.

"We a mighty happy couple tergether, ain' we, 'Pollon?" She wanted his confirmation of her happiness.

"These have been some of the happiest days of my life, Sophie." He had developed the art of lying so perfectly that his words throbbed with sincerity. "I've been happy with you here at Falconhurst. I do hope you will be as happy with me in France."

She looked at him anxiously, but he had said "with me," so her anxiety was allayed. He didn't mean to go alone. She shifted her head, moving it in his lap. The unbuttoned bodice released her breast.

"We a-goin' ter France?" The transport of her joy and the ecstasy of his fingers were almost more than she could bear. Her hand reached for his and she kissed his fingers greedily.

"But of course, my dear. That will be our real honeymoon." His fingers returned to their explorations. "France is my home and now that you are my wife, that is your home too. So, we shall visit France, but we shall have to go to England first. And that reminds me, darling Sophie, there are a few matters we had best talk about, and what better time than when we are here alone together? I do hate to speak of worldly things but. . . ." He raised his head and kissed her, forcing her back on the ground as he did so, kissing her expertly and listening for the little moans that told him of her desire. He would not tell her what those little difficulties were until he was sure that she was more interested in him than in anything he might say. Slowly, button by button, he undid the remainder of her bodice and then guided her hand to himself that she might find proof of his own ardor and his ready ability to please her.

"And, my dear Sophie"—he lifted his face a few inches from hers—"the main one of those little difficulties that I mentioned is money. Let us talk it over and see if we can solve this . . . this so little cloud on the sky of our happiness."

"We got money, 'Pollon, plenty o' money. Le's not talk 'bout money now."

"But the awful thing, dear Sophie, is that we do not have plenty of money. Confederate money, yes! You have it and so do I, but that will not serve our purpose. If we are to get a ship from Mobile—some blockade runner that will take us to Havana or Jamaica—we'll have to have gold. No ship captain in his right senses would consider a passage paid for in Confederate paper, and that's all I have and all you have. So, the one big difficulty we have to solve is how are we going to get the gold to pay for our passage. Once in London we can draw on your account there and I shall be able to get money from France, but now, darling, although we have plenty of money as you say, we are really paupers."

Sophie was sufficiently aware of the lowered value of Confederate notes to realize that there was truth in his statement. Confederate bills had dropped in value, but gold, when it could be obtained, was still supreme.

"And so I was thinking, dear Sophie"—Apollon undid his own clothes the better to accommodate her eager fingers—"that as you have so many jewels—both yours and your stepmother's—possibly we could convert some of them into gold and thus pay our passage to England where we could get plenty of money."

"Cain' sell my pretties, 'Pollon. Goin' ter need 'em if'n we go to France."

"But, Sophie, all my mother's jewels are there and they will all be yours. Why . . . there's a diamond tiara . . ."

"What's that?" Even her groping hands stopped at the mention of diamonds.

"A little crown which you will wear when you go to the Tuileries to meet the Emperor and the Empress."

It was such a beautiful picture—Sophie Maxwell in a crown of diamonds, shaking hands with the Emperor and Empress —that she was still for a moment, savoring it.

"But, 'Pollon, we don' need ter sell my pretties if'n all yo' want is gold. Plenty o' gold right here at Falconhurst."

He thought she was crazy but he kept still, allowing her to explain.

"We got two, three, mebbe four ol' kittles o' gold buried right here at Falconhurst. My Grandpapa he buried them. Don' know jes' where at they are but Lucretia Borgia, she knows. 'Fore he left for de war, my pore papa dug one o' 'em up. Used it ter outfit his company. See, 'Pollon, we don' need ter sell none of my pretties jes' ter git money with."

It could be true. Apollon knew that some of the old planters buried their money rather than trust it to banks. "Are you sure, darling, sure about this gold?"

"Co'se I'm shore. Ain' never lied to yo' yit. Ain' never goin' ter neither."

He believed her and, this point won, Apollon allowed Sophie a few more minutes of dalliance to which she responded with fervor. This Tuesday-morning plum was something she had not anticipated; consequently it was far sweeter than any Saturday night, eagerly awaited though that might be. But her bliss was not unalloyed; Apollon had other business to discuss.

"There yet remain one or two other difficulties, Sophie dear." He seized her hands and held them. "But I'm sure we shall be able to settle them as easily as the gold. First off, of course, we shall have to find the money. Then there's the difficulty of our getting a ship. Blockade runners do not go on schedule, you know. I might locate one in a day or it might take weeks before I could find one. I wouldn't want you hanging around Mobile in this heat, poked up in some little hotel room. Place is full of soldiers, hotels are crowded with all sorts of people, food is scarce, and Mobile in wartime is no place for a woman. I can't have my wife in that sort of an atmosphere while I'm away all day down at the wharves, trying to find a ship."

Despite the pressure of Apollon's body against hers, Sophie sat upright. "Ain' a-goin' ter stay here 'lone if'n yo's goin' 'way, 'Pollon. Cain' set me here at Falconhurst a-worryin' 'bout yo', fearin' yo' sick somewhere. If'n yo' goes, I go too." There was a finality in her words which told him further argument would accomplish nothing.

"But it will be so uncomfortable for you, my dear. Crowds of soldiers, some hot hotel room, nothing to do all day when I am out." Lame arguments, which he knew would accomplish nothing.

"Don' make me no neverminds, 'Pollon! Don' bother me none! Pleasures me to see Mobile anyway. Ain' bin 'way from here since I was in New Orleans. If'n yo' go, I go." She was determined.

He could see her mind was made up and nothing could change her. But that did not mean that he was defeated. He intended to leave with the money and without her. Like a good strategist, he had more than one string to his bow, but further argument would only defeat his purposes. There was still another matter to settle.

"Then there is the difficulty of the money in your bank in London." He released her hands. "We really should transfer it to Paris. It will not do any good for you to have your money in England when we are living in France and you see, my dear, now that you are married to me, I shall have to handle it because in England a husband has to handle his wife's business."

This was far above Sophie's limited understanding. The money to her credit in England had never seemed very real to her. Pounds were not like dollars and she had only a vague idea of what they were worth. Never having had them, she hardly realized that they were there.

"If'n yo' say so, Apollon." In her present desperation for him she was completely uninterested.

"Then if you are willing, dear Sophie"—his lips avoided hers—"We'll go to that lawyer fellow in Benson and have him draw up a paper for me so that I can withdraw your money when we get to London and transfer it to my bank in Paris. It will save you a lot of trouble because you wouldn't want to run all over London attending to it. And we'd better get it done before we leave because we might have to sail the very day we arrive in Mobile."

In her impatience, Sophie agreed. It meant little to her anyway. At this moment, with the assurance that she would go with Apollon to Mobile, she was far more interested in the pressure of his lips against hers. Here, under the soughing pines, where she had initiated so many episodes of sterile passion, she was, for the first time, in the arms of a man who she truly believed loved her—her own husband, her dear 'Pollon. He was taking her to France to be a princess and wear a diamond crown before an emperor. Never before had she achieved such happiness, such ecstasy. Apollon's kisses crushed her lips, his body felt delightfully heavy and strong upon her, and when, with one final, furious burst of passion, he quitted her, she almost collapsed in a delirium of joy.

He helped her with her buttons, gave a hand to pull her up, and then held his hands for her to mount. But before mounting his own horse he leaned his head against the velvet of her thigh.

"Shall we go into Benson this afternoon and see the lawyer?" he asked, and then, as if the matter were of no real importance, he added, "You have made me so happy this morning, Sophie. Love is so much more wonderful here in the daylight under the sky. But we must try it again tonight and see whether we like it better in darkness and in your bed."

This was too much for poor Sophie. Her El Dorado had been achieved. She could only twine her fingers in his hair and remain mute in her exaltation.

After the mid-day meal Sophie accompanied him to Benson and they found the lawyer, who drew up a legal-looking document which turned over to her husband, one Apollon Beauchair, all the monies deposited in Brown's Bank in London under the name of Sophie Maxwell Charnwood, now Mrs. Apollon Beauchair. Sophie signed it quickly in her childishly round handwriting, glad to be relieved of the responsibility and proud of her new name, which she had just learned to spell.

On their return home, before Sophie could prove to Apollon's satisfaction that love-making at night in a dark bedroom was more exotic than love-making in the daytime under the shade of a pine tree, he insisted that she get directions from Lucretia Borgia as to the burial places of the kettles of gold. Lucretia Borgia was not too willing to divulge this sacred trust and even claimed that she had forgotten the exact location. Stubbornly she denied remembering, using as an excuse her old age and the fact that she was forgetful of many things these days. Sophie, knowing full well that the old woman had an unfailing memory, begged, cajoled, and threatened her to no avail, until she herself, recalling that Drummage had accompanied her father on the night he had disinterred one of the kettles, called him in. With the threat of a whipping, which he knew would be forthcoming unless he divulged the knowledge, Drummage revealed the location of the cache by the big rock near Pearl's cabin. Not to be outdone by his revelation, Lucretia Borgia's memory suddenly returned, and she corroborated the information, remembering that there were four kettles buried, as she said, "no'th, south, eas' 'n' wes' of the rock."

Apollon and Kewp set out to locate them. Sophie would willingly have accompanied them but Apollon, with kindly consideration for her, pointed out that there was no need for her to stand around in the darkness while they dug holes in the earth, when she could pass the time to better advantage in prettying herself for their night's experiment.

Drummage accompanied them, trying hard to hide his sullenness through a genuine fear of Apollon. He had already come off the worse in one bout with his master's authority and he did not dare risk another. The next time he might not fare as well. But although they dug steadily for nearly two hours, they were able to locate only two of the kettles. The contents of these, however, glittering in the rays of the lantern, promised Apollon a far richer reward than all of Sophie's jewels. He was determined eventually to get the pick of those also, but now he was overjoyed with this unexpected windfall. Gold—real Federal gold eagles! Now worth many times their original value! He had no idea now many the kettles contained but they were so heavy that it took the combined efforts of all three to carry them back to the house and into his own bedroom.

As Sophie was anxiously awaiting him on his return, befrilled in a cambric nightgown, he had no opportunity to count his new riches. However, he took pains to disparage their value to her. Relying on her ignorance of money, he showed her several of the coins with their dates of forty and fifty years earlier, explaining that they were old coins and as such greatly diminished in value. Maybe there was enough to pay for their passage, he said, although he was fearful, because the blockade runners could charge anything they pleased. No telling how much it would cost, and then there would be their passage money to England from Havana or Kingston or Nassau—whichever port they were fortunate enough to arrive at. Perhaps they might have to sacrifice *some* of her jewelry, but even if they did, there was plenty in France.

Despite his promise to her and the frilled nightgown she had donned, he informed her regretfully and with a masterful quivering of his lower lip that he would be unable to keep the night's commitment. He told her that his exertions in digging up the gold had so exhausted him he feared another stroke. Not but what he was fully prepared; he pointed downward and winked at her.

But Sophie was not to be denied so easily.

"Yo' promised, 'Pollon. Yo' tol' me this mornin' that we'd see which un's better, night or day. Yo' know yo' did, 'Pollon."

"And so I did." He wanted nothing more than to get rid of her, peaceably if possible, but if not peaceably by any other means. "But if I were taken ill again, it would delay all our plans. Bear with me, Sophie. There's another night coming and after all, what I have done is as much for you as for myself. I'll make it up to you. And now, go to your room, my dear, lest you tempt me overmuch and we both regret it, and don't disturb me by coming in later. I do need the sleep, Sophie, and please don't worry about me and awaken me."

She allowed herself to be convinced and relinquished him unwillingly, dreading the loneliness of her room after such high expectations. But he was right, of course. Apollon was always right.

He waited for her to go, trying hard to maintain his expression of disappointment. If only she would go and leave him alone! He had so much to do and so many plans to make. Now, with the money in his hands and the document signed that would give him her money in England, he was anxious to get away. He did not want to hurt her, but he might have to, and it was with this thought in mind that he kissed her.

"Good night, Sophie, we'll meet at breakfast."

She could see there was no use begging, and dutifully, almost mournfully, she returned his kiss.

"Good night, 'Pollon."

He walked with her to the door of her room and then hurried back to his own room where Kewp was waiting.

Chapter 34

APOLLON closed the door and with his finger on his lips and his other hand pointing to Sophie's room, he warned Kewp that Sophie might overhear them. They conversed in whispers.

"Yo' a-goin' ter Big Pearl?" Kewp had witnessed Apollon's dismissal of Sophie. "That Sophie shore got an awful itch fer yo', 'Pollon. She jes' de same wid dat Zanzibar boy. He say she dreen 'im all out, she do."

"Big Pearl's out of the question tonight, Kewp. We've got plans to make, important ones. I want to quit this place tomorrow. I figure we've got plenty of money there"—he pointed to the kettles—"to get us to New Orleans and keep us going for a while. We'll get Mama and Jeanne-Marie and get to hell out of this country. Over in England we'll have plenty more money and then we'll go to France and live like gentlemen. We'll count the money later but it's all gold, and there's plenty there. I'd hoped to get away, just the two of us, leaving Sophie behind, but she insists on going with us. That complicates matters."

"Want ter git away from here mysel', 'Pollon, but if'n we goes, wants ter take Candy 'long too. Likes her, I do, 'Pollon." Kewp winked suggestively. " 'N' if'n yo' likes Big Pearl, yo' shore likes Candy mo'. That Big Pearl she good but"—he rolled his eyes—"Candy she better. She younger 'n' she prettier. Don' min'- sharin' her wid yo', 'Pollon, 'n' yo' know, it come in mighty handy havin' a wench 'long wid us. Mighty handy!"

Apollon appeared not to be listening; at least he paid no attention to Kewp's remark. He was busy thinking, his brain adopting and rejecting various plans. They could leave, right this minute, and get a head start, just he and Kewp in the chaise with the two kettles of gold. But no! Morning would come and they would be missing and he knew Sophie well enough to know that she would instigate a hue and cry after them. They would be hunted down and he could never convince her that he had not abandoned her. Sophie would seek revenge and that would mean prison for him. No, there must be some other way. But what? He removed his shoes and walked back and forth across the room, finally stopping where the iron kettles sat on the floor. Kneeling down and running his hands through them he found that they were indeed filled with twenty-dollar gold double eagles. His hands clutching at the gleaming yellow pieces, he cursed Sophie again for her obstinacy. Suddenly he stood up, snapping his fingers.

"I think I've got it, Kewp."

"What yo' got, 'Pollon?"

"An idea! I don't know if it will work or not but luck's been with us so far, maybe our good fortune will hold out. Now listen! Come closer to me so that you can hear me when I whisper."

Kewp came to kneel beside Apollon.

"Tomorrow morning, Sophie's going to ride with Zanzibar. She doesn't know it yet, but she will."

"How yo' know?"

"I know Sophie. She's been disappointed tonight and she'll have a whole night to think about it. By morning, she'll be wanting Zanzibar if she can't have me. She'll welcome the chance to get away, especially if I suggest it. Here's what I want you to do. As soon as she leaves with Zanzibar, you have a horse saddled and waiting for me. Understand?"

"Co'se I understand, 'Pollon, tha's easy."

"As soon as you see me go, you have big Randy hitch up my horses to the light spring wagon and have them ready, waiting at the barn."

Kewp nodded.

"Here." Apollon pulled out his two carpetbags from the armoire. "We'll put the gold in these."

"What 'bout your clothes, 'Pollon?"

"To hell with the clothes. I can sacrifice them for this." He pointed to the money. "Get the valises into the wagon and get up on the seat and wait for me to come back. The moment I return, we'll leave. Be all set to go when I arrive."

"What 'bout Candy, 'Pollon?"

Apollon considered for a moment. A third person would complicate matters but, as Kewp had said, it would be handy to have her along. He knew that there would be no jealousy between Kewp and himself; they could share her between them.

"Think she'll want to go? Ain' kidnappin' no screaming female."

"She bin a-wantin' ter git 'way from here ever since she come. She say she like me better'n that Drummage. She sick 'n' tired o' Falconhurst 'n' him too."

"Then tell her she can come. Have her sitting in the carriage with you, all ready to go. Tell 'em here at the house it's Sophie's orders."

"But what yo' a-goin' to be doin', 'Pollon, whilst I'm doin' them things?"

"It's all in the lap of the gods, Kewp, but if things go the way I think they will, we'll be away from here tomorrow and Sophie won't be following us, nor will she send after us. She'll be glad to see us go. Here . . ." he stood up and rummaged in a drawer until he found the derringer. "Load this for me. I'll need it tomorrow."

Kewp had never loaded a pistol before but he had seen Apollon do it, so while Apollon transferred the gold eagles from the kettles to his valises, he busied himself loading the little weapon. He could hear Apollon counting as he transferred the money. When he had finished, he buckled the straps and lifted one. The leather handle strained but held. Kewp handed him the loaded derringer, and Apollon slipped it into the pocket of his coat.

"Now you remember what to do tomorrow?"

Kewp repeated his instructions.

Apollon nodded his approval and dismissed him, opening the door to the back stairs for him. Kewp hesitated a moment before leaving.

"Grateful I am, 'Pollon, that yo' a-takin' Candy 'long wid us. Yo' shore a'goin' to like her. Look, 'Pollon, whyn't yo' come up to my room tonight. Candy there 'n' yo' 'n' her git acquainted. Never knows how de coat fits less'n yo' tries it on."

It was Apollon's turn to hesitate.

"Why not, Kewp? Don't feel like sleeping anyway. Too much on my mind."

Together they tiptoed down the back stairs, through the kitchen and up the narrow stairs to the attic. A window at the end of the hall gave a faint light and Kewp pointed to a closed door.

"Drummage sleeps there," he whispered.

312

They continued on to the next closed door and he opened it carefully, closing it behind him as they both stepped inside. It was hotter here than in the second-floor bedrooms and no vestige of a breeze came in through the open window. There was a heavy smell of musk and sweat. A dark figure sat up on the bed.

"Who dat?" Candy could see the black silhouettes of the two men.

"It's me 'n' hush yore mouf." Kewp went over to the bed and laid his hand on her.

"But who dat wid yo'?"

"My masta. He a-wantin' ter pleasure yo' tonight, Candy. Yo' a-goin' ter like him. He better'n me."

"Al'ays admired him. Right glad he come. Whar yo' a-goin', Kewp?"

"Ain' a-goin' nowhere. Stayin' right here."

"Yo' a-goin' ter let him, Masta 'Pollon?"

Apollon laughed. "Kewp invited me, Candy. We three going to be alone together from now on. Might as well get used to it."

"If'n yo' say so, Masta 'Pollon suh, but two's company, three's a crowd."

"Three's not a crowd wid me 'n' 'Pollon, Candy baby," Kewp boasted. "Wid me 'n' 'Pollon round, three's a whole army."

"Uh-huh!" She had already satisfied herself in the darkness that it would be.

Chapter 35

APOLLON'S fingers shook as he replaced the coffee cup in the saucer. The night had been a tempestuous one and now, facing Sophie across the breakfast table, he regretted having yielded to Kewp's invitation. So much depended on today; he needed a clear head for thinking. It would be the culmination of all his plans, and things must go right. Sophie noticed his nervousness and the fact that he had scarcely touched his breakfast. In a way it pleased her, for it proved that he must have been really ill the night before. With the assurance that his inability had been purely due to his physical condition, she was able to content herself and was all solicitude and fussy anxiety. He was aware of her good humor and decided to profit by it.

"I fear I must return to bed today, my dear. All the activities of yesterday were a little too much for me." He looked up at her and smiled wanly. "Yesterday morning under the pines, you know, and then the trip to Benson and the digging. All in all, I didn't sleep very well, so, darling, with your permission, I'll go back upstairs."

Instantly she was all concern. He was so precious to her; his health was more important than anything else. She'd come and sit by him all the morning; she'd fan him; she'd have Lucretia Borgia bake a custard, she'd. . . .

But he shook his head.

"My dear Sophie, you are too good to me. What I need most is rest and there is no reason for you to sit in a darkened room beside me all morning. Look, Sophie, it's a glorious day. Let me sleep and you go out. Take your ride as usual."

"Cain' leave yo', 'Pollon, jes' cain'."

"But I'll rest all the better alone, dear. Now, no more arguments." He pointed to Drummage, who was behind Sophie's chair. "Go out to the barn and tell Zanzibar to saddle Miss Sophie's horse and his own. Have him bring them around front." At Drummage's departure, he stood up and walked around to Sophie. "We'll go upstairs now and I'll stay with you while you change and after you go I'll sleep. Now, is it all settled?"

"Yo' so good to me, 'Pollon. Al'ays thinkin' o' me. Ain' never thinkin' 'bout yo'se'f. I'll go if'n you wants me to. Yes, I'll go."

He sat in her room, watching her while she changed into her riding habit, and a few minutes after she had left he went into his own room, put on his coat, making sure that the derringer was in his pocket, and then ran down the back stairs, through the kitchen and out to the barn. Kewp was waiting for him with the horse saddled and Apollon mounted. Big Randy was busy on the other side of the barn, so Apollon spoke loudly enough for him to hear.

"Miss Sophie and I are going into Benson when she gets back from her ride. Hitch up the spring wagon, Kewp, and have it ready and tell Miss Sophie's Candy that she is to go along too."

"Yas suh, Masta 'Pollon suh." Kewp grinned. He came close to the horse, fumbled with a buckle on the bridle, and whispered to Apollon: "Thought yo'd want Candy ter come 'long. Ain' she better'n Big Pearl? Ain' she, 'Pollon?"

"She is, Kewp. This time I agree with you. Now, don't forget the valises, and you and Candy be ready to leave the minute I come back."

Kewp winked one eye in answer and stood at the barn door, watching Apollon ride off along the same route that Zanzibar and Sophie had taken only a few minutes previously. Apollon guessed where they were headed and he followed their path until he could see the dust of their horses ahead of him. Then he slowed down, keeping close to the woods that ran along the side of the bridle path and later taking a trail through the trees that would bring him to the group of pines by the river. Quite some distance away, he halted his horse and tied the animal to a sapling, then proceeded the rest of the way by foot. As he neared the pines, he saw the two riderless horses and threw himself on the ground. Taking cover in some low shrub, he inched along carefully until he found a place screened by bushes from which he could see the needle-carpeted retreat.

As he had suspected, they were seated in the same spot where he and Sophie had been the day before, but he was hardly prepared for what he saw. The mating of black flesh with white had always been repugnant to him until his visit to Falconhurst. Even in his dalliance with Big Pearl and his last night's orgy with Kewp and Candy, he had justified himself with the excuse that he was a man and as such had the right to take a colored woman. But for a white woman deliberately to seek out a nigger buck as a stud, especially such a *bozal* as Zanzibar, was repulsive to him. And even more repulsive was Sophie's apparent pleasure in exciting her companion, whose stoical indifference seemed to resist all her efforts until she slapped him soundly in her impatience.

"I declare, Zan, ain' yo' got no life 'tall this mornin'? Yo' daid?" Apollon heard her say.

"Cain' he'p it, Miz Sophie ma'am. Guess I jes' daid like'n yo' say."

"Well, yo' better git some life in yo'. A-goin' ter sell yo' ter de first trader what comes along. Yo' bin a-pesterin' some wench over in de New Quarters? Tha's why yo' so lifeless?"

"I'se a-tryin', Miz Sophie ma'am. Tryin'."

"Well, that's better." The results of her efforts were slowly becoming more apparent to her.

Apollon watched, and the longer he watched the more sordid it all became to him. This white woman, mistress of a plantation like Falconhurst, demeaning herself to beg for the unwilling services of a black buck. Supposing, just supposing, he really did love this woman and discovered her in this position. He would kill her and her black paramour with one bullet and not a judge nor a jury in the South would convict him. and now, with the debased acrobatics going on before his eyes, he knew for a certainty he could never again touch Sophie. The memory of her twisting body in that black embrace would make it impossible for him ever to simulate passion for her again. He was glad of what was happening for it suited his plans, but he also thanked God that today was his last day at Falconhurst as an actor in this ridiculous burlesque.

Fascinated in spite of himself, he watched the whole gross performance until it was over and then, as Zanzibar reached for the soiled heap of cloth that was his pantaloons and as Sophie busied herself with the buttons of her bodice, Apollon stood up, his presence betrayed by a crackling of the bushes. Zanzibar, in his black nakedness, stood staring at him with eyes that were chalk dots of fear, knowing full well that the derringer in Apollon's hand meant his death. Sophie, in an awful moment of hesitation, looked first at Apollon and then at Zanzibar. She too saw the gun in Apollon's hands.

"Kill him, 'Pollon. Kill him! He jes' did somethin' awful ter me. Forced me, he did. Oh, 'Pollon, I'se so glad yo' come 'long. Perteck me, 'Pollon, he raped me, he did." She stumbled towards him, holding up the waist of her long skirt with one hand while she tripped over its folds.

"Stand still, Zanzibar," Apollon warned. "And you, Sophie, stay where you are. I'm going to kill this boy, Sophie, but I want you to know he's not to blame. He didn't rape you. You raped him and this isn't the first time either. I'm leaving you, Sophie. No decent man would stay with you after having seen what I have seen."

"Don' shoot me, Masta 'Pollon suh." Zanzibar's face had turned ashen. "I ain' bin a-wantin' to do this. Miz Sophie she made me. She bin makin' me. Ain' bin wantin' to never."

"I know that, Zanzibar. I heard all that went on here this morning but I've got to kill you just the same. I should be killing my wife but I can't do that. Killing you instead." He took careful aim at Zanzibar, pointing at the heaving black chest. He hated to pull the trigger and kill an innocent man but he was compelled to do so to substantiate his repudiation of Sophie and his subsequent departure. She couldn't stop his leaving now.

"Kill him, 'Pollon!" Sophie stumbled a few steps nearer. "Mayhap he didn' make me this mornin' but he did long time ago. Kill him 'n' I swear it'll never happen 'gain wid no one. Wid no one but yo'."

Apollon disregarded her, pitying the shaking black boy. His finger contracted on the trigger but instead of the explosion he expected, there was only the click of metal against metal. He stared at the little pistol in his hand. Kewp had forgotten to put on the percussion cap when he had loaded it.

Zanzibar, with his knowledge of firearms, sensed what had happened. He knew that, for the moment, his life was saved. But only for the moment. Once at the big house, he would either be whipped to death or shot. Crouching now, he darted along the ground to where the horses were tethered. Evidently Sophie realized his purpose, for she screamed—a shriek without words that vainly tried to stop him and at the same time warn Apollon. But Zanzibar had reached the horse and disengaged the long squirrel rifle from his saddle holster—the same firearm which had supplied so much game to Falconhurst and which he always carried whenever he went out to bag stray rabbits or game.

Before Apollon had sensed his danger, the rifle spoke. He heard Sophie's shrieks and felt the impact of the bullet in the side of his head like the dull thud of a mallet. That was the last sensation he ever felt. His knees buckled under him and his body crashed into the bushes. Sophie's eyes turned from the prone figure of Apollon to the fleeing figure of the naked Zanzibar on horseback. Scarcely knowing what she was doing, she stumbled forward a few steps, picked up Zanzibar's pantaloons and went over to where Apollon's lifeless body was stretched out. On her knees beside him she dabbed with the sweaty cloth at the blood from the small round hole in his head. Her moans were hardly human, mere animal sounds, which she was unable in her grief to transform into words. Dumbly she cradled his head in her lap, refusing to believe that he was dead, and continued to stanch the wound until the flow of blood seemed to stop and she imagined she had brought him back to life. In that one joyful moment of hope, she found words.

" 'Pollon, 'Pollon! Never meant ter do it. Didn', 'Pollon, 'cause I loves yo'. Oh, 'Pollon, it's all my fault, my bad blood from mama. She a nigger-lover too. My papa kilt her 'n' now I 'mos' kilt yo'. Kin yo' speak, 'Pollon? Kin yo' speak ter me 'n' tell me yo' ain' a-goin' ter leave me?"

317

But even as she spoke the words, she knew he was dead. Dead! And nothing she could ever do would bring him back to life. His lips were parted, showing his white teeth, and she pressed her lips against his. They were still warm and she could not relinquish them or stop her hands from their frenzied swarming over his still warm body. How long she stayed there, sobbing and caressing him, she did not know, but gradually the paroxysm of her grief subsided and she became more lucid. She could not leave him here. How could she abandon him to the flies that were already feeding on his blood? Who would brush them off if she went away?

Hardly knowing what she was doing she managed to reach her horse and mount him. Without arranging her dress or hooking her skirt, she slashed at the horse with her crop and sent him in a headlong gallop to the house. Drummage, Kewp, and Candy were engaged in some sort of an altercation at the barn, screaming furiously at one another, but what they were saying or doing did not penetrate to her consciousness. Her horse halted at the barn door, unable to enter because of the team already hitched to the wagon. Whatever it was that Drummage and Kewp were quarreling about ceased as she arrived. They saw by her clothes and her streaming hair that something of dire importance had happened and all three stared at her as she slipped down off her horse.

"Wha' happened, Miz Sophie?" Drummage ran up to her, supporting her.

" 'Pollon daid," she gasped, " 'Pollon daid 'n' Zanzibar kilt him. He down by de river." Her mission accomplished, she collapsed in Drummage's arms. Half carrying her, he ran to the house, screaming as he went for Lucretia Borgia.

She erupted from the back door, taking Sophie in her arms.

"Wha' happen, Drummage?"

"Don' know. Miz Sophie a-sayin' that Zanzibar kilt Masta 'Pollon. He daid down by de river. Best I git Brute 'n' go 'n' see."

"Yo' wait fer me. I a-goin' jes' soon's I git Miz Sophie inter de house." Lucretia Borgia and Drummage got Sophie inside and Drummage ran back to the barn, where Kewp and Candy were still sitting in the wagon.

"Yo' git down off'n that wagon, Candy, 'n' git inter de house. Yo' ain' a-goin' wid Kewp. Hear me, yo' gits yo'self inter de house. Miz Sophie done say Masta 'Pollon's daid. He daid so's he ain' my masta no mo' 'n' yo' my woman 'gain." Drummage exulted. " 'N' yo', Kewp, I'm a-going to kill

318

yo'." He made a dive for Kewp, crouching low and springing at him.

Kewp jumped out of the way, vaulting over the seat and landing in the back of the wagon. He yelled to Candy.

"Larrup them horses, gal. Let's git away from here."

She obeyed him, seizing the reins and wrenching the whip from the socket. Drummage had stumbled and nearly fallen but had managed to grab the tailgate of the wagon. Now Kewp kicked at his clinging hands but he held on and, with one knee over the tailgate, pulled himself in, despite Kewp's blows. Once up on the wagon, he grappled with Kewp as the light vehicle caromed around the driveway side of the house. Neither was able to stand and now both were struggling on the floor of the wagon. Kewp managed to get to his knees and from his superior position flailed at his opponent. Drummage, groping for support to raise himself, found the leather handle of the heavy carpet bag. Supported by the firmness of his grip, he managed to lift himself up, only to be knocked down again. This time he fell from the back of the wagon. The bag, pulled out by his weight, fell beside him, breaking open and spilling the gold pieces through its broken sides. Kewp crawled over into the seat beside Candy and took the reins from her hand. They were on the driveway now and he lashed at the horses. Soon they had passed the gateposts and were out on the highway.

Drummage stumbled to his feet, watching the dust of the wagon as it disappeared down the road. He could go back to the barn and saddle a horse and go after them, but nobody told him to do it and he was so conditioned to obeying orders he did not know whether he should go or not. With Masta 'Pollon dead and Miz Sophie dead too for all he knew, he had a feeling he should stay behind. Let Candy go if she wanted to. She was no good to him any more. He had heard the way she had carried on with Kewp and his master last night. To hell with her!

He knelt down and gathered the bright gold pieces together into the broken valise. Suddenly it occurred to him that these were his. Nobody knew he had them. Their value as money meant little to him and yet he realized that they represented many things he had always wanted. He pulled the split valise together as well as he could and, carrying it in both arms, he hid it under a low shrub.

When he returned to the back door of the big house, Lucretia Borgia was sitting on the doorstep directing activities. Big Randy and Sampson were hitching a horse to the

319

buckboard and Brutus was already mounted on the horse Sophie had abandoned. Lucretia Borgia spied Drummage coming around the corner.

"Here, yo' Drummage, come here 'n' help me git up in that there wagon 'n' yo' drive me. Gotta git down there 'n' see wha' happen. Miz Sophie a-sayin' Masta 'Pollon done shot down by Zanzibar 'n' Zanzibar runned."

" 'N' that Kewp boy 'n' Candy, they runned too."

"Good riddance." Lucretia Borgia managed to get one foot on the step of the buckboard, and waited for Drummage to heave her up. He climbed up beside her, following Brutus along the narrow cart path that led through the fields. At the end of the cart path they rode across the fields until they arrived at Sophie's trysting place. Before they stopped they could see Apollon's body, and the sight of it set Lucretia Borgia to keening loudly. When they halted she was the first on the ground, getting out with unaccustomed agility. She did not need to touch Apollon to know that he was dead, the moving incrustation of flies around the wound on his head told her.

Summoning Brutus and Drummage, she had them lift the body up into the buckboard. Suddenly she stopped and pointed to a wad of bloody cloth on the ground.

"Wha's dat, Drummage?"

He picked it up, and it was immediately apparent what the garment was.

"A-thinkin' they's Zanzibar's." Brutus nodded his head slowly.

"Then yo' knows? Yo' knows wha's been happenin' twixt Miz Sophie 'n' dat Zanzibar?"

"We knows, Miz 'Cretia Borgia, ma'am," Drummage answered. "All de hands knows."

"Den yo' don' know nothin'. 'Member dat, Drummage, 'n' yo' too, Brute. Yo' don' know nothin'. Nothin'! Masta 'Pollon done shot 'cause he foun' Zanzibar a-runnin', dat's our story. Jes' foun' 'im a-runnin' 'n' Zanzibar shot 'im. We ain' a-tryin' ter get Zanzibar back neither. Ner that Kewp 'n' Candy. Let 'em go. Don' need 'em. Now yo' all 'members what I tell yo'. Masta 'Pollon got kilt 'cause he foun' Zanzibar a-runnin'."

"But. . . ." Drummage interrupted.

"Ain' no 'buts' 'bout it. Yo' min' what I tellin' yo'."

"Ain' that, Miz 'Cretia Borgia ma'am, but that Kewp done gone 'way wid all de gold. Two bags o' it."

"Don' make no neverminds. Ain' a-tryin' ter git him back.

Miz Sophie's good name better'n all de gold in de world."

When they returned to the back door of the house, Lucretia Borgia had them lift Apollon's body out of the wagon and carry it into the house. They laid it on the couch in Hammond's old study.

"Yo' put 'im there, boys, 'n' I'll wash 'im 'n' lay 'im out. Miz Sophie prob'ly wantin' 'im ter have a black casket wid silver handles from de undertaker in Benson. Cain' bury no white man in a pine box. Time was when we had pine boxes fer de servants 'n' oak boxes fer de white folks. Now, yo' all git outa here now. Ain' fitten fer men ter stay roun' while de daid is washed. That's a woman's job. Miz Sophie cain' do it; she upstairs a-carryin' on somethin' awful."

While Lucretia Borgia and Marguerite bustled around the kitchen heating water and tearing old sheets into cloths, Sophie came down the back stairs, carrying Apollon's best suit, with his starched white shirt and black cravat. She carried them out into the kitchen, spreading the trousers out on the seat of a chair and drapping the coat over the back.

"Wan' him laid out in his best clothes, 'Cretia Borgia. Take off that suit he's a-wearin' 'n' put on this one."

"I'll ten' ter it, Miz Sophie. Yo' go on back upstairs 'n' lay down. See if'n yo' cain' get some rest."

Sophie shook her head. "He a-layin' in there, Lucretia Borgia, stone dead, 'n' it's my fault. I know it's my fault 'n' yo' know it's my fault. I want ter help yo'. Las' thing I kin do fer 'im. Loved him, I did, Lucretia Borgia, 'n' he loved me, leastwise he did 'til this mornin'.''

"It's yore mama's blood in yo'. Ain' Maxwell blood. Yo' tooken it after yo' mama. She 'n' that Mede jes' as bad's yo' 'n' that Zanzibar. But nobody a-goin' to know it. Yo' listen ter me. Masta 'Pollon done caught Zanzibar a-runnin' down by de river. Zanzibar shot him. Remember that!"

Lucretia Borgia lifted a big pan of warm water with both hands, carried it into the study, and placed it on the floor beside the couch. But Sophie would not allow her to touch Apollon's body. Tenderly she undid the buttons and stripped off his garments, wondering at how the warmth had fled, leaving his flesh strangely cold. The sight of his naked body was too much for her and she knelt beside the couch, sobbing.

"He shore was a handsome man. Don' blame yo' fer lovin' him." Lucretia Borgia wrung out one of the cloths and passed it over Apollon's body. With a soft towel she dried him and attempted to turn him over, but his weight was too much for her.

"Yo' gotta help me," she said to Sophie. "He powerful heavy man."

Together they managed to turn him over. Lucretia Borgia gasped and pointed to the black mark on Apollon's rump.

"Ain' yo' never seen dat befo'?"

"Ain' never seen it." Sophie stared with wide-open eyes at the splotch, which looked almost like a crude black hand.

"Yo' know what dat means, Miz Sophie?"

She shook her head, despite the fact that she was well acquainted with the old wives' tale about black birthmarks.

"Means he a nigger. Means he got nigger blood. He jes's niggery's I am 'n' he so high 'n' mighty. No need for yo' ter git a black box wid silver handles fer him. Pine box good 'nuff fer a nigger."

Sophie straightened up and slowly wiped her tears away. Tenderly she touched the black mark which Apollon had taken such pains to hide during his lifetime. Suddenly she turned on Lucretia Borgia.

"Keep yore lyin' mouth shet. Yo' ain' a-runnin' things roun' here, Lucretia Borgia. He my husban' 'n' he always loved me, he did. Worshiped the groun' I walked on, 'n' yo' knows it. Jes' cause he got that li'l black spot don' mean he no nigger. French he was 'n' he came from France 'n' he was takin' me back there too. Makin' me a princess he was with a di'mond crown to say how-de-do to the Emp'rer. If'n yo' ever say he a nigger 'gain, I'll have yo' strung up 'n' stripped down 'n' I mean it. Git his drawers on. Git him dressed. Sen' Brute inter Benson ter git de finest casket they has there. No matter how much it cost. Solid gold if'n they have gotten it 'cause it ain' good 'nuff fer him. 'N' have Drummage go 'long too 'n' tell the Reverend Hazzard ter come out to bury him. He my husban', Lucretia Borgia, 'n' he ain' no nigger 'n' never was. Yo' do's yo're told and never say no mo' 'bout him 'gain. Never!" She fled sobbing up the stairs into Apollon's room, and threw herself onto his unmade bed, burying her face in his nightgown just as he had left it that morning. His scent still clung to it and it seemed to bring him back to her.

BOOK III

Chapter 36

THE WAR was over! General Lee had surrendered to General Grant at Appomattox; slavery in the United States was ended. The armistice was signed several weeks before rumor of it reached the backwater of Falconhurst. It was Drummage who brought the news to Sophie who was, besides himself and Marguerite, the only one left in the big house, and to the inhabitants of New Quarters, which had now grown into a sizable village.

Sophie had received the information as indifferently as she accepted everything else since the loss of Apollon, even the pregnancy which had been so unexpected at her age and was now causing her such discomfort. At New Quarters, however, Drummage's announcement was the occasion for celebration, with a huge bonfire in the center of the village and several jugs of corn which were brought out of hiding. The inhabitants of New Quarters were no longer slaves. They were free men and women and their children were free. Nobody could force them to stand on the vendue table again; nobody could strip their clothes from them that their bodies might be fingered by the prospective buyer or the merely curious. Never again would they need to call a white man "masta." As Drummage said, they were now just as good as any white man or woman. They were no longer animals. They were humans. Such a momentous event indeed called for celebration, and as they reeled around the blazing fire at New Quarters, they shouted at each other, "We'se free! We'se free!"

With white authority suddenly gone, it was to Drummage that they looked for leadership. He lived in the big house and, despite their new status as free men and women, the big house still remained for them a white-pillared symbol of authority.

Yet the once proud Falconhurst had disappeared, never to return; its power was gone. The crowded slave quarters were empty except for the one cabin still occupied by Big Pearl. Even those few slaves whose loyalty had prompted them to remain during the war had now left. Some had gone their own way down the road; others had moved over to New Quarters, built themselves a makeshift cabin, and preempted a few acres of Falconhurst land to eke out their own existence.

Most of the New Quarters men had remained. They accepted Drummage as their leader, young in years though he was. His clothes—what remained of Apollon's and of Hammond's—were better than theirs; he wore shoes while they went barefooted; he was able to read and write; and he had traveled to New Orleans. All these things combined to give him the advantage. But more than anything else, his leadership derived from the fact that he was the only Negro (with the exception of Marguerite who didn't count) who was now living in the big house.

Lucretia Borgia, that power behind the throne, was dead. True to her promise, she had died in the big house. She had gotten out of bed one chilly winter morning, dressed, and gone down to the kitchen to light the fire in the stove. A big pan of corn pone was in the oven; a pot of so-called coffee, made of cracked corn and molasses, was steaming on the stove, and the kitchen table was set for four people, for Sophie now ate with Lucretia Borgia, Drummage, and old Merc the gardener in the kitchen. The table was set and breakfast was ready but Lucretia Borgia never ate it. When Drummage came down the back stairs from the bedroom which Hammond Maxwell and later Apollon Beauchair had occupied and which he had now appropriated, Lucretia Borgia lay stretched out on the kitchen floor, dead. With her passing, the last vestige of Falconhurst, as it had formerly been, was gone.

At Sophie's insistence, Lucretia Borgia was laid to rest in the family plot. Drummage, in his abundant vitality, gave little thought to death. That death should enter and take possession of his strong body seemed impossible. Yet he knew it was inevitable and he was determined when the time came that he and his mother would also be interred in the burying ground along with his father.

Brutus was no longer in the big house, nor did he take

any part in the management of what was left of the plantation. Even before the war's end he had built himself a comfortable cabin at New Quarters, where he had no difficulty in finding himself a woman. He had staked out several acres of the plantation's best land and these he cultivated with far more assiduity and interest than he had ever expended on Falconhurst. For years he had been the most important man on the plantation. Now he asked nothing more than to be left alone with his horse, his two cows, his team of mules, and his pigs, all of which he had taken with him when he left the big house. Sophie had made no objection. Things were going to pieces so fast that the loss of a few head of livestock seemed of no importance to her.

Indeed, nothing seemed of any importance to Sophie now that Apollon was no more. She had become indifferent to her appearance, and spent the days in a frayed calico wrapper, seldom bothering to put on a dress or even to comb her hair. When she was hungry she ate. When she was thirsty she drank. When she was tired she slept. And when she needed a man there was Drummage. She had thought, after Apollon's death, that she would never desire a man again, but the very memory of him aroused her lust. Drummage was the only male available and she had overcome his unwillingness by bribery. Now the child she was bearing so unwillingly was his.

Drummage as a person did not interest her any more than had Zanzibar. But he was a male animal that could fulfill her needs, and by purchasing his services she could find a temporary relief from the memories of Apollon which haunted her. That Drummage's favors had been dearly bought was of little consequence to her. When he demanded Augusta's diamond ear screws, she had given them to him willingly in payment for a month of his nightly attentions. Not only had she given him the jewels, but she had made it possible for him to wear them, by piercing his ears with a needle and a length of white silk thread. Incongruous as the sparkling jewels looked in his dark ear lobes, they reminded her of the pleasure he had given her. The ear screws were followed by other articles of jewelry which, although he could not wear them, delighted him. Since he never lacked for women and did not have to purchase their favors he hid Sophie's jewels away in a tin box which he buried in the same hole in the ground where he had put the torn valise full of gold eagles.

At first, Sophie had tried to sell some of her baubles

through correspondence with jewelers in Montgomery and Mobile, but jewels were a drug on the market and the wads of worthless paper she received for them purchased little or nothing. She might just as well give them to Drummage. After all, he had something tangible she could purchase—something worth far more to her than a mere handful of paper. That she could conceive at her age, had seemed impossible to her. Yet here she was, carrying his child, another hybrid who would be a half-brother or half-sister (she really didn't care which) to a score of naked pickaninnies who wandered the dusty streets of New Quarters.

If Sophie was completely indifferent to the life burgeoning within her, not so Drummage. All his pride, all his vanity was aroused by the thought of fathering a child by Sophie. What if he had had to force himself to the necessary performance, or if his favors had been bought? Sophie was still a white woman and the daughter of Hammond Maxwell, still the head of Falconhurst, a member of that world he had never hoped to enter—a white world which had been as far removed from his own as earth from heaven. He was only Drummage, but she was Sophie Maxwell, with the blood of Maxwells and Hammonds in her veins! And this child that she was carrying would have that same blood along with his own. The child would be born free, would someday be the Master of Falconhurst. He never doubted it would be a son, for most of his offspring had been male.

True, Falconhurst was not the prize it had been ten years ago, when the long dormitories and the slave cabins were bursting with prime "niggers" that would bring thousands of dollars on the vendue tables of New Orleans, Mobile, and Natchez. But to Drummage it was still Falconhurst, the center and circumference of his world.

As the sire of the prospective master of the plantation, Drummage removed his belongings from the little room in the attic he had always occupied to the big room on the second floor which had once belonged to Hammond and Augusta and more recently to Apollon Beauchair. He did not ask Sophie's permission for the move nor would it have mattered to him if she had denied it. He had long ceased to respect what shreds of authority remained to her.

Yet with the knowledge that she was to bear him a son, his attitude towards Sophie changed. He became more respectful and tried to do little things for her that almost amounted to affectionate attentions. His solicitude for her welfare even extended to her appearance, and his coaxing and flattery caused her to renew some pride in her looks. She had Marguerite heat water for her bath; she brushed her tangled hair and arranged it in the "waterfall" style which had been popular in the days of her annual visits to New Orleans. Because of her pregnancy, her pinched-waisted gowns were impossible to wear, but she did discard the soiled calico wrapper and take to wearing her own and her stepmother's dressing gowns, which were far more presentable.

They would no longer eat in the kitchen, Drummage decided. Marguerite could not be expected to cook the meals and serve them too, so he enlisted the services of a boy from New Quarters whom he proceeded to train. The boy had been one of a pair of twins, named Castor and Pollux, whom Hammond Maxwell had purchased from an itinerant slave trader some ten years previously when they were six or seven years old. Castor had died but Pollux survived, having been shunted from pillar to post among the inhabitants of New Quarters, never wanted but only tolerated for the labor that could be wrung out of his scantily nourished body. He was overjoyed at the prospect of a home at the big house, the castoff clothes which Drummage gave him to wear—an old suit of Jubal's from which most of the brass buttons were missing—and above all with three meals a day, such as they were, and the two bits a week Drummage promised him as wages and never paid.

Pollux was a gangling boy, all big hands and feet, but good looking in an Afro-Indian way which revealed that one of his ancestors was a redskin. He had string-straight black hair, high cheek bones, an aquiline nose, and copper coloring, offset by the thick lips, the wide nostrils, and the powerful frame of the Negro. With the rough but regular meals at the big house, he started to fill out, and gave promise of developing into a fine-looking fellow.

So now Drummage and Sophie ate in the dining room, with Pollux in attendance. Although the top of the big table was spotted and stained with candle wax and dried food, although the big fan that hung over it was suspended precariously from one hinge, and the silver on the sideboard was sadly tarnished, Drummage felt he was adding to his own prestige by sitting there. Occupying his master's room, sitting at his master's place at the table, bedding his master's daughter, and being the father of his master's grandson all added up to making him the Master of Falconhurst.

"Goin' ter be a lot o' Union soldiers in Benson right soon," he informed Sophie one evening as they mopped up pot liquor with corn pone from the cracked Sèvres plates. "Man jes' 'rived from Selma a-sayin' so. Sayin' they a-goin' ter have a Freedmen's Bureau too. Was a-talkin' wid him in Benson today. He say colored folk jes' de same like white folk now, goin' ter vote, goin' ter be members o' de Union League." He looked up from under his lashes to see what effect this announcement might have on Sophie.

"Cain' never be de same," she replied with an attempt at hauteur, pushing the crumbs of corn bread into a little heap on her plate and squeezing them together with her fingers to transfer them to her mouth. "Jes' cain' never be de same. Nigger's black 'n' white men's white. How kin they be de same? Ain' possible."

"Don' make no neverminds no mo' 'bout de color o' a man's skin. Black skin jes' so good's white if'n not better. This man, Mista Kendall, he tol' me so. Colored folk's citizens now. They a-goin' ter be 'lected ter Congress. Goin' ter be a colored man president jes' like Mr. Lincoln."

"Yes," Sophie mocked him. "Lincoln a black devil, so's a nigger."

Drummage accepted the rebuff but it did not daunt him.

"This Mista Kendall he say other things too. He say ain' no reason no mo' why colored man cain' marry white woman." Again he peered at Sophie.

"Ain' no white woman ever goin' ter marry up wid no nigger. Ain' fittin' 'n' ain' decent." Sophie bristled.

"Ain' no worse fer a white woman ter marry up wid a colored man 'n' it is fer her ter bed wid 'im." Drummage leaned across the table and pointed his finger at Sophie. "Yo' bedded wid plenty 'n' I knows 'bout dem all. Knows what yo' did wid Zanzibar 'n' others 'fore him. Knows dat Zanzibar's pants were alongside Masta 'Pollon when he kilt. What do dat mean? Means Zanzibar didn' have no pants on when Masta 'Pollon done foun' yo' two. 'N' when a nigger buck 'n' a white woman together 'n' de buck he don' have no pants on, only one thing a-happenin'. Zanzibar tol' me too. Yo' know somethin'? Zanzibar he bin a-livin' over in de New Quarters since de day he shot Masta 'Pollon. If'n yo' wants I kin show him ter yo'. But I don' need to do dat. 'Member how I got dese?" He pointed to the flashing diamonds in his ears.

"White men beds with nigger wenches 'n' white women beds with nigger bucks if'n they wants to." Sophie was righteously indignant. "Zanzibar he belong to me 'n' so do yo', Drummage. Kin sell yo' tomorrow if'n I wants. Think I will too. Think I a-gettin' rid o' yo'."

"Thinkin' yo' won'." He banged his fist so hard on the table that the plates rattled. "Cain' sell a free man 'n' I'se free. War's over. Ain' no more buyin' nor sellin'. Ain' no more ownin'. Ain' no more whoppin'. I jes' de same like'n yo'— citizen o' de United States o' Americky." He stood up and leveled the threatening finger at her again. "Yo' a-carryin' my sucker 'n' yo' a-goin' ter marry up wid me. Understan' that, Miz Sophie. Yo' a-goin' ter marry up wid me 'cause I say so."

Sophie stared at him, scarcely comprehending his words. Never in her lifetime had a Negro so addressed her. It was unthinkable, and yet, even in her horror and fear, she felt a certain pride to think that Drummage wanted her. She had always admired him, always desired him. But he was only a nigger. She could enjoy him but she could never, not for a moment, consider marrying him. She would teach him a lesson. She would have him lashed to within an inch of his life so that he would come crawling to her begging her forgiveness. But there was nobody to lash him. In the old days, a pull at the bell cord would have brought Brutus and with him Big Randy and Sampson and Zanzibar from the barn; would have brought Merc and Jupe running in from the garden. At her word, regardless of any feeling of friendship they might have for Drummage, they would have taken him and he would not have resisted. He would have been dragged over to the old barn, hoisted up by his feet and lashed with whatever number of lashes she directed. They would have killed him had she so directed. It was difficult for her to realize that she no longer had that power.

But one thing did remain to her. She was a white woman. She was the daughter of Hammond Maxwell. Regardless of what Mister Abe Lincoln said, regardless of new laws, new customs, or new attitudes, Drummage was still a nigger slave, not even a human being. He was something to be bought and sold and his body belonged to her to do with as she liked. She rose slowly from the table and stared straight at him.

"Don' yo' go p'intin' yore finger at me, yo' nigger buck. Don' yo' tell me what yo' a-goin' ter do 'n' what yo' not a-goin' ter do. Yo' does as I say 'n' we ain' havin' no mo' talk 'bout niggers a-marryin' up wid white women. Understan'?"

Conditioned as he had been to obey the voice of white authority, Drummage automatically lowered his finger. But only for an instant. He stood up and walked toward her, standing so near their bodies almost touched.

"Yo' ain' a-tellin' me what ter do. Doin' like I damn well please 'n' we goin' to talk mo' 'bout marryin'. Goin' ter talk 'bout a colored man marryin' up wid a white woman, meanin' marryin' up 'tween yo' 'n' me. Tha's what I mean. Yo' a-goin' ter marry up wid me. If'n I'm good 'nuff ter pleasure yo', I'm good 'nuff ter marry yo'. If'n I'm good 'nuff ter knock yo' up, I'm good 'nuff ter be yore husban'. That's the way it's goin' ter be."

Without removing her eyes from him, Sophie raised her hand and struck him across the face.

"Shet yore big black mouth. Ain' a-marryin' up wid yo' now o' never. Pleasures myself wid yo' if'n I wants ter. Births yore sucker if'n I wants ter. Tha' don' make me no neverminds. Plenty o' nigger bastards bin birthed here at Falconhurst 'n' one more won' matter. Mayhap I'll keep it jes' ter have somethin' ter play wid, mayhap I'll drown it if'n I want ter. But I ain' a-marryin' up with yo' o' no other black buck neither." Her raised hand slapped him again.

Strangely enough he did not retaliate, although his anger showed in his eyes.

"Yo' better think 'bout it. I'm a-goin' ter be masta here. Yo' marries up wid me, yo' be de mist'ess. If'n yo' don' yo' be sorry. Ain' 'cause I a-wantin' yo'. Yo' too goddamn old 'n' fat 'n' I don' like white women nuther. But if yo' marries up wid me goin' ter be a lot easier fer yo'. If'n yo' wants yo' kin git de goddamndest heaviest hung nigger buck 'n Alabama ter pleasure yo' 'n' I don' care. Yo' stays on here as mist'ess. What yo' say, Sophie?"

Without answering she gathered her draggled flounces together and swept out of the dining room, pausing for a moment between the tall white pillars that led into the drawing room. She turned and faced him, eyed him from head to foot, and then started to laugh.

"Me marry up wid yo'?" Her laughing continued. "Yo' crazy? Why, yo' goddamn black nigger yo'! Yo' ain' even got a name. Yo' jes' Drummage, that's all. Jes' Drummage, tha's the only name yo' got." Her laughter continued as she swept through the littered drawing room with its faded draperies and its torn upholsteries, and even as she climbed the stairs the echo of her scorn floated down to him, as he stood by the dining-room table. It was true, he thought bitterly. He didn't have a name; he was just Drummage, another nameless nigger.

Chapter 37

FOR SOME MOMENTS after Sophie had left, Drummage remained alone amid the vanished splendors of the Falconhurst dining room. Her sudden burst of anger and her taunting words had brought his true status home to him. He had been deluded by rumors from the North into thinking he was a free man—just as good as any white man. He had been flattered by the attention the men and women at New Quarters paid him because he wore better clothes, because he could read and write, and wore shoes and lived in the big house. He had magnified his own importance because he had bedded Miz Sophie and knocked her up.

But what did it all add up to? Nothing! His skin was still black. No white man from the North with his fanciful tales of equality would ever be Hammond Maxwell or Lewis Gasaway, neither of whom would ever have told him he was free and just as good as any white man. Their opinion would have mattered to him and he would have believed them. The flattery of those ignorant bucks and wenches at New Quarters meant nothing. They were merely trying to insinuate themselves into his good graces because the time would come when they might want to ask a favor of him. And as for his having bedded himself with Miz Sophie . . . hell! That was nothing to his credit. Zanzibar and a half-dozen others had already enjoyed that dubious honor.

Miz Sophie was right! In the eyes of any Southern white woman, Drummage would never be anything but a superior two-legged animal, with a little more intelligence than a dog but certainly not enough to be human. He was just Drummage, whose father had been called Drumson and whose grandfather was called Drum. His mother was a Mandingo wench called Big Pearl and who her father was she hadn't even known herself. He had had a half-brother named Ol' Mista Wilson and another called Benoni. None of them had ever had a name and not one of those goddamned niggers over at New Quarters had a name either. White men called a dog Caesar or named a horse Whirlwind but they didn't give him any other name. They named a cow Bessie or a bull Champion, just to distinguish that animal from the rest when they talked about them. Similarly they named a slave Drummage or Jubal or some other such name, so he would come when he was called. But that didn't mean he had a real name like Hammond Maxwell or Apollon whatever-his-name-was. Having a name like Drummage didn't make you a man any more than a bull called Champion was a man. And when his son was born they'd name him something like Tom or Buttercup or Poker-Face—whatever came to mind first, just like they'd name a puppy or a kitten.

No! He'd be goddamned if they'd name *his* son like that!

He took the glass lamp, from which all but a few of the crystal pendants were missing, from the middle of the table, and walked out into the kitchen. How many times he had passed through that same door with heaping trays and loaded servers, coming and going at the beck and call of white people. Now he was able to sit at that same table and call for Pollux to bring the tray through the door, but the fact that he sat in Hammond Maxwell's place would never make him Hammond Maxwell or anything like him. Hammond Maxwell had been white—he was black . . . maybe not the prune black of the African nigger, but brown, and brown was black. Even bright skins were black. Benoni's mama had been white but she also was black.

Marguerite and Pollux were seated at the kitchen table dawdling over their supper, and he wondered if they had heard the conversation between Sophie and himself. Probably! He'd managed to listen to all the dining-room conversations when he was serving. But it didn't matter. They were too stupid to know what he and Sophie had been talking about. He placed the lamp alongside their lighted tallow dip in the iron candlestick and sat down at the table with them. The food they were eating was nigger food but it was the same that had been served to him in the dining room. It was a far cry from the glazed hams, the tenderly fried pieces of brown chicken, and the other delicacies Lucretia Borgia used to serve to Masta Hammond and Miz 'Gusta. Drummage looked at it in disgust and listened to Marguerite's slurpings as she shoved the food into her mouth and chewed it. Even Pollux was eating like an animal—his elbows spread out on the table, his mouth down on a level with the plate, his hands shoveling the food into his mouth.

No wonder white folks thought of them as animals. They ate like hogs; coupled like goats. That was all they ever thought of—something to put in their belly and a place to sleep with something soft or hard to play with, depending

332

on whether they were buck or wench. And he, Drummage, was just like them. He didn't know exactly how old he was but as long as he could remember all he had ever wanted was food to put in his belly and a wench to sleep with. He'd always kept his belly full and he'd spent few nights alone, but now there was something different he wanted. It was something above and beyond those two primal desires. He wanted to be a man, not an animal.

But if he was going to be a man, the first thing he needed was a name. Not just a name for people to call him by— he already had that—but a name he could put Mister in front of. If Abe Lincoln had freed him and he was just as good as a white man, then he had a right to a name and he had a right to be called "mister." If a white man married a woman, the woman took the man's name. Why couldn't a nigger, if he married a white woman, take her name, especially if he didn't already have one? Why couldn't he? Provided he could find a white woman to marry—and the only white woman Drummage knew was Miz Sophie, who was bigger than ever now that she was toting his sucker. No, damn it! Not a sucker! Niggers had suckers! White folks had babies and Miz Sophie might be fat and getting old but she was white. She'd birth a baby, not a sucker.

Damn her! She wouldn't marry him but she was willing to give him earbobs if he would sleep with her. She sure liked it, she did. Liked it a hell of a lot more than he did. Well, that was only natural. He'd had wenches who had bedded with white men and they had told him that white men didn't know how to pleasure a girl. Only bucks could do it well because bucks were hung heavier than white men, and Drummage was better than any of them. If she liked it so well, why wouldn't she marry up with him? Yes, why wouldn't she? He could make her. He wouldn't pleasure her again, not even if she offered him all her pretties, until she came begging for it on her knees and then he'd tell her she'd have to marry him to get it. That would bring her around.

He wished he had someone to talk to—someone to advise him. Outside of satisfying the demands of his own body, he had never had to think for himself; there had always been someone around to tell him what to do. That was over now. Nobody would ever tell him what to do again and it was up to him to make his own plans. But two heads were better than one even if the other head was as kinky-haired as his own. He'd go and see Brute and Brute would help him. Hot

333

damn! Two nigger heads ought to be able to settle this business of having a name.

"Yo' finished shovelin' them vittles inter yore belly, Pollux?"

"Could eat more, Drummage, but ain' no mo' ter eat." Pollux bent his head over the plate, lapping up the crumbs with his tongue.

Drummage leaned over and snatched the plate away from him. "Yo' eatin' like a goddamn dog, 'n' what I tells yo' 'bout callin' me Drummage. Ain' a-goin' ter tell you 'gain. Still got de paddle down in de barn what we used to whop niggers wid 'n' kin still whop yo' single-handed if'n I wants ter."

"Yas suh, Masta Drummage suh." Pollux grinned.

"Tha's better." Drummage remembered a similar rebuke he had had from Hammond. "Wants yo' should go out 'n de barn 'n' saddle up my horse."

"Yas suh, Masta Drummage suh." Pollux scraped back his chair and stood up, ready to leave, but stopped suddenly, staring toward the door that led from Hammond's old office into the kitchen. Sophie was standing in the door, her wrapper clutched around her.

"Whar yo' goin', Drummage? Ain' yo' comin' ter bed?"

"Ain' got to 'count fer myself no mo','" he answered, as he followed Pollux to the door. "Yo' never asked Master Hammond where all he a-goin' when he wen' out. Don' ask me 'cause I won' tell yo'." He stomped out of the house, following the dim figure of Pollux ahead of him. There was no lantern in the barn, but Drummage, more familiar with its dark interior than Pollux, got his horse out of the stall and told Pollux where to find the saddle and bridle, and together they saddled the horse.

"We free now, Masta Drummage suh?" Pollux buckled the straps of the bridle.

"I'se free," Drummage answered, fitting his foot into the stirrup. "I'se free 'cause I'se de head man round here. 'N' yo' free too but yo' ain' free like I am. I do what I wants; yo' do what I tells yo'. Understan'?"

"Yas suh, Masta Drummage suh."

"Leave de lamp a-burnin' in de kitchen fer me."

He rode out of the barn, skirting the house by the driveway, and down the long tree-bordered drive that led to the main road. The village of New Quarters, built and inhabited by former Falconhurst slaves, was about a mile down the road. Originally it had been built off the road, a series of straggling lanes with crude cabins, but as more and more slaves had left the plantation it had spread out to the main road and now lined both sides of it. The village still depended on Benson for its meager supplies. No store or livery stable or tavern—those three necessary concomitants to all towns—adorned its sagging bleakness, but one building of squared logs, larger than the rest, had been erected by co-operative labor and served as a town center. It was here that itinerant preachers stopped to deliver their sermons. It was here that the social singing and dances were occasionally held and the men of the community gathered in the evening. Although it had never had any merchandise for sale, it was called "the store." It was a clearinghouse for labor, a center for gossip and male companionship—the one place where a man was safe from the nagging of his woman and the confusion of his children.

Drummage figured that he would find Brutus there but, as he passed his cabin—sturdier in construction than the rest, neatly white-washed and with a small porch on the front— he spied Brutus' woman sitting on the porch with others of the village womenfolk.

"Whar Brute?" He halted his horse momentarily.

"He down to de sto'." Beulah-Annie, Brutus' woman, pointed down the road. "Road niggers come a-traipsin' in 'n' Brute he a-parcelin' 'em out fer places ter bide de night."

"Brute he a-lookin' at dat purty yalla gal what comed wid 'em," another woman giggled.

"Brute ain' a-lookin' at no yalla girl." Beulah-Annie was indignant. "Break his goddam head if'n he do. Whaffor yo' says crazy things like dat, Belle? Brute ain' never look at no woman but me. He ain' like Drummage here, a-tomcattin' all over New Quarters every night." She lost her anger in her own high-pitched giggle.

"Ain' out tomcattin' tonight, Beulah-Annie, tho' if'n any of yo' ladies"—it was a new word for him to use and most complimentary to the women, who had never been called anything but wenches before— "wants ter 'commodate me after I gits through, I be glad to 'blige. Only trouble is," he added, "won' be a-wantin' yore own man after yo' tries me."

"G'wan wid yo', Drummage. Yo' jes' a-talkin' big 'cause yo' got Miz Sophie knocked up. Yo' a-lookin' fer a bright-skin sucker?"

"Shore am, Beulah-Annie, 'n' goin' ter git me one, only this un ain' a sucker, he goin' ter be a baby." Drummage left them to a chorus of cackling giggles. He knew he was popular in New Quarters—every man with the possible exception of Brutus, deferred to him, and every woman laughed and joked with him, hoping that she might be the next of his conquests. His reputation had been greatly enhanced by gossip of his prowess.

Laughing himself, he rode on down to the store, where he found a group of men standing around the low doorway. The men opened up a path for him, greeting him vociferously, and he went inside to discover Brutus, Big Randy, and a fellow called Lot seated behind a rough table. Scattered around on the dirt floor, sitting on bundles and ancient carpetbags, there were about ten people, but Drummage noticed first a bright-skinned girl who was standing beside a middle-aged Negro with iron-grey hair. All the rest were older than she was and their drooping fatigue contrasted with her freshness.

" 'Lo, Drummage." Brutus motioned for Lot to get up and give Drummage his chair, which the fellow did willingly. "Jes' in time ter help us. These road niggers come 'long 'bout dark. They ain' got no place ter spend the night nor nothin' ter eat neither. Figures as how we kin help 'em out. They from up no'th near Demopolis. Say the big house on their plantation bin burned by Union soldiers 'n' all the cabins too. Ain' no one lef' dar. Mist'ess done went 'way 'n' lef' 'em. Thinkin' mayhap they kin stay here. They's decent folk. Ain' like mos' road niggers."

"Kin stay," Drummage agreed, appraising the bright-skinned girl. "Yo' tol' 'em, Brute, that if'n they stay, gotta build themselves cabins. Gotta work."

"We right willin' ter work, Mista." The gray-haired man seemed to be the spokesman for the others. "We ain' got nothin' though. Ain' got nothin' ter build cabins wid. Ain' got nothin' ter eat. But come Sunday I'll preach a sermon for yo' all. Preacher I am. Methodist."

"Ain' got much oursel's but mighty 'bliged if'n yo' preaches ter us. Ain' got us no preacher here. We got trees, 'n' we got axes, 'n' we got men what knows how ter fell 'em 'n' build cabins. We he'ps yo'. Yo' he'ps us." Drummage shifted his weight in the chair to face Brutus. "Whyn't yo' parcel 'em out 'mongst de people, Brute, till they gits places fer they'sel's?" Drummage pointed to the girl standing beside the preacher. She had been eyeing him during the conversation. "Who yo'?"

"She Pamela," the preacher answered. "She my kinfolk in a way. She my woman's wench but I ain' sired her. Masta

336

Snodgrass, he done sired her off'n my woman afore de war. She 'tended Miz Miranda in de big house 'fore it burned."

Drummage appraised her again and this time more closely. There was something about her that reminded him of Candy, and her bright beauty had been the principal reason for his wishing the group to stay. Usually he gave scant hospitality to road niggers—those footloose tramps whose new-found freedom impelled them to investigate what lay around the turn of the road from their familiar plantation. But this group—he counted them—of seven men and four women were sober, industrious-looking folk, decently dressed and quiet-mannered. He wouldn't mind having them around, particularly with that Pam girl that was with them. Drummage slated her for his next conquest. Tonight was a little too late to start sweet-talking her. She looked too tired and he had too much on his mind.

One by one the New Quarters men stepped up and volunteered to make places for the new folks in their cabins. Drummage was glad to see that the girl and the old man with her were to be quartered with Sampson. Sampson's woman was so jealous of him that he'd never had a chance to look at another wench; Pamela would be safe there. Soon the new group departed with their hosts, and Drummage was left alone with Brutus and Big Randy. Brutus was about to blow out the lamp and go home, but Drummage restrained him.

"Came over 'specially ter talk wid yo', Brute. 'N' yo' stay too, Big Randy."

Brutus turned up the lamp wick and sat back in his chair. He and Drummage had been together at the big house. No great friendship had ever existed between them, such as there had between Brutus and Drummage's father, but each respected the other.

"Wha' yo' a-wantin', Drummage?"

"We free men now, Brute."

"So they tells me. Ain' servants fer life no longer. Ain' no mo' sellin', no mo' buyin', no mo' whoppin' "—his lips set in a grim line—"though how we a-goin' ter keep some of these bastards in line 'thout slicin' de meat off'n 'em, I don' know."

"Tha's jes' it." Drummage leaned forward in his chair and pointed his finger at Brutus. "Not 'bout the whoppin' I mean but 'bout our bein' free men. We ain', Brute, 'cause we ain' got no names 'n' we ain' married neither. We no better'n cattle, Brute. Stallion see a mare, he mount her. Bull see a cow, he mount her. Rooster see a hen, he mount her. Buck

337

see a wench, he mount her. Jes' like animals, Brute. No names, no marriage, 'n' no names·fer de kids."

"Yo' one ter talk, Drummage. Yo' done more mountin' roun' here 'n anyone else. Bet yo' got twenty kids a-runnin' roun' here at New Quarters."

"Bet I have. Al'ays been horny, I have. But listen, Brute, 's I was sayin'. Yo' calls yore mule Benny."

"Wha' dat got to do wid us bein' free?" Big Randy asked. "Wha' difference it make what Brute call his ol' mule?"

"Tha's what I mean," Drummage answered. "Benny's Benny; Brute's Brute; yo' Big Randy. Tha's all. We ain' got no more names 'n Benny. White men all have names—not jes' names like dogs 'n' horses but real names. I jes' Drummage, tha's all. How we goin' ter git names, Brute?"

Brutus had been slowly nodding his head in agreement. He had not thought about it before, but everything that Drummage said made sense to him. They were named like animals; they copulated like animals; they bred like animals. They were, all of them, as devoid of names as his mule Benny. If they were free men they would have to have names.

"We gotta pick 'em. Pick any name we wants, I guess. Ain' no one ter hender us. Les' see." Brute tipped back in his chair and stared at the smoky rafters. "Wha's name I a'goin' ter take fer myself. They al'ays call me Brute though that ain' my name. My name Brutus."

"Yeah, but Brutus ain' no better'n jes' Brute. Gotta have two names," Drummage insisted. "Yo' Brutus *what?*"

Brutus shook his head in his inability to answer but Drummage could see that the big fellow was thinking. The front legs of his chair came down onto the floor and he pounded on the table.

"Got it! Know now what I a-goin' ter call myself. 'Members onct when Masta Hammond 'n' I in N' Orleans. Useter have me a wench there what live wid a family called Rodney. Done fergit de wench's name but ain' never fergit ol' Masta Rodney. This wench useter let me in de back do' 'n' take me up to her li'l room in de *gar-son-i-yere*. well set-up gal she was too—big tits 'n' plenty o' ass. Well, one night I was a-larrupin' her good 'n' she a·likin' it·so she screamin' her fool head off. I was a-bangin' her so strong I never did hear de do' open but she did 'n' she stop her wigglin'. Ol' Masta Rodney he a-standin' in de do', bilin' over mad. That wench, she so scairt she gave me a push 'n' landed me flat on my ass. This ol' Masta Rodney he a-standin' straddle-legged over me. He say he don' know who I am but he damn well goin' ter fin'" out 'n' have my masta sen' me fer a whoppin' by de city whopper. I tol' him I Brute from Masta Hammond Maxwell's Falconhurst plantation. We in N' Orleans ter get shet o' a caffle o' bucks. Ol' man nearly jump out o' his skin. 'Falconhurst, he say? Yo' a Falconhurst boy?' 'Yas suh, masta suh,' I tells him. Know what dat ol' man did?"

Drummage and Big Randy both shook their heads, enthralled with the story.

"Well dat ol' man, he jes' reach down his hand 'n' took mine 'n' h'isted me up, a-grinnin' all over. He say, 'Go 'head, start pesterin' dat wench 'gain. Goin' ter stay right here 'n' watch yo'. Give it to her good 'n' I gives yo' two silver dollars if'n yo' gits her knocked up. Keep right on a-comin' here. Got me three other wenches 'sides this one. Wants yo' should pester 'em all 'n' git 'em all knocked up. Gittin' me four Falconhurst suckers fer free. Gits 'em all knocked up, gives yo' five dollars.' "

"How'd yo' do, Brute?" It was the sort of tale that interested Drummage. He could feel the hot swelling of his crotch, just picturing Brutus.

"Wen' every night fer 'bout three weeks afore Masta Hammond wen' home. Pestered all four of dem wenches 'n' ol' Masta Rodney he a-watchin' us mos' o' de time. Di'n' know how well I made out till I come back de next year ter N'Orleans. Wen' back to de Rodney house and two of dem wenches had purty li'l suckers—a boy 'n' a gal. Ol' Masta Rodney he sure glad to see me. Prouder 'n Lucifer over dem suckers. Wanted me ter git started on his wenches 'gain 'n' say his neighbor nex' do' had a nice young un fer me, jes' comin' roun'. Gave me five dollars. Dat ol' Masta Rodney de bes' white man I ever knew 'ceptin' o' course Masta Hammond. Thinkin' I take his name. How yo' like dat name —Mista Brutus Rodney?"

"Shore soun' fine, Mista Rodney." Drummage bowed as it had been his custom to do to white men. "Pleased ter meet yo' 'Mista Brutus Rodney. As fer me, ain' got ter do no thinkin' 'bout who I a-goin' ter be. Jes' made up my mind. My name a-goin' ter be Maxwell. That Masta Hammond's name 'n' that Miz Sophie's name what she borned with. Don' know what her name is now; never could 'member that goddamned 'Pollon's name, but I a'goin' ter marry up wid Miz Sophie. That make me a real Maxwell 'n' make me Mista Drummage Maxwell o' Falconhurst."

"Yo' cain' marry up wid Miz Sophie!" Brute was shocked.

"She a pure white woman. She ain' a-goin' ter marry up wid no black buck like yo'. 'Tain' fittin'.'"

"Fittin' fer her ter bed wid me. Fittin' fer her ter have me pleasure her. Fittin' fer her to have that Zanzibar pleasure her. If'n it fittin' fer her to birth my sucker, it fittin' fer her to marry up wid me. 'N' I kin make her too."

"She a-totin' yore sucker makes it different," Brute agreed. "Guess that do make it fittin'. If'n yore sucker a boy, he takes the name Maxwell right like."

"Seem fittin' ter me," Big Randy agreed. "Guess I take de name o' Maxwell too."

"No, yo' don'." Drummage turned on him in anger. "Jes' one Maxwell here 'n' dat me." Drummage half rose from his chair to threaten Big Randy. "Ain' a-havin' no mo' Maxwells."

"Den what I call me?" Big Randy scratched his head. 'Ain' never got no silver dollars in N'Orleans. Guess I jes' calls myself Randy Big."

"That ain' no name." Drummage was disgusted at Big Randy's stupidity. "Got to have us real names. Thinkin' we jes' ignorant niggers if'n we have names like that."

"Ain' far from a name." Brute did not like discussions. "Masta Hammond 'n' I onct sol' two bucks 'n' a wench down Biloxi way to a Mista Biggs. Tha' mos' like Big. Big Randy kin take that name. Mista Randy Biggs. Soun's good."

Drummage nodded in approval and held out his hand to Big Randy. "Pleased ter meet yo' too, Mista Biggs. 'Low me ter introduce mysel'. I Mista Drummage Maxwell o' Falconhurst Plantation at yore service, Mista Randy Biggs."

"Jes' remind me." Randy kept on scratching his close-cropped wiry head. "Ain' thought o' it fer long time but my rightful name ain' Randy. Hit's Randolph. Ain' never bin called dat but dat what it is—Randolph."

"Soun's better." Drummage shook hands with him again. "Glad ter make yore 'quaintance, Mista Randolph Biggs. 'N' now, Mista Rodney, 'n' Mista Biggs, we got us work ter do. Come tomorrow mornin', Brute, yo' git all de hands here at de store. Everyone got to git hisself a name. Kin have any name he wants 'cept Maxwell. Tha's my name 'n' Big Pearl's too. Line 'em all up, Brute, 'n' yo' 'n' I'll write 'em down. Every man take a name. Women takes their men's name 'n' all his kids too. Makes 'em real people. Makes dis village a real village. 'N' once we git 'em all named, that preacher man what come tonight, he goin' ter marry all dem men 'n' women. Goin' ter tie 'em all up like 'n white people.

340

Goin' ter have us a big day tomorrow. Gittin' us all named 'n' gittin' us all married."

"What 'bout all dem kids o' yourn a-runnin' 'bout?" Big Randy asked. "They goin' ter take yore name? They a-goin' ter be Maxwells?"

Drummage shook his head. "They takes de name o' de man what their mama live wid. Ain' goin' ter be but one Maxwell 'n' dat's de one Miz Sophie a-totin'."

"Yo' a-goin' ter marry up wid Miz Sophie tomorrow?" Brute asked.

Drummage shook his head in denial.

"White woman ain' a-gittin' married up by no nigger preacher. White woman a-gittin' married up by a white preacher. Miz Sophie 'n' me, we a-gittin' married up in Benson."

"Yo' mighty biggity 'bout it." Brutus was skeptical. "Nigger preacher good 'nuff fer us, good 'nuff fer yo'."

"Jes' yo' wait 'n' see." Drummage had made a rash statement, and now he couldn't back out of it without losing face. Somehow he'd have to find a way to force Sophie to marry him, but he thought he knew the way—by withholding his favors from her. She'd *have* to marry him. He'd kill her if she didn't, but he wouldn't kill her till after the child was born. "Take time fer a white woman ter git hersel' married up." He temporized. "Got ter git hersel' all prettied up. Got ter git hersel' ready. She a-goin' ter be Missis Drummage Maxwell sure's hell, 'n' my baby . . ."—He paused a moment so that they would understand the full import of the word, and that his child would be a baby and not a sucker—"he a-goin' ter be Mista Drum Maxwell o' Falconhurst Plantation. Jes' wait 'n' see."

Chapter 38

A FULL MOON had risen while Drummage had been talking with Brutus and Big Randy and it silvered the shingles of the cabins, now all dark except for a light in the open doorway of the one occupied by Brutus. Drummage, alone with his thoughts, felt particularly happy. This glow that permeated him was not as physically thrilling as the only variety of happiness he had ever known before—when he was hot after some wench—but somehow it was more satisfying. Of course it was nice to be sweet-talking a new wench, starting queer little spasms of anticipation tingling in his flesh, tightening the muscles of his belly and sending the blood in hot jets to swell his loins. But sometimes, after it was all over and he was buttoning up his breeches, he wondered why it hadn't been as good as he had hoped it would be. Now he felt he had accomplished something far more important than laying a wench in a weed patch. He had made a big step forward and had taken the people of New Quarters along with him. It had been his own idea—he had thought it out himself and not even Brute had helped him. Brute might know how to plant a field and get a day's work out of a field hand, but he could never have thought about the people getting names and getting married like white folks.

Only Drummage could do that.

And with this realization of his own power he saw how easy it was to become a leader. He had given birth to an idea in his own head and had led others to accept that idea. That was all there was to it. It wasn't much different from wenching. He got hot after a wench and sweet-talked her into his way of thinking. That was all it took to get her to spread her legs and that was all it took to get others to do as he wanted them to do. Just sweet-talk them a little. Tonight he had been head man just like Masta Hammond used to be. He spoke and they jumped. It caused a new power to burgeon within him. He had always been a man among women and now he was a man among men.

"Mista Drummage Maxwell o' Falconhurst Plantation, lad-eez 'n' gen'lemen! Lad-eez will kindly line up on de right,' gen'lemen on de lef'."

In this soaring euphoria, he wanted to demonstrate his new power and demonstrate it with a woman. He needed one, and of course the one he needed was Pamela. Any new woman was a challenge to Drummage. With her in mind, he reined in his horse, halting for a moment to think. That preacher man was one of those Jesus-shouting black bastards who wouldn't want any black buck riding his little pet lamb, but Drummage felt he could sweet-talk that goddamn minister. Hell, the way he felt tonight he could sweet-talk that marble woman over Apollon's grave into getting down off her pedestal. He wheeled his horse sharply and turned back to Sampson's cabin. He'd get Pamela tonight just like he'd managed everything else.

Sampson's cabin was dark but the moonlight showed two

men sitting on the bench beside the door. When Drummage rode up one of them stood up and Drummage could see by his height that it was not Sampson—it was the preacher fellow. The other shadow pulled himself up to stand by the preacher.

"Evenin', Drummage," Sampson said softly. "Ain' yo' gone home yet?"

"Got business wid de Rever'nd." Drummage slid down off his horse. "Goin' ter need yo' tomorrow, preacher man. What's yore name?"

"Call me Daniel, they do."

"Goin' ter call yo' more'n that tomorrow. Goin' ter have two names 'cause we havin' us a namin' day tomorrow, 'n' after we gits named we havin' a marryin' day. We goin' ter be people now. Goin' ter have us names 'n' goin' to be married up like white folks. Wantin' yo' ter do de marryin' up if'n yo' will. Ain' got no money ter pay yo' but all de men pitch in 'n' build yo' a cabin, 'n' all de womenfolk pitch in a-givin' yo quilts 'n' pans 'n' sech."

"De Lawd don' brought me here, brother. De Lawd lookin' out fer his stray lambs. Praise de Lawd!" Daniel bowed his head.

One stray lamb goin' ter git hers tonight, Drummage thought, but he bowed his head as sanctimoniously as the preacher before he spoke. "Wantin' ter speak to yo' 'bout dat gal yo' brought. Yo' say she a servant to de mist'ess in de big house whar yo' comed from?"

"She trained by ol' Mist'ess herself."

"Miz Sophie, she de mist'ess at Falconhurst down de road. She jes' a-pinin' way fer a wench ter help her. Askin' me ter fin' one fer her. Ain' dat true, Sampson?"

"Miz Sophie ain' had no one since pore ol' 'Cretia Borgia done up 'n' died," Sampson complied, sensing what Drummage had in mind but feeling that he owed more loyalty to Drummage than to the stranger beside him.

"I a-thinkin' if'n that wench want, kin take her over to de big house tonight. It 'bout a mile down de road. Miz Sophie shore like ter have her. Give her good home in de big house 'n' Miz Sophie pay her two bits a week 'sides her clothes. Miz Sophie right gen'rous, ain' she, Sampson?"

"Miz Sophie fine woman, preacher man," Sampson corroborated Drummage. He had had his eye on Pamela himself, but he knew he could not get far with his wife watching him. Big as Sampson was, he was scared to death of his woman. "Big house at Falconhurst fine place. I live there long time. Miz Sophie treat dat gal fine."

Daniel knew the advantage and the social position that would accrue to Pamela with a position in the big house, and that it would add to his own prestige also. "She a-sleepin' now, Mista Drummage, but I kin sen' her over in de mawnin'."

"Know Miz Sophie likin' ter have her tonight. Help her git to bed. Miz Sophie be mighty grateful. Gal kin ride back wid me 'n' save her walkin' in de mawnin'. No need ter be 'fraid 'bout her. I head man at Falconhurst—ask Sampson, ask Brute, ask any one o' de people here. Ask Sampson's woman. She safe wid me."

"He right, Drummage is." Sampson nodded his head. "She safe wid Drummage, 'n' Miz Sophie look out fer her too."

Old Daniel was persuaded. The prospects of a home here in New Quarters, a flock, a church, and a position in the big house for Pamela were tempting after weeks of wandering. He went into the cabin.

"Dat gal 'bout's safe wid yo', Drummage, 's she be wid a rattlesnake. Betcha yo' a-gittin' it inter her 'fore yo' gits to de big house." Sampson whispered between giggles. "Shore wishin' I was yo'. Could use a li'l piece o' dat myself."

A pale light streamed out of the cabin from the newly lit candle, and soon Pamela came outside. She too was aware of the honor being paid her by this opportunity to serve in the big house and seemed anxious to go. Old Daniel helped her up onto the bench by the door, and Drummage mounted his horse and walked him over to the bench. Sampson lifted Pamela up onto the horse's rump and she sat there side-saddle, holding onto the saddle for support.

Drummage waited in patience for old Daniel's prayerful leavetaking but urged his horse on before the final benediction. "Ain' far," he assured Pamela. "I walk de horse."

Once they were out on the road, he half turned to Pamela.

"Better yo' puts yore arms 'round me. Ain' wantin' yo' ter fall off 'n' break yore leg." He patted her thigh and then brought her hands around his waist. "Yo' shore pretty, Pammie. Yo' color jes' like dem tiger lilies."

"Yo' right good ter us, Mista Drummage suh. Pappy he tell me we a-goin' ter stay 'n' I a-goin' ter be in de big house."

"Tha's 'cause I like yo', li'l tiger lily. I de big man roun' here. Niggers do's I say; white folks too. Everyone tell yo' Mista Drummage Maxwell he de big man. Yo' do like'n I

say, yo' be mighty happy 'cause I a-goin' look out fer yo'."
He pushed one of her hands down into his crotch and held
it there even though she tried to withdraw it.

"Wha's de matter, pretty li'l tiger lily, ain' yo' a-likin' wha'
yo' jes' foun'?" His hand forced hers to remain. "Yo' a-goin'
to fin' somethin' mighty nice ter play wid."

She had started to cry but he still held her hand, bunched
up into a tight little fist, right where he had placed it.

"Wha' my baby cryin' fer? Ain' nobody a-goin' ter hurt
her."

"White man hurt me onct, he did," Pamela sniffled, struggling to free her hand. "White man came on a visit 'n' ol'
Masta he say I got ter sleep wid him. Hurt me awful, that
man did."

"Dat 'cause white man don' know how ter pleasure a pretty
li'l tiger lily like yo'. Only colored boy know that 'n' o'
all de colored boys, I knows best. Slow 'n' easy 'thout
a-hurtin' yo'. Tha's how I does it fer yo'. Make yo' happier
'n yo' ever bin afore."

"My pappy he say it wicked ter let a colored boy pleasure
me 'cause that pleasure 'n' that sin. All right fer a white man
'cause that hurt 'n' sin got ter hurt. He say if'n I sin wid
a white man God fergive me, 'cause I has ter. But if'n I
sin wid a colored man, dat's de debbil 'n' dat's sin what
never fergiven. Yas suh, dat's de awful sin o' fornicashun."
Despite her words, her hand had come unclasped and Drummage felt it open, warmly and tenderly. The action of her
fingers belied her words.

"We gits back to Falconhurst, I shows yo'. Miz Sophie
don' know yo' there, so's she gits herself ter bed. We do
some pleasurin' out in de barn."

"Wishin' yo' a white man 'cause I don' wan' ter sin."
Her sobs had stopped and Drummage no longer had to hold
her hand.

"Yo' ain' a-wishin' I a white man onct we git ter Falconhurst, li'l tiger lily." Drummage's own hand was exploring
behind his back.

The road stretched out ahead, a bright shadow of silver
in the moonlight, and Drummage walked his horse, tantalized
and titillated by the gentle stroking of her fingers and by
his own thoughts, his body moving backward and forward
with the steps of the horse, until he gasped hoarsely yanking
her fingers away as forcibly as he had planted them there.
But it was too late.

"Guess we through 'fore we started," he sighed. "Man

cain' take too much o' he lose everything. No need to stop in de barn now. Got ter wait til 'nother time." Slowly he drew a long breath and expelled it forcibly. For the moment he was no longer interested in Pamela and his thoughts deserted her. Instead of being on horseback on a country road with a nigger wench behind him, he saw himself in a shiny carriage on a wide street, lined with people white and black who were all looking at him and cheering. Major Drummage Maxwell! Congressman Drummage Maxwell! Hell no! President Drummage Maxwell of the United States of America! Beside him was his white wife, ol' Miz Sophie, and sitting across from him was his ivory-skinned son with long black hair curling around his shoulders, who somehow seemed to resemble Benoni.

The quiet of the night, heightened by the hum of insects and the soft *sluff-sluffing* of the horse's hooves in the dust of the road, was suddenly broken by the sound of men's voices coming around the bend. Drummage halted, with a word of warning to Pamela to be still. He held his breath. The voices were those of men, angry and shouting. He was not particularly frightened but he reached in his pocket to make sure that the little derringer was there. He carried it more out of bravado than fear; his position as head servant at Falconhurst gave him a certain cachet in the community among black and white alike. However, there were those among the returning veterans who seemed to resent his good clothes, his horse, his silver-mounted saddle, and the gems that flashed in his ears. One had to be careful these days. Strangers were about on the roads—wandering bands of blacks and whites, slaves seeking their new freedom, deserters from both armies, the ragtag and bobtail of war's aftermath.

"Don' know what's happenin' but better fin' out." He slipped down from his horse and led the animal into a grove of oaks which cast deep black shadows, and tied him there and helped Pamela down, bidding her sit on the ground in the deep shadow of a tree. Slowly, so as to make no noise, he crept through the dark tree trunks, feeling the soft caress of moss streamers brush against his cheek like cobwebs.

When he gained the edge of the little wood he could see out onto the road. Moonlight, flecked with shadow, dappled the road and he could make out four men on horseback, facing each other, two abreast. Now that he was closer he recognized two of the men—one by the large straw hat with the turkey feather sticking in the band and the other by his voice. Leazer and Julian Johnstone—the only two of the five Johnstone brothers who had returned from the war! The others were rotting in the ground at Shiloh, at Vicksburg, and at Atlanta. Only these two had come back to the weed-grown, tumble-down plantation which lay between Falconhurst and Benson. The place wasn't worth working; they had no niggers to work it and no money to hire them with, so they spent their time high-tailing it around the country, getting drunk, fighting, carousing with tavern wenches, and frightening Negroes half to death. They had even been unfriendly to Drummage who had known them all his life, threatening to pull him off his horse and roll him in the dust for being "an uppity nigger."

The other two men were strangers but Drummage could see from the glitter of moonlight on their buttons that they were soldiers—Union soldiers, to judge from the darkness of their uniforms and the small caps which they wore. These were the men who had fought to free him, and as he looked at them the taunts of Leazer Johnstone still rankled in Drummage's mind.

"Le's git that goddam Falconhurst nigger off'n his horse, Julian. Goddam biggity black bastard, ridin' 'long with his goddam black nose up 'n de air. Le's teach him who his betters is, Julian."

But they had done nothing more than frighten him. Perhaps the next time they would act. Drummage not only feared but hated them as he crouched in the shadows listening. He was so near now, he could make out their faces plainly in the moonlight.

Leazer, the elder of the two, was speaking.

"Shore yo' tied them knots good 'n' tight, Jule?"

Drummage looked more closely and could make out a dark line of rope extending from each soldier's neck to the limb of a tree above.

"Whaffor yo' askin' me? Know how ter tie a hangin' knot, I do, 'n' know how to place the knot under their ear. Tied 'em good, I did. Whaffor yo' a-gettin' off'n yore horse, Leazer?"

"Goin' ter lash them Yank's horses. Aim ter see them a-hangin' there. Tha's two less o' them mother-fuggin' bastards—the Captain he's fer Benedict and the corporal he's fer Tommy Joe."

"Too bad there ain' 'nother fer Scott but two's better'n none. Cain' see why yo' a-gittin' off'n yore horse. We jes' rides round in back o' them 'n' lashes out thataway."

347

"Yo' goddam right, Jule. Yo' so goddam lazy yo' 'kin al'ays think o' ways ter do things 'thout gittin' off'n yore ass."

Drummage could hear Leazer cluck to his horse and saw him circle behind the two soldiers.

"Come ter find yo' bastards a-hangin' here in de mawnin', goin' ter wonder what in hell yo' two li'l boys in blue a-doin' way down here in Alabama." Leazer prodded one of the soldiers with his gun.

Drummage's finger twitched on the trigger of the little derringer. Killing a white man was something he had never contemplated since the day he had had murder in his heart for Miz Sophie's man Apollon. He had not dared to do anything then, but now he had the advantage. Leazer and Julian didn't know he was there. He was hidden from them, and by killing one of them he would protect the soldiers. He did not stop to realize that there were two against him or that the little pistol had only one ball. His ego had so expanded during the last few hours at New Quarters and the ride with Pamela that he felt himself invincible. Taking careful aim, he fired. The spit of the explosion rang in his ears, mingled with a yelp of pain from one of the brothers —Leazer he thought it was.

"Got me, Jule. Who t'hell fired that?"

"Ain' waitin' ter see." Julian wheeled his horse, his hand on Leazer's bridle. "Les' git outa here. It's an ambush." Crouching low in their saddles, they galloped down the road. Drummage waited for their hoof beats to recede into the distance, then crept out of the woods, running up to the two men still seated on their horses.

"God bless you, whoever you are, man!" one of the soldiers exclaimed. "You got here just in time. Another minute and we'd been dancing on thin air. Take care," he warned, as Drummage came closer. "Don't start the horses. These nooses are still around our necks."

"How'm I goin' ter git 'em off?" Drummage asked. "If'n I climb up, I scare the horses. Better I go back 'n' git my horse. Kin reach 'em better."

"Don't want to sit here any longer with these things around our necks. Reach up and see if you can untie our hands." The man who spoke had a glint of gold on his shoulders. "Do it slow and quiet-like. If the horse starts up, I'll hang after all."

Quietly, so as not to startle the horses, Drummage reached up in back of the man and managed to loosen the tight thong that bound his wrists together. As soon as his hands were free the soldier reached up and slipped off the noose from around his neck, then untied his companion and relieved him of his noose. Only then did he permit himself a long sigh of relief.

"Guess your prayers saved us, Hobbs." He chafed his wrists to start the circulation again, looking down at Drummage. "Find it hard to thank you for saving us. Don't know how to put such a thing into words."

"Yo' saved me, masta suh, yo' 'n' a lot o' others. Made me a free man, yo' did. Owes it ter yo'."

"Well, we owe our lives to you. You came along at just the right time."

"Jes' a-ridin' home to de big house from de New Quarters. My horse jes' 'roun' de bend in de road."

"I'm Captain Christopher Holbrook, commanding a Cavalry Company in Demopolis." He reached down his hand to Drummage.

Drummage saw the hand—a white hand—extended toward him. It was the first time in his life a white man had ever offered him his hand in a gesture of friendship. He didn't dare to touch it. He wanted to, but he was afraid, afraid that if he reached up and touched that hand with his own the man might kill him.

"Mayhap yo' didn' notice, masta suh, but I'se a nigger. I ain' white, masta suh." Drummage stared up at the man.

"Of course I noticed it, but what difference does that make?" The Captain's hand remained extended.

" 'N' yo' means yo' a-shakin' hands wid me?"

"Good God, man, you saved our lives. I'll kiss you if you want me to. I'd shake hands with the devil himself if he'd done that much for me. After all, I've been fighting three years to free you, why in hell shouldn't I shake hands with you?"

Slowly, and not quite convinced that the man was not trying to trick him, Drummage reached up his hand. He felt it grasped in the warm, damp palm of the other. Emboldened, he squeezed the hand and shook it.

"I'se Mista Drummage Maxwell o' Falconhurst Plantation. I bid yo' welcome, Cap'n suh."

"And this is Corporal Hobbs, my orderly." Holbrook nodded in the direction of the other man, who reached his hand across the Captain's pommel to grasp Drummage's. "Thank you," he said, "we wouldn't be here now if you hadn't come along."

Drummage led them around the bend of the road to where

his horse was tethered and Pamela was waiting. Once out from under the shadow of the trees he could see the Captain better. He was a big fellow, about Drummage's own age, and his hair coming out from under his cap was as gold as the buttons of his coat. The other fellow was older, smaller, darker, and rather insignificant-looking but the Captain would stand out in a crowd. Drummage felt an instant kinship with this man whose life he had saved and whose hand he had shaken. He felt towards him almost the same way he had felt towards Hammond Maxwell.

"We're heading for Benson, Mister Maxwell. Perhaps you can tell us how far it is."

"Ain' so far." Drummage pointed down the road. "But ain' fittin' that yo' go into Benson tonight, Captain suh. Havin' ter pass that Johnstone farm if'n yo' do. Them's the two that were a-hangin' yo'. Wo'thless white trash, they is, al'ays a-rampagin' roun' de country a-makin trouble. Better yo' stays at Falconhurst tonight if'n yo' wishes. Right welcome yo' are ter spen' de night 'n' go into Benson in de mawnin'."

"By Falconhurst, I suppose you mean a plantation?"

"Yes suh, Cap'n suh. Ain' yo' never heard o' Falconhurst? Jes' almost right there. Gates jes' a li'l way. 'Sides, ain' no place in Benson fer yo' ter stay. Tavern there ain' fittin' fer a dog." They had reached the place where he had tethered his horse. He stopped and called out into the darkness: "Pamela, come on out now. It's all right. Lead my horse out."

She emerged from the shadows, leading Drummage's horse. Holbrook stared down at her, standing on the white ribbon of road, as though he had not seen a girl before.

"This here's Pamela," Drummage explained. "She a-goin' to de big house too fer to serve Miz Sophie." He hoisted her up on the horse and mounted. "This way, gen'lemen." He pointed down the road.

The Captain rode alongside Drummage, his horse a step behind so that he was abreast of Pamela.

"Right pretty young lady you got there, Mister Maxwell." The Captain was smiling at Pamela. "She your girl?"

"Not 'zactly. She new here. Jes' 'rived. She goin' ter stay here though. Yo' plannin' ter stay roun' here too, Cap'n suh?"

"We're on our way to Benson to establish a permanent post," Holbrook explained. "All of the state's been put under military rule and this is going to be my territory. Corporal Hobbs and I were riding down this afternoon to find a

350

camp site, find a house for headquarters and another for officers' quarters. We got delayed. Hobbs's horse cast a shoe and we had a time finding a blacksmith. Then he wouldn't shoe Hobbs's horse. Said he'd be damned if he'd shoe a Union horse. Took a little persuading with this"—he patted his empty holster—"to get him to do it. Those two fellows were in the shop while we were having the set-to with the blacksmith. Tried to put in their two-cents' worth but we shut them up. They left and rode on ahead of us."

"How come they catch yo', Cap'n?"

"The oldest trick in the world and I fell for it." Holbrook shook his head angrily at his own stupidity. "When we came along to that place in the road, I saw the body of a man stretched out there. Thought he was hurt or dead, so I stopped and got down. Was just bending over him when I felt a gun in my face. Other fellow jumped out of the bushes and put a gun in Hobbs's back. Then they disarmed us, tied us up, and . . . you know the rest. Again let me tell you how grateful I am that you came along."

"Glad ter help, Cap'n suh. We here at Falconhurst." He turned in at the gateposts and they followed him up the long tree-bordered drive to where the big house gleamed white-pillared in the moonlight. There were no lights in the house.

They rode around to the back and Pamela slipped down from the horse. Captain Holbrook leaned over and whispered to Drummage.

"You say the young lady isn't your girl?"

"Never saw her 'fore 'til tonight, Cap'n suh. Kinda had in mind that she would be though." Drummage paused to make the most momentous decision of his life—a decision which marked a new step in his transition from bond to free, from beast to man. He wanted this girl. He had maneuvered to get her. The interlude on the road had only temporarily quelled his desire for her and now he wanted to satisfy himself completely with her. But . . . he sensed the urgency in the Captain's question. He too wanted her. Drummage did not have to give her to this white man; he was under neither compulsion nor obligation to accede to his requests, and perhaps it was this very reason that caused the change in his thinking. Because he was not forced to give, he was willing to. This man had offered him his hand in friendship, and that meant more to him than an hour of panting, heaving swink with a new wench. For the first time in his life he decided to be generous and give away something he really wanted for himself. He nodded his head in the direction of Pamela. "She pretty, ain' she?"

"She certainly is." Holbrook dismounted and waited for Drummage.

"Yo' sort o' likin' her, Cap'n suh?"

"Well, I don't know." The Captain seemed undecided, "I . . ."

Drummage sensed the reason for Holbrook's indecision. "Yo' meanin', Cap'n suh, cause yo' ain' never before pleasured a colored gal? That what yo' meanin', Cap'n suh?"

Holbrook nodded rather sheepishly.

"Well, let me tell yo' somethin', Cap'n suh. Ain' never in my life shooken a white man's hand afore tonight either. White man's hand no different 'n' nigger's hand. Feel jes' the same. Colored girl no different 'n white girl, once yo' blow out de lamp. Better too, everyone says." Drummage closed one eye knowingly.

"But maybe she wouldn't like me." Holbrook eyed her, hoping for some word from Pamela herself.

"Don' make a goddam bit o' difference whether she a-likin' yo' or not." Drummage pushed her over beside Holbrook. "If'n yo' wants her, yo' takes her. White man a-comin' ter Falconhurst, Masta Hammond always give him a wench ter pleasure if'n he wishes. Masta Hammond gone now so I give yo' wench, 'n' sides. . . ."—Drummage measured Holbrook with his eyes—"she a-wantin' white man. Tol' me so, didn' yo', Pammy?"

Pamela took the one step that brought her to the Captain.

"Ain' no sin a white man pleasures me," she said. "Ain' no sin, 'n' guessin' I like it too." She slipped her arm around Holbrook's waist.

Drummage opened the kitchen door. The lamp was still burning in the kitchen and Pollux was seated at the table.

"Welcome ter Falconhurst." Drummage waved for the captain and Pamela to precede him. "Ain' fittin' ter bring yo' in de back do'. Hopin' yo' don' mind, Cap'n suh." He waited for them to step inside and then, anxious to show off his authority before the Captain and Pamela, he barked at Pollux: "Git up off'n yore fat ass 'n' git out 'n' help that sodjer stable them horses. Jump, boy, when I speaks ter yo'."

Chapter 39

"YO' ET, Cap'n suh?" Drummage pulled out one of the kitchen chairs for Holbrook and seated himself on another.

Holbrook sat down, undecided whether to ask Pamela to sit beside him or not, but as Drummage made no move to invite her or offer her a chair, Holbrook refrained from taking the initiative.

"No, as a matter of fact, Mr. Maxwell, we have not eaten. And," he added, smiling, "we're damned hungry." He glanced up as Hobbs and Pollux came in the door. "You hungry, Hobbs?"

"That I am, sir." Hobbs came over and took the chair which Drummage pushed out with his toe.

"Ain' got much ter offer yo' all," Drummage apologized. "Food mighty scarce roun' here. Kin git yo' all some sweet milk, some cold pone, some clabber, 'n' mayhap kin fin' a jar o' melon rind fer yo'. Ain' much but it'll keep yo' all from starvin'. Better 'n yo' could get in Benson, though." He told Pollux to go out to the springhouse to bring in the milk and clabber while he himself got up to set the table for two. While he waited for Pollux to return he rummaged in the buttery for the jar of Lucretia Borgia's melon rind pickles which had been saved against some emergency. By the time he had found them, Pollux was back to cut up the cold pone and put it on the table. Drummage sat with the soldiers but he did not eat. Pressing the meager victuals on them, he again apologized for their scantiness.

"Thinkin' yo' like ter live here at Falconhurst, Cap'n suh," he said. "Goin' ter fix this place up like it useter be. Goin' ter have me house servants, men in the barn, 'n' men fer the groun's. Goin' ter have me a garden fer green stuff, 'n' git me some hogs, git me some hens. Aimin' ter make this place like 'n it was 'fore the war. Could I git me some paint, would paint it—po'tico needs it. Thinkin' yo' likes livin' here at Falconhurst. Ain' no decent place fer a gen'leman like yo' in Benson. An' 'sides"—He closed one eye in a suggestive wink and leered at Pamela—"yo' gits steady pleasurin' here 'cause Pammy she a-goin' ter stay here 'n' serve Miz Sophie."

"But won't your Miss Sophie have something to say about my staying here?" Holbrook asked.

"Huh! Miz Sophie don' say much roun' here no mo'." Drummage was emphatic. "Miz Sophie don' cut much of a figure here at Falconhurst." Drummage looked at Holbrook, seeing him pause suddenly with a piece of pone half-raised to his lips. Holbrook's eyes were fastened on someone behind Drummage's back.

"Who don' have nothin' ter say round here no mo'?" Sophie's voice took Drummage by surprise. "Guess yo' goin' ter fin' out, Drummage. Who these men here? They Union sodjers?"

Drummage twisted on his chair to face her. She was standing in the doorway that led from the office room into the kitchen and Drummage was relieved to see that she had made some effort to be presentable. Her peignoir of pale-pink satin was clean, her hair combed, and she managed to maintain an air of suzerainty as she stood in the door—some hark-back to Hammond Maxwell.

Holbrook rose from his chair and Hobbs got to his feet. "Captain Holbrook, madam, of the Twenty-fifth Massachusetts Cavalry, at your service, and Corporal Hobbs."

Sophie melted somewhat in the presence of a man as prepossessing as the Captain but she transferred her gaze from him and transfixed the luckless Pamela as mercilessly as a butterfly on a pin. " 'N' who that nigger wench? Yo' ain' a-bringin' no bright-skin nigger wench here ter pester, Drummage. Git her outa here. Ain' havin' her round. 'N' git these sodjers outa here too. Ain' havin' them nuther. This my house, 'n' don' yo' fergit it."

"Ain' my wench, she ain'." Drummage refused to rise from his chair. "She Cap'n Holbrook's wench. I bro't her here though. Bro't her fer yo', Miz Sophie. She trained ter serve 'n' thinkin' yo' need her. Lots o' thanks I git fer thinkin' o' yo."

"Well, I don' care." Sophie tossed her head with a show of arrogance. "Git 'em out! Git 'em all out. Ain' a-havin' Union sodjers. Ain' havin' no truck wid 'em nor their nigger wenches nuther. Git 'em out!"

Captain Holbrook reached for his cap and took a step towards the door, prepared to take his leave, but Drummage put out a hand to restrain him, while he stared Sophie down.

"Keep yore mouth shet, Miz Sophie. Cap'n he a-stayin'

354

here. He a-stayin' 'n' Pammy she a-stayin' wid him 'cause I say so." He banged his fist on the table.

"Who're yo'?" Sophie was not fazed. "Yo' jes' a nigger, that's all. This is my house 'n' ain' no nigger a-goin' ter tell me to shet my mouth."

Holbrook decided to stop the wrangling by leaving. True, he had been hoping to remain, at least for the night, for Pamela was tempting to a man who had not had a woman for three months. Colored girls of the pale shade of Pamela had tempted him before but he had never dared seek them. Now one had come to him without any effort on his part and he hated to lose her. Such an opportunity might not come again. Yet his proper Yankee training surmounted even his desire for Pamela. He bowed low and most correctly.

"I can see that our presence is unwanted, Mrs. . . . ?" He questioned her with a look.

"Mrs. Beauchair." Sophie was quite the *grande dame*. If she could have remembered Apollon's bogus title she would have used it, proclaiming herself a Vicomtesse.

"Mrs. Beauchair?" Holbrook straightened up and regarded her. "Mrs. Beauchair? That is a most uncommon name. I once knew a fellow by that name—Apollon Beauchair. He was from this part of the country too. We were friends at school."

Sophie ran across the kitchen, dropping the folds of her peignoir in her haste. She halted before the captain, clutching both his hands in hers.

"Yo' knew my husban'? Yo' knew Apollon? Yes, he went to school in the No'th. Tol' me 'bout it many times. Boston it was. College by the name of Harvard. Yo' knew him?"

"Tall, dark fellow—handsome! Yes, extremely handsome. Came from New Orleans I think. Yes, Mrs. Beauchair, I knew him fairly well. What a coincidence! That I should come to 'Pollon's house. Is he here, Mrs. Beauchair?"

Without relinquishing his hands, she led him back to the chair, refilled his glass with milk, and turned to Drummage. "Whyn't yo' rouse that lazy Marguerite 'n' git her down here? One ham lef' out 'n the smoke house. She kin git it 'n' fry these gen'lemen a slice. Got us some eggs too. Cain' let frien's o' my husband's go hungry." Without waiting for Drummage to answer, she pushed Holbrook down into his chair. "No, Cap'n, I'se a widow. 'Pollon got killed by a run-'way nigger. But mighty happy ter welcome a frien' o' his ter Falconhurst even if'n yo' a Union sodjer. Guess all o' 'em ain' alike. This yore house, Cap'n. Wants yo' should stay here's

355

long's yo' wishes. Ain' much like it was when 'Pollon here but yo' welcome—right welcome. 'N' yo' kin keep your wench too, if'n yo' likes." she relinquished Holbrook's hands.

"Thank you, Mrs. Beauchair." He pulled his chair up closer to the table. "But don't bother to have anything cooked for us. This will do quite well. And thank you for letting us stay the night. We ride into Benson tomorrow, but if it would not inconvenience you, I would like to return and remain here. Hobbs can stay in Benson, but I feel quite at home here in 'Pollon's house."

Sophie was all solicitude. Even her manner towards Drummage changed. knowing that Pamela was not his and remembering that he had thought of her need in bringing the girl, she smiled at him. Gathering her flounces about her, she sat down at the table with the men, and they told her how Drummage had saved their lives. With a little gesture of affection, she tapped Drummage's cheek.

"He a good boy." She smiled at him and then at the Captain. "He the only one o' all the Falconhurst servants what stood by me. All lef' but Drummage. Git kinda provoked wid him at times but he a good boy. His papa saved my papa's life onct 'n' now Drummage save yourn. Drummage ain' no ordinary nigger, he ain'. He part Mandingo 'n' part Royal Hausa. They de best. Drummage grandpa, he a king in Africa, so my papa tol' me. See that thing he a-wearin' roun' his neck?" She nodded for Drummage to pull the little silver talisman out from the neck of his shirt and show it to them. "Came from Africa, it did. Shows he a king. No suh, Drummage he ain' no ordinary nigger." Her hand moved from his face to his arm and squeezed it.

"We can attest to that, Mrs. Beauchair." Holbrook paid homage to Drummage. He stopped suddenly, noticing the affectionate grip of Sophie's fingers on Drummage's arm. Earlier he had noticed her pregnancy. Now the manner in which she fondled this handsome young Negro and the expression in her eyes told him, plainer than words, that the child she was carrying had been planted by this same Drummage. Strangely enough he did not feel shocked. He could understand how the splendid virility of this personable young fellow might appeal to a woman such as Sophie, whose faded blondeness and bulging waistline would be no temptation to another man. Indeed, she might count herself fortunate to have this Negro who, as Holbrook studied him, somewhat resembled Apollon Beauchair as he remembered him. Beauchair had been a handsome brute. How had he ever

356

happened to marry this woman? To cover his confusion, Holbrook crumbled the pone in his fingers and meticulously swept the crumbs together.

"We have had a rather difficult day, Mrs. Beauchair. One doesn't get saved from hanging every day, and then meet the charming wife of an old friend. All in all it's been an exciting time. Also we have to get up early, so if we might retire . . . ?"

" 'Course." Sophie rose, taking notice of Pamela, who stood behind Holbrook's chair. "What yore name, gal?"

"I'se Pamela but mostly they calls me Pammy."

"Then git yo'se'f upstairs wid me. Show yo' where the sheets are. Kin make up de Cap'n's bed in de guest chamber. He"—she pointed to Hobbs—"kin sleep down here in de office on de sofa." With the same authority with which she had entered the kitchen, she left, with Drummage, Captain Holbrook, and Pamela following her. Upstairs, closets were opened, lavender-scented sheets found, pillowcases unfolded, and soon the beds, both upstairs and down, were made up. Sophie, still in command of the situation, bade good night to Holbrook and waited for him to close his door. She eyed Drummage as he went to his room and then bade Pamela follow her.

The girl helped her off with the peignoir, loosened the pins in her hair, and then turned down the sheets of the bed, awaiting further orders.

"Yo' that Cap'n's wench?" Sophie asked. "Sure yo' ain' plannin' ter sneak in bed wid Drummage?"

"No, ma'am. Cap'n he spoken fer me. Ain' a-wantin' ter bed wid no buck, ma'am. My papa he a preacher 'n' he say it a sin fer me to pleasure wid a buck. Ain' no sin wid a white man 'cause I has ter but wid a buck don' has to less'n I wants. That makes it a sin."

"Certainly does," Sophie agreed. "Then git yo'se'f back there 'fore the Cap'n goes ter sleep. 'N' if yo' stayin' here, yo' keeps yore hands off'n that Drummage. Wenches al'ays after him but yo' keep 'way from him. Catch yo' foolin' around wid him 'n' I'll strip yo' down. We still whops here at Falconhurst. Niggers are still niggers, 'ceptin' o' course Drummage 'n' he kinda special-like 'cause he Mandingo." Sophie held the door for Pamela to leave and watched her go down the hall to enter Holbrook's room. Once the door had closed she went back into her own room, where she paced nervously up and down the floor. Meeting a friend of Apol-

357

lon's had stirred her memories of him. She felt lonely and neglected, longing for companionship.

Drummage, alone in his own room, felt equally neglected. He had kept his ear to the keyhole and had heard Pamela go to the Captain's room and the door close behind her. Now he was cursing himself for his generosity. What a fool he had been to give Pamela to the white man. He had entirely recovered from the episode on horseback and his mental picture of what might be happening in the room across the hall fanned the embers of his desire into a flame. Now he was alone and it was his own goddamn fault. He'd had her right in his hand, or rather, he grinned to himself, she'd had him in her hand, and now he'd given her up. Damn! If he couldn't have her he'd have to get another wench for himself tonight. Couldn't sleep the way he was. He couldn't stand the thought of that pale gold skin being caressed by Holbrook's hand, much as he liked Holbrook.

In his extremity he even considered Marguerite. Hell no! Not if he were dying could he pester her. What wench over in the New Quarters would be available? He'd even be willing to go out and saddle his horse and ride over, but there wasn't a damned one he could think of that he could get without waking up a whole household. In desperation, he took to pacing the floor. Here he was, alone after all his carefully laid plans. No woman around anywhere—nobody but that goddamn harelipped Marguerite and ol' Miz Sophie.

Hot damn! He'd forgotten all about Miz Sophie and she just next door. She wasn't too bad, ol' Miz Sophie wasn't. And she always wanted him. He never had to sweet-talk her into having him. He stripped off his shirt, took off his shoes, peeled off his trousers, and stood in his drawers. Miz Sophie'd be better than nothing, and then afterwards he could sleep. But if he gave it to Miz Sophie tonight, she was sure going to pay for it. Pay plenty too!

With his thumb on the latch, he carefully raised it so it would make no sound. Outside in the hall it was dark, with the white-painted doors making ghostly patches in the darkness. He tiptoed the length of the hall, resisting the temptation to listen at the Captain's door. He lifted the latch on Sophie's door as carefully as he had lifted his own and stepped inside, closing the door behind him. Sophie was in bed, her hand already extended to turn down the lamp. When she saw Drummage she regarded him with expectancy, mixed with a little apprehension. He had never come unbidden to her room before. Previously it had taken her best efforts at cajolery and bribery to get him there. Now he had come of his own accord. Perhaps, she thought, he had been grateful for the complimentary things she had said about him. Well, they were true! Looking at him now, standing like a bronze statue with the lamplight gilding the rich brown of his skin, she knew that she wanted him more than any man, yes, even more than the white man across the hall. Surely no white man could compare with him. The white drawers he was wearing did little to hide his attraction from her. She was well aware of all that was concealed. As she stared at him, he looked back at her through hooded eyes, and when he spoke his words came slowly—thickly.

"Jes' tho't I'd come in ter say good night."

"That all yo' wanted, Drummage?" She heaved herself over onto the other side of the bed, ostensibly making room for him. "That all?" Her voice betrayed her expectancy.

"That all, Miz Sophie, less'n yo' thinkin' ter marry up wid me." His fingers fumbled with the button of his drawers and he peeled them down around his knees until they dropped on the floor. "Jes' a-sayin' good night 'n' askin' yo' 'gain ter marry up wid me. All the folks at New Quarters gittin' themselves named tomorrow 'n' marryin' up. Got a real preacher there now. Taken me a name 'n' now likes ter git me married up regular-like. Ain' thinkin' o' marryin' nobody but yo', less'n yo' won' do it."

"Well, don' think no mo' 'bout it. Ain' marryin' up wid no nigger 'fore no nigger preacher nuther. Yo' say yo' takin' a name? What name yo' takin'?"

"Maxwell! Now I'se Drummage Maxwell."

Sophie sat up in bed and pointed a finger at him. "Yo' cain' take that name. Won' have it."

"Yo' cain' say I cain'. Take any name I wants. Wants de name o' Maxwell 'n' goin' ter take it. My pappy saved yore pappy. Got me a right to take the name. Yo' say yo' ain' a-marryin' up wid me?"

She shook her head emphatically. "Ain' even considerin' it."

He reached down to pick up his garment on the floor. "Jes' came in ter say good night."

"Wait a minute, Drummage. Don' go yet."

He turned to face her. "Better take a good look, Miz Sophie, at somethin' yo' ain' ever goin' ter see again."

"Whar yo' goin'?" she demanded.

"Thinkin' I git dressed 'n' git me over to de New Quarters. New wench jes' came in wid the road niggers tonight. Right pretty wench 'n' she a-wantin' me. Said so, she did. Good night." He opened the door a crack but Sophie called to him, pleading with him.

"Whyn't yo' stay here, Drummage boy? Too late ter go over ter de New Quarters. Wake 'em all up, yo' will."

"Don' make me no difference. She a-sleepin' wid Elkanah 'n' Minnie. Minnie ol' frien' o' mine; she let me in 'cause she think mayhap I wantin' her. Elkanah he sleep like a horse. Done it many times afore." He opened the door wider.

"Drummage." Sophie got out of bed clumsily and stumbled across the floor. "Drummage, stay with me tonight, even if'n it jes' a li'l while. Been a-thinkin' 'bout that Cap'n 'n' that bright-skin wench. Wantin' yo' tonight, Drummage. Give yo' one of my pretties if'n yo' stay."

"Don' wan' yore goddamned dew-dads. Don' wan' yo' nuther. Ain' never wantin' yo' 'gain. Ain' nothin' yo' got what I wants. Tomorrow I'se marryin' me up wid a gal. She goin' ter git what yo' wants now. Goin' ter leave dis house. Ain' never steppin' foot in it again. Goin' ter build me a new house over in de New Quarters. To hell wid yo', Miz Sophie, so take a good look at what yo' goin' to be missin' from now on." Drummage was lying like a trouper but he could see the effect that his words were having on Sophie. " 'N' I'se goin' ter see to it that yo' never gits yo'self 'nother buck from de New Quarters. No buck goin' to pleasure yo' if'n I say he cain' 'n' no white man ever goin' ter have yo' onct he know yo' a-goin' ter have a nigger sucker. I a-steppin' outa dis do' now 'n' yo' never have a man 'gain, white nor nigger, so long's yo' live."

She expected him to leave and slam the door behind him but he remained standing there, bending his knees to get his feet into his drawers, arranging them and buttoning them. As she looked at him, she felt consumed by desire. What would she do if she lost him? No white man would ever touch her again, and such was Drummage's influence with the Negroes that not one of them would ever come near her if he forbade them. Life seemed to stretch out emptily before her. She took a step towards him and fell on her knees before him, circling his legs with her arms, feeling his smooth, strong, warm flesh against her cheek.

"Don' leave me, Drummage," she sobbed. "Don' leave me."

"Ain' never goin' ter have nothin' ter do with no woman 'gain what ain' my wife," he proclaimed righteously, forgetting that only a moment before he had threatened to go to New Quarters. "Got me a name, I have. Goin' ter get me a wife tomorrow, regular-like, preacher 'n' everythin'. Goin' ter live like a white man—man wid a name, man wid a wife, man wid a house o' his own, man wid children o' his own. Sick o' bein' a nigger 'n' a servant. Goin' ter be . . ."—He sought for the word he wanted—"respectable."

She clung more closely to him, nuzzling her mouth against his thigh.

"Supposin' I say I marries up wid yo', Drummage? Supposin' I say I be yore wife. Supposin' I say Falconhurst be yore home 'n' dis baby I totin' be yourn? Supposin' I say all that, Drummage?"

"Supposin' yo' do?" He pried her head away from him.

"Then I do say it. Say it now. Sayin' I marries up wid yo' tomorrow if'n yo' won' leave me ever."

He held her face away from him. "Yo' marries up wid me 'fore a nigger preacher?" He could not quite believe that she would so far demean herself.

"No white preacher marries us. If'n we git married, got ter git married 'fore a nigger preacher or not at all. 'N' 'sides I don' care. Lived wid niggers all my life, I have. Might's well spend the rest of it wid 'em. More nigger'n white I am, I guess, 'n' ain' the first time I marries up wid a nigger. That 'Pollon Beauchair, he a nigger too." She gasped, for she had not intended to disclose her secret.

"He colored, Miz Sophie?" Drummage could scarcely believe his ears.

She hung her head meekly. "So Lucretia Borgia said 'n' she know. Ain' never tol' no one 'fore, but don' make no difference now if'n I marry up wid yo'."

"Den we marries up tomorrow, Sophie." Drummage could afford to express a little feeling now. He drew her head gently back to him, feeling, despite himself, pleasure from her lips.

"We marries up tomorrow if'n yo' stays tonight." She glanced up at him, saw his lips drawn tight and the glazed expression of his eyes. "All night," she added.

He pressed her head more closely to himself.

"All right, Sophie, but le's not stand here. Tired, I am, and want to stretch out."

Later, after Drummage had gone to sleep, Sophie lay awake by his side. Her hand sought the warmth of his flesh in the darkness and she thought of her mother whom she had never seen. Her mother had loved a nigger buck by the name of Mede. Well, at least she was no worse than her mother. Then she remembered the bleached skull in Big Pearl's cabin. That was all that was left of Mede. She

361

knew what her father had done to Mede and now she was glad that her father was dead. He could never do that to Drummage. Her hands wandered over the length of the sleeping body beside her, tangling for a moment with the silver chain, then up to Drummage's face. The warmth of his skin reassured her. This was no lifeless skull. The child within her moved and she was happy that it was Drummage's child.

Chapter 40

THE CLATTER of pots and pans in the kitchen awoke Drummage. It took a moment for him to orient himself. He turned his head and saw Sophie's face, her eyes closed in sleep. Taking care not to wake her, he crept out of bed, relieved himself as noiselessly as possible in the chamber pot, and then, pulling on his drawers, he raced down the hall into his own room, splashed water over his face and body, and dried himself. Eschewing the dark, warm clothes he had worn last night, he dressed in a pair of Apollon's white linen trousers and an old white shirt, and, barefooted, descended the stairs to the office below. Hobbs was still sleeping and Drummage did not wake him.

Marguerite had breakfast ready. With Pollux' help, Drummage laid the big waiter with a white cloth, some of the best china that still remained unnicked, and silver. He poured the imitation coffee into a tarnished silver coffeepot, cut the hot pone into squares, added a pitcher of hot milk and a jug of molasses, and carried it up to Holbrook's room. A knock at the door, and the Captain's sleepy answer gave him entrance. Inside, he glanced briefly at the bed, placed the loaded waiter on the table, and opened the shutters, which let a flood of light into the room.

"Trustin' yo' slep' well, Cap'n suh." Drummage came over to the bed and, pulling the pillow out from under Pamela's head, he tucked it behind the Captain, bolstering him up in bed. Balancing the tray on the Captain's lap, he poured the coffee, added the hot milk and sweetening, and handed the cup to him. Somehow he did not feel in awe of this white man. There was an unexpressed feeling of equality between them. Drummage had loved and respected Hammond Maxwell and he felt that Hammond had cared for him, but not as a man loves a friend, rather with the affection he has for a dog or a horse. With the Captain there was an unexpressed and subtle difference. Drummage felt that this man returned his feeling of love and respect. He needed the support and confidence the white man gave him but the fact that the Captain was his friend and not his master moved him more deeply than he could say.

Holbrook sipped the coffee and made a wry face.

"What sort of a witches' brew is this? I'll see to it that we get some real coffee as soon as the supply wagons arrive. But bad as it is, why none for Pammy here?" His free arm pulled her closer. "Poor Pammy, she's had a bad night."

"She gits hers in the kitchen later, Cap'n. Ain' totin' no tray fer her. Git yo'se'f up, gal! Git yore clothes on 'n' git down to de kitchen. Miz Sophie's a-goin' ter be wantin' yo'."

"Whoa, there," Holbrook held up the hand which had encircled Pamela's neck. "Thought this gal was mine."

"Shore is, Cap'n suh. She's yourn nights. Days she got things ter do here. She Miz Sophie's gal. Don' want ter hurry yo', Cap'n, if'n yo' wantin' ter pleasure her 'gain this mawnin'. Kin come back later."

"Pleasure, huh?" Holbrook shook his head in wonderment. "That's a nice word for it. Never heard it used that way before. We have another word which we use up North which is not nearly as expressive. Must remember 'pleasure'."

"Pleasurin' o' pesterin'—they both the same thing."

"But I think I like pleasuring better than pestering." Holbrook laughed. "If Pammy is needed, I'd better not keep her. After all, I'm only a guest here."

"No, yo' ain', Cap'n suh. Yo' a-livin' here. This yore home. If'n yo' wants, Pamela keep yo' company every night fer pleasurin' o' pesterin'." He waited while Pamela crawled out of bed, modestly turning her back to Drummage while she slipped into her clothes. Once dressed, she leaned over the bed and kissed Holbrook lightly on the forehead, then slipped out the door. Drummage waited for it to close behind her.

"Didn' rightly mean ter send her away, Cap'n suh, but wanted to talk to you 'lone like. Wantin' ter ask if'n yo' do somethin' fer me. Needs yore help, Cap'n suh."

Holbrook set the coffee cup down on the table by the bed and handed him the tray to put on the floor. "Look, Drummage," he said, throwing off the covers and preparing to get out of bed, "if there's anything I can do for you all you have to do is ask. First you save my life, then you give me a home, then you provide me with the most exciting night of my whole life. Good God, man, nobody ever did all that for me before. So, ask away."

"Well, you see, Cap'n suh, it's like this. Goin' ter change my life today. Gittin' myself a new life 'n' wantin' a better life. Wantin' to be like yo'. Knows I cain' be white, knows that, but wants ter act like a white man, live like a white man, talk like a white man. Never been nothin' but a goddam animal. Thinkin' mayhap yo' kin help me get ter be a man. Thinkin' mayhap yo' kin teach me. Thinkin' yo' livin' here mayhap yo' kin tell me what ter do."

"Look, Drummage, if that's what you want, I'll do it and do it gladly. Perhaps I can't give you a bachelor's degree from Harvard, but I'll polish you up so's you'd do credit to a Beacon Street drawing room. Sure, fellow, I'll do it. But you have to study a bit. Things like that just don't happen, you have to work for them."

"Willin' ter work at it, Cap'n suh. Willin' ter do anythin'. Gittin' myself married today I am. Tha's my first step."

"Who's the lucky girl?"

"Ain' no girl, Cap'n suh. Some ways wishin' it was but most ways not. Aimin' ter marry up wid Miz Sophie."

Holbrook laid back on the propped-up pillows and regarded Drummage for a long moment—a moment long enough to die in—and during that moment Drummage felt all his hopes and ambitions dying away under what he considered the other man's disapproval. Then it wasn't true. Niggers were not as good as white men. Even this man, who said he had fought to make Drummage free and who was willing now to help him, did not believe it. Drummage could see it on his face.

"But she's white. . . . !" Holbrook stammered.

"Yes, she a white woman. I know dat. She de owner o' Falconhurst. She de daughter o' my old masta. But I a-wantin' ter marry up wid her jes' because o' dat."

"But she's older than you are, Drummage. Look, you're a handsome fellow. White or colored, you're about the best-looking man I've ever seen. What do you want to tie yourself up to an old woman for. Should think you'd be interested in a cute little trick like Pammy. Certainly you'd be happier in the end. A marriage to a white woman is going to pose problems for you both. Even in the North you'd find yourself in a difficult situation, and you're here in the South."

"Ain' no law agin it, is there?"

"No," Holbrook shook his head, "there are no state laws in Alabama now. There's only military law and I represent that. But think it over, Drummage. what if you should have children?"

"Thinkin' 'bout that. Miz Sophie she a-totin' my baby now. She bin a-payin' me ter pester her." He pointed to the diamonds in his ears. "Gave me these, she did, jes' ter larrup her a few times."

Again there was a long silence on Holbrook's part. Now he understood why Apollon Beauchair had married Sophie. If she was willing to pay Drummage she must have bought Apollon too, and Holbrook knew Apollon well enough to know he could have been purchased. His eyes appraised Drummage and a triple-creased scowl appeared on his brow. He had come to Alabama with every intention of accepting the black man in his new status as a free man. He had been anxious to help this new man raise himself by his bootstraps so that he might take his place in the community, in the state, and in the nation. But the longer he had been in the South, the more he had come to despise the southern white man as cruel, arrogant, and selfish. They had enslaved these Negroes, relegated them to the position of cattle and used them in any way they desired. And now, apparently, it was not only the men who had done that but the women too. This stupid woman at Falconhurst, for instance, with her airy affection of gentility and breeding, had yielded herself willingly to this Negro. Worse than that, she had sought him and had paid him, purchasing his favors as lightly as a man paid for a whore.

At first the thought of a black man marrying a white woman had shocked him. Even his desire to consider the Negro as his peer had not prepared him for this equality. Black was black and white was white. And yet. . . . He remembered the night he had just passed in the clinging arms of a Negro girl. What right had he to be shocked that a black man should take a white woman? What mattered the few formal words that might be said over this juncture of black and white flesh to make it legal? God almighty! Whites had despoiled blacks since the dawn of history. Let the tables be turned. Let the blacks now despoil the whites and he would help them. If this Sophie itched for black meat, let her have it openly for all the world to know about and not just feather-bedded behind the closed door of her bedroom. Let it be known from New Orleans to Richmond that one mating of black and white had been dragged out into the open and legalized. Let North and South both see that when she gave birth to her child—it would be the first to be born legally and not stigmatized as a bastard.

"All right, Drummage," Holbrook said finally. "If you want to marry her, go ahead. But how about her? You can't force her to marry you, you know."

"She willin', Cap'n suh. Jes' tol' me she was."

"And who's goin' to marry you?"

"Nigger preacher over to de New Quarters. He's a-marryin' all the people over there today. Was hopin' ter have a white preacher, but ain' no white preacher a-goin' ter marry Miz Sophie 'n' me."

"How about me?"

"What yo' mean, Cap'n suh, how 'bout yo'?"

"Well, as military commander of this section, I represent the only law here. All civil laws now come under the military. I can marry you legally but not religiously, but I'll do it on one condition and one condition only. Tell me exactly why you want to do it. Why do you want to tie yourself up to her? Do you love her? I can't believe that."

Drummage wanted to answer the Captain's question but he found it difficult to analyze his feelings. Why did he want to marry Sophie? There was no question of love in it. He didn't want to marry her like he would have wanted to marry Candy. Then why did he want her? Why was it important to him that he marry her?

"Don' rightly know how ter say it, Cap'n suh. Don't love her. No, suh! Pleasurin' her bin hard work fer me. Don' like white women. Jes' ter look at one nekkid make me crawl all over, they do. Guess I wants ter be somebody. Wants a name. Wants to feel I am somebody. Marries up wid a nigger wench 'n' has a lot of nigger suckers, who'm I? Ain' nobody. Jes' Drummage, tha's all. Goes over to de New Quarters 'n' builds myself a cabin. Gits me a mule 'n' a pig, Who'm I? Ain't no better 'n de others. Jes' like Brute o' Sampson o' Big Randy. Jes' like all de other bucks. Jes' 'nother nigger. Work all day 'n' raise me a bale o' cotton a year. Tomcattin' all night a-findin' new wenches ter pester whilst I raise a crop o' suckers off'n my woman. Jes' 'nother nigger buck, that's all. Marries me up wid Miz Sophie, I lives here. Makes Falconhurst big 'gain. Brings servants here to de house. Lives decent here. Plants cotton 'n' raises a crop. Makes money 'n' grows more cotton. Paints de house, buys new furniture, goes to N' Orleans 'n' lives in de St. Louis hotel. Maybe goes up No'th. 'Stead of raisin' me a caffle o' nigger kids, I gits me a bright-skin boy off'n Miz Sophie. Sends him ter school up No'th. Dresses him up. He be de Masta o' Falconhurst. Perhaps marries himself up wid a white woman. Ain' goin' ter be no nigger wid a mule 'n' a bale o' cotton."

"But that child of yours will not be white, Drummage."

"Ain' a-wantin' him ter be. But he be part white. He part Maxwell 'n' he part me. I part white too, Cap'n suh. My pappy, he part white. Brute say my pappy he Royal Hausa. Brute say that better 'n Mandingo 'n' I half Mandingo. My mama Big Pearl she pure Mandingo. Heard Masta Hammond onct say when I a boy I bring five thousand dollars but he wouldn' sell me fer ten thousand 'cause ain' no other nigger in de whole South what blooded like me."

"Those bloodlines do mean something, Drummage. I knew you were something special. Look, I'll get you married to your Sophie if you want. I've got to go into Benson this morning and get things started there but I'll come back out this evening before supper and we'll have the marriage then. I'll have to study up on just how to conduct the ceremony like a justice of the peace. Then we'll start in on a course of training for you. Something tells me we're going to be friends. Want to take your first lesson now?"

"Yas suh, Cap'n suh, 'n' thank you suh, Cap'n suh."

"Well, the first lesson is to stop this 'Cap'n suh' business. No more of it: Here at Falconhurst, I'll call you Drummage and you call me Chris. When there are others around I'll call you 'Mr. Maxwell' and you call me 'Captain Holbrook,' but I'm not going to call you 'Drummage suh' and you're not going to call me 'Cap'n suh.' "

"No suh, Cap'n suh."

"Well, I must say you're a hell of a pupil. Can't you remember your first lesson?"

Drummage hung his head. "Hard to 'member. Taught to say 'masta suh' o' 'mista suh' o' 'Cap'n suh' ter every white man. Fergit it 'n' I gits whopped. Seen niggers git themselves stripped down jes' fer fergittin' ter say 'suh.' Kinda scairt o' yo' 'cause yo're a white man but ain' really scairt. Shore admires ter be a frien' o' yourn, Chris." Drummage lifted up his head and grinned.

"Shore admires ter be a frien' o' yourn too, Drummage." Holbrook mimicked Drummage's words with a grin. "Shore a-thinkin' I'm a-goin' ter like my new home here."

"Yo' soun' jes' like some goddam nigger, Chris. Ain' wantin' yo' ter talk like me—nigger-like—wantin' ter talk like yo'."

367

"I'll teach you, Drummage. I'll be able to teach you some things and perhaps you can teach me some too."

"Like what, Chris?"

Holbrook slapped him on the back. "Well, fellow, I always thought I was pretty good with women but I never had one crawling to me on her hands and knees offering me diamonds just to lay her. Do you have some secret? Perhaps you can teach me that, huh?"

"Shore kin try, Cap'n suh . . . means Chris. Shore kin try. But . . ."—he glanced down at Holbrook and snickered—"jes' don' think no white man ever able to pleasure a woman like a nigger kin. White men got lotsa thin's a nigger ain' got —got yalla hair, got white skin, got blue eyes, got lotsa education, got money 'n' got mo' everythin' they wants but ain' hung like niggers. No suh! De Lawd took everythin' 'way from de niggers, gave 'em black skin, gave 'em wool fer hair, 'n' made 'em serve de white men. Den de Lawd fel' sorry fer de poor niggers 'n' he say he goin' ter give them pore black bastards somethin' ter pleasure themselves wid, so he hung 'em twice's heavy as de white men."

It was Drummage's turn to slap Holbrook on the back before he left.

Chapter 41

SOPHIE awoke, sensing that Drummage had gone, and missing him, yet glad to be alone a few moments to consider her situation. As she looked around her room, whose four walls enclosed a barren history of countless nights of frustrated tossing on the big mahogany bed, everything that had happen the night before came back to her. Now the thought that she had promised Drummage she would marry him frightened her and at the same time made her feel happy. She who was always so insecure was secretly thrilled to be under the domination of a man. That the man happened to be a Negro did not trouble her. Quite the contrary. It was only what others might think that worried her.

The fact was that Sophie had lived with Negroes all her life and she felt more at home with them than she did with white people. Outside of her father and stepmother and an occasional guest at Falconhurst, she rarely saw a white person.

Even on their visits to New Orleans they were accompanied by Negroes and spent most of their time associating with them. On their return to Falconhurst, they were again in a sea of black. The servants in the house, the people on the plantation, the workers in the field, the artisans, and the men in the barns were all blacks. Nor were their breeding habits a secret for, despite Augusta's dislike of the subject, it was Hammond's favorite topic, and Sophie was always hearing about the advisability of mating that buck with this wench or this buck with that wench.

Sometimes she would walk down the dusty street between the slave cabins in the early evening when the men were returning from the fields, and, picking out some attractive buck who she had just heard had been ordered to cover some particular wench, she would follow him, in her thoughts, into the cabin, and picture in fantastic detail their mating. Even after she had acquired her own groom, she still envied those women whose mating studs were chosen for them by her father. From the first day that Drummage had come to the big house, Sophie had wanted him more than all others. He was so much handsomer than any of the other bucks, so much more intelligent and attractive, that she had often tried to seduce him but had never succeeded. The more he had eluded her, the more she had desired him, except for that one brief period when Apollon was there. Then, with Apollon gone and Falconhurst slipping into an abandoned plantation, only Drummage was left. Finally she had succeeded in snaring him. And he had lived up to all her expectations, although she sensed that he never really put his heart into it, saving that, she was sure, for the succession of wenches who passed through his hands.

Now this same Drummage, whose body she had bought, insisted on her marrying him. Of course, on the surface it was unthinkable. No white woman had ever married a Negro, a servant, a slave, a subhuman. She shuddered to think what might have happened to a woman in the old days before the war, even had such a thing been possible. The Negro would, of course, have been killed, just as Mede the Mandingo had been murdered for bedding with her mother. But her mother had not married Mede. If such a thing had ever happened, the woman's relatives would have killed her along with her black husband. Even if she had been allowed to live, she would have been ostracized—no other white person would ever have spoken to her and it was doubtful that any self-respecting Negro would either. No, even thinking about marrying Drummage was out of the question. And yet, try as she could to convince herself of the impossibility of it, she had actually already agreed to it and in fact was even now deriving a great amount of pleasure from thinking about it.

The war had changed everything. Not that it had made it easy for a white woman to marry a Negro. But at least Negroes were no longer considered animals. In the eyes of the North they were just as much human beings as the whites. Certainly for the Union captain who had arrived last night, Drummage was the equal of any white man.

Supposing she did marry Drummage—or rather that she allowed him to marry her. What would her position be? For one thing he would be hers, and regardless of what he might do or what wenches he might lust after, she would have the prior claim on him. Her position in the community? What did that matter? There was nobody in the town of Benson or on any of the surrounding plantations that she gave a tinker's dam about or who cared anything about her. Let them say what they would, it was unimportant to her. She would have Drummage for herself and she had rather have him than anything else in the world.

But could she, Sophie Maxwell, daughter of Hammond Maxwell, tie herself up with a nigger slave? After all, that's what he was —a nigger slave. His mother was Big Pearl the Mandingo wench. His father was Drumson, and now she remembered back to a time, long ago, when Drumson had been the object of her devotions. She remembered that day in the butler's pantry when she could not keep her hands from investigating him and how she had thrilled when she touched him. Drumson had given his life for her father. He was buried over in the family plot with a marble stone to mark his grave. Then Drummage's father couldn't really be thought of as a slave because if he had been, he would never have achieved a final resting place beside white folks.

Drummage was different, too. He wasn't like that Zanzibar, who looked like an animal, talked like an animal, and rutted like one. No, Drummage was different. There was something fine about him. He was even kind to her at times—thoughtful, considerate, thinking about her, wanting her to take care of herself and dress up so she would look nice. And more important than anything else, the child she felt stirring within her belonged to Drummage.

The child! What would she do with it when it was born? She couldn't drown the helpless little thing. But if she let it live, what would become of it? It would be neither white nor black and it would not be wanted. But had she ever been wanted as a child herself? A wave of self-pity engulfed her and suddenly she felt a pang of love for the unborn baby. But Drummage wouldn't care anything about it. Nigger bucks never made any fuss over their kids. Yet here again Drummage was different. He seemed to want this child. He would love it, especially if he were acknowledged as its real father.

And yet . . . and yet . . . how could she marry Drummage? Who ever heard of such a thing? But the thought of losing him was even more worrisome. She was all alone. There was nobody in the world to look after her but Drummage.

She shuddered as she thought of living alone in the big house with all the ghosts of the past crowding around her —Papa and Augusta and Lucretia Borgia. Apollon and Kewp and Candy. Drumson and Regine and Benoni. Mede and Big Pearl and Ol' Mista Wilson. Dudley and her two children. All the countless black men and women who had known Falconhurst as their home and were now scattered far and wide.

Panic seized her and she got up hastily, brushed her hair, and put on the pink satin peignoir she had worn the night before. Drummage was not in his room as she passed through it to go down the stairs into the office. But he was in the kitchen, and she heaved a sigh of relief to find him there.

He looked up at her as she came in.

"Good news fer yo', Miz Sophie. Ain' no call fer us ter git married up by that nigger preacher. Cap'n he say he kin marry us up tonight. He a-comin' out from Benson ter do it. Better fer yo' Miz Sophie than standin' up 'fore a lot o' niggers ter git married up."

She looked at him in gratitude.

"Tonight, Drummage?"

"Yes, tonight, Miz Sophie. Guess I better not call yo' *Miz* Sophie no more."

"Then we'll have a celebration tonight, Drummage. There's a little white flour I bin savin', 'n' some sugar too, 'n' raisins. I'll git Marguerite to make a cake—a weddin' cake. Pollux kin clean the silver and that new girl sweep and dust. Everything'll be spic and span by evenin'."

"Thankin' yo' I am, Sophie. Got to git me over to de New Quarters today but I be back time fer de marryin'. Kin use that black suit o' Apollon's 'n' dress myself up."

" 'N' I'll wear a white dress if'n I kin git it roun' me. 'N'

371

I'll use 'Gusta's mantilla fer a veil. We git married up in style, huh, Drummage?"

"Falconhurst a-goin' ter be a Maxwell plantation 'gain, Sophie. Yo' a-goin' ter be Missis Drummage Maxwell o' Falconhurst 'n' I Mista Drummage Maxwell o' Falconhurst. I'se a free man now, Sophie, but yo' knows 'n' I knows I'se nothin' but an ignorant nigger. Cap'n he a-goin' ter teach me, Sophie, but guess yo' gotta teach me too."

"Don' know much myself, Drummage. Only knows it seems right fer me ter marry up wid yo'. Ain' no white woman ever married a nigger 'fore. I'll be de fust. Help yo' if'n I kin, Drummage." She reached out a hand, tentatively, and touchd him.

He accepted the gesture with a smile.

"Yore hand feel nice 'n' cool, Sophie." He took her arm and walked her to the kitchen door. "Gotta go now, but I be back. Yes, Miz Sophie, I be back."

"Whar yo', Marguerite?" she called. "Git that new girl here. Git that lazy Pollux here. We got a lot o' work ter do today." It seemed almost like old times to be giving orders, to be getting the house cleaned up, and baking cakes and roasting ham.

Chapter 42

DRUMMAGE put on a white linen coat of Hammond's which fitted his shoulders and a carefully laundered pair of white linen trousers which had belonged to Apollon and encased his legs even more snugly than they had those of their former owner. The sparkling gems in his ears, his ruffled cambric shirt and carefully tied black taffeta stock, his polished boots (also Apollon's), and his wide, finely woven Panama hat with the black band made him look far better attired than any white man in the region. He had carefully arranged his hair with macassar oil, whitened his teeth with wood ashes and the pulpy end of a green twig, pared his fingernails, and turned himself out as properly and as elegantly as any ante-bellum planter. Mounted on his black horse, with the silver mountings of his saddle gleaming and the black leather quirt around one wrist, he drew envious looks from the men in their rough osnaburg trousers and tow linen

372

shirts when he arrived at New Quarters, but only admiration from the fawning women.

He noticed that Brutus had had the table carried out from the store and placed in the shade of a big pecan tree. Brutus was sitting behind it, dressed in the old black suit he had worn at Falconhurst, and with him were the new preacher and Big Randy. There was an empty chair in the center, awaiting Drummage. Willing hands took his horse, and the people made a pathway for him to the table. He bowed formally to Brutus before he sat down.

"Greetin's, Mista Rodney." He glanced over at Big Randy, " 'N' yo' too, Mista Biggs."

"Greetin's, Mista Maxwell," Brutus answered quite as pompously. "All de people a-waitin' fer yo' ter come. Preacher here say he kin marry 'em couple by couple o' kin take five o' six couple at a time, which'n ever yo' likes. He 'ready taken his name. Say he a-goin' ter be de Rev'rend Jordan."

"After de river where our Lawd 'n' Master were baptized." The minister bowed to Drummage.

"Then it fittin' that we head the list wid de Rev'rend. Write yore name down, Rev'rend. What yore other name?"

"Rev'rend Daniel Jordan—Daniel was de name they gave me; Jordan de name I'se takin'."

" 'N' that make Pamela to take de name o' Jordan too. Write her down 'cause she ain' comin' today. She ain' marryin'. She stayin' at de big house for to serve Miz Sophie, my wife."

Brute regarded Drummage, amazement and wonder in his eyes.

"How come yo' say yore *wife*, Miz Sophie?"

"We to be married up tonight. Married legal too by a cap'n o' de Union Army. Invitin' yo' 'n' Beulah-Annie 'n' Mista 'n' Missis Randolph Biggs 'n' yo' too, Rev'rend, all ter come over to de big house come seven o'clock to de weddin' 'n' stay ter de collation what we to have afterwards." Drummage proceeded to tell them about his adventure of the night before and his rescue of the Captain and Hobbs. They all listened, shaking their heads first in disbelief and then in approval. They were not surprised to hear that the Johnstone brothers were the assailants and they were happy that Drummage had put them to rout.

"Reckon yo' got us a good frien' in that Cap'n." Brutus fully approved of all that Drummage had done, but he withheld his approval of Drummage's marriage to Sophie. Although both he and Big Randy admired him for his astute-

373

ness and daring, there was a certain amount of silent animadversion and censure in their sidelong looks. In the first place it wasn't right for a white woman to marry a nigger. It was all wrong. Moreover, it meant that Drummage would achieve a position far above either of them. Now he would be really the head man, not only by his connection with the white captain but by virtue of the authority conferred on him by his marriage to Sophie.

"Better git started namin' these people 'fore we starts marryin' 'em," Drummage said. "But 'fore we gits started, wants someone ter go ter Falconhurst fer me. Some young buck what ain' a-goin' ter marry up. Who that be, Brute?"

"Could be Valentine. He Enos' boy 'n' right smart too." Brutus stood up and surveyed the crowd of faces until his eyes came to rest on a tall, slender, tobacco-brown boy, to whom he beckoned. "Come over here, Valentine! Mista Maxwell got an errand fer yo'."

The boy made his way through the press, proud of having been singled out, and stood before the table.

Drummage looked up at him approvingly. He was a good-looking, intelligent-appearing boy.

"Kin yo' ride?"

Valentine nodded his head, too tongue-tied to speak.

"Den yo' take my horse 'n' ride over to de big house. Yo' to to de barn 'n' harness up de bay mare to de buckboard 'n' den drive over to Big Pearl's cabin. Know where dat is?"

Valentine nodded again.

" 'N' tell her ter git herself ready ter come over here. Don' fergit ter tell my mama 'bout de namin'. Tell her if'n she wants ter marry up wid any of dese buck what ain' spoken fer, she kin. Lead my horse back 'hin' de buckboard. Yo' 'members all dat?"

A third nod from Valentine, and he walked away, proud at having been chosen for such an important errand by such an important individual as Drummage.

Drummage stood up so that all could hear him and recognize his authority. He paused a moment before speaking, sweeping the assemblage with his eyes.

"Yo' men! Git yore families together. Git yore women 'n' yore kids 'n' come here, family by family, to be named. Hope yo' all got names all picked out fer yo' selves. If'n not we kin help yo'. Picks any name yo' want 'cep' Maxwell. That my name."

There was a hectic passing back and forth as men located their women and as the women corralled the children of

374

their households. Finally, the first family group approached the table.

"Mornin' ter yo', Japheth, 'n' yo' too, Essie," Drummage welcomed them. "These all yore kids?"

Essie hung her head and pointed to a stocky four-year-old, naked as a jay bird. "That big-peckered boy he yourn, Drummage."

"Ain' mine." Drummage shook his head. "Ain' never seen him afore 'n' don' want to now. He yourn 'n' Japheth's, Essie." Young as the child was, however, Drummage could see his own appearance reflected in the boy. "Well, Japheth, what yo' pick fer yore name?"

"Thinkin' we takes de name o' Scott, Drummage."

"Ain' Drummage no mo', Japheth. Mista Maxwell now."

"Yas suh, Mista Maxwell suh," Japheth grinned, hardly knowing whether Drummage was serious or not. "But we a-takin' de name o' Scott. My pappy, what Masta Hammond sold, he named Scott. Thinkin' we take my pappy's name."

Drummage laboriously wrote the name of Japheth Scott under those of the Reverend Daniel Jordan and Pamela Jordan. Then he added: "Wife, Essie Scott."

"What de name o' yore kids, Mista Scott?"

One by one Japheth presented them for Drummage's inspection. "Here Susy-Ruby, 'n' here Catfish . . ."

"Catfish?" Drummage stared at the naked eight-year-old. "Cain' have us names like Catfish. We people now—ain' animals. Gotta change dat boy's name."

"Kin we call him John?" Essie asked.

"Kin." Drummage wrote down the name while Japheth continued.

" 'N' this 'Thusalah 'n' Jenny-May 'n' yore Jock."

"Tellin yo' he ain' mine, he yourn."

Drummage read over the list. "Japheth 'n' Essie Scott— chil'ren Susy-Ruby, John, 'Thusalah, Jenny-May 'n' Jock." He motioned to the next family in line, dismissing the newly christened Scott clan.

It was a long process, for there were some fifty families in the New Quarters. There was also an assortment of unattached males, nubile females, and numerous children whom nobody claimed and who had been shunted from cabin to cabin. These Drummage assigned to family groups and family names.

The people had chosen their names with some regard to gentility. There were names they had heard—Lincoln, Washington, Jackson, Montgomery, Demopolis, Vicksburg,

375

and Lee. Others took the names of crafts with which they were identified—Weaver, Carpenter, Spinner, and Farmer. Some used their given names as last names, choosing a new first name—Napoleon, Caesar, King, Claude, Benjamin, and Jeremiah. A few, lacking in imagination, took familiar names of objects—Wood, Stone, Oak, and House. Drummage ruled out the fanciful and ridiculous—Honeysuckle, Studhorse, Coaloil, and Hammerhead—but allowed such anomalies as Cotton, Plough, Coachman, and Brightday. One unattached teen-age buck, swaggering up to the table alone, insisted that he be called Loverman because that was what all the girls called him, but Drummage, perhaps fearing competition from the rising generation, made him change it and assigned him to a family with the more prosaic name of Brown. Lucretia Borgia's memory was perpetuated in the family and offspring of one Turk Borgia, and one man who had been a close friend of Drummage's half-brother, Ol' Mista Wilson, chose the name of Wilson.

The buckboard, driven by Valentine with Big Pearl, resplendent in starched white, a cerise headcloth and a black Chantilly lace shawl which Drummage had purloined from the big house, arrived, and the men rushed forward to help her down. When she advanced to the table, Drummage rose and bowed as he had seen white folks do.

"Fine day, Mama," he said. "We all a-namin' 'n' a-marryin' up today. If'n yo' ain' wantin' ter git married up wid no buck, yo' a-takin' de name o' Maxwell like me. But if yo' a-wantin' ter git married up, yo' takes de name o' yore man." He lowered his voice, whispering to her across the table. "Who dat buck what bin a-comin' to yore cabin nights, Mama? If'n yo' wants him, yo' marries up wid him today else he not a-comin' no mo'."

"Ain' no buck bin a-comin'.'" Big Pearl denied it with an emphatic shake of her cerise-bound head. "Whaffor yo' shames me 'fore all these people, Drummage?"

Drummage grinned back at her. "Could've bin wrong, Mama, but if'n they's any buck yo' a-wantin' what ain' now spoken fer, yo' kin marry up wid him, 'n' he kin live wid yo'."

"Guess ain' nobody spoken fer Zanzibar." Big Pearl lowered her head coyly. "He right pleasin' ter me. Him 'n' me we match up fine. He mos' as good as yore pappy Drumson. If'n he ain' spoke fer, admire ter marry up wid him."

"Kin have him if'n yo' wants." Drummage saw Zanzibar pushing forward. "Hey, Zan, yo' got a woman?"

The immense black strode up to stand beside Big Pearl.

"Ain' got none but ain' wantin' none 'cept Big Pearl."

"She my mama, yo' know. Gotta be good ter her if'n yo' takes her."

"Admires ter have her if'n she wants me."

"Then yo' a-needin' a name. Goin' ter call yo' Pollon 'cause yo' got rid o' him fer me. Yo' be Zanzibar Pollon 'n' my mama be Missis Pearl Pollon, come marryin'-up time."

It was long past noon when the naming was over, and the women went to their cabins, bringing out cold pone, milk, clabber, and cold meat. Beulah-Annie, now Mrs. Rodney, invited Drummage and Big Pearl and Zanzibar to a hot dinner in Brutus' cabin, and when the meal was over they all repaired again to the pecan tree.

Now it was the Reverend's turn to officiate and at Drummage's suggestion he married five couples at a time, with Brute and Beulah-Annie, Big Randy and his Selina, Zanzibar and Pearl, and Sampson and his woman as part of the first group. There was no laughter or joking during the ceremonies. All took the occasion seriously, realizing that they were achieving a certain status hitherto reserved only for whites. No doubt there would be as much tomcatting in New Quarters as before, but it was good for a man to have a woman who belonged to him and for a woman to have a man who was her own. It was good to know that no white man could ever separate them by selling them, and that their children belonged to them and not to a master. There would be no more annual caffles going to New Orleans. No longer would familiar faces disappear, never to be seen again. They were all people, not beasts of the field, copulating for a white master's profit. They were people with names, married people with children.

When they had finally finished with the marrying and each man and woman had said their "I do's," Drummage stood up and looked them over and bade them be seated again.

"Now we all named 'n' married up. We jes' like white peoples now. Only one thing we needs 'n' that's work. Man got to work 'n' earn money ter keep his family. We bin a-livin' hand ter mouth. Plants us a yam, digs it up 'n' eats it. Raises us a shoat 'n' kills it 'fore it big 'nuff ter breed, jes' 'cause we hungry. Good times, we eats; bad times comes, we go hungry. Ain' no white masta now ter give yo' yore vittles winter 'n' summer, good times 'n' bad. Got to scratch 'em out fer yo'selves these times. Man kin raise mos' 'nuff ter live on but needs boughten thin's too. Has ter have money fer those. Yo' a-needin' money 'n' I'm offerin' yo' work. Brute here a-goin' ter be head man at New Quarters. He a-goin' ter see that yo' all work fer Falconhurst. Yo' wantin' the job, Brute?"

"Yo' a-goin' ter pay hard money, Drummage? Whar yo' a-goin' ter git it?"

"Ain' promisin' ter pay less'n I kin. Yo' all gits yore money. Givin' yo' ten dollars a month ter oversee, Brute. Givin' Big Randy 'n' Sampson seven dollars a month ter be foremen. Givin' all hands a dollar a week. Givin' all women four bits a week if'n we needs 'em. Givin' chil'ren what works two bits a week. All hard money. Up to yo', Brute, ter see that they works."

"They works if'n I tells them ter." Brute nodded. "What work they a-goin' ter do?"

"Falconhurst bin a-lyin' fallow 'bout four years. Ain' bin raisin' no cotton fer 'bout ten years. 'Pears like the groun' rested up 'n' ready ter raise cotton once more. What yo' think, Brute?"

"Think yo' right, Drummage, 'n' if'n anyone kin git cotton outa that groun', I kin. Got to plow first."

"We got some mules over ter Falconhurst 'n' de men here got mules too. Payin' two bits a week fer the use o' a mule. Men work at Falconhurst, women work here raisin' greens 'n' sech till it time fer pickin', den everyone works. Pays 'em every week, come Saturday night." He stood up and regarded the crowd before him. "How that strike yo' all? Every man willin' ter work at Falconhurst hist up his hand. Them not willin' ter work better git ready ter leave. This Falconhurst land. Them that works gits their cabins 'n' their green patch free; them that don' work gits ter hell out now."

A sea of waving hands greeted him and he sat down, talking over details with Brute and the other two men until he once again rose to his feet and held up his hand for silence.

"Falconhurst a-goin' ter be like'n it was in de ol' days. Yo' all a-goin' ter be proud o' Falconhurst come a year or two. Goin' ter be glad yo' Falconhurst people. Falconhurst niggers al'ays the best in the world. Always bring de highest prices. Ain' no mo' sellin' now but wants Falconhurst niggers still ter be de best. Wants yo' ter be proud yo' all Falconhurst niggers. We a-goin' ter show de white trash 'n' de road niggers that we better 'n' anyone else in Alabama. Goin' ter build us a church; goin' ter have us a store; goin' ter make New Quarters better 'n Benson. Goin' ter show de worl' dat black skin jes' 's good as white. How 'bout it, men?"

378

A loud cheer answered him and he waited a moment for the enthusiasm to subside before he continued.

"Falconhurst a-goin' ter be proud-like, we needin' ter keep de big house proud-like. Needin' us some house servants at de big house 'cause I marryin' up wid Miz Sophie come evenin'. Bein' house servant don' pay no more money 'n being a fiel' hand but it finer work. Cain' have no bucks 'n' wenches what married up 'cause they got ter live in de big house 'n' cain' have 'em traipsin' back here to New Quarters every night. Wants all those young bucks 'n' wenches what livin' wid their families ter step up here to de front."

He waited for the young folks to come running up and stand in a half-circle around the table. There was not one of them that didn't want to be chosen, for the magic of the big house and the prestige of being a house servant were still irresistible. Drummage surveyed them, noting the most prepossessing young fellows and the prettiest girls.

"First off, we needin' a kitchen wench. Got us a cook but needin' a wench ter help her. How 'bout yo', Eva?" He beckoned to a pert lass of about fifteen.

"Shore admirin' to serve in de big house, Masta Drummage." She sashayed up to the front with a twitch of her skirt.

"Ain' Masta Drummage no mo', gal. Remember I'se now Mista Maxwell."

"Yas suh, Mista Maxwell."

"We got us a waiter, boy named Pollux which'n yo' all know. Rev'rend Jordan's wench, Pamela, she a-goin' ter serve my wife, Miz Sophie. Needs us now two wenches, one fer de downstairs 'n' 'nother fer de upstairs. How 'bout yo' Dulcy, 'n' yo', Madilda?" He pointed to two giggling girls whose coarse straight dresses did little to hide their nubility. They were of an age with Eva—Dulcy dark of skin with short woolly hair, Madilda a copper color with long curly locks.

"Right pleased ter serve yo', Mista Maxwell." Dulcy, who had already been initiated into making love by Drummage, answered for them both.

"Now we needin' us some bucks. Wants us a well-set-up young feller fer de house. Goin' ter be head man in de house." He scanned the row before him, settling on a strapping young man, darkly negroid but with almost classic features. "Yo' a good-lookin' buck." He pointed to the fellow. "What yore name?"

"I Onan," the youth answered.

"Yo' got two names now, use 'em," Drummage prompted.

379

"Livin' wid Bart 'n' his woman. They tooken de name o' Jonathan. Guess that make me Onan Jonathan."

"Yo' a-wantin' ter work in de big house, Mista Onan Jonathan?"

"Shore do, Mista Maxwell."

"Yo're hired."

Swiftly he picked out several others—a gardener by the name of Jude to help old Merc, a coachman by the name of Godfrey, and a boy for the barn by the name of Zebedee. Drummage passed by the lighter-skinned men, although in most cases they were handsomer than the ones he chose. He did so intentionally because he did not want any men around the house whose skins were lighter than his own pale tobacco-brown.

"After yo' gits to de big house, yo' all got ter wash yo'-selves all over every day. Cain' have no musky niggers round stinkin' up de house. Got ter keep yore clothes clean 'n' jes' so soon as she kin do it, Ol' Aunt Emmy here goin' ter stitch yo' up good clothes. No pissin' outa de windows 'n' no shittin' 'hind de bushes. Knows yo' ain' house-broken so got ter train yo' all. Knows yo' all ignorant but gotta use yo' tonight." He turned to his mother and her new husband. "Yo', Zanzibar, yo' be a-livin' wid Big Pearl. Yo' good wid horses so goin' ter make yo' head man in de barn but yo' ain' a-ridin' wid Miz Sophie no more. Kin go gunnin' if'n yo' wants 'cause we all hankerin' afta fresh meat. Ain' a-fearin' ter let yo' have a gun 'cause guessin' yo' ain' a-aimin' ter gun me down cause now yo' like'n my papa."

"Ain' a-wantin' ter shoot nobody down never 'gain," Zanzibar affirmed. "Ain' wantin' no other woman neither. Married up wid Big Pearl now 'n' ain' wantin' nothin' else."

Drummage was quiet for a long moment as he surveyed the eyes that were watching him.

"Ain' no more whoppin' at Falconhurst. We men now 'n' men don' whop each other. Havin' any trouble wid a man, he has ter leave. Kin take his wife 'n' chil'ren wid him but he has ter git out." He turned suddenly and pointed his finger at the group of young people whom he had chosen to live at the big house. " 'N' ain' no skedaddlin' back 'n' forth from one room ter 'nother. Ain' no pleasurin' in de big house less'n I say so. Boys sleeps wid boys 'n' gals sleeps wid gals. Boy gits horny, he comes ter me 'n' I tells him what he kin do. Gal gits knocked up, out she goes. Ain' a-breedin' here no mo'."

Repeating his invitation to those sitting at the table with

him to attend his wedding that evening, Drummage rose to go. Valentine, the boy whom he had sent over to fetch Big Pearl sidled up to him through the crowd.

"Mista Maxwell suh, kin I be askin' yo' a question?"

"Yo' de boy what fetch my mama?"

"Yas suh, Mista Maxwell suh, name o' Valentine Jonathan, suh, fambly o' Bart Jonathan."

"What yo' a-wantin', Valentine Jonathan?"

"Aim'n' ter ask yo', Mista Maxwell, kin I serve in de big house too?"

Drummage considered the matter for a moment.

"Ain' rightly needin' no mo' bucks over to de big house. Got us Pollux 'n' dis yere Onan. They 'nuff ter work in de big house." He noticed the tears appear in the boy's eyes. "Yo' kin to dis yere Onan?"

"Ain' kin but we al'ays bedded together since I kin 'member. Don' like ter leave Onan 'n' thinkin' Onan he don' like ter leave me."

Drummage thought for a moment. Something about the boy appealed to him. He saw himself as he must have looked to Hammond Maxwell when he first came to fetch him to the big house. He looked over to where Onan was standing and saw him staring intently at Valentine. Drummage remembered Jubal and his own adolescent attachment for him, and recognized the bond between the two. They'd cause him no trouble with the wenches.

"Tell yo' what, Valentine boy. I'm needin' a body servant. Think yo' like that?"

"Likin' it better 'n anything else in de worl', Mista Maxwell suh."

"Den hike 'long wid de rest." Drummage waved a good-by to the New Quarters folks and mounted his horse. Zanzibar and Big Pearl followed him in the buckboard, and then, in a happy, straggling procession came Eva, Dulcy, and Madilda, arm in arm; Onan, Godfrey, and Zebedee. Valentine, seeing the rest leave, ran to the head of the line.

"I'se Mista Maxwell's body servant," he announced to the others. "I goes fust. 'N' Onan, he head man in de house, he come next. Rest o' yo' all follow on behin'."

Chapter 43

DRUMMAGE'S own wedding in the big drawing room at Falconhurst, although in far more elegant surroundings than those at New Quarters, was rather an anticlimax to the mass weddings that had taken place in the afternoon. Despite his fine suit of black broadcloth Drummage was visibly nervous, his hands trembling and his forehead beaded with sweat, as he stood with Chris Holbrook. Sophie at length made her appearance and descended the stairs slowly, clad in one of Augusta's opera gowns of point d'Alencon. She had not been able to hook it around her bulging middle, and wore a China shawl to hide the gaping back. Her blonde hair was elaborately coiffed, she wore a parure of pearls and topazes and carried a bouquet of damask roses from the garden. As she took her place beside Drummage under the chandelier, she sensed his nervousness and tried to reassure him by squeezing his arm.

All that he had hoped and striven for was now about to become his own but the very enormity of the step he was taking frightened him. He was stepping into Hammond Maxwell's shoes as master of Falconhurst—something which seemed so unreal and so impossible that he could not believe it was happening. He, a Negro, was actually marrying a white woman, which was something almost as miraculous as the sun standing still or his skin suddenly turning white over night.

He was not the only one who was nervous. Chris Holbrook's hand also shook as he held a little black book from which he read the civil marriage service. The few invited guests, of whom Hobbs was the only white man, were ill at ease and out of place on the stiff gilt chairs. Of the Negroes, only Brutus had ever been in the big house before and although he was not, like the others, awed by its tarnished splendor, he too stared open-mouthed at the stiff little ceremony, while the Reverend Daniel Jordan, Big Randy, and Sampson, along with their spouses, were transported to another world in which they hardly dared to breathe. They all realized the seriousness of what they were witnessing.

Once the brief ceremony was over, Captain Holbrook was

the only one with enough presence of mind to take over as master of ceremonies and lead the little group out into the dining room. Despite the appetizing food (poor Marguerite had done wonders with what materials she had at hand) and the willing but untrained services of Pollux, Onan, and Valentine, the meal was scarcely a success. The blacks, bewildered by the lace tablecloth, the china and silver, and the cut-glass epergne in the center, did little but stare. Drummage had lost his appetite completely, and Sophie merely pushed the food around on her plate. The Captain and Hobbs, however, did full justice to the dinner. It was only when the wedding cake was brought in with two little corncob dolls atop it, one dressed as a bride and the other as a groom, that the party gained any semblance of jollity, and that was due more than anything else to the decanter of corn which Pollux brought in and served in slender-stemmed wine glasses. Full justice was done to the cake and by the time a second round of corn was downed, the black faces were smiling and even Sophie entered into the spirit of the occasion. Just as they were scooping up the last crumbs of cake, there was a sound of music and, for the first time since Apollon's death, the folks from New Quarters gathered in front of the pillared portico to sing. Their song brought the wedding party out to stand and listen and when it was ended there were shouts of congratulations and good wishes. Drummage and Sophie advanced to the front of the portico and accepted the homage. Captain Holbrook and Hobbs were cheered. Brute, Big Randy, and Sampson got their share of attention, and the wedding day of Falconhurst and New Quarters terminated with a prayer from the Reverend. After that there were prolonged leavetakings and then the noise diminished as the folks from New Quarters left the big house and strolled down the road to their own homes, where the celebration went on for hours.

In the big house, Hobbs repaired to his couch in the office, and Holbrook to the room he had occupied the night before, where he found Pamela awaiting him. Drummage, feeling strangely embarrassed before Sophie, led her up the stairs to her room.

"I sleepin' in here tonight, Sophie," he said, with more tenderness and respect than he had ever shown her before. "Ain' a-sayin' that I a-goin' ter ever' night. Some nights needs ter pleasure me wid colored wenches. Cain' 'splain it, Sophie, but guesses they jes' somethin' 'bout colored wenches fer pleasurin' dat white women don' have. Ain' jes' me! White

383

men likes 'em better fer pleasurin' too. Dat why Cap'n Holbrook he like Pamela. Say he ain' never had no pleasurin' like'n she give him. Ain' yore fault, Sophie, dat I don' hanker ter pleasure yo'. Outside o' pleasurin' I likes yo'. 'N' I a-goin' ter respect yo' too. Ain' goin' ter have no colored wench for ter pester here in de house. Ain' 'lowin' no pesterin' 'mongst the servants nuther. We ain' a breedin' farm no mo'. Goin' ter live respectable-like here at Falconhurst."

The closing of their bedroom door was symbolic; it finished one phase of Drummage's life and started another. No longer was he to be the rather witless, happy person whose life, devoid of responsibilities, had centered mainly around his choice of a partner for the evening. Such choices there would continue to be, as he had told Sophie, but they were merely incidental now, something to satisfy his body's needs. The driving force that now impelled him was his mastery of Falconhurst and his desire to rebuild it.

Everything must be made perfect again. He badgered Sophie into training the house servants. But their work, which passed Sophie's slack inspection, did not satisfy him. He was far stricter with them than Lucretia Borgia had ever been with him. Regardless of the fact that he might have already arranged an amorous tryst with Dulcy or Madilda for the afternoon siesta, he was not above boxing their ears if something was not to his liking. Everything had to be spick-and-span.

The women were dressed in dark-gray calico, made up from a long-unused bolt which Sophie had discovered. Since calico was currently selling for more than damask had sold before the war, the women servants at Falconhurst were dressed far better than most of the white women in Benson. The drabness of their nun-like costumes was set off by brilliantly colored headcloths, cut from worn-out costumes of Augusta's and Sophie's. At first there was no black stuff to make liveries for the menservants, but there were sufficient hand-me-downs from Apollon and Hammond to serve at least temporarily, and these Drummage insisted must be pressed and kept in good condition. A daily bath was obligatory for all the servants —the men in the early morning and the women in the afternoon; in the creek which ran between the old slave quarters and the new house.

Slowly, Falconhurst began to emerge from the limbo in which it had spent the war years. Merc, with the strong hands of young Jude to help him, pruned, cut, and sowed until the grounds achieved a semblance of their old order, and the kitchen garden began once more to furnish green stuff. Out in the fields, Brute marshaled the men of New Quarters behind plows and harrows, breaking up the scrub-infested weed-grown land and laying open the rich furrows. Cottonseed was next to impossible to obtain on the market, but apparently there was nothing which the army of the United States could not furnish, and Captain Holbrook was able to supply the best Petit Gulf seed. Holbrook was a constant source of supply for all the things they had been deprived of during the war—white flour and white sugar, spices, black broadcloth for the servants' clothes, coffee, imported wines, even white lead and linseed oil with which to paint the tall pillars of the portico. As the months passed Falconhurst experienced a renaissance while the other big houses of the South tumbled into ruins, their fields idle, their manpower nonexistent, their gentlefolk hiding the patches on their calico dresses and homespun trousers.

The good gold pieces that Drummage had buried in the ground were now working for him. His laborers were paid weekly in hard cash, which added to the prosperity of New Quarters. He had no lack of resources—money to spend, men to work for him, horses to ride, servants to wait on him, an abundance of food, a white wife to cater to him, even the protection of the army, since Captain Holbrook made his home at Falconhurst.

With affluence, Drummage attained a certain air of authority. His good clothes, his polished boots, his poise and *esprit* lifted him above the other Negroes. His association with Chris Holbrook had done much to change his manners and his talk. He was quick to adapt himself. He listened attentively to Holbrook's pronunciation and imitated his movements, his mannerisms, his way of eating, walking, sitting, and his attitude toward other people. In his spare moments he practiced reading and writing, in which he had had only the most rudimentary instruction. Holbrook furnished the books and Drummage spelled them out, laboriously at first and then more rapidly. Writing was more difficult, but in the end he achieved a fairly legible hand although his spelling remained uncertain.

As Sophie's pregnancy advanced, Drummage avoided her bed as much as possible, insisting that his absence was purely out of consideration for her condition. Thus he was free to keep trysts with Dulcy or Madilda, or some other wench from New Quarters, in the deserted slave cabin, next door to Big Pearl's, which he had fitted up for such occasions with furniture purloined from the attic of the big house. It was a little more difficult to get Pamela over to the cabin since her days were taken up with Sophie and her nights with Chris, but Drummage managed to accomplish this several times while the big house dozed in its daily afternoon nap.

Yet these encounters no longer meant much to him, and sometimes he wondered if he had lost the taste of desire. Yet his companions always seemed anxious for more, which gave him reassurance that he could perform as adroitly as ever. They could not know that even while he was pretending to be at the heights of excitement, his mind was often following the lines of men in the field chopping cotton.

Inevitably Drummage's progress engendered ill will among the white residents of Benson and the surrounding plantations. The gleaming white pillars of the big house, its blossoming fields of cotton, its well-kept lawns were in too direct a contrast to the tumble-down appearance of all the other places. Ill will begat jealousy and jealousy begat hatred, not only for "that biggity Falconhurst nigger what calls hisself Mista Maxwell" but for the white woman he had married. Sophie no longer dared drive to Benson in the polished barouche; the invectives that were shouted at her were too scathing. Drummage himself rarely went out on the roads alone, preferring to ride with Captain Holbrook and an escort of cavalry. The Johnstone brothers had made themselves scarce after their attempt on Holbrook's life, but rumors of their activities occasionally reached Falconhurst. They were now going about the country organizing dens of the new secret society, the Ku Klux Klan, a name which struck terror into the hearts of the blacks and even some of the whites. So far, Benson had not been initiated into the Klan.

It did, however, have a Union League, which was much feared and hated by the local whites. At first the League's membership had been limited to carpetbaggers, those zealous missionaries and self-appointed do-gooders who had drifted down from the North either from a desire to get rich quickly or with some fanatical notion of raising the colored man up by his own bootstraps.

One evening when Holbrook returned from Benson, he brought a man with him whom he introduced to Drummage as a Colonel Bingham, who craved Falconhurst's hospitality for the night. Drummage invited the man to stay, and dinner was served with even more formality than usual. It was evident that Colonel Bingham was impressed by the restored grandeur of Falconhurst. After the meal was cleared away, and wine was served on the portico, it did not take Bingham long to get down to business. He was a pompous man whose every sentence was delivered with mellifluous oratorical sonority, quite as though he were addressing a multitude instead of an individual.

"Mr. Maxwell, sir, I must congratulate you on your establishment. My one regret is that I have not had the pleasure of meeting your charming wife, who, I understand, is expecting an heir to these lordly acres."

"Mrs. Maxwell sends her apologies, Colonel." Drummage's carefully chosen words had a faint Boston accent, traceable to Holbrook. "She thought it better that she dine in her own room. Perhaps the next time you are in our vicinity, we may have the pleasure of entertaining you again."

Bingham sipped his wine and stroked his whiskers. "A pleasure, I assure you, Mr. Maxwell, but it may be some time before I am in the vicinity again. I'm a working man, sir, working hard for the future of our great country and for the betterment of our unfortunate colored brethren. I am, sir, a representative of the illustrious Republican party, the friend of the downtrodden, the builder of the nation, and the only party that has the true interests of the Negro at heart. I have come, Mr. Maxwell, to ask a great favor of you."

"Certainly, Colonel." Drummage was only too anxious to serve such an important personage.

"I was talking with our good friend Chris Holbrook today and I asked him to tell me who was the most important colored man in this section. Naturally"—he bowed toward Drummage, losing his chin in the folds of his neck—"he told me that you were, Mr. Maxwell. Now that I have met you I can commend his perspicacity. It is an honor—indeed an honor—to meet a real colored gentleman of high culture and advanced education. Chris tells me that your parents were slaves, Mr. Maxwell, but I can scarcely credit the fact. In talking with you I would place you as a graduate of one of our great universities."

Drummage reveled in such flattery.

"Yes, Colonel, I was born here at Falconhurst and born in bondage. My father, however, was scarcely a slave, as he was a trusted aide to Mr. Hammond Maxwell, the owner of the plantation. I would say that they were friends rather than master and servant, for my father gave his life to save Mr. Hammond's, and he lies buried in the Maxwell family plot, which was an honor never accorded to a slave. My father was, I understand, of Royal Hausa blood and part white. You, being a Northerner, may not know that we Negroes are proud of our bloodlines. Royal Hausa takes precedence over all other African bloodlines and there are few who can claim it. There may be many Negroes who can truthfully say that they are descended from the Hausa tribe, but there are few Royal Hausas because the rulers of the Hausa tribe were of entirely different blood from their subjects. In addition, my mother was a pure-blooded Mandingo, which is nearly as rare as Royal Hausa. I understand that on my father's side I go back to a powerful African king."

"Blood will tell, don't you agree, Colonel Bingham?" Holbrook raised his wineglass in Drummage's direction. "For as long as I've known Drummage, I've found him a most remarkable person."

"Most remarkable indeed," Bingham agreed, "and that is why, Mr. Maxwell, I am going to make you a most remarkable proposition. The Negroes of your once sovereign state have been freed from the bonds of slavery; they are soon to be enfranchised with full rights as citizens of the United States. Therefore it behooves you, as men of color, to have your own representation in the government, and the only way you can get it is through our own great Republican party, the friend of the colored man. That is the one party and the only party which will give you your rights and lead your people out of the slough of ignorance and despair into which their white masters cast them and where the damned Democrats would now like to keep them. The Democrats would return you to slavery, Mr. Maxwell. The Republicans offer you freedom and representation. But, Mr. Maxwell"—he leveled a pudgy finger at Drummage—"there is only one way you can accomplish this."

"And how is that?"

"By organizing, sir. By union, and by union I mean the Union League—"

"Whose membership is not open to men of my color," Drummage interrupted.

"That's all been changed now." Bingham's voice was unctuous as though he himself had been responsible for the change. He poured himself another glass of wine and stood up to refill Drummage's. "The Supreme Council of the Union League has now opened its doors to its beloved colored brethren and I have come here tonight to offer you a special invitation to become a member of the Council in Benson. We want you to know all our secrets and to take the Union oath along with us. Then, once having become a member, it is my hope that you, as president, will organize a Council here at your village called New Quarters."

Drummage was flattered indeed. No colored man had ever been initiated into the awesome mysteries of the Union League. He bowed to Bingham and then to Chris. "You pay me a great honor, gentlemen."

"We are calling a State Convention of Negroes to meet in Mobile in the not too far distant future." Bingham threw open his arms as though to embrace the whole Negro race. "Before that time, I hope, Mr. Maxwell, that you will have established the New Quarters Council and that as its president you will see to it that you are elected to be the distinguished delegate to that State Convention. Naturally you will be a Republican delegate and as such you will have a big hand in the reconstruction of our sovereign State of Alabama."

Drummage was too overwhelmed to answer; he merely bowed his head in acquiescence.

"Then if we may count on your presence at the convocation of the Union League Council at Benson tomorrow night we will see that you are duly initiated."

"You may count on it," Drummage said solemnly.

For a long moment none of them spoke. Softly, over the rolling acres that separated Falconhurst from the New Quarters, they could hear the sound of singing in the little village. They all listened. The sound seemed to call Drummage away from these two white men, over to the New Quarters where he might feel free and be himself again. He hoped that they would soon be thinking about bed. He had told Madilda to be at his cabin rendezvous and he knew that she was waiting. She would not dare to disobey him. Just now he wanted her with swelling emergency. He wanted to shed this cloak of civilization and rut in the same primitive manner as his African forebears. Madilda would welcome that; the last time she had accused him of being only lukewarm. Well, there was one good way to end the conversation.

"We have a custom here in the South." Drummage smiled at Colonel Bingham. "We believe in doing everything we can to make our guests feel at home.

"Law's sake, you certainly have, Mr. Maxwell. A fine dinner, a delightful evening, and interesting conversation."

"Perhaps Drummage has something more to offer you, Colonel." Chris nodded knowingly.

"That I have, Colonel. You see the rule here at Falconhurst has always been that when gentlemen arrive here unaccompanied by their wives, we try to provide them with a companion for the night. Now we have a most charming young girl by the name of Dulcy. . . ."

The Colonel leaned forward in his chair, breathing heavily.

"A nigger girl, Mr. Maxwell?"

"A colored girl," Drummage made the distinction.

"And pretty too," Chris added.

"And you mean, Mr. Maxwell . . . ?" Bingham wiped his lips with the back of his hand.

"That if you desire, Dulcy will be waiting for you when you retire."

"Good God Almighty!"

"A most delightful custom, Colonel, as I have already proved." Chris rose from his chair.

"Then if you approve, my boy, I shall be forced to sample it. A colored girl! Law's sake! They say they're hotter 'n the hinges of hell. Thank you, Mr. Maxwell, thank you, sir. Getting on in years, I am, but sure can appreciate it. Black titties! Never saw any in my life. This is real hospitality, Mr. Maxwell."

"Then, Colonel, I will let my friend Chris act as host. He will show you to your room while I go to advise Dulcy to attend you. Good night, Colonel, and good night to you, Chris."

Drummage held the door open for them and watched them go upstairs. The Colonel was actually bouncing, and Drummage felt a wave of revulsion at the old man's drooling prurience. Once they had turned the landing he went to the kitchen, where Dulcy was sitting at the table with Onan, Valentine, and Jude.

"H'ist yore ass upstairs to de Cunnel's room, Dulcy." It felt good to lapse back into the familiar vernacular. "Ol' white man a-needin' pleasurin' tonight, gal, 'n' yo' a-goin' ter do it."

She made a wry face. "Dat fat ol' man. Bet he cain' even git it up. Whar Madilda? Why'n she go? 'Druther have yo', I had." She smiled at Drummage.

"Madilda busy. How come yo' a-askin' questions? I say git, yo' git. He ol' man 'n' he ain' goin' ter do much. Now, h'ist yo'se'f up them stairs." He pulled her up from her chair, then turned to Valentine. "Yo' needn't wait up fer me, boy. Kin git myself undressed tonight."

He opened the back door and stepped out into the moon-dappled darkness. After walking a few steps he started to run with all the ardor his Hausa ancestors had displayed on their nocturnal visits to the tamarisk bushes that surrounded their villages. Tonight Madilda would not be disappointed. Hot damn! Could he last till he got there? He ran faster, pausing only a moment to catch his breath at the top of the rise where the ghostly finger of his father's monument gleamed wraithlike in the light. As he passed his mother's cabin, he saw Zanzibar.

"She a-waitin' fer yo', Drummage boy," Zanzibar chuckled. "Bin thar 'bout an hour. She a-pacin' up 'n' down wid her pore li'l heart a-goin' pittypat. Yo' tech a spark ter her, she goin' ter 'splode."

Drummage merely grunted. Being Mister Maxwell of Falconhurst had its compensations but tonight, hot damn, tonight he was just Drummage. Jes' Drummage!

Chapter 44

IT WAS MIDNIGHT. Scudding clouds hid the narrow crescent of a moon, and Drummage shivered as he stood in the darkness outside the closed door of what had formerly been the Benson livery stable. He was alone—Chris and Bingham had gone inside—yet he had the uncomfortable feeling that he was not alone because he could sense that eyes were watching him while he waited there before the rough plank door. Obeying Bingham's instructions, he knocked three times on the door, paused, then added four additional raps. From inside he heard a sepulchral voice. "Who comes there?"

For one awful moment he stood paralyzed with fear. Perhaps they were going to kill him. Perhaps this was a plot against him to take Falconhurst. But no! Chris Holbrook was his friend. But how could he be sure? Chris Holbrook was a white man, and could a white man ever be a friend to a nigger? Or a white woman? Was Sophie his friend as well as his wife? And this Bingham? What did he know about Bingham except that he was a glib talker? Drummage wanted to run for cover, to hide himself, to put all the pretensions of white civilization behind him and seek sanctuary among his own people. He had never felt more alone or more frightened before in his life, and now what was supposed to be the answer to the question from inside came from his parched throat in a hoarse whisper.

"A friend and supporter of the Union," he managed to say.

He heard a loud guffaw behind the door. "That goddamned nigger's scared shitless." And then the sepulchral voice spoke again: "Enter, friend," and the door swung open. Hands reached out to pull Drummage inside and the door banged shut behind him. Inside it was not much lighter than outside. One dim light—the flame of a single candle—was so shaded that Drummage could see almost nothing. The ammoniacal odor of horses still hung about the place and the ghost of their urine was now mingled with the sharp acrid odor of white man's sweat. Drummage felt a hand clutching his elbow, and to his relief a familiar voice whispered in his ear:

"Don't be afraid, Drummage, we've all been through this."

Relieved to hear Holbrook's voice, he was led between an aisle of men whom he could not see although he could hear their breathing. As he approached the light, the paper shade was whisked away from around it and Drummage could see a table covered with black cloth, and on it a number of objects. The light also revealed the form of a man behind the table and although he was masked Drummage could recognize the rotund form and the pepper-and-salt whiskers of his guest of the night before, Colonel Bingham.

"You come seeking admittance to the Loyal Union League, stranger?"

"I do," Drummage answered, speaking more plainly now and wondering why Bingham addressed him as stranger when they had been together so recently.

With his usual pontifical voice, Bingham went into the flowery ritual of the order. One by one he picked up or indicated the objects on the table. First he held the Bible before Drummage, then a sheet of paper which he said was the Declaration of Independence, from each of which he read. Followed then in order the flag, a censer, a sword, a gavel, a ballot box, a sickle, a shuttle, and an anvil. Each was the subject of a long discourse by Bingham and its symbolism was woven into his oration. He explained how these objects had their place in the preservation of liberty, the elevation of labor, the perpetuation of the Union, the maintenance of laws and the security of American institutions. When he had finished exhibiting them one by one, he went into a lengthy discourse regarding the purposes of the Union League in regard to the protection of its members—their persons and their property—and the Union's aim to educate the workingman and to teach him all the duties of American citizenship. He dwelt on the enfranchisement of the Negroes, of their place in the country, and the new freedom which the Union—and the Union alone—had secured for them.

All this sounded fine to Drummage, although the long speech made him fidget. When he was at length asked to take an oath of secrecy, he laid his hand on the Bible and swore that any further proceedings he might take part in or witness during the time he was in the meeting would never be divulged except in the sacred precincts of this or another council of the League. Having made his vow, he was then asked to swear that he would support the principles of the Declaration of Independence; to pledge himself to resist all attempts to overthrow the United States; to strive for the maintenance of liberty, the elevation of labor, the education of all people in the duties of citizenship; to practice friendship and charity to all the order and to support for election or appointment to office only such men as were supporters of these principles and measures—namely those of the Republican party.

Drummage repeated the words after Bingham and when he had finished, more candles were lighted and he was able to recognize the others who were there. Possibly thirty men were in the gathering. Drummage saw several whom he had seen or met before—the head of the Freedmen's Bureau, a schoolteacher from Ohio, officers and privates under Chris's command, and a man from Vermont who had recently founded a bank in Benson. Drummage was the only Negro, but not a single one of the whites were natives of Benson; all were recent importations from the North or soldiers in service.

A pitchpipe sounded shrilly and someone started to sing "The Star-Spangled Banner." Then the schoolteacher solemnly mounted the dais behind the table and harangued Drummage, saying that though the designs of traitors had been thwarted, there were triumphs yet to be secured—complete ascendancy of the true principles of popular government, equal liberty, education, and the overthrow at the ballot box of the old oligarchy of political leaders.

Drummage shifted from one foot to another during the lengthy oration, scarcely comprehending the high-flown hyperbole of the orator. He recalled the old days when he had come here with Hammond Maxwell to take his place with the other bucks on a bench in the back of the stable while his master visited with his white friends. He remembered the crude conversations of the Negro boys, their boastings, their wagers as to their physical prowess, and their lusty accounts of wenching. Abruptly he was brought back to the present when his hands were grasped and pulled behind him. At first he felt reassured by the fact that Chris was one of those who held his hands. But when a black bandana was tied around his eyes and his hands were securely tied with a cord, his fear returned. Blind and helpless, he was led around the room, where he was halted several times, his name was called out and permission asked from the men if he was to be allowed to take the final vows which would make him an accredited member. Each time the answer was in the affirmative. Now once again he was halted, but this time rough hands on his shoulders forced him to kneel, and a prayer was intoned over him, invoking the blessings of Almighty God upon him. Followed then a long silence, marked only by a scuffling of many feet, the moving of some piece of heavy furniture, and, once, the resonant ring of metal against metal. He heard the scrape of a sulfur match and the crackling of fire while a hand was placed on his shoulder. Again he heard the voice of Colonel Bingham.

"Drummage Maxwell, you are once again an African slave, a poor miserable creature, bound with the loathsome fetters of your bondage. You are something to be bought and sold. Your body is not your own but the property of an arrogant master who would take you as a child from your mother's breast and sell you, who would wrench you from the arms of the woman you love and sell you, who would take your children from you and sell them. You are the lowest of all God's creatures and your eyes are blind to the glorious freedom that all other men have enjoyed from the day they came forth from their mother's wombs. And now, Drummage Maxwell, would you escape from your bonds and open your eyes to behold the sacred fire of liberty? I ask you, Drummage Maxwell, do you desire freedom?"

"I do." The thongs on his wrist were hurting him.

"Then where will you look for freedom?"

Drummage thought well before he answered. Where had his freedom come from? From the North of course. He felt he had the right answer.

"From the Union," he said.

"Right well have you answered, Drummage Maxwell. It is the Union and only the Union that gives men liberty and preserves that liberty."

Drummage felt the bonds slip from his wrists and a hand lifted his right hand and placed it on a book. Then the bandage was whipped from his eyes and he found himself kneeling before a ghostly fire whose blue-and-green flames cast an eerie light on the faces surrounding him. In the strange light they looked like the faces of dead men staring at him with strange dark eyes. For the third time he was told to repeat an oath, which he spoke, word by word, after Bingham.

"I swear to defend and perpetuate freedom and union. To this end, I pledge my life, my fortune and my sacred honor, so help me God." At the conclusion, there was a scratching of matches and a click of tinderboxes as each man lighted a candle, filling the room with light.

Drummage was helped up from his knees and underwent a series of handshakes with each of the men present, together with congratulations and good wishes from all. Then the schoolteacher, who was introduced to him as the marshal, instructed him in the secret signs of the order, the famous four "L's." The first was to raise the right hand to heaven, the thumb and forefinger together while he said the word "Liberty." Next he was to drop his hand to shoulder height and pronounce the name "Lincoln." The third was to drop his hand to his side and say "Loyal," while the fourth and last was to catch his thumb in his waistband and say "League." With these signs he became a full-fledged member of the Union League, and as such he was toasted plentifully in corn, to which he replied with answering glasses. By the time he was ready to leave, accompanied by Holbrook and Bingham, he was scarcely able to sit his horse and lurched drunkenly in the saddle. His companions were hardly more sober than he, and with shouts of "Good night!" to the other members, they started on their way back to Falconhurst.

"Tomorrow night, Drummage me laddy buck," Bingham hiccupped, "we'll have a mass initiation at New Quarters. I'll be there to help you with the ritual and we'll get those sons of bitches of niggers into the League and get them all voting for the Republican party, won't we, boy?"

He slumped sideways in his saddle, clinging onto Drummage, who was riding in the middle, for support.

"We do jes' that, Cunnel suh." Liquor had claimed Drummage's cultured accent. "We aimin' to keep them niggers free. But cain' figger out how we git dat fire, Cunnel suh. Cain' figger out how we git it ter burn green 'n' blue-like."

Chris threw his head back and laughed drunkenly.

"Thought that would scare the pants off you, Drummage boy. Scares hell out of everyone, first time they see it. Wish you could have seen your face. Looked just like you'd been buried ten years and then dug up. What you think those colored bucks going to say when you whip the blindfolds off from them tomorrow night?" He swayed towards Drummage. "Want to know what makes it burn like that? Just put some salt on the wood and then sprinkle alcohol over it. Makes the damnedest-looking fire you ever saw."

"Gotta learn how to do it, Drummage." Bingham managed to straighten himself up. "You gotta hold a meeting every week. Gotta get yourself a lot of new members 'sides those at New Quarters. We want every nigger round here to be in the League and voting Republican when the time comes. You'll be 'nitiating every week. Leave you a book I will, with the ritual in it, but just be sure none of those goddamned Rebs get ahold of it. Dyin' to know the ritual, they are."

"Whyn't they join up 'n' fin' out?" Drummage asked.

"Ain' letting none o' those bastards in so they won't never find out. Union League the strongest society in the world today." Bingham was silent a moment, his head bobbing with the footsteps of his horse. Leaning over in his saddle he placed one hand with maudlin affection around Drummage's shoulders. "Glad we're going back to your place, Drummage boy. Think you can spare that Dulcy another night?"

"She shore hot stuff, that Dulcy." Drummage was feeling generous. "Yo' a-likin' her, Cunnel? Hot damn, dat girl jes' take natchr'lly ter pleasurin' like a duck to water."

"Ain't no gal in the whole state of Maine can hold a candle to her. Whoa, there!" Bingham pulled up his horse and pointed down the road. "Hey, boy, what's that light in the sky?"

They were just entering the main street of New Quarters. All the windows were dark, but the whole settlement was illuminated by a strange glow.

Drummage halted. Suddenly his drunkenness left him. He stood up in his stirrups.

"That's the lower nine-acre field," he said. "All prime cotton. Should be ten bales or more in that field. Worth about two thousand dollars." He lowered himself into the saddle and lashed his horse with his quirt. It was only a few yards

396

to Brutus' house and he was there in a moment, yelling at the closed shutters until Brutus and Beulah-Annie both poked their heads out.

"Come on, Brute," Drummage called. "Git the men out. Tell 'em not ter bother gittin' dressed. Nine-acre field a-burnin'. Don' think it gotten much o' a start yet."

"Yo' ride 'n' rise 'em, Drummage. Tell 'em ter fetch shovels, hoes 'n' spades. Got to make us a ditch if 'n we goin' ter save anything." Brutus' face disappeared from the window.

Chris and Bingham were now beside Drummage and had heard Brutus's words. They all dashed off in different directions, riding between the cabins, calling out the men, shouting instructions. Some of the men ran out dressed, others were naked, some clutched a shirt or trousers, but all grabbed a hoe or a shovel and followed after Brutus. Fortunately it was only a short distance to the field. One corner of it was blazing, but more ominous than the crackling flames in the cotton was a huge cross, some six feet high, which reared its fiery outline against the black sky.

"That goddamned Klan," Bingham gasped. "Didn't think they were here in Benson yet." Shots from the darkness answered him and then there was the sound of horses and a glimpse of white riders between the trees. Suddenly they were gone and there remained only the crisp sound of the flames while chunks of blazing timber dropped from the wooden framework of the cross.

Brute and the men set to work with the help of Drummage, Chris, and the Colonel. They all dug furiously, as near to the flames as they dared to go. Throwing shovelfuls of earth on the blazing plants and hewing out a shallow trench some three feet wide, they managed to confine the blaze to the corner of the field, where it soon burned itself out. With the dying of the flames the field became dark again, so that only the glowing embers of the burnt corner could be seen, and with the darkness came rest from their frantic labors. It was a still night without any suggestion of a breeze; there seemed little danger of the fire starting up again.

"Some o' us better stay till mornin'," Brute advised.

"Payin' every man what stays four bits," Drummage announced, whereupon they all volunteered, even those who had left without their clothes. Drummage felt it was safe to leave the field, and he and the two white men, whose faces were now so blackened by smoke that they were scarcely distinguishable from the Negroes, got on their horses and headed for the big house.

"That goddamned Klan!" Bingham swore. "First it was the Black Cavalry, then it was the Knights of the White Camellia, and now it's the Ku Klux Klan. Those bastard Rebs never will give up. We fight them, we lick them, we starve them, we kill them, and the sons of bitches still won't admit that they're beaten. Now you see"—he turned to Drummage —"why the Union League is so important. Those white bastards would like nothing better than to make slaves of you all again, and if we don't fight them tooth and nail they will. Tell that to your friends at New Quarters. Tell them if they want to stay free, they'd better join the League and become Republicans. Tell them it's their only hope."

"What will they do next?" Drummage said. "Tonight they burned the cotton. What will they do tomorrow night? Will they burn Falconhurst?"

"They will not." Chris spoke emphatically. "I'll put Falconhurst under martial law. I'll post sentries."

"Better to rout out the Klan," Bingham shouted. "Get rid of it, lock, stock, and barrel."

"But in the meantime I have to protect Falconhurst. I have no desire to be burned in my bed."

"We've got our work cut out for us, gentlemen." Bingham lowered his voice. "It's either them or us. The League or the Klan. Democrat or Republican. It's either freedom or slavery for you, Drummage. That's why we need you and all your friends at New Quarters. We need your vote. Add black to white and we'll win. We'll put a nigger in the governor's chair; we'll put a nigger in the Senate in Washington; and we'll put them in the House. We'll grind these goddamned Rebs under our feet and it won't make any difference if those feet are black or white."

They turned into the long driveway that led to the big house. When they reached the portico, a dark figure detached itself from one of the pillars and ran down to them.

"Mista Maxwell suh, Mista Maxwell!" It was Valentine, waving his arms in excitement. "Miz Sophie done took somethin' awful. Better yo' ride ter New Quarters 'n' git Mammy Hester 'n' Aunt Kliney. Miz Sophie need midwifin' bad. She took awful hard, Mista Maxwell."

"I'll ride with you," Chris said. "We'll send the women back from New Quarters and then I'll ride into Benson and get our doctor. Don't know if he ever birthed a child before, but at least he'll have medicines and chloroform if it's needed."

"Got de buckboard all hitched up in de barn, Mista Maxwell." Valentine pointed to the back of the house. "I'll drive it ter bring Mammy Hester 'n' Aunt Kliney."

"Le's go." Drummage wheeled his horse and Chris followed him, shouting over his shoulder:

"You might as well go inside, Colonel. Don't know what you can do, but seems to me someone always gets pans of water heating. Why they need so much goddamned hot water for one child I don't know but they always do."

Drummage and Chris galloped down the drive, Valentine following them in the buckboard. Colonel Bingham slowly climbed the steps to the portico and stood there a moment, rubbing his grimy hands. He gazed aloft at the tall white pillars with their swelling Ionic capitols.

"Goin' to get myself a place like this." He spoke aloud. "Goin' to have a big plantation with plenty of niggers to work it and a nigger wench to sleep with. Hell of a lot better than that farm up in Maine and having to sleep with Emmeline every night. Get all these stupid niggers to help me and I'll be governor of the state." With all the dignity his obese figure could muster he walked across the portico and into the house.

Chapter 45

WHEN DRUMMAGE and Chris turned into the gates from their second trip to Benson that night, bringing the doctor with them, they could hear Sophie's screams issuing from the open window of her front bedroom. Colonel Bingham was waiting for them on the portico along with Aunt Kliney, one of the two midwives from New Quarters. Valentine emerged from out of the shadows to take their horses and the three men ran up the steps.

"Thank God you've come," Bingham said. "Poor thing must be suffering badly, the way she's taking on. You the doctor?" He peered through the dim light at the tall spare man who accompanied Drummage and Chris.

"Dr. Gale," the man answered. "You say the woman's bad off? Haven't attended a childbirth for the last four years but guess I haven't forgotten. Don't imagine a colored woman's any different than a white woman when it comes to having a baby."

"Mrs. Maxwell is not a Negro, Doctor. She's white," Chris interrupted.

Gale's eyes opened wide in surprise and he looked at Drummage in embarrassment, while old Aunt Kliney sidled up to them, anxious to assert her importance.

"She tooken awful bad, Masta Doctor suh. She fall down de stairs when dem white men came to de do' all dressed up in sheets. Baby a-tryin' ter come out but he a-comin' ass fust. Ain' good. Me 'n' Mammy Hester bin a-tryin' ter turn he roun' but cain' budge he. Don' know what we a-goin' ter do, Masta Doctor suh. Mayhap yo' kin he'p us. She a-screamin' somethin' awful."

"Where is she?" Dr. Gale took his bag from Drummage.

"She upstairs, masta suh." Aunt Kliney wasn't to be overlooked. "Oh, she a-takin' on awful. Ain' never tended to no white woman afore. Me 'n' Mammy Hester don' know how's to manage her."

"Could be that we're going to have some trouble." The doctor was inside the door and part way up the stairs. "Sounds like a breech delivery and I haven't any obstetrical instruments with me. Never had no need for them in the army but I'll do the best I can." He was off up the stairs and Drummage heard his heels on the floor as he hurried down the hall to Sophie's room.

Drummage stood at the foot of the stairs, wondering at Sophie's screams. Must be, he thought, that white women were more delicate than colored ones. He had attended the lying-in of several Negro wenches and, although he knew they suffered some pain, he had never given the matter any particular thought; childbirth was something one took entirely for granted. The next day most women were up and about. Nigger wenches thought little of childbirth. He had even seen a woman, when her time came, give birth in a cotton field, lying down in a furrow and arching her body while she strained to bring forth her child. Another woman, quite disinterested, stood by, ready to cut the umbilical cord with the sharp edge of a hoe. Consequently he was not too perturbed over Sophie's carrying on, and when her screams died down to hoarse gasps and then became quiet, he felt the worst was over.

"Doc must have given her a whiff of chloroform." Chris took Drummage by the elbow and led him into the drawing room to join Bingham. "Sit down. Guess that corn that we had in Benson has sort of worn off. Always heard that while the womenfolk were heating water, the best thing for the menfolk to do was to get drunk." He walked out into the dining room and brought back a carafe of corn with three glasses on a tray.

"We've all been drunk once tonight, might's well get drunk again, I guess." He filled the three glasses and as he walked across the room to take a chair, his foot hit something and kicked it out into the center of the room.

"What in hell's that?" Chris stopped and looked down at the object—a piece of paper rolled around a stone and tied with a bit of red rag.

"Ain' never seen it before." Drummage stared at it with dull incomprehension. "Le's see it, Chris."

He untied the knot and unwrapping the piece of paper he smoothed out the wrinkles so that he could read what was written on it. With a puzzled look, he handed it to Chris, who scanned it quickly before passing it on to Bingham.

The Colonel held it beside the lamp, the better to examine the crude drawings, reading it aloud with the same sonorous voice he had used at the League initiation.

Hella-ballo Hole, Den of Skulls,
Bloody Bones Headquarters of
The Great Ku Klux Klan No. 1000
Windy Month, New Moon,
Cloudy Night, Thirteenth Hour

Goddamn your soul, Drummage, you dirty black nigger. The Horrible Sepulchre and Bloody Moon has at last arrived. You live today but tomorrow you die, die, die. You are going to learn to stretch hemp if you dare to start a Union League around here. If you want to live, get out of town and take that white bitch whore that you married along with you.

If you don't go, the great High Priest Cyclops will need one black wether and you'll be it. The Great Giantess will need one black barrow and you'll be it. We'll cut off your black nigger balls and let the dogs eat them. The Hole of Hell is waiting for you. Red Hot Pincers are waiting for you. The Castration Knife is waiting for you. Fire and Brimstone are waiting for you. Hell freezes. Leave us. Go. Benedicite. The great Ogre orders it.

By order of the great
Blufustin
K. K. K.

Bingham laid the paper down on the table and looked up at Drummage. "What did that old nigger woman say about men coming here all dressed up in sheets?"

Drummage went over to the doorway, trying to control the trembling in his knees, and pulled the bell cord that hung there. Far out in the kitchen he heard the tinkle of the bell, and a few moments later Valentine appeared in the drawing room.

"What bin a-goin' on here tonight?" Drummage demanded brusquely to hide his own nervousness.

Valentine's eyes rolled. "Bin jes' one awful night here, Mista Maxwell. Fust come de men . . ."

"What men?"

"Don' know jes' who dey are. All dressed up in white sheets wid jes' holes fer they eyes. Come a-ridin' up de drive and a-bangin' on de do'. Onan, he went ter open de do' but de men jes' push pas' him 'n' come inter de hall. They start a-hollerin': 'Whar dat goddam Drummage nigger? Whar he at? We a-lookin' fer him.' Onan, he try ter tell 'em dat yo' not here but dey slaps him down 'n' he start bellerin'. Den Miz Sophie, she hear 'n' she start comin' down de stairs. All de men start a-hollerin' at her 'n' she git halfway down 'n' she faint plum 'way. They keep a-callin' Miz Sophie dirty names but she don' hear dem. Den dey hit Onan 'gain 'n' dey cuff me, den dey all go git they hosses 'n' ride 'way. Den Miz Sophie git tooken bad 'n' Pammy 'n' Dulcy 'n' Madilda they he'p her upstairs 'n' git her undressed. Den we all waits fer yo' ter come home. Jes' mis'ry here tonight, Mista Maxwell suh."

"Did any of these men touch Miss Sophie?" Chris asked. Valentine shook his head. "Dey not a-touchin' her. She jes' see 'em 'n' she keel over. Don' guess she hear none of de things dey call her."

"Did you recognize any of the men?" Bingham asked.

"Cain' reckernize 'em when I cain' see 'em."

Bingham's lips set in a grim line. "Guess we're in for it, Drummage. Don't think there's any Klan in Benson yet, but looks like we're going to have one here soon. This bunch may have come over from Westminster—there's a den there that's been raising hell lately." He downed the glass of corn and held out the empty glass to be refilled.

It was decided that Drummage was not to leave the place by himself. On his trips into Benson he would ride with Chris and a squad of soldiers, and Chris would detail a squad to be at Falconhurst at all times. Neither Onan nor Valentine was to admit anyone to the house without first ascertaining their business. Drummage would post his own men as guards around the barns, the old slave quarters, and the fields, to give an alarm if strangers came on the place. Falconhurst was to take on the aspect of an armed camp.

The carafe was nearly emptied and Drummage sent Valentine for another jug of corn. Now the amenities of the cut-glass decanter and the goblets were dispensed with, and they drank straight from the jug.

Drummage lifted a finger to halt the conversation. Slow footsteps were descending the stairs. Each man turned expectantly towards the pillared doorway to see the tall figure of the doctor, his blue uniform coat discarded, his shirt sleeves rolled to the elbow. He looked first to Drummage.

"You have a son, Mr. Maxwell. A fine boy! Listen, and you can hear him."

The wail of an infant came down the stairs, thin and reedy but full of life and vigor.

"What color is he, Doctor?" Drummage pushed himself up by the arms of his chair and stood unsteadily. "He ain' black, is he?"

Dr. Gale shook his head slowly. "No, far from black. Ivory, perhaps, or sort of weak coffee with a lot of milk in it. He's got gold hair."

"Straight hair or nigger wool?"

"Looks straight, far's I can see."

"Kin I see him?" With a sympathetic gesture, Dr. Gale laid his hand on Drummage's arm. "Before you see your son, there is something I must tell you, Mr. Maxwell."

"Is it Mrs. Maxwell?" Chris asked.

The doctor nodded.

"I'm sorry to tell you, Mr. Maxwell, sorry . . ."

"Yo' mean Sophie's dead, Doctor?"

Again the doctor nodded.

"But the boy's all right?"

"It was a question of one or the other. If I'd only had my instruments here I could have saved her, but there was nothing I could do without them. She didn't suffer any pain, Mr. Maxwell. I gave her chloroform. For a while I thought I could save her but it was hopeless. The nigger women upstairs had given her up before I arrived."

Drummage realized that the three men who were staring at him expected him to show some sign of grief, but in truth he didn't feel any. Sophie was dead. There was nothing he could do to bring her back to life and he didn't know if he would want to bring her back if he could. It occurred to him, even while he was trying to manifest some sorrow, that he'd never have to sleep with her again or listen to her importunings. Never again would he have to think up excuses to absent himself from her. Sophie was dead and that was that. Tomorrow she'd be buried up on the crest of the hill alongside his father and Masta Hammond's folks. Masta Hammond! Sophie had been the last link with Masta Hammond and now she was gone.

Now tears of self-pity welled in his eyes. The others did not know that the tears were for himself and not for Sophie. Drummage was weeping for a familiar way of life that was now only a memory, for a Falconhurst where he had been only a slave and where Masta Hammond reigned supreme. Those had been happy days—days without responsibility. He had not been Mister Drummage Maxwell of Falconhurst then, with a myriad worries on his mind. He was not a member of the Union League and there was no Ku Klux Klan to curse him and threaten to geld him. Poor Sophie had represented security and authority. And now he felt lost without her, lost and insecure.

Chris put his arm around Drummage's shoulder.

"Hard to take, I know, fellow."

Bingham linked his arm with that of Drummage.

"We're your friends, boy, we'll see you through this."

Dr. Gale stepped back out into the hall. "Would you like to see your son, Mr. Maxwell?"

Drummage stared at him dumbly and nodded. With Dr. Gale leading, the four men walked up the stairs. The door to Sophie's room was closed and Drummage wondered what she looked like, lying there on the bed, dead. He wanted to see her and tell her that he was really sorry, and yet the thought of her white body revolted him. He heard a low wailing inside her room and knew that it must be one of the midwives, washing her body, closing her eyes with copper pennies, straightening her tortured limbs, folding her hands across her chest, and brushing the damp hair out of her eyes.

At the door of his own room, Mammy Hester was standing, a swathed bundle in her arms.

"He mighty pretty baby," she was crooning, "he mighty pretty baby, mos' white he is. Mos' white like he's poor dead mammy." She glanced up to see Drummage.

"Got ter fetch us a wench ovah from de New Quarters what got milk. Dat Marlowe's wife, Geraldeen, she jes' birfed a sucker yisterday. She got lotsa milk. De li'l tike a-goin' ter git hongry soon. Better yo' sen' fer Geraldeen quick-like."

"Kin I see him, Mammy Hester?" Drummage extended his arms for the bundle.

She made no move to hand him over; instead she waddled into Drummage's room and laid the child on the bed, unfolding the corners of the swaddling blanket until the infant was exposed.

"Fust mustee sucker I ever birthed. He nice boy. Come look at him but don' put yore big hands on him. Don' tech him."

Drummage gazed down at the infant, marveling that his own dark seed could have produced this nearly white child. Outside of his color, he looked like most suckers except that the scant hair on his head was golden and straight, silky-smooth. The nose was not so big-nostriled as those of most Negro babies and Drummage thought he saw, in the mouth and chin, a resemblance to Hammond. The worm-like sex proclaimed him a male and Drummage wondered if he himself had ever been so tiny. The baby opened its eyes, which were a dark blue instead of brown, stared back at Drummage for a brief moment, then screwed up his face and began to cry. Mammy Hester rolled him up in the blanket.

"He hongry. Better yo' sen' fer Geraldeen now. Bet yo' all hongry too. Better git dat Marguerite to make up some cawfee. Could use some myse'f seein's how we got ter set up wid de daid all night. Aunt Kliney she a-layin' out Miz Sophie. Yo' better git Brute ter make a box ter bury her in, come mornin'."

Drummage turned to Chris, who had been looking over his shoulder.

"Seems like Sophie should have a store box—black wid silver handles like'n she bought fer 'Pollon. Don' know if'n

405

they sell me one in Benson, seein' as how she married up wid me."

"I'll tend to it first thing in the morning," Chris assured him.

They descended the stairs slowly and once down in the hall Drummage dispatched Valentine to New Quarters for Geraldeen, and ordered Marguerite and Eva in the kitchen to make coffee and hot cakes. Then, signaling Chris to follow him, he went out onto the portico. It was daybreak, and as they stood there for a moment in silence, they saw the rim of the sun rise above the horizon. The light, slanting through the tall pillars, struck them full in the face.

"Thinkin' yo' 'n' I frien's, Chris," Drummage said. "Thinkin' I kin talk ter yo' 'bout somethin' what's troublin' me. Mayhap I kin beg yo' a favor?"

"Thinkin' yo' kin, Drummage."

"Yo' ain' no nigger, Chris. How come yo' talkin' like one?"

"Could be 'cause yo' 'n' I'se frien's." Chris smiled.

Drummage shook his head in despair. "Lotsa things happen ter me tonight, Chris. Too many things! Union League 'n' my cotton gittin' burned. The Ku Kluxers comin' 'n' my son gittin' borned. Kinda scared me, Chris, Sophie a-dyin' 'n' all. Ain' got nobody now. I'm all alone. Masta Hammond gone 'n' Sophie gone too. What if the Ku Kluxers git me, Chris? What happen to that baby? What happen to Falconhurst?"

"Nothing's going to happen, Drummage. I'll see to it that it doesn't."

"Might jes' happen though, Chris. Jes' might. Wishin' as how I could fix it so's if anything happen ter me, yo' be here to take care o' . . ." He paused a moment and pointed to the upper floor. "Yo' know somethin'? He ain' got no name."

"You're always talking about your old master, why don't you name him Hammond?"

"No, don' wan' ter call him that. He a-goin' ter be a Maxwell anyway. Wantin' him ter be part me. My name really Drum Major though everyone call me Drummage. My papa, he called Drumson 'n' his papa he called Drum. Ain' many niggers knowin' their grandpappy's name but I do, so thinkin' I call this un Drum. Likin' ter call him after yo' too. Christopher Drum Maxwell if'n you lettin' me."

"I'd be honored, Drummage. But about my taking care of him in case anything happened to you. Yes, I'd be willing to do it, but you'd have to see a lawyer and make a will. Could get the Judge Advocate to do it for you. You could leave everything to young Drum and make me his guardian. I'll look after him and treat him fairly and squarely, I promise you that. He'd be like my own son, but let's not talk about such things. You're a young man, strong and healthy, and nothing's going to happen to you."

"Feel better if'n I know." Drummage reached out to take Chris's proffered hand but suddenly fell to his knees. His hands clutched at Chris and wound around the Captain's waist as he burst into sobs, overwhelmed by a desolate sense of loneliness.

All his life he had had a white person to turn to, to think for him, and tell him what to do; to provide for him, and protect him. Even Sophie had been a prop. Now she was gone and he faced the world alone. In his extremity he clung to Chris. Chris was white and he was his friend. Chris would stand as a protector between him and the world.

Chapter 46

IN THE WEEKS that followed, Drummage was far too occupied to think much about either his past or his future. He attended Sophie's funeral, along with Chris and Colonel Bingham—the only two white persons present except the company chaplain—and followed the ornate coffin to the burying ground with heavy-footed steps. Dumbly he watched the box being lowered into the raw red earth—into a grave between those of Apollon and his own father Drumson. Sophie thus was buried as she had lived, with Negroes. Even her mother's grave contained the bones of a mulatto child. But perhaps Sophie would have wished to be buried with the Negroes. After the clods of dirt were thrown on the coffin Drummage walked back from the dead to the living with a more spirited step.

The child Drum made himself known only when he was hungry for the full breasts of Geraldeen, who, with her husband Marlowe and her numerous brood, had now been moved to one of the deserted slave cabins. At night, she occupied a pallet on the kitchen floor in the big house, to be near in case young Drum cried.

Marguerite, who had established herself as head of the household, became more of a martinet than Lucretia Borgia had ever been. With the authority of her new position, she tried in vain to bribe either Onan or Valentine to separate and share her bed, but when neither yielded to her sweet-talking or her threats she inveigled one of the unattached males of New Quarters—a lubberly adolescent named Rufus —to become her paramour. Without asking permission of Drummage, she boldly installed him in the big house, finding chores for him to do in the kitchen. The change in her disposition, now that she had acquired a man, was so apparent that Drummage grudgingly allowed the fellow to remain. The result was that domestic affairs at Falconhurst proceeded smoothly, with substantial meals on time, a minimum of dust in the corners, and a corps of well-dressed, attentive servants, all under Marguerite's thumb.

Bingham lingered on at Falconhurst, ostensibly to help Drummage found the Council of the League at New Quarters, but equally because he enjoyed the well-cooked meals, the affluence of the house, and the companionship of Dulcy. Then, too, there was sound reason for him to remain. The new bank in Benson was lending money to the impoverished plantation owners to help them pay the arrears in taxes which had accumulated during the war. Inevitably, foreclosures followed, with the result that many of the old families lost what little equity they had in their homes and acres. In this way, Drummage had annexed the Johnstone farm next to his and Bingham had his eyes on the plantation called The Coign, which was even grander than Falconhurst. By waiting patiently until the bank foreclosed (which he had been assured would be soon), he hoped to take over and establish himself there. Already he was making plans which included Dulcy, but in the meantime he was devoting his time to the furtherance of the League.

It was he who organized the Council at New Quarters, coached Drummage in the initiation ceremonies, and officiated at the opening meeting, which elected Drummage President of the Council. Thereafter followed weekly meetings at which men from other plantations were initiated into the New Quarters Council, until it became one of the largest and most influential of the colored councils. Bingham stayed on, giving his support to the assembly, addressing each meeting, and inspiring the men with a sense of their new-found authority and liberty, their coming ability to vote, their duties as citizens, and particularly their responsibility to the Republican party. Drummage had had the name of the Republican party so drilled into him after a few meetings that it took on the aspect of a deity. It was the Republicans who would guarantee his freedom, and give every Negro forty acres of land and a mule. The Republicans would put the Negro on a level with the whites and make a citizen of him. Certainly it was the Republicans, and not the dirty, hidebound Democrats, who would create a veritable Garden of Eden in Alabama and turn it over to the Negroes.

When the time came to elect a representative to the Negro Convention to be held at Mobile, Drummage was nominated and unanimously elected. The other members of the League felt that, with his ability to read and write, his good clothes, and his polish of urbanity, he could represent them far better than anyone else. Drummage felt proud. Mista Drummage Maxwell, delegate to the Convention! Mista Drummage Maxwell, President of the Union League! Mista Drummage Maxwell of Falconhurst, suh! He was somebody —he really was.

There was now no vestige of Maxwell ownership or authority left. Sophie and all she represented belonged to the past. Falconhurst was his. He had prestige among the Negroes. He possessed the friendship of Chris and Bingham and the protection of the United States Army. In order that all this might continue on to his son, he sought out the Company advocate and made out his will, leaving everything to his heir and appointing Chris as his guardian. Some day his son would be as big a man as he was.

Yet, with all his bigness, Drummage was afraid. He was afraid before he left Falconhurst, he was afraid when he boarded the train in Westminster, and he was afraid when he arrived in Mobile, finding himself alone on the streets of the city.

But his fear left him when he reached the home of Major Allison, Chris's friend who had agreed to house Drummage while he was there. Major Allison and his wife were a placid couple, a little past middle age, from Chris's home town of Boston. Long interested in abolition, they had fanatically espoused the cause before the war and carried their fanaticism to the South, where the Major was now stationed. They and their daughter Mary, who also seemed to have no color prejudice whatsoever, welcomed Drummage to their home even more enthusiastically than they would have welcomed a white visitor. It was the first time he had ever been on such intimate terms with a white family, but their graciousness put him at ease.

Drummage was particularly fond of Mary Allison, who,

Chris had hinted, he hoped someday to make Mrs. Holbrook. He entirely approved of Chris's choice. Although Mary certainly was not a beauty according to Southern standards, she was young, attractive, and above all intelligent. Yet he could never bear to touch her, and when, for some reason, she took his arm, he felt embarrassed.

Most of the Negro delegates at the Convention were decked out in castoff finery that had belonged to their former masters; some merely wore the rough osnaburg trousers which they had always worn on the plantation. Drummage, with his finely tailored clothes, his white linen, and his varnished boots, was bound to stand out among them. That he would be nominated as congressman from his district was a foregone conclusion. When the nomination was finally made he was not surprised, although once again he was frightened at the prospect, for he realized that Washington would be a greater test of his abilities than Mobile. That he would be elected was certain, for there were more Negroes in his district than whites and they would all vote for him.

But despite his prominence in the Convention, his weeks in Mobile held little interest for him. If Washington was going to be as boring as Mobile, he dreaded the thought of having to live there. After three weeks without a woman, Drummage was finding his nerves on edge. True, there were Negro prostitutes in the city—hundreds of them—but after one excursion into the street of cribs, which was their domain, he turned away in disgust. He had heard of the loathsome disease which was rampant among them and it frightened him. Then too, the thought of paying for a woman to give him physical relief was repulsive to him. He wanted somebody like Candy to pleasure him.

And then, one day, he saw her!

He was leaving the Convention Hall with William Grooby, a local delegate from Mobile, when he spied her. First he had noticed the smart little calash with the two bay horses, drawn up to the curb. From the calash, his eyes traveled to the woman sitting alone, lolling back on the cushions, her cerise straw bonnet with the soaring white plumes almost hiding her face. There was something familiar in the tilt of the head, in the fluttering of her hands and the set of her shoulders. When he sauntered past to get a better look, he saw the outline of a cheek and he knew that it was Candy. For one moment as he passed their eyes met, but she betrayed no sign of recognition. Instead, her eyes looked past him to the tall and strikingly handsome mulatto who

410

came across the sidewalk, stepped into the calash, and sat beside her with a proprietary interest.

"Dat's Boone Freeman from up Selma way," Grooby snickered. "He ain' los' much time in takin' up wid Miss Candace. He thinkin' he lucky, but he a-goin' ter go home like 'n a picked chicken. Yes suh, dat Miz Candace a-goin' ter git ev'ry picayune dat Boone Freeman have in his pocket. She de mos' 'spensive who' in Mobile."

"Yo' know her?" Drummage watched the calash drive off, seeing the white plumes nodding and noting the protecting arm of the Selma delegate around Candy's shoulders. "Know whereat she lives?"

"She ain' no crib who', that one. Has herself a house o' her own, over on Magazine Street. She come here two, three years 'go; she 'n' her husban', man by de name o' Cupidon Beauchair. Say they free niggers a-comin' fr'm N' Orleans. This Beauchair he have a lot o' money 'n' he a well-set-up young feller too. Buy hisself a nice house, have himself a nice kerridge, 'n' his wife, this Candace, she de queen bee. Den one night they fin' this Beauchair stone daid wid his throat cut wid a razor. Miz Candace a-sayin' that some men come ter rob de house and dey kilt her husban', but most people thinkin' 'tain' so cause 'fore a week go by, she a-steppin' out wid dis free nigger what own a woodyard. She shore not a mo'nin' widder, that one. Pretty soon she git all de money from dis nigger what own de woodyard 'n' out he go. Den she take any man what come along, black o' white o' mulatto, jes' so he have money. Folks say she rich. Say it cost a man twenty-five dollars ter spend de night wid her 'n' there's dem what say it's wuth it. Don' know myself 'cause ain' never had no twenty-five dollars ter spend on pleasurin'. Takes mine where I kin git it free."

But Drummage did have twenty-five dollars and he yearned for Candy as he had always longed for her since he first spent the night with her in Dr. Masterson's home in New Orleans. The money she and Kewp had was undoubtedly those same gold dollars that the iron kettles at Falconhurst had held. His was nearly gone, but apparently Candy still had hers.

The next day, armed with his wallet and ensconced in the faded luxury of a hired coach, Drummage went around the bay to Magazine Street, a short lane of fairly decent houses which seemed pretentious in contrast to the squalid neighborhood which surrounded them. The coachman was evidently familiar with the address and drove up with a flourish before the white picket fence which surrounded the property. Recognizing Drummage as a person of importance —for all those who visited Miss Candace must be of some financial status—he got down off the box and opened the gate for him. The path leading up to the small, white-frame house was weed-grown and choked with branches of crape myrtle, holly, and syringa, but the house itself was well painted and in good repair. Drummage lifted the brass knocker on the front door. A Negress, amply upholstered in black calico, with a spotless white turban wound around her head opened the door. She effectively blocked the door so that he could not enter.

"Who yo'?" she demanded. "Yo' got 'n apertment wid Miz Candace?"

"Don' need none," Drummage answered, "if'n she ter home, she a-goin' ter see me."

"She home but Miz Candace, she mighty perticuler who she a-seein'." The woman continued to block the door.

She was darker in color than Drummage and he cowed her with a look. "Git out o' my way, yo' black slut! Who yo' think yo' be? Yo' jes' tell this Miz Candace, like 'n yo' calls her, dat Mista Drummage Maxwell o' Falconhurst Plantation here 'n' dat he wantin' ter see her. Willin' ter pay fer it too. Now, h'ist yore black ass 'n' jump."

She quailed before him and he went into the small hall and opened the door to a fussily-furnished room. Much to his surprise Candy was sitting in a chair, staring up at him. Evidently she had heard him.

"What yo' wan' here, Drummage?" she demanded sullenly, without rising, affecting an air of elegance by languidly waving one hand.

"What mos' men want what come here?" he answered. "Tha's what I a-wantin' too. Understan' yo' a-gittin' twenty-five dollars fer it now. So . . . I a-wantin' it 'n' I got de money 'n' I a-payin' yo'. My money jes's good's anyone's; jes' so good as Boone Freeman's." He reached into his inside pocket and withdrew his wallet, taking out all his money, which amounted to several hundred dollars. Slowly he counted over the bills, extracting two tens and a five, which he threw down on the small, bibelot-cluttered table. "Ought ter be worth that much to yo', Candy. Thinkin' howsomever yo' ought ter be a-payin' me. 'Member how yo' useter like it, Candy?"

Her eyes were riveted on the money he was replacing in his pocket. She disregarded the bills on the table. Suddenly her manner changed and she rose from the chair, clutching her thin white robe about her, and glided across the floor to where he was standing. Her arms encircled his waist under his coat and her lips reached up to his.

"I ain' fergotten 'yo, Drummage. Ain' no man kin pleasure a gal like yo' kin. Bin a-wantin' yo', Drummage, ever since I lef'. Ain' no man got what yo' got." She released him and placing her hands on his shoulders, studied him carefully—the suit of rich black broadcloth, the waistcoat of sprigged satin with Hammond's gold watch and chain, the immaculate white linen of his shirt, and the satin cravat with the gold stud. "Yo' lookin' mighty peart, Drummage. What I hear yo' sayin' ter Susabelle that yo' Mista Drummage Maxwell o' Falconhurst? What that mean, Drummage honey?"

"Mean that Falconhurst mine now." His words came thickly, because of her nearness. "Mean that I a Maxwell now. Married me up wid Miz Sophie, I did, 'n' now she daid so's all Falconhurst mine now. Fixed up de big house like'n it was when Masta Hammond a-livin'. Got me a whole houseful o' servants. Brute he a-runnin' the plantation fer me 'n' he gittin' in good crops. 'Spect we make ten o' twenty thousand this year from de cotton. I'se a big man these days, Candy; President o' de Union League, delegate to de Convention here 'n' what yo' think—they jes' nominated me fer congressman on de Republican ticket. Goin' ter be 'lected 'n' go to Washington. Den I be de Honorable Drummage Maxwell, Representative o' de Sovereign State o' Alabama to de Congress o' de United States o' America in Washington Dee Cee."

She was impressed, and showed it by her many affectionate little gestures. Her hand reached over and disengaged the gold pin from his stock, which she stuck in his lapel. Then she loosened the cravat and unbuttoned the waistcoat, transferring the gold watch and chain to his coat pocket. Easing off his coat she busied herself with the tiny pearl buttons of his shirt, and soon the white linen followed the broadcloth and satin to the floor. Her lips sought his paps and nuzzled them, while his fingers wandered down to loosen the waistband of his trousers.

"Cain' never fergit a man like yo', Drummage," she whispered, as she turned him around to face another closed door, which opened to disclose her bedroom with a big white bed swathed in a mosquito *baire*. Candy indicated a chair beside the bed.

"Set yo'se'f 'n' take off yore boots, Drummage honey," she whispered huskily. While he stooped to slip off his boots and trousers, she stroked his head. "Yo' say yo' bin married up wid Miz Sophie?"

"Uh huh, Candy baby." He rubbed his cheek against the smooth satin of her thighs.

" 'N' she daid?"

"Uh huh." He could scarcely hear what she was saying.

" 'N' Falconhurst all yores now?"

"Shore is."

"Ain' yo' a-thinkin' 'bout marryin' up 'gain? Man like yo', Drummage honey, got ter have his pleasurin' regular-like. Needs a wife fer that, yo' do."

"Shore am thinkin' 'bout it." He rose from the chair and picked her up in his arms and carried her to the bed. She parted the netting and he dropped her on the mattress.

"Who all yo' a-thinkin' ter marry up wid?"

But Drummage never heard her. He was wasting no more time on words.

Chapter 47

THE SEEMINGLY interminable Convention was drawing to a close, but now that Drummage had found Candy he had lost the pressing desire to return home. There was nothing at Falconhurst that was half as enticing as Candy's nearness in Mobile. These days he spent little time at the Allison house, using as an excuse the last minute business of the closing days of the Convention. But it was not at the Convention, it was at the little house in Magazine Street that he spent the afternoons and evenings. There, in Candy's company, he dawdled over an excellent supper à deux prepared by Susabelle, who was not at all disconcerted over serving Drummage and Candy in the big white bed. Usually when Drummage returned home, the Allisons were asleep, and he would let himself in the front door and tiptoe softly up the stairs to his room. But one night, despite the late hour, as he neared the house he could see the ghostly white forms of the ladies on the veranda, and as he walked up the steps Mrs. Allison greeted him with her usual exuberance.

"Oh, Mr. Maxwell"—she jumped up from her chair and

came across the veranda to meet him at the head of the steps—"we have the most wonderful news. A letter today from Chris Holbrook invites Mary and me to visit him in Benson and," she added archly, tapping his arm with a folded bit of paper which was presumably the letter, "he suggests —but only suggests—that if you were willing, we might be guests at your lovely Falconhurst. Do not think we intend to impose upon you. I am sure we could find accommodations in Benson but . . ." She glanced up at him, awaiting his answer and already sure of what it would be.

He bowed deeply. "Falconhurst would be honored, Miz Allison, at havin' yo' 'n' Miz Mary. Falconhurst's yores ter stay jes' so long's yo' like. Jes' like I bin at home here. Falconhurst yore home." He glanced over at Mary who was sitting in the shadows. "Wonder if this meanin' they's goin' ter be 'nother marryin' up at Falconhurst."

"La, Mr. Maxwell." Mary was properly demure. "Chris and I have been friends since childhood."

But Mrs. Allison was a little more coy. "And perhaps more than friends now, what, Mary dear? He's such a fine young man, isn't he, Mr. Maxwell?"

"Ain' none finer 'n Chris," Drummage agreed. "He right at home at Falconhurst."

"And I'm sure we shall love it too. Oh, it is so good of you to invite us. Chris writes that we are to come with you on the train and that he will meet us all in a place called Westminster with an escort of soldiers. Is it really so dangerous traveling these days—I mean for us Union people?"

Drummage shook his head. "Chris jes' a-showin' yo' all an honor, jes' wantin' ter show yo' he's a sodjer." Drummage wondered if the military escort was for his benefit and then dismissed the thought. Here in Mobile he had been so far away from thoughts of the Klan—so imbued with his own importance—that he had forgotten it. "Convention'll be over in a day or so, three-four days at the most. Kin go then. Goin' ter hate ter leave Mobile," he added. And suddenly it dawned on him just how much he was going to hate to leave Mobile and Candy. Even though he had left her less than half an hour ago, he felt an urge to return to her. It was uppermost in his mind as he said his good nights to Mrs. Allison and Mary and went upstairs to his room. But the room was hot and close. The virginal whiteness of the bed was not inviting. He stared dully at the room, seeing instead the cluttered bedroom with the big white bed in Candy's house. Mechanically he splashed cold water on his face from the china wash basin, dried himself with a towel, and sat down in the stiff-backed chair by the window, hoping for a breeze. It was useless; his whole body yearned for Candy. Why was he sitting here? Why not return to her? Yes, why not go back and spend the night with Candy? There would be so few nights left.

He straightened his cravat, ran a comb through his hair, and then decided to change his black broadcloth coat for a cooler white linen one. And, of course, his wallet! It was necessary if he were to visit Candy, for she made no allowances for their former close relationship. She insisted on payment from him, and he was not unwilling to give it to her. For a long moment he stared at his reflection in the mirror, then smiled. He was better looking than that goddamned Boone Freeman. By God, he was!

The ladies were still on the veranda when he came down and he could sense, both from the tone of their voices and from the nervous flutterings of their fans, that they were surprised to see him going out again so late at night.

"Got ter walk over ter Mista Groober's house." He felt the need of some explanation. "We a-finishin' up some 'portant matters. Guess mayhap I be late in gettin' in. Mista Groober say if it late when we git through, I kin stay over to his house." He smiled apologetically. "If'n yo' all a-writin' ter Chris, o' kin tell him he kin meet us to Westminster Station come nex' Monday. Figure as how everything be over by that time."

Mrs. Allison nodded in agreement. "I'll do just that, Mr. Maxwell. My, but it's going to be nice! We'll all be traveling together and I'll put up a lunch to eat on the train. And Chris will be meeting us! Oh, what a happy trip we'll have!"

"We're so looking forward to going to Falconhurst," Mary added. "We've heard so much about it from you and from Chris, we feel at home there already."

"We'll leave the front door unlocked in case we retire before you return." Mrs. Allison's words followed Drummage down the steps and into the darkness outside the pool of light that came from the open door.

He was glad to be quit of the house with all its gentility and its restrictions. His desire to get back to Magazine Street impelled him to hasten his steps to the corner, where there was usually a cabby waiting. There was one there now, and although the decrepitude of the horse made his journey little faster than if he were walking, he was so glad to be on his way that he allowed himself to sit back on the patched cushions and relax. He'd been with Candy only a few hours before. Now his need for her was greater than ever. Hot damn! He'd spend the night with her this time. He'd not go back to the Allisons'. Spending the night with Candy would be like old times, waking up in the morning and finding her head on his arm.

"Cain' yo' whop up that goddam horse?" he demanded petulantly of the driver. "Might's well be on shank's mare."

"Ol' Miss doin' bes' she kin," the driver grumbled. "Keep yore breeches on. Yo' a-goin' ter Miz Candace's 'n' yo' git there soon 'nuff. Understan' though why yo' in a sweat ter git there. Wishin' I twenty years younger 'n' had de money ter go there myself. Wantin' me ter wait on yo' 'n' bring yo' back home?"

"No, ain' comin' back."

The driver whistled. "Yo' shore a lucky man. Bet it cost plenty ter stay de night." Then, as though in acknowledgment of the importance of the occasion, he flicked the mare's rump with his whip. Not that it accelerated her pace, but eventually they did arrive at Candy's house and Drummage paid off the driver. He ran up the path, tapping the knocker on the door with heavy blows. It was opened by Susabelle and Drummage pushed past her into Candy's little parlor.

"Where she at?" he demanded.

"She right here; a-prettyin' herse'f up in de bedroom. What yo' wantin', Mista Maxwell? Yo' cain' go in there now, Miz Candace, she a-dressin'."

"Seen her dressin' afore when she ain' had nothin' but 'n osnaburg dress." Drummage made a move towards the door of Candy's bedroom but Susabelle interposed her bulk. "Yo' waits a minute, Mista Maxwell, till I tells her yo' here. Sometimes women does pussonal things they ain' wantin' men ter see. Ain' fittin'." She clicked the latch of the door and opened it just enough to let herself in.

"Tell her I wantin' ter see her right quick."

The door closed behind Susabelle and Drummage waited expectantly until, some five minutes having passed, he perched uncomfortably on the edge of a chair. He could hear sounds coming from the next room—low voices which he could not identify. Then he heard soft steps in the hall, which might have been Susabelle's, and the back door open and close. After that there was quiet and finally Susabelle reappeared.

"Miss Candace say fer yo' ter come in, suh." She opened the door wide to admit Drummage. He entered. Candy was

417

propped up in bed, her shoulders covered by a lacy peignoir. Her hands held open the pages of the current number of "Godey's Lady's Book" to one of the fashion engravings.

"Drummage, honey." She smiled languidly up at him. "Wan't 'spectin' yo' back 'gain tonight. Thought yo'd be a-sleepin' soun' after this afternoon. Jes' thinkin' 'bout yo' I was. Know why I bin a-thinkin' 'bout yo'?"

He smiled and made a slight downward gesture.

She shook her head, understanding him but smiling to let him know he was only party right. "Mayhap it could be that too, honey, but this yere picture is what made me think 'bout yo'." She held up the fashion illustration, which showed a simpering bride in white, veiled and with a nosegay of orange blossoms in her hand. "Was jes' a-wishin' I could be a bride and was a-wishin' I could marry up wid yo'."

Suddenly he realized why he had wanted to see her. That was it! He wanted to marry her, so that they would never have to be separated again. Yes, that was certainly it, and why hadn't he thought of it himself? But he would not give her the advantage. She would never know that he hadn't.

"Whaffor yo' thinkin' I comin' back tonight? Tha's jes' what I come fer, Candy baby. Got back to the Allison house 'n' got ter thinkin'. Got ter thinkin' 'bout leavin' yo' here wid me back up at Falconhurst, jes' a-achin' ter have yo'. Got ter thinkin' I got ter take yo' home wid me. Gets us married up 'spectable-like."

Her lips pouted into a little *moue* which she felt was provocative. "Ain' hankerin' much fer Falconhurst, Drummage, but suppose if I a-goin' ter be mist'ess there, ain' so bad's bein' a servant. Awful dead hole tho'. Ain' nothin' goin' on there. Ain' like Mobile. Perhaps better if'n we keeps this house here too. Kin come down 'n' stay sometimes. Then mayhap I sells this house 'n' yo' buys one in N'Orleans. N'Orleans better 'n Mobile. If'n we goes ter N'Orleans, we gits ourselves into society."

"Aim ter be livin' in Washington, come mighty soon. Yo' a-likin' it in Washington, Candy. Me bein' a congressman, we gits ourselves invited to de President's house. We have us a house in Washington too. Keep this 'n if'n yo' wants. Kin come here sometimes. Kin go to N'Orleans 'n' stay in de Saint Louey Hotel if'n we wants." He was already starting to disrobe.

She glanced up at him, seeing the preparations he was making. She wanted him, but she was determined not to sell herself too cheaply. If he wanted her he was going to pay for it.

"Washington shore sounds nice, Drummage honey, but mayhap fust we go to N'Orleans fer our honeymoon 'n' stay at the Saint Louey Hotel. Jes' think, Drummage, tha's where we fust met." She could afford to indulge in a little sentimentality now. "But fust-off we got ter git ourselves married up"—Candy was taking no chances—"ain' we?"

"Aimin' ter git married up at Falconhurst. Miz Allison 'n' Miz Mary, they a-goin' up there come nex' Monday for to visit Chris. We goes along wid 'em 'n' we have a fust-rate marryin' up at Falconhurst. Cap'n Holbrook, he be there, 'n' Colonel Bingham, 'n' Miz Allison 'n' Miz Mary—all white folks. Gits us married up by a white preacher what is the chaplain o' Chris' company. Gits married up in style. Gits us married here in Mobile have ter go ter a nigger preacher." He slipped off his shoes and slid out of his clothes and threw himself on the bed beside her.

"If'n yo' wants," she sighed. "Falconhurst's as good a place as any ter git married up, but cain' go nex' Monday. Law, Drummage, cain' git ready ter traipse off so soon. Cain' go fer another week, 'n' 'sides, ain' wantin' ter go 'long wid no uppity white folks. Everyone a-thinkin' we jes' servants if'n we go 'long wid 'em. Let 'em go on ahead 'n' we kin come a few days later, yo' 'n' me, alone." She retrieved the magazine and found the fashion plate again. Taking his hand, she pointed his finger to the plate. "Got ter git me a dress like this. White satin so stiff it kin stand alone. Take me a week ter git it made. Got ter git me other dresses too. 'N' yo' forgot somethin' mighty 'portant, Drummage boy. If'n yo' come here tonight ter ask me ter marry up wid yo', yo' shore forgot somethin'."

"What I forgot?" Drummage was wanting her too much to pay any attention to what she was saying.

"Gal a-goin' ter marry up wid a man, he got ter give her a di'mond ring. Needin' ter have me one. Yo' got ter git me one o' I ain' marryin' up wid yo'."

"Gits yo' one, Candy baby, 'n' now hush. Le's not talk no more." He stretched his body across hers and reached out one arm to turn down the lamp, but she arrested his arm.

" 'N' yo' got ter git me my weddin' clothes too. Ain' fittin' fer a gal ter buy her own clothes fer her weddin'."

"Git yo' those if'n yo' wants. Ain' needin' ter buy no di'mond ring. Miz Sophie got one's big's a pullet egg. Kin have that one. She got lotsa dew-dads yo' kin have. Oh, Candy baby, wantin' yo' I am. Cain' yo' feel how much I wantin' yo'?"

She could, but she was not ready to submit to him.

"Needs me a hundert dollars to go buyin' things tomorrow." She pulled her hand away from where he had placed it. "Yo' hear me, Drummage. Needs that money ter buy my clothes if'n we goin' 'way."

"Give yo' two hundert if'n yo' jes' shet up." He felt her relax under him as he leaned down to place his lips against hers. The silver amulet he was wearing touched her flesh.

She pushed him away.

"Yo' still a-wearin' that conjure thing? Remember now how yo' always had it roun' yore neck. What's in it, Drummage? Why yo' always wear it and whyn't yo' never let me see what's inside?"

"Ain' nothin' much in it. Miz 'Gusta she gave it ter me. Say I always gotta wear it, 'cause my papa Drumson had it 'n' his papa Drum too. Ain' nothin' inside but a piece o' ol' cloth. Tha's all. Mighty powerful, though. Miz 'Gusta she say if'n I wear this ain' nothin' goin' ter happen ter me."

She reached up and unclasped the chain from the back of his neck. In the old days she had always desired this bit of jewelry, but beg as she might he would never let her have it. Now her innate cupidity demanded it. If he gave it to her it would be a proof of her power over him—it would set the pattern for their marriage.

"Ain' goin' ter kiss yo' less 'n yo' gives me this." She held the little silver filigreed box before her lips.

"Goddam it, take it!" At this point Drummage, consumed with desire, would have given her his right arm if she had demanded it. "Take the fuggin' thing 'n' put out the light."

Her fingers reached out to turn down the wick, dropping the little silver box on the table. His hands possessed her, their lips met, and for a few moments she abandoned herself to him. Suddenly she struggled from his embrace, pushing his head away.

"That di'mond ring o' Miz Sophie's? Yo' say it a big one?"

"Big 'nuff. What in hell yo' keeps runnin' on 'bout di'mond rings. Don' wan' ter talk 'bout nothin' now."

She became silent, arching her body to meet his. Her body responded to him but her mind was far away. She saw herself the center of a brilliant group. She was clad in an elaborate toilette of red satin, with towering plumes in her hair, her ears and throat dripping with diamonds. Drummage was beside her, and as she waved her painted fan she was saying, "Yes, Mista President, we shore would admire to have yo' visit us at Falconhurst Plantation if'n ever yo' come to Alabama. Yes, suh, Mista President."

Drummage's low moan and his gasp for breath brought her back to reality. She heard him mutter something unintelligible.

"What yo' say, Drummage?" she whispered.

"I say le's go to sleep, Candy. Tired, I am." He turned over on his side away from her and in a few moments she heard his deep regular breathing, but for a long time, as she lay beside him, she continued on in her fantasy, changing it from time to time to the King of England, the Emperor of France, and even General Lee. Yes sir, she'd have all the white folks bowing to her, even old Dr. Masterson himself.

Chapter 48

THE WEEK that Candy claimed was necessary to assemble her trousseau extended itself into another week, and still there were more things to do. The wedding dress had been copied from the fashion plate, its stiff white satin meeting the necessary requirement that it stand alone. Along with it was an ashes-of-roses traveling costume of sarcenet with an elaborately beaded bonnet which sprouted plumes of cerise and violet; a ball gown of electric blue velvet with swags of white lace caught up by pink rosebuds around the skirt; and a brace of elaborate peignoirs which were each a froth of lace and gauze. According to Candy, nothing which she already had was sufficiently good; everything must be new. In the meantime Drummage's already thin wallet became flatter and flatter, until he was worried for fear he would not have enough to pay for the railroad tickets between Mobile and Westminster.

He had, however, managed to draw the line at buying jewelry, promising Candy the combined wealth of Augusta's and Sophie's jewel caskets, and she became almost content, remembering their splendor. She herself had a collection of showy paste in gilt settings which, she informed Drummage, was better than anything at Falconhurst, and he in his ignorance believed her. One thing however he refused to part

421

with. He had relinquished his silver talisman to her but he was deaf to her pleadings that he give her the diamond ear-bobs which he had always worn since Sophie had put them in his ears. Candy wheedled, begged, and threatened, but in the end she had to accept defeat.

Candy's horses and calash were sold, Susabelle was put in charge of the shuttered little house on Magazine Street, and the day finally arrived for their departure to Falconhurst. Drummage had intended to write to Chris to announce their arrival at Westminster and have a carriage sent over from Falconhurst to meet them, but he delayed, never having written a letter before, until it was too late. After all, he decided, he could depend on the livery stable in Westminster for a wagon to transport themselves and Candy's innumerable valises and boxes to Falconhurst. The train was due to arrive early in the evening and the livery stable would be open. They would be at Falconhurst before morning. Now that the time had arrived to return he was impatient to get there.

They arrived at the Mobile station in a hired hack, with a wagonful of boxes behind them. Quite unaccustomed to checking baggage, Drummage had to let the hack driver do it for him, much to Candy's disgust. She immediately proceeded to start a scene, declaring at first that all her impedimenta must travel along with her so that she could keep an eye on her things. When she was told that this was impossible, she loudly berated Drummage for his ignorance, insisting that he should have taken over an entire coach for their benefit, such as she remembered his telling about on Hammond's annual journeys to New Orleans. Surely if Hammond could do it he could, too. Wasn't he the master of Falconhurst now just as much as Hammond Maxwell had once been? And wasn't he going to be a congressman? Wasn't that far more important than anything Hammond Maxwell had ever been? Or was he going to continue being an ignorant nigger the rest of his life, and did he expect her to travel in a car with a lot of black niggers and poor white trash? Did he? Well, if he did, she would not go. No sir, she would turn around and go back to Magazine Street.

Her screams began to attract a crowd which increased until finally Drummage, tired of her insults, drew off and slapped her. Suddenly subdued, she meekly accepted the stubs of cardboard, convinced, however, in her own mind, that these worthless things would never bring back her precious boxes.

Thus the first part of their journey, which Drummage had

so anticipated, was passed in a strained silence, with Candy looking sullenly out the window, her lips drawn down in an air of injured martyrdom, and Drummage fuming inside, wishing he knew just how to break the strained silence. There was only one way he could ever handle Candy's tantrums, but unfortunately that was impossible on a train. His hand crept down and sought hers. At first she pulled it away, but he pursued it and caught it, holding it tightly in his clasp. Then gradually her hand relaxed and eventually it returned his pressure, and she turned towards him and smiled. Another crisis was over. Now they could talk again.

Drummage was full of plans for the future but his ambitions, lofty as they were, did not match Candy's. She was aiming higher than he had ever dared aspire. Candy fully intended to become the country's leading colored woman, nay, even more than that, to become the most famous woman in the country—one to whom all knees would bend, all fingers point and all lips pay homage. While Drummage was content merely to usurp Hammond Maxwell's place as the master of Falconhurst, with a pleasant interim of service in Washington, Candy already looked down on the plantation as nothing but a backwater where she would never be able to display her full abilities. It would make a convenient background, true! Mr. and Mrs. Drummage Maxwell of Falconhurst Plantation. But a steppingstone was all she intended it to be. She was not going to spend her life lording it over a bunch of ignorant niggers in the little hamlet of New Quarters. Not by a damn sight! The world was far too wide and her ambition far too great.

It was during their train journey that Drummage first told her of his son by Sophie. Nothing could have been more indifferent than Candy's reception of this news. That Drummage had a half-white son was of no more importance to her than the nigger bastards with whom he had populated New Quarters. Let him talk on about Drum. She was already convinced that Drum, regardless of his color, would never interfere with her plans. Certainly she was not going to be bothered with a child who was lighter than she was, especially one with blond hair. While Drummage talked on of his plans for his son, Candy had already relegated the infant Drum to a life of obscurity at Falconhurst. There would be no place for a squalling brat in Washington and certainly not in her expanding life. But these things she wisely did not mention to Drummage. Plenty of time to manage that when she was in control, as she expected soon to be. Then Drummage would walk the tightrope! She knew she had the power to wind him around her little finger, and wind him she would.

She'd have that white Mrs. Allison and that uppity Miss Mary running in circles preparing her wedding. And this Chris, too, whom Drummage talked so much about. White men were no different from colored men! She'd bet this Chris had had a nigger wench sleeping with him all the time he was at Falconhurst. How was he going to explain that little business now that his white friends had come? Bah! Men were all alike! Regardless of the color of their skins, they only wanted one thing and she had always been able to supply it. Sometimes she wondered why it was so important to them. It wasn't to her. Of course she enjoyed it, but it was never the matter of supreme importance to her that it was to them. Except maybe with Drummage. She sure was a lucky girl to have Drummage! Other girls she had met in Mobile had one man to give them money and another man to spend it on. Drummage was the one man she would have been willing to spend her money on, but fortunately there was no need for that. He could supply her with everything—money, position, and excitement too.

She glanced up at him, admiring his good looks and congratulating herself on her achievement. Not only had she laid the foundations for her future but she had secured the one man she really wanted. Drummage was the only man who could satisfy her completely. Cupidon never had been able to. He was almost as good-looking and his lovemaking had been ardent, but it had never matched Drummage's. Neither had any of the others who had come and gone since Cupidon. Some of them had had money but none as much as Drummage, and certainly none of them had all the other attractions he possessed. She and Drummage were alike. The same blood coursed through their veins. Her own grandmother, Calinda, was his grandmother too. Of course, he was darker than she was because he was half Mandingo, but that made him easier to get along with. Mandingos were just big good-natured slobs, and when he did get mad, that was Calinda's Jaloff blood coming out in him. Fortunately he was more Mandingo than Jaloff. She'd never have any trouble with Drummage, never. She knew how to handle him. Just to test her power over him, she disengaged her hand from his and let it rest on his broadcloth-clad leg. She smiled to herself as she saw his reaction. Drummage would always be easy to handle. Ee-yah!

And he, on his part, was equally satisfied. Ever since the first day he had seen Candy, when she was scrubbing the banquette in New Orleans, he had never really wanted anyone else. Now she was to be his forever, or at least, she would be after tomorrow when they were married up, regular-like. No longer did they belong to Hammond Maxwell. No longer did they have to fear that at his whim of the moment one of them might be sold and they would be separated forever. No, they were their own masters now and nothing could ever separate them. Nothing but death! But Drummage could not envisage death as destroying his flesh.

It was hot and dirty in the train and the cinders coming in the open window blackened Drummage's shirt and smudged Candy's face until she was as dark as he was. The train halted for interminable stops at little stations where baggage was loaded and unloaded, and at each stop, at Candy's hysterical insistence, Drummage had to get off the train and make sure that none of her boxes were unloaded by mistake. At long last, as dusk was beginning to gather and lights in cabins and farmhouses showed through the lowering night, they approached Westminster and the end of their train journey.

When they arrived at the station, night had fallen. The stationmaster, with a swinging lantern, superintended the removal of the baggage, which Candy had to count over several times before she was certain that everything had arrived safely. Even when she was assured that nothing had been lost, she was loath to leave her boxes on the station platform, until Drummage secured the services of a colored boy who promised to watch over them while they went to secure a rig from the livery stable, and to get something to eat at the tavern, before starting the trip to Falconhurst.

However, neither of these things was as easy as Drummage had expected. Accustomed to the attention he had received both at the Allison house and from his position as a delegate to the Convention, he had forgotten that conditions in the small towns still remained practically the same as they had been before the war. Here a nigger was still a nigger—a unique species of animal. That a nigger was well-dressed and apparently had money made him even more obnoxious. Consequently, when Drummage and Candy, whose clothes were far more elaborate than any white woman in Westminster could possibly afford, appeared at the door of the livery stable, where there was the usual crowd of loungers and hangers-on, they were met with hostile stares and angry words.

"Ain' got no rig ter let ter no niggers. Not by a damn sight." The owner of the livery stable tilted back in his chair and spat out the straw he was chewing at Drummage's feet. "Ain' lettin' none o' my hosses out fer a goddam nigger ter drive. How I know I goin' ter get 'em back. Goddam thievin' niggers these days. Cain' trust a one o' the bastards. Too big fer their breeches, they is."

"Always was," another cackled, delighted at his own joke.

"Tha's all there ever was to a nigger anyway," a third added.

Drummage waited for them to finish and then spoke quietly and respectfully, as he had spoken when he was a slave.

"I'm Mista Drummage Maxwell o' Falconhurst Plantation. Hopin' yo've heard tell o' Falconhurst."

"Heard tell of it"—the man spat again—" 'n' heard tell o' the Maxwells too. But the Maxwells white—yo' a nigger. Say!" He let his chair fall forward and sat upright to peer at Drummage, scanning him carefully. "Yo' the nigger what married that Maxwell woman? Yo' the nigger what married a white woman?"

"I married Miz Sophie, yes."

"Then I be goddamned if I lettin' yo' take one o' my horses. Niggers goin' roun' marryin' white women! Cain' have that. Now, git goin', goddam yore black hide. Ain' havin' yo' nor yore black slut a-hangin' roun' here." He stood up and shook his fist at Drummage, and the rest of the men started muttering amongst themselves, but a voice from inside the livery stable called out:

"Hey, Lem, come in here a minute. Tell that nigger not to go. Knows him, I do."

Drummage looked up in surprise and peered into the darkness of the stable. He could not see the speaker, nor could he identify the voice, but, dimly silhouetted against the light of a lantern, he made out the figure of a tall man, slouch-hatted, with a turkey feather stuck in his hatband. The hat and feather seemed strangely familiar but for the moment he could not think who the wearer might be. It bothered him that he could not remember, but he forgot all about it when, a moment later, the owner of the stable came out, nodding his head and smiling. His affability was in such contrast to his belligerence of a moment before that Drummage instinctively distrusted him.

"Man in there a-sayin' that yo' probably a-goin' ter be

426

'lected congressman from this district come election day. He a-sayin' that we gotta treat yo' good if'n yo' goin' ter represent us in Washington. He say we kin trust yo', 'though I ain' much fer trustin' no nigger. Sayin' as how he useter know yo' 'n' yo' ain' no bad nigger. Tell yo' what I'm a-goin' ter do. Goin' ter let yo' have the rig but I'm a-goin' ter charge yo' double fer it 'n' if yo' kin pay it, yo' kin have it. Drive it over ter Benson tonight. Yo' must have some nigger what kin deliver it back tomorrow. Chargin' yo' twenty dollars though I am. 'N' no goddam wuthless 'federate money neither. Yo' got twenty dollars?"

Drummage didn't have, but he looked to Candy who, in her anxiety to save her finery, was willing to advance the funds. She opened her reticule and took out a roll of bills that caused the men to gasp. Carefully she peeled off two ten-dollar bills and handed them over to the proprietor.

"We'll come back fer the rig in half an hour." Drummage was surprised himself at the size of the roll Candy was carrying. "Got ter eat. Ain' had nothin' since mornin'. Goin' over to the tavern 'n' git us some supper. Then we come back 'n' git the rig if'n yo' kin have it harnessed up fer us."

"Kin," the man agreed, but he shook his head. "Ain' doin' yo' no good to go ter the tavern. Ol' George Spooner he ain' servin' no meals ter no niggers. Hates niggers, he do. Better yo' go down the road a piece till yo'gits ter John Lightfoot's. He a nigger 'n' his wench sometimes feeds niggers what passin' through. Will have the rig waitin' fer yo' when yo' comes back."

Lifting her skirts high to keep them from the dust, Candy followed Drummage along the road. Her anger had returned. The long trip, the hostile reception, and now the fact that she would have to eat in some Negro cabin had completely upset her. While she trudged along she berated Drummage, but he, tired also, was too near home to pay much attention to her. He'd be in Falconhurst soon and that was all that mattered. How he wanted to be there! To hell with Washington! He'd never leave Falconhurst again. He'd even be glad to see poor harelipped Marguerite. It would be good to have Valentine attend him again and he wanted Onan to bring him a hot toddy. He wondered if Pamela had changed and where she was sleeping now that the Allisons were there. He'd give anything he possessed if he could only see Lucretia Borgia bustling around the kitchen. Oh, he was almost there —almost to Falconhurst, and he couldn't get there quickly enough. Big Pearl and Zanzibar would be waiting for him.

427

All the folks at New Quarters would be there to welcome him and he wanted to see them all. The unfriendly atmosphere in Westminster had frightened him and he wished now that he had written for Chris to meet him. It would be almost like being at home to see the Falconhurst barouche waiting for him. But he'd be home soon and that was all that mattered.

"Guess they knows who I am here," he boasted to Candy, in an attempt to quiet her with his own importance. "They knows I'se a pretty 'portant man now. They knows they'd better treat me good. Guess yo' kin see that."

"Yo' ain' good 'nuff ter get a decent meal at the tavern," she railed. "Got to go a-traipsin' off ter some nigger cabin ter eat. Tha's how 'portant yo' are, Mista Drummage Maxwell o' Falconhurst. Yo' may think yo' 'portant but yo' jes' a chickenshit nigger here, tha's all. Should've stayed in Mobile. Wishin' I was back there now." Suddenly her anger evaporated and she clutched his arm for support, fright quavering in her throat. "Oh, Drummage, I'se scairt, plum' scairt. Le's get outa here. Le's go back ter Mobile. Le's go to N'Orleans. Le's go where they's civilized 'n' treat us good."

"Now what yo' scairt of? Man promised us a horse, didn' he? 'Sides, 'druther eat at Lightfoot's 'n that ol' tavern. Masta Hammond he say it not fit place ter eat. 'Sides, I know Lightfoot. He's in de Union League here in Westminster. 'Druther go there anyway."

"Dirty, stinkin' niggers!" Candy was disdainful.

"Yo' a nigger 'n' yo' ain' dirty 'n' yo' don' stink. Come on, I'se hungry."

They found the Lightfoot cabin, down along a weed-grown lane which led from the main road. Although the place itself was little more than a hovel it was clean inside, and Lightfoot's woman fried ham and eggs, which she served on scrubbed and shiny tin plates. Candy stuck up her nose and toyed daintily with the food, but Drummage did hearty justice to the meal. It tasted good—like Falconhurst food with a salty tang to the ham and the good ham flavor saturated into the eggs. Once again he realized how glad he would be to get back home and taste Marguerite's food, which was so like Lucretia Borgia's. When Candy got to Falconhurst, she'd get over her highfalutin airs. Falconhurst was far better than anything she had ever had in Mobile.

After the meal, Lightfoot agreed to go back with them to get the horse and then go over to the station platform to help load Candy's boxes. The livery stable man had harnessed a decrepit roan sway-back to a light spring wagon. The horse looked hardly capable of making the trip, but Drummage did not care as long as he could get on the road. He'd wasted two hours now and had a long drive ahead of him. They departed with admonitions by the proprietor to be sure and return the rig the next day.

"If'n this ol' nag kin make it," Drummage said. "Look as though he a-goin' ter die on the way."

"Tha's a val'able critter." The livery man bristled. "Yo' hurt that horse, yo' a-goin' ter pay fer it."

"Already paid fer it," Drummage answered. "Twenty dollars buy a dozen ol' dog-meats like this'n." He lowered his voice. "Ain' argufyin', mista. Ain' wantin' ter do nothin' but git started. Got me a long way ter go tonight." He helped Candy up onto the seat and then jumped up beside her. Lightfoot climbed up on back. Drummage picked up the reins and clucked to the horse but the proprietor put his hand on the bridle.

"Jes' wan' ter ask one question, nigger," he said, leering up at Drummage. "That white woman what married up wid yo'? She do it 'cause she wanted ter o' 'cause yo' a-makin' her?"

It was on the tip of Drummage's tongue to tell the man to to to hell, but he choked back the retort. Diplomacy was the best policy. Lick the man's boots if he had to—just get started towards home.

"If'n yo' knows the Maxwell family, Mista," he said, smiling to make a joke of it and not offend the man, "yo' know that nobody ain' makin' a Maxwell do anythin' they don' wan' ter do. Miz Sophie married up wid me 'cause she wanted to." To corroborate his statement, he pointed to his ears, where the diamonds glistened in the dim light of the livery man's lanterns. "Gave me these she did fer a weddin' present."

The man released the bridle and sidled along the shafts, stepping in around the wheel and coming up close to the side of the wagon where Candy was sitting. His hand reached out, clutched at her ankle, and then slid up under her skirts.

"Goddam pretty wench yo' got there, nigger. Ain' never laid a nigger wench what had on silk stockin's. Got a mind ter take her in the stable for a spell 'fore yo' leaves. Nice soft hay in there." His hand slid further. "How about it, gal?"

Drummage reached for the broken whip in the whipstock and lashed the horse. With more agility than he would have credited the ancient animal with it reared up and bolted, giving the livery man just time to get out from between the

429

wheels. With Lightfoot waving to them, they caromed down the rutty street to the accompaniment of the livery man's oaths.

Chapter 49

ABOUT AN HOUR after Drummage and Candy left Westminster, the moon, which had been partially hidden behind a scudding mass of clouds, emerged to light the road with pale silver. Patches of sky, brightly pin-pricked with stars, appeared where the clouds had raced. The one burst of energy which the horse had made back in Westminster had apparently been his best effort, for now he plodded along at a snail's pace. The scuffling of the beast's feet in the dust, the montonous creak of an ungreased axle, and the soft warmth of the night lulled Drummage and Candy into a state of lethargy, somewhere between waking and sleeping.

Candy lay curled up on the seat, her head in Drummage's lap, while he, stretching out his long legs as far as the dashboard permitted, nodded his head in cadence with the jolting of the wagon. Neither spoke, although when Drummage passed the spot where long ago Nero had been hung for the murder of Regine and Benoni, he shuddered as if cold fingers had touched his spine. He could still see the twisted bodies of Regine and Benoni on the ground and the swaying form of Nero on the end of the rope. Faintly, across the fields, he saw the light from the Getty farmhouse and wondered if they knew that their Jubal had crossed the ocean to England.

If it had been daytime, he would have been tempted to stop and tell them the news. Even now he wanted to drive to the door of the farmhouse and ask permission to spend the night in their barn. But no, Candy would be mad. Imagine her sleeping in the hay! Yet it would be better than this seemingly endless night with its slow inching toward Falconhurst. Ah well, things would look better in the morning. What a fool he had been not to write to Chris! They could have been speeding along the road now, comfortable in the big old barouche with the black team trotting the miles away.

He lifted Candy's head with one hand and eased it into a more comfortable position on his thigh. She turned slightly to look up at him.

"Whar we now, Drummage? We mos' home?"

"Long ways yit, Candy baby. Why'n yo' go ter sleep? Yo' 'member Jubal? That his home over there." He pointed to the light across the fields.

"He that black boy what was wid yo' in N'Orleans when yore ol' Masta Hammond bought me?"

"Uh-huh! Jubal he a right nice boy but kinda funny-like. Went off ter England wid Miz Sophie's kids. Wonder what he a-doin' now. Pleasure me ter see him 'gain, it would. Masta Hammond shore tried ter git a sucker outa Jubal but never did. That boy he jes' plain scairt o' women. He go limp's a rag when he get on one. Masta Hammond always a-sayin' he a-goin' ter sell Jubal 'cause he ain' got no sap in him, but li'l Masta Warren he take on somethin' awful. He right 'tached to Jubal, that li'l Masta Warren, so Jubal he don' never git sold though he never made a single sucker."

"Never did like that boy." Candy snuggled her head on Drummage's leg. "He not natcherl."

"Reason yo' never liked him 'cause he didn' like yo'. Tha's why." Drummage yawned. "But yo' sure liked that Kewp boy what come wid 'Pollon. Yo' know somethin', Candy? That 'Pollon he a nigger too."

"Knowed it. Kewp tol' me."

"Yo' loved that Kewp, Candy?"

She shook her head and he could feel its negation through the broadcloth of his trousers. "Jes' wanted ter git 'way from Falconhurst, tha's all. Sick o' stayin' there then. Wanted ter git back ter N'Orleans 'n' 'Pollon 'n' Kewp a-goin' ter take me. Like dat 'Pollon better 'n Kewp. He sure a handsome man." Her hand caressed Drummage's leg. "But he not so well-set-up's yo', Drummage." She echoed Drummage's yawn. "Thinkin' I go to sleep. Yo' wakes me up when we gits ter Falconhurst."

He was almost asleep himself. The reins fell slack in his hand, his eyes closed, and he dozed, while the horse, one slow step after another, leisurely plodded along the silver strip of road which led to Falconhurst.

Drummage's thoughts were a strange jumble. Nero and the dead Regine and Benoni. Nero hanging from a rope and now buried in the sandbank by the river. Benoni with his pretty face and his head of dark curls. Jubal with his shyness and his adoration of Drummage. Apollon and Kewp and the sleeping Candy beside him. Masta Hammond and Miz 'Gusta and then Sophie and the mustee baby back at Falconhurst. Big Pearl, his mama, and the bleached skull of Mede on her mantelpiece. Big Olly with his tender hands. And now Chris —good, solid, dependable Chris, and Miz Allison and Mary. Brute and Big Randy and Sampson and old Lucretia Borgia. But he would be home soon and Valentine would be running down the steps to meet him, with Onan standing before the open door on the portico.

Falconhurst! So many things had happened there, and he enjoyed remembering them—like the day they had returned from New Orleans and Lucretia Borgia had trapped the abolitionist and how proud he had felt to ride to Benson for Masta Hammond. He'd stopped at the Johnstone farm. Little he thought he'd ever own it. The Johnstone farm! Good God! Now he knew the tall figure with the slouch hat and the turkey feather. Leazer Johnstone!

Yes, that was Leazer Johnstone back there in the livery stable in Westminster. Drumson sat upright, pitching Candy forward and waking her. She clung to the seat to keep from falling off and stared at him with sleepy stupor as he reached for the whip and tried to increase the slow plodding of the horse. His repeated lashings finally spurred the beast into a loping canter, which gave promise of halting each time he let up on the whip. Leazer Johnstone! The name beat against Drummage's eardrums as though it were being shouted into them. Leazer Johnstone! He was a big man in the Klan these days. That much Drummage knew, and he also knew that Leazer Johnstone hated him more than ever since he had bought the farm.

They crossed the big bridge over the Tombigbee, the hoof beats of the horse making a resounding tattoo on the loose planking. Once they were on the other side of the river Drummage breathed easier. They were halfway to Falconhurst. Halfway! He relaxed in his seat until he rounded the first bend in the road.

And then he saw them!

They were waiting for him. They were waiting, silent and motionless, sitting astride their hooded horses—three of them, in white, red, and sable robes. They were three abreast, effectively blocking the road, and even as Drummage stopped the horse, grabbed Candy's hand, and started to jump, he realized it was useless. A number of white-robed riders, their robes ghostly-pale in the moonlight, appeared from the shadows of the trees and rode alongside the wagon. Slowly, the horse walking again, Drummage approached the grim trio until the horse stopped of its own accord.

The black holes cut in the colored hoods stared straight

at him. Candy screamed—one high-pitched shriek—and sought the security of Drummage's arms. But he had no strength to protect her though she clung to him, sobbing. The riders beside the wagon rode closed in until their horses brushed the wheels and Drummage could hear the restless champing of the horses' bits and the creak of leather in the saddles. One of the three riders confronting him advanced his horse a step.

"Are you the nigger Drummage?" The voice issuing from the folds of the hood sounded sepulchral. "Answer me, are you the nigger Drummage what useter live at Falconhurst Plantation?"

"Still live there," Drummage managed to stutter.

"Answer the question." There was an edge of anger in the voice. "Are you the nigger Drummage?"

"I'se Drummage."

The hooded figure slowly nodded and the second of the three horsemen—he of the black robe—got down from his horse, took the few steps necessary to bring him to the wagon, and climbed up on the seat, pushing Drummage over and taking the reins from his limp fingers. "Git down on the floor, niggers," he commanded, "yo' all cain' sit 'side o' a white man."

Quietly the two remaining horsemen turned their mounts, leading the third horse. The man on the wagon seat slapped the reins down on the nag's back and the wagon started. Now Drummage could see that the sides of the road were lined with robed figures on horseback, who joined the slow procession two by two, bringing up the rear.

"Whar yo' a-takin' us?" Drummage, crouched on the floor beside the seat with Candy, clawed at the knee of the black-robed man.

"None o' yore goddam business, nigger." The driver brushed Drummage's hand aside. "Yo' ain' askin' no questions now 'n' yo' ain' gittin' no answers neither. Open yore trap again 'n' yo'll feel my fist in yore face."

Drummage knew better than to speak again. They proceeded in ominous silence about a quarter of a mile up the road and then turned off the main road onto a side lane—a mere rutted path across the fields. He recognized the black silhouette of the ramshackle building that emerged from a sparse clump of pines. Before the war they had occasionally brought cotton here for ginning and baling. It was about ten or twelve miles from Falconhurst and, although Hammond Maxwell had always preferred to use the nearer gin in Benson, they occasionally sent a wagonload of cotton here. Drum-mage remembered riding over once with Hammond to arrange for the ginning of some cotton.

"Whaffor they a-takin' us here?" Candy whispered. "They a-goin' ter kill us?"

"Course they ain'." Drummage tried to sound reassuring but he was too terrified himself to inspire Candy with much confidence. "Guess they just wantin' ter scare us a little."

They neared the gin and now Drummage could see other figures gathered there and the dark shadows of horses hitched under the trees. These white-robed men were as silent as the rest. When the wagon halted, several of the men came over and reached up to get hold of Drummage. He struggled, his strength gaining him a momentary victory, and as he lashed out with arms and legs he had the satisfaction of hearing a yelp of pain when his boot caught one of the hooded figures in the head. But his struggles gained him nothing more than a string of curses from the injured man. Strong arms pinioned him from behind and other strong arms lifted him from the wagon and carried him away. Others took Candy and bore her, kicking and screaming, beside him. They were both half carried and half pushed to the dark wall of the gin. There was a sputtering of matches and tinderboxes and a lighting of lanterns, until the yellow light of candles and oil flames dispelled the silver of the moon. Behind a plank that served as a table, supported by sawhorses, the three robed and hooded figures sat silently—white robe, black robe, and red robe. The white one, in the center, spoke first, asking the same question that was asked on the road.

"Yo' the nigger Drummage from Falconhurst?"

Drummage could only nod. He had lost the power of speech.

"Answer me!"

His tongue dry against the roof of his mouth, he mumbled the one word, "Yes."

"Who that wench wid yo'?"

Drummage swallowed hard and managed to speak.

"She's Candy. I'm a-goin' ter marry her come tomorrow."

"Niggers don' marry," Red Robe said.

"You are here to answer charges against yo'." Black Robe was speaking now.

"What I done?" Drummage asked. "Ain' done nothin' ter hurt nobody. I'se a citizen o' de United States. I'se got rights, I has. Ain' aimin' ter harm nobody 'n' ain' aimin' ter have nobody harm me."

White Robe disregarded him.

"Didn' yo' git a warnin' from the Ku Klux Klan ter git outa this part o' the country?"

"Got a letter thrown inter my house the night they burned my cotton."

"Then why didn' yo' go 'n' stay away?"

"Falconhurst my home. Lived there all my life. Ain' aimin' ter leave it."

"Yo' 'member what that letter said?" Black Robe questioned.

"Lot of stuff I didn' know much 'bout."

"What's a barrow?"

"Barrow's a pig what been nutted."

Red Robe pointed to Drummage. "Needs us a black barrow."

"What's a wether?" Black Robe asked.

"Wether's like a barrow, 'cept it's a ram."

"We needs us a black wether." Black Robe pointed to Drummage.

"Yo' a-goin'. . . . ?" The very enormity of the thought that entered Drummage's mind caused his knees to buckle under him. He sank to the ground, his arms outstretched, but the three at the table remained impassive. Strong arms under his armpits lifted him up and supported his sagging knees.

"Did yo' force a white woman ter marry up wid yo'?"

"Didn' force Miz Sophie. She a-wantin' ter marry up wid me."

"Did you steal the farm of one of your neighbors?"

"Bought the Johnstone farm from the bank in Benson, I did. Paid money fer it I did."

"Less 'n ten cents on the dollar." Black Robe crashed his fist against the plank.

"Did yo' conspire wid the Union League to rob, pillage and plunder the rightful inhabitants of this land?"

"Ain' wanted ter rob nobody. Jes' minded my own business. Ain' got nothin' 'gainst no white folks. Never had. Mista Hammond Maxwell, he always say I'm a good boy. My papa, Drumson, he die ter save Masta Hammond. Masta Hammond he buried my papa in the white folks' buryin' groun'."

"Hammond Maxwell al'ays did spoil his niggers. Makin' out they 'most human. No wonder they got ideas like this bastard here." Red Robe turned to White Robe. "High time we taught this nigger a lesson. Time we put the fear o' God inter his goddam black heart. Teach all the rest of the

435

niggers that they ain' white folks. Come on now, what do yo' all say."

"Kill the nigger!" The voices joined as one.

"Gotta take a vote on it." White Robe held up his hand to stop the angry mutterings. "Got ter do all this legal-like. Klan stands fer law 'n' order in the South. This nigger cain' say we didn' warn him. Tol' him ter git outa town. Tol' him ter git the hell away from here. 'N' what did he do? Hikes his black ass down ter Mobile a-tryin' ter raise rebellion 'mongst the niggers. Tryin' ter git schools fer niggers; tryin' ter pass laws that niggers kin marry up wid white folks; tryin' ter git the niggers ter votin'. Gittin' himself sent up ter Washington fer a congressman. Organizin' Union Leagues. Raisin' hell wherever he goes."

" 'N' now he come back here, draggin' his black fancy wench wid him." Black Robe shook his fist at Drummage. "Say he a-goin' ter marry up wid her. Say he a-goin' ter sashay roun' like Lord McGull. Takin' the Johnstone farm fer his own. Time come he a-goin' ter come round a-buyin' yore farms. Time come he goin' ter pay yo' ten cents on the dollar fer 'em. Time come he a-goin' ter come up to yo' men 'n' say, 'Yo' better h'ist yore ass over ter Falconhurst 'n' pick my cotton. My niggers gettin' tired o' pickin cotton.' That what yo' men a-wantin'? Well, that what yo'all a-goin' to git if'n we don' teach these nigger bastards a lesson. We a-goin' ter let the goddam niggers git away with it?"

There was a screaming, furious chorus of "no."

"Then we all a-goin' ter vote on it. Each man walk up here 'n' cast his vote. Majority vote rule. Head Goblin—write down the yeas; Head Cyclops write down the nays. Grand Kleagle he count the votes." Red Robe sat down and White Robe and Black Robe followed him.

A straggling line of hooded and sheeted men—all except those who held Drummage and Candy pinioned—formed at the right of the plank table and one by one they passed by it. Invariably they passed by Black Robe and stopped before Red Robe, calling out their "yeas" in a loud voice. Not a single one halted at Black Robe and said his "nay." When they had finished, White Robe stood up and pointed his finger to the men holding Drummage and Candy. "Yo' all ain' voted. What say yo' all?" To a man they answered, "Yea."

White Robe waited for the clamor to die down, and came out from behind the table to stand before Drummage.

"Yo' jes' bin tried, legal-like, nigger, 'n' the votin's

436

unanimous that yo' die. Yo' got anythin' ter say fer yo'se'f 'fore yo' dies?"

Drummage recognized the voice of the man talking to him. He had been trying to place it, and now he realized it was that of Lewis Gasaway, Hammond's old friend. How many times had he heard that voice at Falconhurst? How many toddies had he mixed and carried on a silver tray to this man? How many times had he held the stirrup for him to mount his horse?

"Whaffor yo' a-wantin' ter kill me, Mista Gasaway?" Drummage found it difficult to form the words between his sobbings. "Ain' never done nothin' ter harm yo'. Never have. Yo' a frien' o' my Masta Hammond's. Yo' know Masta Hammond al'ays say I a good boy. Masta Hammond never sell me. He say ain' 'nuff money in Alabama ter buy me. Right fond o' me, Masta Hammond was. Oh, Mista Gasaway, don' kill me, don'!"

"Goin' ter kill yo' anyway. Hammond Maxwell'd killed yo' jes' like he killed that Mede nigger years ago if'n he'd known yo'd been actin' up with his daughter. Fond o' that Mede nigger too but he killed him jes' the same. If'n he here tonight, he vote ter kill yo' too. Yes, yo' gotta die, Drummage, but I'm sorry fer yo', I am." White Robe walked back to his place behind the table. "Yo' useter be a good nigger onct. Spoiled now, 'though." Lewis Gasaway turned to the assembled white robes. His voice had an edge of sadness as he looked long and searchingly at Drummage.

"This here nigger has been given a fair 'n' legal trial at a duly convocated meetin' o' the Ku Klux Klan. Yo' all assembled Klansmen have 'spressed yore verdict. The nigger has got ter die. But I'm a-goin' ter leave yo'. Up ter yo' all ter finish off the job." He walked a few steps into the shadows toward a horse that was tethered to a sapling. Whipping his white robe up over his head, he mounted his horse and cantered off without looking back.

There was a moment of silence while he rode off; then came a bustle of activity.

"What the hell we a-botherin' with these goddam nightdresses fer?" Red Robe whipped off his scarlet sheets and revealed himself as Leazer Johnstone. Black Robe slipped out of his and appeared as the minister from Benson—the same who had married Sophie and Apollon.

"Come on, boys," Leazer shouted, "there's a-goin' ter be one less nigger tonight, so le's have some fun with the fuggin' bastard." He advanced around the table to stand in front of

437

Drummage, who was still being held. Johnston's hand whipped up to Drummage's face and Drummage tensed, expecting the slap that never came. Instead Johnstone's fingers reached for the lobe of one of his ears, grabbed at the flashing stone, and yanked hard. Drummage screamed as he felt the thin gold shaft tearing through his flesh. Then the same hand, clutching the diamond in its bit of bloody flesh, reached to Drummage's other ear and pulled the stud, along with the ear lobe. Leazer held up the two gems.

"Got what I wants, boys. Yo' all kin help yo'se'ves to the rest. Damn fine clothes this nigger buck's a-wearin'. Go ahead 'n' he'p yo'se'ves."

" 'N' he got more in the wagon," a voice from the perimeter of the crowd called. " 'N' that wench o' his too. Goddam pretty dress she a-wearin'."

"Goddam pretty wench too." Leazer wiped the earbobs clean of shreds of flesh and slipped them in his pocket, scrubbing the blood from his hands on his trousers, "Feelin' like a bit o' nigger tail myself. Thinkin' mayhap we takes them pretty clothes off'n her and pleasure ourselves a little while we lets this son of a bitch look on 'n' see how white folks does their pleasurin'. Better tie him up fust. Cain' have him rampagin' roun'."

"We ain' a-goin' ter tie this one." The Reverend Hazzard had a fanatical light in his eyes. "The Jews done crucified our own sweet Jesus 'n' he innercent. Thought we a-goin' ter crucify this un. Thought we a-goin' ter nail him."

Through the stinging pain in his ears, Drummage heard the words. His knowledge of religion was rudimentary, but he had seen pictures of the crucified Jesus and had marveled at the nails in the hands and feet. Was that what they were going to do to him? Could it be? Oh no!

Abjectly he crawled on his knees, pulling the men who were holding him towards the Reverend Hazzard. "Whaffor yo' a-wantin' ter kill me, Mista Minister Man? What I ever done to yo'? Let me go, Mista Minister Man. Let me go 'n' I take Candy 'n' git out. Yo' all kin have the things in the wagon. We go away from here 'n' never come back. Jes' let us go." He glanced at Candy, crumpled on the gound and wailing beside him. "If'n yo' wants her, take her 'n' let me go. Don' care jes' so yo' lets me leave. Please, Mista Minister Man. Please let me go. Oh, let me go."

"Don' leave me, Drummage! Don' leave me here wid these men." Candy was struggling to reach him.

"He ain' a-goin' nowhere, 'cept maybe ter hell." The Reverend Hazzard was dancing in his excitement. "He a sinner! He a black sinner wid a black soul 'n' he got ter pay fer his black sins. He bin a-settin' hisself up like a white man 'n' that a sin. Bible say that the whole tribe o' Ham cursed. Ain' fittin' fer no cursed black nigger ter set hisself up like a white man, fornicatin' wid white women, dressin' hisself up in white man's clothes, makin' hisself better 'n a white man. Goes 'gainst the Bible it do 'n' that's a sin. Bible say that black men gotta be slaves to white men 'n' what the Bible say is true." He pointed down to the huddled figures of Drummage and Candy on the ground before him. "Brethren o' the Klan," he shouted, "we got ourselves a sacred duty ter do tonight 'n' we a-goin' ter crucify this yere black nigger. We a-goin' ter nail him on the cross. We a-goin' ter light that cross so it blaze in the sky. We a-goin' ter burn the fiery cross tonight, but tonight it goin' ter have a nigger nailed on it. We a-goin' to put the fear o' God in the hearts o' these black niggers. What yo' say, brethren?"

"Nail him up."

"He make a good fire, that one."

"Well, le's git started. We got any spikes?"

"Got 'em."

"Got us a sledge hammer?"

"Got it."

"Then le's git started."

" 'N' we a-goin' ter pleasure ourselves wid his wench too." Leazer Johnstone made a grab for Candy and pulled her, sobbing, screaming, and struggling, towards him. "Ain' had me no black pleasurin' fer a week. When I gits through, yo' all kin have her. All yo' what wantin' some black tail, jes' line up 'hind me."

"Git him on de cross fust." The Reverend Hazzard was insistent. "Let 'em hold onto her so's she won't run. Plenty o' time fer her when we finishes wid him. Strip them clothes off'n him. They took the clothes from our sweet Jesus 'n' they cast lots fer them. Strip them fine clothes from this nigger 'n' yo' kin parcel 'em out."

Willing hands grabbed for Drummage and lifted him. He felt his boots being pulled off and he could see that Leazer Johnstone had seized Candy and was carrying out his threat on her. A man was holding up Drummage's boots.

"Who want to wear a nigger's boots. Store-made ones they are 'n' mighty fine."

"Been wantin' me a pair o' store boots all my life 'n' don'

439

care if'n they is nigger's boots. Pass 'em over." Gnarled red hands reached up for them.

" 'N' here's the fugger's coat. Fine coat, made outa broadcloth. He a big fellow. Seemin' that coat 'bout fit yo', Rafe." Drummage's coat was thrown to a big lout, who clutched it out of the air.

"Thinkin' I like them pants he got on." A red-bearded man ripped the buttons from the waistband and pulled them off Drummage. "Smell kinda niggery but sight better 'n these I got. Well, look at that! The son of a bitch's a-wearin' drawers. 'Magine that! Goddam nigger wid drawers on. Who a-wantin' 'em?"

"I'll take 'em home fer my old woman. She ain' never had no drawers in her life, 'cept those made outa sackin'."

" 'N' here's his shirt. Right fine one too. 'N' here's his neckerchief. Real black satin. 'Pears ter me the Reverend ought ter have these. He the only man what wear a white shirt. Kin wear it nex' Sunday while he a-preachin' 'n' a-tellin' the folks how we sent this goddam nigger ter hell."

The hands that had lifted Drummage while they stripped him of his clothes released him, and he sank to the ground again, too weak to stand, too terrified to speak, too convinced of the uselessness of pleading to sue for mercy. Fear had numbed his senses, and the awful unreality of his plight seemed to fill his thoughts so completely that he felt his head would burst. All this could not be happening to him! Masta Hammond would not allow it! Miz 'Gusta would not let it! Chris would not permit it! He heard himself screaming and yet the screams sounded so far off, so unreal, that he could not believe it was himself. And now he heard Candy's screams mingled with his own and he saw Leazer Johnstone reappear, adjusting his trousers and pulling his wide leather belt tight in the buckle. But what happened to Candy now was unimportant in comparison with the enormity of what he knew was going to happen to him. Instinctively his hand felt around his neck for the silver talisman that had always hung there. It was gone! And as a temporary wave of oblivion blotted out his thoughts, he knew that nothing could ever save him now.

The mercy of his escape from reality lasted only a moment. He returned to the awful present and felt himself being lifted by many hands. There was no use to struggle, and his body became limp while it was carried on the shoulders of the men to a crudely formed cross, nailed together from the beams of the old gin. He felt them lower him to it, sensed the roughness of the wood along his back; they were holding his arms outstretched, and he felt the iron grip on his wrists.

But he was not prepared for the piercing pain when the spike was driven through his palm. Once again he was screaming and he heard his screams echoed by the mocking laughs of the crowd. He tried to move his impaled hand but the pain was intense and the movement tore at his flesh, so he did not try again. And now they were on the other side of him, and before he had had time to recover from the first shock he felt a stab of pain in the other hand and heard the ring of the hammer on the metal as the spike cleaved the bones and sinews of his other palm. Now he was screaming wildly, begging for mercy, and even through the shrieking intensity of his yells he heard the muttered prayers of the Reverend Hazzard, condemning his soul to hell.

The group of men moved from his hand to his feet, pressing one foot flat above the other, and the pain ripped through both feet. The blows of the heavy hammer did not always hit the head of the spike, but smashed against his toes, cracked his insteps, and broke his ankle bones, pounding his feet into masses of bloody flesh.

The tumult passed and suddenly he was alone. The hands that pressed down on him were gone, and slowly the timbered cross moved upwards, pushed by a score of willing hands, and as it rose he felt the strain on his hands, and his whole weight sagged from the cruel nails. Waves of unconsciousness passed over him, deadening for a moment the torture, which then flooded back on him in surges of torment. Through his eyes, as through a clouded glass, he could see what was happening below him, and his mind cringed from the evidences of further torture as he saw the men piling green pitchpine boughs around the base of the cross. The pain in his hands and feet was excruciating but, bad as it was, he feared the flames even more. He realized that he had stopped screaming and that the shrieks he heard were no longer his own. In the brightness of lantern light at his feet, he could see Candy's outstretched limbs and the bestial plunging of the men who possessed her one after the other. He was able to hear their ribald shouts, mingled with the taunts of his own tormentors as they piled the branches that were to be his pyre.

Leazer Johnstone stood near Drummage's feet, so close that if Drummage had been able to move his foot he could have touched Leazer's chest. A grinning man came up to

Leazer and handed him a knife. While Leazer was testing the edge of the blade by slicing the pine needles, the man spoke, pointing up to Drummage.

"Thought yo' a-sayin' we a-goin' ter have a black wether tonight. Thought yo' a-sayin' we a-goin' ter have a black barrow. Ain' yo' a-goin' ter nut him 'fore yo' burns him?"

"Aimin' ter." Leazer looked up at Drummage's tormented body. "Jes' waitin' fer them boys what hasn't had the wench yet. They a-wantin' ter see it but they too int'rested in her now. What's yore hurry? We got all night."

"That nigger hung awful heavy, ain' he though?"

"Won' be when I gits through wid him."

"Bet yo' a-wishin' yo' had one like that, Leazer."

"Got better. Mine's white. 'Sides no white man a-wantin' nothin' like that. All niggers like that—tha's why they jes' animals, like a bull or a stallion. Men—white men—ain' like that, thank God."

"Still, I kinda like ter be. Bet my old woman like it." He reached up and touched Drummage. "Come on, Leazer, le's see yo' do it."

"Jes' might." Leazer laughed and reached up with the knife. "Jes' might take a slice now. Not 'nuff to spoil it fer the others, but jes' a little."

And then it happened!

Drummage heard the sharp explosion of the gun, cutting through the brawling shouts and simultaneously with it he felt the impact in his chest. It was more powerful than the blows of the sledge hammer on his feet. For one fleeting moment, he wondered what new torture this might be, for the pain was far more excruciating than anything he had suffered before. It was unbearable. He could stand it no longer and mercifully he did not have to, for a black curtain of oblivion descended, blotting out pain, canceling all consciousness. His body, its tensions relaxed in death, slumped down, its weight tearing one hand free from the spike, and then the additional weight of his unsupported body tore the other hand loose and his body pitched forward, tearing the pitifully crushed feet from the spikes, and plunged head first to the ground.

With something of awe, the men looked down at Drummage's dead body, and even those who were standing in line, awaiting their turn at Candy, turned from their slavering contemplation of her writhing limbs and faced the now empty cross.

"Who done that?" Leazer Johnstone bellowed, the glinting

blade still in his hands. "What son of a bitch shot this nigger daid?"

A figure emerged from the darkness, a long-barreled squirrel rifle in his hand.

"I did."

Leazer dropped the knife and strode belligerently towards the man, pushing aside those who were standing between them.

"What yo' wantin' to do that fer, Lewis Gasaway?" He shook his fist in Gasaway's face. "Yo' said we could have our fun. Yo' said we could do jes' as we wanted with this nigger. We were a-goin' ter geld him 'fore we burned him anyway. Now yo' up 'n' shot him. Thought we was goin' ter make a 'zample outa him. How 'n hell kin we make a 'zample out o' a dead nigger?"

"We already have." Lewis Gasaway spoke slowly, sickened by the lust and brutality in the eyes of the men around him. "He's dead, ain' he? Ain' that 'nuff?" His eyes regarded Drummage's body on the ground, then came to rest on Candy's body, where the grass had been ploughed into red dust by the boots of the men. Briefly he indicated her. " 'N' she's daid too?"

"Yeah, she's daid." A burly young giant prodded her body with the toe of his boot. " 'N' it were my turn next, damn her. She up 'n' died under Enoch."

Lewis Gasaway ignored him, his eyes searching the crowd of men until he had located the particular men he desired. One by one he called to them.

"Ethan Bellingham! Floyd Colton! Zach Grandin! Herb Atherton! Yo' all come over here with me. Yo' don' belong here no more 'n I do. We're decent men. What we a-doin' here? I joined up with the Klan like yo' all 'cause I thought it would help us; 'cause I thought it would save the whites. I thought we could settle matters round here with the Klan. I wan't 'gainst killin' Drummage ter set an example fer the other niggers, that they don' get too biggity 'n' marry up wid white women, 'n' own property, 'n' git 'lected ter Congress. Gave my permission, I did, that Drummage be killed. But never said he was ter be tortured. Cain' see no animal tortured be it dog, horse, nor nigger. Had an idea these men a-goin' ter torture him so's I left 'n' rode away but I sickened 'n' had ter come back. Cain' see no animal git tortured. Drummage's dead. If'n he had a soul, I'd say God rest his soul but he nothin' but an animal 'n' he ain' got no soul 'cause he's a nigger. I'm glad he's daid—it was a rightful thing. But torturin' him weren't. What yo' say, Ethan? Yo' a-goin' ter stay j'ined up with a bunch o' men what tortures animals?"

"Don' like it myself, Lewis. 'Most puked I did, seein' what they was a-goin' ter do to that nigger. I'm a-gittin' out too."

" 'N' I'm a-goin' wid yo' too, Lewis. We Coltons never lashed a horse; never beat a dog. Horse break his laig, we shoot him ter put him outa his misery. Dog git old, we shoot him so's he don' suffer. Cain' stand makin' no beast suffer 'n' a nigger's nearer human 'n a dog."

"Klan started out ter be a good thing," Lewis Gasaway said, "but now it nothin' but a bunch of hoodlums. We useter be decent folk. Some of us still are 'n' we don' hold with such goin's-on. I'm a-gittin' outa the Klan. Who's a-comin' with me?"

Grandin and Atherton walked over to stand beside Gasaway, and one by one others detached themselves from the crowd and joined them. Silently they turned and walked to where their horses were hitched, mounted them, and rode away. Those remaining were silent, shamefaced like little boys caught in a dirty act. Even Leazer Johnstone lost his bellicosity and, mounting his horse, rode off into the night. The last lantern was extinguished, the last hoofbeat sounded on the rutted road, and where there had been shouting and brawling, all was quiet. Where there had been the flickering flames of lantern light, there was nothing now but the serene moonlight which silvered the ground, highlighting with its cold radiance the bodies of Drummage and Candy.

Epilogue

ALL THE LIGHTS were out in the big house at Falconhurst except one which remained in the upstairs room where the baby Drum slept. Then that too was extinguished. The big house was dark; the barns were dark; the slave cabins were dark. Falconhurst slept and Drummage, too, slept, just as he had planned, alongside Candy, but not where he had planned, alongside his father.

The moon, which had witnessed Drummage's agony of the night before, had not risen, and there was nothing to relieve the over-all blackness except one tiny light which bobbed along the path that led from the new house to where the old house had stood.

Zanzibar, who was carrying the tin lantern, walked slowly, and Big Pearl followed him, moaning and sobbing. She carried a bundle wrapped in cloth in her arms, and she cradled it as though it were a child. At the little arched bridge, Zanzibar stopped and waited for her to catch up with him, then preceded her across the bridge and up the slope on the other side to where the stones of the burying ground made a white blur in the blackness. Pearl had some difficulty in getting over the wall, and Zanzibar had to set his lantern down on the ground to help her. Once inside she indicated, by the feeble rays of the lantern, a spot midway between the marble shaft that marked Drumson's grave and the raw red earth that marked Drummage's.

"Dig here, Zan." She pointed to the ground. "A-goin' ter burry this Mede boy right here. Time he got buried afta all these years. They all dead 'n' buried now, Zan. Fittin' that Mede be buried too. More fittin' fer him ter be in the groun' dan in my cabin. Lucy she set a store by Mede 'n' didn' want him buried. Mos' fergittin' 'bout him, I am, Zan, but 'members now how pretty that Mede was. He jes' so pretty's Drumson 'n' jes' so pretty's Drummage. Drummage my boy, Zan, 'n' now he daid, jes' like Mede 'n' all the rest." She laid the cloth bundle on the ground while Zanzibar's spade dug into the earth. When he had excavated a deep hole, she laid the bundle in it and he shoveled the dirt back. Gently, she smoothed it with her big hands.

"They all daid, Zan. Ain' no one lef' but me. Ain' no one now ter 'member the folks that was at Falconhurst. Masta Hammond gone 'n' Miz Blanche 'n' Miz 'Gusta. Miz Sophie she a-gone 'n' that pretty man o' hern, Masta 'Pollon, what yo' kilt, Zan. My Ol' Mista Wilson's gone 'n' Drummage too. 'Cretia Borgia's done lef' us 'n' Mama Lucy. Meg 'n' Alph they gone long since. Now my boy Drummage he bin taken. Ain' no one lef'. Buryin' Mede here, Zan, so's when I go, he be taken care of. This ain' no white buryin' groun' no more, Zan, 'n' hopin' when I dies, yo' burries me here, Zan."

"How come yo' talkin' 'bout dyin', Big Pearl?" Zan reached down and helped her up. "Yo' strong's 'n ox 'n' 'sides"—he pointed in the direction of the big house—"ain' all daid. "Yo' got yo'se'f a grandson, Big Pearl. Yo' got a new Drum."

"Don' seem like no kin 'o mine, Zan. He white. He a-goin' ter be brung up like a white man. Masta Chris he say so. He say ter me dat he 'n' dat Miz Mary a-goin' ter marry up 'n' that li'l Drum be like their own. He a-wantin' ter comfort me, I guess. Hard fer me, though, Zan, ter figger out how come that li'l Drum so white-lookin'."

"'Pears white, Pearl." Zanzibar helped her over the wall. "But don' be fergittin' somethin'."

"Wha's that, Zan?"

"White's he is, he's still part Mandingo."

FAWCETT CREST BOOKS
ON TOP WITH THE BIG BESTSELLERS

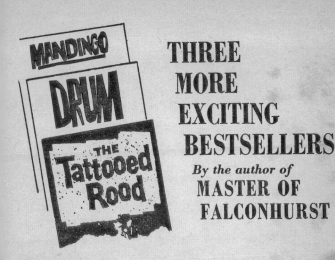

THREE
MORE
EXCITING
BESTSELLERS

By the author of
MASTER OF FALCONHURST

MANDINGO . . . M630 95¢ • The novel that shocked the nation . . . an uncensored abridgment of Kyle Onstott's best-selling novel about slave-breeding plantations in the old South, where men and women were mated, bred and sold like cattle. *"It has taken America nearly a century to produce the great novel on slavery."—John Henry Faulk, CBS*

DRUM . . . M658 95¢ • An explosive novel that sweeps away the myths of the ante-bellum South—the benevolent master, the fragile Southern belle and the humble happy slave . . . *"Compelling and powerful . . . a shameful slice of American history."—Bridgeport Post*

THE TATTOOED ROOD . . . T809 75¢ • Kyle Onstott with Lance Horner. The lusty adventures of a brash young soldier-of-fortune during the Spanish Inquisition . . . *"Shocking."—New Haven Register*

CREST
BOOK

Wherever Paperbacks Are Sold
FAWCETT WORLD LIBRARY

If your dealer is sold out, send only cover price plus 10¢ each for postage and handling to Crest Books, Fawcett Publications, Inc., Greenwich, Conn. Please order by number and title. If five or more books are ordered, no postage or handling charge is necessary. No Canadian orders. Catalogue available on request.